Elizabeth Knox was born in … is the author of eleven nove… *Vintner's Luck*, won the Deutz Medal for Fiction in the 1999 Montana New Zealand Book Awards and the Tasmania Pacific Region Prize. *The Vintner's Luck* has been published in seven languages and is being made into a film. In 2008, *Dreamquake* was awarded a Michael L Printz Honor by the American Library Association.

She is also the author of *Glamour and the Sea*, *Treasure*, *Paremata*, *Pomare*, *Tawa*, *The High Jump*, *Black Oxen*, *Billie's Kiss* and *Daylight*, which was shortlisted for the regional division of the Commonwealth Writers' Prize.

Elizabeth lives in Wellington with her husband and son.

PRAISE FOR *DREAMHUNTER*

'This fully imagined world will surely lure readers back for multiple readings' *Publishers Weekly*

'Readers pining for a fantasist to rival Philip Pullman or Garth Nix may have finally found what they seek in New Zealander Knox'
Booklist

'Knox's writing is rich and interesting. A highly original exploration of the idea of a collective unconscious'
The Horn Book

'The plot is intricate but always clear and the skilfully choreographed action sequences make [*The Invisible Road*] a likely future project for Peter Jackson . . . Elizabeth Knox has fashioned a brilliant two-volume masterpiece' *Christchurch Press*

'This time next year, we'll all be queuing for the sequel'
New Zealand Listener

'closer to Pullman's style . . . Knox's world is beautifully realised'
The Observer

'sure, literary prose, nuanced characters and fully realized Edwardian setting, but even more so for its original, surprising imagery and plot . . . unfolds with spectacular brilliance'
Toronto Star

Praise for *Dreamquake*

'Knox's haunting, invigorating storytelling will leave readers eager to return to its puzzles — and to reap its rewards' *Booklist*

'Knox's new novel, *Dreamquake*, follows Laura's quest to conclude "The Dreamhunter Duet" in a gripping, urgent pursuit that raises the pitch of its predecessor . . . a forceful tale . . . a classic coming-of-age story' *The Independent*

'Knox bravely draws her story to a grand finish in a way so surprising I can't immediately think of another fantasy where something similar happens'
Shaken and Stirred

'Knox's whole detailed construction will enchant daydreamers, right-brain thinkers and creative visualizers everywhere'
Times Colonist, Canada

'. . . an audaciously imagined and ingeniously constructed tale that transplants old-world myths into new-world soil to stunning effect . . . Reader, the earth moved.

Knox's uncanny talent for literalising metaphor and for metaphorising the real world is on full display here: feet of clay, hearts of stone and glass, singing hills, roads and rails to nowhere, burning passions, and everywhere, true grit. Stylistically, Knox favours the plainest verbs in the toolbox and is not much given to scene-setting, but nonetheless constructs a world that is alluring and convincing.

The plotting is staggeringly good . . . Knox not only generates a riveting mystery and a forcefully original myth of place, but raises some challenging questions about power and freedom, artistic licence, the role of the storyteller, and the way that both history and the future are constructed around dreams and fantasies of one sort or another' *NZ Listener*

DARE TO SLEEP ... DARE TO DREAM

The Invisible Road
Elizabeth Knox

HARPER
Voyager

Harper*Voyager*
An imprint of HarperCollins*Publishers*

First published in Australia in 2005 and 2007 as *Dreamhunter* and *Dreamquake*
This edition published in 2008
by HarperCollins*Publishers* Australia Pty Limited
ABN 36 009 913 517
www.harpercollins.com.au

Copyright © Elizabeth Knox 2005 and 2007

The right of Elizabeth Knox to be identified as the author of this work
has been asserted by her in accordance with the *Copyright Amendment
(Moral Rights) Act 2000*.

This work is copyright.
Apart from any use as permitted under the *Copyright Act 1968*, no part may
be reproduced, copied, scanned, stored in a retrieval system, recorded, or transmitted,
in any form or by any means, without the prior written permission of the publisher.

HarperCollins*Publishers*
25 Ryde Road, Pymble, Sydney NSW 2073, Australia
31 View Road, Glenfield, Auckland 10, New Zealand
1–A, Hamilton House, Connaught Place, New Delhi–110 001, India
77–85 Fulham Palace Road, London W6 8JB, United Kingdom
2 Bloor Street East, 20th floor, Toronto, Ontario M4W 1A8, Canada
10 East 53rd Street, New York, NY 10022, USA

National Library of Australia Cataloguing-in-Publication entry

Author: Knox, Elizabeth.
Title: The invisible road / author, Elizabeth Knox.
Publisher: Pymble, N.S.W. : HarperCollins, 2008.
ISBN 978 0 7322 8731 3 (pbk.).
Subjects: Dreams – Fiction. Family life – Fiction.
Dewey Number: NZ823.3

Cover design by Darren Holt, HarperCollins Design Studio
Cover images: woman courtesy of Getty Images; all other images courtesy of Shutterstock
Typeset in AGaramond 12.5/15pt by Helen Beard, ECJ Australia Pty Ltd
Printed and bound in Australia by Griffin Press
70gsm Bulky Book Ivory used by HarperCollins*Publishers* is a natural, recyclable product made
from wood grown in sustainable forests. The manufacturing processes conform to the
environmental regulations in the country of origin, Finland.

6 5 4 3 2 1   08 09 10 11

To my son, Jack Barrowman

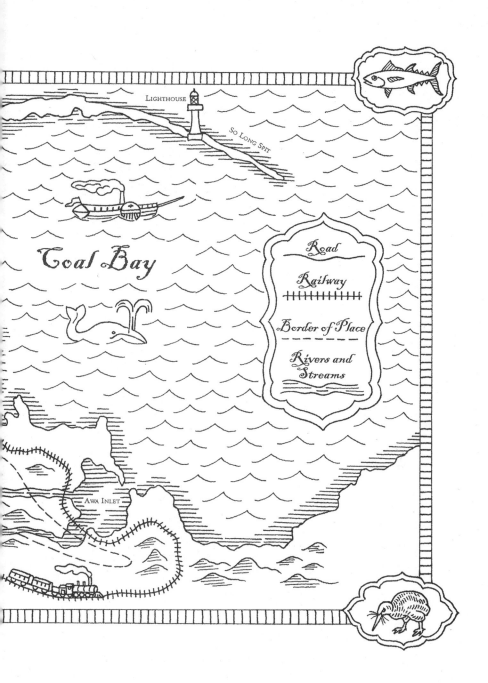

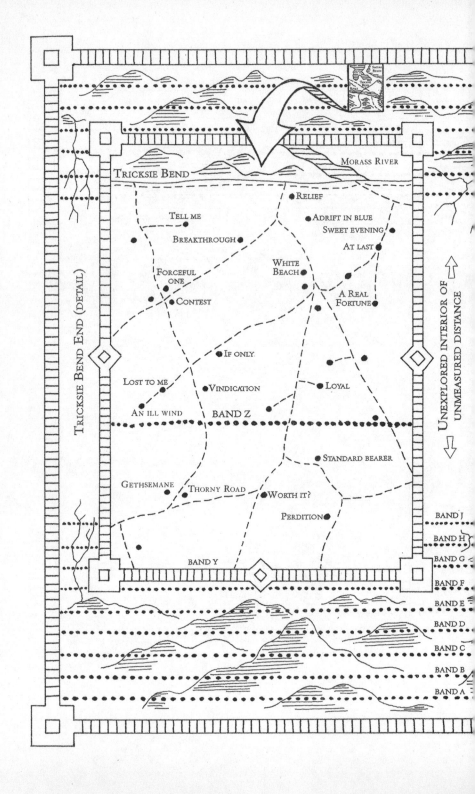

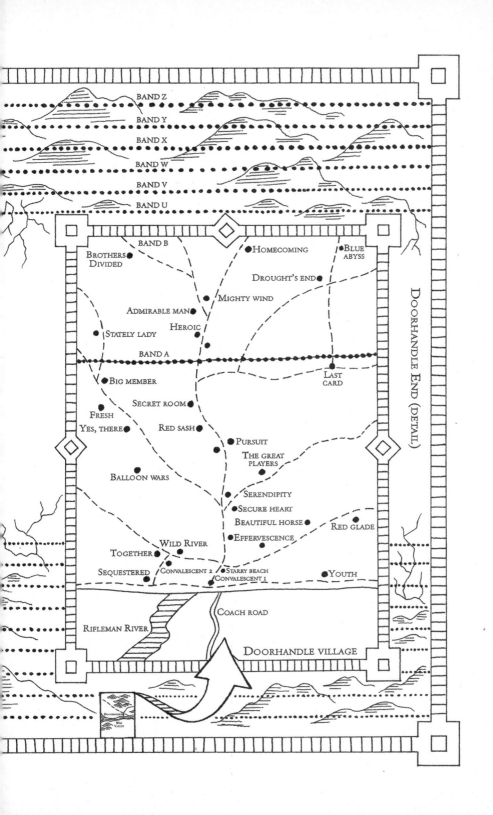

Prologue
1905

On a late winter night, the Isle of the Temple lay quiet, streets empty and shimmering. The moon was at the top of the sky, and the dew had set as frost on copper roofs, iron railings and window glass. But the roof of the Rainbow Opera was clear of frost, and lit from without by tall gas beacons that rose, a crown of flame, from the coping around its dome.

Inside the dream palace all was silent. Its central pit was illuminated by low nightlights, and by a mix of moonlight and the unsteady gas jets shining through stained-glass. The Rainbow Opera seemed deserted. But behind the doors that lined the four tiers of its balconies were bedchambers, all occupied, and all with their padded doors shut fast. Each bedchamber was at an equal distance from a dais that rose in the centre of the pit, a platform upholstered in white silk.

The dreamer's bed.

It had been a hard winter, the kind that kills the old, the ill and unlucky infants and, at the Opera that night, the great dreamhunter Tziga Hame was performing his most famous dream — Convalescent One.

Tziga Hame lay on his back in the dreamer's bed, his sleeping face serene, paralysed by his dream and holding all the Opera's patrons still in its priceless healing spell.

. . . the invalid had been gravely ill, but was better and was to be allowed out. He was to take the air. But he wasn't just lifted into a

bath chair and wheeled into a garden. Instead, he was bundled up and taken by carriage to a small country station. There he was transferred to a white canvas pavilion which had been built on the roof of a railway carriage. His attendants joined him, and picnic baskets were passed up to them. The train pulled slowly away from the station. It went on quietly, its motion only fast enough to raise a pleasant breeze. It was a late afternoon in summer, the air balmy, the light gold.

The train took them through tunnels of elms and black beech trees, a cool green and red gloom. It ran along cuttings with its roof at the level of meadows. Young horses galloped beside the train, sometimes plunging through the trailing banner of the engine's white steam. The train passed over a viaduct, high above the meadows, then ran alongside a canal, passing barges with bright paintwork. It picked up its pace a little on a winding, graded stretch of line that took it through pastures where rabbits grazed and crouched, washing their black noses and ears in the evening light. The train ran along beside low sand dunes, and showed the invalid the sea, the sun setting over its quiet surface.

The scalloped edge of the white cotton sun-shelter fluttered in the breeze. The invalid's attendants handed him strawberries, each the size of a child's fist, firm fruit with foamy white cores. They gave him milk sweetened with honey.

The train ran on to a causeway, a narrow strip of land, only wide enough to carry one set of rails. The causeway went out across the water. The train seemed to glide over the sea itself. Everything was peaceful, the air cool and caressing. The invalid lay in the safe embrace of his bed, yet there was space all around him, open air and flaming light . . .

Almost as one the Rainbow Opera's patrons breathed in deeply, and out slowly, and seemed to melt into their beds, let gently down into a deep, restoring sleep.

But Tziga Hame opened his eyes. He looked up at the fluttering light filling the air. He listened to the auditorium's dedicated hush. Nothing had disturbed him. He had roused himself.

Like other dreamhunters, Tziga Hame could edit any dream that needed editing *as he caught it*. He'd wake himself up before the dream managed to load him with any distressing dark turn. But he had never managed to learn how to edit Convalescent One in the catching. And so, when the dream reached the point where the train moved out on to the causeway, Hame had trained himself to wake up. To ease out of sleep without hauling his audience with him. Their dreams would trail off with the train into the beautiful sunset. There would be no dark turn.

For the dream went on. The train slowed because there was work being done on the line. Men stood on the stony trackbed, their hands hanging idle, while the train glided by. The invalid looked down on their upturned, grimy faces. He saw that the legs of their trousers were gathered at the ankles, as if tied there. The invalid was innocent and curious. He didn't know why, in looking at the exhausted men, he felt frightened by them, and unhappy for them.

But the dreamhunter Hame had caught and performed Convalescent One many times and had understood long ago that the invalid felt frightened because the men looked up at him with eyes full of menace and a kind of hungry expectation. And that their trousers were gathered at the ankles because their legs were in chains.

Hame had begun to suspect who the men might be, and that their presence in the otherwise beneficial dream was not a mistake, but a *message*.

That night at the Opera, after frost-fall, Hame lay gazing up at the dome high above him as a drowning man looks back at the surface, the underside of the world of air. He lay under silence like the weight of water and thought: 'What do they want *me* to do? Tell their story? Or break their chains?'

Part I
A Talented Family
1906

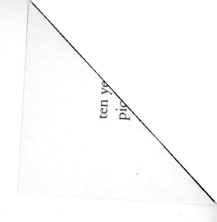

One

On a hot day near the end of summer, Laura Hame sat with her father, her cousin Rose and her aunt Grace against the fern-fringed bank of a forest track. She watched as her uncle Chorley and the rest of the picnic party passed out of sight around the next bend.

Chorley turned and waved before he disappeared. Laura stared at the empty, sun-splashed path. She saw black bush bees zipping back and forth through the air above the nettles, and heard the muffled roar of Whynew Falls, where the rest of the party was headed.

Laura and Rose, Laura's father Tziga and aunt Grace were sitting under a sign. The sign read, 'CAUTION: You are now only 100 yards from the border to the Place.'

'The falls are loud today,' Tziga said. 'It must have poured up in the hills.'

They listened to the cascade pound and thump. Laura, who had never been allowed near the falls, tried to imagine how they would sound up close.

Her father said, 'Think how startled Chorley would be if one of these girls suddenly skipped up behind him.'

Aunt Grace squinted at Laura's father. 'What do you mean?'

'Come on, Grace. Why don't we just get up and wander along that way?'

'Tziga!' Grace was shocked. Laura and Rose were too. The family had owned a summer residence at nearby Sisters Beach for

...s, and at least once a year they would go with friends for a ... up in the old beech forest. Every summer those who *could* ...ould continue along the track to see the falls. And, every summer, the girls were forced to wait at the sign with their dreamhunter parents. Tziga Hame and Grace Tiebold couldn't go and view Whynew Falls themselves because, one hundred yards from the honest and accurate warning sign, they would cross an invisible border. They would walk out of the world of longitude and latitude, and into a place called simply the Place. Tziga and Grace could no more continue on to Whynew Falls than Laura's Uncle Chorley could walk into the Place. Uncle Chorley, like almost everyone else, couldn't go there. Tziga and Grace were part of a tiny minority, for whom the rules of the world were somewhat different.

'Come on, Grace,' said Tziga. 'Why should we make the girls go through all the ceremony of a Try? It's only for the benefit of the Regulatory Body, so they can see their rules enforced. Why can't we just find out *now*, in a minute, in private?'

Rose wailed, 'It's against the law!'

Tziga glanced at Rose then looked back at Grace. He was a quiet man, self-contained, secretive even — but his manner had changed. His *face* had. Laura thought that looking at him now was like peering into a furnace — its iron doors sprung open on fire. Her father was a small man. He was a mess, as usual, his shirt rumpled and grass-stained, his cream linen jacket knotted around his waist, his hat pushed back on his dark, springy hair. Laura's aunt Grace wasn't any better turned out. Both dreamhunters were thin, tanned and dry-skinned, as all dreamhunters became over time. Rose was already taller than her spare and weathered mother. Rose was white and gold and vivid, like her father Chorley, and like Chorley's sister, Laura's dead mother. Laura had, unfortunately, not inherited her mother's stature or colouring. She was little and dark, like her father. But — Laura thought — her father, though small and shabby, still had the aura belonging to all great dreamhunters. Laura liked to imagine that the aura was a residue of the dreams they'd carried. For, when Tziga Hame and Grace Tiebold ventured into the Place, dreams were what they brought back with them. Dreams that were more forceful, coherent and vivid than those supplied to all people by their sleeping brains. Dreams they could share with others. Dreams they could perform, could *sell*.

Laura's father was saying, 'We were pioneers, Grace. You didn't "Try", you crept past the cairn beyond Doorhandle early one morning when there wasn't a soul on the road. Do you remember? That moment was all your own. There wasn't anyone standing by with a clipboard and contracts.'

Laura saw that her aunt had gone pale. Grace stood up. Laura thought Grace meant to walk away, back towards the road, to go off in a huff and put an end to Laura's father's crazy talk. But then Laura saw Grace turn to look up the track towards the border.

Laura's heart gave a thump.

Laura's father got to his feet too.

Rose didn't move. She said, 'Wait! What about our Try? You've even bought us outfits — our hats with veils.'

'Rose thinks she's a debutante,' Laura's father said.

'I do not!' Rose jumped up. 'All right, I'll go! I'll go now! I'm not scared. I was only trying to remember the law. But if you don't care about it, why should I?'

'Good,' said Laura's father. He offered his hand to Laura. She looked at it, then took it and let him help her up. She busied herself brushing dry moss from her skirt. The others began to amble slowly along the path. Laura caught up with them and gave her hand to Rose, who took it and squeezed it tight. Rose's hand was cold, much cooler than the air which, even in the shade of the forest, was as marinated in heat as the open paddocks, the dusty roads and the beaches of Coal Bay. Rose's hand was chilly, her palm coated with sweat.

Around the first bend was another, very similar. The track was flanked by black beech trunks. The sun angled in and lit up bright green nettles and bronze shoots of supplejack.

'I guess we won't see the Place until we're there,' said Rose.

'That is right,' Grace said. 'There's nothing to see. No line on the ground.'

Tziga said, 'The border is around the next corner.'

They didn't slow, or hurry. Laura felt that their progress was almost stately. She felt as though she were being escorted up the aisle, or perhaps on to a scaffold.

She didn't want to know yet. *It was too soon.*

In two weeks Laura and Rose were due to Try. Any person who wanted to enter the Place for the first time had to do so under the eye of an organisation called the Dream Regulatory Body. The Body had been set up ten years before. It employed 'rangers' — those who could go into the Place but couldn't carry dreams out of it — to patrol the uncanny territory and its borders. The dream parlours, salons and palaces in which working dreamhunters performed had to obey laws enforced by the Regulatory Body and its powerful head, the Secretary of the Interior, Cas Doran. The parlours, salons and palaces were businesses, and had to have licences. Dreamhunters, too, had to have licences. A Try was the first step on the road to a licence, and a livelihood.

The Body held two official Tries a year — one in early spring and one in late summer. Each Try found hundreds of teenagers lined up at the border. It wasn't compulsory to Try, but many did as soon as they were allowed, because dreams represented a guarantee of work, and the possibility of wealth and *fame*. Any child who showed an inclination — vivid dreaming, night terrors, a tendency to sleepwalk — was thought, by hopeful families, to have a chance at the life. A dreamhunter or ranger in the family was another indicator of talent. More boys than girls Tried, since parents were more permissive with boys, and the candidates were, by and large, in their mid-teens.

The *earliest* age for a Try was legally set at fifteen.

Rose and Laura had celebrated their fifteenth birthdays that summer.

Walking along the Whynew Falls track, hand in hand with her cousin, Laura felt desperately unprepared for an impromptu Try. She felt unprepared *whatever*. Every night that summer, as she'd put her head down on her pillow, she had mentally ticked off another day — the time narrowing between her and her life's big deciding moment. She had felt as though she were hurtling down a slope that got steeper and steeper the further she fell.

For Laura knew that, after her Try, she would either be in her father's world, or would remain at her school — Founderston Girls' Academy. She would have a calling, or be free to continue her education, to travel, to 'come out' when she was sixteen and appear at every ball in that season. If she was free, Laura knew she'd inherit the Hame wealth — but not the Hame glamour. And, free, she would lose Rose, because *Rose* fully expected to walk into the Place, fall asleep there, dream and carry back her dreams intact, vivid and marvellous. For Rose had already been into the Place, had been a number of times, because Grace Tiebold had gone on catching dreams when she was pregnant with Rose. (Grace had just laughed when her sister-in-law Verity said to her, 'Did you ever think that you would go there and leave the baby behind?' Grace had put a hand on her stomach and laughed at Verity — also pregnant — saying, 'Oh! Darling! What a bloody thought.')

As Laura approached the bend around which her father had said the border would be, she began to drag her feet.

Rose gave her hand a sharp tug. 'Come on,' she whispered. 'Stick with me.'

'Tziga,' said Grace, 'just tell me this — why now? We could have tried last year, or the year before, or when they were only ten. We could have whipped them across quickly when they were really tiny, and they wouldn't even have known where they were. We would have learnt whether they could cross or not, and just waited to make it official.'

Laura saw her father shake his head at Grace, but he didn't answer her.

'Why do you need to know *now*?' Grace asked again.

Laura gave a little sob of tension. Then she crashed into her aunt, who had suddenly stopped in her tracks. 'Jesus!' Grace said. They all stepped on one another. When Laura righted herself, she saw a ranger walking towards them along the path.

The man came up to them. He looked, in quick succession, surprised, suspicious and polite. 'Mr Hame, Mrs Tiebold,' he said, respectfully. 'Good day to you. Are you going In?' Then he looked beyond the adults at the two girls. He stared, pointedly.

'No, of course not,' said Grace. 'We are just waiting for my husband and our friends. They went along to the falls.'

'I see,' said the ranger. He stood blocking their path. He cleared his throat. 'Perhaps it would be wiser to take these young ladies back to the sign.'

'We do know exactly where the border is,' Grace said, frosty. 'It isn't as if it moves.'

'It *is* very well signposted,' Tziga said, neutral. 'We're not likely to make any mistakes.'

'But you can't always keep your hand on your children near the border — best not to go too near.' The ranger was quoting a bit of the Regulatory Body's official advice, saying something he had no doubt had to say to many people on his patrols. But, because he was addressing the undisputed greatest dreamhunters — one of them the very first — he at least had the decency to blush. 'I'm very sorry,' he said.

'We're not dopes, you know,' Rose said, indignant. 'Laura and I are Trying in two weeks, for heaven's sake. Why would we spoil that by sneaking across now?'

'It is better to be careful,' the ranger said. He focused on a point above Rose's bleached straw sun hat and composed himself into a stiff state of official dignity. He looked block-headed.

'Come on, girls,' Grace said. She turned Rose and Laura around and propelled them back along the track.

Laura swallowed hard to suppress her sigh of relief.

The ranger hovered for a moment. He seemed to realise that Tziga Hame meant to stay put, so followed Grace and the girls.

At Whynew Falls, Laura's uncle Chorley Tiebold filmed the other picnickers as they requested. He shot them pointing up at the waterfall, wet from spray. He filmed them jostling and giggling at the pool's edge.

When he was finished Chorley packed up his movie camera, hoisted it on to his shoulder and followed his neighbours back along the track. He was itching to get back to his workshop in Summerfort, the family's house at Sisters Beach. He wanted to see whether he'd managed to capture on film the scales of shadow pushing down the white face of the cascade. Chorley picked up his pace to catch up with the others. He passed the orange-painted circle of tin tacked to a tree trunk — the border marker. He went on a few steps then, for some reason, glanced back. He saw the track, tree ferns, grey knotted sinews of a red-bush vine. Then he saw a flicker of colour and shadow in the air, and his brother-in-law Tziga materialised on the track behind him.

Chorley flinched. He had filmed this phenomenon — of people passing into and out of the Place at its busiest border post, the cairn beyond Doorhandle. It was Chorley's best-known film; he'd sold copies to all corners of the world. Everyone wanted to know just what it looked like — and that it didn't look like trick photography. It didn't. It was a quiet, unfussy, terrifying sight. The only time Chorley had seen it and hadn't felt frightened was when, shortly before they married, he and Grace had played a stalking game in the long grass on the bluff above the river at Tricksie Bend. Grace, inside the Place, hadn't known where Chorley would be outside it, and he hadn't known where she would emerge. She jumped back and forth, sometimes startled to find he was close by and could grab her. It had made Chorley anxious, made his heart ache to see Grace come and go like that — to go where *he couldn't follow*. But it was magical too.

'There you are,' said Tziga. 'You always come last when you're carrying your camera.' Tziga stepped around Chorley and walked ahead of him, turning back now and then to speak. Looking up, for Chorley was quite a bit taller. 'You know — there's far too much interest in Laura and Rose's Try,' he said.

Chorley couldn't remember anyone mentioning the girls' Try at the picnic. Not even Rose, who was more excited the nearer the event came. Chorley said, 'I may be following you, Tziga —' he poked his brother-in-law with the legs of his camera '— but I don't follow you.'

'There's too much interest in the *outcome* of their Try. That's all I'm saying. I don't want them besieged with publicity, or contracts.'

'That's why we've bought them hats with veils; to keep their faces out of the newspapers,' Chorley said. 'To keep it all as private as possible. We could, at least, all agree to do that much. You *do* realise that I've been trying to talk to you — and Grace — about this for months now?'

'I know. But there was never any question that they'd Try as soon as the law allowed.'

Chorley took one hand off his precious camera to grab Tziga's arm. '*I* questioned it,' he said. 'The law can say what it likes, but I think they're still too young.'

'They *want* to Try,' Tziga said. He looked very unhappy.

Chorley said, 'Rose wants to — Laura just doesn't want to be left out.' He watched Tziga's face go remote. Even Chorley, who knew his brother-in-law better than anyone, couldn't tell if Tziga was offended, angry to be told something about his own daughter that he should know himself, or whether he had just dropped down into a colder and deeper reach of his usual sadness. 'Tziga,' Chorley said, and gave the arm he held a little shake. He was annoyed with himself for poking the chisel of his complaints into this crack in Tziga's certainty. 'Look,' he said, 'it'll soon be over. It'll be decided one way or the other.'

'Yes.'

Chorley told Tziga to get a move on. The others would wonder where they were. 'You do know it will be all right whatever happens,' Chorley said, as they went along. 'I'm not a dreamhunter and I'm all right. Grace and you are dreamhunters, and you are too — all right, I mean. Aren't you?' Chorley gave Tziga yet another chance to confide in him, to tell him why, lately, he'd seemed so *hunted*.

Tziga just made a faint affirmative noise, then asked his brother-in-law if this was the camera he wanted him to take into the Place.

Chorley immediately forgot his worries. 'Yes,' he said. 'Are you saying you will? Finally?'

Tziga said yes, he'd take Chorley's camera In tomorrow.

Chorley was rapt, and for the next hour, long after they caught up with the others, he talked. He gave instructions, advice, almost gave a shooting script for the film he most wanted to make, but couldn't make himself.

Tziga only interrupted once, when they reached the cars, which were parked at the gate of the farm beside Whynew Reserve. Tziga said to Grace, 'There he is,' and tilted his head in the direction of a man in a brown dust-coat, a shadow against the tangled trunks of the whitey-wood forest.

'He's seeing us off,' Grace growled.

'Who is it?' Chorley asked.

'A ranger,' said Rose.

Chorley saw Grace give Rose and Laura a sharp look. The girls got into the car. Chorley said to the dreamhunters, 'Do you think that ranger is watching you?'

'Of course not,' said Grace.

'Yes,' said Tziga, 'I'm being watched. The Regulatory Body has a big investment in me. Contracts. That sort of thing.' Tziga made one of the gestures peculiar to him — a gesture of crumbling something in his right hand and casting it away into the air. Then he went around the front of the car to crank it for Chorley.

Two

The ranger came in at the end of the day and shut himself in his hotel room. It was a room without a sea view, but looked along the Strand towards the hill at the western end of Sisters Beach, and the gates of Summerfort, the Hame and Tiebold beach house. The ranger opened his windows — dragged an armchair across the room and sat facing the view. He pulled a crumpled paper from his coat pocket. It was a letter containing his instructions. He looked again at the figures pencilled on its back. He had been doing sums, figuring how best to spend his extra cash.

The letter told the ranger to tail Tziga Hame.

> *. . . the dreamhunter has failed to register the location of a dream about which I have grave concerns. Keep close to Hame at all times. As he is concealing a site, it is reasonable to suppose that he will attempt to enter the Place on a quiet section of the border, and without registering his intentions at a rangers' station. Follow him and find out where he goes.*
>
> *And — this cannot be stressed enough — do not sleep when or where Hame sleeps.*

The ranger had spent that day lurking in the beech forest near Hame's picnic party. The picnickers fortunately hadn't any dogs and the ranger had been able to position himself between the group who went up the track to admire the Whynew Falls, and the two dreamhunters and their unTried daughters. He hadn't expected to run into the four right by the border. He'd been just as surprised as they were. It was an awkward moment.

As he sat at the hotel window, the ranger decided that he would not report today's incident. He was afraid that he'd be taken off his lucrative job, a job he was no longer the best man for, now he had been seen by his quarry. If Hame spotted him again, the dreamhunter would know for sure that the ranger hadn't just stumbled upon him. He would know he was being followed. The encounter near the falls was unfortunate, but the ranger decided that he would not let it ruin his opportunity to earn some good money.

He produced matches from his coat pocket and tore the letter in half, kept the portion with his calculations and set a burning match to the other half. He held it while it flared up, then released the flaming fragment on to the evening breeze and watched it blow away, shedding threads of floating embers.

Three

Laura dragged herself out of bed early and went downstairs in order to see her father off on his latest foray into the Place.

As she pushed through the padded doors to the kitchen Laura heard singing. The song was strange, and the sound of it made her scalp prickle. She reacted to the music before she recognised the singer's voice. It was her father — singing something disturbing and incomprehensible.

When Laura appeared her father stopped in the middle of a phrase. The air in the room smelt of porridge, and brown sugar, and something else — moisture and electricity. It was as if her father had been joined for breakfast by a thunderstorm.

Laura pushed a chair up next to his, sat down and leant against him. She said, groggy, 'Has someone left a door open? Is it going to rain?'

He put his arm around her. There were two places set at the table, two empty teacups and one empty porridge plate. Tziga's plate was still full. He had gathered the glutinous oatmeal into a mound and had shaped the mound into rough, mealy sculpture, *a face*.

Laura picked up a napkin and wiped her father's fingers clean. 'Who is that supposed to be?' she said.

Tziga smiled. 'Someone bran-knew,' he said.

Laura giggled. 'Bran new and feeling his oats,' she said. Then, 'What were you singing, Da?'

Laura's father rested his cheek against her hair. '"The Measures",' he said. 'A song my great-grandfather taught me. Or, rather, *tried* to teach me. He was always trying to teach me and your aunt Marta the old folk songs he knew. I was too young and callow then to understand that the songs were our family inheritance. The songs, and stories, and — *other* things. I used to say to the old man that I hadn't time for that ancient stuff, that I was expected to earn a living, and that nobody in the fashionable places wanted to hear "Of His Name" or "A Stitch in Time".' Laura's father sighed. 'So I never did master "The Measures". I've been trying to remember how it goes.'

'I didn't understand a word of it.'

'You wouldn't. It's *koine*, demotic Greek, the common tongue of the Roman Empire. Or rather, half the song is in *koine*, the rest of it is just sounds, what doctors in insane asylums would call glossolalia — articulate, nonsensical noises — noises like words. A priest would call it "talking in tongues". So — perhaps "The Measures" might be described as a mixture of *koine* and tongues.'

Laura leant away from her father to take a good look at his face. She asked him whether his great-grandfather ever told him where *he* had heard the song.

'Do you know the story about how the survivors from the island of Elprus first came to settle in Founderston?'

This was something Laura had had in her history classes. She knew that Elprus was an island depopulated some 200 years before by a catastrophic volcanic eruption. Most of the island's population were poisoned and buried when the volcano in its centre vented corrosive gas and a burning cloud of ash that filled the air for fifty miles and fifteen days. The survivors were either from the island's fishing fleet, or merchant traders — those who were at sea when the volcano blew. They were gathered together by Laura's ancestor, one John Hame. The history books said that this John Hame took the Elpra far across the seas to Southland, finally to settle in Founderston, then a small pioneer settlement around a fort and river port. But, before they left their island, the survivors excavated their main holy site, the tomb of St Lazarus. (Lazarus of the gospels, whom Jesus raised from the dead, had apparently spent most of his long, miraculously restored life on Elprus. There he had married, fathered children, worked his own miracles, written his own gospel, grown old and died — *again*.) John Hame and the other Elpra dug down through the ash to the saint's tomb, removed his bones and carried them away.

Laura said to her father, 'I know the story. Our ancestor brought the relics that are now in the Temple.'

'Yes. "The Measures" was passed down through our family. It's the oldest of all the Hame songs. Legend has it that John Hame was a descendent of St Lazarus. That's why "Lazarus" is a family name.'

'Is that true?'

'Well — it's a story I inherited, not one I made up.'

Laura pulled a face and said, 'But it can't be proven, right? It's what Uncle Chorley would call unscientific.'

'History, unlike science, doesn't need *repeatable* proofs. A story can be true if its sources are sound. The gospels are a good source of things Chorley would call unscientific. Saint Lazarus's gospel mentions a song he heard in the tomb. But the Gospel according to Lazarus is the only *documentary* source. All the rest of it is lore — family lore.'

Laura gave her father a worried look. 'I would have thought that all St Lazarus heard in the tomb was Jesus telling him to come forth.'

'Yes — to return to the land of the living. But perhaps Jesus was singing.' Laura's father blushed and pressed his lips together. He'd said something blasphemous, and was embarrassed by it.

'Da, you'd better stop before Uncle Chorley comes back. You wouldn't want to offend his *irreligious* feelings.'

Tziga laughed. 'Chorley's getting the car out and putting his camera in it. And, probably, fifty pages of instructions. Perhaps, when I come back, I should pretend I forgot to remove the cap on the lens. See what he does.'

Chorley Tiebold was hard to tease, even-tempered and too quick to fool easily. But the fact that Chorley was so hard to tease meant that it was a challenge — a challenge which his wife, children and brother-in-law frequently took on.

'No one thinks you're *that* vague, Da. And you shouldn't start acting vague in case you do forget something important, like coming back in time for my Try!' She let go of her father and drew back so that she could hold his gaze.

'You *will* make sure to be back in time, won't you?'

Tziga nodded.

'You can just go In and get something therapeutic for the old ladies who go to matinees at The Beholder. A nice dream for the afternoon naps of vacationing biddies. *Promise*,' said Laura.

'Sweetheart . . .'

'Just promise.'

Tziga put his hands, still slightly tacky with porridge, on either side of Laura's face. He said to her, 'Darling — do you want to be a dreamhunter?'

'Yes!' She was surprised, but answered instantly. 'And before you ask me — no, I *don't* mind being tired all the time; being in and out of different worlds; being weirdly imperilled. I've heard you say that to Aunt Grace — "weirdly imperilled". And she always says, "Some things are worth the risk." I am very nervous about my Try, but dreamhunting *is* worth the risk — isn't it?'

Laura's father sighed. He looked sad. 'Yes,' he said, 'it is. But not to supply tonics for old ladies at matinees.'

'But, Da, that's just *this* week. So you'll be back in time for my Try.' Laura kissed her father on his cheek. Then Chorley came into the room, grinned, said, 'Good girl, I'm glad you got up,' and ruffled her hair. Then he began to hustle Tziga out of the house. Laura went with them. She carried her father's bedroll. Chorley carried Tziga's pack and water bottles. They put everything in the car and Laura stood, dew soaking the hem of her nightgown, waving until the car disappeared down the drive.

Four

A week after Laura's father had left on his latest expedition, she and Rose lay bundled up beside a fire on the beach beneath Summerfort. They had a pile of firewood near at hand and were nursing the flames stick by stick so that they would provide a pleasant heat. Rose had scorched her blanket earlier in the evening, and when her father came to check on them before he went to bed, he noticed the black-edged holes in the material and said, 'If you can't be more careful then you'd better put out your fire and come indoors.' They'd promised to be more careful and, before he left, Chorley had filled a pail with seawater so that they could douse the fire and decamp any time they wanted.

All the other beach fires had been put out. The stars were coming clearer as the land cooled and the forest on the high headland to the east finished breathing out a day of sun in the form of heat distortion. Those stars at the zenith were steady, cold, and piercing.

The sea was calm. The tide had turned only an hour before. The girls could hear an occasional flipping splash as a small fish feeding on insects was startled up into the air by a larger fish hoping to feed on it. Laura, who lay facing the curve of the bay, could feel heat on the back of her neck radiating from the rocks at the skirt of Summerfort's headland. There was flax growing on the rocks, and Laura could smell its baked black flowers, and the perfume of the tea tree scrub.

Earlier in the evening they had done a round of other fires, chatting with this and that friend — people they saw only in summer. They cooked potatoes in the embers of their own fire — then peeled them in the shallows and let seawater cool and salt them. They baked clams open on a sheet of tin, then balanced a pot on the embers to brew black tea. They toasted marshmallows and scalded their lips with molten sugar. They sang songs and cooled their overheated feet in the sea. Now they were tired, and taking slow turns to speak about what they had ahead of them.

The trip back to the capital, Founderston, was quite a journey, ten hours by rail, for when the railway line to Coal Bay had been built, fifteen years before, it was built to safely skirt the borders of the Place. The family travelled back on an overnight train and their arrival in Founderston always seemed an abrupt end to the summer. Founderston was inland, and colder. Their house, the Tiebold town house, was grand but old, built of stone, not timber like Summerfort. It faced the river, the bright Sva, but its windows were small, leaded and composed of tiny panes of greenish, uneven glass. The house had electricity, and a fireplace in every room, but seemed close and gloomy. Its walls and doors were thick, and anyone closed in a room alone felt alone.

For seven years the end of summer had meant for Laura and Rose a return to the old house, and to school — Founderston Girls' Academy, where they had begun at eight years of age, after two years of patchy learning with day tutors. These tutors were always being encouraged to go home early by either Laura's father or Rose's mother. The dreamhunters might arrive back home at any hour, leather coats covered with the white dust of the Place. Over-excited by the dreams they had caught, Tziga and Grace would want company, and cuddles from their daughters, before they had to go out and sleep, in Tziga's case at a hospital, and in Grace's at the Rainbow Opera.

At the end of every summer, the girls often found themselves anxious about going back to school, because, every summer, they had been drawn back into the family culture of late nights, broken sleep and napping during the day. The girls often arrived back at school as dazed and feverish as their dreamhunter parents, and full of irregular habits they had quickly to give up. This year Rose and Laura were more nervous than ever because, *this year*, it was possible that they would not be returning to the Academy at all.

On the last day of the term before the summer holidays Laura and Rose's classmates tried to talk to them about what would happen. The other girls needed to talk — Rose was very popular, and would be missed, and her friends were aware they might have to do their mourning before the fact of her departure.

After the final assembly the girls' class gathered in their favourite meeting place, the peach tree in one corner of the quad. Everyone swapped gifts. Laura and Rose passed out their presents — carefully chosen gifts for the girls they really liked, and beautifully wrapped, pricey soaps, perfumes and manicure sets for those they liked only diplomatically. Mamie Doran was one of these, and, as Rose handed her a ribbon-festooned tray of soaps, Mamie said, 'How will we manage without you, Rose? In the choir, and in goal at hockey? And who will counsel Jane when Miss Melon is stern with her, or console Patty when she breaks out in blisters again?'

'You could take up the slack, Mamie,' Rose said. 'And it's not as if we're going to the other side of the world!'

'But it's such a different life. A life apart,' said Mamie, falsely sentimental, and as though to suggest that this was what Rose and Laura in fact thought. As if Rose and Laura were disdainfully shaking the dust of some provincial place off their feet.

Rose, being Rose, moved into Mamie's attack rather than away from it. 'Mamie,' she said, 'I promise to blow you kisses when you're eating ice cream on the balcony of your father's suite at the Opera.'

Mamie Doran's father was the Secretary of the Interior, a man whose power and influence were, according to some, now greater than the President's own. Mamie wasn't popular, like Rose, but she had her followers and, when she could be bothered, she was very good at managing the opinions of others. Now Mamie seemed to be determined that everyone should discuss the possibility that Rose and Laura wouldn't be coming back to school. Like the cousins, almost every girl in their group had attended the Academy for seven years. Founderston Girls' Academy was their universe, a universe in which, year by year, they all rose nearer to the exalted status of seniors. Some were already the womanly heroes of the cricket and hockey pitches. And soon they would play the leads in end-of-year productions, edit the yearbook, chair the school council.

One girl, a girl too dependent on Rose's morale-building presence, and made bold by Mamie's chiselling, said, 'How can you think of leaving?'

'Aren't you scared?' said another girl.

Mamie looked keenly at this girl, then smirked at Rose and Laura.

Mamie Doran, unlike the other girls, was prepared to talk about where the cousins were — or *might be* — going. She knew something about dreamhunters. Ten years before, when they were all little, Cas Doran had headed the government commission that produced the legislation that controlled what dreamhunters did. The Dream Regulatory Body reported to Mamie's father. So Mamie could talk about 'the industry'.

'Well,' said Mamie, 'dreamhunters are an independent and unmanageable group of people — I can see the charm for Rose.'

Rose said, 'Money's the charm.'

Mamie turned pink. For a moment she held her breath, then she said, 'I'm surprised to hear you say that, Rose. Dreamhunters must also have professional ethics. And they have to think about public safety.'

'Oh, I can do all that and think about money too,' Rose said. 'And fame. And what outfit to buy for my début at the Rainbow Opera.'

'All right, be facetious,' Mamie said. 'But at least I'm actually talking about dreamhunting, not just going "Aren't you scared?" like Patty.'

Laura turned to Patty, and touched her arm. 'We don't know what will happen. I can't think yet about missing school. I can't think what I'll wear at my début at the Rainbow Opera either. It's all too far away, and uncertain.'

'Well, at least Laura is taking it all seriously,' Mamie said, and managed to sound as though she were criticising Laura as well as Rose.

'Laura's seriousness sounds like seriousness,' Rose said, 'and mine does not.'

Rose and Mamie might have gone on fencing, but Laura discovered one unclaimed present in their basket, looked at the card and realised that a classmate — a quiet, mousy girl — was missing, and they all had to go in force to look for her and fuss over her.

Lying on Sisters Beach, after midnight, Laura was thinking about that last day of term. 'Rose?' she said, then freed her arm from her bedroll to poke another stick into the flames. The driftwood caught and, for a moment, its salt-saturated timber burnt green. 'Isn't it strange not to be thinking about school?'

'But you *are* thinking about it. You just mentioned it,' said Rose.

'I just realised I hadn't thought about school all summer. I've only been thinking about our Try.' Laura listened to her cousin's silence. Finally Rose stirred, her blankets rasping softly in the hollow she'd worn herself in the sand. Rose said, 'I'm trying not to be impatient for the time to pass. These last days at the beach are always so special.'

Laura, frightened by the prospect of her Try, and not wanting to be alone in her fear, asked her cousin, 'Aren't you nervous? I'm miserable with nerves whenever I stop to think.'

Rose was unperturbed. 'But we're so lucky, Laura. We have Ma and Uncle Tziga as guides. We don't get pushed off into the Place in the company of rangers and a gaggle of poor, piss-pants kids with fortune-hunter parents.'

It seemed that Rose hadn't considered that she wouldn't go. That, like almost everyone, she wouldn't be able to enter the Place, but would be left standing on the everyday road. 'But —' Laura began. She was about to say, 'What say you don't go there?' Then she stopped. She could feel Rose's confidence like the noonday sun, Rose's confidence shrinking and blackening Laura's doubts. If Laura were to say, 'What say it doesn't happen?' she would sound mean. Laura felt the difference in their expectations like a poison between them, a contamination that only she was aware of. She decided not to say anything. She felt that her cousin's confidence would contaminate her own luck — but only if she spoke, and spoiled it for Rose.

'It'll be an adventure,' Rose said, as though she were reading Laura's mind.

'An ordeal,' Laura thought. But her father would be there. Her father, at least, would understand her disappointment if she didn't succeed. Laura was quiet for a time. A breeze had got up. They were sheltered from it by the rocks, but Laura could hear the flax bushes clapping. That, and the clucks and groans of roosting gulls.

'Wasn't Mamie a pain, though?' Rose said, sleepily. 'All her false sentiment about how the school will do without us.'

'Without *you*,' Laura said.

'Oh yes. Perhaps she thinks I'm flattered. But the way she talked about our Trying, as if it's never bravery we're showing — it's only pride. Implying that we are horribly confident. We're forward, so, if we fall on our faces, then it serves us right. And the other girls, saying "I don't know how you do it", and "I'd never have the nerve".' Rose hissed with contempt, 'It isn't admiration — it's an effort to control us. To make us see sense, or show fear — or something!'

Laura could see Rose's profile, her cocked elbows. Rose was gazing up into the stars and Laura knew her eyes would be wide — she'd be wearing her fighting look.

'They're so transparent,' Rose said. 'Honestly.'

Laura realised that Rose, in taking her friends' concern as their attempt to make her feel fear, must be resisting fear. At some level Rose was nervous, too. As soon as she'd thought this Laura felt the late hour, the long day. She felt herself slipping, falling down into the soft dark below the clear black of the open air. 'They're your friends, Rose,' she said sleepily. 'They care about you.'

'I know. But they want me to stay with them, at school. They want me to fail.'

'Not you,' Laura said, and fell asleep — and into dreams, her own dreams.

Five

The ranger lay concealed in a thicket of brown gorse by the dry riverbed. His view of Tziga Hame was unimpeded by haze or shade. The scene was saturated with light, as though the sun had dissolved, whitening the air. It had taken the ranger hours to creep close to his quarry. The Place was silent, so there were no sounds to mask his approach, no birdsong, sawing insect chorus, or wind. For each movement he'd made the ranger had had to wait for Hame to make some covering noise. He'd been patient, and was now in a good position.

Tziga Hame knelt in a damp excavation in the dry riverbed. He had unwound the bandages from his hands in order to use them. His injuries were troubling him, and it was his pained gasping that had served to mask much of the ranger's stealthy rustling. His hands were now gloved with a mixture of blood, blue clay from the riverbank and silver river sand. He was sculpting. A form was beginning to emerge from the long mound of sand beside his excavation. He worked quickly, as if against a clock, or in a competition.

This impression jogged the ranger's memory. He remembered Hame's picture in the *Summertime Weekly*, the newspaper of Sisters Beach. The ranger had seen the picture among other photos taken at an annual sand-sculpting competition. In the picture, Hame, barefoot, his trousers rolled, stood behind his daughter and niece — girls really too old for buckets and spades — and their competition entry, the recumbent form of a man made of sand.

It occurred to the ranger that this was what Hame was busy sculpting now — a recumbent human figure. Hame's work was quick, but not crude. It seemed he had practised.

The ranger was puzzled, and attempted to make mental notes for the report he would have to give. A verbal report, since the man for whom he was tailing Hame wouldn't want anything committed to paper.

For the last seventy-two hours the ranger had been chewing a grainy paste of Wakeful, a narcotic that dreamhunters and rangers used to stave off sleep. The ranger knew he was no longer at his best and hoped his watch would end soon. It must — for Tziga Hame had put his first wad of the drug into his own mouth forty-eight hours before. Hame would need to sleep soon. He hadn't any time to muck around, yet here he was, digging, patting, shaping sand, like a child at play — except that he moaned as he worked. For, as he worked, Hame was driving dirt into the wounds on his hands.

The ranger had picked up Hame's trail the day after the picnic. He followed Hame into the Place. The dreamhunter had led him deeper into that silent wilderness than he'd ever been on his normal patrols. Hame was hard to follow — he'd been followed before, by claim-jumping dreamhunters back in the days before the Place was patrolled. The dreamhunter was wary, and slow, and the ranger had kept nearly overtaking him. Hame was burdened with the usual provisions, food and water and a sleeping roll, but he also carried a movie camera, a big instrument with a collapsible crank and telescopic brass legs. Chorley Tiebold's movie camera.

Hame had led the ranger deep into the pressing silence of the Place. And, as he walked, the ranger worked on his verbal report. He composed it in his head, and rehearsed it. It was terse. 'I followed Mr Hame fifty-two hours In. He made camp at a place with a ruin, a burnt timber-frame building of some considerable size, standing at the edge of what appeared to be an expanse of dry seabed. Hame set up his camera, pointed its lens at the building and cranked its handle for two minutes by my watch. After that Mr Hame ate, then settled himself to sleep. He caught a dream.'

A bad dream the ranger could add, were he able to find some way of describing what he had seen.

The ranger had watched Hame struggle in his sleep, moving violently, but as though constrained, as though he were beating his forehead, elbows and knees against invisible walls. The ranger's report would have to include an explanation of the wounds on Hame's hands. But how to put it? Perhaps like this:

Mr Hame appeared to be distressed by his dream. He tore at his own hands with his teeth. I could not say for certain if he was asleep or awake when he inflicted these injuries on himself.

A report was required to give directions, to record actions, to measure the duration of events. The ranger had stayed under cover and watched Hame suffer some horrible, mysterious ordeal. He had trembled with the effort of remaining still and hidden, of not rushing to the dreamhunter's aid. He had never felt more alone — alone with his task and its limitations. Still he composed his notes. 'At fifty-seven hours Hame broke camp and carried the camera back to grid reference Y–17.'

Back on to the known map. But how should the ranger describe what he was watching now, at grid reference Y–17? When Tziga Hame began to dig in the riverbed the concealed watcher had thought that perhaps Hame meant to bury the camera, or the cartridge of film. He saw Hame's hands bleed, and listened to his hoarse breathing. He saw mad purpose in the man's actions.

'At grid reference Y–17 Hame dug a trench . . .' thought the ranger, attempting to compose his report, to shape it, as Hame's hands were shaping the long mound of sand — making a man of it. Hame was using clay as well, to fashion forms too delicate for sand to hold. He made hands from the clay and laid them at the ends of the arms. The shape he'd sculpted on the riverbed was that of a man with a broad torso and powerful limbs, a man half again Hame's height.

The ranger cowered in the tunnel of dry gorse, his shirt collar clutched over his mouth, although the vegetable dust he'd stirred up had long since settled. He watched Hame scrape the blood and soil from his hands and use this paste to form a face for his sandman. Hame took his time, and took care. But *why*? This waterless crease of unpopulated land, this most remote of remotenesses, was no place to pursue a hobby or perfect an art.

Hame sat back on his heels and surveyed his work. He nodded slowly to himself. He took out his water bottle and splashed the last of his water over his hands to wash them. His injuries oozed blood through scabs of sand. Hame raised his hands up over his head, to ease the flow of blood, the ranger supposed, though Hame seemed to be praying. Indeed, the ranger imagined he heard Hame *singing* softly.

For long moments Hame remained in this incantatory position and the ranger, tormented by puzzlement and gorse prickles, was only able to get a little relief by formulating a final sentence, at last allowing himself to express an opinion: 'Hame's behaviour was highly irrational and I believe he requires further close observation.'

'I've warned them,' thought the ranger, though he hadn't. He was miles and hours away from the end of his task — the delivery of his report — and alone with crazy Hame.

Hame finished his appeal to the gods. He put his hands down and stooped over his figure once more. He hesitated, one finger pointed at the figure's face. Then he leant closer and wrote with a fingertip on its sandy forehead.

The ranger could have sworn that the air became suddenly humid, as on certain sorts of summer days the sun uncovers itself and creates a heat sink from the water vapour in the air. But it wasn't waterborne heat that thickened the parched air. It was something else. Something as stifling and invisible as humidity, but not made of water.

The figure, the man made of sand, got up out of the excavation. It stood up before Hame — stood up to face its maker. It shimmered, its surface blurring, the sand there in motion like smoke rising.

The ranger gasped and flung himself back through the tunnel in the gorse. He rolled free of the thicket, out into the open and ran. He heard Hame call out — an angry summons, or perhaps an order.

The ranger was fit and fast, and there were times, as he fled, when he imagined he'd finally been able to outstrip what followed him — till he caught again its soft approach, the hissing, sifting sound of its walk.

Six

The first thing Laura saw when she opened her eyes was a seabird, a shag, standing in the shelter of a big log at the high-tide line. It stood with one wing tucked into its side, and the other drooping, tip trailing in the sand. The bird was injured. Laura wriggled out of her bedroll and crawled towards it. She came closer, but it seemed not to see her, didn't even turn its head until she was right beside it, and her human shadow was at its feet. Then it looked at her, dazed and exhausted, and shuffled a few feet away from her. It moved slowly, stumbling as it went.

Laura shook her cousin awake. For the next quarter of an hour they discussed the bird, what to do about it, what might have happened to it. There had been a big blow four nights earlier — perhaps the bird had been hurt then. They were planning to catch it in a blanket and carry it up to the house, when Rose's father appeared.

The girls had lain awake talking and thinking until dewfall, then until the cool perfume of dew gave way to the smell of bread from the two bakeries along the seafront of the resort. They'd had only a few hours' sleep, so it was easy for Rose's father to talk them out of their plans of rescue. He asked which of them knew how to set a broken wing? And, if the wing was only wrenched, perhaps the bird might still gather its strength and fly away. He suggested that, if they wanted to go to bed till lunchtime, he could check on the bird now and then.

Rose and Laura went up the beach yawning. Chorley bundled up their bedrolls and picked up their picnic basket. He doused the grey but still smoking coals of their fire.

Once his daughter and niece were in bed, Chorley went back down to the beach to find the shag lying face down in the sand. Its head was turned and its smooth feathers and round shoulders made it look like a sleeping baby. Chorley picked it up and carried it down to the water. The tide was still going out, and if he threw the bird far enough the tide would carry its body away. He would tell the girls that it had been gone when he'd checked. He wouldn't lie for Rose, who would think that the bird's death was a shame, and might wonder whether or not it might have been better off if she had taken it up to the house — she'd wonder, but she was tough-minded, and the bird's death wouldn't trouble her. Chorley disposed of the small corpse for Laura's sake. Laura had said, 'How lonely it looks. How tired.' Laura was sensitive, and her uncle had the habit of protecting her from upset whenever he could.

Laura was the only child of Chorley's dead sister — his only sibling. He loved his daughter, naturally, but Laura was all he had left of Verity.

Verity and Chorley Tiebold had been inseparable, and so, after they married they combined their households. The brother and sister were support for each other in their mutual peculiar marriages to the great dreamhunters. Grace and Tziga were friends. Friends who went away for weeks at a time, foraging for dreams. When the girls were born their care naturally fell to Verity and Chorley. It had *made sense* for them all to live together. To throw in together, financially.

But, when Verity's marriage was only five years old, and her daughter only four, she became ill, and it became apparent that she wouldn't recover.

The family, so dedicated to one another, and to their unconventional lives, had found themselves facing a slow, creeping disaster. They were already financially overextended by Chorley's ambitions to restore the Tiebold estates, refurbish the Tiebold town house and build a beautiful summer residence at Sisters Beach. They had to struggle to keep up payments.

Yet, while Grace scaled up her dreamhunting to meet the family's commitments, there came a time when Tziga would only leave his wife to catch the kind of dreams that might help restore her health. Later, he caught the kind of dreams that might prolong her life. And, at the last, he sought and pursued the kind of dreams that might help ease her dying. Tziga caught and performed for nobody but his wife. Every night, for Verity alone. She and he would disappear together into her darkened sickroom, and into his dreams. Apart from his hurried forays into the Place, Tziga was always with Verity. His savings ran out. Chorley and Grace supported him, and his neglected daughter. To Chorley it seemed that his sister, in dying, was taking her husband with her. He imagined that Verity would die in her sleep — in Tziga's sleep — and that neither would wake.

In the end Chorley begged his sister to stop Tziga. He was in anguish, torn in two, but he said to her, 'Please, dear, you must refuse his help now. You must ask him not to go to the Place again. Please — can you *please* try to go from us awake? Forgive me. But please, Verity, don't let Tziga go with you in his sleep.'

Verity promised to do what her brother asked. 'But only when my time has come,' she said. She postponed her sacrifice, while Tziga worked to banish her pain and stave off her death. Little Laura asked her Uncle Chorley, 'Is Daddy sick too?' Even the child could see how it was — that her father was desperately active, but fading.

Tziga went away to get another dream. 'It's only overnight,' he promised his wife. 'Be brave.' When he'd gone Chorley told his sister what her daughter had said. Verity asked to see Laura. They had a little talk. Then Verity kissed her daughter, and sent her off to play. She summoned Chorley and Grace. She said she wanted to get up. She put on a robe and they helped her out on to the terrace. She sat watching the river traffic go by in the afternoon sunlight. An hour later Chorley and Grace carried her in, unconscious. They called the doctor, and watched by her bed, and, in the small hours, Verity Hame died without ever coming around again.

Tziga carried his dream home, and found a hearse parked at his gate.

Verity's funeral was held three days later. Tziga stood at his wife's graveside, his eyes sunken in circles of bruises.

He refused to sleep or eat, took nothing at the funeral breakfast and sat in the chief mourner's chair oblivious to the approaches of friends and relations, who steeled themselves to come up to him and offer their sympathy; oblivious to his daughter, who was ruining her black velvet dress by lying on the floor under his chair.

When the guests had gone, and the girls had been carried off to bed, Tziga prowled about the house. Chorley got out of bed at dawn to find Tziga in the kitchen yard, his head held under the stream from the pump. 'You can't stay awake for ever,' Chorley told him — though he could smell the spice of Wakeful in Tziga's sweat, and see that his lips were stained mauve from the drug.

'This dream isn't anyone else's,' Tziga said. 'It was for her. The best yet. The best I've ever caught.' He raised his wet, white face and glared at his brother-in-law. 'You can bury me with it,' he said.

By the next morning he was swaying and stumbling. He stumbled on the stairs and sat on the landing with his head hanging. Chorley followed him about. Tziga called him a vulture, and threw things at him. Grace sent the servants away and sat with the girls in the nursery. She read to them, sang lullabies and put them in their beds. She listened to the house. Rose's bright, sleepless eyes regarded her mother through the white mosquito net around her bed. Laura poked her head out of her netting — sat veiled in it, like a little communicant. At sunset Chorley found Tziga holding himself up against a doorframe, on which he was rhythmically beating his head. Chorley inserted his hand between the bloodied moulding and Tziga's oozing forehead. Then Tziga collapsed and Chorley picked him up. Tziga was light, worn thin by walking inland after the consoling beauties of the Place, by watching, by keeping himself awake. Chorley carried Tziga to his and Grace's bed.

Tziga woke in the morning — at the same time as a whole city block woke weeping with joy at a dream so powerful and beautiful that it altered each one of its dreamers for ever, a dream caught to carry a beloved, pain-racked woman into paradise. Tziga woke, weeping himself, and saw that Grace was beside him, and Chorley beside her, looking over her shoulder with pouring eyes, and between them were the little girls, Rose laughing at her dream with nervous, puzzled delight, and Laura calling alternately 'Mummy!' and 'Rosie!' — as though she wanted to share some wonderful news but didn't know who to tell first. Tziga could feel his dream echoing in the city like a thunderclap. He lay floating in breathing light. Grace cupped his wet face in both her hands, and Chorley's hands covered hers.

Tziga wasn't good for much after that. He rested, and the bills mounted up. Grace, meanwhile, foraged deep into the Place, looking for wonders and novelties, overwriting one dream with another till she got something she knew she could sell at a very high price. Sometimes she would encounter dreamhunters who had abandoned their own plans in order to wait for her, dreamhunters who would offer to empty their heads for her. She was exhausted — so they might also offer to carry her out. They'd carry her out, and delete their own dreams, replacing them with what she had — not so that they could part from her and peddle their poor copies of her dreams, but so that they could act as amplifiers, dream in unison with her, lie down with her, share the dreamer's bed and a small part of her fee. For, remembering with what force her presence in Tziga's sleep had amplified his last dream, Grace was ready to accept these offers.

Chorley was busy. He reorganised the family's finances — budgeting and juggling due dates on payments. He kept Tziga company — Grace had been very clear to him about this. 'Tziga has to get well,' she'd said. 'He's worth more than we are. He is the beauty of dreamhunting. He is the good of it.'

Chorley had the girls to care for. Grace was clear on that score too. 'Watch poor Laura. And you know, love, I can work, and work, and work, so long as Rose is happy.'

Chorley did all that he had to — and he failed to notice things. He didn't see the dubious looks people had begun to give him in the street. He didn't hear the odd, stifled snigger in acquaintances, or see how an embarrassed, fastidious look would appear on the faces of certain friends whenever he spoke about his wife.

One evening he took Tziga out drinking, to shake him out of his misery. At six in the morning, Chorley and Tziga decided to go quietly — or as quietly as a couple of scuffling, giggling drunks can — through the stage door of the Rainbow Opera. They had decided to wait for Grace in one of the galleries (this was before they owned private suites). They'd carry her off for breakfast. They'd go to a café and eat a pile of potato cakes and sour cream, just like they used to. 'She must want a change of scene,' Chorley said. 'She spends half her life in this place — or the Other.'

Chorley and Tziga stumbled up the back stairs to the first-floor gallery. The Opera was silent. The men of the fire watch, who were sitting one level above and opposite, leant out to gesture, fingers across their lips. Chorley mirrored the gesture. He put a finger to his lips and shushed Tziga. Then he tiptoed to the balustrade and looked over.

Chorley Tiebold saw that his wife was asleep in the Opera's dais bed and that there were two strangers lying on either side of her.

The Dream Regulatory Body was set up under a piece of legislation known as the Intangible Resources Act. The Body came into existence six weeks after Chorley Tiebold's discovery and, in a way, owed its existence to him. For Chorley had caused a scene, he and the fire watch had come to blows and some furniture was broken. Grace, hearing her husband's drunken bluster, flung herself and everyone else out of sleep. Several hundred people woke up abruptly, before the happy conclusion of their dream. It was, one man later told his cronies, like being thrown into an icy pond while in the act of love. Behind the Rainbow Opera's padded doors people surfaced shouting, gasping and gagging.

There were complaints to the Rainbow Opera, of course. Some patrons demanded the return of their ticket price. Others cancelled their season tickets. The police considered charging Grace Tiebold with criminal negligence. But no current law quite covered what went on in dream palaces.

The newspapers reported the incident, then refused to let the matter drop. For ten years fastidious fear, suspicion and disapproval had been brewing about dreamhunters and their performances. Even when dreams were only a therapy, even when Tziga Hame was the only one able to broadcast a dream wider than a room, there were people who said that dreams were wicked seductions, that dreamhunters interfered with people's souls and that the Place was alien and unhallowed. The public was ready for a moral panic, and the newspapers whipped up the public's fears.

The President called a special meeting of Congress. This was the meeting at which the young Deputy Secretary of the Interior, after making a number of alert and thoughtful remarks, was appointed head of a commission of inquiry.

Over several months the commission called its witnesses, asked its questions and discussed the testimonies. The commission gave its report and its head, Cas Doran, wrote a draft Bill based on its findings. Doran's Intangible Resources Bill proposed that a body be set up: to regulate traffic In and out of the Place, to police the Place and its bordering countryside, and to act as a licensing body for dream parlours and palaces — deciding where they could be set up, and how they would be run. 'The Place is not a mirage that will disappear,' Doran wrote in the commission's report. 'It is a valuable resource belonging to our nation and, as such, it cannot be an ungoverned frontier.'

When the Act was passed, and the Dream Regulatory Body set up, and its regulations written, almost everyone was satisfied.

Chorley Tiebold was not. He complained to his wife that nowhere in the regulations did it say that a dreamhunter wasn't allowed to sleep in the same bed as any amplifiers she used. The legislation got its start in public concern about public morals. Where was that reflected? All the government seemed to care about was that they got *control*.

Chorley Tiebold stood on the beach, watching the dead shag floating a foot under the calm surface of the morning sea, slowly drawing away in the ebb tide. Chorley was thinking about the life of a dreamhunter. Not 'the beauty of it', as his wife had said to him about Tziga all those years before, but its dangers. His daughter and niece might congratulate themselves on having lived in a liberal, adventurous household, but really they'd led sheltered lives.

Chorley had led a sheltered life too — and was very grateful for it. He wanted to see the girls grow up surrounded by pleasant, civilised people. Grace, in her fantasies about Rose's future, couldn't seem to see past that magical moment on the border, at a Try, where one child in a hundred walks out of the world everyone can see. Dreamhunting had brought Grace everything — fame, wealth, pride in her work. But the girls already had everything they could ever need. They were well off, and well informed and confident. They didn't need a job that would see them limping home haunted and hollow-eyed, as Tziga often did. *Increasingly often.* If the girls went into the Place they would be going where Chorley couldn't walk after them, couldn't look for them if they got lost. And he was the parent who'd *done* those things, who'd rounded them up at dusk from the safe little park a few streets from their house in Founderston, who'd called them in from the beach below Summerfort. He was the one who was always there at bedtime. Chorley didn't want his daughter and niece to Try — especially not Laura, who was small for her age, and always had at least one serious cough every winter.

He didn't want it, he'd argued against it, but he hadn't stood a chance against everyone else's wishes. For a while it had seemed as though Tziga was in two minds about his daughter's Try, but now he was in just as much of a hurry as everyone else.

Chorley lost sight of the dead bird. The sea dazzled him. He trudged back up the beach to Summerfort, where he stood listening in the lower hall. There was no noise from upstairs; the girls had fallen asleep.

Seven

The ranger thought he was finally safe, with the balding earth and pale, trampled vegetation of the border before him. But he still jogged on, his feet dragging and sweat dripping past his belt. He was gasping for breath, and making a lot of noise, but when *it* came, he still heard it. He heard the whisper of his mineral pursuer.

The ranger put on a burst of speed. The nightmare that was chasing him must belong to the Place, he reasoned. Once he was across the border the monster would vanish.

He felt the creature's heavy, semi-solid hand drop upon his shoulder. He let out a raw scream.

The hand solidified enough to grip, and jerk the ranger about. He faced the creature, its dry, lumpish face and the horrible swarming attention in its holes-for-eyes. The ranger felt the creature fumbling at him, and imagined that it was searching him. As he tried to tear the creature's hands from him, the ranger's own hand found the remnant of his letter of instruction. He took the paper and stuffed it in his own mouth and began to chew. At the same time he threw his weight backwards, and hauled himself away towards the border.

The sandman's muddy, fused-together fingers separated. He poked two into the ranger's mouth.

The ranger tried to swallow the letter and began to choke. He and the sandman rocked back and forth, fighting, but moving ever nearer to the border.

The ranger bit down on the fingers. His mouth filled with loose sand. Sand packed down the partly chewed letter.

The sandman released the ranger, who saw the monster's bitten fingers reform, grow from a trickle of sand running like veins down the surface of its arm. He saw the fingers lengthen, till the hand was whole.

The creature was holding a fragment of the letter.

The ranger saw all this before he staggered, gagging, through the border, into the heat and colour and noise of the world.

The noise was that of running horses, and iron-rimmed wheels rolling on sun-baked earth.

The ranger turned towards the sound, and threw up his arms to ward off what instantly overwhelmed him — the Sisters Beach stagecoach, which had come, at full tilt, around a bend in the road above the village of Tricksie Bend.

Eight

The day after their camp-out, at around four in the afternoon, Laura and Rose were on the infants' beach. For the last few weeks of that summer the cousins had made a daily visit to this sheltered spot. There was a lifeguard they liked to look at. The girls tried not to be conspicuous in their admiration, so would park themselves at the edge of the ranks of for-hire sunbeds. The beds were usually empty at that hour — the infants and their minders having packed up and gone home. The sun was well past its zenith and the sun umbrellas cast their streaks of shade along the sand behind each slatted bed.

That day the handsome lifeguard wasn't at his station, but was prowling up and down before the shallows in the shelter of the breakwater. Rose and Laura ambled as near to him as they dared, finally settling down partly concealed behind a sunbed.

The bed they chose was occupied, but Rose and Laura were looking elsewhere, and scarcely noticed its occupant. He was quiet, reading. But, as the sun settled towards the horizon, and the shade of his umbrella thinned and swooped eastward, the girls moved to stay in its shadow.

Eventually, they were lounging on the sand to one side of the bed.

Rose craned and squinted. She shuffled a little closer to the sunbed. Then she said, 'We have that book in school.' She turned to Laura. 'Well, next year we do. It's Dr King's *A History of Southland*.'

Laura peered at the book. People usually read magazines on the beach, or didn't read, but draped their faces with them.

Rose said, 'He's up to chapter sixteen, "Tziga's Fall".'

The occupant of the sunbed grunted. He sat up, swung his feet down on to the sand and looked at Rose. He looked to be a few years older than the cousins. He was already sporting a small, experimental moustache, a thin strip of brassy whiskers, a shade darker than his hair. He was fair skinned and freckled — and very pink.

Laura said to him, 'You're getting a sunburn.'

'I'd say, judging by your colour, that you are a little more practised at beach holidays than I am. This is my *first*, and I'm making the most of it. I hired this sunbed for the afternoon, and I'll not leave it till the afternoon is over.'

'I can never read on the beach,' Laura said.

'I'm not at leisure to choose when I do my reading,' said the boy.

'Won't you at least take my towel?' Laura said. She rolled off it and held it out to him.

'That's hardly necessary,' he said.

Rose said, 'You could get off your sunbed and drag it into your shade. Your shade is oozing away from you — it doesn't seem to understand that it's been hired for the whole afternoon.' She asked him where he was staying.

'My uncle has an apartment in Bayview.'

'Oh!' Rose said. 'Someone was killed there last year! A pot plant fell from the terrace on the sixth floor and killed a man on a first-floor balcony. It was dreadful!' Rose mused for a bit. 'But they did manage to re-pot the geranium,' she said.

The boy stared at Rose, baffled and sceptical at once. 'What are you girls doing on the infants' beach?'

Rose tossed her head. 'I am the mother of one of those infants, naturally,' she said.

'Only *one*?'

Laura asked, 'What are *you* doing on the infants' beach? Can't you swim?'

'I thought I'd get some peace and quiet — get away from youths stuffing sand down one another's fronts. All those splashing, dunking, shrieking, *sidling*, *flirting* nuisances.'

'Laura and I are only interested in what you're reading,' said Rose.

'Really?'

Laura said to her cousin, 'He's here to Try. He's doing research.' Then she asked the boy, 'Are you Trying at Tricksie Bend?'

The official Tries took place at two locations. One was at the village of Doorhandle, an hour and a half by coach from Founderston. The Try at Doorhandle took place on a strip of land cleared from the forest a mile out of the village. The clearing followed the border for a short way before letting it go in the thick woods that — with patrolling rangers — helped to guard it. The second location was some fifteen miles away, across Rifleman Pass, on the Place's seaward border. There the candidates Tried in a meadow that sloped up to a bluff above the river at Tricksie Bend.

'No,' said the boy, 'I'm going back to Founderston tonight and I'm Trying at Doorhandle.'

'Uh-huh,' said Laura. Then she asked him, 'Do you have that book in your school?' She wanted to establish how old he was, and where he went to school.

'We *had* this book at my school.'

Laura and Rose exchanged a look — he was perhaps more a young man than an oversized boy. 'What school?' Rose asked. Founderston Girls' Academy's annual ball was attended by the seniors of several boys' schools and military academies. Rose was trying to place him on her social map.

'A school in a town south of The Corridor.'

The Corridor was a wide valley that cut through the mountains which divided their country. The south was all plains and grain, vineyards, small towns, pasture and cattle. The north had the capital, Founderston; the nation's next largest city, Westport, with its mines and industries; forested mountains; and beautiful Coal Bay. The north also had the Place.

Rose said, 'What does Dr King have to say about Tziga's fall?'

The boy leant his forearms on his knees and opened the book. 'He seems to be saying that it was no accident. And I keep feeling sorry for Hame's sister, Marta. She's "just folks" in this story. Everyone else is special and involved.'

'Yes, poor her,' Laura said, of her Aunt Marta. She was fond of Marta, whom she never saw often enough. It was Laura's impression that her father didn't invite his sister over because she and Chorley didn't see eye to eye. Marta was very religious, and Chorley, a firm atheist, was rude about her beliefs. He wasn't rude to her face, but Aunt Marta seemed to be able to tell that Chorley said things behind her back.

Rose wriggled a little closer to the boy, put her finger on the corner of the book and pushed it down so she could see it. Laura hoped Rose wasn't going to do her show-off's upside-down reading. Rose could read upside-down in mirrors too. 'So,' said Rose, 'you live in the south, but I suppose you've shared dreams.'

'One or two. My uncle is a dreamhunter.'

'Which one? Is he famous?'

'George Mason. He usually only works in hospitals. Pike Street, and St Thomas Lung Hospital.'

'Well — that's good,' said Rose, in the tone of someone thinking of something nice to say.

'I think we might have King's history at home, in the library,' Laura said.

'You have a library so large that you're not sure what's in it?' For some reason the boy seemed to find the idea of a large library offensive. Or perhaps it was only the idea of a large library largely unread by girls who had access to it.

Laura could see that Rose would strike back at the boy's remark; she had sparks of white in her blue eyes. 'Actually we have *two* libraries too large to know what's in them. One here, and one in Founderston.'

Laura said, '*Rose!*'

'Rose,' said the boy. He said it as if he had a pen and was writing it down.

'My cousin has had too much *afternoon* this afternoon,' Laura said.

Rose said, 'We can look for the King if you'd like, Laura — and check his history against the facts. You know, I don't think I've ever *read* about dreamhunting.'

When Laura and Rose were four they had been told what Laura's father and Rose's mother did for a living. That simple explanation went something like this: 'Laura, your father and, Rosie, your mother go to the Place to catch dreams. Other people pay to go to sleep with them and share their dreams in hospitals and dream palaces.' The little girls had accepted this explanation because they were very happy with the arrangement. Laura's Da and Rosie's Ma were only sometimes at home in the evening, and so Laura could climb into bed with her Ma, and Rosie with her Da. There was room in each adult bed for *two* girls, if that's what they felt like. But, for Laura, who had this lovely privilege explained to her only a few months before her mother fell ill with the cancer that killed her, her knowledge about what her father and aunt did for a living became connected in her mind with the terrible changes that came later. She had questioned how things worked in her world, and then things changed for the worse. Laura was careful about asking questions after that. She kept looking at her life, her family — her *happiness* — only out of the corner of one eye.

The boy's jaw had dropped. He was staring at the cousins as though they'd grown horns. After a moment he collected himself, and glared. 'You're a Tiebold,' he said to Rose. 'You're Grace Tiebold's daughter, aren't you?' Then he turned, with a different expression, to Laura, 'So you must be . . .'

'Gosh, it's nice to be famous,' said Rose.

'Honestly, you girls are just playing with me, aren't you?' said the boy. 'Saying "What does the book say?" as though you really are infants. Big joke on the country boy, right?'

Rose tilted her nose in the air. 'No,' she said, 'my motives are completely pure. I only wanted to pilfer your bought-and-paid-for shade.'

He stood, shut the book with a snap and picked up his towel from the sunbed. He stepped through the cousins and began to walk away.

'Hey!' Laura called. 'Good luck!'

He spun back. 'I suppose you expect me to wish you good luck too? But *you* don't need luck. After all, like everything else, I'm sure it's not what you know but *who* you know.'

'No, it's who you *are*,' Laura said, plainly.

He turned away and stalked off.

'That was interesting,' said Rose, looking after him. 'If we say who we are we're boasting, and if we don't we're sneaky.' Then she said, brightly, 'Let's go for another swim.'

Half an hour later a wind got up on the beach. It bowled sun umbrellas, flipped picnic rugs and made the wide brims of fashionable sun hats take on unfashionable shapes. Everyone began to abandon the shoreline.

The cousins were very quick to pick themselves up off the prints their wet bodies had made on their hired towels, and sprint up the steps to the Strand. Because Laura and Rose spent three months of every year at the beach they knew that when a westerly set in around five it was bound to blow until the early hours of the following morning.

The girls hurried across the Strand to the corner of Main Street. They tumbled through the glass and brass doors of Farry's, the confectioner, and stood shaking sand from their knitted swimsuits and printed cotton kimonos. Rose, seeing her favourite table emptying, made a dash for it. She came around from one side as the previous occupant was leaving by the other. Rose slid into the warmed iron chair and the woman who had just left it looked back at her, rather startled. Rose didn't notice. She was issuing orders to the countermen: 'I want my usual — chocolate and ginger ice-cream with candied apple and cream.' She repeated her order to the waiter who'd come over to clear the table. Then, as he made space, transferring plates from the marble tabletop on to his tray, she stretched her tan, salt-silvered arms out of the sleeves of her kimono and laid them on the table. She said, 'Do you think my skin looks dry?' She pinched the taut flesh on her sharp elbow joint.

'If you like, Miss Tiebold, I can give you a bit of butter to rub on your elbows.'

'I asked for your opinion, not for assistance,' said Rose.

The waiter said, 'Ah.' Then, 'I'm sorry to have to admit that my experience of female elbows is rather limited.'

Rose dismissed him with a wave of her hand.

Laura was up at the counter, choosing a cake.

Farry's had two curved counters at the back of its round room. Behind the glass front of one, sweets were displayed — marzipan in the shape and flavour of every fruit, and filled chocolates, bitter dark chocolate, milk chocolate and white. There were glistening fruit jellies, and thick slabs of marshmallow dusted with sugar. There were caramels, and fudges, peanut brittle, sugared almonds, sherbet in paper envelopes with liquorice straws, and hokey-pokey stacked high like gold bars in a treasury. The shop smelt of sugar and fresh cream. Behind the glass of the other counter, glittering beneath the light of electric bulbs, were huge slabs of ice and, nestled between them, steel tubs of Farry's famous ice-cream.

Laura saw that an assistant was waiting for her order. She was having trouble making up her mind. She felt vague, stupefied by sun, weak and watery from swimming. She told the man she'd have the same as her cousin.

'Again,' said the man.

This was a little rude, but the girls had practically lived at Farry's every summer of their lives and, Laura supposed, the staff were entitled to remark on their habits. 'Again' was true. Laura was in the habit of following Rose, of letting Rose make arrangements, shape their days, choose their food. The man was telling Laura off. Teachers would do the same. They'd say, 'Laura Hame, if you don't come up with your own topic we're just going to have to separate the two of you.' Or they'd say, 'Miss Hame, could you please show a little more initiative?'

It was easy for Laura to follow Rose. Rose always made headway, whichever way the wind was blowing. And following Rose left Laura free to watch what was going on around her.

As Laura walked back to the best table in Farry's big bay window, she looked about, her mind floating, unburdened by decisions. She saw a woman come in the front door shepherding a wind-tossed flurry of girls — of three different sizes, but in the same white flounced dresses, their straw hats clapped flat to their heads by their lace-gloved hands. Laura saw the matron take in Rose, slouching in her chair at the front table. Laura saw the woman assess Rose point by point: Rose's damp kimono, her gold hair clumped in salt-dulled rat-tails. She clicked her tongue against her palate, went 'tich' like an angry thrush. Then Laura looked past the woman and saw, through the window, across the road, the manager of the stagecoach posted out on the pavement, looking at his watch, then up Main Street towards the rise to Rifleman Pass.

Laura glanced over her shoulder at the clock above the door to Farry's kitchens. She saw that the coach was already more than half an hour late.

Half an hour, in a four-hour journey.

'Look,' said Laura to Rose, pointing at the clock, then the anxious manager.

The waiter returned. He carried a tray with a plate of ice-cream and pink curls of candied apple. He put the tray down on the table, shook napkins open and dropped them on to the girls' laps. The girls leant back to let the linen settle.

Rose dug into her ice-cream, then immediately began to talk around her spoon. 'Perhaps it's broken an axle,' she said.

'I don't think so.'

'You're a ghoul, Laura.'

'I'm the ghoul? It'd be pretty gruesome to break an axle above the bluffs in Rifleman Pass.'

Rose shrugged. She said she was going to get a conversation cake too. 'Do you want one?' She jumped up, dodged the matron's table and the waiter carrying the matron's tea, and ducked under the brass rail before the cake display case. She draped herself on its glass. She gave a moaning sigh, pressed one pink cheek against its condensation-covered surface.

'Miss Tiebold,' said the assistant.

'Two conversation cakes. With cream and lemon curd.'

'Certainly. Will that be all?'

'And a pitcher of mint tea.'

Rose brushed the glass with her nose, leaving a smear. She came back to the table. She didn't say thank you.

The matron's daughters were all managing to sit straight in their chairs and eat with their cake forks. They were a contrast to the cousins, who sat in Farry's prime spot and were clearly visible from the street, dusted with crumbs of baked egg white, licking their fingers and staring fixedly, rudely, at the people waiting at the stagecoach stop.

Laura said, 'It's nearly *an hour* late.'

'Come to think of it,' Rose said, 'you haven't even *seen* the bluffs at Rifleman.'

'Your Da took us up to the trig station near there. Remember? It was one of his educational outings. The trig was right on the border to the Place.'

'Did *your* Da know about this?'

'Uncle Chorley lied about it. He said we'd stopped at Tricksie Bend.'

'I remember *that*. We bought honeycomb.'

The three girls at the next table had removed their gloves to eat. Between each bite they dabbed at their lips with Farry's white linen napkins. They were so ladylike, so poised and mild that they only raised their heads when Laura and Rose suddenly dropped their teacups into their saucers and jumped up, shoving their chairs back so hard that one fell over with a clang.

The stagecoach had appeared behind other traffic on the long avenue of Main Street. Its driver was standing up in his seat, his whip flicking and biting above the backs of his horses. The stagecoach sounded its horn, then kept sounding as it made its way through Sisters Beach's shallow settlement to the stage post. The stagecoach pulled up — a noisy emergency.

The cousins rushed out of Farry's and across the road. Rose's kimono billowed open in the wind — its cord detached itself and, unnoticed by her, went away leeward, travelling along the pavement like a thin, side-winding serpent.

The girls plunged into the little crowd and pushed to its front in time to see the stage doors open and passengers spill out.

A man and woman were clasping each other. She had a handkerchief stuffed into her mouth. Rose leant back on the jostling crowd. She called out, 'Driver! Have you lost someone?'

The driver and passengers all looked at her.

It did happen that, every so often, an adult might vanish by the cairn that marked the border on the road beyond Doorhandle — might melt from the coach. It would turn out that this person hadn't, for whatever reason, chosen to Try at fifteen. Hadn't attempted before to pass across into the Place.

Rose called out her question, and the crowd hushed. People looked from the stage post manager to the driver, to the girl in a kimono and bathing suit. 'Because —' continued Rose, managing and informative, '— you should go straight to the telegraph office at the station and send a wire to Doorhandle.'

Most of those who fell were missed right away and, when they emerged, were recovered. Some, disorientated, wandered in the wrong direction, deeper In. Rangers were dispatched to find them.

'Have someone send a ranger,' Rose said. She gestured at them to hurry.

The driver lifted his hand, the hand with the horsewhip gathered in it. He pointed with his whip, showing something to his employer, the bossy girl in beachwear and the gathered crowd.

Laura saw what was fastened to the roof rack among the luggage on the top of the coach. A long, limp, blanket-wrapped bundle.

She backed out of the crowd.

Uncle Chorley's cream and chrome motor car had pulled up by Farry's. Laura's uncle was at the confectioner's door, his hands cupped by his eyes and his face pressed to the glass as he tried to see inside. He peered, then took a step back and opened the door for the matron and her daughters. They nodded their thanks, then clapped their hands on to their hats and turned into the wind coming up from the beach. The sand lying on the road rose to make a sparkling golden stream at knee height, in which the woman and girls seemed to be paddling.

Chorley caught sight of Laura and waved.

She ran across the road to him.

'I've been looking for you, Laura.'

Laura interrupted him. 'There's been an accident. Someone is dead.' She pointed at the crowd around the coach. 'Rose wanted to help,' she said, as her uncle opened the car door and handed her into its back seat. 'She wanted to take charge,' Laura added, currying favour — she knew that Rose's father was sometimes irritated by what he called 'Rose's prefect manner'.

Laura watched her uncle walk away from her across the road. She saw him stop on the edge of the crowd and crane across the people's heads.

The wind dropped and the sand settled. The girl heard Chorley asking questions. The crowd became quiet. The wind gusted again and sand rose in one place, in a humped wave. Laura watched as her uncle, the driver and the manager climbed on top of the coach to inspect what was tied there. They removed some of the wrappings. Chorley put his face down, close to the wrapped corpse. His hand went into the wrappings where Laura knew a head would be. He straightened, looked at something he held. He showed it to the manager, then they both climbed down. Several men from the crowd clambered up to help the driver unfasten the body and lower it to others on the ground, who carried it into the stage post.

Laura's uncle came back across the road, leading her cousin. Rose got in beside Laura. Her expression was sober, and she didn't say anything. Chorley released the brake and the car rolled away from the kerb. He raised his voice above the engine noise. 'Your father is back, Laura. But they've sent a special train for him.' He sounded sympathetic.

Laura put a hand to her throat — she felt breathless, as if the air in her lungs had set hard.

A special train meant that Laura's father had one of his rare, priceless dreams — a dream that was contracted to the government and would be commandeered for the public good. He would be performing it for as long as it lasted — a week to ten days. The girls had once asked Rose's mother — who was always more open about her profession and its mysteries — where exactly Laura's father took these dreams.

'Insane asylums and the like,' Grace had said.

In the car, on their way to the railway station, Laura said to her uncle, 'But Dad has to be *here* a week from today. He *promised*.'

'The Body has him under contract — and that's a promise too,' Chorley said, patiently explaining what Laura already understood. 'Sorry, darling,' he added.

'Why didn't he avoid getting a dream they'd want? He knows where his dreams are!'

'I don't know what he was thinking,' Chorley said.

'He can't make it to my Try!' Laura wailed.

Laura's uncle didn't say anything, but she saw him clench his jaw.

Rose looked at Laura and blushed, then bit her lip. Laura turned away from her cousin. She didn't want to see Rose concerned for her, Rose excited by concern, alive with it.

The Strand was almost deserted. A few people walked, tilting forward or backward, against the wind. The waves were still small, but tipped white. There were flags flying on the twin turrets of the resort's dream palace — The Beholder — long green pennants, Grace Tiebold's sign.

'Mother's back too!' Rose said. Her mother had gone In three days before.

'She's dreaming tonight,' said Chorley.

Rose squeezed Laura's arm. 'That's something to look forward to, at least.'

Nine

The stretch of the platform that was under cover from the sun was crowded with passengers, all keeping an eye on the luggage trolley, the smoking porters and their train, which sat in a siding five hundred yards up the line, breathing wisps of steam. The Sisters Beach Express was waiting for the special train to leave so that it could pull into the station.

The special train was up at the far end of the platform. Only one or two brazen travellers had wandered up to have a look at it. The special train had only two carriages — a luxury coach and a guard's van. Its engine was new, bull-nosed, and black. The train flew red flags, two on the engine and two on the guard's van — danger signals.

A group of officials waited by the train. They all wore dark suits and city hats. Several were mountainous, broad-shouldered bodyguards in the guise of civil servants. Also attending on the train was a famous and flamboyant physician from Sisters Beach. Doctor Wilmot was resplendent in grey pinstripes and a gold cravat. He was playing with a monocle; it flashed as he twirled it.

Grace and Tziga had come straight from the Place and were dressed in linen shirts and trousers, leather jackets and supple leather lace-up boots. Grace Tiebold wore a dustcoat over her clothes, and Tziga Hame had bandaged hands. He carried a handkerchief with which he sometimes dabbed at his mouth.

The special train had a full head of steam. Steam escaped from all its engine's valves, wrapping the black iron in a tissue of white vapour.

The passengers waiting for the delayed Sisters Beach Express saw Chorley Tiebold's car pull up, the two girls jump out of its back seat and sprint along the platform past them. Chorley hurried too, but was less headlong.

Long-legged Rose was the first to reach Tziga. She clasped him around his chest and leant close to issue a warning: 'Laura's mad with you!' Then she let go and drew back and noticed how he held his hands clear, so that his blood-spotted bandages wouldn't foul her clothes. She saw his hollow eyes and scabbed lips. Then Laura barged in and Rose stumbled back, too surprised to stand her ground.

'Goodbye, Rose,' Tziga said. 'Good luck.'

Laura had begun to talk, low and accusing. Her father didn't meet her eyes, but took her arm and walked her along the platform away from the others.

Laura let her father lead her away. She knew that she would cry. She collected her thoughts and tried to tell him how she felt. She said, 'You've always talked as though you'd be there for my Try. I expect you there. You should understand that, Da. Don't you know that all my life people have looked at me as if they imagine they can see something in the air around me? Dreams. It might be *you* they are thinking of, but it's *me* they're staring at. *Hame*, those looks say, like someone sighing when they're in love. How do you think that's made me feel?'

Laura stopped walking: she dug her heels into the platform's rust-browned bitumen and her arm slipped through her father's hand. He gave a sharp cry and snatched the bandaged mitt of his hand back against his chest. He hunched over, cradling it.

Laura wiped her eyes and looked at him. She saw his torn lips, and the red seepage on the white linen. She forgot the rest of what she'd meant to say. She said, 'What happened to your hands?'

'I bit them,' he said. He straightened and gathered her in an arm and hustled her along the platform again. This time Laura took in the movement he had suppressed, a glance back at the officials by the waiting train.

'I'm afraid,' Laura said.

Her father didn't look at her, but he said, 'What are you afraid of?' He was brusque, sounding not so much impatient but as if his question were a formal challenge. Laura's father's tone did not say that there was nothing to be afraid of, but that he didn't have any time for her fear.

'When you come back, it'll all be over. That's what I'm afraid of,' Laura said. 'It'll be decided.' She shouldn't have to explain — he should know. 'My whole life will be decided.'

He had walked her to where the platform began to slope down to the trackbed. He stopped, and Laura, looking for an expression of understanding and sympathy, saw instead a look of desperation cross his face. Beyond them the silver railway lines, siding and waiting express all shimmered in the hazy middle distance.

Laura said to her father, 'You should have told those people "no"!' She pointed back at the officials and the special train, keeping her eyes on her father's face. She was crying now. He should at least say sorry. At least dry her tears. 'Rose will go there,' Laura sobbed. At last she let it show — all those weeks and months of being slowly crushed by Rose's confidence. Rose was her mother, Grace, all over again — fearless and full of appetite. Rose had hung at the front of the crowd that day to look at the corpse, while Laura flinched and fell back.

Laura cried, 'Rose will go and I won't!'

Her father sighed. 'Don't be so soft-headed,' he said.

'It's how I feel!' Laura said. She heard herself, her aggrieved whining.

'As if confidence can affect the outcome,' her father said — cold and impatient. Then, 'Laura.'

His voice had acquired some warmth and urgency, so she looked at him. He was frowning back along the platform. There was a figure apparently wading towards them through the fluid of heat haze, one of the black-clad officials, his hand on his hat, head down into the wind.

Laura's father grabbed her arms and leant down to look into her face. Laura could feel the bandages and his fingers beneath them, held stiff so that his palms took the pressure of his grip and not his injured digits. He said, 'Do you remember any of the songs I taught you?'

Laura was so surprised by this question that she didn't answer.

Her father gave her a little shake. 'The old family songs. I sang them to you night after night when you were small.'

'The bedtime songs?' Laura said. '"The Hame inheritance"?' She was unimpressed.

'Do — you — remember — them?' her father demanded, separating each word.

He was frightening her. Only the fact she was frightened stopped her from breaking away and shouting at him, 'What is all this!' She did manage to mutter, sullen, 'Why should I bother to remember any old songs when you aren't going to take the trouble to be there for my Try?'

Her father's eyes were wide, his face so pale that Laura could see, very clearly, that the wounds on his lips were crenellations, the marks of teeth, his own upper incisors having bruised and broken the skin on his lower lip. And she saw that his teeth were streaked with blood, as though he'd further wounds inside his mouth.

He shook her again. 'The songs,' he said.

'"Button Thread", "A Stitch in Time". The *baby* songs. Yes!' Laura shouted at him. She'd heard her aunt calling, far away at the other end of the platform. Aunt Grace yelled, 'Tziga! It's time to go!'

Laura's father's grip loosened. He whispered, '"Of His Name".' It was the title of a song.

'Yes,' Laura sobbed. 'That nonsense.'

'Noun sense,' said her father. Laura felt his wadded hands on her hair, the sticky edges of the bandages catching at her curls. Her father asked her if she could just say the words for him.

'The words of ?'

'"Of His Name".' Tziga Hame glanced again at the hurrying figure of the official — the nearest one, and all the others coming hard on his heels, Uncle Chorley with them, his pale coat flying. 'Quickly,' Tziga said. 'Please, Laura.'

She couldn't sing, her voice was too choked. She recited it, the nonsense nursery song.

> The final measure is his Name.
> Four letters, and four laws.
> The first gives life, the last speech,
> though they are the same.
> Two letters remain within,
> death and freedom.
> Make his name his Own and he is.
> If your Will departs he will.

Laura's father released her. She stood, her eyes squeezed shut, weeping. She could hear the running feet, the hard shoes of the first official, and a scattering of footfalls following him. She didn't open her eyes. She didn't know if her father was still standing near her or not. But then he said, from a short way off, 'Those are capitals. Name. Own. Will.' Then, 'Name,' he said again. 'Remember that.'

'Mr Hame,' said the official. He sounded breathless.

Laura heard her father say, 'I've been trying to explain how little time I have.' He addressed this remark to the official but seemed still to be speaking only to her. Then Chorley arrived and wrapped his arms around her. Laura smelt the bergamot in his hair oil. It was a smell that always made her happy. She opened her eyes and looked over her uncle's shoulder at her father, who was standing beside the official, looking shabby, rumpled and small.

'For heaven's sake, Tziga! Is it really necessary to browbeat the child?' Chorley said.

Laura's father said that Doctor Wilmot had given him a shot so that he'd stay awake throughout the journey. 'I'm over-medicated, I think,' he said.

'He won't be here for my Try!' Laura said, aggrieved, to everyone but her father.

'I know, honey,' Chorley said. 'But your Aunt Grace will take care of you.'

'Mr Hame,' the official said again. He had a grip on Tziga Hame's arm. Laura's father turned away with the official and began back down the platform. Chorley put his arm around Laura and they followed, walked up to the others, Laura's Aunt Grace and Rose. They went along together, all of them touching Laura, while her father walked ahead. Laura noticed the moment the official collected himself enough to release her father's arm.

They reached the special train's private car. Inside it a maid was lowering the silk blinds against the glare of the low sun. Laura could see tables, white linen, silver, a steaming tea urn.

'Tziga,' Chorley said, 'where's my camera?'

'I had to leave it,' Tziga said.

Chorley flushed and compressed his lips.

'It won't be rained on, at least,' Tziga said. Then he held up his wounded hands, reminding his brother-in-law.

Chorley blinked. He seemed distressed. He glanced about him at all the men from the Regulatory Body and swore.

'Look, Grace,' Tziga said, 'Chorley's camera is at the stream with the blue clay bed. The cutting.'

'I know the place,' Grace said, to her husband. 'Don't worry — I'll drag some ranger along to carry it for me.' None of that country's pioneering film-makers had yet been able to build a camera light enough for a person Grace's size to carry with comfort.

It was Grace who first put a hand out to Tziga. She squeezed his arm. She said she'd mind Laura at the Try. Rose kissed his lapel — and shot him a stern, disappointed look on her cousin's behalf. 'Bloody government contracts,' she said, quite audible to the officials. 'I won't be signing any.'

'Our loss, I'm sure, Miss,' one of the officials said.

Tziga Hame opened his arms for his daughter.

She made him wait, nestled against her uncle, the ever present, constantly attentive and affectionate Chorley. Then she conceded and went to him. He pressed her into his shirt front and kissed her hair. Was he asking for forgiveness, or forgiving her? It was more than just a going-away embrace.

'So —' Laura said, 'when I see you next, it'll all be over.' She rubbed it in.

Her father whispered, 'I'm sorry.' He said, 'Goodbye, darling.' And then he let go and climbed the folding steps into the train. Dr Wilmot and two officials swung up behind him into the private coach. The rest went in the guard's van. The stationmaster blew his whistle and waved his flag and the engine shot out a blast of steam, then it drew slowly out of the station.

The delayed passengers saw, with relief, the special train pass the detained express and that train begin to shunt out of the siding. The porters wheeled their luggage trolleys up to the red line where the baggage car always came to a stop. More attendants appeared with linen for the sleeping car and foodstuffs for the dining car.

It had all been very interesting — especially those final moments when the men from the Dream Regulatory Body ran to retrieve Tziga Hame from the end of the platform. It had been interesting, but it was late and the passengers had a ten-hour journey ahead of them. Some were thinking 'Hurry up', others, though late, were content to go slowly, happy to see the smokestack of the special train recede up the line. 'Let it get well ahead of us,' they thought. 'Let us not catch it up in the two-mile tunnel. Not in the dark. Not with our heads down on starchy railway pillows. Not *asleep*.'

Whether impatient or prudent, whether thinking 'Hurry up' or 'Let it get ahead', the passengers were all looking up the line, measuring the distance between one train and the other. They all saw the dark girl, the Hame daughter, shrug off the adults who were comforting her. She slipped back through them. She was looking down at the tracks, or at something on the tracks. The girl jumped down on to the sleepers between the rails, then stooped and picked something up.

Her cousin shouted, 'Laura!'

Her uncle rushed to the edge of the platform.

The dreamhunter Grace Tiebold ran the other way, yelling, 'Stop the train!' and waving furiously at the driver, in his cab at the far end of the shunting express.

The driver hadn't seen the girl jump, but did see the woman waving. He put on his engine's brakes and sounded its whistle. The brakes caught and sparked as the engine slowed. The wheels locked, but the engine kept sliding, pulled on by the momentum of its freight.

Chorley Tiebold jumped down on to the tracks, picked up his niece and rolled her back on to the platform. He didn't have time to scramble up himself, so he threw himself across the rails and tumbled down the slope on the far side.

The train passed between him and his family, and finally came to a stop.

Chorley got up and tramped around the back of the halted train. The driver climbed down from his cab. The stationmaster dropped his flags and hurried up the platform. Some of the passengers followed.

Grace was shaking Laura, who knelt on the platform, hunched over something she had in her hands. 'Put it down!' Grace was saying. 'Are you mad?' She was furious.

Chorley clambered back on to the platform, restrained his wife and got his niece to her feet. He moved her away from the converging driver and stationmaster and flung out an arm to ward them off. Then he gathered Rose to him too and strode away towards his car.

Grace faced the stationmaster and, before he could speak, said, 'Just name your amount, your fine for Laura's stunt. Go on, give me a figure.' She gripped the stationmaster with one brown hand, and put her other hand into her dustcoat and produced a wallet.

The stationmaster blustered, 'You think it's enough to offer me money? This is a serious incident. That child needs a good talking to, at the very least!'

Indeed, the child, the curious onlookers thought. What had she seen? Some dropped treasure, or injured animal? They imagined the extravagant childishness of a spoilt rich girl. They peered at her as her uncle hustled her past, pale and tear-stained. And some saw that what Laura Hame had in the fist curled to her chest was a large rust-stained rock. A rock from the trackbed.

Ten

When the special train pulled away from Sisters Beach station something very strange had happened to Laura.

She was walking along the platform with Rose, Grace and Chorley. She was dragging her feet, feeling defeated. Her father had gone, and she felt that he had *left* her. She felt abandoned, resentful, deeply anxious about her Try. And then — all at once — she felt all these things as a howling emptiness, like extreme hunger. Hunger without exhaustion. It was as though a gap opened within her, and yawned wide. For a moment Laura felt the emptiness of this open chasm, then something rushed to fill it. Something was suddenly *in* her — it felt like sorrow and need and power too.

Laura stumbled. Then she came to a stop and her family went on for a few paces without her. Laura looked over her shoulder, back along the line, through the haze at what she thought was the back of the receding special train. Then her gaze drifted down, and she found herself staring at the rocks between the bright rails. She looked at one in particular. It occurred to Laura that, if she picked up that rock, the thing that had rushed to fill the gap inside her, the weighty, cold, roaring thing, would jump out of her and into the rock. It was a mad thought, but it seemed true. True and urgent.

Laura jumped, and caught up the rock, and turned, meaning to fling it after the special train. She could see only the back of the guard's van — like a black door in the heat-distorted air. But, of course, what she really saw was the express bearing down on her. The rock stayed in her hand. *In fact*, it seemed to stick to her hand.

Then Chorley jumped down beside her. He lifted her up on to the platform, and Aunt Grace took her arm by the wrist and shook her hand hard, twice, to make her drop the rock. Grace was shouting at her, but Laura kept her fist clenched.

Then Uncle Chorley intervened, he put an arm around her and urged her to go with him. He and Rose had hurried her along the platform. They walked her out of her shoes. They seemed not to notice that she'd lost them. The soles of her feet were scorched by the hot pavement. Then she was back in Chorley's car. She was crying. She sat beside Rose, who put an arm around her and kept quiet — which must have cost some effort.

Laura felt that her family were thinking she'd behaved badly — but were sorry for her, and so wouldn't say anything about it, would let her forget it. Except Rose, of course. Rose, who held her with one firm, friendly arm, but vibrated with suppressed excitement.

Back at Summerfort the norwester was combing all the grass clippings missed by the gardener's rake out of the new-mown lawns, and was scattering them across the polished floors of downstairs rooms. Grace went around closing the doors. She sent Rose and Laura upstairs to bathe.

In the upstairs bathroom Laura climbed into the bath and turned on the taps. Tepid water splashed her feet. She pulled the chain that diverted water to the shower head and stood in the downpour. The water coaxed a saner self back into her body, so that when she got out and wrapped herself in a towel she began to wonder about the rock.

She went into her bedroom and found the rock where she'd put it, beside her jewellery box on the dresser. It was quarry stone, a lump of crushed granite. Its edges were still sharp, although its whole surface was softened by a velvet of accumulated dust, the iron rust that slowly salted from the rails, ground away by the wheels of trains. The rock had made a mark on Laura's dresser, as it had marked her palms. She stared at — a dirty stone.

Rose came to the door of the room. She stroked it with her knuckles. 'May I come in?'

Laura put the rock into her jewellery box and closed its lid. She carried a string of amber beads to her bed and put it down on the outfit her aunt had laid out — some of the extravagant sleepwear fashionable people wore to dream palaces.

Rose came in, kicked off her beaded slippers and sat on Laura's bed. 'So —' she said, 'we're on our own.' Rose said that the girls — Summerfort's two servants — had gone for the night. 'Ma is doing something with chopped egg and chives and bread.' (Dreamhunters ate sparingly before each performance of a dream, enough for comfort, but no more.) 'Dad's threading the projector. He's screening his film of the sand-sculpting competition. He finished it this morning when we were asleep,' Rose said, then asked, 'Shall I brush your hair?'

Laura dropped her towel and got into her pyjama trousers and jacket. Her pyjamas were pale yellow, her robe pale green with a broad band of dark pink around its hem and collar. Laura sat on the edge of the bed and let her cousin tame at least the surface of her bushy hair. Rose made noises of effort — and once or twice clicked her tongue, as the matron at Farry's had done.

After a moment Rose said, 'Have you still got that rock?'

'I put it in my jewellery box.'

'Is it like — a memento?' Rose was cautious.

'No.' Laura was happy for Rose to think that her feelings were Rose's business. She did want to be checked on and worried about. But she didn't know how to explain herself.

'Maybe "memento" is the wrong word, since a memento would be to remind you of a time you treasured,' Rose said. 'Just a reminder then. But, Laura, your Da let you down. He did. I'm really mad at him. *I* won't need reminding.'

'I was going to throw it at the train.'

'I see. But if you'd thought to throw your *shoe* instead you wouldn't have had to jump down in front of the express. I bet Ma and Da are worried that you meant to kill yourself.' Rose hurried on. '*I* know you wouldn't do that — but I'm still pretty puzzled by what you *did* mean to do.'

Laura turned around and stared at Rose. 'Why would anyone think I'd do something like that? Try to kill myself.'

'You jumped down in front of a train.'

'It was still a way off.'

'Laura, it was close, and you were dithering on the tracks.'

Laura gathered her hair out of Rose's hands. She began twisting it into a thick, crackling rope. 'I had to pick up the rock, because something was in me and when I saw the rock it occurred to me that, if I picked it up, the thing that was in me would go out of me and into the rock.'

'That's crazy,' Rose said — though not as if she disbelieved Laura. '*What* was in you? And why *that* rock and not the one next to it?'

'I think it could just as well have been the one next to it,' Laura said.

Rose asked whether she could see the rock and Laura pointed at the dresser and her jewellery box. Rose wriggled off the bed and took out the rock and gave it a serious inspection. She said, 'So — what do you think you put into it?'

'I don't know. Bad feelings. Disappointment. And I meant to *throw* it. But I got mixed up about how many minutes had passed. I thought the express was the special train still pulling away.' But, Laura thought, she hadn't thrown the rock. She couldn't release it. And, although she was angry, what had seemed to pour from her into the rock was more longing than anger. Longing for what she believed she deserved from her father — his undivided loyalty, and love in any measure she asked or needed.

Rose caught Laura's eye and gave the rock a little shake. 'So you want to keep this?'

Laura nodded. Rose put it back in the box, then came back to sprawl on Laura's bed. 'You know, you Hames have always been kind of peculiar about dirt and sand and stones. Uncle Tziga is always feeling the soil, as though he's a farmer planning to buy some land. You do that too. You love sandcastles, and do you remember all your little earthworks in the kitchen garden at

Founderston? "Mucky Laura" the cook used to say. There's a word for it — all that fiddling with dirt.'

'There's a word for people who *eat* dirt,' Laura volunteered.

The cousins gazed at each other, grimacing, and trying to remember what they'd learnt from a book they'd sneaked a look at. A girl had brought it to school. The girl's father was an asylum doctor. It was a book about mental aberrations. Rose turned pink then gave a shriek of laughter. 'I can only remember the sex disorders!'

They swapped a few words and definitions, and had a good giggle. Then Rose changed the subject. 'Did you get a look at the body tied to the top of the stagecoach? Did you hear what the men said?'

'I didn't manage to keep my place in the front. I didn't push hard enough.' Laura sounded prim, even to herself.

'Oh, blah,' Rose said, impatient. 'Please show some interest, Laura.'

'I'm listening,' said Laura.

'Being sullen doesn't suit you,' Rose said, annoyed.

'You sound like your mother,' Laura said, 'telling me to be "ladylike". No one ever says that to you! They think you won't need to be.' She lay down and began to cry. 'They think you'll succeed and I won't. I'll have to be "careful of my station in life", like the women in novels about women who make mistakes and end up miserable.'

'Laura,' Rose said. She stroked Laura's back. 'You've got it all wrong. They don't say those things to me, because I bite their heads off. Instead they do this thing of pretending to be brightly positive about me and all my habits. "Rose is a big, robust, forthright girl," they say, as if by describing me I'll start feeling properly selfconscious and pull my head in. It isn't anything to do with our Try and what they think of our chances. Your Da never tells you to be ladylike. Nor does mine. Your Da is too artistic, and my Da is a *real* gentleman and a lot less worried about being proper than poor nervous Ma and our teachers. Our teachers have had to think about being *respectable* to get on themselves. And Ma was *poor*. She's had to put up with all sorts of snubs since she got rich and married Da. Ma's worried about *both* of us, but only *you* ever listen to her when she gets on to how we should be ladylike.'

Laura had stopped crying to listen to Rose. She kept still and let Rose pet her. After a moment Rose said, 'I'm bursting to tell this story.'

Laura lay quiet. This was enough of an invitation to Rose. 'The dead man tied to the top of the Sisters Beach stage was a ranger. The driver said he staggered out of the Place — not in the safe spot beside the old telegraph pole, but in the middle of the road, right in front of his horses. The man was trampled and died on the spot. Or almost.

'When they picked him up he was still "making mouths", the driver said. And when the driver, stage post manager and Da climbed up on top of the stage and unwrapped the ranger, Da discovered that the man's mouth was full of sand — fine, silvery sand. And in the sand was a fragment of paper, with fragments of words written on it.'

Laura rolled over, sat up and swept her hair back from her face. 'That's what your Da was saying under his breath when he got into the car. Fragments of words.'

Rose nodded. 'I got a glimpse of the paper,' she said. 'The phrases were separated and stacked.'

Laura scrambled off the bed and found a notebook and pencil. She gave them to Rose.

Rose wrote. She then said, 'I'm pretty sure there was a gap between "as" and "D". And I think the D was a capital.'

They put their heads together and looked at what they had:

ours
as D
ecre

'The "as" is the end of one word, and the "D" is the start of another,' Rose said.

Laura said, 'Should we check this with Uncle Chorley to make sure we have it right?'

Rose shook her head. 'He was angry with me for being so nosy. Or bossy.' She wriggled her shoulders, shrugging off her father's disapproval. Then she slid off the bed and bounced up. 'That poor ranger,' she said, bringing the talk back to the dead man briefly, only to dismiss him.

'The border can be dangerous. It's like diving into a river when you can't see the bottom,' Laura said. 'He was only a few feet off the safe path, and unlucky in his timing.'

'The sand is a puzzle, though,' Rose said. 'How did it get in his mouth?' She rubbed her stomach. She was thinking about dinner. She gave her cousin a hand and hauled her up. 'Eggs and toast,' she said, and led Laura downstairs.

Chorley's film was less than ten minutes long. He'd filmed a sand-sculpting contest held six weeks earlier on the beach. Grace had been asked to judge it, and there was a lot of footage of her with the mayor and several other dignitaries, going about the entries and asking the competitors questions. Grace holding her sun hat and bent at the waist to speak to sand-caked children. Grace inspecting shell-studded ramparts. All in ghostly black and white — the small waves flickering in, soundless, and a little too fast.

Grace told Chorley he should put this footage together with his balloon flight and his film of whales stranded on the western shore of So Long Spit. He should hold another public screening.

Chorley had held a number of public screenings. His most recent hit was a film of a state funeral. People were grateful for the record — for film's power to capture a real event, and to repeat it infinitely.

'People like to see themselves,' Grace said. 'A newspaper can only report.'

'Miss Laura Hame and Miss Rose Tiebold, the niece and daughter of the competition's judge, whilst not eligible to enter the competition, were still able to join in the fun,' Rose said, imitating a newspaper's social events page.

On the screen a sandy Rose and Laura were sculpting sand with butter knives. Laura's father stood between them, his feet bare and his trouser legs rolled up. He was giving the girls advice. 'Miss Hame and Miss Tiebold's "reclining man" was admired by all the other competitors,' intoned Rose.

Chorley had caught the moment when Laura's knife slipped and the sandman's nose collapsed and crumbled down his cheek. The black-and-white Rose burst into silent giggles, Tziga Hame's hands flew up in mock horror. Black-and-white Laura paused, then smoothed the sandman's face with her knife, like someone spreading icing on a cake, till the mouth and eyes had gone too.

The film ran out, slipped off the end of the reel and spun flapping in the projector. The room filled with radiance from the screen.

Grace got up and opened the curtains on the dusk. She went out to make a pot of tea, and Chorley switched off the projector and packed his film away. He said it was a shame that he couldn't make a motor to crank the camera so that the speed of the film would always be even, and lifelike. Or at least, he hadn't yet been able to make a motor light enough or with a portable source of power. He'd shown his balloon film to the Government Surveyor, who was interested, but not in motors to crank a camera or batteries smaller than hatboxes. 'No,' Chorley said, 'this will continue to be a rich man's hobby until I travel to remote places and film horned whales and witchdoctors' ceremonies. That should get more people interested.'

Rose yawned to interrupt her father's complaining. 'Mother can catch horned whales, a dream of horned whales. Dreams have sound and sensations, colours and tastes. Films don't.'

'So you think films are only a novelty?' Chorley asked his daughter.

'No — but they're for recording *facts*. They can't do fiction, like dreams can.'

'Has anyone been able to establish that dreams are fiction rather than fact? They may all be true. They might be like a mirage — a strange image of a distant place, some spot in the world very like here. No one knows what they really are.'

Grace came back in with the tea.

Laura said, to her uncle, 'Is that the sort of thing people discuss when they write about dreamhunting in books?'

'What kind of thing?' said Grace.

'What dreams really are,' said her husband.

'Oh — that.'

Rose said, 'There was a boy on the infants' beach reading Dr King's *A History of Southland*.'

Chorley looked interested. 'Some kind of prodigy?'

'No, a boy around our own age,' said Rose. 'He's Trying.'

'If he was so trying why did you talk to him?' Chorley asked.

'Da!'

'The boy said his uncle is a dreamhunter named George Mason,' said Laura.

'Is this boy's uncle, this Mason, respectable?' Chorley said, to Grace.

'You're such a *father*,' Grace said. 'It's very sweet. Mason's perfectly respectable. He's a Soporif — the surgeons at Pike Street Hospital use him to enhance their anaesthetic. If you're in the same room with him when he drops off, he can knock you out.'

Chorley was shaking his head. 'You're all terrifying,' he said, 'you dreamhunters. You do know that, don't you?' And then, as if the action were somehow related to his remark, he took two extra sugar lumps for his tea.

In the half-hour between tea and her family's departure to the dream palace, Laura went into Summerfort's library. She found Dr King's book in the shelves devoted to encyclopaedias and Chorley's science journals. She took the book down, and curled up in a chair with her feet tucked under her.

Eleven

Excerpt from 'The Invisible Road', a chapter from Dr Michael King's *A History of Southland* (1904):

> It is difficult to convey to anyone beyond our shores the extraordinary influence of dreamhunting on the life and culture of Southland. Since the arrival of the first settlers nearly two hundred and fifty years ago much has been made of the tyranny of distance, the fifteen hundred sea miles between ourselves and our nearest neighbour, and five thousand between us and the great centres of civilisation. Ours is a productive but isolated country. Southland can export wool and leather, but not meat or milk; wine, but not fruit; grain and linen, steel, tools and machinery — but not dreams. Dreams are a highly perishable commodity and are yet to be sent offshore.
>
> Dreams are found in a territory in the north west of our country, a territory known simply as the Place. Certain facts about the Place have been hard to establish — for example, when did it first appear? Southland is a landmass without a native people, and so there are no songs or legends for us to consult. Has the Place always been there, its borders concealed in the rugged terrain of the forested Rifleman Ranges? Did it remain secluded because only a very few people were *able* to go there? For dreamhunters and rangers, those able to enter the Place, represent only a tiny proportion of the population — perhaps one in every five hundred people.
>
> We do know that Wry Valley, the fertile land between the Heliograph and Rifleman mountain ranges, was first settled in 1750. Sparsely settled, but I imagine that were the Place present there would be some record of it, if only of the occasional 'disappearance'. Timber has been cut in the Rifleman Ranges since first settlement. In the 1790s the

bullock trails used by foresters to haul timber linked up with the road from Founderston to the Wry Valley. And yet I have found no reports from that time of the kind of mysterious disappearances that would indicate that the Place was there.

By the middle of the nineteenth century Sisters Beach in Coal Bay had become a summer retreat for the wealthy. The Bay's visitors arrived mostly by sea, but the road from Founderston was improved, and in 1860 the Sisters Beach stagecoach made its first run from the capital. And still there were no disappearances. It wasn't until 1886 that the Place first made its presence felt — for that was when Tziga Hame vanished from the Sisters Beach stagecoach.

Tziga Hame, a seventeen-year-old violinist from Founderston, was making his first journey outside the capital. He and his elder sister Marta had been hired to play at the summer assemblies at Sisters Beach. The Coal Bay railway was, at that time, still only a plan on paper — a plan that had to undergo a radical alteration after the discovery of the Place. The young Hames chose to travel overland, so booked seats on the stagecoach.

It was early summer, 15 November, and the weather in the mountains was wet. Tziga Hame gave up his seat inside the coach for his sister's cello, which was particularly vulnerable to damp. Hame rode up on top of the stage, on the box seat at the back.

Halfway through its journey the stage made its usual stop in Wry Valley, at the village of Doorhandle. Marta Hame got out to stretch her legs. When she climbed back into the coach moments before it departed from Doorhandle, Marta Hame saw that her brother was in his place on the box. Yet, when the coach arrived at Sisters Beach four hours later, Tziga Hame was missing. Marta Hame, desperate with worry and sure that her brother had fallen, tried to raise a search party at the stage post. She was still making her arrangements when a summons came from Doorhandle for a surgeon. A farmer from that village had discovered the young man lying on the road.

Marta Hame travelled back to Doorhandle with the doctor, a holidaying Founderston physician, Dr Walter Chambers.

Tziga Hame had broken his left leg. It was a serious injury and a cause of grave concern to Dr Chambers. The doctor knocked Hame out with ether and set the leg as well as he was able. And, while Hame was unconscious, he had a dream. In fact, Tziga Hame repeated the dream he had first had when he fell from the back of the stage.

The road through Wry Valley had been wet and green, but the ground on which Hame landed when he fell wasn't even a proper road, he later said, only a track, a streak of bald earth showing through parched grass. Hame said that he fell because his seat suddenly 'wasn't there'. One moment he was on the box at the back of the coach, the next he was apparently sitting in the air, and the next he lay on the dry track with his thighbone shattered. 'At first I didn't understand that I was injured. But when I sat up and looked I saw a tear in the cloth of my trousers and the broken bone jutting blue against my skin,' he said. Hame fainted at the sight. He lost consciousness and had a dream.

All famous dreams have names. The dream that came to be known as Convalescent One can be found in a stable dream site directly across the border of the Place beyond the village of Doorhandle. For the first seven days of Tziga Hame's convalescence in Doorhandle he repeated Convalescent One till, eventually, the whole village had managed to sleep when he was sleeping and share his dream. Its effects were noticed. A girl who had coughed all winter finally had a good night's sleep and woke with colour in her cheeks. A troubled man woke feeling the dark haze lift from his mind. The people of Doorhandle felt invigorated and at peace. Eventually, comparing their experiences, they realised that, over the course of the week, they had all had the same dream, and many had had it several times.

Hame's dream faded. He was on the mend. His sister Marta was paying their board by playing her cello in the inn parlour. The Hames' father sent money for their passage back to Founderston — they were to make the journey once Tziga's leg had healed well enough for him to travel.

Tziga Hame was distressed by his father's orders, for he and Marta had failed in their plan to spend their summer earning their fees for a final year at Founderston's Music Conservatory. Without their fees the brother and sister would be unable to attend.

Dr Chambers passed through Doorhandle in late January on his way back to the capital. He removed the plaster from Hame's leg and told the young man he must exercise it to unthaw its stiff knee joint.

Tziga and Marta Hame returned to Founderston. Throughout late summer and autumn Hame exercised his leg. He climbed up and down the six flights of stairs from the family's rooms in their tenement in the old town. He walked the streets. When a number of weeks had passed he visited Chambers in the doctor's rooms at the front of his residence on the west bank of the Sva River. Hame showed Chambers how, when he planted his feet to play reels, his bad leg would tremble. Chambers told Tziga Hame that although he could still expect some improvement his limp was with him for life.

Hame was cast down. After seeing the doctor he took to his bed for a time, using the winter's first cold snap as an excuse not to exercise.

Hame lay in bed and did some thinking. He thought about the dream he had had, night after night, in the first week after his accident. Hame felt that the dream had helped him to heal. He reviewed what had happened to him. He'd had a fall and had broken his leg and, while unconscious, he had caught a *dream* as one catches a cold. When he'd caught his dream, he'd seemed to be in *another* place — somewhere dry and silent, a place whose trees had bark that was peeling in sooty strips; somewhere unlike the road through lush Wry Valley.

Hame later explained that he would never have known that he had gone into another place had the farmer who found him come from the Doorhandle direction. Fortunately the farmer was coming from the coast with a cartload of seaweed for compost. Hame, crawling back the way he had come, slithered from the dusty trail on to the muddy road and heard a cart coming up behind him. He looked over his shoulder and saw the farmer coming around the bend of a road *he hadn't crawled along*. The farmer stopped and looked Hame over, then picked him up and tried to carry him to his cart. But Hame simply dropped out of the farmer's arms and fell back through what he called 'a fold in the map'.

'I've always imagined the Place is a whole territory hidden in a fold in a map. Everything on the map apparently joins up, the roads, rivers, mountain range — but the map can open wider, and show a whole concealed country.'

The farmer, finding his arms empty, to his credit did not immediately decide that Hame was a ghost and flee. A calm and practical man, the farmer waited on the spot at which Hame had disappeared until the young man managed to collect himself and crawl out again. The farmer saw Hame's arms break through the air. He said later that it was like watching a calf born from an invisible cow. When Hame appeared the second time, the farmer led his horse past the spot where Hame lay and *only then* picked the young man up, and put him in the cart.

Hame, lying in his attic room in Founderston's old town, discouraged and in pain, thought about his fall and came to a conclusion. He concluded that he had caught his dream in *a place* he might be able to find again. A place on the road beyond Doorhandle. And so he pawned his violin, and bought a seat on the Sisters Beach stage as far as Doorhandle. He found the farmer and asked the man to accompany him to the point on the road where they first met. The farmer was quite clear about the location of the spot where he'd found Hame — a section of road shadowed by a mature hawthorn tree.

It was late afternoon when they reached the spot. The road was narrowed by drifts of fallen leaves. There was a cloud of midges under the hawthorn — but the road was otherwise an empty, everyday road. Hame and the farmer crept under the tree, their hands held out before them. Then Hame disappeared — and the farmer walked on a little alone. A moment later Hame reappeared out of the air and asked the farmer to build a cairn by the tree to mark the border. And then he went back In.

It is possible that, having injured himself on his first arrival in the Place, Hame had been pushed into a certain kind of adaptation to its weather. I will use that word 'weather'. Sailors talk of winds, of Trades and Variables, Doldrums and Roaring Forties. Just as different vessels are adapted to different weather conditions, so each dreamhunter is adapted to sail down different winds of sleep. Directly over the Doorhandle border is a band of 'dream weather' full of powerful, beneficial dreams. Tziga Hame emerged from his second, deliberate excursion into the Place with the dream now known as Starry Beach. Starry Beach is a less effective dream than Convalescent One. It is soothing rather than healing. The dream did make Hame feel better, but it wasn't enough in itself. Hame decided to use it to somehow bargain for better medical treatment. He hoped to persuade Dr Chambers to do something more for him.

Tziga Hame took the dream back to Founderston and to Chambers. He asked the doctor if he might spend the night in the doctor's house. Hame attempted to explain, but Chambers wasn't of a mind to listen. It was totally out of the question, Chambers said, *preposterous* — what was the young man thinking?

Hame left the doctor's residence, but returned at nightfall and camped on the area stairs. He went to sleep with his head resting on the back doorsill.

Walter Chambers later reported what happened that night. He said that he had a wonderful, refreshing sleep and a blissful dream. The following morning over breakfast his wife told him about *her* dream. The doctor recognised his wife's description of the warm sea, golden beach, the fish baking in crumbling white coals, the sunset, kind friends, campfire singing. Chambers recognised the dream's air of languid wonder, and its mysteries he'd marvelled at, like the sight of a line of lights moving through the forest behind the beach. He and his wife had had the same dream. And, it turned out on further investigation, the couple's daughters, and their household staff, had all shared it. The whole household was in a gentle mood so that when the butler appeared to tell the doctor that the young man from yesterday was back, and refused to be seen off, Chambers was welcoming. He hurried out to Hame and the young man explained what had happened to him.

Chambers was amazed, but could immediately see advantage for himself in Tziga Hame's gift. The doctor took the young man on an overnight visit to one of his wealthy spinal patients. Chambers later gave an account of this first experiment. He said that, as he sat by his patient's bed he'd watched something in the sick man's sleep, but more effective than sleep, smoothing the man's tense face.

Hame spent a week in the rooms of several of Dr Chambers' chronic patients. Much to the families' puzzlement the doctor turned up when no crisis was anticipated, but in the morning the patients were better, one even saying she felt she'd been bathed in a whole summer overnight.

When the dream faded the doctor gave Tziga Hame money so that he could return to Doorhandle, and the strange territory it seemed only he could enter. This was Hame's first commission — his third dream, for which he was paid only expenses and meals. The young man was still proving what he could do, and neither he nor Dr Chambers had yet thought to put a price on what they regarded as a miracle and a gift.

But, of course, a cure is a saleable commodity. Two years after his fall Tziga Hame had subscribers — sanatoria, and private and charitable hospitals. He was taking his dreams to any sizeable town within two days' travel by sea or rail.

He had given up his violin, but paid his sister Marta's way through the Conservatory. He had bought himself and his family houses. He was a wealthy man.

News spread quickly about the help Tziga Hame had brought to the suffering. And of the fortune he was making. Others were inspired to try to see if they could do it too — pass across the point where the everyday road met another: an invisible road which would lead them to goldmines of dreams. These early adventurers came alone to face their failure privately: that moment when they turned to look back at the piled stones of the border marker. Some came in groups, egging one another on. A group of clerks from a bank. A group of weavers from a textile factory. A mixed group of philosophy and divinity students. They arrived noisy, and stayed noisy if none of them passed through, or were quickly silenced if one of their number was swallowed whole by the innocent air.

All who came to Try and found themselves able to enter the Place assumed that, like Tziga Hame, they would be able to follow the remains of the road a few hours In from the border, lie down and catch a dream. This was not the case. Most caught a little sleep, but nothing else. But some went In often enough to be able to give their friends — or the newspapers — a better description of that territory so few were able to see. They reported that the Place was vast, much larger in its interior than the territory it seemed to encompass in the Rifleman Ranges. They reported that it was never dark in the Place, although no sun could be seen in its luminous, white sky. There, they found, no flame could be kindled. Only humans could cross the border, so no one could take In a horse and cart, and any supplies had to be either carried, or wheeled In on hand barrows. And, because no flame could be kindled, machines driven by steam power or internal combustion didn't work.

The explorers boasted, or complained, about their hard rations, the dry, cold food and cold beverages on which they lived. They reported on the uselessness of compasses. Some were so curious about this uncanny, exclusive Place into which they — special people — had been admitted, that they carried in surveying equipment and began to make maps. They formed a club, first meeting in the big parlour of the inn at Doorhandle. Some, poor and keen to work, offered themselves as porters to those others who, like Tziga Hame, could catch and carry dreams.

The people of Doorhandle were probably the first to notice the changed appearance of those who made repeated trips into the Place. The mapmakers, trailblazers and porters got the look that anyone who kept going In did. They grew thin, rangy, dry-skinned. The dreamhunters took on this look too, but their eyes changed as well. Whereas the 'rangers' — as the mapmakers and porters had begun to call themselves — developed crow's feet from squinting into bright distances, the dreamhunters gradually all came to wear a strange stare, as though the distances into which they looked exhausted them, were full of terrible battles or tormenting mysteries.

The dreamhunters were making their own discoveries. Many had begun to emerge from the Place with dreams for which there was no existing market. They began to advertise these dreams in the classified section of Founderston's daily newspaper. Some pooled their resources and rented one of the small hotels on the Isle of the Temple, a city district of Founderston. These small consortiums of dreamhunters would dream to paying, sleepover audiences — audiences that were growing quickly as more and more people sampled and were enthralled by these astonishing shared dreams. Dreams as coherent, full and physical as lived experiences — but in which no one was ever themselves, so that the timid could be brave, the infirm could be well, men could be women, and women men, and the old could be young again.

Dreamhunters organised themselves for their growing market. They printed posters and flyers. One might describe his dreams as outdoor adventures; another, in a careful code, as 'Dreams for Sporting Gentlemen'. One might offer battles and football matches; another dreams 'soothing to the mind'.

An industry had begun.

* * *

Within eighteen years dreamhunting has become central to the domestic economy and cultural life of Southland. To any historian, the activity has even more the appearance of an apparition than those other appearances that can make the past seem not quite continuous with the present: the invention of the printing press, the discovery of the New World, the invention of the steam engines that drove the Industrial Revolution and — if for a moment I can play prophet instead of historian — those fragile flying machines that are now literally casting their makers' fortunes to the wind. But, unlike all these world-expanding inventions or discoveries, dreamhunting is a discovery itself based on *an apparition*, the apparition of the Place, which was in one historical moment not there, then *there*.

In fact, it has often seemed to me that the Place appeared in time to welcome its discoverer, to welcome Tziga Hame and give him his crippling injury. Hame is still indisputably the greatest dreamhunter. He has the widest zone of projection, a four hundred-metre 'penumbra', to use the language of the profession. He can 'overdream' any other dreamhunter — if he and another have freshly caught dreams, his will cancel theirs and erase it from their systems. Can it be a coincidence that Hame is both the first and the greatest dreamhunter, and that the Place first appeared to our knowledge when Hame first entered it? It is as if the Place was locked, and Hame was the key that unlocked it. It is as if the Place appeared where and when it did because *that* was where it happened to find Tziga Hame.

Twelve

In a house near the trestle railway bridge at Morass River a man and his wife were eating their dinner. They looked up at each other, their spoons poised, when they heard the approach of a powerful engine. The express and milk trains never took the bridge at such speed. They listened to the engine's thunder transmitted all the way along the valley by the resonating timber structure of the bridge. Then the engine was across, safe. The man set down his spoon, the woman sipped from hers. They began to count carriages. One, two —

Silence from the bridge, the roar and rattle receded. The man crossed himself. Two carriages. A special train from Sisters Beach. The great dreamhunter brimful with powerful medicine.

Later the train slid past the little town at the foot of Mount Kahaugh. A boy baiting hooks on a line wound out from a boat in the sea below the mountain saw the train, its windows reflecting the setting sun in long and short flashes as though transmitting a message as it turned and slowed into the spiral. The boy felt the train was signalling to him — a message of farewell. He glanced up now and then to watch for the train's reappearance, to see it come around the curve of the mountain, labouring now, on the inner spiral, two hundred yards above the village. The light it gave back, window by window, was barely gold. Coal Bay had sunk in blue shadow and only the summit of Kahaugh had fire in its crest of forest.

The train passed through the tunnel that pierced the shoulder of the mountain. It picked up speed, heading east and inland.

It blasted through town stations, hauling the loose leaves of evening newspapers in its slipstream. Stations wired ahead in a relay and, at each, stationmasters came out to see the train hurry through. Stationmasters and porters, and passengers early for later trains, caught glimpses of the figures within the luxury coach — the two men playing cards, the portly man in a bright waistcoat, a white napkin tucked into his open collar. And, alone in the brightest part of the carriage, the slight figure in dust-covered clothes.

The train turned from east to south to west again, the railway line making its miles-wide circle around the place where the Place was.

Near Founderston it travelled sluggishly through a crossing where signs said 'Slow' and work was being done on the line. A small girl, waiting with her mother at the barrier, said, 'Ma, a man in that train is singing.'

'Yes, he's singing to keep himself awake,' the mother said. She listened to the voice, light, hoarse, carrying, and identified the song. She said to her daughter, 'It's an Old Town song — "A Stitch in Time".'

The train had gone by. The girl asked, 'Do you know it, Ma?' And her mother, who had a repertoire of folk ballads and hymns and old prophecy songs, sang 'A Stitch in Time' as the crossing guard winched the barrier back out of their way.

> If I could, I would, my dear,
> stitch the next happy hour to our good time here,
> sew up the whip, the cell, the noose,
> till that time's a false pocket that lets
> no true terror loose.
> A stitch in Time can save us, love,
> now closed between then and then,
> a charm to work and spell to prove,
> a door to shut and dream to end.
> But I am just a tailor,
> my art with cloth and thread;
> not a dreamer dressed as jailer,
> or a saviour as the dead.

At Founderston railway yards the train stopped to fill its water tank, and the physician got out and walked along the railway line, from sleeper to sleeper, and up on to the platform. He went into the concourse and bought a carnation for his buttonhole, and a newspaper. He checked his watch by the station clock. It was twelve thirty a.m. — they were still three hours from their destination. He hurried back to the train, and was hauled on board by one of the men from the Regulatory Body who had come out scouting for him.

Tziga Hame looked sleepy. The shot of stimulant Dr Wilmot had given him eight hours earlier was finally wearing off. The physician went and sat opposite Hame. It was his job to keep the man awake till they reached Westport.

The train left the yards at Central Station. It crossed the iron bridge upstream from the Isle of the Temple. Its occupants looked out on the black river water, the moonlight caught only where its silky surface was flawed by current.

Dr Wilmot read items from the paper to Hame. 'The Grand Patriarch has been sermonising against you again, I see,' said the physician. 'Not you personally, Hame, dreamhunters rather. He is troubled by dreamhunter terminology.' The physician read: '"They speak of a dream's range as its penumbra. This is a word borrowed from astronomy. A penumbra is the shadow the moon casts on the earth during a total eclipse. It is the course of a shadow."' Wilmot sniffed. 'Perhaps he would rather you called it a blast zone. Or, if we're describing circles, perhaps a bubo, like the boils of plague.'

Hame's head, which was propped on his hand, slipped. He jerked awake. He'd been asleep for a second and in the narrow tenements beside the tracks, in people's sleep, shapes sprang up — people in black, a group of pale-faced mourners — there for an instant, then quenched, sucked down into the graveside earth again.

'Stay awake,' Wilmot snapped, and slapped Hame across one cheek.

'Be careful with him,' one of the officials cautioned the physician.

Hame got up and began to walk, steadying himself on the long polished table in the centre of the carriage. An official opened a humidor and offered Hame a cigar. Hame shook his head.

The train sped through the small hours towards Westport.

Westport was a big industrial city, a city of mines and mills and shipyards, mostly privately owned. But its richest coal mine belonged to the government. The mine's shaft penetrated a hill to the north of the harbour, a hill wearing skirts of glittering slag. Below the hill and extending out into the harbour was a causeway that, halfway along its length, became a pier. At the end of the pier stood a huge, grim, ironwood structure — Westport's Shore Prison. The prison supplied the coal mine with labour. Every day, in two shifts, prisoners were conducted in a shuffling column along the causeway and up a cinder-covered road to the mouths of slanting mine shafts. Twelve hours later a shift returned, blackened and bowed down with exhaustion. Every day barges heaped with high-grade coal would set out from the shelter of the causeway to the foundries across the harbour. Or the coal was loaded into trucks at the railhead and taken away, inland, to Founderston and other settlements, where it was sold for domestic use. Good coal, it burnt quite cleanly, its smoke slower to accumulate as stains on city walls and trees.

The special train arrived at the railhead at four in the morning. The officials jumped out on to the platform. There was a flurry at the station. Someone ran a red flag up a flagpole. The physician climbed from the luxury car and put his hands up to assist his patient down on to the platform.

Tziga Hame looked around. He saw a ground mist softening the stones between the rails, and goods wagons seeming to float on thin white vapour. He saw the men waiting for him — prison guards in black, brass-buttoned uniforms, and the prison governor in a coat with a fox-fur collar. The governor's breath smoked like a dragon's — he'd been drinking hot tea.

Tziga said to the people nearest him that he'd like to stretch his legs, to walk before he slept. He'd make his own way along the pier to the prison.

There was a whispered consultation between officials. The prison governor attempted to shake Tziga's hand then flinched back when he touched the bandages.

Some of Hame's escort climbed into cars. Others walked with him. The walkers went down from the platform on to the causeway. They left the lights of the railway yard behind them. It was easier to see where the tide lay on the beach, the water striped one way by electric light and the other by the setting moon. The tide was right out, the seabed bare, stinking not of seaweed but of the sulphur in coal. The beach was coated in a silt of coal dust.

Tziga Hame saw that one wing of the prison was lit up. A light burned in every cell. They had kept those prisoners awake all night — after working them all day. As he watched, the lights began to go out. Now the prisoners could sleep. Now that he was coming.

He was asked, 'Have you had enough to eat?'

'Yes,' Tziga said, 'I've had enough to eat.'

He'd had enough. Enough of his work, his weakness, his mistakes.

He had scooped a cavity in the chest of his sandman, and had hidden his letter to Laura there. He'd put the sand back in and had smoothed the place over. The whole time he'd been singing, softly, the song of making. ('It's called "The Measures",' Tziga's great-grandfather had told him and Marta when he taught them it. 'It's music and mathematics and prayer too.')

A letter of apology was all Tziga had to offer as a heart for his daughter's servant. He hadn't been able to write, 'Laura, if I don't come back . . .', and offer a proper explanation. Or any reasonable advice. His mind was filled with murky guilt and misery. He was a fallen man, he knew, and ghostly, as though his sins had sucked the life out of him.

He had practised 'The Measures', and played with sand, and felt the facility of magic fizzing in him — but he hadn't been sure he could make a sand servant. Until the moment when it came to life and stood up before him, his experiments with 'The Measures' and hopes for the old Hame magic had seemed only a desperate wish, a wish for someone stronger than himself, someone fit, to whom he could pass his unbearable burdens.

Laura would go to the Place. She would find her servant and Tziga's film of the gutted building — the site of the dreadful dream. She would discover what he and other wicked adults had done. The dream would make it clear to her. She would stop sulking and mooching and living in Rose's shadow. She would catch the dreadful dream, the dream with the great, eclipsing penumbra. She would blot out the sun.

Tziga Hame limped between his watchful retinue to where the causeway became pier and their footsteps sounded hollow. Perhaps he pulled a little ahead of them, despite his limp. They imagined he was eager. How could they imagine *that* — they, who had all taken care to sleep earlier that day, or to chew some Wakeful, who had all done whatever they could to avoid sleeping with him?

Tziga didn't want to sleep. He didn't want what was before him, the strict prison of his dream, nine nights of torture for himself, and for the hand-picked prisoners who would share his dream — unrepentant murderers, and the men who persistently threatened public order then, when locked up, started prison strikes or riots. Tziga wanted the horror of the dream *out of him now*. He wanted to break himself open and have it leave him at once, and for ever.

Hame's escort saw him draw a little ahead of them. They heard him say, 'Enough.' Then he veered to one side, limping but swift — a slight man, and fit from twenty years of walking inland in the Place after dreams. He ran to the edge of the pier and flung himself off it, head first, like someone diving into deep water. Except that the tide was right out, and there was no water, only slick black stones at the base of the thirty-foot piles.

Thirteen

The family entered the dream palace by the dreamer's door only fifteen minutes before it was time for the patrons to retire to their rooms.

Grace stopped in the hallway before the stage door, which led to the oval floor of the palace's amphitheatre and the dreamer's bed, under the huge central chandelier and painted silk canopy. Grace kissed her family. Her clean, plain face was shining with excitement. 'You wait. You just wait,' she said to her husband. 'I don't know whether you'll run off with the woman in love, or with her jealous brother. I like them both. I particularly like the way the brother feels everything in his lips.' Grace touched her own mouth.

'Oh dear,' Chorley laughed. 'But I have your assurance that no one is me.'

'Of course not.'

He wiped his brow in mock relief. Rose and Laura smiled at each other. They knew Chorley was referring to a time before he and his wife were introduced, when Chorley's friends had alerted him to the fact that his face was appearing on the heroes in the dreamhunter Grace Cooper's romantic dreams. Chorley was disgusted. It was an invasion of his privacy, he thought. Not only had Grace Cooper been eyeing him up, she was now using him like a mannequin and dressing him up in her dreams. He confronted the dreamhunter, who at first claimed that his face appeared in her dreams as a result of a poll she'd taken among the society women of Founderston on who they thought was the town's most eligible bachelor. She went on to point out that she'd changed things about him — for example, in her dreams he never spoke. 'Your function is simply to be handsome,' Grace had said. And she said, 'The heroes who look like you dress differently too — for instance, they would never wear such *big* cufflinks.' At this point in the interview Chorley decided the dreamhunter was teasing him, and retaliated by asking her out. The story of how Chorley Tiebold's face turned up on the heroes in Grace Cooper's dreams was Rose's parents' story of how they met.

To Rose and Laura, Grace said, 'This really is at the upper limit of what you're allowed, girls.' She was warning them not to be shocked, and reminding them how lucky they were. 'You'll be the youngest here.'

'That's so silly, Mother,' Rose said. 'Next week we'll be in the Place, and I'm sure *it* makes no fine distinctions about what's suitable for young ladies.'

Laura opened the door for her aunt, who stepped out into shouts and applause.

'She's so excited we'll all be lying awake for hours,' Chorley said.

'It'll be worth it,' said Rose.

Chorley and the girls climbed the stairs and emerged on to the first-floor balcony through a door in a mirrored panel.

Laura looked up at the massive crystal central chandelier. She squinted through its dazzle at the two tiers of balconies, upon which the wealthy visitors to Sisters Beach strolled about or sat on padded benches. People were keeping an eye out for their friends, waving to one another across the space. Most people were in sleepwear — pyjamas, nightgowns and dressing gowns, all in brilliant colours and rich fabrics. The women wore their hair threaded with ribbons, or caught up into silk bags and loosely turbaned around their heads. The only people not in sleepwear were waiters, who wove among the patrons carrying refreshments — or, now, rather more empty glasses. People craned over the balconies to watch Grace Tiebold speaking to the dream palace's manager. He handed her up the steps to her dais, and its huge bed.

A bed like an altar. (Laura had overheard one of her teachers say that — in a disparaging way — to one of her classmates.) Grace climbed into her cloudy bed and sat, looking small and businesslike. She looked up at the crowded balconies and tucked her hair behind her ears. Chorley kissed his hand to her and one of his friends called out that they hoped that he, Chorley, wasn't on the program tonight. Chorley laughed. He turned away from the pit of the stage and opened the door to the Hame suite. He stood aside for Laura and Rose. 'You girls can go in together, so that when Grace joins me for breakfast we won't have to put up with your chatter.' He went through the door to the Tiebold suite.

Most of the other rooms were just that — hired rooms — sometimes double, sometimes for families, but all with numbers on their doors and, like the rooms in hotels, used by different people at different times. At the Rainbow Opera in Founderston the President of the Republic had a private suite, reserved for his use alone, as did the Speaker of the House of Representatives, the Secretary of the Interior and several very rich men. The Hames and Tiebolds also had suites in the Rainbow Opera, and were the only people with suites in the Beholder — a dream palace only half the size of the Opera.

Laura closed the door. She shut out the sound of the crowd, and of the bells calling the Beholder's patrons to turn in for the night.

Rose asked whether Laura would mind if they left the room-wide sliding door open between them.

'You can come in my bed if you like,' Laura said. 'Or we could both curl up in father's bed.'

So it was that the girls lit the branch of candles in the master bedroom, and climbed into Tziga's bed (Tziga sometimes had time to catch one of someone else's dreams when his own latest dream had been discharged). The girls lay diagonally on the bed, with their feet touching. Laura felt very close to Rose — Rose sleepy, Rose muted and blinking slowly like a cat. Rose told Laura that one thing she'd miss would be sharing all her mother's dreams. 'Because my emptiness won't always coincide with her being full. It'll be like being a child again, and not being allowed to share every dream. Do you remember what that was like?' Rose said.

'We'd come here only once in a blue moon, to enjoy one of those nice, vivid, plotless dreams of your father's.'

Laura thought of the dreams her father had caught that she had been permitted to share — how *well* they'd made her feel, though she was already whole, healthy and young. Laura had understood for a long time how valuable her father was. He was valuable, so she saw less of him than she'd like to. How *naïve* she had been to imagine that when it came to something vital — her Try — her needs would come before the needs of the ill, mad and dying he ministered to.

A moth had come in through the open window that faced the promenade and the sea. The moth grazed a candle flame and fell, to flop about on the polished table top. Laura closed her eyes. Some time passed and Rose was quiet. Thoughts were sliding through Laura's head, some bright like sparks in a storm — she wondered where the special train was now — and some obscure — a face she had glimpsed in the audience tonight, a bearded man, someone she didn't know but for some reason was thinking of as a good person, solid and equitable. Laura yawned and let the incongruous thought fly away. The wings of the maimed moth whispered on the carpet. Then Laura was walking down the long staircase in the tower at Summerfort, walking backwards in the dark.

Her parents were dead, and she had been left in the care of her older brother. He always kept her close, as though he, and he alone, should be enough for her. But the day had come when she had to go against him — or give in to him for good. She was in agony, she had to make a choice. Her brother had told her that she must either send her suitor away, or go away with him. She sent him away. She was too ashamed to look into his face, as he'd stood before her begging her for an explanation, for a word. But they weren't alone. Her brother was by the door, bristling with power, compelling her to be quiet. She didn't look into her suitor's face, but at his hands, his slender fingers and clean cuffs.

He fell silent, and walked away from her.

That was the moment into which, it seemed, she was born. The moment when her brother left the room to see her suitor to the door.

She looked up after them, through the doors to the hallway, at the tall arched window on the landing. She heard the front door close. She discovered that she had to look at her suitor's face once more. If she did not, it seemed that he'd only ever appear to her in memory turning away.

She ran after him, out of the room and down the stairs.

From the window on the landing she saw him crossing the lawn to the stables, to where a groom stood ready, holding his horse. She ran into the lower hall. Someone spoke her name. The hall was full of light and the reflections of light. The servants who tried to hamper her flight appeared only as silhouettes. Her brother's stern voice sounded behind her. She didn't pause. She opened the door and sprinted out under the deep portico, down its steep steps, looking back once at the house, its sandstone pillars and pediment.

There was a gale blowing outside, from behind the house, and she was swept up into it. She saw that her suitor's horse was already at the foot of the hill, at the iron gates to the estate.

She didn't take the path, but ran across the close-clipped green grass. The wind was frightening and forceful. The tall eucalyptus trees were shedding their dead branches. Bark was flying from the trees in strips like tattered canvas. It was on the ground everywhere, threatening to trip her. She had to run. She must get to him before he was gone. She must have him touch her cheek again. She sped with giant steps down the steep lawn. A tree branch fell in front of her.

She dodged to avoid the fallen limb and lost her footing, dropping on to one knee on the springy grass. As she got up again she looked to one side and noticed that someone was building a new garden wall. She saw red dust, and raw new bricks. She saw labourers in shapeless, grey clothes — their trouser legs gathered at the ankles. Then she was on her feet and ready to run again. Her suitor would never hear her call out to him against this wind. She ran.

The heroine ran on, leaving Laura Hame standing on the lawn of the heroine's house. She didn't see a woman run away from her. She only saw the wind, one last fierce gust that flattened her silk robe against the backs of her legs, bent the trees and cleared a corridor in its own debris. Then the wind stopped blowing, and the garden was silent, but for the insects ticking like a cooling engine.

Laura went to look at the wall the labourers were building.

It was a long wall with arches that made a frame for the view. It was the sort of wall on which gardeners train climbing roses. The men were making bricks. Laura saw a clay pit, and the frames for shaping slick red clay. She saw a kiln with a blackened chimney. She watched a man stamping the drying, unfired bricks, marking each with the flat of an arrowhead. She saw that, while the clothes the men wore were grey and stained with brick dust, they too were marked with arrowheads in a darker grey. And she saw that it was shackles that gathered their dusty trouser legs at their ankles.

Only one of the men seemed to see her. He straightened from his work — mixing mortar — and looked at her. He glanced about him, furtive, perhaps looking for an overseer.

There was no overseer in sight.

The man put his trowel down and came over to Laura. He walked stooped over, seemed at once cowering and eager. He kept looking about him — but none of the other prisoners noticed he'd abandoned his task.

Laura leant towards him.

He opened his mouth. A trickle of silver river sand spilled from it. His mouth stretched wide. It was packed with sand. He thrust his fingers into the sand in his mouth. The day grew suddenly dark, as though thick cloud had crossed the sun. The garden turned the colour of prison clothes — and cold. The world was leaving Laura. She was dying out of it. She reached out to the man and grabbed his arm. It felt soft, like sand, and yielded, creaking, beneath her fingers.

The man had fished something out of the sand in his mouth. A crumpled paper. He unfolded it for Laura to see, raised it to her eyes.

Before the world grew dark Laura read the few lines at the foot of the page. She was able to read it because the words assembled themselves around a core of letters she'd already encountered:

Yours
Cas Doran
Secretary of the Interior

The light faded. The words, paper, prisoner, all the world sank away.

* * *

Laura opened her eyes on the Hame suite. The stumps of the candles were bearded with melted wax. Rose breathed peacefully beside her. Rose's eyes moved under her lids, back and forth, scanning some beautiful thing.

Laura lay on her back and looked at the warm pool of candlelight on the ceiling. She knew she couldn't climb back on to the dream that had tossed her and taken off without her. She could feel it still, like the beginnings of a fever. She was reluctant to go to sleep again, but didn't want to disturb Rose, so got up and left the room.

The Beholder kept a fire watch, a group of men who patrolled the dream palace's balconies and stairways on their soft-shoed feet. Men with keen noses for smoke, who kept the sand buckets filled and their eyes on a board of switches which, if flipped, would set an alarm bell ringing in each room.

At three a.m. the dream palace was hushed, its guests breathing softly, sleep troubled only by the emotions of the dream. Grace Tiebold lay on her back in the dais bed, her face softly visible in the light of the dimmed chandelier. The dreamer wore her heroine's brother's face, and was frowning sternly in her sleep.

The eight men of the fire watch were at their station in a cosy room on the second tier of balconies. The room was like those that opened out on to ballrooms, where chaperones sit to keep an eye on the antics of young people on the dance floor. The fire watch's window opened on to the silent auditorium.

The men spun around, startled, when Laura appeared at the door. 'Am I dreaming?' said one of the younger men — a bit of a joker.

The girl blushed. She asked where the manager had got to. She said she was looking for someone to take her home.

The men exchanged glances. One cleared his throat and one scratched his head.

'He's asleep,' the girl guessed.

'I'm afraid so, Miss. You see — no one ever wakes up.' He wasn't apologising. She was the one at fault, since no one ever woke.

'Dream too rich for your blood?' said the joker, and arched an eyebrow. He'd just finished doing his rounds, had pressed his ear to several doors and had been excited by the sounds of a male curse and female sigh.

One of his workmates clipped him over the back of the head. 'Sorry about him, Miss Hame. He has terrible manners. Would it be acceptable to you if one of us walked you?'

'Yes,' said Laura, 'but not him.' She didn't even glance at the joker as she said this. He found himself blushing.

'I'll see you home myself,' said the oldest man. He took off his jacket and draped it over her shoulders. He found a lamp and lit her way down the back stairs to the stage door.

The Strand was empty, its streetlamps pale in the moonlight. The westerly had dropped. The girl walked quietly beside her escort. Now and then she turned to look at the regular flashing light on the end of So Long Spit, miles away across the bay. Laura thought about the dream. It wasn't the first time she had strayed inside one of her aunt's dreams before. She had never mentioned it to Grace. Laura didn't want her aunt to feel that she'd somehow failed to keep Laura's attention. The dream had been exciting, and Laura couldn't see why it hadn't kept her in its grip, why her dreaming self would choose to show more interest in prisoners building a wall and — most of all — why the dream should give her *Mamie's father's* name. A name formed around the letters on the fragment of paper Uncle Chorley had fished from the mouth of a dead ranger. Did it mean anything? *What* did it mean?

It seemed to Laura that the faraway flashing light was tapping on her eyes, as though asking to be let into her head. But Laura was tired, and her mind remained dark, and puzzled.

They reached the gates to Summerfort. The house was above them, hidden by the bulk of the hill, but the man could see the driveway running through flax and tea tree. The drive was paved with broken scallop shells, which shone in the moonlight and slithered noisily against each other when the girl stepped on to them. 'I'll be fine from here,' she said.

'Goodnight, Miss Hame,' said the man. He stood at the gate holding his lamp high, till she disappeared around the bend in the drive.

Fourteen

Grace appeared with the breakfast tray. She carried the morning paper tucked under her arm.
Chorley saw that his wife looked pleased with herself, so didn't hurry to comment on her dream. He sat up in bed and stretched out his arms. Grace peered at him speculatively and tossed him the newspaper. He opened it and settled back on the pillows.

The room was quiet. Chorley could hear the sea and the cheerful sound of sugar lumps dropped into hot tea and the crisp crusts on rolls pierced by a buttery knife.

Grace handed Chorley his coffee and climbed into the bed. She put the buttered rolls down between them. The Tiebolds began to fill the bed with crumbs — only Grace giving a momentary thought to the person whose job it was to clean up after them. (She still remembered having to clean tobacco dust and pipe ash off the counter of her tobacconist father's little shop.)

Husband and wife swapped pages of the paper and murmured to one another about the news. For instance, the buzz about who would be the new Speaker of the House of Representatives. They agreed that one man in particular struck them as a good choice. 'Solid and equitable,' Grace said.

'Yes,' Chorley agreed, 'though, for the life of me, I can't think of anything *else* I know about the man.' He shook his head, and put the paper down, stretched his legs and said, 'Grace, why must I always fall into your villains' heads? I never seem to have a choice.

And I can't say that I enjoyed being that jealous brother. He spent the whole dream breathing in clean air and breathing out smoke.' He pulled a face and Grace for a moment saw the luxurious fury of her heroine's controlling brother.

'He's light-headed all the time from holding his breath,' Grace said, and kissed her husband on his slightly scratchy morning jaw. 'I like that.' Grace sighed and shrugged and nestled down in the bed.

Rose burst into her parent's room. 'Laura got up and went home last night,' she said. She was waving a note about. 'She writes that she couldn't get back to sleep.'

'I thought so,' Grace said.

Chorley looked down at his wife, worried. Grace's tone was so strange, so knowing. 'Laura was very upset yesterday,' he said. 'No wonder her attention wandered.'

'No,' said Grace, '*she* wandered. She's done it before. She wanders about my dreams as if —' Grace screwed up her face. 'I was about to say, "as if they're her own", but when I catch my dreams I follow them faithfully.'

Chorley was shaking his head at his wife.

'Listen,' she said, 'what Laura does — no one does that. Not even Tziga can do that — go exploring, as if it's a world, not a dream.'

'Mother?' said Rose. She was disturbed by her mother's tone.

'I thought so,' Grace said again, brooding. 'I felt her taking a tour backstage.'

'Hang on, Grace,' said Chorley. 'At one time, for months, you imposed my face on the faces of all your heroes — whatever other faces they wore in the dreams you caught.'

'It's not at all the same as your face appearing in my dreams,' Grace said to Chorley.

'But when you did that you were *changing* something, Grace, even if it was unintentional. All Laura does is *change* things a little.'

'I don't go rummaging in other people's cupboards,' Grace said, softly. Then she dropped the subject.

But Rose wasn't about to let it drop. She felt that she could make a better job of defending Laura than her father had. 'You mustn't be mad at her, Ma. Laura doesn't mean to be annoying. She's like that at school — always drifting — and teachers think it's insolence. Only sometimes she isn't able to pay attention to what she's supposed to be paying attention to. It's like Da says, her mind wanders. She used to get dreadful marks in Comprehension because she was always supposing that the questions were trick questions and there was some less obvious answer that the teachers really wanted.'

Grace shook her head. 'I'm not angry at her, Rose.'

'Good,' said Rose. 'At least she's not making your heroes look like anyone else — like, for instance, that handsome lifeguard on the infants' beach, who we think is a smackerel.'

'What on earth is a smackerel, Rose?'

'Oh, you know, a smashing mackerel, which is to say a miracle,' Rose explained.

Chorley frowned at his daughter. 'This isn't George Mason's nephew we're talking about again?'

'No!' Rose was disgusted. 'He was brassy and parboiled. The lifeguard is a god!' Then she said that if her parents had finished arguing she would leave them in peace. But only if they had.

They found themselves making promises as if she was the adult and they children, then they watched her raid half the contents of their breakfast tray and swan out of the room. For a moment they stared at the closed door. Then Grace said to Chorley, 'Laura isn't just wandering around behind my scenery. Dreams don't have a backstage. It's all real, and it goes on and on, a big world in a small box. Every dream is like the Place itself, vast, and no place to wander alone.

'Look — it's a good day's walk between Doorhandle and Tricksie Bend, but in the Place you can walk for weeks and still find nothing you can recognise from the other side. Tziga and I talked about doing a transverse trip. Our talk inspired a group of rangers, who set out with a lot of food and water, and a stash of Wakeful.' Grace paused to take her husband's hand. She said, 'They were never seen again.'

Part II
The Try

One

The main autumn Try took place on the road west of Doorhandle. It was always a circus. At Doorhandle there were dozens of officials overseeing the registration of candidates from around five in the morning. Police were present as crowd control. Marquees and refreshment stands were set up for the sightseers, journalists, the candidates themselves and their families. At the end of each Try day the grass in the forest clearing was trampled flat. Hundreds Tried at Doorhandle.

At Tricksie Bend the Try was usually a quiet event, for Coal Bay was a small catchment area, despite the summer population of holidaymakers at Sisters Beach. At Tricksie Bend, on the morning of Laura and Rose's Try, the Regulatory Body had only to register forty-five nervous adolescents, and two adults.

Laura and Rose arrived with only half an hour to spare. They came with Chorley. Grace was acting as an official, and had gone ahead of her family.

As their car passed through the village, Laura and Rose had turned to look back through the window at the downhill view of its houses. They exchanged a look.

The time had come. It seemed that within a day they had gone from not being allowed to do something to being pushed into it. For fifteen years they had steered clear of the border, now they were steering straight for it.

Chorley turned the car off the road. It bounced up a hill towards the meadow on the bluff above the river. Other vehicles had already flattened a trail through the dry grass. A small crowd of onlookers was clustered around parked cars and carriages. The candidates were already in formation further up the slope, standing knee-deep in golden late summer grass, along a line marked by a shiny blue satin ribbon. The ribbon was strung between two stanchions and extended right across the meadow.

Laura said, 'Does that mark where the border is?'

'They line you up along the ribbon,' Chorley said. 'The border is several paces beyond, I think.'

The cars, carriages, horses in nosebags, the small crowd milling under the shade of hand-held umbrellas, the short line of candidates and the finishing-line ribbon were all humble and unceremonious. Rose was disappointed. 'It's not what I expected,' she said.

Her father told her that Tricksie Bend was favoured by parents who supposed their children might suffer from stage fright — who were afraid that stage fright might affect their candidate's performance. 'Of course your mother and I know that's nonsense. But Tricksie Bend is more private. That makes it better for you.'

Laura thought that there were quite enough people for her — even the small crowd was intimidating.

Grace came to meet the car. She put her arms on the sill of the driver's window and leant in. 'We were right to delay, Chorley,' she said. 'There are several reporters up there. They have cameras.'

Chorley told the girls to put on their hats and lower their veils.

Laura and Rose's hats were new — bought to match their first full-length dresses. Before now the girls had worn skirts that stopped at the top of their boots, halfway between knee and ankle. The hats' wide brims supported veils of bunched organdie. Laura and Rose realised that it was with this moment in mind that they'd got their new outfits.

Chorley said to Rose, 'You do see now why we wanted you to Try on the quiet side?'

'Yes,' said Rose.

'Thank you,' said Laura.

'I'm going to stop by the registrar,' Chorley said. 'As soon as I stop, you two get out and go straight to his table.'

Rose and Laura nodded. They turned away from the windows of the car and towards each other. Laura saw Rose's eyes, wide and shining behind the lilac gauze of Rose's veil and through the pale yellow of her own. Over Rose's shoulder she saw a photographer's assistant drop a burning match into a pile of magnesium in a flash pan he held aloft. There was a white flash and a puff of smoke rolled up from the pan. Laura's vision filled with a shining cloud of green light. (And, a day later, there was her face in the paper, her black eyes huge and fearful. The caption took the tone of the article, which disputed the wisdom of letting girls Try at such a tender age. The caption read, 'Age of Consent?')

The car reached the registrar and abruptly stopped. 'Out,' Chorley said.

The girls clambered out and hurried to the registrar's table. Grace waited for them, holding two pens — their forms were already filled in, and only lacked signatures. Grace pointed at each page, showed Rose and Laura where they must sign. Laura's hand shook and the pen dropped blots beside her signature. Rangers had crowded around the two girls, jostling the newspapermen away from the table. But they let Chorley through. Chorley signed too — the forms required the signature of both parents for Rose, and two guardians for Laura.

'Laura!' a newspaperman shouted. 'Do you have anything to say about the objection lodged to your candidacy?'

Laura looked around at the reporter, but the registrar was speaking to her. He told them to please make their way up to the line. They were holding up the proceedings. Laura looked around. She tried to catch her aunt's eye to ask if she'd heard the reporter's question and what it meant. But Grace had her head down over the permission forms.

Chorley repelled another camera and shouted, 'Please! Let these young women collect themselves!'

'That's right, George,' said one reporter to another. 'Mustn't put the girls off their game.' Then, in an insinuating way, 'It's an inspiration seeing these girls going on the game.'

Chorley Tiebold gasped and lashed out. He knocked the reporter's hat off. The man's comb-over came unstuck and lay in oily tatters against his neck.

Grace grabbed the girls and thrust them before her, around the registrar's table and up the slope to the line. Behind them they heard the registrar shouting, 'Only dreamhunters, rangers and candidates are allowed past this point!'

Space had been reserved for the girls roughly in the centre of the line. Grace positioned them standing more than an arm's length apart, and about three feet from the blue ribbon.

Rose hauled off her hat and dropped it on to the flowing mass of thick grass behind her. She raised her face to the breeze. Laura copied her cousin. Once she had abandoned her hat she could hear clearly, but she was still breathless and her heartbeat was shaking her body.

While Grace and the other officiating dreamhunter and rangers conferred, the registrar locked his box and left his table. He made his way up the hill, holding his coat tails free of the seeding grass. He was carrying a stopwatch — as if it really was a race that the candidates were about to run. He stopped on the slope and straddled one end of the ribbon.

Grace came up to her daughter and niece and touched their shoulders. 'Don't anticipate the signal, or you'll look silly.' Then she said, 'See you shortly.' She stepped over the ribbon, and disappeared into the air. The other dreamhunter and rangers did the same — as though showing the candidates how it was done.

It was the first time Rose and Laura had ever seen the phenomenon that they had known about all their lives and had always accepted without giving it any thought. Seeing the people disappear came as a shock. Rose called 'Mother?' — tears springing into her eyes.

'Candidates! At my signal,' the registrar bellowed.

Downhill the crowd was hushed. Up the slope, towards the blue air over the bluff, Laura saw a pair of skylarks start out of the grass and go up, singing. There was a thistle in the grass directly in front of her. It was a big, healthy thistle, with three bright purple flowers and a woody stem. Grace, oblivious in her sturdy walking boots, had positioned Laura where she'd have to take her few paces through that thistle.

Beside her Rose said, 'Laura!' Urgent.

Laura looked around. The registrar had dropped his handkerchief. It fluttered, snagged on the grass. The whole line was a pace ahead of Laura and Rose, already pushing the ribbon with their legs. Rose had waited for her, but was leaning far forward, as though she meant to throw herself on to the ground. Laura picked up her skirts and approached the thistle. She stepped gingerly over it, then jumped forward to catch up with the ribbon.

Where was it? She was too far behind. Laura let her heavy skirts drop — must she spend the rest of her life dragging about in all this cloth? She let out a sob of frustration. The skylarks had stopped singing. She couldn't find the ribbon. The ground was bad. The grass had gone grey.

Laura came to a dead stop. She looked around. There was no ribbon, no candidates, no crowd of carriages, no village, no river, no quiet box beehives, no birds singing and no Rose. She heard feet running on hard earth. She saw the rangers converging on her — one girl out of that whole line. They came up to her — but Aunt Grace ran right past her, without a word or glance.

Rose walked on, pushing the line. She turned when she sensed Laura failing, saw how sick she looked. Laura was a walking corpse. Then she was a spectre. Then she was gone.

Rose stopped, and the shiny blue line of ribbon was carried off by the others ahead of her. One by one the other candidates came to a stop. Some abruptly, some gradually as if slowed by the drag of the grass. Some doubled back to pass again through the place where the Place should have been for them. Rose did too. She went and stood where Laura had been, where Laura's trail of parted grass came to an end.

Rose felt numb. She didn't know what she should do, so looked up to see how the other candidates were dealing with what had happened — or had failed to happen.

The staggered group, no longer in line, had all stopped walking forward. All but one. One girl carried the ribbon away. It flowed behind her trudging form, a blue V of wake. She began to run, knock-kneed, up the meadow.

'Hey!' Rose shouted. Then she went after the girl, tapping the next nearest candidate, a boy of her own age. 'Help me,' she said.

The girl was running, blinded by tears, towards the bluff above the river. Rose and the boy pursued her. The boy overtook Rose and tackled the girl. They went down with a crackling thump in the grass and Rose threw herself down beside them.

'There's a cliff,' said the boy to the girl, who clapped her hands over her face and burst into loud sobs, her flesh quivering in her too-tight cotton dress, and her buttons shivering on their rusted wire posts. Everything the girl wore was made over, Rose saw. And Rose understood the difference between this girl's dashed hopes and her own disappointed expectations.

'I can't!' the girl moaned, 'but I have to.'

'None of us can,' the boy said. 'And if we can't we can't.'

The girl paused to listen, then continued to weep.

The boy said, 'We're hidden in the grass here and the grown-ups can't see us.'

Rose leant up on an elbow and craned over the heads of the grass. She saw the dark trails the candidates had made, and the wind pushing at the rest of the meadow, making ripples of shadow. She saw her mother appear and spin to face uphill, searching for Rose. Her mother spotted her almost immediately and started forward — forgetfully, for she rushed straight back out of the world again.

Rose laughed. It struck her as funny.

Her mother came back, wringing her hands, and began to patrol an invisible line.

Rose decided to let her mother wait. Let Grace think about it — that her daughter was sitting somewhere where she, Grace, couldn't ever reach her. The land between Doorhandle and Tricksie Bend, though open to almost everyone, was closed to Grace. As closed as the Place was to Rose.

Rose was angry with her mother, who, it seemed to her, had never encouraged her to consider the possibility that she'd fail her Try. Grace had wanted Rose to become a dreamhunter. Grace was clearly distressed — but was she upset for Rose or her own disappointed hopes? 'I'm not going to cry,' Rose thought. 'And I'm not going to put up with *her* crying.' She lay in the grass watching her mother's misery and feeling a kind of spiteful satisfaction.

Rose's father detached himself from the onlookers, skirted the barrier of officials and went to Grace. He didn't offer his wife any comfort, but appeared to speak sharply to her. Then he pushed Grace forward, firmly, away into the Place again. He dropped his arm once Grace had disappeared and strode up the hill to Rose.

Rose's father sat down with them. 'That was quick thinking,' he said to Rose and the boy. He took the boy's hand and gave it a brief, approving shake.

The weeping girl spread her smeary fingers and glared at Rose's father through them. Chorley reached into his jacket and pulled out a Farry's toffee tin. He opened it and offered it around. Rose and the boy took one each.

Chorley said, 'There's plenty to be done by people who don't spend their lives stupefied by one dream after another.'

The girl sat up, and thrust her blotchy face into Chorley's. 'That's all very well for you! You're rich. And she's beautiful.' She pointed at Rose.

'And you're ambitious,' Chorley said, calmly. 'Stay that way.'

'I've always been frightened of dreamhunters, anyway,' the boy confessed.

'Me too,' said Chorley. 'But I rather like being frightened.' He stood up and helped the tear-stained girl to her feet.

She accepted his help, but told him that he was an idiot.

'Our people are waiting for us,' the boy said. He was frowning downhill. 'I bet mine are miffed.'

Chorley took Rose's hand. 'I'm not disappointed in Rose,' he said.

'I hope you're disappointed *for* Rose,' said Rose, her voice brittle.

'Yes,' Chorley said, and looked at Rose as though waiting for something more.

'*I won't cry,*' Rose told herself again.

The girl was eyeing the ribbon. She said she wondered who got to keep it.

Chorley bent down, bundled it up and gave it to her.

Laura squatted in a circle of rangers. She crumbled the grey-white grass in her hands. She rubbed the turf bald. The grass would never grow back. A fire could have removed all the vegetation, could have inhaled and taken it. But, in the Place, it was impossible to strike a spark or kindle a flame.

Laura was wondering, her brain broached by the silence. 'Shhhh,' she said to the shuffling, murmuring rangers. Her hands were covered in dust. There was an idea in the silence. As she grew still, and the rangers hushed, the bubble of sound that insulated them collapsed and the silence swamped her. It had almost come to her, the thing she must think.

Then Laura thought, 'Rose.' The name was a blow that bruised her heart. She was alone. Moments ago she was a point on an axis, one child in a line of children — one beater on the heath, one soldier in the column. Now she was alone.

The shuffling circle of rangers parted to admit Grace, who knelt beside her. 'Welcome, Laura,' Grace said.

Above their heads the rangers murmured it too, 'Welcome.'

'We have to go out now, and get busy,' Grace said.

Laura recalled that there were formalities, full registration, the appointment of a guide and — later — a trip to an outfitters. Laura got up and followed her aunt, out of the dry, colourless brightness.

Into colour and sense and sound. The meadow was abuzz. Families who had hung back during the Try had reclaimed their children. They stood about in little groups, consoling one another. Laura saw Rose, her face pressed into her father's lapels, her gold hair rippling as she cried. Grace broke away from Laura and hurried to them. Laura stopped. How could she move? She had always followed Rose. Rose stepped out, and Laura went after her. Even today. Rose stepped out, then stopped and put out a hand to Laura.

Now a curtain of nothing more than air — or time perhaps — had brushed Rose from Laura as Laura had gone through it. They were two pips in the core of an apple. But someone had cut the apple. Just now. The voices in the meadow above the river were the sound of a blade hitting a chopping board. Rose and Laura were cut apart. Laura stood, wounded and exposed. Then the rangers came through after her, and they stopped too, stood by her, a retinue for the day's sole successful candidate.

Two

Following the Try, Laura's days were taken up by a whirl of appointments. It was scary and celebratory at the same time.

The family went back to Founderston. On the train Rose, quiet and red-eyed, retreated behind a barricade of bags and travel rugs, drew up her feet and seemed to sleep. The family was late home and went straight to bed.

Every day, for the next three days, Laura was up early. She went to the head office of the Regulatory Body to sign forms. She visited shops on the Isle of the Temple — dreamhunter outfitters. Grace bought her walking boots, trousers, silk socks and shirts and a fawn dustcoat. Laura went to a hairdresser to have her hair cut. Laura was out early and in late. She scarcely saw Rose. She wanted to talk to her cousin, but didn't make an effort to do so. She was afraid she'd start to tell Rose about all the exciting things that were happening to her — and news, like how that boy from the infants' beach was among the ten successful candidates from the Try at Doorhandle. Laura had passed him in the doorway at the offices of the Regulatory Body and had managed to give him a polite 'Good day'. But, when Laura did see Rose, Rose's silence silenced her. It was a neutral silence — Rose wasn't punishing her. But it suddenly seemed that, having shared everything, the fact that they didn't now share everything meant they had to learn how to talk to each other again.

* * *

Four days after the Try, Laura and the season's other successful candidates were conducted into the Place for their first testing sleepover. They went In at Doorhandle, but were first briefed by the Chief Ranger at the Doorhandle headquarters of the Regulatory Body. The headquarters were in a large, two-storey timber building with a veranda that wrapped all the way around its ground floor and was the usual congregation place of rangers who were on their way In or had just emerged from the Place. The ground floor was full of desks, clerks and filing cabinets and, in fact, looked like any ordinary office. The top floor was taken up by a small locked armoury, and several large meeting rooms.

It was in one of these meeting rooms that the Chief Ranger briefed the eleven potential dreamhunters. He had given this talk many times before, and his tone was one of impersonal efficiency. As he spoke, the eager and restless candidates began to settle, even to sag a little in their chairs. They were tired, and the Chief Ranger's manner was a bit of a comedown after all the fuss of their last few days.

The Chief Ranger began by telling the children that each must carry their own food, water and bedding. He said that it wasn't necessary to take a change of clothes — for one thing they'd only be In 'overnight', for another they couldn't expect any rain, or dewfall or any variation in the weather. They wouldn't be getting wet: the Place was permanently set at what most of its travellers agreed was noon under a layer of thick white mist. A mist that hid the position of the sun, but never touched the ground, nor moistened the air. 'The only reason anyone might take a change of clothes was if they were walking many hours In and cared to come out smelling sweet. You won't find any water there,' he said. 'You have to carry it. Water is the weight you won't ever dispense with. Even if you get rich and hire a ranger to carry things for you, he'll still be burdened with his own supply.'

The Chief Ranger had packages of food on the table before him, which he held up, item by item. He showed them the strips of dried meat, cakes of pressed, dried fruit, strongbread loaded with nuts and chocolate, and 'dreamhunters' bread' — wafers made of rice flour and powdered milk. 'You'll learn to live on this,' he said. He cast his eyes over the eleven — eight boys and three girls. Several looked soft, were children who had never had to carry anything much heavier than a football or book bag. He took note of the two bandy-legged slum runts, and the remaining nine, who were only a little fitter. Behind the candidates were their guides, rangers and dreamhunters leaning on the briefing room wall, all thin and hardy from the repeated hikes into the Place.

'Well,' the Chief said to the candidates, 'you'll all build up to something better, I'm sure.' His eyes lingered on the two who were clearly from wealthy families. They were already ostentatiously outfitted in walking boots and dustcoats. The girl had even had her hair cut short, which the Chief Ranger thought was rather tempting fate. After all, what the majority of these children would discover on this first trip was that they wouldn't become dreamhunters. Just because they could penetrate the veil of the Place, it didn't mean they could catch dreams or, even if they could, that they could do so with sufficient vigour to make their dream saleable. Most of these children would find employment as rangers — but the Chief Ranger knew of very few women who took up that option. The girl had sacrificed her hair to her vain hopes. He hoped she wouldn't regret it too keenly, for he thought she was still rather pretty under her helmet of glossy curls.

He resumed his briefing. 'You will each take one of these kits, in which, among other, more self-evident items, you will find a signal whistle and a book about its use. I recommend that you study the book and master all the signals before you even consider going In on your own. Which, I might add, you have no hope of doing until you are licensed. And, to be licensed you must satisfy the Body that you will not be a hazard to yourself or anyone else, either in the Place or out of it, with any dream you manage to catch.' He looked at each of the children sternly and then went on to talk about the futility of attempting to light a fire in the Place, the importance of consulting maps, and of reporting any *changes* in the landscape. As he talked his eyes roved over the whole assembled group. He wanted to make sure they were listening to him. He looked into each of their faces — and was satisfied by their looks of respectful attention. But, as his gaze moved, he found himself looking more often and longer at that pretty, attentive girl.

Grace Tiebold arrived at the door of the meeting room. The Chief Ranger waved to acknowledge her and watched every head in his audience — even his own rangers' — swivel to the door.

'Mrs Tiebold,' he said, 'I have just finished with the generalities. I'm afraid that, at the moment, these young people are looking on their trip In as an exercise in orientation — which it is not. Perhaps you would like to explain its purpose? I think a dreamhunter will do a better job of explaining than any ranger.'

Grace Tiebold said, 'Thank you, I'd like that.'

The Chief Ranger yielded his place, but stayed at the front of the room, watching both the famous dreamhunter, and that increasingly — it seemed to him — attractive candidate.

The girl was smiling at Grace Tiebold — who smiled back, a brief, warm look, then moved her gaze to take in all the expectant, admiring young faces.

Grace began by pulling down the Chief Ranger's chart. Several of the candidates gasped.

Grace Tiebold said, mildly surprised, 'Have some of you not seen a map of the Place? You're shocked. Of course, any map of the Place will be shocking to anyone with any understanding of geography. As you can see, this is a map of no *earthly* geography. It is an interpretation of an unearthly geography by the discipline of earthly mapmaking.' She looked around at the Chief Ranger and asked if he had a pointer. He found her one and she returned to the map and tapped it with the pointer. 'As you can see, parts of this chart correspond in many ways to normal maps. There are topographical measurements. These hills and valleys have been surveyed.' The pointer pattered on the canvas of the map. 'Here is a forest,' Grace said. 'Here is a dry watercourse, here are roads, and ruins. Yes — *ruins*. And then *here* are markings only to be found on maps of the Place. These shadings indicate bands of certain sorts of dreams. And these spots — little dots that on a normal map would show the position of a village or town — here mark the sites of certain famous stable dreams, dreams that any dreamhunter can catch, that are always consistent in their content and intensity.'

The Chief Ranger's eyes wandered over the large labels of the famous stable dreams. He spotted Convalescent One and Two, Starry Beach, Balloon War, The Great Players, Beautiful Horse and Big Member — a title he wished was rather less prominently visible to these children.

Grace rested the tip of her pointer on one spot. 'This is Wild River — the dream on which you will be tested.'

It wasn't the first time that Laura had seen a map of the Place, and she knew that it wasn't the bands of colour, or the phantom villages, or even Big Member that caused the candidates to gasp — it was the whole *shape* of the map. The interior of the Place couldn't be measured in relation to known lines of longitude and latitude. Because, Laura knew, the land in the Place represented a much bigger space than the fifteen miles between Doorhandle and Tricksie Bend. Also, the Place had only parallel borders. No attempt to follow the border on the inside had ever resulted in tracing a line from the marker just inside the border at Tricksie Bend around to the one near Doorhandle. The Chief Ranger's map of the Place consisted of two horizontal ribbons of borderland, separated by a feathering of details supplied by those who had travelled deepest In from either side. Between the feathering was a broad blank space. No map of the interior of the Place could be set inside one of the surrounding country — as a maritime map of a coastline can be set against a corresponding map of what lies inland from that coast. And that was because the border to the Place was only continuous from the *outside*, not from within.

Laura's Aunt Grace was saying, 'This is where we are taking you today. It's a dream site at map reference A–8. As you can see, the map is labelled in bands A to E from the Doorhandle side, and Z to X at Tricksie Bend, where the Place hasn't been quite so fully explored. I always wonder if we'll eventually have to adopt letters from another alphabet when we find there are actually more bands in the hinterland than there are letters to label them.' Grace

Tiebold paused and made a thoughtful humming noise. Then she said, 'But enough of that. Yes?'

A boy — one of the bandy-legged runts — had put up a hand. He asked, 'What's it for?'

'A–8?' said Grace.

The boy blushed and subsided in confusion.

Laura knew that her aunt had purposely misinterpreted the boy's question. He had probably just asked for the first time that perpetual, teasing question: what was the Place for? Why did it exist?

Grace continued, 'A–8 is the dream Wild River. It is highly likely you know it already.'

Many of the candidates nodded.

Laura had shared the dream before, a perennial favourite performed at least four times each year in the Rainbow Opera. It was a dream to which older children were permitted to go — a harmlessly exhilarating dream. Anyone who shared Wild River found themselves as either a young man or a young woman — depending on which point of view they fell in with — taking a ride with friends in a sturdy boat down a river. A very beautiful river with a series of increasingly thrilling rapids. The dream always ended with the boat's safe arrival, and stately progress, into a calm lake.

'Wild River is a highly consistent, benign dream. It's ideal for you to cut your teeth on. What we're looking to see is, *first*, whether you can catch and retain it at all. *Second*, how strongly and for how long. *Third*, whether any of you will be fortunate enough to catch the split dream, to carry off both protagonists' points of view.'

There was a murmuring among the candidates, who must all have been aware that anyone who caught the split dream would have their fortunes made. There were only eight dreamhunters who could catch split dreams — of that eight, Grace was by far the most powerful.

'Even given that you're all sleeping in the same place, so boosting one another — this a true test, because you all get the same advantage. The test takes account of that. After the test you'll walk out and catch a train back to the capital. You'll be taken to the head offices of the Regulatory Body where you will each individually perform your Wild River for the examiners. Because Wild River is consistent it's possible to grade the quality of your catch.' Grace asked if they had any more questions.

The bandy-legged boy put up his hand again. 'Miss,' he said — rather betraying his charity school education — 'aren't all dreamhunters different? Is the river dream one any dreamhunter can get?'

'Yes. That's why we use it. If you can catch a dream at all, you will catch Wild River. We don't really learn much about what sort of dreamhunter you are unless you catch the split dream. In this test we will only measure your strength and the dream's longevity, and get some sense of your powers of projection.'

Another hand went up and a boy whispered, 'What say you're afraid of water?'

'The dream supplies another *self* — you know that. Though it does happen sometimes that a dreamhunter can change the appearance of a character in a dream so that they resemble someone in the dreamhunter's life.'

Grace Tiebold went on to tell the boy who was afraid of water about other exceptions to the rule that the dream supplied all its characters. 'There are a few talents who are able to make *substitutions*. To supply faces and bodies to order. For instance, the dreamhunter Maze Plasir makes half his income from the sale of "bespoke dreams" to solitary clients. He can make the characters in his dreams look like people his patrons desire and can't have, or like people they've lost. Plasir makes wishes come true. And he resurrects the dead. His is a very rare — and, I think, rather *dubious* — talent. I'm sure you — all of you — will find that you're one or the other same old characters in the usual old boat.'

'That's to be hoped,' the Chief Ranger added, seeing the disappointment on several of the young faces. Some of the candidates, having joined an exclusive club, now wanted to be singular among the exclusive, to find their own strangely configured niche and sit in it like saints.

'Any further questions?' asked Grace Tiebold.

There were none.

* * *

The head ranger thanked Mrs Tiebold, and she spread her hands to herd the candidates from the room — out to the road and the short walk to the border. The rangers fell in behind her. The Head Ranger was surprised to see Grace Tiebold collect a pack from her car, shoulder it and set off along the road with this latest clutch.

The Head Ranger had, years before, stopped bothering to check the newspapers to see who had passed at each Try. The successful were always named in the same breathless, gossipy tones in which the social pages reported on who attended the Founderston Cup race day. It wasn't worth following. He'd only notice them when they either became dreamhunters or came to work for the Body as rangers. However, on this occasion, the man did go back and ask one of his clerks for the day's log to see the name of those who went In. The unlicensed eleven were easy to find. And there were only three girls.

'Laura Hame,' he read. That sombre, pretty child was the daughter of the dangerous Tziga Hame.

Grace and the dreamhunter guides left the eleven guarded by rangers at an encampment at A–8, under a group of trees from which the bark hung in blackened strips. The children spread their bedrolls on ground rubbed bald by successive visitors. Grace and the other hunters walked off out of range. The eleven had something to eat and drink, then lay down.

Laura slipped a black silk eye mask over her face. For the next few hours she listened to the ludicrous sound of coughs, sniffs, shuffles and giggles as the stage-struck eleven tried to settle. Someone got up to pee, then everyone did, including Laura. Once they'd done that — a mutual acknowledgement of nerves — the eleven settled somewhat. Laura noticed the sounds thin out as, one by one, the young people fell asleep.

She felt a lurching drop. It was as if she had been walking and had lost her footing on a tilting stone. She knew the feeling. It was what she always felt when she was in a dream palace and the dreamer fell asleep before she had. There was a moment when she teetered, and either fell in after them, or not — and the feeling would pass. Laura very nearly removed her eye shade and sat up to see who the real dreamhunter was, the one who just fell so hard into the Wild River. But she didn't sit up, she continued to lie still and breathe deeply. She would go too. She could feel the Wild River beneath her, rushing by under her bedroll. 'Ah,' Laura thought, with relief, falling asleep, dropping through dream water and white bubbles, 'here it is —'

For a moment it seemed to the fleeing convict that he had fallen asleep on his feet, and had dropped through his weakness into a cold, stifling substance, like water. He found himself lying, gasping for breath, on the leaf litter of the forest floor.

The man knew he was finished. He was sick and tired. He couldn't keep up with the others, who could coax but not carry him.

It was black dark in the forest. He and the others from the mass breakout were running, strung out along a ridge.

The man was glad at least to be out. He got up from the ground to struggle on to the clearing he could see ahead, a thinning of the trees on the ridge's spine, where he'd be free of the forest and under the sky.

Another convict took his arm to help hurry him along. It was the young man from the cell next to his. They'd scarcely ever spoken, but had always stood together at the tubs to wash off the mine's black grime. The young man hauled him along. Then the failing convict stumbled and was dragged a little further, skidding on his knees.

Several of the men nearest him in the ragged line stopped when the sick man fell in the clearing. They waited for him. But he looked up at the star-filled sky, and remained on his knees, swaying.

The man who had helped him began to call out to the others — his voice croaking. He was parched. He made no words, only a sound, a rattling scream. Back along the ridge a line of torches moved through the trees. The pursuers. Their dogs would be bounding ahead of them, nosing along through the dusky forest, following the warm trails of the desperate convicts.

There were other fires burning, a long way down on the coast. Stationary fires, the convict thought. Bonfires maybe, bonfires on a beach. He imagined company, singing, fish baking in glowing embers.

He turned full circle, looking one last time at all the open horizons, before running down to the trees again. He saw why the man beside him had cried out in despair. He saw that both coasts were visible from the ridge and that he and the other prisoners were being driven along a narrowing peninsula. He saw that, as the pursuers came on, their line grew tighter, the lights closer together, and that it would be impossible for any of the escaped convicts to double back to break through that line. He saw that the only real choice was to be swept along by that net and eventually be gathered up into it. He saw what was going to happen, and yet he ran.

He felt the raw surfaces of bone grate in his bad knee. He swung his leg out from the hip at each step as though meaning to fling it away from him.

The continuous line of light was closing on him. His fellows were scrambling ahead of him, grubby shapes in the acidic undergrowth of the dry forest.

He was all in, worn out by labour. For years he'd broken stone, and hauled stone. His hands were permanently cramped as though clutching a pick. He couldn't run any further. He lay down to wait. He pressed his face into the leathery leaves on the forest floor.

A dog found him and leapt about, barking and snapping at the air over his head. One of the pursuers arrived and pushed it away. The light of the torches held over him made the long, dry gum leaves on which he lay look like dim flames and their shadows like a bed of coals. He heard one pursuer say to another, 'This is the first. But what should I do with him?'

An overseer answered, 'I'm tired of even feeding these people. They're all ill-conditioned and I'm not going to trouble myself driving the worst of them back.' He kicked the convict in the ribs. 'Do you hear me?' he said. 'There's nowhere to take you animals back to. When you set fire to the prison you burnt your own bridges.'

The convict realised he was about to be killed. The man was working himself up to it. The convict held out his hands, asking for mercy. In the torchlight he saw his clawed fingers, his broken nails. He couldn't believe what he saw. Was this it, then? Was this all? How could it be? 'This isn't me,' the man thought. 'This isn't what I've come to.'

He remembered being a boy at the lighthouse on So Long Spit — his quiet, isolated life with his father, tending the light. He remembered how he had liked it when ships had come along the Spit, stopped and offloaded supplies on to the platform his father and the other keepers had built out on the level sand at the low-tide line. The convict remembered being a boy, running on the sand, alongside a schooner that was sailing up the ocean shore of the Spit. He ran on the unending, smooth sand, and waved at figures lining the ship's rail. He ran into the wind, the same steady wind that bellied out the schooner's sails. The boy waved. A group of four low-flying gannets passed between him and the ship, faster than both, scooping the air back with their black-tipped wings. The gannets flew on towards their colony, far away at the end of the Spit where — to the boy's eyes — the sand vanished in the sea horizon so that only the colony itself was visible, a thin line of shimmering black and white drawn between the sparkling water and the blank sky.

The flying gannets overtook him easily, but he made an effort, sprinted, breasting the wind, trying to keep up with the ship. His shadow ran beside him, and sometimes he was paced by his reflection too, on sand made wet by waves. Reflection, shadow, boy — running, and all keeping up.

Three

The head office of the Regulatory Body was in a tower built on a spur of reclaimed land, formerly swamp, at the upstream end of the Isle of the Temple. The tower stood by itself in a walled park, whose grounds were planted with water-loving willows and cypresses. From the gallery that circled its upper storey there were views of the city, the wide pavements of the west embankment, and, on the east bank, the walls of narrow houses stained by the outfall from jutting privies. Upstream, back along the island, the white marble dome of the Temple itself — St Lazarus — seemed to hang in the blue air, hazy and weightless, like a daytime moon.

The examiners were waiting in the ring room, some walking about stifling yawns. One complained to another that he was dead on his feet. This season's little clutch of unlicensed dreamhunters had arrived back at the very end of the period he was rostered on. The woman walking with him had only just arrived and wasn't at all sleepy. In fact, she felt quite perky. She glanced at one of the clocks. It was three hours yet to sundown.

On their arrival the tired children had been escorted into inner chambers at the base of the tower, where they bathed and were given something to eat. Once they were clean and fed they would get into night clothes. Shortly the examiners would take their places, two to each child, in the dream-testing rooms, cabins that lay in the park around the tower like seed dropped from a tall flower. Indeed, at the moment when the sun vanished the doors in the walls of the antechamber opened and messengers appeared to summon the examiners into the core of the tower. A stair spiralled down to the ground floor and the doors out to the garden and its carefully spaced, isolated cabins. The messengers seemed to want the examiners to hurry. There was an air of urgency in their gestures as they gathered the examiners towards the doors from the room. They kept glancing back towards the elevator. Apparently they were expecting someone. Their glances were surreptitious, and they checked as often on each other as on the examiners they were herding. The perky examiner guessed that they had been asked to get themselves out of the way too. She refused to be hurried. She feigned some trouble with the heel of her shoe. She stopped and fussed with it. A messenger came forward and took her arm, helped her to her feet and hustled her towards the door. She heard the elevator open. She and the messenger hesitated, and looked. They saw three men. Two were dark-suited Regulatory Body officials — men from records, or registry. The third was still wearing his topcoat and hat, so had come from outside the building.

As she was pushed through the inner doors and out of his line of sight, the examiner recognised the man. It was the Secretary of the Interior, Cas Doran.

'Now why,' thought the examiner, as the door swung to between her and the Secretary, 'should these functionaries be in such a hurry to clear everyone out of Secretary Doran's way?' Doran was responsible for the Regulatory Body. It was in his portfolio. He had every right to be in the Body's offices. 'Is he coming now to lie in on one of these candidates' examinations?' thought the examiner. 'Even so,' she thought, 'why should his interest be a matter of any secrecy?'

Several hours later the examiner emerged, feeling rather deflated, from a ghostly, muffled experience of Wild River. She decided to take a walk around the garden to clear her head.

She strode swiftly away from the cabin she'd been in, careful to avoid meeting the eyes of her fellow examiners — though she was sure they'd agree with her about the poor quality of the dream. As she walked she thought about how she would word her unenthusiastic report on the feeble dreamhunter whom she would *pass* — but whom she should, in all justice, discourage from taking up the life.

The examiner ducked through a grove of dripping golden ash trees. She caught sight of some dark-suited figures hurrying ahead of her towards the tower. She was sure that one of them was Secretary Doran.

She stopped under the trees and waited till the group was out of sight, then went on cautiously towards a hubbub she could hear through a hedge of hydrangeas.

A crowd was milling around the open doors of a cabin, their shoes making dents in the damp lawn. The examiner saw two of her colleagues sitting on the cabin's veranda with their heads on their knees. And she saw the dreamhunter Grace Tiebold leaning on a veranda post, pale, her hand held over her mouth.

The examiner thought better of her walk. She retraced her steps through the garden, and took her usual route into the tower.

Grace had sent a wire to Chorley from Doorhandle. In it she had said only that she and Laura were back and she'd be lying in on Laura's examination. Going by the wire, Chorley thought he could expect them both back home the following day.

That day arrived, and Grace and Laura didn't. For that matter, neither did Tziga, who'd been gone for two weeks now, long enough to have exhausted even his most enduring dream. Chorley had expected Tziga to appear about the time Laura set off on her first overnighter. They had all hoped he'd be back before she left and would be able to take Grace's place as Laura's guide. He hadn't arrived in time and Grace had accompanied Laura. Tziga was still absent — and Chorley hadn't had word from him.

The next day Chorley had another telegram:

LAURA MUST GO BACK IN STOP PROBLEM
WITH EXAMINATIONS STOP WILL GO TOO
STOP SORRY BUT IT IS ME OR SOME
STRANGER STOP WILL TELEGRAPH ON
REEMERGENCE GRACE.

Chorley was concerned. He took himself to the head offices of the Regulatory Body to make his own enquiries.

He was shown to the Director's office. Chorley simply asked what the problem was with Laura's examination. 'And do you — by any chance — have news of Tziga Hame? We did expect him back several days ago, before Laura's examination.'

The Director summoned underlings and sent them off to find answers to Chorley's questions. The Director had his secretary bring in a pot of tea. He poured and chatted and — Chorley thought — acted oddly nonchalant.

Chorley had thought it strange that, when he had first appeared in the Director's office, he had got the feeling that the man had been expecting his visit, and had even known what it was about. The man was — Chorley thought — now walling himself up behind this bricks and mortar of chatter. The Director had acted helpful, and sent people running, but all his showy activity seemed to Chorley to conceal something.

By the time Chorley's second cup was cool the underlings had returned with answers — and with documents.

The Director read them while Chorley waited. The Director made a neat stack of the pages and rested his folded hands upon them. He looked up at Chorley.

'Apparently your niece caught a nightmare. However, she didn't describe it as such to the rangers who escorted the season's candidates back from the test site. No one for a moment imagines Miss Hame was being *dishonest*, just a little shy, and backward. She did manage to let the rangers know that she'd caught something *different*, and unexpected. Her examiners were chosen very carefully, and there were more than the usual number. Your wife insisted on lying in with the girl too — so, unfortunately, the effect of the nightmare was rather amplified.' The Director paused and smoothed the pages with his fingertips. He cleared his throat and continued. 'It was decided that it was *imperative* that Laura overwrite her nightmare. There were no dreamhunters in Founderston with any dream suitable, or sufficiently strong, to do the job. The child had to be taken back In. Your wife went with her. Mrs Tiebold can steer her niece into calmer waters, I'm sure. I'm sure they will both be back directly.'

The Director smiled. 'As to Mr Hame. According to our records he went back In seven days ago, after registering his intentions at the ranger's post at Doorhandle.' The Director paused, then asked, 'Did Mr Hame not go home first?'

'No,' Chorley said. 'And, since he wasn't there for his daughter's Try, we expected him to turn up as soon as he was able. Why would he go back In?'

The Director frowned. 'I have no idea,' he said. It seemed to Chorley that the Director looked *expectant*, as though waiting for him to begin making excuses for Tziga. As though by hearing what Chorley would say the Director would supply himself with explanations for Tziga Hame's behaviour. Not — Chorley suspected — because the Director was disturbed and *needed* Tziga's behaviour explained, but perhaps because the Director wanted an answer to offer *other* people.

Chorley leant forward, he put his hand out for the papers and asked, 'What were Tziga's recorded intentions?'

The Director sorted one sheet from the pile and passed it to Chorley. He said, 'That's a carbon.'

Chorley looked at the paper then, sharply, up at the Director. The form wasn't written in Tziga's handwriting.

The Director seemed already aware of this. 'The ranger on duty filled in the form,' he said, and waved a hand, as if to wave away any suspicions Chorley might have. 'Mr Hame only signed it. That's not unusual, especially for the great dreamhunters. They are often helpless about anything practical.'

The space on the form where the dreamhunter was meant to write his planned destination had only one word in it. The ranger who'd supposedly filled in the form for Tziga had written: 'Across'.

Chorley saw that the paper in his hand was trembling. He put it back on the Director's desk, but kept his hand upon it. Chorley's ears were ringing. He was in shock — a shock that was several parts rage. He wanted to lean across the desk and take the Director by his collar and shake him. But Chorley knew that showing what he was feeling wasn't wise till he'd got away from the office and had a chance to think. Chorley had a suspicion that the document was *forged*, not 'filled in' for Tziga. He was sure that something was being covered up, hastily and messily, just ahead of his enquiries. He was sure, too, that if he didn't pursue the matter *at once* the cover-up would sort itself out and tidy itself up and form a solid front.

Chorley Tiebold was a man who'd got his own way almost all his life. His whole life experience, and his forceful nature, told him to challenge these lies and whatever lay behind them. His character and knowledge shrieked at him to *attack* — now, decisively. But something else — an instinct deeper than experience — was telling him to let it go, and not let this man know how suspicious he was. For, as he sat there in the office of the Director, Chorley was at last being forced to face a fear he'd had but kept secret from himself. Worries that he'd shaken out of his head whenever they intruded. The fear was *this* — that Tziga, his sad, secretive friend, had been involved in dangerous things. Dangerous things possibly sanctioned by the Regulatory Body, but things that Tziga was ashamed of and wanted to keep from his family.

Something had gone wrong. The danger had overwhelmed Tziga.

And, until Chorley discovered exactly what that danger was, and that it only threatened Tziga and not his family too, Chorley decided that he had better keep his new understanding from anyone who had anything to do with the Dream Regulatory Body.

The Director cleared his throat again. 'We can't know how Mr Hame was *in himself*. If he was joking, for instance. Perhaps he wrote what he did only to imply that he didn't like to be asked where he was going. I mean — the great ones in their exploratory phases are often secretive about their sites.'

'Yes,' Chorley said. He looked at the paper again, at that word 'Across'. He didn't imagine for a second that Tziga had intended to make a crossing.

The Director said, 'I'm sorry that, at this point, I can't be of more assistance. But if you have further cause to feel concerned — that is, if Mr Hame doesn't appear within the next few days at Doorhandle, as usual . . .'

Chorley said, 'Thank you,' and put the paper back on the Director's table and got up.

'I'll have the post at Doorhandle send a wire as soon as Mrs Tiebold and Miss Hame emerge,' the Director said. He stood too. They shook hands and Chorley left.

Laura and Grace were back within three days. A car dropped them at the front steps of the family's house in Founderston. The driver carried their hats and coats and knapsacks into the hall, then Grace closed the front door on him in a definite but not ill-tempered way. Rose ran down the stairs and hugged her mother and cousin, crushing them together in her embrace.

'Sorry for being away so long,' Grace said to Rose. 'Laura needs a bath.' She pushed Rose and Laura towards the stairs. 'Please see to it, Rose. I'll organise a meal.'

Chorley had already organised a meal and baths, but didn't like to talk over the top of Grace, who clearly had urgent things to say to him. She was more tired than he'd seen her for years. She was pale and had shiny concavities of dry skin on her lower lip.

'Go on,' said Chorley to Rose and Laura.

'Where is Da?' Laura said.

'I told you not to expect him,' Grace said, testily.

'Why shouldn't I expect him? He should be here,' Laura said.

'He's not here, Laura,' Chorley said. 'We'll discuss it later.'

Laura looked from uncle to aunt. 'I see,' she said. 'Once you've got your stories straight.'

'Sweetheart, we'll tell you everything we know, once we've had a talk and between us — yes — sorted out fact from — from other stuff,' Chorley said.

Laura glared at them, but let her cousin lead her away.

Laura lay in her bath, peeling a mandarin. Several other mandarins floated around her, bumping against her body and the sides of the bath.

Rose was sitting on the floor, her back against the full-length mirror, her hair clinging to its misty surface.

Laura had just come to the end of her account of her first dream.

'More convicts,' said Rose.

'Yes. That's three dreams we know about. Two of them mine and one that Da made a point of mentioning.'

Rose looked puzzled, then said, 'Oh! You're right! The labourers at the end of Convalescent One are convicts.'

'Convicts mending the railway line, convicts building a wall, one convict with a letter in his mouth —'

'From a real person, the real Secretary of the Interior.'

'And convicts on the run after a mass prison break,' Laura finished. She dropped peel on the tiled floor and began to feed herself a mandarin, segment by segment. She grimaced. 'I have mouth ulcers.'

'Ma and Uncle Tziga always get mouth ulcers,' said Rose. 'And so it begins for you too. The stereotypical silent and secretive dreamhunter just has a sore mouth.' Rose gave a barking laugh then said, 'The things I know — I should write my memoirs.'

'We should probably keep Cas Doran under our hats,' said Laura, as if she thought Rose was serious about her memoirs. 'When we were on our way back to Doorhandle your Ma told me that Secretary Doran lay in on my examination.'

'Well, you are a Hame.'

'I don't like it,' Laura said. 'It gives me the creeps. That letter — the real letter — was really in a dead ranger's mouth.'

Rose wondered aloud whether their classmate Mamie Doran, Cas Doran's daughter, had any opinions on convicts.

'Mamie has an opinion on everything.'

'Except hair ribbons and other stuff she's above thinking about,' Rose said.

'Poor Mamie's just making the best of being a girl — the best of a bad lot.'

Rose said, determined, 'I'm not going to be like that. I'm not going to start telling myself I'm *settling* for anything.'

Laura batted a mandarin away from her chin and sank down in the bath. 'Why do I dream about convicts?' she said.

'The Place is trying to tell you something. Remember how Da said to us that perhaps the dreams are true stories? If they're true then some of them *matter*.'

Laura looked very worried.

Rose sat up straight. Her damp hair detached from the mirror and dropped on to her shoulders. 'The real question is this: Who is using dreams to tell stories?'

'Da would say "God",' said Laura.

'And *my* Da would say "Nonsense!"'

Grace and Chorley were shut in his workshop. She had just finished a detailed account of Laura's first dream and was attempting to eat something. She had trouble with a bit of scone she was trying to swallow and spat it out into her hand. She dropped the chewed mess on to Chorley's workbench and put her face in her hands. 'I'm so tired,' she said. 'I feel as though I'm nowhere.'

Chorley ran the tea towel that had wrapped the scones under a tap and handed it to his wife. He said, 'The convict in Laura's nightmare remembered being a boy on So Long Spit. Her dream was set in *our world*.'

Grace was nodding. Then she knuckled a tear out from under her eye.

Chorley went to Grace. He sat beside her on the workshop's lumpy, developer-stained sofa. He stroked her hair. 'Look,' he said, 'I'm sorry to have to worry you any more, but Tziga has disappeared. The Body says he went back In to hunt another dream. The Director showed me a carbon of his page from the intentions book.'

'I saw it when I was signing myself,' Grace said. 'I think the signature is a forgery — I've seen the real thing often enough over the years in intentions books. I think the Body is keeping things from us. We have to decide what to *do*, love. We have to think about what it means that we're being encouraged to think Tziga did something as crazy as attempting a crossing. And we have to think of Laura.'

Chorley drew a deep shuddering breath. Then he said, 'Do you have any idea what it was Tziga was up to?'

Grace let go of him and drew back. 'No,' she said. Then, 'Yes. Maybe. Not exactly.'

'Which is it?' Chorley's voice was stern. 'Yes, no, or maybe?'

'Dear, I know there are things about dreamhunting that you disapprove of. You think some of it is a bit distasteful. Tziga and I never discussed certain things in front of you. Things we felt you might find offensive.'

Chorley gestured for her to go on. He was too angry to speak. Grace was blaming his *attitude* for her secrecy.

'You know that there are different types of dreams — different classifications. There are healing dreams, and adventure, romance, achievement, enlightenment, indulgence — the dreams where you find yourself sitting down to eight-course feasts . . .'

'Yes,' said Chorley.

'There's a type of dream the Body classifies as a "think again" dream. Tziga catches them to take to prisons. "Think again" dreams are a tool in reform programs.'

'And how would this get him into trouble?'

Grace's eyes wandered. She looked down as if she was ashamed. Ashamed of what she knew, or suspected, Chorley thought. She said, 'I can't see how Tziga might have got into trouble with the Body. He's always trusted their judgment. But, Chorley, those dreams were *bad* for him.' Grace bit her lip, then went on. 'I thought about it a lot this summer, because he seemed more sad and shut into himself than ever. "Think again" dreams may well do wonders for hardened murderers, but Tziga performs them over and over, and so he's the one learning again and again that he's a *sinner*, a bad person.'

'So — these dreams are unpleasant?'

Grace looked up into Chorley's eyes. 'They're nightmares.'

Chorley got up and paced. He made several circuits of the workbench before he spoke again. Then he said, 'You should have told me.'

'Why me and not him? He's *your* friend. *He* should have told you. I only had suspicions and figured it out — he never actually talked to me about it.' Grace raised her voice; she was fighting back. 'And you made it quite clear to me that you only wanted to know so much and no more about what we did. About where the money came from, for God's sake! All summer you've chiselled on about how you didn't want the girls to Try. They came of age and suddenly you were full of prejudices about dreamhunting. But Laura and Rose were never going to turn into Tziga.'

'Laura is exactly like him!' Chorley yelled at his wife. 'And the first time she goes In to catch a dream she catches something frightening. If that's not like Tziga then what is?'

Grace began to cry again. 'But Laura won't get mixed up in the Body's contracts. We'll tell her not to. She and Rose always had very definite opinions about government contracts, if only because they saw Tziga being whipped off from Sisters Beach several times every summer.'

Chorley closed his eyes and tried to calm himself. 'If Tziga was so troubled by his nightmares, why did he *keep on* delivering them?'

'I don't know. If I'm right about it — and how bad it's been for him — I can't imagine what would induce him to keep on. Perhaps he believes he's doing good. He has always tended to think of himself as some kind of saviour.'

Grace patted the sofa beside her. 'Sit down, please, Chorley. We have to decide what we're going to do.'

Chorley relented. He came and sat beside Grace and she retrieved his hand and held it hard. After a while she said, 'If Tziga is supposed to have disappeared — according to the Body — then I should get together an official search party. I have to do that so that the Body thinks I *believe* its story. I just don't trust it. If it's covering things up I don't want to give it reason to think it has to cover up any further. We do want to find him.'

'Something has happened to him,' Chorley said.

Grace nodded.

'What about Laura?'

Grace was silent for a long time. Then she said, 'Perhaps we should try to persuade the Body to withhold Laura's dreamhunter's licence. They're already alarmed by her talent — alarmed and fascinated in equal measures, I think. We might be able to put them off her.' Grace thought for a little longer, then she told Chorley her plan.

Four

Laura was relieved when her aunt and uncle finally admitted to her that her father was missing. She'd known for days that they were hiding grave concerns about him, and waiting to know more before breaking the bad news.

Laura learnt that Grace was getting up a search party to look for her father. She pinned her hopes on her aunt's search and tried to put her fears out of her mind. She had remarkably little trouble doing it.

Since first entering the Place Laura had changed. She seemed to be able to put all her feelings further away from her day-to-day self. It was as if she'd developed an inner hinterland, and, having entered the Place, she'd taken on some of its characteristic distance, silence and dryness.

Besides, she hadn't really had time to talk to Rose properly. She felt much of what was happening to her was suspended and unreal till she could talk it all over with Rose.

The Body kept her busy. She was out for only one sleep in her old bed before being taken In again and to the site of another of those stable, benign dreams. She caught Beautiful Horse and Aerial Picnic. She went to sleep with examiners in the cabins in the garden of the Regulatory Body, airy buildings built of polished timber, with wide porches screened by white-painted louvres. She was tested again and again — but no more convicts appeared in her dreams.

On her way out with her fourth dream, a seasonal favourite called Great Players, concerning football, Laura met the four of her clutch who had been successful in catching Wild River. They were standing around the potbellied stove in the hall of the post, consulting charts. They were clustered together, talking in loud, self-important voices and glowing with excitement. Around their necks, proudly, outside their clothes, they were wearing the copper tags that were their licences.

The little group spotted Laura and began to whisper among themselves. Then, as one, they shuffled over to where she stood waiting for her guides to complete their paperwork.

The tallest boy — the boy from the infants' beach — extended his hand to Laura. 'Sandy Mason,' he said.

Laura took his hand and shook it.

The bandy-legged boy asked her, 'How's it going?'

'Slowly,' said Laura. 'They tell me that they need to know whether I'll provide dreams of consistent quality.'

The other girl in the clutch, who had succeeded in catching Wild River, said, 'Why won't they just licence you and see how your dreams do on the market? I thought the market sorted out the weak from the strong.'

'It's not a matter of weakness. It's not *that* kind of problem with quality.'

'You don't think they're making allowances, perhaps, letting you retest because you're his daughter and they just can't believe you're a fizzer?' the bandy-legged boy said, smirking at Laura.

'My Aunt Grace often says that dreamhunters are envious and competitive. It seems to be true of you,' Laura told the boy. 'I caught a nightmare and the examiners say that's a safety issue.'

'Right,' said the boy, dubious.

An adult approached Laura and the clutch. An expensively kitted-out dreamhunter with red hair and a taut-skinned, pale face. 'Children,' he said, 'I realise it's early days yet, but I'd like you to be aware of your options.' He pulled a silver card case out of his breast pocket and flicked it open. He passed them all his card. 'I often have occasion to hire dreamhunters as amplifiers. It is a very good way for novices to earn while they're learning their trade and building up their own client base. What people don't tell you — while they're filling your head with visions of mastery, of ranging hunts and magnificent new dreams — is that you have to learn to out-walk and out-wake dozens of other keen hunters. Fit, seasoned dreamhunters. The drug Wakeful is a very bad habit to acquire at your age — and you will be tempted to take it up. There's so much pressure to succeed quickly. I'm sure your families are very keen for you to start earning your fortunes.' He looked from face to face, his expression inquiring. 'Yes? Are you feeling the pressure already?'

The clutch all looked down at the card he'd handed them.

'I don't usually solicit children,' the man said. 'But I happened to be passing A–8 when you were there with your less successful fellows catching your first dream.'

'Catching it and skinning it,' the bandy-legged boy said, boastful and gloating.

'Very good,' said the man, and smiled at the boy. 'A ranger on picket duty told me what was up and steered me away, but not before I felt one of you fall asleep — crash! Like a hangman's trapdoor. I said to myself, "I'll look that one up later. There is a dreamhunter among dreamhunters. I'll offer him work."'

'It was me,' said the bandy-legged boy. 'I'm the one.'

'Good for you,' said the man, and gave the boy's arm a squeeze.

'I know who you are, sir,' the boy said.

Laura knew too, and she wasn't about to open her mouth in his presence. This was Maze Plasir, about whom her father and aunt always spoke with stiff disapproval.

The boy was saying, 'My brother sampled you once.'

'And he told you all about it?' Maze Plasir shook his head and laughed.

'Yes, he did.' The boy had coloured up, his face and neck suffused with blood, his earlobes purpled, jutted, actually throbbed. He glanced around him at the clutch, then seemed to decide to put them all aside. 'Never mind this lot,' he said. 'They're all nice kids from good homes — you know what I mean. My brother, he came home off his ship and he had a dose. He had to stay away from his girl, but he was — you know.'

'I know,' said Plasir, po-faced and sympathetic.

'So he went to your place and tried your dream — Fresh.'

'Ah,' said Plasir, 'I have Fresh tonight.' He smiled and tapped his head with a forefinger. 'It's a favourite with my clients.'

The boy's jaw dropped, so that all the others could see the glistening strings of spit strung between his tongue and the roof of his mouth.

Plasir said to the boy, 'Think about this: after you've caught your very first dream your brain changes. Your mind becomes an amphitheatre in which any other dreamhunter can perform. Empty, you're an amplifier. The greater the talent you have — the more capacity — the greater that amphitheatre is. You can make a good dreamer of a poor dreamer, and a great dreamer of a good. I'm a good dreamer, unique, versatile and — this is the important point — willing to experiment.'

The boy was hooked, he was nodding as though he was sitting on a horse at a trot. He folded his chart and put it away.

'Would you like to come with me?' Plasir said. 'Would you like to provide an amphitheatre for me to perform in? You can earn good money, and learn a thing or two.'

'Am I *allowed* to?'

'Don't you know that a licensed dreamhunter is no longer a minor? That's an allowance the law makes to get around the child-labour laws, the law that says you stay in school till you're sixteen. But this —' Plasir flicked the copper tags on the boy's chest. '— this says you're an adult.'

'Great,' the boy said. 'You're on. I'll go with you.'

Plasir put an arm loosely around the boy's shoulders and grinned at the others. 'You keep those cards, children. Think about it,' he said. He conducted the boy out to his car.

'That man has nearly lost his licence many times,' Laura said. 'My father says Mr Plasir has reached some accommodation with the Body so it overlooks his excesses.'

'I'm sorry about your father,' the girl said to Laura. 'You must be worried.'

Laura shook her head, not to deny that she was worried, but just because she felt that if she gave any sign of assent she'd be assenting to the fact that he had disappeared.

Sandy Mason said, 'Fresh is something nasty about a beautiful young girl. I may come from a "good home" but I've heard talk. I never imagined I'd meet anyone who actually *wanted* to be Maze Plasir. But that guy did.' The boy tossed Plasir's business card on top of the stove where it humped, went brown, then burst into flame and flew up like a tiny black bird. 'Everyone else wants to be your aunt,' Sandy said to Laura.

'Even me,' said Laura.

'That kid's a liar too — and I don't know why it suited Plasir to believe his boasting.'

'Maybe Plasir just likes to collect corruptible youth,' the girl said.

Mason pulled a face, then he said to Laura, 'Anyway, as I was saying, it wasn't snot-face who went down like the gallows' trap. My guide was feeling for me, because my uncle is a dreamhunter who, when he has a dream, falls asleep with such a hard hit he knocks out whoever is in the room with him. Doctors sometimes use him instead of a general anaesthetic. That's his special talent. My guide knew to look out for it in me. And I didn't disappoint her, I did go hard — perhaps you felt me? Or maybe you felt snot-face from the slums, who my guide says nearly dumped her like a shaky stepping-stone. But you went after us all, Laura, and it was you who was Plasir's "gallows' trap" — except my guide described it as a landslide. It was a near thing, she said. She's just a ranger, like the others there, and she reckoned half of them nearly fell in after you.'

'No one told me that,' Laura said.

'No? Anyway — *I* believe you about the "safety issues" stuff.' He put out a hand. 'And I want to wish you good luck.'

Laura took his hand again, and shook it. She took the other hands she was offered.

'Dreamhunters aren't all envious and competitive,' the girl said to Laura, gentle and reproachful.

'Only competitive, maybe,' said Mason, grinning. Then he took Plasir's card from Laura and wrote his own name and address on the back of it. 'Keep that,' he said.

* * *

Grace organised her search party. They set out, herself and six rangers. They walked eleven days In from Doorhandle, a day beyond the marker left by an earlier — surviving — expedition. They found no sign of Tziga Hame. They turned around and walked back out. Twenty-two days it took them. They emerged, thin, dehydrated, and several with suppurating blisters on their feet.

Grace had slept, so had caught and overwritten thirteen dreams altogether. Several were new to her, and some were unpleasant. She was forced to go off by herself to one of the dreamers' retreats in the forest near Doorhandle, there to rest up and rid herself of the cacophonous jumble of incidents, characters and settings. She slept for hours at a time, woke only to feed herself, or draw water at the well, or sit on the veranda in the autumn sunshine watching wood pigeons with their bellies full of fermented berries, bumbling drunkenly from branch to branch and sometimes dropping out of the trees altogether.

She wrapped herself up and slept in the sun, gradually ploughing her monstrous mix of dreams back into the air.

Grace left it to Chorley to tell Laura that the search party hadn't found her father.

'They didn't find him *dead*, either,' Laura said. 'The intentions book may say "Across", but how do you know that "Across" wasn't his name for a dream?'

'Darling, they didn't find any sign of him, and he hasn't turned up anywhere. It's been nearly five weeks.'

'But couldn't "Across" be a dream?'

Laura wanted to cling to the last thing her father had done that seemed to her fully *sane*. Sane and reliable. She didn't count his impatience with her on the station at Sisters Beach. She went looking in her memories and found herself in summer again, at the sand-sculpting competition. Her father was helping her and Rose make a reclining man from the sand on the beach below the Strand. 'Dad?' Laura said to her memory, peering back through time at his face, in the shadow of his sun hat. 'Dad? What is it?'

'Laura?' Chorley shook her. She was sitting in a chair in the parlour of the Founderston house, staring off up into the corner of the room. She came to and crumpled. 'Where is he?' She was pleading.

Chorley held her. 'I don't know,' he said, in tears too.

'Where's he gone?' Laura said.

Rose was kneeling on the rug behind her father, who was on his knees before Laura, holding her to him. Rose wrung her hands and pressed them against her mouth. She was afraid to speak, afraid to interfere, afraid to join in their grief.

'I don't know where he's gone,' Chorley said, again.

'Why didn't he come home?' Laura said, childish and dogged.

Rose scrambled across the floor and embraced Laura too.

'I want him to come home,' Laura said, sobbing.

Five

The offices of the Secretary of the Interior, pressed for space, had reclaimed the attics of the Palace of Governance, a building which, in former days, had been one of Founderston's grand residences. The attics had been servants' quarters, and narrow back stairs still ran all the way down from top to bottom of the four corners of the building. The stair on the east corner was enclosed for all its length, and the doors on every floor were fastened by locks, and by several coats of paint. At its foot this back stair opened on an alley beside one of Founderston's brackish storm drains. At its top the staircase ended in a plain, panelled door. On the far side of that door was the office of the Secretary of the Interior, Cas Doran.

Doran's large, low-roofed room had two old oval windows, whose solid frames bulged above and below the window glass like swollen eyelids. Through the windows Doran's visitors could appreciate keyhole views of the tower of the Dream Regulatory Body — one of Secretary Doran's most tightly controlled departments.

Doran sat with his back to his view. It was his visitors who should be reminded that they were looking out at his domain. Those visitors whose appointments the Secretary scheduled for the early morning also could hardly fail to notice how Doran's windows focused the low sun into his room like a burning glass.

Secretary Doran was an early riser. The people in his outer office were early risers too, because of the pressure of his expectations.

They knew that the Secretary always asked certain people to come early. People he wished to catch on the hop.

It was just after seven when Dr Wilmot arrived in Doran's outer office. The doctor was still pink from his bath. His hair was so freshly and heavily oiled that its scent was causing his eyes to water, so that he had several times to pop his monocle out of his sweaty eye socket and polish it. Wilmot was on time, but had to wait. He polished his monocle so often that it was smeared with cloudy iridescence.

The musical tinkle of a bell by Doran's door signalled that the Secretary was ready for his next — or, Wilmot hoped, his *first* — appointment of the day.

The doctor was shown into Doran's office.

The Secretary of the Interior did not get up from behind his desk. It was a desk like an altar stone, as heavy as carved masonry, but made of some tropical hardwood. Doran had one paper on this slick, dark desktop. Wilmot recognised his own letterhead.

'Good of you to come,' said Doran, and gestured at a chair.

Wilmot took a seat. The chair was comfortable, but from this angle Doran was now only a silhouette against light striking up from the zinc roof of the assembly rooms one floor below.

'This death certificate . . .' Doran began.

'Esteemed Secretary . . .' said the doctor.

Doran raised a hand. The doctor fell silent.

'A certificate signed by one Dr Grove — you mention it in your letter.'

Dr Wilmot had not *mentioned* the death certificate in his letter — the death certificate was the *whole subject* of his letter. Wilmot said, 'Dr Grove is the consulting physician at Magdalene Charity Hospital in Westport.'

'You have written that here,' said Doran.

'Secretary, indeed. It is all there, I believe. I have seen the certificate. I have a copy of it in my private records. I thought that was best. I was sure that was what you would want. The *substance* of Grove's findings are in my letter, Secretary.'

Doran read out, 'Tziga Hame expired on 10 March this year, as the result of injuries to his skull sustained in the Westport railway yards on 2 March. That is the substance?'

'That is what Dr Grove's certificate says. And, from my own examination of Hame directly after his fall, it is the result I expected. Though he did last a little longer than I thought he would.'

'He *lasted* — while you returned to your practice.'

'There was nothing to be done for the man. My further attendance on him would have been conspicuous.'

The doctor could have sworn that he felt Doran's gaze, the Secretary's eyes, shifting from item to item of his clothes, appraising him. Dr Wilmot was dressed as a successful man should be — a successful man who also prided himself on being something of a *character*, an *identity* at the resort in Sisters Beach. The doctor flushed. He said, 'Hame was best left where he was, an anonymous beneficiary of the tender care of the good sisters. I'm sure you agree.'

'Yes, I do agree,' Doran said.

Wilmot sagged with relief.

'However,' said Doran, 'your letter, while reassuring in many respects, lacks some vital information.'

'Sir, how can I help you?'

'I don't want your bedside manner, Wilmot. I want intelligent compliance with my needs.'

Wilmot swallowed, and waited.

Doran gave a small sigh. 'I have a letter about a certificate. You have the certificate in your private files. But, tell me, Doctor, does Hame have a grave?'

The blood left Dr Wilmot's head so swiftly that his bald spot grew chilly.

'This distresses me,' Doran said. 'I dislike having to apply for this sort of information myself, but I have done so and can tell you that your discreet Groves and the sisters at Magdalene Charity cannot tell me what was done with the man's remains.'

Wilmot opened his mouth, but could think of nothing to say. His jaw was trembling with tension. His open mouth made popping noises.

'You silly fish,' said Doran. He sounded like a parent at the end of his patience and about to resort to disciplinary measures.

He crumpled the letter in his hands. 'You can be in Westport in three hours if you take the next train.'

Doctor Wilmot got up and left the Secretary's office.

In the evening Cas Doran's oval windows opened on to a dark blue late autumn dusk in which only a few lights showed, attic windows in the roofs of the Isle's hotels and dream parlours, and the beacon on the top of the tower of the Regulatory Body.

Doran and his friend were sitting in easy chairs at a fireplace on the far side of the room. They were enjoying a glass of wine.

'How is your Mr Gregg?' Maze Plasir asked his friend.

John Gregg was the new Speaker of the House of Representatives. Various people, including the President of the Republic, would have been alarmed to hear Gregg referred to as *Cas Doran's* Mr Gregg.

'Highly satisfactory.' Cas Doran mused for a moment, then he asked, 'How do you do it, Maze?'

'You don't want me to answer that. The less you know the better, probably.'

'I'd like to know.'

Maze looked into the fire. 'It's more difficult to do than it is to explain. So — briefly — the process. Your latest request was that anyone with any influence should favour Mr Gregg for the job of Speaker of the House. You wanted people to imagine that, for some time, they'd had a good opinion of him?'

Cas leant forward.

'First I caught Admirable Man. Then I grafted Mr Gregg's face and voice and gestures on to the subject of the dream. I let the dream degrade a little over several nights. Then I loaded what was left of it — its strongest emotions and impressions — into my apprentice. My apprentice attended performances at dream palaces: the Beholder and the Rainbow Opera. He was induced to go into his trance once the patrons of the palace had retired, and he insinuated a few ideas and impressions into them when they were on the verge of sleep. He cast his colour out on the shock wave of Grace Tiebold's big penumbra. He caught all the right people. And a week later Gregg won his appointment.'

Doran raised his glass to Plasir. 'You make it sound very matter of fact.'

Maze shook his head. 'It isn't. And I'm afraid I'll be unable to colour any more of the public's opinions for the next while. My apprentice has had a breakdown. They do. But I have found a suitable replacement. The last Try turned up an excellent child.'

'And what is it that makes this child so excellent?'

'He's very impressionable. I am letting him in on mysteries — my most delicious dreams, and certain "mental disciplines". He laps it all up.'

Doran refilled Plasir's glass. 'When will he be ready? I'd like to think that, if I find myself in need of some good propaganda, all options are available to me.'

'The colouring of dreams has limited use as propaganda. Did you see the papers this evening?' Maze asked.

'What in particular?'

'The Temple claims to have ten thousand pledge-takers.' Maze sat up straight and put his hand over his heart. He quoted, '"I swear I will not partake of dreams . . ." Cas, we can't colour the opinions of people who won't sleep with a dreamer.'

They were quiet for a time. A log in the fire fell apart. The flames covered its coals in a blue and orange membrane, and they tinkled like breaking wires.

'I'd like to know what your plans are, Cas. If I know more I can think about what dreams to catch and how to alter them to suit your purposes.'

'My plans, as far as they concern you and your new boy, involve a series of adjustments in the attitude of the general public.' Doran mused for a time. Then he said, 'It's impossible to have an effective government when it is constantly checked by a very poorly drafted Constitution. For instance, my projects would benefit greatly from a longer term in office.'

'I see.'

'Maze, we are a country that has always found reasons to congratulate itself. Material reasons — our production of wheat and beef, iron and coal. And *moral* reasons — our tradition of democracy. Now, I'm a patriot. Any patriot has sometimes to think like a farmer — a farmer who takes out his gun to kill a wolf, and who builds a fence around his water supply.'

Plasir said, 'I'm not sure who the wolves are, Cas. Though I think I'm getting your drift about the water. I guess you're talking about Shackle Island and its copper mines. I read the editorial your friend wrote, about the islanders' greed and our needs.'

'There's no copper on the mainland,' Cas Doran said. He leant forward, excited. 'When we were using it only to make things like warming pans and carriage lamps, its cost wasn't a problem.' He pointed at the light fitting above his head. 'Now we have countless vital uses for that flexible, conductive metal.'

Plasir nodded. 'And it's easier to present arguments for an invasion to people who have been somehow prepared to hear them.'

'I don't like that word "invasion". If the islanders all had a share in the mines' huge profits, things would be very different. But they don't. No — our need is making only a few of them rich. The inequalities on Shackle Island are unjust, and offensive to any decent society.'

'Cas, you're a visionary.'

Cas Doran cast his eyes down. 'No, just a practical man who is prepared to think about the future.' He turned his hands palm up, seemed to examine them for stains. He said, 'I have plenty of work for you, Maze. I have big plans. But, things aren't going as smoothly as they should.'

'Hmmm?' Plasir made an encouraging noise.

Cas Doran looked up at his friend. 'Tziga Hame has no grave. The man was a meteor and no one can show me where he fell.'

Six

It was late at night, and the house was quiet. The only sound was from the river — a barge passing under the echoing arches of the nearest bridge.

Grace and Chorley were in bed, clinging together for comfort. They were talking, softly, trying to refine their plans.

Chorley said, 'I have to make the Director think that if he lets me have my way I won't be any bother to him in the future.'

Grace said, 'And he has to imagine that if Laura isn't licensed and goes back to school she'll never bother the Body again either.'

'If only Laura *wanted* to go back to school,' Chorley said. 'She's developed her taste for dreamhunting rather quickly, hasn't she?'

'She knows she's good at it. Talent has its own needs, you know.'

'So I've been told. And I've been told that God is in Heaven, and that Jesus died for my sins.' Chorley gave a rude, sceptical grunt.

Grace ignored this. She said, 'There is one thing we can do to make Laura *want* to go back to school. But it's hard on Rose.'

'Rose is resilient.'

'Yes, she is. She's probably tougher than all of us put together. My thought is this — we could send Rose away, have her board at the Academy, get her out of the house so that Laura hardly ever gets to see her. We can put Rose in as a boarder for a term, but tell her it's for an "indefinite period".'

'That is hard.'

'Yes. Hard on me too, Chorley. Rose will think I've lost interest in her since she isn't a dreamhunter.'

Chorley nodded. His chin brushed his wife's hair. They were quiet for a time, then Grace said, 'I don't want to sleep. I still have bits of my raggedy mess of dreams. I think I'd better get up and read, then go to bed once you and the girls are awake.'

'Is Laura expected to go In again soon?'

'No. The Body is making its deliberations. Its decision. And Laura is in mourning, of course.'

'*He's not dead*,' Chorley said, suddenly. 'He *can't* be dead.' Grace heard his jaw make a pneumatic creak as he clenched his teeth. Other than that he was motionless — but she could still feel turmoil in his body, his anger, and fear, and suppressed sorrow.

'We could send Laura to her Aunt Marta's for a day or two,' Grace said. 'She should see Marta. And with Laura gone we can tackle Rose and have her off to school before Laura gets back.'

'All right,' Chorley said. 'I'll put Laura on the train tomorrow.'

'When I'm asleep,' Grace said. 'Sorry, Chorley, I know how it's been — Tziga and me out at all hours and sleeping when you were awake. Awake and on top of things while we were out of our heads, or full of nonsense. Sorry — I'm saying sorry.'

Chorley sighed. 'When Tziga was courting Verity I used to call him "my sister's creepy suitor". He was the first dreamhunter I ever met. I never went to dreams. Tziga was this black-eyed, limping, spooky man who managed always to be *there*, watching my friends and me as though we were a pack of happy dogs — which we were. I never knew what he was thinking, but, at the time, I thought he saw us all as shallow and simple. But, the strange thing was that, as time went by, I got to like being rubbed up the wrong way. I liked to feel that he was judging me, because I liked his attention. I'd say to Verity and my friends, "I suppose that damned Hame will be there as usual", but I'd want him to be there.' Chorley made a choking sound, then added, 'I want him to be *here*.'

'I know,' said Grace, and put up her hand to stroke his hair. 'I know.'

* * *

When Rose's father told her that she was being sent away to board at Founderston Girls' Academy she didn't react at first. She was quiet because she was wondering why her Da looked as though he was steeling himself for an ordeal. Did he expect her to explode? He certainly looked set to endure shouting, accusations, tears — all kinds of girlish unpleasantness.

Because she didn't immediately react to what he'd said, Rose had a chance to reflect. Why would her mother and father want to send her away? Her father was transparently distressed. Was this only her mother's idea? Was her mother really *that* disappointed in the result of her Try? Would her father let her mother act on disappointment? Rose thought, 'They want to protect me from something. Or I'm somehow in the way of their concentrating on Laura. But *I* can look after Laura better than anyone can.'

'So —' said Chorley, 'that is acceptable to you?'

'Are you holding your breath?' Rose said. 'Do you think I'm going to start shouting at you?'

'You're being very mature, Rose. It's admirable.'

'Why are you doing this?' Rose said.

'It suits us.'

'That's the most cold-blooded thing you've ever said to me, Da.'

Rose watched the colour leaving her father's face. She watched him control himself — not his temper, but perhaps his desire to confide in her. She said, 'Why don't you just tell me?'

'We don't have to explain ourselves. All you need to know is that, at the moment, it *suits* us to have you board at the Academy. For goodness' sake, Rose, when you were younger you girls used to ask to board. You thought it would be fun.'

'I remember,' said Rose. 'And what about Laura? What's Laura going to do when she comes home and finds me gone?'

'That's our concern. You're just going to have to trust our judgment.'

Rose shook her head. 'Uncle Tziga set out to walk across the Place and you expect me to trust your judgment?'

'Act as though you do, then. Don't give us any trouble.' Chorley took a step away from the library fireplace, a step towards her. He put out his hand, but didn't touch her. 'You're behaving admirably, darling, and I appreciate it.'

'A gold star for Rose,' said Rose.

Chorley called on the Director of the Regulatory Body.

When Chorley arrived the Director got up from behind his desk, came around it and took Chorley's hand in both of his and gripped it with great solemnity. 'I'm terribly sorry about Mr Hame,' he said.

'Thank you. I did get your letter of condolence.'

The Director took a chair opposite Chorley, out from behind the barrier of his desk. He crossed his legs and twitched the crease in his pin-striped trousers till it sat in the centre of his knee. 'How can I help you, Mr Tiebold?'

'I'll get straight to the point. I would like the Body to refuse Laura her licence. I understand that you do have reservations about her suitability as a dreamhunter.'

The Director pursed his lips and inclined his head. 'We do feel it would be wrong to let her out on her own too soon. Her ability is so very far ahead of her maturity. We have concerns for her safety, and her mental health. We are also obliged by law to protect the public. *However*, our lengthy deliberation about Miss Hame does not reflect our sense of her worth as a dreamhunter, or our desire to help her take up the life. We'd just like to set her on the right path.'

'I'd like to see her go back to school,' Chorley said.

The Director covered his mouth. He smoothed his moustache. From behind his hand he said, 'There are problems with that. You are aware, I hope, that in giving your consent to your niece's Try you have consented to the examination process? And that, once her licence is issued, you and your wife are no longer her guardians? That, in effect, the Body is her guardian till she comes of age? The law was intended to protect young dreamhunters from family ambition. Each dreamhunter represents so much potential earning power, and they come from all walks of life, including families who are not at all accustomed to managing wealth.'

'Yes, I understand all that. But my request is very different. The Body doesn't need to protect Laura from my desire to exploit her. I've no ambitions for her. I only want her to be safe.' Chorley leant forward. 'Laura is the only child of my only sister. Her father has come to harm. I have always had my reservations about my niece and daughter Trying. *Always*. But it was their wish to Try. And it was Grace's wish. Grace doesn't know I'm here, making this request. This is between you and me.' Chorley leant further forward and took the Director's hand. 'Sometimes sentiment is more important than the law. I cannot bear to give Laura up to the madness that has swallowed her father.'

The Director's eyes flashed with appetite and interest. 'Do you think that Mr Hame went mad?'

Chorley lowered his eyes. He tried to seem stricken. He hoped that the Director would swallow his act. 'Yes,' he said, hushed, 'I'm terribly afraid for Laura.'

'I see. But, Mr Tiebold, what is your wife's opinion?'

Chorley frowned. 'My wife is not Laura's blood-relative. If it comes to a confrontation between us about Laura's future I have the greater right. However, I don't want to openly oppose my wife's wishes. That's why I've come to you. I'm very happy to reimburse the Body for the trouble it has taken with Laura.'

'Are you asking me if you can *buy* the Body's refusal?'

'Of course not.'

'Miss Hame could return to her studies, but she isn't the same person she was before she caught her first dream. She won't be able to sleep near another, loaded, dreamhunter without amplifying their dream. She will have to be very careful, all her life.'

'Yes, I know.'

The men studied each other. One was imagining that his wish would be granted, and the other was thinking, happily, of how many *other* people would believe that Tziga Hame had been insane at the time of his disappearance.

The Director got up. He made a circle of one arm and invited Chorley to stand up into it. He gripped Chorley's shoulders and squeezed gently. 'Leave this in my hands,' he said.

Chorley thanked him and went home to wait for Grace.

* * *

'This might work,' Grace said. 'Laura has never been strong on initiative. If someone decides things for her she'll simply accept it. With a few tears.'

'I'm prepared for tears. And I'm sure she'd really rather be with Rose,' Chorley said.

'I'm glad the Director was so receptive. I don't think I could have staged a public quarrel with you, dear. And I'm sure it would be bad for Laura to think we'd quarrelled over her.'

'I hope we haven't over-reacted. I hope we're doing the right thing.'

'Me too.'

Four days later, when Chorley and Grace were sitting quietly, holding hands across the gate-leg table in the sunny bow window of their library, Laura burst into the room. Her eyes were puffy from days of crying, but she was smiling. Around her neck, flashing and clanking faintly, hung the fresh copper tags of a dreamhunter's licence. 'Look,' she said, 'they let me pass!' Then, 'Where's Rose?'

Part III
The Sandman

One

Rose, ten weeks after her Try, was sitting in a classroom in the Academy. The window she sat beside faced the playing fields and the high brick school walls. Beyond the walls Founderston showed only its rooftops, attic rooms and smoking chimneys. A late autumn sun was declining in a sky the yellow-white of whey. It was the last class of the day.

Rose was bored. The teacher was pacing up and down before the blackboard, firing questions at her class. Questions about a chapter in their history text — Dr King, at last. Rose had done her reading, digested the lesson, remembered everything, as usual. She'd allowed herself to answer her customary four questions and left the rest to the other girls, who were halting and routine in their replies. Rose had soon lost interest in what they had to say. She looked out of the window, and watched the day die.

She was brought back to the room by the sound of Mamie Doran's cool, smart voice. Mamie was disagreeing with what both the teacher and Dr King had to say about the balance between individual rights and 'the common good'. Mamie was eyeing Miss Melon, her head turned sideways like a bird. Her posture was intensely sceptical, and insolent. 'Miss Melon,' Mamie said, her voice chiming, 'do you not think that people can act in ways that lose them their rights? Convicted criminals, for instance. One citizen takes another's life, and the law deprives them of their liberty. The law won't let them vote. Rights are something we earn by being *good* citizens. Criminals *haven't* earned, they have fallen into debt to society. And you know, Miss Melon, it's impossible to feel much sympathy for people like that. After all, we all know what we have to do to keep on the right side of the law — that is, *obey* the law.'

Miss Melon had gone pink, but tried to sound tolerant. 'But, Mamie, you can't argue that it is reasonable to make new-born babies subject to rules they haven't invented. We aren't *born* into a contract with society. Our relationship to society is something we negotiate — or rather is negotiated for us by other people, all sorts of people, reformers and lawmakers and artists and so on.'

'Yes, just anyone, in fact,' Mamie said. 'Which is very charming — the charm of democracy. But the point is that we all do inherit the law.' Mamie was squinting at her teacher. She clearly thought Miss Melon was dim and illogical.

Miss Melon lost her temper. 'Well, Mamie, you should perhaps consider that the law is *all* that some people inherit. They don't inherit money, or privileges — only duties, and duress.'

'We all inherit the law *and its protection*,' Mamie said, cold and nasty. She said it suggestively, as if to imply that, were she not contained by school rules, and the respect the rules demanded she show her teacher, then she *would* show Miss Melon a thing or two.

'Mamie Doran, you are a girl fortunate enough to be born with many personal advantages, and into privilege — I doubt you will ever have reasonable cause to call on the law for protection.' The teacher was sharp and final.

Mamie opened her mouth to say something further and Miss Melon said, 'That's enough from you, Miss Doran.'

The bell rang. Miss Melon dismissed the girls. Chairs scraped. Rose's classmates all filed out while Miss Melon busied herself wiping the board with a duster. After a minute or two she turned around and saw Rose, who was still in her seat. 'Rose!' the teacher said, startled.

Rose could see that although Miss Melon was going calmly about her tasks, internally she was licking her wounds. She had thought she was alone. She rallied. 'What can I do for you, Rose?'

'Mamie only behaves that way because she's easily bored,' Rose said.

'I don't mind when my girls are lively. Or when they debate. And I hope I don't take a disagreement on the meaning of a text as a challenge to my authority. I hope I'm a better teacher than that,' said Miss Melon. 'It was Mamie's *opinions* I objected to, Rose, not her persistence in voicing them.'

'But she does play devil's advocate when she's bored.'

'You think so?' said the teacher. 'You think she's debating a point, not stating a position?'

'Well — yes,' said Rose, 'and she is the smartest girl in the school.'

'And so I should appreciate her?'

Rose shrugged. Then she said, 'Mamie annoys me too, but at least she's not timid. If I wanted to, I could talk to her.'

Miss Melon came and sat in the seat beside Rose. 'And what would you talk about, Rose?'

Rose shrugged again and shook her head.

'How are you enjoying being a boarder?' Miss Melon asked, not bothering to disguise the fact that it was a pointed question.

'Every fortnight I arrive at my own home with a trunk, like a visitor,' Rose said. 'Boarding isn't bad. The girls I share a room with are nice. But having been sent away is *horrible*.'

Miss Melon put her hand on Rose's and squeezed it.

Rose went on. 'Laura only answers some of my letters and then just scribbles a few lines. I think she doesn't want to let on how much she's enjoying herself. She thinks I'll be *jealous*, or I'll judge her harshly for being able to enjoy something with her Da gone. I wouldn't do that, and I don't want my feelings spared. Sparing my feelings just hurts them, actually. I don't get to *see* Laura. She has a room in a boarding house in Doorhandle and keeps going In to get dreams just to build up her stamina, Ma says. I go home and Ma and Da spoil me. We go on outings. I even went up in a balloon. But they won't consider changing my boarding arrangement — as if it matters that they'll lose the fees. They say, "The arrangements have been made for the half year and we don't want to trouble our good relationship with the school." They're inflexible, though they're very sweet to me. But

I feel as if Ma's lost interest in me now that she knows I'll never be a dreamhunter.'

'I see,' said Miss Melon. 'And feeling that your mother has lost interest in you puts you in some sympathy with unattractive Mamie Doran?'

'Yes, it does.'

'As for Laura — you know she has a lot on her plate. And, Rose, you must be aware that Laura, when asked for four pages, would often only turn in two. She doesn't like putting pen to paper.'

'That's true.'

'And do you think that your mother and father and Laura based their opinion of you on your own ideas of your future?'

'Yes,' said Rose, quietly, 'I was so confident.'

'You're the same person you were before your Try,' Miss Melon said. 'All that has happened is that you have lost a fixed idea of your future.'

'And I've lost my Uncle Tziga — coincidentally.' Rose sounded dry, but she was telling her teacher off.

'Well — yes — and there hasn't been a funeral yet, I gather. That must be difficult for all of you.'

Rose drooped. 'Yes, I suppose Ma and Da are in limbo about that, and they're not thinking how the weeks are stretching out for me. But they *should*.'

'If you can't change their minds, or really know what they're thinking, you just have to be patient. Patient and charitable.' Miss Melon quoted scripture: '"Faith, Hope and Charity — and the greatest of these is Charity".'

'The new translation says "Love" — "The greatest of these is Love".'

'It does, and I understand that "Love" is supposed to be more accurate. But it was always better translated as "charity" because "charity" reminds us of what we owe, not what is owed to us.'

Rose lifted her head and smiled at Miss Melon, who said, 'I know that you are a wise girl, Rose.'

'Thank you,' said Rose. 'Now, about Mamie, I suppose I want to ask you to think about being a little bit more *charitable* towards her.'

'If you like, dear, I'll make more of an effort. But is it doing

Mamie justice in the long term to let her get up on her high horse?'

'I don't know. Shall we experiment?'

The teacher laughed. 'That's better. That's the Rose we all know, and treasure.' Miss Melon patted the hand she held, then got up. She said, 'You should go now, dear, or you'll miss your tea.'

That evening Rose went to look for Mamie Doran. She found her at a table in the school library, reading a novel behind a barricade of atlases.

Mamie didn't look up from her page. She said, 'What do you want, Rose?'

'That stuff you were saying today in history, do you get it from these books?'

Mamie laid her book face down on the table. 'What do you think?'

'I don't know. I'm just interested.'

'In our house the dinner-table discussions are often wide-ranging and philosophical,' Mamie said.

'You must miss it,' Rose said. Mamie had been boarding for over a year, although, like Rose, her home was nearby.

'Miss Melon is no substitute for — for example — father's friend Wilkie,' said Mamie. She looked at Rose archly. Then sighed. 'Garth Wilkinson, the President,' she said, as though she were attempting to educate someone very much her junior.

'What's he like?'

'Gentlemanly. And he likes to do card tricks.'

Rose tried to imagine the President of the Republic doing card tricks. 'Who else?' Rose asked, curious about Mamie's father's friends and allies.

'Senators and so forth. And —' Mamie's eyes flicked up to Rose's face. '— recently we had a particularly interesting man, Mr Gregg, the new Speaker of the House.' Mamie watched Rose with shrewd interest. 'Do you know who I mean?'

Rose was surprised to discover that she did know who Gregg was, and even more surprised to find she had an opinion of him. 'Yes, I do know Gregg. He's solid and equitable,' Rose said. 'Someone must have told me that.'

Mamie gave a strange, nervy laugh and picked up her book again.

'Well,' said Rose, 'I just wanted to say that I liked the way you stirred things up in history today.'

'You surprise me, Rose.'

Rose sat down next to Mamie and leant towards her, speaking eagerly. 'Don't you get tired of everyone being so timid?'

'Timid towards *you*, Rose? Is that what you mean? Of course they're afraid you're going to cry.' Mamie studied Rose for signs of tears. 'The trouble with you, Rose Tiebold, is that there were a whole lot of things that it never occurred to you to think about.'

'For instance?'

'For instance, why did none of your classmates consider Trying?'

Of all the girls at Founderston Girls' Academy who had turned fifteen in the last twelve months only Rose and Laura had Tried. 'I guess their parents didn't give them permission,' Rose said.

'That's right,' said Mamie. 'They come from well-bred, *scared* stock. Their parents probably told them that it is something they can do, if they *must*, when they reach their majority. Like attending the University. Jane wants to attend the University and her parents say she can, but only once she's twenty-one. You and Laura were expected to *choose* to Try. But my mother says dreamhunters are just fortune-hunters — even though Laura's father's dreams enriched her father, Grandfather Chambers. It's easy for all our classmates to avoid Trying — all they have to do is avoid the road through the Riflemans' between Doorhandle and Tricksie Bend. When they go to Coal Bay, they catch the train. Trying is something that *other people* do — not them. You and Laura did what *other people* do — and then *you* came back to school. They're not going to talk to you about it, Rose. They're embarrassed for you. You'll never be one of them again.' Mamie stopped speaking and stared at Rose expectantly. She seemed to want a fight.

'Thank you for telling me that, Mamie,' Rose said.

'You're welcome. And, now that you have Tried and come back I can tell you something. I had my fifteenth birthday six months before yours. About a year before that my father bought some land at the back of Awa Inlet in Coal Bay. That's where we have our new holiday house. It's very isolated. It's also not a place any dreamhunter can go, because it's across the line. When we were building everyone in the family but me went up and had a look at the progress. I wasn't allowed to. Father didn't want to involve me in one of the official Tries — he said it wasn't necessary for his daughter. So we did it privately. The day after my fifteenth we sailed up Awa Inlet with some officials from the Regulatory Body. We walked up from the landing place to our house. We crossed the line. Then we all had a nice lunch and sailed back. It was only a formality, really. No one ever thought that I would go into the Place. And I was very glad that I didn't. I have no particular plan in life — and that's something I rather like. Most things that people do seem to me to be rather dull and silly. In my ideal life I'd be left alone to read.'

'So — I guess I should leave you alone,' Rose said.

'This book is wonderful. But, Rose, I've always quite enjoyed talking to you. You aren't *dim*, like Jane and Patty and Anne. Also, I'd like to ask you who you thought was right, me or Miss Melon?'

'I'm not sure. But the thing is that you *cared* about your argument. Jane and Patty and Anne are only interested in what Melon says when it earns them lots of ticks in their margins.'

Mamie nodded. 'Ten out of ten — that's Jane. It's like she washes, dries and presses history instead of studying it.'

Rose laughed. Mamie looked startled then pleased to have made her laugh. She said, 'You can stay put if you like, Rose. But you'll have to find something to read.'

'That shouldn't be hard.' Rose looked around at all the bookshelves.

'Go and find *The Mill on the Floss* — that might do you some good,' Mamie said.

Two

There was a gate in the high brick wall at the far side of the playing fields of Founderston Girls' Academy. It was always locked. On the other side of it was a narrow night-cart lane. Early one wintry morning a pupil slipped out of her dormitory, and hurried across the field to the barred arch in the wall. Another girl waited on the far side of the gate, holding the bars.

Rose collided with the gate so hard it clanged. She thrust her arms through and gathered Laura against the bars. Their smoking breath mingled. They both started to cry, and for a time just clung together with the cold iron between them.

'Why didn't you answer most of my letters?' Rose asked.

'I couldn't. It was too difficult. I couldn't think what to write. I can't answer for your mother and father. They say they've sent you away while we regroup. You think that means you're not necessary to the new grouping. But that's not what is going on, Rose. There is something going on. Uncle Chorley and Aunt Grace are afraid for me, I think. And no one is behaving properly. For instance — you do know about their fight with Aunt Marta?' Rose shook her head. 'It's about a memorial service for Da. Aunt Marta talked to the Grand Patriarch, apparently. And then he refused Grace and Chorley the use of St Lazarus. It doesn't make any sense. If someone had asked me what I thought would happen if my father went missing and was declared dead, I'd have sworn that Aunt Marta would be the one to want the ceremony, and Uncle Chorley, at least, would have dragged his feet. First, because he's not religious. Second, because he'd be happy with the excuse of no body so that he wouldn't have to bury Da.' Laura began to cry again.

'Shhh,' said Rose, stroking her cousin's curls.

'I've had this dream — a real dream of my own, I mean. I keep sitting up late in my room at the boarding house. I'm trying to be tired to go In and catch something. I'm no good at staying awake. I nod off in my chair and then Da is standing beside me and he says, "It's time you went to bed, Laura." And I look around and he turns to smoke and vanishes.' Laura pressed her forehead against the gate and sobbed. 'I'm just waiting. I'm going to wait and wait for him to come back. I can't stop. I can't help it.'

'I want to look after you,' Rose said. 'Why won't they let me look after you?' She let go of Laura and jumped back from the gate to look up at the top of the wall. She measured it with her eyes and even flexed her legs like a cat rocking on its haunches before making a jump. She moaned and flung herself back at the gate and clutched Laura again.

'Your Da is nearly as bad as I am,' Laura said. 'Every time I see him he cries.'

'Every time *I* see him he puts on a brave face — he's Mister Sunny,' Rose said, disgusted. 'I've been trying to eavesdrop on them. I climbed down the shaft of the dumb waiter, just like we used to when were little. I listened, but all I could make out was your name, by turns, in things they said. "Laura" in his voice. "Laura" in hers.' Rose told her cousin that she'd wanted to beat on the walls of the shaft so that they would know she was there. She said she'd felt as though she were attending her own funeral, as if she was listening to her loved ones from inside her own coffin.

'I keep feeling that I'm not in the middle of their hearts any more. As if I'm not the same person I was, so they can't love me the same way.' Rose clenched her teeth and turned up her eyes. She was trying not to start weeping again. She looked fierce.

Laura pressed her face against the gate to kiss Rose's cheek. 'I didn't answer your letters partly because I felt they didn't want *me* around, either. I was pushing at you, being silent, to see if you meant to leave me too.'

'Oh, Laura,' said Rose.

'Da did leave me,' Laura said. 'He did.' Then she shook herself. 'But I mean to find out exactly what he left me for. What he was doing. He was doing something he shouldn't. He knew something would happen. He kept trying to remind me of old family things that he'd tried to teach me when I was little. I just thought he was being weird. And it is kind of weird what he thought was worthwhile passing on.'

'What?' Rose asked.

'Old Hame songs and stories. I've been thinking about them. It's driving me crazy. It's like I'm being haunted by all this old stuff instead of ordinary, everyday life. Just Da being ordinary — sitting on the veranda at Summerfort and chewing his fingernails.'

The sun came over the top of the roofs on the other side of the night-cart lane and threw Laura's shadow and the shadows of the gate's bars on to Rose. The light was bright behind Laura's head and her face was in shadow. Rose leant even nearer till she could smell the tea and oats and apricots on Laura's breath.

Laura said that she had been scared to go off on her own and hunt dreams. Twice, she had been caught following another dreamhunter, lying down near them, so that she got what they got. 'They said I was poaching. But I wasn't. I was trying to avoid getting something odd, like lying down at Wild River and catching fleeing convicts.' Since her first sleepover she'd had the feeling that there was a big fuss going on around her, a fuss she knew was about her, but which she couldn't make sense of. 'I'm tired of it,' Laura said. 'I'm tired of being miserable and lonely and well behaved. I want to know what really happened to Da. No one in this family really believes he suddenly decided to traverse the Place. I have to try to find out what happened. I'm going to catch the train to Sisters Beach today. I'm going to find Uncle Chorley's camera and remove the film from it. I want to see what Da shot on his trip in from Tricksie Bend.'

'Uncle Tziga told Ma at the station that he'd left the camera in a dry stream bed about two days In,' Rose said.

'I knew you'd remember. That's what I came to ask you.'

Rose sighed, then said, 'Well, I'm glad something made you come.'

'I'm sorry,' said Laura. 'Look, I thought I should also tell someone where I mean to go. I don't want to go In at Tricksie Bend or fill in my intentions, just in case I find something to follow up. I don't want rangers poking their noses in.'

'Already the secretive dreamhunter,' Rose said.

Laura didn't respond to this. She said, 'I'll go In along the track to Whynew Falls —'

'Hey!' said Rose. She'd made a happy discovery. 'I can see the falls now! I always *hated* having to stop. Especially the year Da kept going on up there with Caro Bax.' Rose scowled at the memory. She disliked Miss Bax, a Sisters Beach neighbour who had hung on her father's every word through two summers.

Laura smiled at Rose's excitement. Then watched Rose get even more fired up. 'You know your dream, Laura? The one where you solved the "ours as D ecre" puzzle? "Yours, Cas Doran, Secretary of the Interior".'

'What about it?'

'I'm making friends with Mamie Doran. I'm cultivating her. I've been telling her how neglected I am. How I can't talk to the other girls — which I have to say is true. Anyway, I'm hoping Mamie will invite me to her house.'

Laura was surprised, and filled with admiration. But this was Rose, her clever, calculating, controlled cousin. Rose was shut out of the Place, of her family home, of Laura's new life — but she'd found something to do, some way to connect.

'I hope to be able to give Secretary Doran a good looking-over and see if I can find out why his name should appear pulled out of the sand-stuffed mouth of a dead ranger, and a convict labourer in a dream.' Rose waggled her eyebrows at Laura, pleased with herself. 'So —' she said, 'how long do you think this trip will take you? I should know, if I'm standing in for the Tricksie Bend intentions book.'

'About five days. I'll send a wire from Sisters Beach when I'm back.'

'You do that.' Rose kissed Laura once more, clumsily, through the bars, then relinquished her grip.

'Oh — can I borrow your coat so I look a little less like a dreamhunter on the train?' Laura said. 'The new kids only ever work the Doorhandle end, and I don't want to be too conspicuous.'

Rose took off her coat and fed it through the bars. Laura put it on. She was shorter than Rose and it came down to the tops of her mid-calf length walking boots. Rose said, 'Please be careful.'

'I will.' Laura stepped away from the gate, waved, settled her pack on her shoulders and walked away.

A cold evening at Sisters Beach. Each wave made a hard, definite sound on the sand, against the winter silence. The seafront was empty, grilles fastened on the windows of shops, the hotels blind, all their seaward shutters closed.

Laura went up the scallop-shell drive between flax bushes on whose blades dew was beginning to set as white frost. She found the hidden key and let herself in through one of the glass doors of Summerfort. She found the house icy and close, all its curtains drawn on the sunny winter weather, the rooms prematurely chilled. The house was dry, but all the empty and unwashed flower vases were dank — the grates swept, but not spring cleaned.

It was horrible. But Laura had the hard work of a long walk ahead of her the next day so she didn't sit down and cry — for her father, for the family, for their last summer. She swallowed the urge and folded the sorrow back into herself.

Three

Laura saw only one ranger near the border. She was following a fence through farmland when she saw him emerge from the border of whiteywood scrub at the head of the track to Whynew Falls. Before he had turned her way Laura crouched down in the wet grass and ducked her head. The skirts of her coat spread out around her, making a creased bell. The coat was an old salt-stiffened oilskin she'd found in the room by Summerfort's main hall, a room that was stuffed with badminton rackets, coats, croquet mallets and hoops, picnic rugs, fishing rods and tackle, and all the other props of the family's idle attempts at living life in the great outdoors. The coat smelt like old copper coins, but it did the trick, it made the crouching girl look like a large rock. Laura didn't dare turn to watch the ranger but, after a moment, she was alarmed to hear a tread and breathing behind her. Breathing, a sound like a bellows working and thumping footfalls. Laura squeezed her eyes shut and tried to think of what to say, of an excuse, of who else she could be but Laura Hame.

Something stirred her hair. She turned her head and a cow blew a cloud of grassy steam into her face. There were several cows, they'd come over to see what she was doing. They surrounded her, snuffling and whipping their back legs with their yellowed white tails. They sniffed, then began to lick her coat. They fell to, licking, pushing at her, thorough and luxurious. They were black and white cows, with mottled pink and grey tongues. They were very happy to make the most of this source of salt that had kindly stopped in their field.

Laura held the coat up over her head and reflected that at least it was unlikely that the ranger would suppose that the cows were clustered around a trespassing dreamhunter — or indeed that anyone was at the bottom of this scrum of salt-hungry animals.

After some time Laura pushed the cows away and got to her feet. Her coat, shoes and bare hands were covered in swipes and strings of glue-like spittle. The ranger was a long way off, already out on the farm road and heading on to the gentle downhill towards the coast. Laura took her coat off and shook it, then dragged it along the grass. The cows plunged away from her when she flapped the coat at them. She held it over her head, up in the breeze, to dry as she walked.

Laura entered Whynew Falls reserve in the late afternoon, through a half-acre of regenerating forest, all indigenous evergreens, whose pale, twisted trunks formed a sunlit filigree before the rest of the forest. Laura climbed a stile over the last farm fence and went on to the track.

An hour later she was walking between mature mountain beech, on the track that was just a trough of bare ground surrounded by a confetti of tan beech leaves. The air was filled with their savoury perfume. The track had climbed above the stream bed, and Laura could see the water downhill between black, velvety beech branches and the dry boulders of the wide stream bed. She came to the sign: 'CAUTION: You are now only 100 yards from the border to the Place.' She stopped. Despite the height of the stream, and the damp brilliance of the vegetation — despite all the signs that it was winter — for a moment Laura imagined that the rest of the picnickers were about to catch her up, to come around the corner with their sun hats and baskets and their jackets tied around their waists. Laura could hear the falls, from this distance an endless deep sighing sound, only another quarter-mile away. It was here, on last summer's walk, that she and her father, Grace and Rose, had sat down on the bank while the rest of the picnic party went on.

Laura stepped past the sign. She walked on, turning several corners till the sound of the Falls grew louder. She came to a tree that had a circle of orange-painted tin nailed to its trunk. She passed the tree. The sound of the falls faded and stopped. Laura stepped into the dry, open country of the Place.

The track went on before her, buff-coloured, bared earth running through grass with the white sheen of candy floss. Laura stood at a T-junction. There were three paths Laura could choose. To either side of her the path branched off to follow the border. On her left it led to the main thoroughfare from the ranger's post at Tricksie Bend. On her right it went on for miles, for days, gradually becoming less definite, less travelled. The path before her feet, the tail of the T, led on deeper into the Place.

Laura was headed In, but didn't really want to encounter anyone. So she went on straight ahead for a time then, when she came to a tree twice the height of a tall man, she left the track. She picked her way through the meadow away from the path. When she could only see the very top of the tree she straightened her course and walked on, parallel to the path, but — she hoped — invisible to anyone on it. Every now and then she stopped to consult her map, and to listen. She listened to the silence then went on. The brittle grass hissed and crackled as she passed through it. It didn't close behind her, and as she went she left a wake of snapped stalks.

Laura had heard her father say that the Place was driest at its perimeter. Like a wound, he had said. Laura wanted to find the stream bed she had heard Grace and her father speak about. It was marked on her map. It was a two-and-a-half day walk In from Tricksie Bend, and two days from the Whynew Falls track. According to marks on the map the stream bed showed the first signs of what rangers called 'remaining moisture'. 'There are places where you can dig down and find damp earth,' Laura's father had once told her.

Laura had often wondered, idly, how that could be. If it hadn't rained in the Place for — to the best of anyone's knowledge — twenty years, how could there be any groundwater?

Since first coming to the Place, Laura's idle wondering about how it worked had become sharp speculation. She had made the investigations that she knew other dreamhunters and rangers must have made many times before. She'd tried carrying a burning match across the border, or striking a light once there. She had found that nothing would burn. She'd experimentally snapped twigs off the trees and seen the sappy gristle at their hearts. She'd seen that the trees in the Place were not like those struck by earthly droughts. Trees in the Place had leaves, sere, on branches that hadn't had a soaking in living memory. The Place was full of vegetation that wasn't dead, but wouldn't revive. It seemed somehow to continue right at the point of death, year after year, as if time had simply stopped.

The landscape was stripped of all animal life — even insects — but was without corpses too, without empty chrysalises or the brown skins of cicada nymphs, without transparent, scale-printed, cast-off lizard skins. There were no piles of rotted fleeces, the remnants of sheep corpses left after a cold spring in earthly fields. There were no bones, no empty birds' nests, no cold eggs.

Because of what it lacked the Place looked like a modelled mock-up. But it was too vast, and too detailed, for anyone to have made it. If it wasn't a model, or a living landscape, what was the Place? Were dreams its inhabitants? What kind of place had no mortal remains but dreams?

Laura went over all this once more as she walked. And she wondered whether, if someone did perish in the Place, would the Place, after a time, somehow tidy their remains away? Laura thought of her father, and abruptly sat down in the dusty grass to cry. She cried hard, but in the dry air her tears hadn't even reached her chin before turning to stiff salt trails on her skin.

She got up again and went on.

Laura concealed her trail by struggling through little copses, and by climbing a hill to step along the raised nubs of its stony backbone. Sometimes she came upon signs of traffic — boot toe-sized steps kicked in a bank, a smooth place where the bark had been worn from a tree branch by the hands of people helping themselves up a steep slope. She hurried through these places, breathing hard. She made her winding but definite way towards the highest rise she could see, a hill whose contours she recognised from her map. From the hill's crest she believed she would be able to see where the land was creased by the stream, somewhere in band Y, in whose dry bed her father had left her uncle's camera.

Laura had to call it a day before she reached the summit of the hill. She had been walking for eight hours by her watch, eleven if she was to count the walk from Summerfort to the Whynew Falls track. She had stopped several times to have a drink and snack. But now she knew she must sleep.

She pushed her way into a stand of thorns and lay down on a patch of springy heath, there unfastened her bedroll and crawled into the bag of blankets. She lay on her side, munching on a few handfuls of scroggin, washed down with a mouthful of water from the copper spout of her water skin. She coated her lips with wax salve and put on her eye mask, then lay still and listened to the hushed flicker of the tiny leaves of the heath sifting down through the twigs beneath her bedroll. She heard the blood in her ears. She lay still, waiting for sleep to come up over her; she lay secret and solitary under a tide of sleep.

The only dream she had was her own. She woke up and could recall only how it ended. In the dream Uncle Chorley had sent her out to see if her father was coming. When she reached the gate of Summerfort her father had just turned to climb up the track from the beach. She saw him against the evening light, his shoulders rounded and walk tired. She saw the moment he noticed that she was there, waiting for him — the moment he recognised her and picked up his pace, began to hurry to meet her.

Laura woke up knowing she had dreamt something she'd seen, her father hurrying towards her, pleased to see her. She found that she was in tears again, weeping with grief and gratitude. For weeks she had been worried that a deeper sorrow was lying in wait for her — some sort of predatory, crippling sadness made of regret and guilt. She knew that she hadn't fully felt her father's loss — that loss had been absorbed into her global grieving for her old life, her home, Rose, her school routine, a time when all her decisions were made for her and she had only to go along with them. How *kind* of the dream to remind her that, when he saw her waiting for him, her father would hurry forward! Her father — who had gone, who had left her — but who, after all, had loved her.

The stream, where Laura first came to it, was in a narrow gorge and bordered by tree ferns with slender trunks and startled tops. The fern fronds were limp and curled, as if they had died just a few days ago. Laura went down between the ferns, her hands skinning the trunks of their furry bark. She walked along the bed, heading to her right, moving still further from the main road and its traffic. She wasn't sure that this was the right way, but thought it likely, given her father's constant questing after new dreams.

Laura walked for another hour, stepping from boulder to boulder. The gorge grew gradually shallow and opened out. The boulders became stones, and the going easier. The vegetation changed too. There was scrub growing back from the bank and weeping willows at the edge of the stream bed, willows with the occasional bare wand, leaves stripped away by the touch of passing human hands. The stream bed flattened out, became a trench through fields dotted with thickets of gorse and tea tree. The stream had been the meandering sort, and in places had undercut the bank so that blue clay showed beneath fringes of grassy turf, grass roots exposed to the air and the same colour as the dry stalks above. Gleaming swathes of very fine river sand appeared between the stones, and Laura made her way between them. The sand was easy on her feet, though now she left a trail. She made progress. She stopped to drink, standing in the middle of the dry bed where the vanished water had formed a smooth eel of silver sand.

When Laura lowered the water skin from her lips she saw a gleam some distance ahead of her. She saw the brass and oak legs of Chorley's camera, its black concertina lens and shining, lacquered crank handle. Her heart jumped and her throat grew suddenly tense. Laura's training forced her to stand still at least to screw the cap back on her water skin, then she sprinted to the camera. It was lying just beyond a patch of disturbed sand, an excavation she jumped over to reach it. She fell to her knees beside the camera and was for a moment completely still, staring at indentations in the sand under the camera's gathered legs, the imprints of the knuckles of a hand. Laura knew that her father's hand had made the mark when he laid the camera down.

She didn't want to disturb his signs. For a moment she knelt, her hands pressed to her mouth, rocking. Then she took a deep breath, and began carefully brushing sand from the box that she hoped contained an undeveloped film. She knew what to do — she would make sure her hands were clean, then would pull her oilskin over her head to form a tent over the camera while she unwound the wing-nuts on its case, opened it and retrieved the film without exposing it to the light. But first things first. She sat back on her heels, unbuckled the flap on her pack and found the film canister. She put it down carefully on her knees and thrust her sandy hands under her coat and into her armpits to wipe them clean.

Something moved in the shadow of the overhang on the bank nearest her. Laura started — then instantly recognised the movement, or explained it to herself, as an earth fall, the bank giving way.

Then, suddenly, she was up and running.

The earth hadn't fallen, it had collected itself and had stood up out of the shadow.

Laura rushed across the stream towards the far bank. She jumped at it, and caught hold of two handfuls of grass. They came away in her hands, roots and all. She fell backward, but on to her feet. She dodged the grey, blurred bar of an arm — an arm! — that snatched at her as she scrambled away again. The sand, a welcome softness after her long tramp on hard earth, was now treacherous; it yielded behind her boots, offered no resistance from which she could launch herself at speed away from the thing that was chasing her.

She looked back, saw a huge, heavy, glittering mass looming after her, moving forward with great fluid strides. Laura screamed and veered for the bank again. She ran at a ramp of fallen sand and tufts of turf. She waded up it, then jumped at the lip of the bank. Her feet came down on the edge. She saw a crack appear before her. A seam of grass roots ripped opened, the lip broke off and she was dumped back in the stream bed.

There was no air between her and the monster, no open space. Laura scrabbled along the raw earth of the undercut bank, then was cut off by more earth — earth in motion, and in the shape of an arm. The monster set its arms on either side of her body with a thud that shook the bank and sprinkled her face with gobs of turf. The creature's chest loomed above her like a stone lid. She saw the grains of sand on its torso seething like smoke, rearranging themselves into the shape of muscles under skin. Laura screamed again and turned her head. 'No!' she howled, and 'Please!' She closed her eyes.

She was sitting in a warm puddle. Her bladder had let go, and the urine had pooled on the inside of her oilskin. Laura moaned and whimpered, now only able to make inarticulate sounds. Then she broke out again, as a rodent cornered by a cat will, alternately bolting or frozen in fear. She battered at the arms and chest and felt her hands sink some way into the yielding sandy stuff then — horrible — the sand come to life and consolidate to force her fists out of it. She screamed and thrashed until she was covered in sand. It seemed she was buried in the creature itself. She fought to a standstill, and was still miserably conscious, gasping for breath, gagging on sand, spitting it out of her mouth.

Once she was still, the monster released her, only hovered again, hemming her in. Laura lay motionless. She gave herself up — but then nothing further happened. The monster was there, still and silent. Waiting.

After a time Laura stirred. She looked up at the monster's arms, to see if there was a chink it might let her slip through. Then she shortened her focus to look at the tombstone lid of its chest again. It didn't move. It let her make these slight movements, and didn't act to suppress her.

Finally, Laura looked up into its face.

It was a lopsided, lumpish face — and very solemn. The sand and clay from which it had been formed was crusty and uneven, and stained red, as though mixed with blood.

Laura saw that the monster was watching her, and waiting for something. She saw letters scored into its sandy forehead. Three letters. 'NOW'

Now she was finished, Laura thought. *Now* she had gone too far, asked too much. She had struck out on her own at last and *now* she was going to get it.

Laura cowered from the creature. 'Don't hurt me,' she begged. 'Please. Please let me go.'

The monster simply watched her and waited.

Then a thought came to Laura, as cool as rainfall — a memory, a song.

> The final measure is his Name.
> Four letters, and four laws.
> The first gives life, the last speech,
> though they are the same.
> Two letters remain within,
> death and freedom.
> Make his name his Own and he is.
> If your Will departs he will.

Laura remembered her father, the last time she had seen him, on Sisters Beach station. He had said, 'Those are capitals: Name, Own, Will, Name.'

She remembered the song, and her father's words. She stared at the letters on the monster's forehead and her right hand drifted up towards them. It was as though her hand had a mind of its own. She stretched out her forefinger and, for a moment, in the spell of her terror, she nearly used it to erase the W in NOW. But, as soon as her fingertip touched the letter Laura understood that erasing the W wouldn't make the monster disappear. Laura somehow understood that the monster would be wholly invulnerable till she had finished the spell that made him. She must first write a final N in the sand of his brow. Understanding seemed to rush down her finger, hand, arm, and fill her body. Laura simply knew that there was a NON, that there was an *end* to the spell, but that first she must supply a second N, a final letter which — the song said — would give the monster 'speech'.

Laura wrote with a trembling hand on the creature's forehead. She knew as she did so that she was opening her father's Will. For, as she altered her father's handiwork, and added to his spell, Laura experienced a deeper form of recognition. Some kind of music — more than the remembered song — flowed from her into the sandman. A soundless music made of calculations. The single letter formed by her fingertip was, she knew, a compressed phrase of information, instructions, laws.

Laura lowered her hand. The word, the name on the sandman's forehead, now read 'NOWN'.

The sandman moved. It sat back, and then knelt before her. In a low, harsh, arid voice the sandman said, 'Laura Hame, I am your servant.'

Four

Laura had no spare trousers, and no water in which to wash. She shrugged off her coat, abandoned it and sat in a patch of dry sand some distance from the creature.

She watched it. It didn't move, but turned its head to watch her in return. She saw that while the front of its body and its face were, in their texture, like the crudely clawed-together sand around the excavation, from the *back* the creature was shapely and statuesque. Laura wondered whether the sandman had been formed like the sculpture she and Rose had made for the Sisters Beach sand-sculpting competition. If so, then only its face and the front of its body would have been formed by its maker's hands. And, she thought, perhaps the creature's back bore the stamp of the spell alone, not its maker's hurried efforts.

Its maker — her father. When Laura had opened her eyes and read the monster's name she had recognised it from a song her father had taught her. And when she had finished her father's spell it was as though she had heard his voice — singing, a music made of calculations.

Laura pulled her pack to her and put it on. She crouched over the camera and picked at the wing-nuts with weak fingers. Her body was still trying, as though only by reflex, to complete her task and carry her out of there, away from the creature. She was crying. Her corded velvet trousers clung, clammy, at the back of her thighs. She fiddled ineffectually with the camera, then stood up.

For long moments Laura Hame simply looked at the sandman. Then she said, 'Come here,' and, as it got up and moved towards her — with heavy, thumping steps and a dry hiss of sand on sand — she backed away. She pointed at the camera. 'Pick that up,' she said.

The sandman stooped, like something being poured. It seized the camera, and the tripod's splayed legs closed together with a 'clop'. The sandman swung the camera over its shoulder.

'I want you to walk ahead of me,' Laura said. 'Walk along the stream bed.' She pointed the way.

It moved ahead of her and she followed. She wanted to keep it in sight.

Laura didn't pause until she had reached the crest of the highest hill. She walked for hours and her thighs were chafed and stinging.

'Go in among that brush,' she told the creature, pointing at a stand of low trees. The creature pushed its way into them.

'Stop,' said Laura. 'Put the camera down.'

It put the camera down, carefully.

'Sit,' Laura said.

It sat, so she was able to sit too. Her head was swimming. She unfastened her bedroll from her pack and spread it out on ground that was gritty and covered in sinewy tree roots. 'Nown,' she said, naming the creature, 'my name is Laura.'

'My dear Laura,' said Nown.

Laura flinched. She told Nown not to say that. Then she told it to sit still.

It was sitting still. She didn't like to look at it. When it had spoken she had seen the back of its mouth, a shallow cave, without tongue or teeth or any physical equipment with which it could produce its voice — its harsh, low-pitched whisper. She knew she wasn't looking at a body, but at a conglomeration of earth and magic.

Laura had to sleep. She was afraid to close her eyes but her eyes were closing. She had slumped on to the bedroll. Her thighs were burning — probably breaking out in a blistered rash.

'We're hiding,' Laura explained to the creature. 'You must be very quiet. People may come.'

'There are no people,' the creature said. 'Or I would see them. People are very easy to see here. Only people burn. Everything else is dead. The trees give off no soft fire. People shine through the dead forests and grasslands. If there was a person I could see them. Someone has stopped here before. They have dropped the salt of their fire. They have dropped waste.'

Laura listened to this. Her eyes had closed. She felt herself slipping, felt herself melt her way through the surface of sleep, felt the world turn from solid to liquid grease round her. She was afraid of Nown, so before she lost consciousness she said to it, 'Don't hurt me.'

Laura slept for a long time. When she woke she found that, at least, her trousers had dried. Nown was sitting in exactly the same place and position, with the clenched legs of the camera inclined against him and its boxy head drooping behind his own. Laura bundled her bedding and scrambled up. The sandman didn't get to his feet until she told him to. She told him to follow her, and set out herself.

On any journey in the real world, as often as not there would be something to welcome, the sun coming up over the eastern horizon perhaps, or the heat going off the day. In the Place there was only ever a sense of covering a distance to reach a goal, either In or out. Laura and her servant moved their way across the landscape, leaving a trail of broken grass in their wake.

Laura was in shock. All she was able to do was head back to the border. She held to her original plan: to find out what was on the film her father made, and then decide where to go from there. There would be clues on the film to instruct her, Laura hoped. But instead of clues — or as well as — her father had left her this. This creature coming after her with its steady, hissing gait.

It occurred to Laura that, having gone looking for knowledge, she should recognise it when she found it walking softly behind her. She understood that she should ask the sandman some questions. She paused to let him catch up with her. But as soon as she stopped, he stopped too.

They were on the lower slopes of a hill, winding their way through parched thorn bushes. There was room for Nown to walk beside her, so she told him to. She didn't like him standing so near to her, but understood that she could, without embarrassment, tell him to keep up with her, but to maintain a certain distance between them.

When Laura had the sandman where she wanted him, she began to interrogate him. She said, 'Were you waiting for me?'

'In the stream bed?'

'Yes, in the stream bed. Were you waiting there?'

'Yes.'

'Is that what my father told you to do?'

This time Nown answered at once, readily. 'All your father told me was to chase a spying ranger, and find out who had sent him.'

'So you chased him — the poor man?'

'He ran fast, and he wouldn't tire.'

Laura said, 'Do you know you killed him?' As soon as she said it she realised that, in fact, they were talking about the ranger who had been killed when he appeared on the road right in front of the Sisters Beach coach.

Nown didn't answer her.

Laura wanted to know what sort of creature he was. How dangerous he was. What he might do, what he was capable of. So she probed some more. She asked him, 'Do you not *mind* that you killed him?'

Nown was still silent. After a while Laura looked at him — an impassive object. She said, 'I asked you a question. Why don't you answer me?'

'I was considering your question,' he said.

'And your answer is?' Laura demanded, feeling a little thrill of power.

'I wasn't told to kill the ranger.'

'Then it's lucky for you that you *didn't*,' Laura said. Then she explained to the sandman how the ranger had been killed when he had stumbled out in front of the coach.

They walked on for a time in silence. Laura weighed the sandman's silence, his hesitation before speaking. She looked on it as a guilty one, then she looked on it as puzzlement. Then she tried to see it as profound consideration.

Laura tried to come up with another question. She needed to think about the way Nown expressed himself as much as the answers he gave. She asked, 'Are you *glad* that you didn't kill him?'

Nown was silent.

'Are you considering my question again?' Laura asked.

'Yes,' he said.

Laura wondered whether he was stupid. Slow, obdurate and earthy. Then she thought about what he'd said earlier, when he was trying to explain to her how he knew there were no other people about. She said to him, 'How do you know the difference between the forests here, in the Place, and the way that forests are *supposed* to look if you've only ever been here? You *have* only ever been here, haven't you?'

Nown said, 'I am the eighth of myself.'

'Do you mean that you are the eighth Nown?'

He didn't reply.

'Were none of the others called that? Nown?'

'No one has ever called me Nown.'

'But that's what it says.' Laura pointed at his face, the four capital letters scratched into the sand above his brow bone. Then she realised that she had been saying 'noun' — like 'noun, verb, adjective' — not like 'known' without its silent K. She asked Nown whether he remembered what the other sandmen had done. He told her he did.

Laura thought about this. She asked, 'What did people call those others?'

'Servant.'

'Who were they, these people?'

'Hames. The Hames who could sing true.'

When she had touched the sandman Laura had felt an ancient, complex music in him. She was sure that she'd heard it before. Her father had been singing it the morning he left Summerfort. He was, Laura remembered, playing with the cold, glutinous oatmeal in his plate; he'd made an oatmeal face and was singing over it. He'd called the song 'The Measures'. He'd been practising —

practising a spell, singing 'true'. And he had made a point of mentioning all the songs his great-grandfather had wanted to pass on, and how foolish he'd been when he was young not to value them — his Hame inheritance.

Laura said, 'My father's dead, isn't he.'

'No,' said Nown. 'If he were dead, I would be undone.'

Her father was alive. Laura said it to herself, over and over, 'He's alive, he's alive.' She was so happy that for a while she hurried, and Nown stumped along behind her, and the camera he carried rattled as he walked.

Laura wiped her eyes and looked at her servant. She wondered whether he could only answer the questions put to him, couldn't voluntarily expand on an answer. Then she recalled again that he had expanded his answer about the dead forests of the Place and the 'soft fire' that plants and people gave off. He'd spoken as though he was explaining something surprising to *himself* as well as to her. Laura racked her brain for another question, one that might yield another telling answer. Then she had it. 'Did you catch the ranger?' she asked.

'Yes.'

'I thought so. He had sand in his mouth.'

'He bit off my fingers.'

'What were your fingers doing in his mouth?'

'He was eating a paper.'

'A letter from Cas Doran?'

Nown said, 'I don't know.' And then he unfolded one of his hands from the camera's legs and touched his own chest. He began to work his hand slowly into his chest. This looked horrible, shocking, as though he had begun to scratch in a very private place. Laura told him to *stop it at once*. He withdrew his hand, returned it to the camera's legs. Laura watched this with relief, and then remembered the camera. She asked Nown whether he had been with her father when he was making his film.

'No.'

They walked along for a while without speaking. Laura kept licking her lips in order to keep them moist and flexible enough *to* speak. She couldn't leave her servant alone. She had to worry at him. Again a sense of her own power came upon her, like a wave of heat, like faintness, like liquor. It was a new sensation to her, a physical sensation of force and weakness mixed together. Laura Hame asked her sandman whether he had to do anything she requested.

'Yes.'

'*Anything?*'

'Anything I am able to.'

'And what would *stop* you?' Laura asked. 'Scruples?'

'Oceans, high walls, strong locks, swift rivers.'

Laura stared at him. She asked him what he would do if he didn't *have* to obey her.

'That I can't know,' he said. He was quiet again, apart from the sound he made as he moved — almost the same sound Rose made when she was wearing her best silk pyjamas and walking briskly — a silky susurration. Laura supposed he had finished his reply, and was about to ask him another question, when he said, 'I am not the one who need not obey you.'

Laura went over this in her mind. *I am not the one who need not obey you.* 'Who is the one?' she said, baffled. She couldn't understand what he was saying. Was he talking about some other person? Or some other monster *she* might be able to make? Then Nown further surprised and puzzled her by making a remark, rather than merely replying to her question. 'Perhaps you will introduce me to him,' he said. 'The one who need not obey you.'

Laura found herself squinting at Nown. 'Did you just make a joke?'

'I hope I made a prediction,' Nown said.

Laura said that since Nown was supposed to *obey* her she should at least be able to understand what he was saying. She was beginning to enjoy questioning him, as though it were a game they were playing. She was tired, but Nown was distracting her from her tiredness, and from the stinging rash under her trousers. She wished she had some Wakeful — but at least the conversation was keeping her going.

Then, dizzy with vanity, Laura asked him — this creature compelled by his nature to be wholly honest to her, and who, in the absence of her father, owed its existence to her — 'What do you make of me?'

He didn't answer.

'Are you considering my question?'

'I am making sure that I am, truly, unable to answer you,' Nown said.

Laura, peering at him, could see that he was thinking. She could see thought in the busy swarming of the grains of sand in the sockets of his eyes. 'I am thinking till I am sure that I *cannot* think of an answer,' Nown added.

'So — you don't make anything of me?'

'I might,' he said. 'I can't say. It's not my business to make. I have been made, Laura. It seems to me a great step from being made, to making.'

'It's just a figure of speech, Nown,' Laura said, in exasperation. Then she thought that *that* was what he was, a figure of speech and sand. She tried again, this time saying, 'I mean — what do you *think* of me?'

'I think you are tired,' he said. 'I think you are keeping yourself alert with this game of questions.'

Laura felt that he was an adult, and she was a child. She hated the feeling. Yet though she hated it she had to admit that it was probably true. For Nown was a being who had been made eight times, and could remember his earlier selves. He had appeared in time, in history, on eight occasions. He had lived with Laura's distant ancestors. He must have experienced things, unimaginable things.

'Like *himself*,' Laura thought. '*He's* an unimaginable thing.' It was possible that the sandman might have only been made in emergencies and not *kept*. But, still, he must have seen a great deal — and so he could make Laura feel like a child.

Laura's thoughts went on for a while gnawing at this least of their differences. She yawned and scrubbed her face with both her hands. She sneezed — her feet and Nown's were raising dust as they walked, a dust made of dry earth and of the grass that disintegrated when they stepped on it. Then Laura thought of another question. She was tired, and it was vague, lazy, general. It was the sort of question that infants ask their mothers when they want to be talked to, but have nothing to say in return. 'What else do you think?' she said, then added, 'About me?'

'I *see*,' he said. 'My mistress is walking beside me. I look at her and she burns before me in a world in which everything else has lost its working heat. I see Laura Hame, the daughter of my maker Tziga Hame. I see another Hame whom I must obey. I see another Hame, not so different from all of them.'

'But a little different?'

'Younger. The first girl, who asks more questions. Who gives fewer orders. Who has not yet thought what I am good for.'

Laura glowered, then yawned so hard that her jaw clicked. 'So — what are you good for?' she demanded.

'I could carry you as well as the camera.'

Laura actually flinched from him. Her heart began to hammer. 'No,' she said. 'No, that won't be necessary.'

Five

Despite the fresh day and hard frost, the gymnasium at Founderston Girls' Academy smelt as usual of sweat and sour dust. The gym was a big, echoing room with knotted ropes hanging from its high roof-beams, and all its walls lined with climbing frames. The windows were at the very top of the walls, transoms operated by dangling chains, several of which were fouled in their pulleys. The day's earliest classes had stood in steaming huddles in their skimpy gym clothes till spurred into activity by their instructors and group leaders. No one had minded the jammed windows, but by midmorning the gym was airless. The sun was cutting right through the upper third of the huge room, and a ceiling of warm air had begun to drop down at least to head height.

The girls were doing folk dancing, for exercise, rather than practising for a performance. The hockey field was deemed too dangerous for play — till its frost-stiffened grass and frozen puddles were fully thawed.

Rose was in charge of one circle of dancers, and was trying to persuade one of her classmates to be nice. Patty and Anne had had a falling out. Patty had a ball of candle wax, and had moulded it into a sheaf sheath around her right index finger — the only part of her body she would allow Anne to touch. Rose normally had no trouble sorting out this kind of thing, but she was having trouble today. The easiest option would be to find Patty another partner

— but no one must be permitted to reject even pinched, prim Anne. Founderston Girls' Academy had a motto — 'Fidelity, Equality, Justice' — and Anne was going to bloody get all that from Rose.

Rose coaxed Patty into handing over her wax finger-stool. Surely it was unhygienic for both of them, Rose argued. Rose took the wax to the rubbish bin and came back to find that Anne was being danced about, but that Patty had hauled down her sleeve to cover her hand. Rose held her breath and began to count.

She was saved from temptation to violence by the gym teacher, who called her name.

Rose went over to the woman, who was leaning on the piano, where Mamie — the most musical girl in the middle school now that Laura had gone — was playing a country air. The gym teacher said, 'Rose, could you climb up there and see if you can open a few more of those windows?'

'Sure,' said Rose.

'Sprightly, sprightly!' Mamie said to Rose, obviously imitating the gym teacher's remarks about her own piano playing.

Rose smiled at Mamie, then edged her way through the spinning cogs of the two groups of dancers, reached the wall and began to climb. She went up the centre of a frame, where the varnish had been worn away from its timber rungs. She climbed into warm air, and then into the sunlight.

The windows were rheumy, coated with dust and crusted with cobwebs. But Rose didn't need an outlook. As soon as her face was in the sun, she was instantly happier. She perched on a windowsill covered in the corpses of flies and moths, and played with the window catch. She took her time, and did some thinking.

Rose's teachers relied on her to take the lead and show other girls what they ought to do. No problem was beneath Rose's notice. She was patient and firm, she would always find time and ways to talk the other girls out of silliness, or to help them articulate real problems to those who could solve them. She had been an advocate, had stood up beside others, steadied them when they had to explain themselves to housemistresses or to the headmistress. 'Rose will go with you,' others would say. It had been a very great privilege — especially for a day pupil, a girl who hadn't shared everything with those who offered her their trust. But Rose's patience had run out. Why should she go on doing what everyone expected of her? Be nice to Patty, Anne, Jane and so forth, and be obliging to teachers? Why should she? It seemed that the less *trouble* Rose was to the school, and her parents, and her so-called friends, the more they seemed to feel that it was perfectly acceptable to leave her *alone*.

Far below, the gym teacher called out, 'Rose?'

'This chain is badly caught,' Rose called back, 'but I am making some progress with it.' She bent her head, turned away into the light. She rattled the catch. Then, to her surprise, the window came open with an awful squawk, and its top whacked Rose on her forehead.

The teacher called up to her, 'Oh, good, you finally managed it! You can come down now. You've only ten minutes to change.'

Rose wondered what they'd all do if she refused to come down. But now wasn't the time to make experiments in rebellion. She wanted to find a mirror and look at her forehead to see if the window had left a mark.

She clambered down the frame and sprinted across the now-empty gym into the noisy fug of the changing rooms. She pushed through the pink and pale bodies. Then she came to a baffled stop before her spot. There was a junior sitting on the bench under her clothes on their hook. The junior was holding Rose's laundry bag on her lap.

'Are you waiting for me?' Rose asked.

'For ages,' said the child. 'Miss wouldn't let me into the class. She wasn't *listening* to me. I'm late. Your father is waiting for you in the head's office.' The child was peering at Rose with an expression of keen curiosity. 'He's wearing driving goggles on top of his head and kind of stomping his feet,' the child added.

Rose stood still and frowned at the junior. The school encouraged parents to make appointments. Of course in an emergency any parent could appear at the school and ask for their child to be pulled out of class. But normally Rose's father and mother would observe the school's protocols. Was there a family emergency?

Rose dismissed the messenger, stamped her bare feet into her shoes, stuffed the rest of her clothes into the laundry bag and pulled her blazer on over her wool shirt and shorts. Then she sprinted out of the gym and through the school to the administrative building.

Rose's father wasn't in the head's office. He had clearly already spoken to the head and had permission to see Rose. He was standing in the open arch under the gatehouse. The porter was holding the gate open, and her father's car was parked by it. The sun had just looked over the roofs but had not got past the eaves of the building opposite. Rose's father was in shade still, and his head was haloed with a cloud of his breath. Rose reached him and touched his arm. She was worried to see how tense he looked.

He didn't acknowledge her touch, but only walked through the gate, tipping the porter. He held the car door open for Rose. She got in and he walked around and climbed in beside her.

'What is it?' Rose said.

'Where is Laura?'

Rose considered telling her father that she didn't know where Laura was. She did stall. She said, 'Why?'

'Rose!' He was angry, and very anxious. 'We've had her landlady at Doorhandle let us know when she comes and goes. A week ago Laura was with us. But when she left Founderston she *didn't* go back to Doorhandle. *A week*, Rose!'

Rose swallowed. Her father took this as further reluctance to report what she knew and leant towards her, gripped her shoulder and gave her a quick, hard shake.

'Ow!' said Rose. 'Let go! Laura has gone to Sisters Beach, to go In at Whynew Falls and recover your camera.'

Chorley removed his hand from Rose's shoulder and sat back in his seat, staring through the windshield with the expression of a man confronted with a frightening obstacle.

'Is Laura in danger?' Rose asked.

He didn't answer. He just reached across her and opened her door so that she could get out.

'She's probably out again by now, Da — resting at Summerfort. She told me she'd send me a wire. She made sure someone knew where she was. Me. I hope you don't think I should have told her not to go?'

Chorley gave Rose a cold, bleak look.

'Look,' Rose said, 'someone had to get the film out of the camera.'

'Your mother was going to do that.'

'When? It might hold clues, you know.'

'Yes, we know.'

'Well, why take so long about going In to get it?'

Rose's father didn't reply. He shut his eyes and shook his head.

'I wish you would tell me why you're so worried about Laura,' Rose said.

'Tziga disappeared.'

'It doesn't follow that you should be worried about Laura.'

Chorley muttered something about Laura's 'state of mind'. It sounded pretty feeble, Rose thought.

She closed her door again. 'Come on,' she said. 'I'm going with you. I'm sure I can be of *some* use.'

Chorley opened his eyes again. He nodded to the porter, who was waiting to crank the car. The man stooped behind the bonnet, cranked the motor and the car rocked — he cranked again and it caught and ran. The porter stretched his back and gave them the thumbs up.

As Chorley pulled away from the school gate he said to his daughter, 'What did you do to your head?'

He had noticed. Rose felt a little less neglected. 'There was a stuck window. I got whacked by the frame.'

'Doesn't the Academy employ a caretaker?'

'Certainly. And since I'm not going to be a dreamhunter I've apprenticed myself to him.' Rose waited for her father to glance at her and gave him a 'you deserved that' look.

Six

In the small hours Summerfort was dark and still, glittering under a seal of frost. Laura let herself and her servant into the house. She lit a lamp and led Nown to the kitchen. As he followed her down the hallway, Laura looked back to see if he had trailed sand indoors, as Grace was always telling her and Rose not to. Laura saw that his feet left no mark on the floor, that the prints of her feet, damp from the icy grass, were the only ones visible, as if she was alone. It seemed that Nown's sandy soles were thirsty and had mopped up any moisture. He left nothing of himself behind.

In the kitchen Laura showed Nown the wood box. She opened the iron door of the range, made balls of paper with the yellowing pages of last summer's *Summertime Weekly*. She struck a match and put a flame to the paper, then sprinkled wood shavings on the first thin flames. Laura told Nown to keep the fire going. The wood range was a wet-back stove and Laura hoped that, in an hour or two, the fire would have heated enough water for a bath.

Nown squatted by the hearth. Laura stood behind him, swaying with tiredness. 'What am I going to do with you?' she said.

'You could send me to fight your enemies,' he said. Prompting her, she thought.

'I don't have any.' Her head was swimming. She imagined enemies, in silhouette, like shadow-puppets. She imagined her sandman tossing them left and right. She had a little glimpse of what her life might be like if she asked Nown to throw his weight around.

'I think, for now, I should keep you secret,' she said. She was too tired to think. And that was what her father, aunt, uncle and teachers had always instructed her to do — 'Use your head', 'Be responsible'.

Laura left the kitchen, found a blanket, wrapped it around herself and went back to doze by the stove. She wasn't disturbed by Nown's movements as he went back and forth between the wood box and the range. After an hour, the moon cleared the steep hill at the eastern end of Sisters Beach and shone through the kitchen's latticed windows.

Laura was hungry, but unwilling to stir. She wondered whether she might be able to ask Nown to find something for her to eat. She imagined him buttering slices of bread, and presenting her with a sandy sandwich. She laughed and opened her eyes.

Nown had the range door open and was using his hand as fire tongs, rearranging embers in order to put in more wood. The flame strained up through his fingers, didn't wrap them — it was as though the fire knew that there was nothing in him to satisfy its appetite. Nown stayed squatting by the open range peering in at the flames.

Laura asked him what he saw. Was that fire at all like the 'soft fire' of trees and people?

'It is brighter than creature fire,' Nown said.

Laura asked Nown what else he saw — for instance, how did he make his way around obstacles that had no heat that he could see?

'I see spaces and shapes. Objects like myself manufactured by people, and objects nature has made.' He touched one of the roughly hewn blocks of the hearth. 'This stone is made of many things lying quietly together. But inside each thing, everything is in motion. Nothing is wholly solid.'

Nown could see things that Laura could not. He could see *inside* the stone. Laura questioned him further and discovered that he couldn't see colours, and that he had no idea what colours were. She tried testing him by pulling faces and asking him what he could see. She tried a smile, and what she hoped was a sceptical expression, she tried a frown, and a look of fear. He was able to guess most of her expressions. But Laura was determined to sort out, if not their *differences*, at least the things that she felt made her *superior* to him. She said to him, 'A frown means what? A smile means what?'

Nown's impassive face changed — there was a perceptible upward flow in the smoky grains of sand. 'A frown means you're frowning. A smile means you're smiling,' Nown said.

Again Laura had the strong suspicion she was being teased. She frowned at him.

'But I will watch your face for frowns, Laura, if that is what you want,' Nown said.

'You would do *well* to,' Laura said, tartly. 'For now you can fetch me the biscuit tin.' She pointed at the pantry. 'The tin with the kittens on it.'

She watched Nown cross the room and thought that even exhausted and numb as she was — even *surprised* by him — somehow *having* him seemed natural to her.

Nown came back and put the biscuit tin into her hands. She took it from him but was staring past him at the cut-crystal knob of the pantry door. Was it her imagination, or had the crystal clouded, marred by his abrasive touch? Laura got up to take a closer look, then lost her nerve — was she really ready to know that her servant could unconsciously destroy things at a touch? *No* — that was more than she needed to know right now. She decided that she must not confuse her servant, overburden him with trivial questions and instructions. It was important that he respect her, *and* her judgment.

She left the room, trailing her blanket but trying to look queenly. She called out to Nown to follow her. She led him upstairs. She showed Nown her room and told him to make a fire there — then remembered to add, 'In the hearth, please.' She took the biscuit tin into the bathroom, put the plug into the bath and turned on the taps. She sat on the edge of the bath and crunched her way through five dry macaroons.

The bathroom filled with steam. Laura closed, then locked its door.

The steam formed skeins, seemed to bale itself up near the ceiling. Condensation appeared on the inside of the bathroom windows and droplets ran, zigzagging, down their bobbled glass.

Laura shed her filthy clothes. She kicked them into a corner. She stepped into the hot water, sat, then slid down. She left the taps running for a while and the water chimed in a rising tone as the bath filled to its rim. Laura floated down the bath and turned the taps off with her toes. She submerged her head, then came up for a breath and rested her head on the bath's rim while water drained, sizzling, out of her short hair.

Laura managed to eat another biscuit, this time dipping it in her bath water, then draping it — a biscuit-shaped paste — on to her tongue. She thought of the open door of the kitchen range — she hadn't told Nown to close it. She thought of the camera on the kitchen table — she hadn't thought to ask Nown to carry it upstairs. Her thoughts were fragmentary and helpless, her limbs heavy in the hot water.

When Laura woke up the bath was still warm, but only just. She woke abruptly, slipped down in the water then lifted her head to listen for a noise she was sure had woken her. She tried to sort the sound out — whatever it was — from the wash and slap of the little waves her sudden movement had made in the bath water. She was looking up at the ceiling, and saw the swinging squares of pebbled light appear there as the headlights of a car swept across the glass of the bathroom windows.

Summerfort was nowhere near the road — the car must have come up its driveway.

Laura held her breath. She sat up in the lukewarm bath water and listened to the still house, the wintry grounds.

She heard car doors slam, and then the latch on the front door making its familiar musical rattle.

Laura flung herself out of the bath, slipped and slithered across the bathroom floor to the wicker cabinet where towels were kept. She grabbed a towel and draped it over her shoulders. She fumbled with the lock on the bathroom door. The bolt was slippery with condensation. It gave way suddenly, and Laura skinned a knuckle.

She opened the door and looked around it. She saw lamplight, and the crown of her cousin's glossy golden head appear — Rose was coming up the stairs.

Laura dashed down the hallway to the door of her bedroom. Rose had reached the top of the stairs. She saw Laura and called out to her. Their eyes met. Rose looked relieved. She was holding a lamp, but raised her other hand to gesture — she seemed to be saying something about Laura's towel. Then she turned and spoke to someone over her shoulder. It was Uncle Chorley, of course.

Laura wrenched open her bedroom door, went into her room and leant against the door to close it. She stayed there, a puddle of water forming around her feet.

Nown was standing by the fire. When she came into the room he turned and looked at her. In the firelight his eyes were hidden under the deep shadow of his gnarled forehead.

There was *no lock* to Laura's bedroom. Laura gripped the doorknob in her slippery hand and held it closed. Rose was now on the other side. 'Laura?' Rose said.

'In a minute,' said Laura.

'Rose, what is it?' Chorley was there too. That was his hand slapping high on Laura's door.

'Go away,' said Laura.

Laura panicked. She abruptly released the doorknob and crossed the room in several bounds, leaving her towel behind her. Then she was next to Nown, beside the fire, its flames warming the water on her chilly skin. For a moment she was closer to her servant than she had been since he'd cornered her. He was looking down at her with calm expectation. All the fine, crystalline river sand in his form was alive in the firelight — *alive!* Laura was quick. She put up her hand and caressed her servant's forehead. She did what she had known how to do since she'd first touched him. She didn't think of what she wanted, or 'Will it work?' but simply acted on the information she'd gleaned from that touch. She erased the W in his name.

Nown collapsed with a gentle, mineral sigh.

The door burst open behind Laura.

* * *

When Rose came into the room she found that her cousin was naked. Rose saw Laura's towel at her feet. She picked it up and carried it over to Laura, held open ready to drape her. Before dropping the towel on to her cousin's shoulders Rose turned back briefly to her father, in the doorway. She frowned at him, and made a little movement with her fingers, sweeping him away.

Rose's father had frozen, his mouth open. Rose was angry with him, and embarrassed on Laura's behalf. She wished he would just take the hint and step out of the room. Rose's father hadn't quite caught up with the fact that she and Laura were young ladies now.

Rose turned her attention back to her cousin. She settled the towel around Laura, meaning to mask her breasts and backside, and then to dry and warm her. It was only then that Rose saw that her cousin's face, shoulders, breasts, stomach and thighs were coated in sand as though a blast of wind had blown it at her. Rose saw that Laura was standing up to her ankles in a mound of sand. She saw that Laura's hand was raised at the level of her head, and that Laura's fist was clenched as though she had been knocking on an invisible door.

Rose took a step back. She stared at the mound. The sand was mostly smooth, but was in places mealy with lumps of clotted clay. Rose saw, peeking out of the pile, what looked like the fingers of a clenched, clay hand.

Chorley came up beside his daughter, then he touched his niece's arm. Rose stepped forward again, so that she and Chorley flanked Laura. They began to speak, to try to talk to her. They spoke over one another.

'Laura?' said Rose.

Chorley said, 'Take a hold of your towel, dear.'

'Are you all right, Laura?' Rose said.

'What is all this?' said Chorley, pointing at the floor.

Rose didn't understand what her cousin was up to, she simply helped Laura hold her towel.

Laura's eyes slid sideways. She looked at her uncle. She looked wild and furtive, then she dropped on to her knees and began to scrabble through the mound. Perhaps she had seen something. Something buried in the sliding mass of silver. She was moving the sand about with all the messy diligence of a digging puppy. It was Chorley who first saw what Laura was looking for. He saw the corner of an envelope sticking out of the sand. He bent and picked it up. Laura jumped to her feet, dropped her towel and made a snatch at it. Her sandy skin rasped against her uncle's clothes. Chorley reeled back, holding the envelope up over his head.

'Give that to me!' Laura said.

Chorley held off his niece with one arm, brought the envelope down to his eyes and shook the sand from it. The letter was addressed in Tziga's hand — 'Laura' it said. The letters of her name were faint, the ink scratched away, the surface of the envelope itself distressed and furry — as though it had been rolling around in sand. But, since the letter was addressed to Laura, Chorley surrendered it to her.

As Laura waded out of the mound, clutching her letter, one of her feet hooked free another paper. Laura didn't notice it, but Rose picked it up. Laura went over to her bed and wound herself up, sand and all, in her eiderdown. She tore her letter open. Chorley watched his niece's eyes go back and forth, climbing down the page, reading. He became aware of Rose, beside him, making crackling noises as she unfolded the other piece of paper. He looked over her shoulder at a large fragment of a letter. He and Rose read:

> *. . . it is reasonable to suppose that he will attempt to enter the Place on a quiet section of the border, and without registering his intentions at a rangers' station. Follow him and find out where he goes.*
>
> *And — this cannot be stressed enough — do not sleep when or where Hame sleeps.*

Chorley was surprised to hear his daughter saying, under her breath, 'Yours, Cas Doran, Secretary of the Interior.' Then Chorley thought of the fragment of paper he found in the mouth of the man run over by the Sisters Beach stagecoach. The fragment had read: 'ours as D ecre'. The paper Rose was holding was another piece of the letter whose *partial signature* he had pulled from the sand-stuffed mouth of that dead ranger, three months ago, on the day that he last saw Tziga.

Rose understood more than *he* did, Chorley realised. He and Grace had been protecting their daughter from knowledge she already had. She'd been keeping secrets — not her own perhaps, but Laura's.

Chorley tried to catch Laura's eye. He said, 'What does your father have to say?'

Laura looked up from the page only to say, 'Get up.' She appeared to be speaking to the mound of sand. She said, 'Pull yourself together.' Then she laughed, a ragged, unhappy sound.

'My dear Laura,' the letter began. Laura, reading it, heard Nown speaking, not her father. 'My dear Laura,' Nown had said. Later she had seen him working his hand into his chest — to fetch out this letter, she now knew. The letter had lain against his heart, or had lain inside his chest alone, instead of a heart. Laura had asked Nown about her father — she had requested information, and Nown had reached for the letter. *If only*, Laura thought.

> *My dear Laura,*
> *Please excuse this clumsy scrawl. I haven't much time, and my hands are hurting me. I'm writing only to tell you what I must.*
> *I've made a mess of things. I'm afraid I intend to leave my mess for you to tidy up — a shameful thing for any father to do.*
> *Laura, you must listen to what the Place tells you, what it **will** tell you if it speaks to you as clearly as it has to me since the beginning. I wasn't ever prepared to listen to it. I should have let it make something of me — what it **needed** me to be. Instead, I took what I wanted from it. I really always knew that the Place wanted me to do something for it. What I wasn't able to understand was that it was warning me, warning me what I must not do.*
> *Laura, I've made terrible mistakes. I don't want to tell*

you what I've done because I know that, if I try, I will betray myself even further by defending my actions when, in fact, they are indefensible. Indefensible and unspeakable. Can you blame me if I can't speak about it? But see — I am defending myself. Maze Plasir, who is as guilty as I am, would not try to make excuses for his part in our crime. Plasir, it turns out, is a more decent man than I am.

This is my excuse, Laura — for the little it's worth — I loved your mother for too long before she consented to be my wife. I loved her too much, till it wasn't love, till it was only excessive sentiment and miserable longing, as lonely a habit as habitual drunkenness.

I must stop this. I must remember everything I have to tell you.

Your Aunt Marta knows 'The Measures'. It may be that you will find need of them, though I have given you someone — **this** someone. He will be able to help you, to carry you places where you wouldn't be able to walk on your own. His patience, his stamina and his loyalty are infinite. I hope that you will make good use of him, and that his usefulness to you will make up for my failings.

Laura, I have left you with a terrible task. But you need only do it once, if you do it properly. When you're ready catch the dreadful dream. Overdream someone with the right-sized audience — your aunt in the Rainbow Opera. Pick the right occasion, then break and enter, break and enter their minds. Make them see that the dreams are ghosts. That the Place is a tomb — the tomb of the future.

Laura, love, I am so sorry for involving you in my ludicrous life.

Laura twisted the page in her hands and tucked it out of sight under the bedclothes. At that moment her confusion was the only reason she had for not answering her uncle's question, or simply handing over the letter.

Her father's last line was like the darkness following a lightning flash. The letter had dazzled Laura, but after reading it, only its final line stayed with her. She couldn't understand it. Laura was her father's child — had he 'involved her in his life'? *Ludicrous*. What a word — it was too deflating, too bleak, too adult for her to understand. There had been a moment — a moment between Nown's collapse, and this — when she thought she would get an explanation, receive instructions, be released from the lonely prison of her puzzlement. But Laura found her father's letter unfathomable. And she was *ashamed* of it.

'Well?' said Chorley. His voice sounded like a grating hinge.

Under the covers Laura had begun to tear the letter into pieces. Her uncle saw what she was doing and dived at the bed. Suddenly he had one corner of the paper, and Laura was rolling around over the other fragments, kicking, and slapping him with her free hand. She shouted at him, 'It's *my* letter!'

Rose came to Laura's aid. She took her father by the arm and hauled him away. She yelled, 'Let Laura keep it!'

Chorley shook his daughter off. He said to her, 'She *isn't* keeping it, she's tearing it up! Why won't she let me *help* her?' Then, to Laura, 'Why won't you trust me?'

Rose, seeing Laura in tears, began to cry too. Laura was still shredding the paper, tearing it into smaller and smaller pieces. 'Dad wouldn't want you to see it,' she said to her uncle.

'Let *me* be the judge of that,' Chorley said. 'You're still only a child, Laura.'

'You don't need to know.' Laura shook flakes of paper off her ink-blackened fingers. She and her uncle stared at each other, each looking through tears on the other's anger, pity and compassion. They didn't look away till Rose said, 'Where did all this sand come from?'

Part IV
Open Secrets

One

Chorley had to leave his car at a garage in Sisters Beach. Laura couldn't be taken back through Rifleman Pass where, for her, the border was. So they caught the train. They went in their usual style, and had a compartment to themselves.

Laura refused to answer their questions. After a time she found it easy to disregard them. She felt chilly and light-headed. Her hair hadn't dried properly after her bath, and her scalp was damp. She inclined her head into the padded corner of her seat and let her uncle and cousin talk. At one point she found herself telling her uncle a *story*. She said that her father had left her a sandcastle — that he had built a sandcastle in her bedroom at Summerfort. She'd only just found it. 'It fell apart when you hammered on the door,' Laura said.

Her uncle's face was like the reflection of the moon on water, pale and unstable. Laura couldn't seem to look at it properly. Chorley was reminding her that her father had been *dead* before they had left the house at Sisters Beach, two days after her Try. He said, 'You're just being insolent, Laura.'

Rose said, 'Laura, when I asked where all the sand came from, why did you lie down on your bed and pull the covers over your head?'

Laura slid further down the seat. She heard Rose say, 'She has beads of sweat on her top lip. I think she's unwell, Da.'

The seat beside Laura depressed as Chorley sat down. He prised her out of her corner and felt her forehead. Laura said to him she was going to have her dream about the mice — she always dreamt about mice when she had a fever, dear little mice running all over the place so that she couldn't lie down anywhere. Beneath her uncle's hand her head felt like a teapot stowed under a cosy — something was brewing there. Rose seemed to be counting the stops between Sisters Beach and Founderston — but weren't they on the express? They were discussing where they might have the train stop. She heard Rose say, 'Do you think she is very sick?'

'She's very hot. But I want to get her home. I'd rather not hand her over into anyone else's care.'

'No,' said Laura. She was agreeing with her uncle, she wanted to be taken home. She tried to explain that she was only knocked back because she'd walked so far. Her water was in her pack, wouldn't someone *please* give her water?

There was a little flurry around her, as if the mice had arrived. Then someone put a cup to her lips, and she took a few sips of cool water. Her teeth hurt. She heard Chorley say to Rose, 'Do you have any idea what she's been up to?'

'I told you — she went to get the film from your camera.'

The camera. Laura asked them had they remembered to collect it from the kitchen. 'After all my trouble,' she said. She saw Rose frown and slap her forehead. They had forgotten it.

Laura said she wanted to lie down. 'Let me,' she begged. Then she said, fearful, 'You stay over there. Stay where you're put.' Then she called his name, 'Nown!' and began to cry, and put her right hand — her writing hand — up into the curling column of the music that had appeared around her, and was smoking away from her body, the music she had felt singing between Nown and her when she gave him his voice.

A week later Laura's fever had gone, but had left her as worn out as her ordeal of walking.

The doctor had been in that morning. Before he'd left her, she'd asked him to tell her aunt and uncle not to tax her with questions. He'd said he would do that for her, but in a few days she'd be as right as rain. He was the family's doctor and specialised, he'd said, in exhausted dreamhunters, but he was distressed to see one exhausting herself so *early* in her career. He had got up to leave, and patted her foot under the covers. He'd said, 'You'll be back on your feet in no time. If you're anything like your father, you're as tough as a bug.'

Her illness and its dispensations couldn't last for ever.

Rose appeared in Laura's room after lunch. She was flushed, as if she'd been running, and was wearing her school coat and hat. When she saw Laura looking at the coat Rose took it by the lapels and gave it a little shake. 'When Da went back for his car and the camera I remembered to tell him to look for my coat.' Rose came and sat on the end of Laura's bed. 'They're sending me back to school. Da is developing that film — they mean to have a look at it tonight, I think. I'm being kept out of everything, as usual. I know you're not going to say much to them, but, Laura, you *are* going to talk to *me*, aren't you? They keep bushwhacking me — they told me the cab would come at two, but it's here already. I have to go. But look, I figure that, if they're in such a hurry to send me away, then there's still something they're frightened of.'

Laura grabbed Rose's hand. Then she had a fit of coughing.

'We only have a minute,' Rose said. She looked over her shoulder at the door. Then she helped Laura sit up and gave her a sip of water. 'Tell you what —' Rose said. 'You let me know what's on the film. Put it on a postcard. Then meet me Wednesday week, in the sculpture room at the museum. I have the day off.' Rose leant over Laura's pillow and kissed her.

'Bye,' Laura rasped. 'Wednesday week, the sculpture room.'

There was just over two minutes of film, showing, in ghostly black and white, the remnants of a burnt building. A ruin sketched as if in black ink against —

'Is that water?' Chorley said to Grace.

'No, it's sand,' Laura said.

'A dry seabed, I think,' Grace said.

The first shot came to an end, then a second began, the same view, but the camera was unsteady.

'He's picked it up,' Chorley said.

The camera turned, slowly rocking, through one hundred and eighty degrees, till it showed a range of grey hills.

'That's the view back the way he came,' Grace said. 'That's a kind of map.'

The film came to an end, the projector flicking through what was left on the reel — Chorley's cataloguing marks — and lighting their faces in flashes.

Two

Six days later Laura was back in Doorhandle. She dropped her bag at her boarding house, and asked her landlady to lay a fire in her room. Then she went out again.

She ran along Doorhandle's plank pavement towards the rangers' station. It was raining heavily. She ducked through fountains from jutting downpipes. The duckboards were slippery, the spills of summer oozing out of their timber — dog piss, liquor, horse shit, ice-cream. The boards seemed coated with saliva, not rain, a surface on which even Laura's rubber-soled walking boots sometimes slithered. It was dark, the guttering on all the verandas drooped, and dribbled fringes of rainwater. Everyone was indoors. There were no people or animals in Doorhandle's streets, but still those streets were noisy with drumming, splashing, splattering, never-ending rain.

By the time Laura reached the rangers' station the rain was through the shoulder seams of her coat. The station was warm; its rooms were steamy and smelt of wet wool. It was crowded, and everyone there seemed set to head In. There were queues before the counter in the supply depot, and all the customers were cradling ration packets and the bottled lime juice they used to keep their water sweet. The shelves were thinly stocked. The station had been like this for days, as everyone who had the option of escaping the awful weather packed up and walked off into the only reliable dry Place.

Laura didn't plan to go In that day. She would spend a night at the boarding house, climb into her bed and listen to the rain on the iron roof of her gable room.

But first, she had to buy a special kind of map.

Laura already had a book of charts, what she was after now was a book of *profiles*. These books contained views of the landscape of the Place from the points of entry at Doorhandle and Tricksie Bend. The pages in books of profiles were made of semi-transparent paper, so that the next view of hills appeared faintly through the view on the page before it, as it would to anyone shifting their focus from the hills in the foreground to a range further away. The profile books were essential to anyone who planned to penetrate deep into the Place. Because the pages were transparent, the reader had only to flip the book over, and go back through it, in order to plot a course back out again. Each newly issued book of profiles represented the landscape of the Place for as far as anyone had journeyed In from either end. The latest issue — the one Laura wanted — was entitled simply *Profiles: Seven Days In from Tricksie Bend*. Laura wanted to see whether she could plot a course to the dry seabed of her father's film using a combination of his shot of the hills back the way he had come, and the landforms in a book of profiles.

The books were an expensive item and Laura had to join the queue in order to ask for one at the counter. As she waited her turn, she looked about at the gathered rangers and dreamhunters. Even after all her trips In, and her examinations, Laura wasn't quite used to the sight of this collection of thin, fit, brown, crop-haired people. They were the *other* family to which Laura's father and Aunt Grace belonged. As Laura mused over this family likeness she noticed a boy trying to catch her eye. He was a few bodies behind her in the queue beside hers. He had been staring at her till she felt it, and looked back at him.

He was one of the boys who had been examined with her, the boy from the infants' beach, the one who had written out his name and address on the back of her copy of Maze Plasir's business card. Laura had lost Plasir's card, and couldn't remember the boy's first name. She gave him a small smile of acknowledgment and looked away.

His line was shuffling forward faster than hers; he would soon be beside her. She racked her brains. His name was Mason. What Mason? Something Mason?

'*Sandy!*' Laura thought, and giggled with relief at the very moment that Sandy Mason finally fell into step with her.

'What is so funny?' he said, and grinned.

Laura told him she had only just remembered his name and that she been running through the options. 'It's Sandy Mason, isn't it?'

'Alexander,' the boy said.

'But you wrote "Sandy" on Plasir's card.'

The boy blushed. 'Sandy isn't a good professional name,' he said.

They reached the counter at the same moment. He deposited his armload of rations, and watched carefully while the clerk added up the total. Laura paid for her book and an oilskin satchel in which to keep it. They came away from the counter, Sandy with his purchases in a flour sack, Laura with a sealed and wrapped package clutched to her chest. Sandy licked his lips. He said, 'Have you earned anything yet?' He was looking at the book, longingly.

'No,' said Laura. 'But I am writing an article for the *Ladies Journal* — "My Winter Dreamhunting".'

'Really?'

'No,' said Laura.

Sandy Mason's blush spread up into his ears. 'I suppose it *was* rather a rude question,' he said.

'Yes,' said Laura.

'Do you always put people on the back foot?' Sandy was clearly preparing to defend himself.

'Well — if it helps them get their other foot out of their mouth,' said Laura.

For a moment they continued to stand dumbly in the middle of the store, clutching their purchases and getting in people's way. Then Sandy showed what he was made of by trying to continue the conversation. He said, 'How are you, then?'

'Not bad,' said Laura. 'And how are you?'

'I don't know. Still Trying, it seems. I've been working at Pike Street Hospital, amplifying my uncle — I told you about him, the one who works with the surgeons, supporting the anaesthetic.'

Laura nodded.

'But apparently I am not "opened" enough yet to be much of an amplifier. My uncle says I should spend a few months catching different things and "opening" myself. He's sponsoring me, which makes it easier.'

'Good,' said Laura. 'Plasir didn't seem to mind taking that boy unopened.' A moment after she had said it, Laura realised that it could be taken two ways. Sandy was looking shocked. She clapped her hand over her mouth, and then apologised. 'I was only trying to use your term — "opened". I mean — I didn't mean anything else.'

Some rangers went past them, one saying, 'Excuse me,' pointedly.

'We're in the way,' Sandy said. He gestured with his chin at the door, beyond which was a wide veranda, littered with umbrellas and covered in muddy footprints. Laura followed him out.

It was cold outside, and the street was uninviting beyond the veranda's beaded curtain of dribbling rain.

'I really didn't mean — you know,' Laura said again.

'Good. For a moment I thought you were one of those girls who'll say anything for a laugh.'

Laura, irritated again, said, 'What *can* such girls be thinking?'

Sandy lost his temper with her. 'You're impossible to talk to — you're so scratchy!'

'Well — if I agreed with absolutely everything you said, that would be scratchy too, believe me,' Laura told him. 'I had a friend like that. He was very accommodating — and very abrasive.'

'You *had* a friend?'

'Amazing, isn't it?' Laura said, then, 'He's gone now. But not because I was impossible to talk to.'

'Do you mean your father?'

'Fathers aren't friends,' Laura said, impatient.

'No, they're not. My father is more of an opponent. He made me wait two years past the legal age to Try. He set impossible conditions — which I met, actually.'

'I thought you were nearer my age,' Laura said, though she knew he was not. She didn't want him talking down to her.

'Do I *look* your age?' Sandy said. It seemed his disgust in her was complete. 'No, I do not. I look as though I should be doing *better* already. I should be a brown-skinned veteran with speciality dreams and keen clients.' Sandy was shifting from foot to foot, a picture of frustration and impatience. He said he had a thirty-five-metre penumbra already, unopened, and his uncle should be working for *him* by now.

Laura was surprised. 'Who measured your range?'

'The examiners. They do that. Didn't they give you your figures?'

'No, they didn't.'

'They're supposed to. Why wouldn't they? You know, that was what was behind the trouble we had with that boy who went with Plasir. *Range*. After our examination he was nagging everyone else for their results, *their figures*. It was like the bloody changing sheds —' Sandy remembered he was talking to a girl and blushed again.

'That boy seemed to think he knew what Plasir wanted,' Laura said. She was wondering about Plasir, whom she knew she'd have to talk to. Her father had mentioned Plasir in his letter. He said Plasir knew things. Laura hadn't even begun to think how to approach the man.

The boy was saying, 'Plasir's penumbra — his *range* — may be tiny, but he can overdream almost anyone.'

Laura suddenly realised that there was a great deal she didn't know about differences in talent. Her father and aunt had almost always talked as if it was all a matter of *degree* — great and small. She tried to explain her thought to Sandy, and then said, 'You'll have to give me a full rundown, I think.'

'Sure. But, you know, it really isn't surprising that your father and aunt didn't go into a lot of detail. For them it was a case of *them* and everyone else. Your aunt's a split dreamhunter, as catchy as flu, and has a three-hundred-metre penumbra. And your father once overdreamt eight dreamhunters who all had his own Starry Beach, *and* on their first night with it. His penumbra was estimated at somewhere between three-fifty and four. He was a god, basically — if you don't mind me saying. Even if he only ever caught single point of view dreams.'

'I'm going In tomorrow to catch Starry Beach,' Laura said. She watched Sandy swallow, and try to collect himself. He began to apologise. He said he realised that it might be hard for Laura to hear people talk about her father. Laura saw that he thought she had changed the subject because her feelings were hurt.

'My uncle is organising a memorial service,' Laura said. Then she put out her free hand and touched Sandy's upper arm. She had a moment of surprise at how little her fingers were able to encompass — how big his arms were compared to her own. Then she remembered she had meant to say something, had only touched him to get his attention. 'Don't be sorry,' she said. She removed her hand and they stared out at the rain. After a time he told her that he'd taken a room at Mrs Lilley's.

Laura's room was at Lilley's too — no surprise, really. Lilley was the kind of landlady who kept an eye on her lodgers, so her house was often recommended to the parents of young dreamhunters. 'Shall we go, then?' Laura said. She didn't wait for him but held her package up over her head and darted down the station's steps and out on to the plank pavement.

They arrived at the boarding house wet and breathless to find that another lodger was entertaining his parents in the parlour, and Mrs Lilley's daughters were setting the table in the dining room. They had nowhere to go but to their respective rooms. Laura noticed that Sandy seemed to feel he had to make something up to her. He climbed backwards up the stairs in front of her, beginning several sentences, clutching his side — he had a stitch — and getting nowhere.

Laura interrupted him. 'Do you have a fire?'

'No,' he said.

'I can give you some coals in my warming pan,' Laura said. She unlocked her room, left the door ajar and him outside — mindful of the house rules which said that there were to be 'NO visitors in lodgers' rooms at ANY hour'.

Laura took the warming pan from its hook and used the poker to roll some coals out of her fire. She called Sandy in to pick the pan up. Then, as he hesitated in the doorway, she said, 'My feet are wet. I want to change before tea.'

'Dinner,' said Sandy.

'Dinner at teatime,' Laura said.

'And there's the difference between us,' Sandy said. 'You're used to having *tea* while I am having my *dinner*.'

Laura told him to go away. She closed the door on him and sat on her bed to remove her wet boots and socks. She put her boots on the hearth and hung her socks from the mantel by placing her parcel on their tops. She was feeling irritated, but happier. She'd been preoccupied with her big problems — her father's letter, what he had meant, who she might confide in once she *understood* what he meant — so was grateful to be presented with a minor puzzle, Sandy Mason's behaviour.

Sandy was as displeased and contrary as Rose could be when things weren't going well for her. Most of what Laura said seemed to offend him, yet he seemed troubled if she let him know he'd offended her. He seemed to want to prove to her that his *manners* were better than hers. Or, if not his manners exactly, then his morals. Sandy thought he was somehow *better* than she was, more mature, more realistic. All his carry-on seemed to imply that, since she wasn't trying to make money, she was only playing at being a dreamhunter, perhaps in an effort to make herself seem more substantial to herself. Perhaps he thought she was some kind of dabbler — and that it was significant that she came from a household where dinner was served at eight. But, Laura decided, she would let Sandy think what he liked. He could imagine she was a posh girl with a hobby if that's what he wanted to imagine. Laura didn't like being alone — when she was alone she felt all bent out of shape by her burdens. Squabbling with Sandy Mason made her feel human, nearly as human and alive as she had felt while asking her sandman questions.

Three

In the morning the rangers at the border post beyond Doorhandle were having trouble with some youths throwing stones. They were locals, who had decided to alleviate their cabin fever by winding up rangers. They had hidden themselves in some bushes by the roadside a little way beyond the stone cairn. In fact they had removed some stones from the cairn as ammunition, and were now throwing them at anyone who came near the landmark.

The rangers couldn't catch them. They couldn't get past the border without crossing over into the Place. Stones were sailing through the air at them from a spot only twenty yards away — where they couldn't ever walk. The rangers had sent someone to the sheriff's office for help, and were loitering about just out of range, with a gathering of dreamhunters intent on going on In that morning. The dreamhunters were feeling the cold. It was still raining, and they had umbrellas, but they had left their heavy winter coats back in their rooms — they wouldn't need them once they were across the border.

Time passed, and the gathering of dreamhunters clustered under their umbrellas like mourners at a rainy graveside. There was no sign of the sheriff. Doorhandle was having a delightful moment — letting the employees of the Regulatory Body, who had virtually taken over the village ten years before, feel *its* power for a change. The news of the stone throwers made its way back to the shelter, so the dreamhunters who had been filling in their intentions stopped there, where there was a fire in the stove. They waited to hear that the problem had been sorted out, the culprits chased off or collared.

The rangers near the cairn were therefore quite surprised to see a couple of dreamhunters come scampering up the road after word had been sent to the shelter and the flow of people stemmed. They were more surprised when the two rushed past the tortoise-back of joined umbrellas and ran on, headlong, towards the cairn. The two had their packs held up over their heads. When stones began to fall around them, making pockmark splashes in the mud, the big one, the boy, pushed the girl behind him. They continued on that way, like an engine and its carriage, into the shelter of the cairn. They crammed together there, laughing. The boy picked up a stone from the cairn and tossed it into the bushes. It was answered by a furious volley. Stones clapped and thumped on the far side of the cairn. The two put their heads together and had a consultation. They filled their hands with stones. He ducked out into the road, she followed, threw her handful, then dived through the space beyond the cairn, and vanished. Stones splattered into the puddles where she had been. The boy poked up his head, feinted, provoked another volley of stones, which he ducked. Then he jumped to his feet, threw his handful and plunged through after the girl.

There was a burst of clapping from the watching dreamhunters. Others were inspired to make a dash for it and, after a few more minutes, the wet road was pimpled by flung stones and littered with mangled umbrellas.

When the last of their followers had overtaken Sandy and Laura, greeted them and hurried on in squelchy shoes, they found themselves alone. Their jackets steamed, and their dripping trouser legs left trails of clotted dust behind them on the road.

Sandy had asked Laura that morning whether she minded if he went along with her. He'd felt surprised — and surprisingly happy — when she said she'd welcome his company.

They walked to where the road forked, into road and track — the track beaten and scoured of dead grass. There was a sign on a tree; it told them they were only an hour from Starry Beach.

'I set my alarm and got up really early,' Laura said. She stretched and yawned. 'I'm ready for a nap.'

Sandy had kept himself up late. He'd read old issues of the *Founderston Monthly Illustrated* that Mrs Lilley kept in piles in the hall. He had scoured the magazine's pages for any mention — or better, any pictures — of Hames and Tiebolds. The whole time he had been skimming and swooping, Sandy had felt he was studying for an exam. In what subject he didn't know.

He had already done the Hames and history. He knew — for instance — that they were one of five families who had come to the country from the island of Elprus after a volcanic eruption. The Elpra who crossed the seas all settled in Founderston — then a jerry-built settlement around a fort and river port. They were welcomed for their highly cultivated skills in silk making — and for the relics, the bones of St Lazarus. The relics were housed in the Temple. The islanders stayed together as a people in the streets they built, in what, over the centuries, became Founderston's Old Town. In fact, up until eighty years before Sandy was born, the Old Town was predominantly peopled by the dark-skinned, curly-haired people, and would be still, were it not for a cholera epidemic, and the two contaminated wells in the Old Town which caused more than half the epidemic's deaths.

The Tiebolds were another story. Sandy had encountered plenty of Tiebolds in his history courses at school. They were impossible to miss — the histories were full of them, sometimes scoundrels, but usually worthy citizens. The family appeared as politicians and soldiers, scientists and churchmen — the current Grand Patriarch, Erasmus Tiebold, was a cousin of Chorley Tiebold's father.

Of course, the most *famous* Tiebold was, in fact, a Cooper. Grace Cooper was only eighteen when she first entered the Place and discovered she could catch dreams. Her father owned a tobacco shop, and her family hadn't the resources to rent rooms, and so Grace was at a loss how to sell what she caught. But she had always been an avid reader of the social pages, and it was her knowledge of who was who in society, of the habits, hobbies and tastes of the rich — as reported in *Founderston Monthly Illustrated* — that helped her form an idea.

The story Sandy had heard was this: Grace Cooper had turned up one day at a famous dressmaker's when a certain racy lady of fashion was there for a fitting. The dreamhunter told this perfumed person, 'This is what I can do for you.' She was invited to turn up at a house party at the woman's country place. The woman said to Grace, 'You shall be my rabbit in the hat.'

On her first night in the country house, full of a dream she had caught only two days before, and ready to sleep deeply — because she had deprived herself of sleep in order to keep the dream fresh — Grace lay down and filled forty rooms with her dream. The guests found themselves fleeing cross-country, night and day, as two lovers pursued by enemies who wanted to keep them apart. Grace set the sleepers afloat in boats down dark streams fringed by bulrushes. She laid them down in an embrace in the sweet damp summer grass. Some of the male guests found themselves in the head and body of the woman as she watched her lover defy their pursuers, filled with fear and admiration for him. Some female guests found themselves in the mind and body of the man as he lay over his lover touching her tenderly and gazing into her face. Some sleepers moved from one to the other. And all woke moved, refreshed, excited by their thoughts and their bodies. They could talk of nothing else all the next day. It was beyond anything that any of them had experienced, or even heard reported.

At breakfast their hostess pulled her rabbit out of the hat — she introduced her guests to her young dreamhunter.

Grace Cooper was an overnight sensation. From then on she was very much in demand in certain circles, at some houses, though it must be said that there were mothers who would keep their daughters away from any house at which Grace Cooper was to be a guest. Grace was the toast of — as the newspapers said — 'the fast set.' Grace Cooper and her dreams were disturbing to polite society in a way that Maze Plasir was not. Plasir conducted his business with privacy and discretion, and could only project his dreams into rooms right next to his own. Grace Cooper, despite the frivolous content of her dreams, had powers of projection rivalled only by those of Tziga

Hame. When she dreamed, her dream was shared by as many people as could be packed in comfort into some two hundred square metres of space. Many people tasted her dreams, and her influence was great. For instance, it was for Grace Cooper that the first dream palace, the Rainbow Opera, was built. Shortly before the Opera was completed, Grace Cooper had married the dashing, but debt-laden, Chorley Tiebold.

As Sandy walked along beside Laura, this Tiebold/Hame, he wasn't feeling too star-struck. In fact he felt he could be of some use to Laura, who, after all, had been a sheltered schoolgirl up until only a few months ago. There was so much that Laura didn't know and should, Sandy thought. She had become a dreamhunter naturally, but haphazardly. Her father and aunt hadn't bothered to explain the life, had possibly only ever talked about it in a vague, self-glamorising way. Her father may even have hoped she wouldn't become a dreamhunter — the fact she had attended Founderston Girls' Academy suggested quite different ambitions. Laura Hame was adrift, dabbling, wasting time and money, buying the texts like a good schoolgirl, wearing the correct uniform, but — to Sandy Mason's mind — she was adrift. After all, what had she said about catching Starry Beach — that she wanted to 'have a look at it'? As though the Place was a big store, and she was a lady of fashion out shopping with a fat purse.

'So —' Sandy said, breaking into the perfect, uncanny silence of the Place, 'you want to catch Starry Beach to "have a look at it", but not to sell it?'

'There's something I want to learn.'

'About Starry Beach?'

Laura said, 'Have you ever shared it?'

'No. I told you I come from south of the Corridor. I only shared dreams once I came north to stay with my uncle.'

Laura nodded. Then she seemed to decide to confide. 'In Starry Beach the friends around the bonfires wonder about a line of lights moving through the forest on the hills above them. I caught a dream where I was *among* the lights on the hill. My dream was a reverse view of Starry Beach. Starry Beach is a healing dream and my dream was a nightmare. I guess I'm just checking all the angles.'

Sandy was perplexed. 'You mean,' he said, 'you want to know what the two dreams *mean* in relation to each other?'

'Yes.'

'That's a very strange approach to dreamhunting.'

Laura shrugged.

'And that's your plan?' Sandy said. He thought she was very odd — one of those people with an impractical amount of intellectual curiosity.

'Ah,' she said, 'my *plan*. I also want to learn how to walk for days and days. And I want to learn how to make something.'

'Make what? Are you talking about the material world? You know dreamhunters don't really deal with the material, except money, water and shoe leather.'

Laura Hame wore an airy, secretive look. She said that all the girls at her former school were making beaded snoods for St Lazarus's Day gifts.

'What the hell is a snood?' said Sandy.

'A woven bag to wrap around loosely bundled long hair,' Laura said, informative.

They walked along in silence for a time. Sandy, who felt he was being teased with stories about snood-making, tried again. He said, 'You know, I think it's pretty slack of the Body not to have given you your figures.'

Laura said, 'They might have, I may not have been paying attention. I don't pay attention sometimes.'

'You drift,' Sandy said, pleased to have one of his own views confirmed.

She didn't answer. She had the look of someone who was listening, trying to identify some distant sound. Then she stopped, squatted and touched the ground. She seemed to pet the surface of the road.

'What are you doing?'

'I don't know,' she said. 'Whenever I come In, for the first hour or two I get a funny feeling.' She stood up again and resumed walking. 'It's as if it's telling me something.'

'You hear the Place talking to you?' Sandy tried not to sound too sceptical.

'I don't hear it. I begin by knowing I'm being talked to, then I get a very strong feeling. I feel I want to *console* the Place, as if it's crying. Or — or I have to *save it* somehow.'

Sandy told Laura that all that meant — probably — was that she had an affinity with healing dreams. 'They are all around here. If you feel you want to *stop the suffering* it's because those dreams are here. Perhaps you're a healer, like your father.'

'Maybe.'

This was enough of an invitation for Sandy. He went on to explain some things to Laura, to educate her about affinities. She listened to him with interest. He was right, she had only a sketchy knowledge of what was what — the pedigrees of dreamhunters.

There were Soporifs, Sandy told her. Soporifs like his uncle, who could send people off to sleep. Sandy told Laura he thought she might be a Soporif, if the way she'd nearly knocked out the rangers at Wild River was anything to go by. There were Novelists, Sandy went on. Novelists were very rare dreamhunters who could catch split dreams. Laura's Aunt Grace was the most celebrated example. 'Wild River is a split dream, but none of us caught its split version,' Sandy said.

'I didn't even catch Wild River,' Laura said. 'I told you that.'

Sandy ignored this. He knew she'd caught a nightmare. But he figured that, since the Body had licensed her, it must have been an isolated episode. He told her about Healers, with their affinity for healing dreams, and Hames — any dreamhunter with a big penumbra. 'A whole class of dreamhunters is named after your father!' Sandy said. 'Imagine.'

There were Mounters, who may not have big projection zones but could easily overdream others. 'Your father was a Mounter, too. So is Plasir — he is also what is politely called a Gifter and impolitely a Grafter. Depending on your point of view, he either grafts real people's faces and bodies on to characters in dreams, or he gives people what they can't have, or what they've lost.'

Lastly, Sandy said, there were Colourists. 'Colouring is illegal. I have heard a Colourist can infiltrate dreams and suggest things. They're secret persuaders.'

Laura was staring at him, apparently horrified. 'What do they persuade people to do?'

'Alter their opinions, invest their money, sell their houses, vote a certain way, leave town, get married, change their will, like or dislike someone, form suspicions — all that.'

'But how? How can they catch dreams to do all those things?'

'I don't know. Because it's illegal no one talks about Colouring.'

Laura was quiet, thinking. Sandy let her think — he'd told her enough to be going on with.

After a little they reached Starry Beach. The dream site was in a clearing between trees with polished white limbs. The patch of ground between the trees was dusty and interrupted by hollows where people had been bedding down for the past twenty years.

Laura and Sandy were stopped short of the clearing by a couple of rangers. The men were sitting together and swigging from a bottle. They were surrounded by dirt-caked picks and shovels. They had been digging a new latrine, they said. They were having a break before closing and covering the old one. 'There's a couple of dreamhunters at the site already. They're asleep. Men from St Thomas's Lung Hospital. You'll have to wait till they wake.'

The rangers finished their meal and went back to their digging, off behind a screen of trees. Sandy and Laura waited quietly. Sandy hadn't run out of conversation, or *lessons,* for Laura, but while he was making his lesson plan he became distracted by something the girl was doing.

Laura was playing with the dirt. She was sitting cross-legged, scraping the dusty earth together until she had a small mound before her. Sandy was reminded of his neighbour's daughter making mud pies on the back steps of her house. Laura pressed the mound together and patted it smooth. Then she began to shape it. Sandy saw her form deep eye sockets and a rough, flattened nose. While she worked the dirt her face was blank and dreamy.

From the far side of the clearing came the sound of stirring bodies, coughs and murmurs. The dreamhunters were awake. They sat up, one scratching his head. They looked about them with slitted, blissful eyes, then yawned, stretched, got up and shook the dust from their bedrolls. One spotted Sandy and Laura and said, 'It's all yours, kids.'

Laura's head jerked up, she stared at the man, startled. As she got to her feet she knocked her dust sculpture to nothingness with her knee.

The dreamhunters stuffed their bedrolls into their packs. Sandy and Laura came into the clearing and stood waiting for them.

'Is it still raining?' said one man.

'When we left it was,' Laura said.

The dreamhunters shouldered their packs, waved and left. Laura and Sandy spread out their bedrolls at the base of one of the skeletal trees.

They didn't catch Starry Beach. When she lay down to catch her first dream Laura had run off on her own with the fleeing convict, while her successful test mates plunged together into Wild River. By himself, unsupported by other dreamers who were catching the predictable dream, Sandy Mason had to go where Laura Hame went. It really was as though the Place was determined to communicate something to Laura through her dreams.

Later Sandy came to name the dream and make it part of his repertoire, once he had caught it a couple more times and had learnt to wake up before it changed, turned from an 'achievement dream' into a nightmare. Sandy registered the dream as his own, and the following year, in the latest issue of the charts, the dream appeared in small print under the still stable Starry Beach. The map reference read: 'The Water Diviner — Alexander Mason.' The dream's name was coupled with Sandy's name because it was his claim, and he first performed it. It didn't fall under the description of 'dreams for the public good', so wasn't commandeered by the government. Sandy had an exclusive on the Water Diviner for a year and he made good money out of it — but only once he had learnt to wake himself in time.

The boy went out in the afternoon and cut a forked branch from the hazel tree by the stables. He stripped off all its leaves and twigs and took it out to the lip of the crack — the relic of an earthquake half a century before — a scar on the home paddock, filled with blackberry brambles. The boy did what he had seen the water diviner at the agricultural produce show do. He balanced the branch between his spread palms, fixing it in place with his thumbs. With the hazel rod held that way the boy paced along the edge of the crack. He only walked with the rod, didn't point it. The water diviner had shown him how to go slowly and hold the rod loosely.

The boy circled the crack and the rod failed to move, so he went on up the hill behind the house and stables, among the rocks, and there, after an hour walking back and forth, the hazel rod suddenly flipped down in his hands and pointed at a patch of rocks and ferns. The boy put the rod down and moved the stones with his hands. He pulled out ferns by their roots, dislodging more rocks.

Water bubbled out, at first in little pushy knuckles, then in a steady trickle. Clear water, though it came out through a crack lined with coal.

The boy's father had been worried about water, his plans for the farm constrained by a shortage of it.

The boy poked the rod into the coal crack to mark the spot, then ran off to find his father. His father would be so pleased with him, and proud of him. 'At last!' he thought. 'At last I'll be praised. At last I'll be noticed for the right reason.'

The boy couldn't find his father, who wasn't at the house, or in the stables. A stockman said his father had gone into town.

The boy set off down the road, which passed through fields where the stubble had been burnt off after the harvest. The slope beside the boy, undisturbed by rain or wind, was charred still, black against the white sky, and as glossy as an ember. The boy was running, and he startled several crows that were picking over the burnt field. He didn't see them until they separated themselves from the silky black slope and flew off. It was as though fragments of the hill had broken off and fluttered away into the sky.

The road turned down towards the town. The sun was low, setting into a band of smoke from the burn-offs. In its light the sandstone of the town shone clear gold. The new bridge spanning the slow, green river looked like something built by spirits. The boy could see the builders, though, still at work, the mason presiding over his labourers who were busy on the bridge rail mortaring the mason's strange, unlearned carvings into place.

The boy searched for his father at the post office, the butchers and the general store. He told people about his find, bubbling out of childish shyness and his usual silence like a spring released from a seam of coal.

He crossed the bridge, between the convict labourers and their guards, who lounged against the finished coping, their rifles pointed skyward. The guards were keeping a close eye on the men, whose chains had been removed so that they could clamber over the outside of the structure without risking falling into the river, and being dragged down and drowned by their leg irons.

The setting sun made the smoke pall lovely, lit it up in layers of crimson, vermilion and tangerine. The light went pure orange, the orange of orange oil.

The boy came to the church, whose sandstone glowed. The church was locked, so the boy wandered about the churchyard. He was no longer really looking for his father, but only turning around staring at everything, in awe of the light. The tombstones turned from rose to flame, as though each one were staring a bonfire full in its face. The air was close and reeked of wood smoke. All the birds had stopped singing.

The boy reached a place where there was a tree stump among the tombstones. It was the stump of a giant eucalyptus, recently felled, brought down by saw and axe, and then its remnant chipped at and reduced in size. It was still huge, and still gave off the fiery perfume of its resin. The stump was like another tomb in that light, a mausoleum, scarcely redder than the stones, though its bleeding timber would be red in any light.

The boy climbed up on to it. He got sap on his hands and feet. He stood on the stump and looked about. The sunset was so violent that it should have been making a noise. The light cast the shadows of the far hills upward across the sky, bristling rays of opaque blue in a huge, bright, slicing pane of orange light.

There was a noise in the churchyard. It was not the sort of noise the sun might make, or a bird inspired by the sunset. It was a moan. It *might have been a human sound, only there was no human consciousness, or intelligence or character in it. It sounded as though it came from a very dark place. It was a sound of absolute despair.*

The boy climbed down from the felled tree. He followed the moan, creeping softly among the tombstones.

The sun went down. The billows in the sky seem to roll and swell as they filled with purple shadows. The light went blue.

The boy stopped. He listened. He heard the sound again, a muffled rustling, then a terrible, raw-throat moaning.

A little way off, between two tall headstones, the boy could see a pile of colour — colour still, even in the blue twilight. It was a heap of white, red, yellow and purple flowers. The boy crept closer. He saw a fresh grave, piled high with late summer flowers and wreaths, laurels painted black and gilt. Nothing stirred, but the ground moaned again, then shrieked, thumped, scraped and rustled.

The boy stood staring, his hands spread as though he held his hazel rod, it wavering in his loose grip, and turning — turning down to what he had divined.

Four

On the day Rose had arranged to meet Laura she had some difficulties. It was still raining, and she had Mamie Doran in tow. Rose had been rather startled by her success in cultivating Mamie's friendship. Mamie Doran was usually cool and offhand. She never showed any sign of needing to be liked, all her actions said: 'You can take me or leave me.' Rose had wooed Mamie, had recommended her for choice parts in play readings. She'd asked for Mamie's help in sorting rags for one of the school's church-related charity drives — had kept her good company and plied her with paprika chocolate cookies from one of Farry's jumbo-sized biscuit barrels. When Mamie got chilblains, Rose bought her lavender-scented hand cream. When Mamie had a cold, Rose sat on the end of her bed and read to her. This was an unexpected pleasure. Rose didn't really approve of Mamie's manner, her sour talk about people, but Mamie was better read than Rose and had a more adventurous taste in books. Before the second term was halfway over other girls were speaking of Rose and Mamie as they had once spoken of Rose and Laura. So it was that Mamie naturally assumed that they would spend their free day together.

Rose had tried to discourage Mamie by making her plans sound as dull as possible. Her attempt to do this was complicated by another girl from the dormitory, a girl Rose rather liked, who tried to invite herself along too. 'We could take a tram to Kirks,' the girl said. (Kirks was a big department store with a cavernous, overheated tea room.)

'We could go to a matinee,' Mamie suggested, speaking only to Rose.

Rose didn't know whether Mamie meant a play or a dream. She was so distracted by wondering she nearly asked which — then remembered she didn't want anyone to go anywhere with her.

'I'd like to do that too,' said the other girl.

Mamie had her back to the girl, and didn't look at her when she spoke.

Rose was uncomfortable. She nearly said, 'Of course you can come!' But then she'd be committed to company. Instead she said only that she was *determined* to go to the museum. She tapped her sketchbook with her gloved hand. Let them think she was a swot and trying to get ahead of everyone else in their art class.

'We can do your thing, Rose, and then do mine,' Mamie said. She was still giving the other girl her cold shoulder.

The other girl gave up and drifted off to sit in the bay window of the common room.

'Only if you're sure you'll not be bored,' Rose said to Mamie.

'Of course I won't. So we agree — the museum, then a matinee? And we could have lunch at Kirks — to honour certain people in their absence.' Mamie glanced at the girl she'd driven off and gave one of her sly smiles.

When Rose and Mamie came out of a street on to the west embankment's wide pavement they saw that the Sva River was the colour of over-brewed coffee and only a few feet from the bottom of the arches of the nearest bridge. It was an alarming sight and they were relieved to turn away from the river to climb the zigzag steps that led to the plaza before the National Museum.

They left their coats and umbrellas in the museum's cloakroom, showed their school passes and went in.

Rose checked her watch. It was half an hour to her rendezvous with Laura. She should just take Mamie to the sculpture hall and start sketching something.

The sculpture hall was in a covered courtyard in the centre of the building. It had been roofed only recently, by the same architect who designed the glass dome at the Rainbow Opera. It was a lovely, light-filled room that mainly displayed copies of classical statues. When Mamie and Rose arrived they found the roof was leaking, and that several curators were marking the spots of the leaks — one standing, her head thrown back to regard the failed lead seal far above her, while her toe tapped, keeping time with the drips that fell into the puddle by her foot.

Two guards appeared with buckets. Rose and Mamie hesitated in the entrance and were told, 'Just mind the puddles. It's quite dry everywhere else.'

Mamie said to Rose, 'Are we quite sure this is a *nice* thing to do?'

Rose only pointed with her pencil. She set a course between the statues in search of something she could sketch. The splish-splash behind them changed into a tock-tock of drops hitting the bottom of zinc buckets.

'I wonder if the Opera is leaking,' Rose said, then, 'What kind of matinee did you mean, Mamie? A play or a dream?'

'Rose, you forget that some of us aren't allowed to go to dreams yet. My mother says all but a very few dreams are *too strong* for girls.'

'Oh,' said Rose. 'Do you believe her, Mamie?'

'It isn't a question of whether I believe her. I'm obedient to my parents' wishes. Aren't you?'

'Um,' said Rose. Then she stopped dead.

Laura was standing at the other end of the hall, with her back to them. Laura had her hands on the naked back of a male statue and was caressing its contours, thoughtfully, down from the shoulders to the buttocks.

Mamie sniggered.

Rose hurried towards her cousin — before the museum guards could notice what she was doing. As Rose approached, Laura removed her hands. She turned and smiled, then lost her smile when she spotted Mamie.

Mamie was smirking, looking from Laura to the statue. 'I suppose you had a previous arrangement to meet your cousin here, Rose,' Mamie said, 'but why didn't you just say?'

'I wasn't sure she'd show up,' Rose said. She widened her eyes at Laura, trying to tell her cousin that she was lying — to convey the *necessity* of lying to Mamie. Then she asked Laura, 'What were you doing?'

'Waiting,' Laura said. 'I came in out of the rain when the museum opened.'

'Not that!' Rose snapped. She gestured at the statue. She was furious with Laura for embarrassing her in front of Mamie Doran — for being so peculiar, doing something so *dirty*, then being vague about it.

Laura seemed baffled, so Rose pointed at the statue.

'Oh,' said Laura. 'Um.'

'Oh? Um?' Rose fumed.

'I was thinking of making a sculpture.'

'You could have taken an interest in the little bronze ballet dancer over there,' Rose said.

'I studied her too, before you arrived,' Laura said. She now sounded smooth. She had assumed a polite, public face again.

Mamie was showing some tact now too. She had moved a little way off and was studying another nude — a saint clothed in her long hair.

Rose took Laura's arm and drew her aside. 'Are you well?' she asked. 'We haven't much time. I promised to spend the day with Mamie.'

'Why on earth?'

'Shhh!'

Laura sighed. She said she was fine. She'd spent a few days In, where it was warm, catching dreams to 'open' herself. 'Me and Sandy Mason — the boy from the infants' beach. I went to catch Starry Beach but managed to get something else with convicts. The last one was a bad dream that ended well. This was a rather lovely dream that ended horribly — though not for the convicts. Honestly, Rose, I'm sick of those bloody convicts. Anyway, I erased it myself, overwrote it with Convalescent Two. I have a few nights' work boosting one of the resident dreamers on the medical ward at Pike Street. I got the job through Sandy's uncle.'

Mamie joined them. 'Perhaps we should all just go to Kirks? The air is clammy in here.'

Rose looked around the room, at the light from the overcast skies shining coldly on the frozen figures, on dark bronze and pale marble. 'All right. Lead on, Mamie,' she said. She tried to sound friendly.

Mamie took Rose's arm and looked across her at Laura, who Rose already had hold of. 'Isn't this nice, Rose?' Mamie said, 'Your old friend on one arm, and your new on the other.'

Rose got lucky at Kirks, where Mamie ran into her mother and some other society ladies. Rose had to endure a few uncomfortable minutes when Mamie not only introduced her to Mrs Doran, but delivered a speech in praise of Rose's achievements.

'Well,' said Mrs Doran, when Mamie finally finished, 'cream rises to the top.' She looked around her circle. 'Don't I always say that? Cream rises to the top.' To Rose she said, 'I'm hoping that one day Mamie will be made prefect too.'

'I'm sure she will,' said Rose.

'And this is Laura, Rose's cousin,' Mamie added.

The ladies smiled nervously at Laura.

'We won't join you,' Mamie said to her mother.

'But you *must*! Rose dear, take your cousin and Mamie up to look at the selection. Choose whatever you like. It'll be my treat.'

Mamie went red. She glared at her mother. Rose saw her chance to have a moment alone with Laura. She took her cousin by the arm and led her away to the cake counter, where the glistening creams and glazed fruits shone up through the glass into their faces.

'You've sure hooked and landed Mamie,' Laura said.

'I know. Now I only have to scale her, bone her, cook her, and eat her.'

Laura pulled a face. Then she said, 'I can't wait for your next free day to talk to you properly. Have aunt and uncle relaxed at all?'

'Not to the extent of having me live at home again. But my board is only paid for this term. I doubt they'll send me back after St Lazarus's Day. I don't feel they're scheming any more.

Perhaps they gave that up once you got your licence. They're indecisive and depressed and soggy now. Ma is working much harder than she needs to. Escaping into dreams, really. Da is still tussling with your Aunt Marta about the memorial service.'

Laura said, 'People in Doorhandle — rangers and villagers — keep being friendly and helpful, and it turns out that they are all doing Aunt Grace favours.'

'Yes — they are keeping tabs on us. The headmistress stopped me in the corridor yesterday and said, "I've just had such a nice chat with your father." I waited to hear about the chat — but that was all she had to say. Da had called in and been *terribly charming* to her, and she just couldn't resist sharing her good luck.'

'They're avoiding us because they're so bad at being secretive,' Laura said. 'If they saw more of us they might just blurt out their fears.' Then Laura told Rose what they had found on the film in Chorley's camera.

Rose said, 'Why did your Da film the view back the way he had come? Was he leaving directions?'

Laura shrugged.

Rose stared at her suspiciously. 'Directions for you?' she said.

'I don't have the stamina yet for a journey like that.'

'Good,' Rose said. Then she asked if Laura could stomach Mrs Doran and her friends. 'Can you sit and be a friendly nonentity?'

'Yes.'

'Can you, Laura? Can you remember I'm cultivating Mamie, and just eat cake and keep your mouth shut?'

'No, I can't eat cake if I have to keep my mouth shut.'

'Ha ha.'

'What I can't do, Rose, is wait for your next free day. There's someone I have to go and see. Someone creepy. I'd rather you went with me.'

'I'll cut class. I'll climb the wall, if I have to. Who is it you have to see?'

'Never mind that now, just meet me on the steps of the Temple. Two o'clock, Friday.'

Rose reached for Laura's hand and held it. Her heart turned over. If she could only get Laura alone for a few hours she knew she could fully unthaw her cousin. 'I'll be there,' Rose said. 'So — are you ready to brave the ladies?'

Laura nodded.

'You be bland and I'll be duplicitous. Lovely word that — duplicitous. Sounds like a prehistoric animal. *The lame duplicitous was pursued by the ravening erroneous.*'

Laura folded into her funny, panting giggle. And Rose felt tears come into her own eyes because she had made her cousin laugh. Happiness had never been like this before. Now it came like sun showers, the sun and the rain together. Happiness was happier than it had been, sharp, piercing and snatched, like a breath while swimming in surf.

Five

The Isle of the Temple was a lovely mirage of stone domes and spires standing in the stream of the Sva River. The Isle's temple, St Lazarus, was a site of pilgrimage. All the hotels, guesthouses and convents on the Isle had, for over a century, accommodated pilgrims. But by the time Laura's father fell from the Sisters Beach coach, business wasn't what it had been. *Faith* wasn't what it had been, and there were fewer pilgrims than in former times. The hotels had needed custom, and welcomed dreamhunters as guests. It was an ideal arrangement. Over the years the streets, and alleys, and winding staircases of the Isle had filled with dream parlours and their customers. Of course there were rumbles of disapproval from the Temple and the throne of the Grand Patriarch. The church preached against the 'houses of unholy worship' and 'strangers sleeping together'. But it had made sense, for safety reasons, for dream parlours to be set up with the broad, swift waters of the Sva between the dreamers and the overcrowded buildings of the Old Town on the east bank, and the promenades before the white houses along the west.

By the time Tziga Hame's daughter had become a dreamhunter the Isle was as full of the commerce of dreamhunting as it was of the business of the Orthodox Church. The offices of the Dream Regulatory Body stood at one end of the Isle, and the temple, St Lazarus, stood at the other. Between them, as well as several charity homes and hospitals and church libraries, there were countless shops that outfitted dreamhunters, in work clothes and their opulent nightclothes. There were sleepwear emporiums for dream palace patrons. There were saunas with steam rooms (dreamhunters and rangers all suffering as much from sinus complaints as mouth ulcers, due to the arid air of the Place). There were small, specialist dream parlours, and larger salons, with shuttered windows and high, boasting, perimeter fences. (The dreamers who performed in salons didn't have dangerous projection zones, but they put up fences to *imply* that they did — it was a form of advertising.) And, finally, there was the Rainbow Opera, looming above its high fence, its perimeter patrolled by guards who regularly cleared away loitering, hopeful dream-pilferers.

Maze Plasir's dream parlour wasn't easy to find. Rose and Laura wandered about looking for forty minutes before Rose thought to buy a newspaper and look for his listing. The girls put their heads together and searched the three columns devoted to advertisements for salons and parlours on the Isle. They found it — 'Maze Plasir: Adventure, Satisfaction, Solace. Dreaming *Feast after Fasting* tonight, 9 p.m.' Below the description was a street address.

Laura and Rose set out again. They hurried and clung to the walls. They were the only young women abroad in those streets, and felt conspicuous. They were so nervous and rushed that they missed the head of Plasir's street on their first pass. They turned back and went more carefully, then found it, a narrow, doglegged alley. It was dry and clean, though, and not too forbidding. This passage led to a narrow path beside the river, with only an iron rail between them and the high brown flood. The path passed around the water-stained basements of several houses then plunged between two, down a tight, short passage to a private door. A black timber door studded with bright copper nail heads.

Rose pulled the chain that hung above the door, and they heard a bell ringing somewhere in the house.

The door was answered by the bandy-legged boy who had tested with Laura. His appearance had improved — he'd filled out, his skin was clear, his hair slicked back with pomade, his clothes new and neat. He looked at Laura with lowering suspicion, and his top lip lifted. 'What are *you* doing here?'

Laura said, 'Mr Plasir gave me his card too.'

'And what about her?' The boy looked Rose up and down.

'We're keeping each other company on our errands,' Rose said.

'May we come in?' Laura said. The boy stood aside and let them in. He said that Plasir wasn't in, he was taking his exercise, he would be back shortly.

The boy showed them into a sitting room lit only by the coal fire and the slivers of light that came through its fixed shutters. There were several wingback leather chairs and a massive leather sofa. There were brass ashtrays on stems beside every seat. There was a gate-leg table, in its centre a silver platter holding sparkling balloon glasses and a cut crystal decanter filled with brandy. The walls were decorated with a frieze of dancing eastern maidens, prancing horses, pheasants, peacocks and gilded palms. There was a clock on the mantelpiece, all its workings visible, fidgeting and glittering under a glass dome. The room smelt of tobacco and furniture polish. The house was hushed.

'Are you here alone?' Laura asked the boy.

'Not this minute. The cook's come in to make me and Mr Plasir our lunch.'

'And how are you?' Laura asked.

The boy began to boast. He had been apprenticed to Mr Plasir. They went into the Place together, where the boy was able to catch some dreams that Mr Plasir said were special only to him. The boy said he didn't just have casual work boosting Plasir — no, he had an *affinity* with Mr Plasir's sites. And Plasir was teaching him some amazing, special mental disciplines, things that most dreamhunters knew nothing about.

Laura said, 'From what I hear Mr Plasir wouldn't require boosting.'

'Then why are you here if you haven't come to take up his offer?' said the boy.

'My business is with Mr Plasir, not you.'

The boy shrugged. His eyes went back to Rose, and again he scanned her from top to toe. He swallowed nervously, licked his lips, then said he had to go back to his studies. 'I'm studying the dream almanac.' He left Rose and Laura alone.

They sat down, hip to hip, on the sofa. Rose said, 'I don't like people who breathe through their mouths.'

'Yes, revolting,' Laura said.

Half an hour later the girls heard the street door, and the clatter of the boy's footsteps as he rushed from somewhere else in the house to the hall to speak to Plasir. Their voices murmured a moment, then the door opened and Plasir came in, with a look of cool curiosity on his pale, taut face.

Laura and Rose stood up together. Plasir said, 'Please,' gestured to the sofa and took a seat himself opposite them. The girls sat down again. Rose put her arm around Laura's waist. Plasir had not offered to shake their hands.

'To what do I owe the honour of this visit?' Plasir said. 'Are you considering my offer?' He smiled at Laura.

'I am dreaming Convalescent Two in concert with the resident dreamers at Pike Street Hospital,' Laura said. 'I have work enough.'

She was at a loss. She had hoped that once she got here she would think of some way of picking Plasir's mind while giving nothing away herself. She was afraid just to ask. But asking was all she *could* do. She said, 'I want to ask you some questions about my father.'

Maze Plasir looked surprised. Then he looked at Rose.

Rose said, 'Laura didn't think she should come here on her own, so I agreed to go with her. I'm only here to keep her company — so you shouldn't look to *me* for clues. I haven't any idea what she's going to say.'

'Anything I can tell Laura concerning her father concerns you too — since you're Chorley Tiebold's daughter.'

Laura could feel Rose looking at her; they were sitting so close that she could even feel Rose's breath on her cheek. Laura knew that Rose wanted to consult with her, to say with a look, *Wasn't there something funny about Plasir's remark, something suggestive?*

Laura thought there was too, but she would think about it later; she wasn't about to be swerved from her purpose.

'Come then,' Plasir said.

Laura said, 'My father left me a letter.'

'You mean — a suicide note?' said Plasir.

'Not quite,' said Laura. 'In the letter he mentioned your name in a way that made me think you might know something about what he was *doing*. The things he was doing that he never talked about.'

Plasir's expression said, 'Is *that* all?' He leant forward. 'You *know* what he was doing, because he did it publicly.'

'You're only saying that to make me feel stupid,' Laura said. 'If you don't intend to tell me anything, just say so. Otherwise, won't you please just *tell* me?' Laura was begging him.

Plasir made dampening signals with his hands.

'My father disappeared. He got on a special train at the end of summer and we didn't see him again.'

'Yes, I read the papers. But the papers said he attempted a crossing. To attempt a crossing — alone — is insane, or suicidal.'

Laura didn't answer.

Rose said, 'When we were staying in Summerfort, Mother and Uncle Tziga would go In from Tricksie Bend. That end of the Place was less explored. They wouldn't have to walk so far to find new dreams. Mother would catch a dream, and sometimes she'd get the express to Founderston, to play at the Rainbow Opera, but mostly her audience followed her to Sisters Beach, and The Beholder. But, at least three times each summer, a special train came for Uncle Tziga.'

Laura said, 'My father always said that dreams travel better in summer — because there are longer hours of daylight.'

Rose said, 'We would be on holiday and they'd be working hard.'

Laura said, 'But Da was never *happier* in summer. He *should* have been, but he wasn't. *We* were all happier, we were on holiday. Aunt Grace was happier, catching new things . . .'

Plasir interrupted Laura. 'You want to know where he went. Where the special trains took him?' He looked at them with raised eyebrows.

Laura nodded.

'Most of what I'm about to tell you is public knowledge, or part of the public record,' Plasir said. 'You could put it all together from newspaper reports, if you wanted. It's not often discussed, though, or discussed in any detail.'

Maze Plasir waited, gauging their attention, their *need*. He said, 'For years dreams have been part of a program of prison reform. Your father was one of a handful of dreamers who were able to catch dreams that could inspire and *improve* people. Dreams like that are rare and precious. They are never dreams for the open market. They are classified under the Intangible Resources Act as "dreams for the public good". The Department of Corrections took your father and his dreams to prisons.' Plasir looked from Rose to Laura, checking their expressions, making sure they understood him. 'The prisons supply labour for public works,' he said. 'You must have seen convicts building roads?'

Laura shook her head.

'Or perhaps you don't travel anywhere off the beaten track?' Plasir said.

'*I've* seen convict labourers,' said Rose. 'Laura sleepwalks. She never notices anything.'

'When the government first came up with the scheme its merits were debated in the newspapers. This was six or seven years ago. You wouldn't have been reading the papers then.'

'Is that all?' Rose said. She seemed to be hoping he had finished.

'I too have a contract to perform dreams in prisons,' Plasir said. 'Dreams as rewards. If Tziga Hame worked in rehabilitation, I offered rewards and incentives — and education.'

Laura was shaking her head, trying to hear the sense in the thick of his words. There was something implied in this talk of incentives and rewards.

'And, of course, as a Gifter I am able to alter dreams. For instance, I can catch a dream about a killing, and then change the face of the victim to fit a certain crime, a particular criminal. Many a murderer has been brought to a better understanding of what they have done by my dreams. Imagine a criminal being able to experience what his victim suffered. You can see how *effective* it might be. How educational.'

'I see,' Laura said. 'You worked on rewards and education, and my father was working in rehabilitation. He gave prisoners inspiring dreams.'

'Yes,' said Plasir. The way he said it, the word sounded open, like 'Yes, *and . . .*'

'Then why did he never talk about it? And why, in his letter, did he say he'd done terrible things?'

Plasir said, 'I am unwilling to be the person who casts a shadow on your memories of your father.'

If Laura hadn't been given a task to complete by her father she would have listened to Plasir's warning. She would have ended the interview, got up, called Rose to follow her and gone away. She hadn't *promised* her father, after all, she had only opened his letter. But the letter was part of a bigger legacy, a legacy she wanted. She suddenly understood this, as she sat facing Maze Plasir in his darkened parlour. She knew now, for sure, that she wanted to put her hands into sand and shape it, she wanted to sing to the sand to make it get up and speak to her. Speak to her again. Laura felt, that to take what she wanted, she must accept her father's whole legacy. Besides, she really did need some clues about why convicts kept appearing in her dreams. She said to Plasir, 'I need to know.'

Plasir seemed to settle deeper into his chair. He said, 'The Department of Corrections subscribes to dreamhunters in order to reward prisoners for their cooperative labour. But if prisoners don't cooperate, the Department of Corrections uses dreamhunters to *punish* them.' Plasir stopped and waited for his listeners to react. When they didn't, he went on. 'It has been noted by prison reformers in other countries that, in our prison system, convicts are well clothed and housed and fed. They're not whipped, or starved. Foreign prison reformers hold up our system as a kind and humane ideal. But, given the nature of criminals, there are always agitators in any prison population. And there are always prisoners who are prepared to protect agitators.' Plasir spread his hands, palm up, and said, 'Well — imagine.' He waited.

'My father took nightmares to the prisons,' Laura said.

'Yes.'

Laura was aware that Rose, beside her, had put a hand over her mouth. Laura said, agonised, 'But why would he do that? He always earned enough. He was famous, and celebrated. Why would he agree to do that? He couldn't possibly have believed it was right.'

Plasir said, 'Was there something he didn't have, that he badly wanted?' The way he asked it, he seemed almost gentle. Again he waited, but Laura said nothing.

'When it was first suggested that uncooperative convicts might respond well to the threat of nightmares, Tziga and I were already under contract to the Department of Corrections. He was already selling his inspirations to the prisons, and I was selling my rewards. We both had an affinity with nightmares — but for some reason he could find many more than I. More and worse. But, as I say, we were both under contract, so it was suggested that I go to Tziga and offer him an inducement — a very strong inducement — to help him get over his misgivings about the scheme.'

Rose jumped to her feet. She yelled at Plasir, 'Don't tell her!'

Plasir glanced at Rose, and shook his head. 'You're a clever girl,' he said, then, to Laura, 'Do you know that your father and I were once friends? I knew him before he became socially ambitious. Before his eyes lit on those beautiful Tiebolds. In fact, I was with him when he first saw Verity Tiebold. I watched her too, and spoke to her. She made a strong impression on me — too.' He watched Laura, he looked sad. 'Do you see?' he said. 'I had *several* dreams that worked. The one he liked best was Stately Lady.'

'That's enough,' Rose said. She put out a hand to her cousin, then withdrew it again, apparently afraid.

Laura felt surprisingly alert — but not agitated. Had Plasir's words injured her? She wasn't sure. If there was pain it was coming slowly, raining on her, changing her temperature. She said to Plasir, 'You gave him back my mother. And, for that, he agreed to sell nightmares. The Department of Corrections paid you both for this work. That's it. That's all of it.'

'What were you expecting, Laura? A criminal conspiracy?' Plasir said. 'I think you will find that the public supports the penal system *as it is*. The public knows what goes on. They may not want to be bothered with the details, but they know. The general public isn't fond of details. They know that this is a civilised nation, where no one is tortured, or lives in squalor. That's all they want to know. There's no scandal here, Laura. No crime. If you made a fuss, your father's reputation might suffer, that's all. As it is people regard him as a kind of saint — a scary saint, one who came out of the invisible realm carrying beautiful visions.'

Laura found herself trying to work out, quite cool-headed, if Maze Plasir hated her father or not. She said, 'There's nothing to be done then?' She said that, but she thought *When you're ready, catch the dreadful dream* and *Your Aunt Marta knows The Measures*. She thought of her father's instructions, and his story about the song St Lazarus heard in the tomb. Then she asked Plasir if he had ever seen the convicts *in dreams*?

He looked surprised. 'No,' he said. 'Have you? What are they doing, these convicts?'

'They're waiting to be seen. They're waiting to be heard,' Laura said. She got to her feet. 'Thank you for talking to me,' she said. She put her arm around Rose's waist.

'Yes, yes,' said Rose, 'let's go.'

But Laura had one more question. She asked Plasir whether he still took his rewards to the prisons.

'I'm still under contract. My business alone won't support me. My parlour is very exclusive, at most I perform for five clients a night. They pay very well. But even five wealthy customers a night will not keep me in style.'

Plasir was making excuses, Laura thought. He was saying 'needs must'. But *he* knew what he was doing was wrong — whether the public cared or not.

'Please, Laura. I want to leave,' Rose said.

'We'll let ourselves out,' Laura said, as if this were an ordinary visit, as if Plasir had politely stood up to see them out, as good hosts do when their guests get to their feet. Laura led Rose from the room, and from the house.

Part V
The Measures

One

Marta Hame, the retired director of the choir of St Lazarus, and sister of the dreamhunter Tziga Hame, lived in a large timber house a half-hour walk from a railway station twenty miles south of Founderston. The house was surrounded by orchards that belonged to it, but were worked by a neighbouring farmer. The retired choirmistress was still several months short of her fortieth birthday, but dressed like an elderly widow, in black from neck to ankle, her only adornment a small gold crucifix. Marta Hame was a very religious woman and, despite her retreat to the country, she was still involved in church work. She was on the boards of several church charities and was known to be a close confidante of the Grand Patriarch himself. The local postman could testify to this — for letters were exchanged, often daily, between the Palace at the Temple, and the house in the apple orchard.

The postman was waiting for the train that came through at eight in the morning. The eight o'clock train came and stopped, didn't just snatch the mailbag in passing from the hook-topped pole beside the track.

Four passengers got off this train. A farmer jumped down from the steps of a third-class carriage and his wife handed down their baskets, then herself. Another man stepped down from the second-class carriage on to a box the conductor placed for him — this man was a travelling salesman with a sample bag. The passenger who climbed down from first class on to the platform wore a beautiful camelhair coat. He was tall and had gold hair and, for a moment, the excited postman imagined he was witnessing one of the Grand Patriarch's rare visits to his friend. But the Grand Patriarch generally arrived by car, and with some followers, and this man wasn't even carrying luggage. Besides, as the man approached, the postman saw he was too young to be the Grand Patriarch. Too young and clean-shaven, and unaccompanied — but very like His Reverence, Erasmus Tiebold. *Of course!* the curious postman thought to himself. Then, as an experiment, he said to the man, '*Good morning*, Mr Tiebold.'

Chorley said good morning to the postman, slightly annoyed that he'd been recognised. This was silly of him, really. How many other men of fashion got off at this country station? Chorley had never learnt to be inconspicuous, to dress modestly, to travel cheaply. He hadn't managed to do those things even when — as a young man — he couldn't afford to do otherwise.

Chorley left the railway station and tramped on up the road. The postman rode past, and peered at him. The bike's front wheel wobbled, then the bike tipped in a rut, dumping the postman on to the road beside Chorley.

Chorley helped the man to his feet. He picked the bicycle up. Its chain had come off.

'Thank you,' said the postman.

Chorley retrieved the mailbag. It was dripping mud. He held it out to the postman, who said again, 'Thank you, Mr Tiebold.'

'Do you have any mail today for Marta Hame?' Chorley asked.

The postman explained that he hadn't sorted the letters yet. He usually sorted the mail at the station but —

But today he was in a hurry to see where I was going, thought Chorley. '— and sometimes I sort the mail *at* Miss Hame's. I have a cup of tea with her. She's a friend.'

'I see,' said Chorley. 'I only meant to offer to carry Miss Hame's letters — if you have any for her. To spare you the trip, since you've torn your trousers.'

The rip was in the worst possible place. The postman found it, blushed and went knock-kneed in an effort to conceal it. He explained that a third of the mail was usually *for* Miss Hame anyway.

Chorley gestured at the torn trousers. 'That — and the broken chain on your bike — need immediate attention.' He looked about at the railway line and the farmland, then back at the postman. 'What *will* you do?'

The postman answered with dignity, 'I will make my way slowly up to Miss Hame's and seek assistance there.'

Chorley put out his hand for the mailbag.

The postman clutched it to him. '*With* the mailbag,' he said. 'It's my responsibility.'

Chorley shrugged, tipped the man a salute and strode on up the hill.

Chorley recognised the house from Tziga's description — a description given offhand, but so detailed and interesting that Chorley had felt the question he had asked was being answered: *Why do you spend so much time there when Laura's here?* (Chorley *had* meant, 'When we are *all* here,' but didn't want to make any demands on his own behalf.) 'It's very peaceful,' Tziga had explained. 'And there's no other place near it.' Tziga had described Marta's house — and his description was an explanation. He'd explained everything — without burdening Chorley with the truth. For, as Chorley stood where Marta Hame's driveway turned off the road up to the house, he knew he was looking at the place where his brother-in-law had hidden with the tired fragments of the final days of each of his terrible nightmares.

Marta Hame's house was handsome, but it looked haunted.

As he crossed its yard Chorley heard singing, a light, low voice singing not a melody, but a complex, modulated chant. The singing was accompanied by the sound of a stick thumping on a wooden floor. Marta was giving a lesson.

It's only a lesson, Chorley thought, though the chant seemed to pull him about inside. It made him feel queasy.

When he knocked at the door the singing stopped, and a dog began to bark. Chorley heard the bark coming closer as the dog raced to the door. He heard its nails skittering in the hall, and then Marta hushing it.

Marta opened the door. She was clutching her woolly-coated boyar by his collar. She hauled him back out of Chorley's way. She looked stern — at the dog — and amazed to see Chorley. 'I'll put him out,' she said. She shuffled around him, pushing the dog out with her legs. She closed the door on her dog, who barked briefly, then whined a little, then yawned while still whining, then fell silent and trotted off into the yard.

'Can I take your coat?' Marta said. She was a short, broad woman with her grey and black hair wound into a tight knot at the nape of her neck. She had Tziga's deep-set, dark-circled, black eyes.

Chorley gave her his coat and followed her into the nearest room, a sunny front room, with a piano, and a cello leaning on a chair, and with *Laura* — Laura was there.

Chorley asked his niece just *when* she had planned to tell him and Grace where she was. 'You told us you would be sleeping at Pike Street, dreaming with the resident dreamhunters, but we had hoped you might come *home* during the day.'

Laura got a stubborn, defensive look. 'I spent two of those days with Rose. Didn't she mention it?'

'No,' Chorley said.

'But perhaps you haven't *seen* Rose,' said Laura, with transparent false nonchalance. 'But that's all right, I guess, since you always know where she is — where you've *left* her.'

'Please do not speak to your uncle like that,' Marta said. She was standing in the bay window, facing the yard. She said, 'Laura, would you please go out and rescue the postman from Downright?'

There was barking outside. Laura went out to deal with the dog, and Chorley joined Marta at the window. He saw Laura running towards the postman, who had put his broken bike between himself and Downright's doggy enthusiasm. Chorley looked at Marta. He caught her eye. 'I knew I hadn't long before the postman descended on us with his broken chain and torn trousers.'

'What *on earth* did you do to him?' Marta said.

Chorley lost his temper. Laura's criticism had stung him and he wasn't going to take a telling-off from Tziga's sister. 'Why would you imagine I've done something to the man?' he said. 'What do you think I am?'

'A Tiebold,' Marta said, coldly. She turned away. Her profile looked like a portrait on a medal, cold and minted. 'Your sister tormented my brother,' Marta said.

'What are you talking about? Verity loved Tziga!'

'She tormented him for years before she would marry him,' Marta finished her sentence.

'She was *afraid* of him!' Chorley shouted.

Marta flinched. She stared at Chorley, her eyes wide, while he glared back at her.

Then, all at once, Chorley saw how hopeless it was, his having come here to *beg* Marta to cooperate with him and Grace in organising the memorial service for her brother. There was too much between them — too much made of too little. Years of neglect on his side. He had taken her brother — one of only two surviving relatives, counting Laura — and made him part of *his* tribe, the Tiebolds. He hadn't discouraged Laura from regarding Marta as her 'dull auntie'. He hadn't invited Marta to family celebrations — and neither had Tziga, but then Tziga would *never* remember to host family celebrations anyway. If Chorley ever remembered Marta and felt uncomfortable, he would remind himself that Marta had her church and choir. Marta was respectable. (That was another thing Laura had always called her, mockingly — 'My *respectable* aunt'.) Grace and Tziga hunted dreams and wore themselves thin, while Chorley stayed at home with the girls and was *loved*. He was the one who got the love. He had been neglectful and disrespectful and he didn't deserve Marta's help. And he *did* deserve to have Laura answer back when he started his ineffectual nagging.

Chorley folded, he slumped down on the window seat, bent over with his face in his hands. He said, 'Please, please, for God's sake, let us hold this service. Help us do it.'

Marta put her hand on his shoulder. She said, 'Chorley Tiebold, you don't believe in God.'

'But *you* do,' said Chorley, muffled. Then he jumped up from under her hand and went across the room to lean on the fireplace. He gripped the mantelpiece with both hands, but couldn't prevent his shoulders from shaking. 'The only reason you won't help us bury Tziga is that you think he's still alive,' Chorley said. His words were strangled, but audible. He listened to Marta's silence and supposed she hadn't heard him. But then she asked, 'Why would that thought upset you?'

Chorley heard her footfalls, she came close to him. He tried to get a grip on himself. 'If Tziga was alive, why wouldn't he let his daughter know?' Chorley said.

'Or *you*,' Marta added.

He hadn't said it. He'd kept his mouth tightly shut.

'You — his best friend,' Marta said, rubbing it in.

Chorley dropped his head till it pressed into the jutting shelf of the mantelpiece.

'Do you think Tziga's dead?' Marta said.

'I don't know what I think. What I think changes every hour. But I know it's wrong to let Laura go on hopelessly hoping.'

Chorley heard her move closer, then her voice at his shoulder. '*Think*,' she said. 'Think why you're so determined to hold a memorial service.'

'I want it settled somehow for Laura,' Chorley said. 'For all of us. And Tziga was a great man. A public figure . . .'

Marta interrupted him. '*No* — I mean, why do you want to be *seen* holding a service?'

Grace and he had agreed, months ago, that it was vital to have some public show of their belief in the official story of Tziga's fatal disappearance. Grace had said, 'If *they* — whoever they are — imagine that we think they've *lied* to us then they'll never relax enough for us to learn anything. A memorial service will, perhaps, make them drop their guard. Besides, I'm scared that, if we don't somehow discourage her, Laura is going to go looking for him days In from Doorhandle. She isn't strong or experienced enough to do that.'

Chorley wiped his eyes on his sleeve and faced Marta. 'So — you won't go along with our plans for a memorial service, even for the sake of appearances?'

'I'm a religious woman; I never pray for the sake of appearances,'

Marta said. 'And — who knows — *I* might be holding out a foolish hope.' She shrugged.

Chorley stared at her for a long moment, then said, '*Where is he?*'

The question hung between them in the quiet, plain, sunlit room. Marta put out a hand, a shy hand, but one without the slightest tremor, and laid it on Chorley's. 'Listen,' she said. Her hand was warm. 'I'd like you to go out and help the poor postman restore the chain to his bicycle. Now, don't protest, I know you're a mechanically minded man, Chorley Tiebold. While you do that I'll write a letter for you to carry to my friend. He will tell you what to do.'

Chorley sat on the steps and restored the chain to the bike. He got some grease on his trousers. The postman sat in a cane chair, at a wicker table, sorting the mail. Every so often he would look expectantly along the veranda. He clearly hoped tea would appear. Downright the dog sat at his feet, sighing.

Laura came and sat near Chorley. He asked her whether Aunt Marta was giving her singing lessons. Despite her impressive piano playing Laura had never shown much interest in learning to sing.

'I wanted to learn some more of the old songs,' Laura said. And then she sang one of the Tailor's, a short song:

> The past is a purse;
> the future a note of promise.
> Past blights are poison in the ground,
> rotted crops or living corpses. Against the time the debt falls
> due is time itself, and only time. The dry seconds are sand in a
> glass, and a servant made of sand.

'That wasn't what you were singing when I arrived,' Chorley said. 'It was something older. Something foreign.'

'It's in *koine*, demotic Greek, with some additional Cabbalist-type words. It's a song they say St Lazarus heard in the tomb.'

'Sing it,' Chorley said.

Laura got up and backed off from the steps till she stood in the centre of the yard. She clasped her hands, as if it was important that each hand held the other still. She began to sing. She was still practising the chant — that much Chorley could hear, because her voice faltered sometimes. The chant was made of complex, shifting tonal patterns, of strings of words that didn't sound like sentences, because each word sounded like a *new* word, as if no word was used twice, as if the language of the song had no use for 'and' and 'to' and 'it'. Laura scowled in concentration. Chorley even saw sweat start on her face, swelling beads of it, big enough to tremble as a breeze got up. For, as she sang a wind did get up and sweep around the yard, around and around, till it had raised a little dust devil which danced for a moment about Laura. At the same moment that Laura lost her place in the chant and broke off with a coughing sob, the dust devil collapsed and vanished. 'Damn it,' she said, panting.

'That was pretty impressive,' Chorley said, then added, 'Sweetheart.'

Marta appeared. She held out her letter. Chorley wiped his greasy hands on his trousers and took it. The letter was in a sealed envelope. The envelope was addressed to 'His High Reverence, Erasmus Amon Tiebold' — the Grand Patriarch.

Laura and Chorley stayed one night at Marta's. The adults enjoyed a diluted version of the young dreamhunter's Convalescent Two — in its ninth night no longer saleable, but strong enough to be felt. Uncle and niece caught a train back to Founderston together, in what each thought was a friendly silence.

Laura didn't wonder about the oil-spotted, unopened envelope her uncle carried, or notice how his hand went to his jacket pocket now and then to check that the letter was still there.

Chorley didn't notice how Laura sat, her face turned to the view of paddocks and poplars and ditches filled with blackberry bushes, or how her lips moved and fingers flickered as she mouthed the chant and counted its measures.

They failed to notice what they should have noticed; that Chorley was nursing his hopes, and Laura her secret resolve.

For Laura was planning to make herself a sandman.

Two

Laura spent several days at the house in Founderston. She let her aunt and uncle fuss over her. Grace was at home during the day, but sleeping at the Rainbow Opera, where she was dreaming Balloon Wars. During those days Grace made plans for what they would all do in the summer, 'as a family'. Chorley and Laura nodded and made attentive noises. Chorley wrote a letter asking for an audience with the Grand Patriarch. And Laura practised 'The Measures' in the bath, in her bed at night, whenever she was left alone.

When she was ready Laura took her pack, maps, food, money, bedroll — and one other thing. She left a note for her aunt and uncle and caught a train to Sisters Beach.

She went on up the track to Whynew Falls, and trudged for two days through the silent country to the dry riverbed.

The sand disturbed by her father's digging, and by her flight and struggle, hadn't settled. With no wind or rain to erase them the signs stayed. Laura looked at the imprint of Chorley's camera, and the marks where her fingers had clawed at the bank and, lastly, at the excavation, which looked like a shallow grave. She tried to imagine what her father had seen when he sang a body up out of that grave.

For the first time Laura let herself really think about what she planned. It seemed to her that she had been drawn back to this place by a series of unconnected impulses. She had asked her Aunt

Marta to teach her certain old songs that Marta and Tziga were taught as children by their great-grandfather. She had memorised and mastered one song — a long, complex chant Marta called 'The Measures'. Before she left Founderston, Laura had removed something from her jewellery box — the rust-stained rock she had picked up from the trackbed six months before. She had kept her hand closed around the rock in her pocket as she rode on the train to Sisters Beach. She had mouthed 'The Measures' at the carriage window, and her hand felt her heart beating in it, as though the rock in her hand was a heart.

She had been planning this for weeks, the plan like a pulse in the back of her mind. She'd fondled the statue in the museum, touched it in order to feel how to *shape* it. Laura had formed a strange notion. She felt that she wanted to learn who Nown really was — if he really was somebody in his own right, not just an occasional powerful wish wished by a succession of powerful Hames. Laura was planning a kind of experiment that, she thought, would let her look on the *real* face of her sandman. She had realised that she didn't want to look on a face like the one she and Rose had formed in the sand of Sisters Beach during the sand-sculpting competition, a face with the marks of their tools in it, clumsily made. No — Laura wanted to look into her sandman's *true* face.

Standing in the dry riverbed at map reference Y–17, Laura was about to attempt something that no Hame had attempted before. She *knew it* too, knew it in her body and brain, and in her mouth, where the words of 'The Measures' seemed to sit on her tongue and fizz like sherbet dissolving.

Laura took her coat off. She put down her pack, and the heavy water bottles she had carried and scarcely touched to drink herself — for she might need water for her work. She found an undisturbed patch of river sand, and began to dig. She dug with one of Grace's narrow gardening trowels, which she had taken from its hook on the porch of Summerfort. It wasn't a very effective digging tool — Grace only ever used it on Summerfort's potted plants — but it did spare her hands.

When she had cleared a long, wide trench, and had dug down to damp sand, Laura rested and had something to eat. Then she excavated some sticky clay from the bank of the stream. She wet her hands and worked the clay till it was firm but plastic. She spent an hour carefully fashioning two hands, hands nearly three times the size of her own, with long, thin fingers, big knuckles and backs marked by branching sinews. She did her best. Art was one of two school subjects at which Laura had done well. (The other was music.) The girls at the Academy had often crowded around her table in art class to admire her work.

When she had finished making the hands Laura looked up to check the light. It was a reflex — but of course the light hadn't changed, no sunset would come to hurry her along.

Laura washed the clay from her hands. She stepped down into the excavation and began to scrape the damp sand together. She bulldozed with her palms. After a time she had scraped together a long mound. She stood up and walked around it, measuring it with her eyes. Then she knelt once more and began to work.

She disappeared into her work. She became invisible to herself.

Laura shaped a pair of long, sturdy legs. She shaped square heels, round ankle bones and a thick Achilles tendon. She modelled squared calf muscles, strong thighs and a narrow pelvis. She made a form remembering the statues she had looked at, and the one she had been moved to touch, much to Rose's embarrassment. *How could Rose have known?* Laura thought, as she finished with the buttocks and began to shape the small of the back.

While the back was still only roughly shaped, Laura put her sandman's heart in place.

Nown had had her father's letter hidden in his chest. It had served him as a heart. Laura fished the rust-stained rock from out of her coat pocket and pushed it through the sandy back. She shoved it deep into the body she imagined lay before her, with its knees, feet, hipbones, chest and face — *its own true face* — all hidden in the sand. She withdrew her empty hand and closed the hole, smoothed the place over. She then shaped the symmetrical trapezoid muscles and shoulder blades. She fashioned wide shoulders and strong arms. She made sure the elbows were level with the waist, and wrists with the top of the thigh. She got his proportions right. She laid the clay hands at the end of the arms, backs down and curled fingers up. She blended the join between sand and clay and sprinkled a coating of dry silver sand on to the still damp blue clay so that — when he was dry — his hands would be the same colour as the rest of him. She made a powerful neck and as shapely a skull as she could fashion.

Laura sat back and began to laugh. She'd forgotten to make ears. She looked at the clay on the bank, and at the place both she and her father had dug, and felt too tired to move. So she wrapped her coat around her and lay beside the face-down, earless figure, and went to sleep.

There was no dream at that place in the riverbed. Nothing marked on the map, and nothing even for Laura.

When Laura woke up she opened a tin of condensed milk and poured it on top of several dry rounds of dreamhunter's bread. She looked at the face-down figure. It was beginning to dry in the air, its surface turning a soft, granular silver. Laura was careful as she moved around it. She didn't want the vibrations of her footsteps to shake any sand from the figure, making cracks in his skin.

Laura went to the bank and scooped out two balls of clay. She fashioned each into an ear, a left and a right, like the hands. She had to dampen and remould the sand of the figure's head in order to attach the ears, though each had a cupped back, like a shell, that held them firm.

Laura lay down once more to gather her strength. She had been in that place for sixteen hours by her watch, through a sleep and two meals.

She began to sing, lying there, looking into the sandman's ear. She didn't feel any need to get up and lift her hands to the mist-covered skies. She sang in a quiet, clear, intimate voice. An unfaltering voice. And, as before, on other occasions when she'd managed to get through 'The Measures' without making a mistake, Laura began to feel the spell build, a force like a wind funnelling up around her body. Nothing moved, though, her clothes and hair stayed still, and no dust devil got up to dance for her as it had when she sang in Aunt Marta's yard. The force sucked at her, like air pressure so low it was almost a vacuum. Laura grew cold. She finished her song shivering. She shut her mouth. The air began to shimmer.

Laura lifted her own cheek and ear from the riverbed. She leant up on one elbow and bent over the back of the figure's neck. There, on the bumps she'd made to suggest vertebrae, Laura scratched the letters with the tip of her finger. She wrote his whole name:

NOWN.

The cold, shimmering, sucking force around her leapt into her body and out again through her finger. She heard the spell again, a whole song that seemed to shout only this: *Soul of the spell! Come out of the earth! Wake! Speak! Obey my will, and know your name!*

Laura flopped back, exhausted.

Nown's arms moved up from his sides, turned palm down, and pressed. Laura was only feet from him. His hand brushed by her as it moved. She saw the back of the head she had shaped stir, a crack appear in the sand where what she had shaped came to an end, and the earth itself began. Laura watched Nown lift his face from the riverbed. He came up shaking off clots of sand. Only not *all* the sand fell. Instead it sorted itself out, some grains rising like steam against Nown's face, settling there and shaping it.

He turned towards Laura, his skin of sand still rearranging itself. She saw his skin move to make sharp ridges of eyelid. She saw his nostrils become dark and deep, then flare, as though he drew breath. She saw his lips split in two, and teeth rise up before the hollow of his mouth, and sand run from the hollow, leaving only enough for a tongue. She saw thin gaps appear in the fence of his teeth, but nothing in his eyes, no lines to represent an iris, no hole for a pupil. His eyes stayed smooth — widely spaced eyes in a face as handsome as that of a classical statue. Except that, having no human model, the face was too symmetrical.

Nown got up, separated his sandy self from the sand of the river bed. He stood above Laura, looking down at her. He opened his mouth again — and this time didn't dribble sand. He said, 'Laura Hame. I am your servant.'

Three

Laura had done what she wanted to do. She had made her own Nown. That done, she was left with only her duty. She had to follow her father's instructions. She felt that, if she followed them faithfully, she might somehow find him again. Sometimes this was what she felt, and sometimes she thought it was silly and crazy to have feelings like that, and that her father was lost to her for ever.

Laura knew where she had to go next because the film her father had left had shown a view of a burnt building. Laura believed that she would find her father's 'dreadful dream' near the building. The film had shown its black beams flickering like the shadows of twigs stirred by a breeze, against a bay of naked sand. The film had stopped, then started again with the building, shot from her father's shoulder. He had held the camera and turned himself about, one hundred and eighty degrees, to show the view back the way he had come, and hills like a page in a book of profiles.

Laura was looking at those hills now from the other side. She could see them rising in the distance, above the scrubby country across the dry stream bed. She knew that, beyond the hills, she would find the ruin, and the dream she had to catch and carry.

For over three months, Laura had gone about her business as if turned side-on to her own intentions. From the moment she had read her father's letter she had meant to do what he told her. She had felt that if she followed his instructions she could conjure *him* too, and make him reappear. But she had not thought clearly about what following her father's instructions would actually entail. She hadn't thought about catching the 'dreadful dream' and overdreaming her Aunt Grace.

Laura tried to make plans as she lay on the ground looking up at her sandman. But any thoughts about what she should do next were driven out of her head by the sight of him — the *fact* of him.

She — Laura Hame — had raised a thinking, speaking being from nothingness, or time, or family tradition. It was very confusing. She had made *a person* out of river sand in the Place, and the rock she'd kept. She had made her sandman out of longing and disappointment and indecision. She had made him as though she were making her own father, rather than a replacement for her father's servant.

Laura had made someone to look after her. And here he was, big and strong, and *wise* — she was sure of it — and looking at her to see what she would ask him to do. Waiting for her to make decisions.

Laura was too exhausted to move, and couldn't decide what to say to him.

Hello again. I missed you. I needed you.

Looking up at Nown, Laura felt she had finished everything she *wanted* to do. She felt safe, not just because he'd arrived again to protect her, but because she'd put something of herself into him — where it was safe for now — something she felt she was too young to use wisely.

Laura realised that she needed to sleep. So great was her need that, when she closed her eyes, she immediately fell asleep.

Laura woke when she turned over and snuffled up a little sand. She sneezed and sat up. She was thirsty, and needed to pee. Time had passed. Nown stood as he had before. He was looking out over the low bank of the riverbed and through the curtain of grasses at the hills Inland.

Laura asked him what he was doing.

'Listening,' he said.

Laura crawled over to her pack and found her water bottle. She took a long drink, not bothering to ration it. Nown could carry her out again.

This thought came to her calmly. He had suggested it once, and she had shied away from him. Now she couldn't see anything wrong with the idea. Perhaps *this* Nown was less uncanny — more hers. She looked at him again and began to laugh.

Nown had no nipples, or navel, or whatever lay under the fig leaves on the copies of classical statues at the Museum. Laura had studied her favourite statue before making this Nown. She had studied the most beautiful statue she could find, but it had had a fig leaf. Laura had made her Nown face down, hoping to discover his true face — but she also wanted to find out what was underneath the fig leaves on statues. Of course she had a vague idea — she'd seen plenty of small children of both sorts, girls and boys, running about naked on the beach. But she was quite sure men were different from little boys.

Laura finished laughing and wiped her eyes. She imagined sharing the joke with Rose — then sobered up when she remembered just how much she'd have to explain first.

Nown had watched her laugh. But when she was quiet he lifted his head again and listened.

'Is someone coming?' Laura said. She clapped her hand over her mouth, regretting having laughed so loudly.

'No,' Nown said.

'Then what are you listening to?'

'I am listening to it. It is listening to you.'

Laura shivered. 'The Place?' She said. 'Is the Place listening to me?'

'Yes. I can hear now. I am nearer to myself than before.'

Laura stared at Nown for so long that her neck began to hurt. She climbed to her feet, and stood rubbing it. Did Nown mean that each new Nown was *better* than the one before? That he was made to make progress towards some *perfect* sandman? Is *that* what he meant by being nearer to himself? He couldn't mean that, could he?

'What do you mean?' Laura said.

'I can hear now. I am here with myself,' Nown said.

'How?' Laura asked, then realised it wasn't the right question.

'I don't know.' Nown answered her anyway.

'Are you more yourself? More your *true* self?' Laura asked, then blushed — feeling she had asked for a compliment, or a show of gratitude.

Nown was looking at her intently. She knew it by the way the gleaming black grains of iron sand sorted themselves out from the mix in his face and flooded his wide open eyes, till his eyes, brows and the bridge of his nose were banded with glittering black. He answered her. 'Yes, I am.'

Laura was pleased to have helped Nown. Pleased with her own speculation. She didn't for a minute consider that her servant might have spoken obscurely.

Nown stood, his face striped black with the force of his attention, and waited for his mistress to help him understand what he sensed. Then she was talking again, and his desire to understand disappeared into the flow of time, for her will was the flow of time for him.

She said, 'My father wrote in his letter that I must listen to the Place. He meant the *dreams*. He meant me to do something about the convicts in the dreams.'

'Yes,' Nown said. 'I think that is what he wanted.' He touched his chest, wherein he had once carried Laura's father's letter — or where, at least, the *eighth* him had.

Laura saw that he remembered the letter and was curious to know if he knew what she'd put into him. When she asked he said, 'It's a rock you wanted to throw at your father. To throw at the train that took him away. It is anger and unhappy love in a rock.'

Laura began to cry then. She covered her face with her hands — sore, raw under their nails from scraping sand — and sobbed. Her sandman made no move to comfort her, and after a time she simply finished crying.

Nown was listening again, it seemed. Perhaps he was even embarrassed. Laura imagined that it might be embarrassment that made him look away through the grass to the hills Inland.

Laura told him to pick up her pack. He did. Then she told him to pick her up.

His arms were faintly warm, like sand under a winter sun. They softened to accommodate her. She rested her head on his chest, heard a faint creak of sand moving on sand — but no heartbeat. 'Back to Summerfort first,' Laura said, 'for provisions.'

Nown began to walk back the way Laura had come.

Four

Chorley's appointment with the Grand Patriarch was on a Sunday afternoon between the masses at noon and three. On Sundays the Isle of the Temple was quiet. All dream parlours and palaces were closed till sundown. By one the cafés were open and serving whatever it was possible to prepare in an hour.

Chorley crossed from the west bank on the enclosed iron footbridge slung under the railway bridge. He was early. He stopped at a café for coffee, and crêpes with honey and nuts — a Sunday favourite. The café was in a colonnade across the square from the Temple. Chorley ate, and watched pigeons fossick for crumbs among the iron table and chair legs. Then he paid, stored a coffee-soaked sugar lump in one cheek and crossed the square. He went around the Temple to the gates of the Grand Patriarch's palace. He presented his appointment card. The guards, men in long embroidered capes — beneath which they cradled repeater rifles — let Chorley in. An usher led him upstairs and along galleries under high vaulted ceilings covered in frescoes. Their footsteps echoed.

Chorley had expected to be taken to an office, or an audience chamber, but instead the usher took him to the Grand Patriarch's private rooms.

The Grand Patriarch was just finishing his lunch. He was sitting at one end of a long, polished table, and tilting his plate to spoon up the last of his soup. There were a few slices of black bread and a pot of tea in front of him. When Chorley appeared the Grand

Patriarch called over the solitary servant in the room and had him pull out a chair for Chorley where a second cup and saucer sat waiting for him.

Chorley sat down. He turned this way and that to check how many people there were in the large, gloomy room, and whether they were near enough to hear him if he spoke. There were two guards, one by each door, the servant and a young priest who stood closer.

The Grand Patriarch set the plate back on its base, laid his spoon down and removed the napkin he'd tied around his long beard to keep it clean. He wiped his mouth. His beard, dented where it had been tied, began to spring back into shape. For the next few minutes, while they talked, Chorley watched the beard expand, bristling, and restore itself to its square, golden magnificence.

The Grand Patriarch held his hand to Chorley, palm down. He offered his ring for Chorley to kiss — but Chorley only took the hand and shook it. The Grand Patriarch smiled faintly.

'Cousin,' Chorley began. 'I will call you cousin because I am not a parishioner, and I intend to presume upon our relationship.'

Erasmus Tiebold took up the teapot and poured Chorley a cup.

'Er — thank you,' said Chorley.

'How was my friend when you saw her?'

'That was more than a week ago,' Chorley said — he couldn't resist telling his kinsman off for not responding more quickly to his request to see him. 'Marta was well — a week ago,' Chorley added, then took the sealed letter from his jacket and gave it to his kinsman.

The Grand Patriarch broke the seal and read the letter. It wasn't a long letter. Erasmus Tiebold finished and looked at Chorley over the top of the page. Then he gestured to the young priest, who came over. The Grand Patriarch handed the young man the page, then said, 'No, don't read it.' Then he gestured at the branch of candles in the middle of the table. The young priest held the corner of the page to a candle flame. The paper flared up. The Grand Patriarch pointed to his empty soup plate, and the young priest laid the paper there to burn and backed away from the table.

Chorley watched this and realised that, if his family really had found itself on the wrong side of something — a secretive, sinister something that had to do with the Regulatory Body — then this secret, sinister something had *opponents*. This man, the head of the Orthodox Church, and his father's cousin, was an opponent. This man — and other men and women. Marta, for instance. Chorley realised that he wasn't just here to look for Tziga, he had come to show that he was willing to sign on to some sort of *resistance*. If they would have him.

Chorley actually had no idea what Cas Doran and the Body were up to — but they had taken Tziga from him, he was sure of it. He blamed them. They were his enemies. And his enemies' opponents were his friends.

Chorley leant towards his kinsman, his eyes fierce. 'Tell me what to do,' he said.

The Grand Patriarch laid his hand on Chorley's. 'Only this, for now,' he said. 'You must take passage to Sisters Beach by sea. Catch the packet boat from Westport. The schooner *Morningstar*, which sails every week. You must leave the *Morningstar* at the first place she stops.'

The Grand Patriarch lifted his hand and leant back. He took up his teacup and sipped, raising his brows to urge Chorley to taste his tea. 'Don't bring anything back with you,' he added. 'And I hope to see you on your return.'

Grace sat on the bed and watched her husband pack.

'I won't be back till the day after St Lazarus's Day,' he said. 'I have a table booked for us at Bacchus. The booking is for six-thirty. And Rose wanted to go skating in the afternoon.'

'Goody,' said Grace, who didn't like skating.

'She won't expect you to take her,' Chorley said.

'Still, I had better take her. She won't mind if I'm groggy.' Rose would know that her mother would be tired. Grace performed a dream called Homecoming on the evening of Saint Lazarus's Day, every year. The site of Homecoming was three days In from Doorhandle, and Grace was setting out herself the following day.

Grace didn't like watching her husband set off somewhere before her, or in this case without her. Nor did she like how *small* his suitcase was. Chorley wouldn't usually travel anywhere overnight without a selection of clothes and a case of toiletries. He liked to look his best.

'What are you hoping to find?' Grace asked.

'I'll tell you what I do find,' he answered, 'that's all I can say.' He changed the subject. 'Does Laura know you expect to see her on St Lazarus's Eve?'

'Yes. Rose has spoken to her. And she sent us a postcard from Tricksie Bend.'

'She's at Summerfort again?'

'Yes, Chorley — she's looking for clues. She got the camera, but she's still looking.'

Chorley put on his coat and picked up his suitcase. 'Well — maybe soon she won't need to look any more.'

Grace watched her husband's slow, growing smile. He looked like a man with a confident hope in his future happiness. Grace couldn't share his hope. As she watched him standing there with his suitcase she felt that he was leaving her. Leaving her alone with the lonely affliction of her fear.

Five

A week before the feast of St Lazarus, Nown carried Laura, her pack and provisions, up the Whynew Falls track and into the Place.

The sandman loped along, his stride and speed almost unvarying. Sometimes Laura asked him to put her down so she could walk for a bit. 'To get my blood moving,' she told him. She walked and raised a sweat and the dust of chaff stuck to her face and prickled in her nose. Nown could run with her without raising sweat, or tiring — of course. She had him hurry when she was sleeping. She hoped he would run her right through dreams.

They had passed the stream Y–17 before she was quite ready to sleep — Nown had carried her there in ten and a half hours. Nearly thirty hours after that Laura fell asleep in his arms, on the upward slope of a crumbling, fissured hillside. And Nown *did* run her through dreams.

Laura dreamt she was a young man who had found a place above a waterfall where he could look down and see the picnickers who came and bathed. She dreamt that he was waiting at the end of the summer, on a day when the track was quiet, and a certain girl came to the pool in the company of his sister. Laura left the young man waiting. She then dreamt she was a hunter, walking through brush at evening beside a ravine from which a terrible smell was coming.

Laura woke up, moaning. They were at the foot of the far side of the hill. 'Nown! Stop!' she complained. 'You hold the heat so. You're like a hot stone. Put me down.'

Nown put Laura down and she staggered about till he steadied her. She asked for the water bottle and sat on the ground to drink. 'I had the beginning of a dream about a man in too-tight trousers,' she told Nown, then laughed. '*Funny* feeling. And I had a nightmare.' She shivered.

Nown said nothing. He didn't even tell her she should eat. Not that she needed telling.

Laura got out her strongbread, some nuts and an apple. She looked around herself as she ate. They were in a narrow valley between hills that were more like dust heaps in a midden. Laura almost expected to see human rubbish — old bike wheels or bits of broken bedsteads smeared with ash. It was a horrible place, and if there had been any wind Laura was sure she would be breathing dust.

It had been windy when she and Nown had crossed the paddock before Whynew Falls reserve. Nown had been impervious to the wind, which had left him as untouched as a rock — when she had expected him to smoke in the gale like the crest of a dry dune.

Laura couldn't tell, from where she sat at their base, whether the hills were the same shape as those in her father's film of the backward view from the burnt building. She hoped they were the same. She hoped these were the last of the hills. She and Nown couldn't go around these because they were so crumbled away that the ravines between each hill were choked with boulders and heaped shingle, all harder going than the climb.

Laura pitched her apple core at the next hill. 'What am I doing?' she said.

'Eating,' said Nown.

'I keep forgetting just how literal-minded you are,' Laura said. 'I keep imagining you're marvellous.'

Nown was silent.

Laura looked up at him. 'Would you like to be able to eat?' she asked. She wondered whether he was envious of things he might know she could do, like taste food.

'I have watched eating often. Vitas Hame asked the fifth to hold up the arch by his fireplace for many years. The fifth could see the dining table. Vitas Hame often had guests. Feasts.'

Nown was telling her that some ancestor of hers had had him play statue and support the roof.

Laura asked Nown to show her how he'd stood.

He put his feet together and stretched his arms up over his head, the heels of his hands horizontal as though pressing a great weight upward.

'How unkind,' Laura said.

'It was the service asked.'

'I won't ever ask anything like that,' Laura promised. Then she had Nown pick her, the pack and water bottles up again. She told him not to let her fall asleep till they got to where they were going. 'I want to be ready to sleep when we get there.'

They went on, up the next hill, Nown climbing on two legs and with one hand. The arm that cradled Laura had lost its elbow joint and had become a flattened sling. Her pack and the water bottles rested in a hollow Nown had made in his own back.

At the summit they found lesser hills below them, a rucked cover of vegetation, dead pasture on hills any wind would have made bald, grass like a haze, and more hills piled in the hazy distance.

Laura walked for a time. Nown broke a path for her; he parted the grass.

Sixty-five hours in, by Laura's watch, they came to where more sky was visible than at any place in the Place. The sky was still white, but like steam gathered under an immense high dome. They looked down from a low hill on to what appeared to be a wide harbour, a seabed of sand and rocks that shelved down to several deep, branching channels. On a spur of land with an apparently man-made, straight-edged shoreline, was the remains of a huge timber-framed building.

'There,' Laura said. Nown let her down and she went ahead. She held his hand as if she were leading him, though he was the one anchored on the slope.

They climbed all the way down and walked to the head of the causeway — for Laura could see now that that was what the squared headland was, a wide bank of hewn stones, mortared together, the bank paved on top. The ruin stood on a hammerhead of embankment at the end of the causeway. Its main beams were of tree length and girth, the surfaces of their wood scabbed and glossy black.

Laura took her pack from Nown, untied her bedroll and spread it on the ground. She was thinking *Whatever the nightmare was, it should relate to the fire, to this particular place.* She imagined being penned in by smoke, and herded by flame.

She squatted by her bedroll and drank and ate a little. She said to Nown, 'I'm afraid.'

He made no sound, no comforting noises, not even a grunt of acknowledgement. He didn't offer encouragement, or remind her that having come so far she *must* want to find out.

'My father wanted me to do this,' Laura said.

Nown was silent.

'Is he still alive?' Laura asked. She needed to know now. If she couldn't ever expect to see him again then she didn't need to do this, she didn't need to sleep here.

'I don't know if he's alive,' Nown answered. 'The eighth knew that. I am the ninth. I only know whether *you* are alive.'

'Know, or believe?' Laura imagined her father standing in the shadow of a passionfruit vine that grew over the arch of a gate. The gate to a garden in the afterlife.

'I can't believe. I can only know,' said Nown.

Laura thought about that. She said, 'There's a nightmare here that my father caught to take to the men in prisons. Something to frighten them into obedience. Something worse than the worst sermons about hell. My father wanted me to catch it too — and show it to other people, so that they'll know how bad it's been for the prisoners. It's like the little children working in mines and factories a hundred years ago — everyone knew about that, but they didn't feel how heartless it was till people wrote describing the conditions. Then public opinion changed the law. If people experience what the prisoners are forced to, then they'll be shocked, indignant, and — I hope — compassionate.' Laura was wiping her hands, which were covered in oil from the peanuts she had eaten. She said, 'Anyway, that's what Da said I should do. He always thought that, with any encouragement at all, most people will behave kindly.' Laura mused for a moment, then said, 'I should probably tell the newspapers too. Write them letters explaining what I know.'

Nown said, 'Your father had injured his hands. Shall I hold your arms?'

It was a practical suggestion. And given what she knew about his nature, Laura was surprised that Nown had offered any suggestions. But it was *coldly* practical, and Laura felt like a condemned criminal sitting out his final night with a polite warden. She lay down. She looked up at Nown and said, 'All right. But gently.'

She couldn't stop shivering. She was afraid to close her eyes. 'Is it cold?' she said.

'I don't know.'

Laura yawned and her jaw shuddered. She was tired after all. She listened, but there was nothing to hear. She was adrift in her body, in the quietest place in the universe.

Weak from a long sickness, heavily encumbered with what he did not know — perhaps the bedclothes — the man moved. He came to and moved. With no result. His eyes were open, but it was dark. Pitch black, as though death had pressed its thumbs into his eye sockets. He turned his head. A thin cloth pulled tight against his face as he turned. He opened his mouth and sucked in air to call out, and the cloth came into his mouth, a bubble of lily-scented satin and air that smelt of damp earth.

His hands stirred. He meant to lift them. He meant to pull the cloth from his face. His hands moved up only inches, and were pinned by pillows of satin, an upholstery over hard walls. His hands scraped and slithered. He heard the noise his nails made.

He heard the box.

He began to scream. The reverberations of his screams gave him the whole shape of the box, narrow-walled, low-roofed, unyielding. Its lid was screwed down hard and would not give. Earth was piled above the lid, airless earth, pressing down hard.

He screamed and moaned, he fought the box, in a frenzy of terror. He struggled and scuffled, strained his head up so that it beat against the coffin's lid. He chewed his shroud, took it into his mouth to tear it, to get a little more air. Any more. He bit at his lips, and through his lips, and through the shroud. He managed to make a hole in the shroud, and yet still stifled on the condensed vapour of his own breath. He bent his hands back and pressed upward, clawed till the satin tore and he was through to the wood. He beat on the lid of the coffin. He strained till his wrists cracked.

Then he stopped. He made himself lie still and listen. He forced his panic back. He thought he heard birdsong. He thought he heard the world above him, daylight and the open air. He listened. He listened. He listened. He hoped to hear someone coming, someone who could help him. He hoped. He listened. Then he burst out of his hope, as he couldn't burst out of the coffin. He went mad with activity, he convulsed. His bowels let go and the trapped air went from bad to worse. He scraped at the lid till his nails ripped way from his fingertips, then till his fingers were broken. He didn't feel it — he only felt the grip of the box.

He forced his hands up as far as his face, to find flesh that did yield, his own mouth the only space he could thrust his fingers through. His lips were in tatters, and his broken hands were full of his own torn hair.

He kicked and thrashed.
It was dark.
It would not break.
It was dark.
He was shut in, shut in, scuffling on in the stifling dark.

Laura woke and reared up. Her head collided with something above her, on top of her. She screamed.

Nown released her hands and they flew out making rents in his arms and shoulders, bashing sprays of sand out from his body. The sand flew wide, stopped in the air, then rushed back into Nown's body.

Laura scrambled up and away from Nown. She stood, shaking her arms and howling. She had bitten her lips and blood was dripping from her chin. She cried like a child, in terror and despair. She had caught the dreadful dream. She would find herself buried alive, if she slept, when she slept, night after night. It wasn't over.

The dream went on. Laura knew that it did. The buried man suffered. He waited to die in a mess of blood and filth. He hadn't any hope. He was a penned thing.

Laura walked back and forth, shaking her hands and crying. Her arms were aching. She could see bruises and sandy welts on her skin. Laura pulled up her sleeves and showed Nown the marks he had made. She roared at him, and shook her arms under his nose.

Nown got to his feet.

Laura rushed at him, put her arms around him and pressed her head into his creaking chest. 'Be human!' She begged.

Nown said, 'How?'

Laura continued to cry. Nown was unrewarding to cling to. Stony, then yielding. If she pressed his sand it cracked and shifted.

Suddenly he picked her up, his hands under her armpits. He lifted her up, then lowered her. Lifted her up again, then lowered her. He swung her gently from side to side.

Laura was shocked, she hung from his hands, stiff and stunned. Then she realised that he'd seen people do this to coax their small children out of crying. She was being dandled, like a baby. She stopped crying. 'Nown?'

He lifted her to his eyes.

'I'm not a baby,' she said.

He put her carefully down.

Laura packed up her bedroll. She had water, then set Nown walking in front of her, towards the hills.

As they went she thought about her father on the platform of Sisters Beach Station — his gnawed lips and bandaged hands. She wondered how her father had managed not to think of her as a child. As *his* child, whom he should protect at all costs. But between the nightmare and the station her father had shaped and sung his Nown into existence. Laura thought that she must judge her father now like God, not like a girl of fifteen.

In springtime Laura had often been late for school because she would stop to pick woolly bear caterpillars up off the path. Rose called her a soppy thing. Laura was softhearted, but now would have to do what her father had asked. She would take the dream to those who profited from their willingness to terrify other people with it, and dreams like it. They would all be there — on the evening of St Lazarus's. The President would be in his suite with his family. The Secretary of the Interior in his, with his family. Government secretaries, and deputy secretaries, captains of industry — they would all be there. Laura had no doubt at all that she could overdream her aunt. She was the same size as the dream now. It was packed into her, tamped down, compacted under tremendous pressure, like a huge, horrible charge.

Six

On a sunny Saturday, two days before the official first day of spring — the feast of St Lazarus — a shop assistant at Farrys' looked up to see Laura Hame. He smiled. 'You are the first of your family I've seen this season,' he said. 'Welcome back.'

'I'm here alone,' she said.

The man was puzzled. He watched the girl touch her hair — the ends of her curls that showed under the red velvet hat she wore. Her hair was damp, freshly washed — and short.

Of course — one of the inseparable two had passed and the other had failed. He had read that in the newspaper. She was thin, he saw, and had lost none of her summer tan. She was beginning to look like a dreamhunter. 'What would you like, Miss Hame?'

'I'd like a hazelnut log. And some toffee shells and musk cream. The cream in a jar, please. I'll make the musk creams up myself.'

'For Miss Rose,' the man said. He knew each girl's favourite sweet. 'Yes, a saint's day present. Could you put the shells and the hazelnut log in pretty boxes?'

Her tongue was mauve, the man saw. She was already chewing that drug they used.

As he assembled the boxes and punnet of musk cream the man thought about everything he had read in the papers. He'd forgotten it all when he'd first seen her. He'd seen her and smiled, as he would at the first cherry blossoms or daffodils. She'd made him think about summer. He'd always liked those girls.

As he put the boxes in a bag he said, 'I was sorry to hear about your father.'

'Thank you,' she said, and took her package from him.

At that time of year, off season, the Sisters Beach train had only two coaches and a mail car. It was never an express. The conductor had an easy job. He kept his eye on the third-class carriage, since there were people on and off it at every station. But he had only two people in the private compartment of first class — and those two had tickets all the way to Founderston. In fact he only looked in on them once, to ask them if they would like their beds turned down. The compartment was a sleeper and the beds were next door.

The girl was nearest to the door. She told the conductor no thank you. 'My father will do it,' she said, and gestured at the man in the seat beside her. The man was huge, bundled in a coat and travel rug and wearing a broad-brimmed hat.

'Shall I turn up the heat in here?' The conductor asked.

'Would you?' she said. 'Father feels the cold.'

The man didn't acknowledge the conductor. He didn't turn from the window. It was dark outside; there was nothing to see.

'Can I do anything else for you?' the conductor asked. He raised his voice to reach the man.

'No. That will be all, thank you,' the girl said.

The conductor moved away from the door before sliding it shut. As he did so he let more light into the compartment, whose lights were turned down low. The light from the carriage passage made a reflection appear in the carriage window. A reflection of the man's hidden face. It gave the conductor a fright for a moment — though it must only have been a trick of the light. The conductor closed the door. He walked off shaking his head, telling himself he hadn't seen — couldn't have seen — the face of a statue, stone, but with eyes full of a seething glitter of aliveness that wasn't quite like life.

Laura wanted to sleep in order to escape her memory of the dreadful dream. But she knew that, once she slept, she would be back in that stifling box. She dared not close her eyes, but there was nothing to look at. It was night and the carriage window was black.

Laura slid along the seat and huddled against her sandman's bundled form. She said, 'There's nowhere else — nowhere to go.'

Her servant turned to her. She peered up into his face. It was statuesque and superficial and offered her no comfort. 'I hate this dream,' she said.

'And you are going to give it to other people,' Nown said.

Laura stirred uncomfortably. 'I'm doing what my father asked me to do,' she said. 'We need to make people see what it is like for the prisoners. To make them feel pity.'

'Do people who are frightened feel pity?'

Laura considered, then said, 'The dream frightens me. But it does make me feel sorry for the prisoners, and responsible.' She gripped the sleeve of the coat Nown was wearing. 'You must stop acting as if I'm a child and you're an adult. You're not an adult. You're not really a person.'

'Do you think you should be talking to an adult about what you plan to do?' Nown said.

'You're doing it again!' Laura pushed herself away from him. She retired to the opposite corner of the compartment and glowered at him.

'Laura,' Nown said, 'why do you think it is that the Hame servant cannot be undone until after its final N has been inscribed?'

Laura remembered how she'd undone the eighth Nown — wiped him out of existence. She recalled with horror the dry sigh of his undoing. 'I'm sorry,' she said. 'I'm sorry I did that to you. Or the eighth you.'

'That isn't something I have feelings about,' Nown said.

'Do you have feelings?'

'I find I feel afraid for you, Laura. No Hame can undo a servant without first giving it a voice so that it can talk to its maker, give its maker an account of what it has done, what it has been asked to do.'

'I *have* to do this, Nown,' Laura said, desperate. 'This is what my father wanted me to do! The only thing he asked me to do!'

'Your father said to me, "Laura isn't very good at thinking for herself."'

Laura cried at her servant, 'Stop! You're *hurting* me!'

Nown fell silent.

Laura turned away from him. She put her eye to a gap in the compartment's curtain and watched two men standing in the train's corridor and smoking pipes. They looked peacefully involved, and very human.

Laura wiped her eyes on her sleeve, then put a wad of Wakeful into her mouth — her fifth in three days. Her tongue went numb, then, a moment later, the drug roared into her head like oxygen and electricity and fury.

The train slowed into the first turn of the spiral at Mount Kahaugh.

Seven

At high tide, late in the afternoon of St Lazarus's Eve, the schooner *Morningstar* tacked towards the ocean shore of So Long Spit, where it put in to its first stop, an ironwood platform built at the low tide line, beside the lighthouse.

The head keeper and his son waited on the platform. They had tied up their boat and were ready to catch the line thrown to them from the deck of the schooner. Between them, the seamen, the head keeper and his boy brought the schooner alongside the platform. They were all practised at this monthly manoeuvre, and it was easy on a day like this — a day with a calm sea and only a light breeze.

The seamen delivered the lighthouse supplies: boxes of canned food, barrels of flour and rice, and whale oil. All were winched over the side in a rope net. The head keeper and his son guided the net gently down on to the platform.

The captain of the *Morningstar* was supervising the unloading and passing the time with the keeper, handing on the news, wishing the man and his family a happy St Lazarus's Day. When the captain had done that he glanced over his shoulder and leant closer to confide. He spoke in a loud whisper — for the deck and platform were separated by eight feet. 'We have a visitor for you,' the captain said.

'Someone from the Keepers' Service?' the head keeper said, worried.

'I don't know his business. He just asked to be put off — though his passage is paid all the way to Sisters Beach.' The captain looked over his shoulder again. 'Here he comes,' he warned. 'I told him to stay out of the way till we had finished unloading. I wanted to let you know.'

The seamen unrolled a ladder. The passenger appeared beside them, a tall, well-dressed man sporting a hat with earflaps. One seaman passed the man's bag over the rail. The head keeper stood under the ladder as the passenger straddled the rail and lowered himself on to it. The keeper helped the man on to the platform, and then ignored him for the next several minutes while the *Morningstar* cast off. Then the keeper's son jumped down into their boat, and his father began to pass the barrels and boxes to him.

The visitor didn't offer to help — which was fine by the keeper, who thought inexpert help slowed down any job. They were finished in only a few minutes; then, 'Sir,' said the keeper's son, and practically snatched the visitor's bag from him.

'Careful, boy.' The keeper understood that his son was in a hurry. His boy always liked to race the *Morningstar* along the shore for a little way. It was a game he had played for some time now.

The keeper handed the visitor down to the boat. He was feeling a little awkward by this time since he had tried a number of times to catch the man's eye and had been avoided. Nor had the man made any attempt to introduce himself.

The keeper and his boy took an oar each and pulled to shore — not quite straight, since the boy was too keen and was putting a little more into each stroke. They bumped on to the sand, and the boy jumped over the side and waded in to hold the bow as the visitor made a well-timed leap up on to the beach, beyond where the waves were breaking. The keeper and his son ran the boat a few feet up the beach and began to unload.

This time the visitor offered to help.

'Oh, no, it only takes a few minutes,' the boy said. His eye was on the schooner, whose sails were set and filling as she came around to head along the Spit and a little out to sea.

The keeper and his boy went back and forth with boxes and barrels across the short stretch of sand between the water and the first clumps of spinifex, marram and pink flowering ice plants. As the keeper worked, he spoke to the visitor. 'We have inspectors from the Lighthouse Keepers' Service who visit. We have surveyors, and birdwatchers, and the parish priest, Father Paul . . .'

None of this inspired the visitor to volunteer his name or mission. He watched the keeper. His face was tense — and tender around the mouth, as though he were near to tears. 'Come on up then,' the keeper finally said.

He led the man to the sandy track up on to the crab grass, and under the wind-tortured pines that had been coaxed to grow in soil hauled in by carts from the farm at the base of the Spit. The keeper pointed out the three houses and said, 'There are nine of us here permanently. Myself and my wife, my boy and my two girls; the second keeper and his wife — they have a baby on the way — the third keeper and the reserve man.' The keeper shot a glance at the visitor, trying to read him.

The priest, Father Paul, had asked the head keeper to stay quiet about 'the reserve man' — the man who had come five months before and was now fit for a few duties like cleaning whale-oil smoke from the lamp. Whale oil burnt bright, but not clean, and it took eight man-hours every day, seven days a week, to keep the crystals clean.

The head keeper had taken the reserve man in as a favour to Father Paul — and it wasn't the first of that sort of favour. The reserve man was called Mr Thomas — but he wasn't the keeper's first 'Mr Thomas'.

Of this latest Mr Thomas, the keeper knew only this: that he had been injured in an accident in the railway yards of Westport, and had been given up for dead by a dandy of a doctor. For weeks he had occupied the bed nearest the door in the crowded men's ward of Magdalene Charity Hospital. He had lain with the curtains drawn around his bed, and the sisters waiting every moment to sew him into his bottom sheet. For weeks he lay still, balanced on the border of life and death — and then lived. No one came to claim him. And, when he was waking — but not yet awake — the sisters claimed that he somehow disturbed the sleep of their other patients. It was the sisters' unwillingness to keep him on the ward that brought him to Father Paul's notice perhaps. Father Paul took an interest in him, and when he had improved enough to travel, Father Paul brought him to the lighthouse to convalesce. Mr Thomas. And all Father Paul's *former* Mr Thomases had been in hiding from the law.

Chorley could see that the new lighthouse was built only a little way from the base of the old one — a wooden structure whose timber had rotted. The new one stood on four steel legs and was of plate steel, like the hull of a ship. The lighthouse had a widow's walk at its top, around the windows that let out the light.

As they came up the track Chorley caught sight of a man standing on the widow's walk, wiping his hands on a smudged rag. Chorley shaded his eyes to get a better look, but couldn't see for the scintillating dazzle behind the man — the setting sun reflected in the crystals of the lamp.

Chorley hadn't known what to say — or who to trust. The keeper had mentioned a 'Father Paul' among their visitors. Father Paul might connect this place to the Temple.

Chorley had followed the Grand Patriarch's instructions. He had got off the schooner at its first stop.

There were several huts in the lighthouse's windbreak, Chorley saw, but only one that had a porch. The sun coloured the salt-silvered weatherboards of the huts. The ground under the pine trees was as russet as oxidised iron. The setting sun was warm on Chorley's back.

'Wait,' said the keeper, and touched Chorley's arm. 'Look.'

Chorley looked where the man pointed and was in time to see the last sliver of the sun disappear below the horizon. Then he noticed the keeper's boy, who was some distance along the shore, sprinting, apparently racing the schooner.

'That's a regular game of his,' the keeper said. 'And look —' He called Chorley's attention away from the boy.

Chorley turned, stunned into obedience.

The shadow was climbing the lighthouse. It was the shadow of the sea horizon, the shadow of the world. And when the sun vanished from the very tip of the tower a sliding glitter showed in the tower top, then a bright flash as the light came around to probe the open sea.

'Now my boy will turn back,' the keeper said. Sure enough the boy was looping back. The *Morningstar* had changed her heading to sail away from the Spit.

'He always does that, you say?' Chorley said.

'Yes. We lead very quiet lives here, and he's learnt to find a lot of pleasure in little things.'

Chorley hadn't shared Laura's first dream, had only had it described to him by Grace. But he knew that the man in Laura's dream, a convict, broken by hardship, had remembered being a boy racing the schooner along the shore of So Long Spit. The convict in Laura's dream had remembered being *this* boy. And so Laura's dream had taken place in a time *further on from now*. Laura's dream was about something that would happen *in the future*.

The keeper said, 'My lad is bound to pepper you with questions, sir, the moment he reaches us.'

'Sorry,' Chorley said. 'I haven't introduced myself.'

'I did think you might be another Mr Thomas,' the keeper said.

'Mr Thomas?'

'We have had several Mr Thomases here. Named after the apostle Thomas. Doubting Thomas.'

'You mentioned a Father Paul.'

'Yes. But I shouldn't have mentioned anyone without knowing who you are.'

'I think I *am* another Thomas who has his doubts,' Chorley said.

The keeper smiled. He said, 'None of us here knows anything much. We're only hospitable. *We have all been the world's guests, and we must pay for the world's hospitality.*' This last thing he said as though quoting someone. He took Chorley's bag from him, and they turned back to the light. The boy came up behind them, his bare feet thumping on the crab grass. He eyed Chorley, panting.

Another person appeared ahead of them on the path. A person in shirtsleeves with a grubby rag slung across one shoulder.

Chorley cried out and ran up the short slope. He pulled Tziga to him and held him. Then, horribly, Tziga jerked back in

Chorley's arms and began to flop about. Chorley lost his grip, and Tziga dropped at his feet. Tziga's jaw was clenched, his breath hissing through his nose, his legs and arms trembling spasmodically.

The keeper and his boy hurried to help. The keeper pulled a rubber bung out of his pocket. He forced Tziga's mouth open, and wedged the bung between his teeth. The keeper said to his son, 'Run and tell your mother that Mr Thomas is having another of his turns.'

Chorley fell to his knees beside his brother-in-law. He was afraid to touch him.

'He has these fits,' the keeper said. 'It's because of his injury.'

Chorley had had no trouble recognising Tziga. He had appeared above them on the track, his face indistinct in the dusk, but his stance instantly recognisable. Chorley now saw the changes in Tziga's appearance. Tziga had one mutilated ear, dents and lumps of shiny scar tissue on his forehead, one eyebrow smeared nearly out of existence by scarring, and one cheekbone caved in. All the injuries were on the right side of his head. Chorley found the courage to touch Tziga again. He helped the keeper, who was gently restraining Tziga's quaking arms.

The tremors gradually quieted. 'He will come to shortly,' the keeper said. 'He's always very tired and disorientated after these fits.'

Chorley asked how often Mr Thomas had fits.

'Every few days. It's very hard on him.'

A woman arrived with the boy, a lamp and a blanket. She spread the blanket over Tziga and put the lamp down on the turf beside them.

'It's best not to move him till he is awake,' the keeper said. 'I have to go and fetch the boxes up from the beach before it's completely dark.' He and the boy went back down to the water, leaving Chorley alone with his wife and Tziga. After a time the woman got up too. She said, 'The men will be back and forth. Let them know if he wakes up before I return. I've left my girls minding the cakes, and I don't quite trust them.' She turned back towards the house with the porch.

Chorley could smell the cakes, their cinnamon and sugar. He could smell pines, eel-grass on the ponds among the dunes, and the sap from the green claws of the ice plants he had stepped on. He imagined he could hear the waves on both shores of the Spit — the ocean, and Coal Bay.

Tziga was lying curled like a sleeping dog, his arms stretched out in front of him. Chorley put his head down to listen for Tziga's breathing. It wasn't yet quiet; it still sounded as though Tziga were recovering from a steep climb. Chorley felt Tziga's sweat-slick face and ran his fingers over the scar tissue. Then he touched Tziga's throat, and tested his weight by pushing up his frayed shirt cuffs to clasp his bony wrists. Chorley lifted a hand and kissed it. The hand smelt of charred benzene spirit — whale oil.

Tziga's eyelids fluttered.

'Wake up,' Chorley whispered.

Above them the beam of light probed the dusk. A warning, and comfort to all within its thirty-mile range, it too seemed to say, silently, urgently: '*Wake up. Wake up.*'

Part VI
The Rainbow Opera

One

On St Lazarus's Eve in 1906 over one thousand people were at the Rainbow Opera to share a traditional feast-day dream. A dream named Homecoming, performed by the dreamhunter Grace Tiebold.

Grace had told the Opera's manager that she'd been having trouble falling asleep, and that it wouldn't do to keep her audience awake and staring at the ceilings of their bedchambers. She'd arranged for another dreamhunter, George Mason, to lie in with her. He had caught Homecoming too and so would boost her already famously powerful performance. Also, Mason was a Soporif. He often worked in hospitals, enhancing the effects of anaesthetics. He would enter the operating theatre before the surgeons and their assistants, and bed down near the prepared patient, for anyone who was close to a Soporif when he fell asleep would fall asleep with him.

The Opera had a full house that evening. Founderston's fashionable people were all in attendance. The manager was happy and, at the time, looked on the dreamhunter's change in the evening's arrangements as a good thing, a guarantee of his customers' satisfaction.

Shortly before the performance began, when most of the patrons were already inside and in their sleepwear, the guards at the Rainbow Opera set out to patrol the Opera's perimeter. It was generally a dull, everyday job. It had been years since anyone had succeeded in parking himself near enough to the Opera to pilfer a dream. These days guards were mostly for show. The Opera's prices were such that it wasn't a likely haunt for drunks and troublemakers. On St Lazarus's Eve things were only a little different. Busier. Security a little tighter.

There were more cars and carriages than usual parked in the space around the perimeter. The President of the Republic was at the Opera, so his guard of honour — a dozen military men with sabres and pistols — were standing to attention by the President's vehicles, while the chauffeurs and grooms of other rich patrons lounged about smoking.

The Opera's guards always patrolled in pairs. Each pair was responsible for one section of the Opera's blind outer wall. The two men who were in the best position to raise the alarm that night had been assigned the quietest section, a forty-yard stretch that faced the river at the far side of the perimeter from the main gate. This stretch of wall was interrupted only by the dreamer's door — a stage door by which the dreamer entered the Opera — and, right beside the dreamer's door, a drinking fountain in an alcove.

The men set out, making their way around their stretch, one swinging the padded club he carried. When they came to the alcove they stopped. They stopped and stared. Where there had been a drinking fountain, there was now a statue.

A statue of a man, a little bigger than life-sized, was crammed into the alcove. A beautiful, bald-headed figure, who should have been posed like a sentinel, but instead was stooped and had his head over at an angle in order to fit into the arch of the alcove.

The guards were curious. One tapped at the statue with his club, while the other ran his hand down the figure's muscled side. The statue was finished, but not polished, he noticed — its surface was still gritty. One man called the attention of the other to a cloth that had been crammed behind the statue. He crouched down to try to pull it free. It was a worn, gabardine cloth — perhaps a workman's drop cloth. He couldn't free it, but as he was working on it he noticed that the drinking fountain was still there behind the figure, and that the statue seemed to have been posed as though sitting on the bowl of the fountain. The guard pointed this out to his companion. They spent a few minutes puzzling over this whimsical addition to the Rainbow Opera's decorations. Then they walked on, one pausing to check the lock on the dreamer's door as he went by.

The four oval balconies of the Rainbow Opera were full of the Opera's patrons. Many were wearing the latest spring fashions in sleepwear. The men wore quilted crimson or grey robes, and the women were mostly in white and darker grey, floating silks trimmed with swansdown. The people milled about in the balconies, and up and down the red-carpeted staircases, visiting friends. Waiters wove between them carrying trays of sweet wine or chocolate liqueur mixed with fresh cream.

The people paused in their talk to applaud as Grace Tiebold appeared under the dome, and began to climb the spiral stair to the dreamer's bed.

At the Rainbow Opera the dreamer's bed was on a raised platform in the centre of the auditorium, and at the same height as the second balcony. The long train of Grace Tiebold's embroidered robe trailed after her around the turns in the stairs. Despite her elaborate costume the dreamhunter looked girlish, small and thin, her light brown hair bobbed, her wrists, neck and ears bare of jewellery. At the top of the stair she turned to make a curtsy to the President of the Republic. He was on his private balcony, isolated from the rest of the second floor by locked doors. Grace bent her knee and inclined her head, then raised her arms to the rest of the public, who clapped and cheered. Then, as she always did, Grace turned and blew kisses towards the balcony before the second-floor private suites belonging to her family. The crowd looked where she threw her kisses, to see that, this evening, only the dreamhunter's daughter and niece were in attendance. The girls were, as usual, the two youngest people at the performance. The patrons noticed that Rose Tiebold was fulfilling every expectation people had of her by growing more beautiful with each passing month. 'But she won't be out this summer, though,' one society matron said to another, consolingly — they had girls coming out that season, and the competition for good husbands was always hard enough without the added complication of half the eligible men falling for the same girl.

Cas Doran wished the President of the Republic a good night and retired to his private balcony. His son Ru had ordered some more chocolate. Ru was posted at the rail, looking out over the auditorium and waving to his friends. Doran said, 'Ru, I'll be back out shortly, save me some of that chocolate.' He went into his suite and shut its padded door. The sound of the Opera's crowd retreated completely.

Maze Plasir was waiting. Plasir had his new boy with him. The boy stared at Doran with wide eyes, then looked to his master for a cue as to how he should behave. Plasir nodded faintly, and only then did the boy extend his hand. Cas took the limp, sweaty hand and shook it.

'Gavin knows that he must regard this as a very great privilege,' said Plasir. He looked at the boy, 'Don't you, Gavin?'

'Yes, Mr Plasir.'

'I've been telling Mr Doran what a talent you are,' Plasir said.

'And I had heard already from the examiners,' said Doran.

Maze Plasir seemed to be taking a great deal of pleasure in their little act of patronage. He said to the boy, 'Now, Gavin, you are Mr Doran's guest, but you mustn't bother his *other* guests.'

'Yes, Gavin. You must keep your room.' Doran waited for the boy to agree.

The boy swallowed, then nodded.

'You'll be very comfortable. The room will be my daughter's when she is old enough to attend these things.' Cas Doran put his hand on the boy's shoulder and walked him to the bedroom. 'Sleep well, dream well,' he said. He closed the door on the boy.

'They'll be ringing the bells in fifteen minutes,' Plasir said. He began winding his scarf about his neck and buttoning his coat. 'I came up the stairs from the dreamer's door. I could still smell Grace Tiebold's perfume in the stairwell.' Plasir smiled to himself.

'And you persuaded your boy to think that he's here only for the benefit of the experience?' Doran asked.

'He's the best I've ever had,' said Maze. 'But simple — or single-minded. He believes every bit of flattery he hears. He's hungry for it, and totally credulous. That's the profile of an ideal Colourist. I can guarantee that he'll go into his trance when he hears the turn-in bell. He'll catch everyone when they're dropping off. Hopefully he will still be performing his little repetitions by the time Grace Tiebold falls asleep, so that, in the first minute of her dream, he might be able to get his ideas out to her whole audience. Even if he isn't able to do that he will manage to colour the dreams of everyone in the suites on either side of this one, and yours, of course.'

'I don't mind that. I look on it as quality control. Your Colourists are very convincing, Maze. I still find myself congratulating myself on my judgment regarding Mr Gregg and what a fine Speaker he's made.' Cas Doran laughed. 'I find myself thinking, "What a decent, fair man." And I hope I'll wake up tomorrow thinking how wonderful Garth Wilkinson is. How he should be enshrined. How desirable it would be that he remains in office beyond his second term.'

'Knowing what I know,' Plasir said, 'I'd discount *any* idea I had while dozing off in a dream palace.'

'You and I are the only ones who know how good you are, how *priceless*,' Cas said — a cool man, but passionate in admiration.

Maze Plasir smiled. He finished buttoning his coat. He said he'd leave when the balconies had cleared. They went to the door together, Doran saying, wistfully, that he hoped his son had left him some hot chocolate. 'Sleep well,' said Plasir. 'Dream well.'

Ru Doran was leaning over the balcony rail. When his father joined him he turned, eyes bright, and said, 'Is that Mamie's friend? That beautiful girl?'

Rose stood straight and held her head high. For a moment she could feel all eyes on her. The attention was like a hot spell of sunlight on a dull day and, heated, Rose put up a hand to lift her hair off the back of her neck. The stares had made her self-conscious, but her gesture was unselfconscious, it was innocent and arresting — and, of course, it only encouraged various people to stare harder at her. Out of the corner of her eye Rose saw some hulking boy on the balcony of the Secretary of the Interior's suite imitate her mother and blow a kiss her way.

'Who *is* that cocky so and so?' Rose muttered to Laura.

Laura seemed even more dazed than she had all afternoon. She was still sucking on one of Farry's raspberry lollipops. She had arrived at lunch with one in her mouth already, and her dustcoat's pockets stuffed with a dozen more. Her lips were stained red — and looked raw now — though when she'd appeared in the restaurant she had only looked childish.

'Laura!' Rose said, and turned her cousin's head so that she would look across the space at the balcony opposite them. Rose felt Laura's jaw clench under her fingers.

Laura said, 'That boy?' exuding raspberry-scented breath. 'Well, he's with Cas Doran so perhaps he is Mamie's older brother.'

Rose decided that she would have to share some news she'd been withholding *now* if her cousin was going to be able to appreciate why it might be uncomfortable to have Mamie's brother kissing his hand at her. 'You know I'm spending the first two weeks of the summer with the Dorans,' Rose said. 'On Mamie's invitation.'

Laura shrugged. Rose had expected Laura to laugh — to see right away that she could hope to hear some *good stories* as well as Rose's views on Cas Doran's character, opinions and interests. The whole point of Rose's campaign of making-friends-with-Mamie had been to get near enough to Mamie's father to make an assessment of him and his associates. Yet, when Rose was at the Dorans over the coming summer, making her assessment of Mamie's father, there might be *other* intrigues for her to share with Laura — like, for instance, how Rose would manage to cope with Doran junior's flattering attention.

But Laura didn't laugh. She only stared at the Doran men and the President, her eyes shiny and dull at once, as though another skin had grown over their surfaces. Laura hadn't even waved to Grace. She was slumped on one of the ottomans by the balcony rail, side-on to the amphitheatre and hunched down as though she wasn't happy to be seen.

Laura had been vague and absent at lunch — but friendly enough. She had remembered to bring Grace and Rose Lazarus's Day gifts. Rose was rather surprised at this — since it was normally the sort of nicety that slipped Laura's mind. Laura had turned up to lunch with two beautiful packages of Farry's finest confections — a hazelnut log for Grace, and Rose's favourite sweet, musk creams.

Rose had her package open on her lap, and had already eaten three. Her lips were greasy and her mouth perfumed. She would save the rest till they were in bed and could share them — though Laura seemed content to stain her mouth with those cheap boiled lollies.

Rose flipped her hair again and stood up, stretched and took a deep breath. The tall gas flames around the coping of the Opera's dome sent unsteady light down through the stained glass. The house lights began to dim by stages, a little at first to hurry the patrons to finish their conversations, wine, chocolate, cups of roasted rice tea, and at least *think* of retiring to their rooms. As the house lights dimmed the fluttering, multicoloured radiance that came through the dome grew stronger, till the whole auditorium began to look as if it were under water.

Rose spotted another young man — this one on the third floor. He was leaning over the balustrade opposite and waving at her. She waved back. She said to Laura, delighted, 'I am beginning to see what my life's going to be like!'

Laura merely asked her whether she was sleepy.

Rose wasn't. She'd got up early that morning but wasn't tired at all. In fact she felt jittery — either picking up her mother's performance nerves, or wound up by all the attention she was getting. Rose didn't answer Laura, because she caught sight of the latest male admirer making his way down the staircase to their level.

The lights dimmed another notch. The crowds on the balconies began to thin. People called out to one another, 'Goodnight. Dream well.' Some of the padded doors were already fastened. The waiters were gathering empty cups and glasses.

Rose grabbed Laura's arm. She pointed, wanting to show her cousin the man hurrying up to them.

Laura said, apparently to herself, 'I like things the way they are.' She sounded very definite — and as though she were arguing with someone — though not with anyone there with them on the balcony. But then she *did* speak to Rose. 'I love the way the torchlight shines through the roof. Your mother looks like an enchanted, sleeping queen.'

Grace wasn't asleep. She was propped up on her elbows and eating an apple.

Laura looked up at Rose then, and said, plaintive, 'I always liked the Rainbow Opera.' She was talking, Rose thought, as if she had just discovered a plot to burn the building down.

'What is it, honey?' Rose said, concerned. But before Laura could answer the young man appeared beside them. 'Hello,' Rose said, and held out her hand. 'I'm Rose Tiebold.'

'Pleased to meet you.' The young man was briskly polite. '*Again.* Alexander Mason,' he said, and shook her hand.

'Oh, you,' said Rose. It was the boy from the infants' beach. He had done some growing. He seemed friendly, too, but only looked at Rose for a moment before turning to Laura. He offered Laura a bright, eager smile.

'Oh — Sandy!' Laura said. 'Sandy — *what are you doing here?*' It sounded like a lament.

Alexander Mason frowned. 'You're not happy to see me?'

Rose thought he was risking an even worse rebuff. She was impressed.

Laura showed more life than she had all day. She jumped up and grabbed Alexander Mason's hands. She gripped them hard and drew him to her, till they stood chest to chest with their locked hands between them — rather like, Rose thought, singers about to perform a love duet. Rose took a closer look at Mason's heavy, freckled face, and thought that he wasn't really her idea of handsome. But Laura looked inspired. Then she looked confused. She released Mason's hands. Rose heard him draw a sharp, shocked breath.

Rose said, 'The Hames can be very dramatic.' She patted Alexander Mason's arm. 'Don't let it worry you.'

Mason glanced at her, frowned again, then said to Laura, 'Have you been chewing Wakeful?' He sounded stern and paternal. If

Laura hadn't been behaving so badly towards him herself, Rose would have been tempted to kick him.

The lights went down another notch. The turn-in bell began to chime, the balconies to empty.

'No, I've been sucking a lollipop,' Laura said. She didn't seem at all offended.

'That would be one way of disguising Wakeful,' said Mason.

'Why would I? I'm going to sleep tonight, to dream,' Laura said. Her voice was dull.

'I'm here with Uncle George,' Mason said. He addressed Rose this time — and changed the subject, she was pleased to see. She wasn't used to being ignored. 'Your mother asked my uncle to come and help her. She's been having trouble falling asleep.' Mason looked over the rail. 'There he goes,' he said, and pointed to the balding, burly man climbing the spiral stair to the platform. 'Since your father's away,' Mason said, to Rose, 'he can't object. Besides, Uncle's a portly old gent.'

'She's so sly,' Rose said, of her mother. 'She loves being boosted. Da would have a fit. Your uncle isn't palsied and doesn't carry a cane — so Da would *still* object.'

Rose imagined that she could hear people murmuring, even above the bells. She looked about and saw — yes — they were pointing Mason's uncle out to one another, then looking her way. She resisted an urge to thumb her nose at them.

'Everyone will fall asleep at once,' Laura said. 'Since your uncle is a Soporif. They'll go down and stay down.' She looked about, turned her body and her head, as though searching for an avenue of escape. Then she froze, staring.

Rose followed Laura's gaze and saw that her cousin had caught sight of a pregnant woman. But why should Laura look frozen with fright at the sight of a pregnant woman? Rose reached for Laura's hand, and her hand collided with Alexander Mason's — he had reached for Laura too.

Laura turned away from them. 'I'm going in,' she muttered. She walked away into the Hame suite and — much to Rose's surprise — closed the door.

'I'm always upsetting her,' Mason said.

'Oh, poor you,' Rose gushed. Then she said, sharp, 'And you only sometimes mean to.' She had decided to blame him for Laura's peculiar mood.

His face went dark. 'You girls,' he fumed. 'You think you own the world.'

'I shall,' Rose said, with as much hauteur as she could muster — which was a lot. 'You had better get back to your nice little room, Alexander.' Rose said. She turned on her heel and went into the Tiebold suite. She knocked on the connecting door.

Laura opened it, but stood blocking the way through. She said, 'I'm going to go to bed by myself. My sleeping is all over the place these days. I don't want to spoil it for you.'

'All right. If you like.'

'Have you got your musk creams?'

'Yes.' Rose produced the box and opened it. Half the creams had gone already. 'Take one,' she offered. 'They're very good, though the taste is a little different from the last box I had.'

Laura took one. She said she would eat it in bed. She leant towards Rose and kissed her cheek. Then she closed the door. And Rose thought she heard the sound of the lock turning.

Rose got into bed with her box of creams. She turned the lamp down low. She took one sweet and slowly excavated the musk cream from its cup of toffee. She was cosy, but not at all sleepy. She had too much on her mind. For instance, she'd connected three things in her thoughts — Laura's sudden inexplicable fondness for raspberry lollipops, her agitation on seeing Alexander Mason and her horrified look at the pregnant woman. '*No*, no, *no*,' Rose said to herself, shaking her head. She had been reading too many 'educational books'. (Founderston Girls' Academy had a secret club — the Educational Books Club — which circulated novels that girls their age were not usually allowed to read. Novels in translation with stories where married women had affairs then killed themselves.)

Rose was more excited than worried by the thought that her cousin had 'got herself into trouble'. After all, if something like that happened they would all look after Laura. Nothing like that could make the family falter in their love. However, Rose's father might *murder* Alexander Mason . . .

Rose's thoughts circled, excited and — it seemed to her — loud. Time passed. She finished her musk creams. She tossed and turned. Finally she got up, found a book and turned up the lamp to read. It was one of her father's books, bought to research a trip the family had planned and hadn't taken. It was about castles in France.

For a time Rose was lost, floating down a famous river with a guide who delighted in stories of witch trials and walled-up wives. She heard the clock on Temple Square strike midnight.

By midnight the Opera's four tiers of balconies were empty. Waiters had finished gathering up the cups, liqueur glasses and bonbon trays from the little tables and ottomans around each balcony. Everyone was in bed — all but the President's and Secretary of the Interior's bodyguards, and the men from the fire watch, who were either patrolling balconies and backstairs in their soft-soled shoes, or at their post in the window of the Rainbow Opera's control room. The fire watch was awake and vigilant. The building was secure and peaceable. A stage was set in the thousand drowsy heads of the Opera's patrons.

Grace Tiebold lay under the thick, down-filled quilt of the dreamer's bed. She could hear Mason breathing quietly. She waited to fall through the trapdoor of his sleep into their shared dream. It was nice at least not to have to worry about when she'd drop off.

Instead, Grace worried about her husband, Chorley. Chorley had packed a bag and left the house a week before, and hadn't told her where he was going. Grace worried about Rose, who had been boarding for two terms at Founderston Girls' Academy, a school that was less than a mile from her home. She worried that Rose, having been sent away by her parents, wouldn't want to come back and live with them again. Grace wanted to do something to reassure her daughter that they were interested in her. Perhaps she should arrange for Rose to come out at the next Presentation Ball, instead of having to wait another year and a half.

Grace worried about her niece, Laura. Since Laura's father had disappeared earlier in the year, Laura had been quite distant from her family. But at lunch that afternoon Laura had behaved beautifully. She was polite and affectionate. She had even remembered to bring her aunt and cousin St Lazarus Day gifts — the kind of nice gesture that was usually beyond her. Not that Laura *wasn't* nice — only solemn and wrapped up in herself. At lunch Grace had watched Laura smiling as Rose opened her box of musk creams. Grace had thought: 'She's finally growing up.' Rose, even when biting into a sweet and moaning loudly in delight, didn't give her mother a moment's doubt about *her* maturity.

As Grace waited to fall asleep she mused on that lunch. She fretted. True, Laura had brought gifts and behaved herself, but, as Grace gazed into her memory and studied the face across the restaurant table, she could see that Laura had a look in her eyes, a dangerous look — like those her dreamhunter father had often worn — a kind of dark haze made of desperation and determination and power.

Lying in the white cloud of bed at the pinnacle of the Opera's dais, Grace thought: 'What is Laura planning?' She turned her head and looked over at the second storey balcony, and the doors to the Hame and Tiebold suites, where Laura and Rose were sleeping. Firmly fastened, the quilted doors gave Grace no clues.

A moment later she was drifting. Something passed through her mind, a proud happiness about her home, her city, her country, the golden age in which she was living, the fine people she'd chosen to manage her world. The thought pleased her — and amused her too, since it was so unlike her. Why should she be thinking of President Wilkinson when she had so much on her mind?

Then Grace saw the crisped, brown, late-summer leaves of oaks in a grove by the road that would take her *home*. George Mason had fallen asleep and had dropped her into her dream.

Sandy Mason's room at the Opera was one tier above and across the auditorium from the Hame and Tiebold suites. Sandy lay, his eyes fixed on the unadorned ceiling, and thought about Laura Hame.

When Laura saw him that evening she had seized his hands and said his name, as if he was really something to her, more than a friend. Her hands were shaking and Sandy was sure she'd been chewing Wakeful, the highly pigmented drug dreamhunters used to ensure they didn't sleep till they were ready to broadcast the dreams they'd caught. But if Laura had a dream, she shouldn't have been at the Opera. A dream would interfere with the sleep of people in rooms near to her, and possibly contaminate the dream her aunt would perform. Laura had made excuses, she'd said that her mouth was only stained from sucking lollipops, but Sandy was sure that she was lying.

Laura had lied to him, but she'd grabbed his hands and pulled him close, and gazed up into his face as if looking for salvation.

Sandy sat up abruptly, pounded his pillow a few times, then flopped back down again. He decided that he'd rather stop thinking about Laura Hame. She was too difficult, a sad and secretive girl. And despite the fact that they were both dreamhunters, had first entered the Place at last autumn's Try, earned their licenses only months apart, despite all they shared, they were from very different worlds. Laura was wealthy. When her father, the famous Tziga Hame, had disappeared some months ago, he was missed by dream palace patrons and *mourned* by all the invalids he had helped to better health. Laura's aunt was on the Rainbow Opera's dais and about to deliver a vivid and perfectly clear print of Homecoming to the audience of a dream palace that had been built for her. Even Laura's non-dreamhunter uncle, Chorley Tiebold, was famous — a figure of fashion and talented hobby inventor. Laura was *somebody* by pedigree while Sandy — Sandy was the middle child of seven, whose family lived in the provinces, and whose father was the foreman of a factory that made flax matting. Sandy's father thought that dreamhunting was fortune-hunting. He'd said to his son, "Most dreamhunters wind up like wizened, squinty-eyed old gold prospectors, and the rest are corrupt or crazy." Sandy's father saw himself as the salt of the earth. He scorned his dreamhunter brother and was disgusted that any son of his should want to take up the trade, "if you can call lying around in a stupor in silk sheets a trade," he'd said. Sandy's father saw dreamhunting the way that much of the population of Southland did — those too far from the Place for dreams to travel fresh. The majority of Southlanders thought dreams were a luxury, a drug of idleness. And though Sandy wanted more than anything to become a great and famous dreamhunter, a star like Grace Tiebold, or a magician like Tziga Hame, part of him felt his father's squeamish mistrust of dreamhunters.

Sandy bashed his pillow some more and told himself sternly that he was *not* falling for Laura Hame. He was only star struck and infatuated with the idea of her family.

Sandy felt his Soporif uncle fall asleep and for a moment he resisted the cozy wave of weakness; breathed through it as though it were a spasm of pain. He held to his memory of Laura Hame's pale face and dark eyes, her stained lips and the mauve cave of her stained mouth. Then he felt himself slipping, and then he was asleep.

. . . he woke, an invalid, weak and encumbered in sheets, wrapped in smooth cloth. Why was it so dark? He took a deep breath and sucked in a bubble of lily-scented satin.

A shroud was covering his mouth.

He flung out his hands. They hit the soft quilting that lined the sides of the casket, beneath which he found the hard wood of the box itself. The box — narrow, and irresistible, and dark . . .

Shortly after midnight the two guards were ambling past the alcove and dreamer's door, as they had countless times that night. They had just met another pair of guards and exchanged reports. All was well.

The moon was up, its light pulsing through gaps in fast-flying cloud. The wind was higher in the upper atmosphere than on the ground, though the river's surface was ruffled, its ripples not black, but speckled with the same grey light as the cloud. The torches on the Opera's roof had become fluttering banners of fire. They gulped and snapped above the men. The ground was wet and reflected the moon and torchlight.

The light was unsteady but came from everywhere, and so shone into the empty alcove, shone on the water fountain where the men *had* seen a statue.

The guards stopped. They gaped at the empty arch, and the fountain. There was nothing there, even the bundled cloth had gone.

One guard clutched the other's arm. He pointed. The dreamer's door hung off its hinges, and the carpeted stair within was sprinkled with broken glass from the first of the electric candles.

As the men stood staring they heard another smash, and the faint light shining down the stair diminished. They heard something heavy vaulting up the stairs. Beyond that, from the building's interior, came the sound of screaming — of a multitude of people calling out in an agony of terror.

The guards shouted for help then ran inside. They sprinted up the short staircase to the first floor, their boots crunching over broken glass. The light ahead of them receded as lamp after lamp shattered. They plunged on.

The Rainbow Opera was oval in shape. One of its longer curves faced the River Sva, the other a paved, crescent-shaped plaza. The building and plaza were enclosed in a high fence, built to keep out anyone hoping to get near enough to the auditorium to pilfer dreams. But the Opera patron's chauffeurs and coachmen parked overnight in the plaza could go to sleep if they needed to, for dreams very rarely spilled beyond the Opera's walls.

A dreamhunter's projection zone was known as his or her 'penumbra' — a term borrowed from astronomy, where 'penumbra' describes the partial shadow the moon casts on the face of the earth during a total eclipse. (The 'umbra', or totality, was the dreamhunter him or herself, asleep, and haloed by the shade of a dream.) Grace Tiebold's three-hundred-and-seventy-five-yard penumbra could comfortably fill all the Opera's rooms and spill only a little beyond its walls. If one of the Opera's security men, patrolling between fence and walls, did happen to hunker down and doze off, he might well find himself involved in one of Grace Tiebold's dreams. Grace's brother-in-law, the great dreamhunter Tziga Hame, had had a four-hundred-and-fifty-yard penumbra. Dozing guards or chauffeurs could find themselves immersed in any dream Tziga Hame performed at the Opera. However, city ordinances and cautious supervision by the Dream Regulatory Body had, for years, guaranteed that none of the households above shops in the streets surrounding the Opera would *ever* feel the faintest bit of colour from any of the Opera's performances.

That was until the early hours of St Lazarus's Day, 1906, when sleepers in those houses found themselves snagged by the rim of a great screeching wheel of nightmare. Only its edge — and although they woke with their hearts pounding, and gasping for breath, their distress quickly passed, to be replaced by something else. Fear. They sat up in bed and strained to hear. Some ran to their windows and threw them open and looked towards the festively lit Opera, from which came the sound of screams — a hellish howling that filled the still, chilly spring night.

Rose was startled out of her book by the eruption of screaming. She heard her cousin call out in horror and despair. Rose heard Laura above the horrible cacophony of the others. She jumped out of bed, and ran to the connecting door. It was locked. Rose hammered on it and called to Laura. Then she rushed out onto the balcony to try the outer door to the Hame suite.

That door was locked too. Rose gave up twisting its handle. She looked around her and listened.

The first thing Rose saw was her mother — thrashing about in the wavering light that came through the dome. Grace was clawing at her own face and throat— the ends of her fingers were black in the light; black with her own blood.

Grace Tiebold knew that she was caught in a nightmare, and wasn't really in her coffin. She was a skilled and experienced dreamhunter who'd had to free herself from nightmares before. She fought to be free of this one. At first she fought it on its own terms — she struggled with the shroud, tore at the padded satin lining of the coffin, and finally with its undressed wood. She made the futile repeated movements — the clawing, thrashing, hammering — of the person she was in the dream. *In the dream*, she reminded herself, and kept in mind as the spark of her experience, her mastery of other dreams, brought her back to herself.

Grace finally burst right out of the battered limbs and welter of blood and filth — out of that miserable, suffering self. She jumped like a spectre out of the trapped body, the grave, the dream. For a moment she was paralysed by sleep, then she struggled free of the silk quilt, panting, and found that her face was smarting and her fingertips were slick with blood. She fell off the bed, got up, and looked about the auditorium.

The balconies were empty. Electric candles around the walls of each tier, and the unsteady glow of the gas jets beyond the stained glass dome, showed Grace her beautiful Rainbow Opera — just as it always was, but as though turned inside out. Its beauty looked ghastly. The men of the fire watch looked monstrous. George, lying rigid, his face contorted, mouth alternately straining open and snapping shut, looked monstrous too.

Grace picked up the water jug and tipped it over him. For good measure, she slammed the jug itself down onto his chest. The Soporif woke, then rolled onto his side to spit out blood and a piece of cracked tooth. He struggled to rise, but kept flopping back as if stunned.

Grace shouted at the fire watch to sound the alarm bells. She could barely hear her own voice over the storm of screaming that came from the fastened bedchambers.

Grace saw her daughter Rose leaning over the balcony, her hands gripping its rail. Grace felt herself swoop towards her daughter. She nearly jumped from the dais, stopping herself only just in time. As Rose's face came into focus Grace saw that her daughter was pale and confused, but not bloodied or maddened.

Rose had looked at her mother, then away. Grace followed her daughter's gaze and saw someone running towards the fire watch control room.

It was a man in a long coat and broad-brimmed hat. He moved fast, but as though he was skating, his limbs seeming to stretch and blur. As he ran he struck out at each light. Grace saw the hot fuses quenched beneath his fist. She saw the spraying glass, and heard each bright smash.

The man reached the control room, and leapt into it, among the fire watch.

Then, it seemed, Grace momentarily lost her grip on wakefulness, and the dream came back to change the shape and sense of events she was trying so hard to follow. She saw the coat and hat float to the control room floor. Had the ceiling collapsed? The men of the fire watch appeared to have been knocked flat and were struggling under something that had fallen on them — something dark and heavy. Then one body got to its feet, although it seemed to be covered from head to foot in some crumbling substance, as if it had been in the ground and had emerged contaminated by earth. The body moved towards the alarm board, put out a hand, and was suddenly caught in a cascade of blue sparks. The control room went dark. The bells didn't sound.

George was still struggling to get up. Grace couldn't wait for him to recover. She left the dais. The turns in the spiral stairs forced her to lose sight of her daughter several times as she descended. When she was only halfway down, she felt the dream leave the building. It didn't disperse but departed all at once, like a flock of birds breaking from a stand of trees.

Grace reached the bottom of the dais, and sprinted across the auditorium to the nearest staircase. She ran up it. From above her came the sound of timber splintering.

Halfway up the stairs Grace was knocked back against the wall by a phalanx of men — the President's bodyguards. They were carrying President Garth Wilkinson on their shoulders, like a body on a bier. Bloody foam spilled from Wilkinson's gaping mouth.

Grace Tiebold was used to being treated with respect, to being *somebody*. It was years since she had been shunted aside by anyone. These men did just that — shoved her aside. Worse, she *was* noticed by the last man. He was rushing too, but he stepped aside to avoid bowling Grace down the stairs. Then he recognised her. His face filled with disgust, and he struck her across the mouth. It was an open-handed slap, but it knocked her down. She clung to the hand rail, her ears ringing. She thought: 'He thinks the nightmare was me.'

Once she'd had this thought, another followed it: 'If it wasn't me, then who was it?'

Then, '*Laura,*' Grace thought, though she couldn't think where her niece might have gone to catch a nightmare like that. It was like something from 'the shadow belt' — a region in Band X, four days' walk Into the lifeless desert of the Place. Grace knew that an eight-day walk In and out again was beyond Laura's stamina, that her niece was simply too small and weak to carry enough water for a journey of that length. So where had the nightmare come from? How had Laura managed to catch it? And *why* would Laura bring a dreadful thing like that to the Rainbow Opera on St Lazarus's Eve?

Grace collected herself and went on. She reached the top of the stairs and saw her daughter. Rose's jaw went slack, and she took a step back, apparently appalled at her mother's appearance. Grace ran to Rose, took her hands, and scanned her face. Rose was unhurt — her lips were mauve but, Grace recalled, that was the stain of the musk creams she had been nibbling since lunch.

The terrible howling had stopped. Behind the Opera's doors people had begun to call out for help — a sane, human clamour. A few began to spill out onto the balconies. The door of the Hame suite opened and Laura emerged, slowly and unsteadily. She looked tiny, with her thin limbs and short, sweat-soaked hair clinging to her skull. She looked childish in her white pyjamas with forget-me-nots embroidered on the collar. Laura was clumsily unwinding bandages from her hands. There was blood on her lips.

Grace said, 'Laura!'

Laura looked up at her aunt, her expression closed and remote.

There was a loud crash from the auditorium. Grace turned and saw that George Mason was in trouble. A group of men were making their way up the spiral stairs, with murder in their eyes. George had hurled his own water jug at them. For a moment the men fell back, shielding their faces with their hands, then they continued to climb.

The control room was dark, but the alarm board was cascading sparks, by the light of which Grace could see several of the fire watch leaning across the sill of the window that looked out over the auditorium. They appeared stunned and battered. Grace ignored the sounds behind her — of breaking glass, and her niece calling to someone — and shouted across the auditorium to the fire watch. 'Please help him!' She gestured towards Mason. A long moment went by. The Opera's rooms disgorged retching, staggering people. Grace yelled some more. She still had hold of Rose, who was trying to pull away. Grace hung on to her daughter but kept her attention on the control room and fire watch. She urged them to do something. In another moment George would be overwhelmed. The dais was so packed now that Grace imagined she could see it swaying. Finally the fire watch pulled themselves together and, lit by blue flashes, began to move, and act.

When her mother turned away to help George Mason, Rose kept her eye on Laura. Laura had glanced briefly at her aunt and cousin, then had begun to shout. Rose couldn't make any sense of what her cousin was yelling, though she was able to hear Laura clearly, since the screams behind all the Opera's padded doors had, for the most part, subsided to sobs. What Laura yelled was maddeningly ridiculous and, briefly, Rose felt like joining in — adding, 'Verb! Adjective! Adverb!' Because Laura was shouting, 'Noun!'

Then a shadowy male figure appeared. He burst through the doors from the private balcony of the President's Suite, leaving the doorframe bristling with shards of wood.

What Rose saw was a massive, glittering, silvery statue. A statue that moved, and looked about with eyes banded black, as though encrusted with tiny flakes of jet. The calm, noble face turned her way, then swung towards Laura as she stretched out her arms to him.

Rose tried to tear herself away from her mother. She tried to struggle free and go to Laura. To *save* Laura.

Laura held her arms out to the statue. It swooped on her, caught her up and rushed away into the nearest stairway — the one that led down to the dreamer's door.

Grace finally lost her grip on her daughter, who broke away and rushed to the stairs that led to the dreamer's door. There she stopped, clinging to the door frame, and peered down into the dark. The lights seemed to have failed in the stairwell. 'Rose!' Grace called, and her daughter turned and came back. 'Are those stairs clear?' Grace asked — she was thinking how they might avoid the angry crowd.

'No. Laura went down there. *It* took her,' Rose said. She was stammering with shock. 'Did you see it?'

Grace frowned at her daughter and touched her forehead. 'Darling, we have to hide,' Grace said, gently. Then she grabbed Rose and propelled her towards the President's balcony. Grace was hoping that, since the President had been carried to safety, his bodyguards hadn't bothered to close the door behind them when they fled.

The door was not only open, but broken and hanging from one hinge. The balcony was empty but for an overturned chair. Grace hustled her daughter into the suite. She pulled the door closed and bolted it.

For the next five minutes Rose and Grace hid, cowering, as an enraged crowd beat on the bolted door. Then they heard police whistles.

Rose tried to talk in stops and starts. She said to her mother, 'Did you see it? What was it? Why did Laura want *that*? Why was she calling it to her?'

And to these incoherent questions Grace could only reply, 'It was a dream, darling, only a dream. It must have seemed like that to Laura, too. Just a dream. She's not like you and me.'

Nown held Laura close, his body almost curled round hers. He took the stairs at a tumbling run, but kept his feet, for, wherever they fell, the sand from which they were formed spread and shifted and held him balanced.

They erupted into the moonlight; Nown landing with a jarring thump on the pavement. He straightened, and then very deliberately turned and seized the broken dreamer's door by its handle. He lifted the door back into its frame, and pulled it shut. It was just a gesture, for the closed door did nothing to dampen the noise of crashes, sobs, and frenzied shouting from inside the Opera.

Over her sandman's shoulder Laura saw light blooming in the streets around the Opera as curtains were pulled back and people looked towards the festively lit building, the source of the hellish howling that had woken them. Those houses nearest the Plaza were normally safely beyond any dreamhunter's maximum range, but Laura saw that the.people leaning out the windows of these houses were brushing at their faces, over and over, as though trying to remove an obstruction only they could see.

The scene blurred and tilted as Nown began to run. He made for the gate in the Opera's perimeter fence. It was open and there were men clustered around it. Two stricken chauffeurs had stumbled through it and were on all fours on the road, retching. Opera guards still seemed to be trying to control who came and went, while two of President Wilkinson's uniformed bodyguards stood over them shouting. One bodyguard was waving a revolver back and forth as though it was a hose and he was watering a lawn. He was trying to clear a way for the President's car. Laura recognised the car not only by the armed men standing on its running boards but because she caught a glimpse of Garth Wilkinson himself, his face stark white and his chin and starched dress collar smeared with bloody foam. The car slid through the gate, sounded its horn, and sped away.

Nown followed it. He plunged through the gap in the crowd, then lurched left, towards the river. Over his shoulder Laura saw bristling beams of pressure lamps at the head of the main street into the plaza. She heard pounding footfalls and police whistles. Then she caught sight of the man with the gun, his arm extended, sighting along his gun barrel. 'Nown!' Laura yelled. She drew her legs up and ducked her head down between her shoulders. Nown jerked sideways and stumbled. A spray of sand stung Laura's ear. Nown flung himself onto the ledge between the perimeter fence and the river, ran for a few steps along its narrow course, then lost his balance. Laura felt him falling and flung out her hand to grasp the fence. Her hand closed on a bar, then, in a desperate snatch, his did too, only inches above hers. For a moment Laura had held them both — a moment in which she'd learned he was too heavy for her to hold. They swung above the river, and Laura saw a thin stream of sand fall from Nown's shoulder and disappear hissing into the water, followed by a smoking stone, the bullet.

Nown flexed his elbow and drew them both back against the bars. He let go his grip to prise her locked fingers free. He was speaking to her. She could feel the low muffled reverberations of his voice in his chest, but her ears were deafened by the sound of the shot, or the screams, or even by the horrible hiss of his dry vitality dropping away into the river. She'd heard *that*, why couldn't she hear him speaking?

Laura released her grip and Nown bundled her close to him again and sped away along the ledge, fearless, his balance and momentum unimpaired. They skirted the Opera and sprinted through the Isle's alleyways. There were people behind them blowing whistles, and others closing in from the right — people everywhere, the whole Isle apparently awake and blundering about the streets.

The harrying calls came nearer, and beams of light that ran along the eaves of the buildings they passed between. Their pursuers had entered the street they were on.

Nown paused and looked about, then he stooped and rolled Laura into a dark alcove by the door to a coal cellar. He pushed her up against the padlocked door and pressed himself into the space after her. Laura saw with horror the moonlight and fleeting torchlight closed off. The sand of her servant's body creaked, and then it was seeping around her. She was sealed in.

Laura stuffed the heel of her hand into her mouth and bit down. She hadn't any bandages to protect her. She thought of the clamour in the Opera, the cries of distress. She thought of the polished paint and glass of the President's car marred by bloody handprints. She thought of the long, raw claw marks on her aunt's face and neck.

It had happened. She had done it. She hadn't been able to spare her aunt Grace — the dreamer she'd had to mount. Or Sandy Mason — who she hadn't imagined would be there — or any of the other innocents. She hadn't spared the pregnant woman, the sight of whom had appalled and very nearly stopped her. She'd gone through with it. She'd followed her father's letter, kept faith with him, done what he said must be done. She'd stuck to her resolve.

But, early that morning, before her train had come into Founderston, and after she'd seen Nown off it — pushing him onto the track near the muddy river bank — Laura had sat down to mix Wakeful into the jar of Farrys musk cream before spooning it into the toffee shells. She had done it so that Rose, *Rose at least*, would be spared waking up in her coffin.

It was over. And *now*, for now, she'd do this — bite on her hand till blood ran down into her sleeve. She could hear her pursuers right beside her hiding place. Their lanterns would be passing over Nown, balled into the alcove like a big stone stopping the mouth of a tomb.

The men passed on, and Laura was safe. Buried, but safe.

Two

Secretary Doran wasn't carried off by his bodyguards. For one thing he had only two of them, men in opulent silk dressing gowns worn over evening dress, who might be mistaken for his guests. For another, unlike President Wilkinson, Cas Doran wasn't incapacitated by the nightmare. He'd sampled nightmares before.

Once he managed to drag his consciousness and his intelligence free of it, Doran first checked on all his people — his bodyguards, who had been awake throughout, and who had stationed themselves at the door to the suite, where, they reported to their employer, they'd heard someone smashing through all the doors that sealed off the row of private balconies. Doran checked on his son, Ru, who was vomiting into a basin in the bathroom. He checked on Maze Plasir's apprentice, who had been invited to the Opera because Plasir had loaded him with a dream doctored to colour the few moments of sleep before Grace Tiebold's dream commenced, to fill the Opera patrons' drowsy brains with the impression that they were in the hands of a very good government — an *irreplaceable* government. Doran found the young Colourist uninjured, but rigid with fright — he had wet his bed. The boy was too shocked and ashamed even to attempt an apology. He stood by the bed, shivering so hard that the silk of the drooping crotch of his trousers made a wet flapping noise. Doran stripped the quilt from the bed and wrapped it around the boy. He took him into the suite's sitting room and sat him beside Ru, who had stopped being sick and had some of his colour back. One of Doran's bodyguards told him that his lips were bleeding and passed him a towel. Doran pressed it against his mouth and went to the door of the suite, where he stood listening to shouts and breakage and pounding feet. Then, distant at first, but coming closer, police whistles.

Doran and his bodyguards exchanged glances, then Doran unbolted the door.

The balcony was empty, but the doors at either end were wrenched out of their frames, timber splintered around latch and hinge. A phalanx of blue uniforms was thrusting its way up the spiral stair of the dreamer's dais. The stair was packed with struggling bodies in torn silk nightwear. Doran spotted several members of the Opera's fire watch among them, on the stair and trying to defend the platform on top of the dais. George Mason was on his stomach on the dreamer's bed. Two men had hold of his kicking legs and were dragging him towards the maw of the crowd. Mason clung with both hands to the headboard.

Another cluster of police emerged from the main staircase into the auditorium and fought their way through, striking at all about them with their black truncheons. In their midst Cas Doran glimpsed the slight form of Grace Tiebold. The dreamhunter was hustled out of the building.

The police on the dais had secured Mason. They threw a quilt over his head and gathered themselves around him and defended the bed till reinforcements arrived — another fifty or so constables who erupted into the auditorium through every entrance. Several were carrying rifles.

The mêlée blew apart everywhere the armed police appeared, people scattering from the sight of the guns and truncheons, those who were staggering suddenly fleet. The crowd began to press out of the Opera into the surrounding streets.

Doran turned to his bodyguards, his son, and the shivering Colourist. 'I think we might venture out now,' he said.

Rose emerged from behind the door of the President's suite, where she'd hidden with her mother for a terribly long time it seemed—

though it was perhaps only five minutes. The police had appeared and carried Grace off. The mob had poured away after them.

Rose took a seat on an ottoman on the balcony. She was quietly beside herself. Her mind was in good working order, but her feelings seemed to have gone to sleep. She'd been shocked before in her life, when she'd failed her Try and found she couldn't enter the Place and wouldn't become a dreamhunter. But this, she supposed, was what it was like to be *in shock*.

She had discovered that her cousin Laura was on friendly terms with a monster.

Laura had called on the monster's help and had fled the Opera wrapped in its glistening, inhuman arms. This discovery was such a dislocation in Rose's sense of what she knew about Laura — never mind *the world* — that Rose had the impression that, if the world wasn't quite itself, then she wasn't herself either. Any moment now she'd do something strange, like poke out her own eyes or jump off the balcony. She would do so solely out of a crazed urge to check that what she had always thought was true — Rose and Laura, Laura and Rose, together in a world without monsters — was *still* true.

To make matters worse, it seemed that Rose's mother hadn't seen the monster. Grace had been too intent on the fire watch and George Mason. When Rose told Grace that a monster had carried Laura off, her mother had touched her forehead as though testing for fever.

Rose wound a lock of her long hair around her fingers and dragged on it. The steady pressure made her tilt her head, then stoop. She concentrated on the fiery patch of pain. Then someone near her said, 'It's Rose, isn't it?'

Cas Doran and his party made their way from the balcony of his suite, through the smashed, skewed doors of the suite belonging to the Speaker of the House, and onto the President's balcony. There they found a girl sitting slumped and knock-kneed on an ottoman and tugging severely on a lock of her long golden hair. Doran removed the towel from his bleeding mouth and said, 'It's Rose, isn't it?'

Rose Tiebold was a friend of his daughter, Mamie. The girls were in the same class at Founderston Girls' Academy.

Rose let go of her hair and her head bobbed up. She straightened and looked at him, his son Ru, the bodyguards, Plasir's apprentice. 'The police took my mother away with them,' she said.

'For her own protection,' said Doran. 'But — did they just leave you here alone?'

Rose glanced over her shoulder at the door to the President's suite. Its surface was dented and gouged. 'The crowd followed the police. They were throwing things at Ma. Mostly only their slippers, thank God. I was behind the door when it opened. Suddenly everyone was gone.' She rubbed at her scalp. 'Ouch,' she said. 'I think I've pulled my thoughts into line.'

'I'm glad to hear it,' said Doran. The girl was a little hysterical, he thought. It was to be expected. He caught her under her elbow and helped her up. She flopped against him, then said, 'Oh — Mamie's father.' She sounded as though she were making a note of it, her tone musing and cautious.

'We'll get you out of here,' Doran said. 'Come along.'

The building was emptying. There were ambulances in the plaza. People were being seen to, bandaged, offered blankets and sweet tea.

Doran took a blanket and draped it around Rose. He got the attention of a captain of the police and called him over.

'I'm rich in witnesses,' the captain said, 'but of course they all want to go home. I have my men taking names and addresses.'

'Good,' said Doran. 'Were there any serious injuries? Or arrests?'

'There were people who couldn't be calmed down. We took some into custody. Others were taken in ambulances to Pike Street Hospital. I imagine the Regulatory Body will want to interview witnesses?'

'Yes.'

'The dreamhunters have gone to the city barracks. They'll be safe there. I have to say, Secretary Doran, some of what I'm hearing sounds like plain nonsense. Half these people were running around while still asleep, I think.'

A dishevelled youth, blanket floating behind him like batwings, barged past the police captain shouting, 'Rose! Rose!'

'Sandy!' Rose said.

The police captain seized the youth by the collar of his pyjamas.

'Where's Laura?' the young man asked. His eyes stayed on Rose's face while his fingers grappled with the policeman's hand, slipping, for they were covered in bleeding bite marks.

Doran spotted the copper tags that swung flashing through the gap in the front of the young man's pyjama jacket. He said to the police captain, 'This is another dreamhunter. You should make sure you catch any who were here. It's almost certain that the nightmare has printed itself on them. They'll be reproducing it in a diminished form for the next few nights.'

The young man looked at Cas Doran then, his eyes wide. He moaned.

'Sandy, your uncle is with my mother at the police barracks,' Rose said.

Cas Doran thought: 'This is George Mason's nephew, asking after Laura Hame, desperate with worry.'

'Where is she?' Sandy Mason said again.

Rose's eyes flicked sideways — met Doran's gaze — then returned to Sandy's face. 'She ran off. She was scared. I had bare feet, there was glass on the stairs.' Rose was explaining how she and her cousin had become separated.

Cas Doran knew — because it had been described to him — that the nightmare he had just experienced was Tziga Hame's Buried Alive, a dream Hame had caught for the first time the previous spring and had performed in prisons in a couple of week-long stints in spring and early summer. Hame had had Buried Alive the night he jumped from a pier while walking under escort between the Regulatory Body's special train and Westport's Pier Prison. Hame's family seemed to accept the fiction that he had disappeared while attempting a solo crossing of the Place. The story — the cover-up — wasn't Doran's idea. He knew nothing about it until it was done: a sloppy deception, a forged signature in the Intentions Book at the ranger station in Doorhandle. Hame's sister-in-law Grace

Tiebold had organised a search party and had taken it In looking for a body.

There was no body. No body mummifying in the Place, nor, in fact, where it *should* be, in a pauper's grave belonging to Magdalene Charity Hospital in Westport. But Hame's family seemed prepared to accept his passing without a body to bury. They were even planning a memorial service. Cas Doran knew all this, and he also knew that Tziga Hame's sister, Marta, opposed the planned service. Marta Hame was a very religious woman and — Doran figured — the only reason she could have for not wanting the proper ceremony was if she thought her brother was, in fact, still alive.

Cas Doran looked back at the Opera, its walls blackened by heaving, magnified shadows. He looked at all the tattered fingers and clawed faces and thought: '*Hame is alive.*' Hame's nightmare had not been felt in the world since he disappeared. And yet tonight, when the Opera's patrons were expecting a seasonal performance of Homecoming, here it was, bursting out of an unknown grave — *Hame's grave* — like a blood-soaked revenant.

Doran set his hands on Sandy Mason's bullish neck and held him hard. 'Who was Laura Hame with?' he demanded.

Sandy looked baffled. 'She was with Miss Tiebold. That's why I'm asking Miss Tiebold where she is.'

'Laura was in bed with me,' Rose said.

Cas Doran studied Rose's face and saw that she was much more composed than she had been only moments before.

'We didn't sleep. We were talking. When the screaming started Laura got scared and bolted down the stairs to the dreamer's door,' Rose said, looking from Doran to Sandy.

Sandy was stricken. He writhed out of Doran's grip. 'We have to find her!'

'Oh — yes,' said Rose. She laid a hand on Cas Doran's arm. 'Secretary Doran, could you please have someone take me home? Laura will have run there.'

'No. I won't feel clear in my conscience unless I take you home with *me*, Rose. Mamie's mother wouldn't forgive me for failing to do so. I'll send some people around to your house to find your cousin. I'm sure you're right and she's there.' Doran regarded Sandy. 'As for you, Mr Mason — the police and Body officials are gathering exposed dreamhunters so they can be quarantined. It's a matter of public safety. I'm sure you understand. And you will need some easing through it.' Doran patted Sandy Mason's shoulder. 'We'll let you know how your friend is as soon as we locate her.'

Sandy slumped, but nodded.

Doran signalled to a bowler-hatted Regulatory Body official. The man came to him.

'I have a dreamhunter here,' Doran said, one hand resting on Sandy in a proprietary way, 'and Maze Plasir's apprentice is standing over there with my son. Also, Miss Tiebold tells me that her cousin — the dreamhunter Laura Hame — will have run home.'

'She didn't sleep,' Rose said again. 'We were talking.' Then her eyelids fluttered as if she were about to faint and she began to laugh, semi-hysterical again.

The official took hold of Sandy and escorted him away.

'Your cousin's beau?' Doran asked.

Rose stopped laughing and said, 'I'm sure *I* wouldn't know,' every inch a Founderston Girls' Academy senior asserting her sense of what was proper. And Cas Doran realised with a small shock that he knew very well what her life was like. Rose Tiebold had the kind of agile spirit to be found in those who straddled very different worlds. She attended a fashionable school, had all the manners of a nice young lady — in other words, she prickled with barbed boundaries — but she was also from a dreamhunting family, and party to the daily phantasmagoria of life with dreamhunters, to their frequent exhaustion and feverish wildness.

These dreamhunters — they were *his*. His responsibility, his study, his stock-in-trade. But Cas Doran was not a dreamhunter, nor was anyone in his family. He lived a regular domestic life in a household run by a refined woman — herself a graduate of the Girls' Academy. And that is how Cas Doran knew what Rose Tiebold's life was like: how contradictory it must be. Because, even given the differences in their age and occupation, this girl was in some ways *like* him.

Rose was squinting against the headlamps of his car, which his chauffeur had driven slowly and expertly through the thronging people. The chauffeur put his hand on the top of the windscreen, stood up and called to Doran. 'Sir!'

'Good work!' Doran called back. He took Rose's arm. 'Come,' he said, tenderly. 'There's no need for you to try to think it all through now. I'm sure we'll find your cousin and she'll be all right. Your mother will be perfectly safe at the police barracks, and cared for — I'll see to that myself. We'll send for your father — wherever he is. You must be worn out. If, as you say, you didn't sleep, it is safe for you to sleep now.'

Rose went with Secretary Doran. He spoke soothingly, said that everything would be all right. He handed her into the car. Its interior smelled pleasantly of new leather. Rose realised that there had been some terrible smells, as well as terrible sights, in the plaza.

The car began to move again, easing its way through the thronging people. There were seething shadows in the plaza, interrupting the lights from streets and houses. Rose stared at Doran's profile. In the light ghosting over his face Doran looked grim and intent, like someone making ready for a fight. Then he turned and smiled at her.

Rose knew she'd do everything she could to keep people from guessing that it was her cousin's nightmare. Before too long she'd speak to Laura, then she would know why her cousin had done it. There would be a reason, some kind of sense. Rose suspected it was something to do with the letter Laura had torn up, a last letter from her missing father.

The letter had, for some reason unfathomable at the time, been partly buried in a large amount of sand in Laura's bedroom at Summerfort. Laura had been Into the Place illicitly, looking for clues as to why her father had disappeared. When Rose and Chorley turned up looking for Laura she had shut herself in her bedroom and stood against the door. Then, when she had finally let them in, they'd found her standing up to her ankles in a pile of sand. The envelope that held the letter was sticking out of it.

Sand!

That very night — St Lazarus's Eve — when the howls of terror had wound down, Rose had seen her cousin emerge from the Hame suite, and stand for a moment unwinding bandages from her hands. Laura had looked up at Rose, then seemed to dismiss her. She began to call. What Laura shouted sounded like nonsense, but it was a name. At her call a monster had come running. A great statue in the shape of a man — beautifully muscled, nobly serene. A man apparently made of sand. The monster had swept Laura up in his arms and run to the stairs down to the dreamer's door. And Rose, straining after Laura, had seen something. She saw the name Laura had called was scored in the sand on the back of the monster's neck. Four letters: N O W N.

Rose was trembling. Secretary Doran touched her arm and said, 'How are you, Rose?' Then, 'We'll be home shortly.'

There was no one in the world Rose was closer to than Laura, but Rose had known nothing of any of this — the nightmare, or the monster. She felt herself shrinking. She didn't *know* anything. All her schoolmates thought she was a bit of a hero, but she wasn't. She was baffled, and in the dark.

Three

Laura and Nown left the Isle of the Temple by the railway bridge to the east. Nown carried her. He walked from board to board along the top of the bridge, over the running water that was deadly to him.

He cradled her, his arms so long in comparison to her body that he could warm her bare feet in one hand — a cold hand, but it kept her toes from the night air. He held her as he could hold heat, and her breath blowing against his fake collarbone warmed him all the way to the back of his neck.

Nown strode on, stepping on every third sleeper on the track, passing beneath the barred windows of the houses that backed on to the railway line in the Old Town. There was no one looking out of those windows. Not a soul to see them go by.

It had been raining and the sleepers were wet, the rainwater sitting on spills of engine oil. But Nown's sandy soles never slipped, and their progress was smooth.

They passed through the Old Town and into the suburbs, over crossings whose striped warning barriers were up, saluting the sky. Nown stepped aside for one train. They went on past backyards where damp work clothes and aprons and nappies hung from clothes lines. They passed properties where dogs erupted from their kennels only to baulk, whining, then scuttle back into shelter again.

Nown carried Laura beside ditches choked with brambles, and banks covered in newly planted trees — budding birches and willows.

The railway line would, eventually, take them to the stop near Marta Hame's house. That was where Laura had asked Nown to carry her.

She lay quiet. She didn't stir till they reached the country. Then her head moved from where it rested against his shoulder to look around at the slender birches that clacked and ticked in the night breeze.

'Nown,' she said, 'in the train last night, did I tell you to stop talking to me?'

'No.'

'I think I did.'

'You said, "You're hurting me." You had told the eighth, "Don't hurt me."'

Nown had let himself be guided by an order she'd given his earlier self. He'd tried to help her, and she'd silenced him.

Laura hitched herself up in his arms. She felt the smooth bandage of sand that wrapped her feet separate, and round out into fingers once more. She climbed Nown, flexed her legs so that she could get her arms up over one of his shoulders. Laura looked behind him — not back along the track — but at the back of his neck. She looked at the letters of his name. NOWN. She thought of the words of the song her father taught her: '*Two letters remain within, death and freedom. Make his name his Own and he is.*'

She reached around and used one finger to erase the first N in his name. His name now read: 'OWN'. She knew that, if she properly understood the way the spell worked, she had just set her servant free.

Nown hesitated; he broke stride. He faltered, but he didn't stop walking.

Laura sank back into the cradle of his arms, and he once again picked up his pace, kept on steadily striding along between the rails.

Shortly before dawn it began to rain. Laura watched the big drops absorbed by Nown's sandy skin. She saw the rain spots join together to become dark patches. Nown stooped his shoulders, and bent his head over Laura to shelter her from the rain. His face was near to hers.

She said to him, 'You might melt.'

And he said, 'If I melt, you can make me again.'

Part VII
The Isle of the Temple

One

Laura's sandman carried her all night. He walked for twenty miles, following the railway line south-west from Founderston, travelling along the track bed with long, rocking strides. Laura was careful to keep her eyes open. She was afraid of waking up in her dream again, of opening her eyes on blackness and the chilly embrace of a satin shroud.

They left the railway tracks at the small station near Marta Hame's house. They didn't follow the road, for it was getting light, a dull twilight rinsed by drizzle.

As Nown clambered up a hillside Laura heard sheep pattering away from them. She saw the flock pour down a slope together and flow into the groove of a gully, like raindrops on a large leaf spilling to pool at the stem.

Nown pressed down the top wire of a fence and the whole thing strained, twanging along its length. He stepped over it.

At the edge of Aunt Marta's yard Laura told Nown to stop. She slid from his arms and he steadied her till she found her feet. She said, 'You hide yourself. But stay near.' Then she recalled that she had set him free.

Nown had helped her do what her father had asked in the letter he left for her. Laura hated having to catch Buried Alive, and overdream her unsuspecting Aunt Grace. But it did seem the only way of letting people know that prisons were using nightmares to subdue convicts. As Laura had gone about catching and delivering

Buried Alive, she had come to understand that her sandman had doubts about what she was doing. When he tried to speak to her she had silenced him.

She had made him, he was her servant, bound to obey her by rules she knew she didn't fully understand. But she did understand the most simple rules of the spell that had made him. She knew that if she erased the W in his name, made it NON instead of NOWN, he would fall apart, as her father's sandman had. And she knew that if, instead, she erased the first N in his name, he'd be his own — free. With Nown's help Laura had completed the task her father had set her. Then she found that what she wanted next wasn't obedient help, but guidance and wisdom — and to be cherished.

So it was that, a few hours before, in the dark of night, when frost was first forming on the timber sleepers of the railway line they walked along, Laura had leaned over her sandman's shoulder and scratched out one letter on the back of his neck, the first N in his name. She'd freed him. And he didn't leave her (as her father had) — instead, he gathered her close and kept on walking.

'You hide yourself, but stay near,' she told him, then stood for a moment stupefied by the thought that since she'd freed him he didn't need to obey her. Then — 'I'm soaking wet,' she said, 'I must go in. Will you wait for me?'

'Yes,' said Nown.

Laura approached the house. She went up the steps to the porch. As soon as her foot touched the top step barking erupted from within. It was Downright, her aunt's dog. She heard the dog coming till he was on the other side of the door, his nails clicking on the timber floor as he danced about.

Laura called through the door, 'It's me, Laura!'

Downright paused to listen then began to bark again.

The stained glass around the door lit up as a lamp was carried to it. It was Mr Bridges, one of Aunt Marta's elderly servants. Laura heard the man speak sharply to Downright. Then Marta joined him, calming her dog with praise. 'There's a good boy, settle down now.' The bolt rattled, the door opened, and two people and the dog all stared at Laura.

Downright surged forward, and his collar jerked free from Marta's grip. He brushed past Laura, ran outside, and began to track back and forth across the lawn with his nose down. He reached the long grass at the edge of the mown area and stood stiff-legged, silent, pointing. Then his ears went back and he hunkered down on his haunches, made a tight turn, and scuttled back across the lawn. He pushed past the people in the doorway and vanished into the dark dead-end below the main staircase, where he cowered, whimpering.

Marta looked at her dog, frowned, then drew Laura indoors. She released her niece and looked at her wet hands. 'What is this?' she said. 'Where have you come from? And what on earth are you wearing?'

'I walked here. I'm wet through,' Laura said.

Marta made a small sound between grunt and gasp, more exasperated than shocked. She took hold of Laura and hustled her up the stairs, issuing instructions over her shoulder about breakfast.

Marta's bedroom was warm, last night's fire smoking still. She gave her niece a nightgown and told her to change out of her wet clothes and get under the covers. Marta poked at the fire, put on more coal. Laura stripped off her silk pyjamas, which weren't evenly soaked — no, her back and seat and one shoulder were dry, for they had lain against the shelter of Nown's body. Laura could see that the pattern was incongruous, so she crumbled the silk into a wad so that the very dry patches blotted the wet. She dropped the bundled pyjamas and put on her aunt's nightgown. Her bare feet tingled with the blood coming back into them. She climbed into her aunt's bed, but remained sitting. 'I mustn't sleep,' she said.

Marta got up from the hearth and stared at Laura. 'What have you done?' she said.

'I showed them.' Laura shivered.

Marta put on her dressing gown and stood at the mirror to brush out her plait. She wound her hair into a coil, and pinned it. She was silent throughout, and it was as though she hadn't heard Laura. But then, without turning, she met her niece's gaze in the mirror and asked, '*What* did you show them, Laura?'

'What happens,' Laura said. She opened her mouth again to add, 'The dreams they take to the prisons,' but something inside her interrupted. It wasn't like being interrupted by her own thoughts. She recognised it as different from her, a fragment of planted intelligence, something that had come to her with the dream. It seemed to say, 'What *has* happened,' to warn, 'What *will* happen.'

'Laura.' Aunt Marta was sitting on the bed beside her, hands gripping her shoulders. 'Lie back, girl, you're faint. Your face is completely white. You can sleep if you need to. No one in this house is about to go back to bed.' Marta began to muse. 'Though, really, if your dream is that dire, I will have to have you moved elsewhere.'

Laura put her head back on the pillow. Her shivering began to subside. She closed her eyes. A moment later she felt her aunt lift the covers. Marta said, 'You weren't wearing any shoes, but your feet are clean. Who brought you here? Who else knows you're here?'

'No one,' Laura said. 'I came on my own.' In her mind she saw the three remaining letters on the back of Nown's neck. She flicked her thumb against her forefinger and felt the sand packed under her fingernail.

Her aunt said, 'Why did you choose to come here?'

'I haven't anywhere else to go. Everyone will be angry with me,' she said, and thought: 'and it was raining.'

She had been wet and cold. But if, when the day came, the sun had appeared too, then she might have asked Nown to keep on walking, to carry her away somewhere, as if a spell held her together, instead of all her regular needs — food and shelter, clothes and money.

The bedroom door closed. Aunt Marta had gone out. Laura opened her eyes and looked around at the plaster decorations on the ceiling, the white ropes of leaves and flowers gathered at four corners of the room by big bows borne by birds in flight.

Once she was warm Laura got out of bed and stood at the window. It was a grey morning, not much more light than the dawn had been. Laura saw Mr Bridges hurrying off down the road, patting one pocket as he went.

The bedroom door opened. 'Get back into bed,' Marta said. 'I've sent Mr Bridges to the telegraph at the station. I feel the need of some advice. You were always an honest girl, Laura, and open — without having picked up that habit the Tiebolds have of broadcasting constant reports on their mental weather . . .'

Laura got back into bed, remained sitting, but drew the covers up to her chin. She listened to her aunt mutter about the shortcomings of the rest of her family. Marta was opening drawers and rattling coat-hangers in her wardrobe as she spoke. 'You were honest, but now I see you're heading down the same path your father took. You have to understand that you shouldn't abuse your gift for any reason. Not for any reason.'

'I'm not. You'll see.'

Marta shook her head, bundled her clothes in her arms and went out of the bedroom again.

Half an hour went by. Mrs Bridges came in with breakfast on a tray. She too told Laura that her husband had gone to the station's telegraph office. 'Miss Marta has asked her friend the Grand Patriarch to send a car — "immediately" is what she wrote.'

It appeared that Laura had come all this way only to be carried back to Founderston.

Mrs Bridges shovelled more coal into the grate, then said, 'You should tuck in, dear. You must be famished. Here, let me take the top off that egg.' The woman came and did that, and then stood making soothing noises over Laura as she ate. 'That's right. Get that down you,' she said, and, 'Have some more toast. My quince jelly turned out particularly well this year.'

When Mrs Bridges finally left, Laura eased the tray off her legs and got out of bed. She posted herself at the window and waited. Mr Bridges came back along the road and turned in at the gate. Once he was indoors, Laura pushed up the sash and thrust her head out. It was dull full daylight outside, but Laura couldn't see where Nown might have hidden himself. She called his name — in a loud whisper.

Behind her the bedroom door opened. 'Get away from that window!' commanded Aunt Marta.

Laura took her knee off the sill and shuffled back to the bed. Her aunt's nightdress was too long for her.

Marta closed her wardrobe doors. She turned the key in the lock, removed it and put it in her pocket. 'I have nothing that would fit you anyway. You'd be swimming in all my dresses,' Aunt Marta said. 'And this way you won't think of setting out cross-country again.'

'Mrs Bridges told me you asked the Grand Patriarch to send a car.'

'That's right. Upon reflection I've decided that I can't turn the Bridges out of their beds just because you're carrying a nightmare.'

Laura's aunt stood straight-backed, with one hand pressed flat to her pocket as though she thought the key might leap out of it. Her face was stern and full of suspicion. 'While I am pleased that you think you can come to me, Laura,' she said, 'I'm afraid that this is all a bit beyond me.'

When Laura had last visited Marta, she'd had her aunt teach her 'The Measures'. Laura had told her aunt that she had been talking with her father about 'The Measures' and other old Hame songs the last times she saw him, at Summerfort and on Sisters Beach station before the special train carried him away. She'd told her aunt that her father said the songs were his only real family legacy, and that she should know them. Marta Hame had, till recently, been the choir mistress at the Temple in Founderston. She was a musician, a music teacher and a Hame — the ideal person for Laura to ask about the family music. But Laura hadn't been collecting songs to remember her father by — no, she had wanted to learn 'The Measures' because it was a spell, a recipe for making a servant out of earth. Now, looking at her aunt, Laura wondered how Marta could know the chant and not know what it could do.

Laura's aunt said, 'Erasmus will tell me how to handle you.'

Laura laughed and shook her head, partly out of a sense of absurdity — her aunt had such faith in her friend and spiritual guide, the Grand Patriarch of the Southern Orthodox Church. But the Grand Patriarch was always speaking out against dreamhunters and dream palaces. According to him, the Rainbow Opera was a place where people indulged in 'a second-hand education of the senses' and 'acts without consequences'. What kind of advice could the Grand Patriarch offer a law-breaking dreamhunter? All he believed in was abstinence. Besides, Laura hadn't wanted advice, she'd only wanted to *get the job done.*

Marta pulled the window closed before she left the room. For a long time Laura didn't dare to stir. She was sure that her aunt was just beyond the door, listening for movement. Laura waited. She became drowsy, and it was her drowsiness that frightened her out of the warm bed and across the room. For a minute she stood pressed against the window — her face turned to the door. There was a light in the hall, a candle perhaps, its wavering radiance lancing through the keyhole. Laura watched it, and the strain of watching was so great, and she so still, that everything seemed to come to life around her, the bedroom furniture, the plaster garlands carried by plaster birds, the patterns on the carpet — everything became animated and seemed to watch her back. Laura felt like a wild animal; she ached for escape.

After a long time she turned back to the window.

Nown was standing on the lawn looking up at her.

Laura pushed the sash open and swung her legs over the sill. She stepped out onto the cold, corrugated iron of the veranda roof. She walked as far as she could, to where the curve began to plunge down to the guttering.

Nown stalked nearer, till he stood at the veranda rail, directly beneath her.

Laura looked down into his black-banded, statuesque eyes and thought that it wasn't really any wonder that she'd imagined the bedroom furniture had come to life. Nown was made of inanimate matter, sand all the way through — and yet here he was, waiting to hear what she wanted. She said, 'My aunt has sent for a car. She's taking me back to Founderston. Not to the authorities though, I think.'

Nown didn't move, show surprise, nod to acknowledge he'd heard, or make any noise to encourage her to go on speaking.

Laura looked around the misty farmland. She saw a pine plantation — trees black in the mist — growing on the curve of the nearest hill like the neatly cropped mane of a cavalry horse. She pointed. 'Wait for me there, in that forest. Can you do that? I'll be back as soon as I'm able. I don't want anyone to see you.'

Nown didn't reply — he didn't say 'I'll do that.'

'Please,' she said.

He lifted his arms and held them out. He didn't say anything, but the gesture meant, 'Jump!' It meant, 'Jump, and I'll catch you.'

From the room behind her Laura heard her aunt, shocked, shouting, 'Laura! What are you doing out there? Come back inside this instant!'

Laura took one last look at her sandman's open arms, his black-banded, brilliant eyes, then turned and made her way carefully back to the open window and stepped into the warm bedroom.

Two

The day before — St Lazarus's Eve — when Laura's overnight train had arrived in Founderston at nine-thirty in the morning, she had pushed three envelopes into the postbox on the concourse of the station.

The letters were collected and sorted at the Central Post Office. None made the ten-thirty delivery. All three went out at noon.

One landed at twelve-forty in the basket of the assistant to the Director of the Regulatory Body. It was still lying there unopened when the man put on his coat and hat at 1 p.m. — the beginning of his half-day holiday — and went out to meet his wife at the People's Gardens.

The second letter was delivered to the Temple at noon, but the Temple was always busy over the feast of St Lazarus, and the letter didn't find its way into the hands of Father Roy, the Grand Patriarch's secretary, until seven the following morning. When the Grand Patriarch returned to the vestry after the celebration of early mass he was met by Father Roy, with the letter, and a telegraph from his friend Marta Hame asking him to send a car to her house. The Grand Patriarch read Marta's message and despatched a car. He read the letter, then handed it back to Father Roy and said, 'Perhaps this explains the crowd at mass. Much more than the usual Lazarus Day throng. There were people wrapped in blankets standing at the back, and lining the aisles. They looked as if they'd wandered in from a disaster.'

The Grand Patriarch went back to his apartments and sat down to breakfast and the morning paper. The paper carried a red 'Stop Press' report of the riot at the Rainbow Opera.

The third letter found its way to the mail room of the *Founderston Herald* shortly after noon on St Lazarus's Eve, then languished among dozens of other letters to the editor because the paper was being put to bed early that day — printers into double time to get out the holiday edition, a paper full of advertisements, announcements of engagements and the Ladies' Supplement's thoughts on hats and tango heels. At midnight on St Lazarus's Eve the skinny, seedy little man whose job it was to sift through letters to the editor burst out of the nearly deserted *Herald* offices and into the street to jog several blocks and over a bridge to the Isle of the Temple. He arrived in time to see bloodied people spilling out of the Rainbow Opera, and the first constables pushing their way in. Despite his protests he was turned away from the Crescent Plaza by the police. It was hours before he managed to find the *Herald*'s editor, who was at home by then, cleaned up, but still grey-faced, and with fresh scabs on his scalp from where he'd torn at his own hair. The skinny, seedy man handed the letter to his editor, who peered at the elongated, backwards-sloping handwriting, and read:

> Dear Sir
> Please publish this letter. It has come to our attention that the Dream Regulatory Body has been using nightmares to terrorise and subdue the inmates of this nation's prisons in order to guarantee a co-operative labour force to work in mines and factories and on road and rail projects.

The accusation was all in one long, mad, bad sentence. The editor frowned, and read on:

> The public may already be aware that dreams are used for education and rehabilitation in prisons. But the public does not know that instead of sharing dreams about the wages of their sins the prisoners are forced to endure frightful nightmares from which no one could learn anything.

'The author of this letter has a large vocabulary, but is semi-literate in my opinion,' said the editor.

> The nightmare broadcast in the Rainbow Opera on St Lazarus's Eve is one such dream. We have overdreamed Grace Tiebold's Homecoming so that the public will know that this is what it is like for those prisoners. We did it in order to wake the public conscience.
> Stop the torture!
> Lazarus

'I'll deal with this,' said the editor to his assistant. He saw the man to the door then sat down to compose a note to his friend Cas Doran, the Secretary of the Interior.

The police handwriting expert peered at the two letters, the one that began 'Dear Sir, Please publish this letter' and the other beginning 'The time has come for the Regulatory Body to submit to judgment'. He said that the writer was left-handed, and secretive. 'Look at those backwards-sloping letters.' He said that the stationery was the same for both letters, but that one page was more yellowed than the other, perhaps the top sheet of a pad that had sat around in sunlight for some time. It was export-quality linen paper, manufactured in a certain paper mill in the south. The letters had probably been written at a desk equipped with a writing set, because the ink was blotted with sand. The handwriting was highly distinctive, fluent and not, the expert thought, a disguised hand. 'But it seems to me that the handwriting is more mature than the composition — the bad grammar and poor punctuation.'

Having given his opinion, the handwriting expert was shown from the room. Cas Doran, the detective inspector from Founderston Barracks and the director of the Regulatory Body were left alone.

The detective inspector said, 'Before we ask Grace Tiebold in here we should think about charges.'

Doran closed his eyes, saw darkness, winced and opened them again. His mouth and jaw were sore. It hurt him to speak. 'What can she or Mason be charged with? There is no crime of "Grievous Mental Harm".'

'Perhaps there should be.'

'Certainly not,' said Doran. 'We'd then have this Lazarus and his allies bringing criminal charges against the Regulatory Body and the Department of Corrections.'

At this the detective inspector merely cleared his throat. Then he said, 'So, you believe this Lazarus has allies?'

'Yes. The letter says, "*We* have overdreamed", and "It has come to *our* attention". But I doubt that "we" is George Mason and Grace Tiebold.'

'Mason and Tiebold could be charged with disturbing the peace,' said the detective inspector.

Doran shook his head. 'There are regulations that cover safe practices in Dream Palaces, just as there are regulations that govern how many fire escapes any new building must have. But the regulations haven't thought to ban Soporifs from sleeping in Dream Palaces. Though — believe me — that's about to change.'

The detective inspector sighed. He would have been much happier if he had been closer to an arrest.

The director of the Regulatory Body said, 'Shall we speak to these dreamhunters now? Mason first, I think.'

George Mason was cooperative — and no real help at all. He spent only half an hour in Doran's office, then was sent to join the dozen other dreamhunters who had been at the Opera. They had all taken a print of Buried Alive. They were to be transported to Doorhandle and then Into the Place so that they could attempt to overwrite the nightmare with something harmless.

When she was shown into Cas Doran's office, Grace Tiebold was still wearing her dreamhunter's finery, though the peacock-print train of her gown had been trodden to tatters by both the police and the people the police had protected her from. Doran saw that Grace had a bruise on her jaw, as well as the now familiar self-inflicted scratches on her cheeks. And, of course, it hurt her to speak.

The first thing Doran did was push one of the letters across the desk and under her nose. 'Is this *your* schoolgirlish false officialese?' He asked. Then, in mocking imitation, '*It has come to our attention . . .*' He waited, then said, 'I believe you left school at twelve to work in your father's tobacco shop?'

The dreamhunter's eyes flicked up to his face. She showed fright. Then she stared at the letter and looked puzzled. 'I don't recognise the handwriting,' she said. She seemed surprised.

'Should you?' asked the detective inspector.

She hesitated. Then, 'No,' she said, finally.

'And how does this letter strike you?'

'It's demented, fantastical,' Grace said. 'The writer is defending an act of terror. An act of spectral terror. But apparently, according to the letter, you people deal in terror too.'

'You *know* what we do,' Doran said. 'There's nothing you don't know about what we do.'

Grace looked into his eyes. She was exhausted, bleak, but seemed to have recovered from her moment of fright. She said, 'I doubt that.'

'The Intangible Resources Act provides for the use of certain sorts of dreams "for the public good", including nightmares — punishments that cause pain but not injury. I'm sure we can agree that this is something you already know.'

'I know it,' Grace said. She gestured at her own nail-marked cheeks, then at Doran's injured mouth. 'But — is *this* pain without injury?'

'There were no precautions. No restraints.'

'So you strap your prisoners down, then give them nightmares?'

Doran leaned back in his chair. 'Mrs Tiebold, are you defending yourself? You seem to be saying that inflicting a virulent nightmare on the general public is no different from the controlled use of nightmares on convicted criminals.'

'It wasn't my nightmare!' Grace Tiebold's eyes blazed. 'This Lazarus used me! Me *and* George.'

The Director of the Regulatory Body spoke up then. 'Why did you ask the Soporif George Mason to lie in with you?'

'I've been having difficulty falling asleep. George went In with me to catch Homecoming. We even have a witness. Jerome Tilley was at the site with us, catching it too. Jerome had a booking in Westport for a feast-day performance at the Second Skin Theatre. George and I walked back to Doorhandle with him, and George drove us all to Founderston. He dropped Jerome at the station, and me at my house. Three hours later I met my daughter and niece for lunch, then we went home, changed and came out to the Opera. I'm sure George can account for all *his* movements that afternoon too. We didn't hike back In — *days* In — and catch that nightmare. We are not Lazarus. I'm very sorry that this person chose to spill his nightmare out on my penumbra. And I'm sure George is very sorry that he made it difficult for everyone to wake up.'

Doran made a steeple of his hands and gave Grace Tiebold a little pinched smile over the top of them. 'That wasn't your penumbra — it was Lazarus's. Perhaps five hundred yards. Lazarus wanted your *audience*, Mrs Tiebold, not your powers of amplification. Lazarus is very probably a more powerful dreamhunter than you.'

'Where has he been hiding himself all this time?' Grace said.

'*Has* he been hiding himself?' Doran said, as though she knew whom they were talking about.

'Tziga's dead,' Grace said, and dropped her gaze. 'I'm tired, Mr Doran. I don't know anything more. I want to go In and erase this, if I can. And first I want to go home to wash and change and check on Rose and Laura.'

'Rose is spending today in the company of my wife, and Mamie,' Doran said. 'The girls go back to school tomorrow.'

Grace glared at him. 'You might have mentioned that first. And if Rose is with Mamie, where is Laura?'

Doran spread his hands and shrugged. 'I thought you might know.'

'Laura will have the nightmare too. She might not realise it until she falls asleep.'

'Your daughter told me that Laura didn't sleep. But we are looking for her,' Doran said.

'Good,' said Grace, and turned her face away.

'That will be all for now,' said the Director of the Regulatory Body. 'Some of my people will escort you to your house, then take you on to Doorhandle.'

'Thank you.' Grace Tiebold got up and nodded to the detective inspector, who said to her that he'd like her to come and see him once she was back. At the door the dreamhunter turned and asked, 'How is President Wilkinson?'

'He is recovering well,' Doran said.

'I'm glad to hear it. We need him,' Grace said.

Doran smiled again, his mouth performing a kind of spasm of involuntary glee that opened the wounds on his lips. Here was evidence that, despite the nightmare, Plasir's apprentice Gavin Pinkney's little bit of 'colouring' had been absorbed and remembered. Doran risked saying, 'Yes, we do need Wilkinson, and it's such a pity his term is nearly up.'

'Yes.' Grace hovered in the doorway, frowning. 'Eight years does seem far too short a term for such a constructive President. Or, at least, that's what *I* think.'

Grace was feeling very foggy when she left Cas Doran's office, but once she was out in the cold morning air she remembered something she'd noticed while she was there. Something much more important than what a shame it was that Garth Wilkinson was shortly to retire. She had recognised the stationery on which Lazarus's letter was written. The paper was expensive, and probably plenty of well-off, or very particular, people liked to use it. It was expensive and elegant, like everything of Chorley's — for it was Chorley's. Grace's husband wasn't much of a letter writer and tended to make all his plans on drawing paper in his workshop. So the stationery sat in a boxed block on the desk of Summerfort's library, in full sunlight, often for weeks — and for months once the family packed up at the end of summer and went back to Founderston. The paper of the letter had been yellowed, and printed with a paler mark, a star shape — where Chorley's fossilised starfish paperweight had sat while the sun shone and turned the page yellow around it.

'Laura,' Grace thought, again. For the letter showed her niece's lack of punctuation and, as Doran had so descriptively put it, her 'schoolgirlish false officialese'.

But the handwriting was not Laura's.

Three

It was afternoon when the car sent for Laura and her Aunt Marta reached its destination. It passed through an open arch into the courtyard of the Grand Patriarch's palace. Laura had a glimpse of Temple Plaza — of sunshine on damp cobblestones, and people strolling about in their feast-day finery. She could hear the music of an accordion coming from one of the cafés in the plaza. These signs of life came to her through a hot mist of fever and exhaustion.

The running boards of the car were slick with mud from country roads. Laura climbed out carefully. She had slippers on her feet and one of her aunt's coats over the borrowed nightgown.

There was a priest waiting to meet them. Aunt Marta called him 'Father Roy'. Marta and the priest fell into step, their heads together. As they were climbing the steps to the side entrance to the palace, Father Roy turned and gave Laura a sharp, wry look. Laura was led into a chilly room with dark, wood-panelled walls and ceiling. Father Roy asked her to wait. He and Marta went out. A few minutes went by, then Laura heard several people hurrying back along the passage. Father Roy returned with a couple of black-clad religious sisters. They got Laura up and conducted her out of the room. Aunt Marta was nowhere in sight.

Laura was marched up several flights of stairs, along corridors, then out of a door onto a rooftop walkway, which crossed from the roof of the palace to that of the Temple, and a small door beneath the deep masonry lintel around the base of the dome. One of the sisters behind Laura tapped her back to urge her forward. Laura stooped and went through the door. It led into a short tunnel, at the end of which Laura glimpsed a grille, and beyond that a place she recognised, the gallery that ran around the inside of the dome, which was as far up as she'd ever been on visits to the Temple with her schoolmates. The sister behind Laura seized her arm and turned her in the narrow space to face a dark opening in the wall of the tunnel. 'Wait,' the woman said. Laura heard a match struck. The sister pushed past Laura, carrying a candle, and stepped up into darkness. She was standing on a stone staircase that disappeared upward in a tight spiral. She gestured for Laura to follow her.

The dome of Founderston's Temple was eggshell smooth, but was set into a four-tiered crown of decorated masonry, and topped by an ornate turret. The turret had blind arches, window-shaped recesses filled with mortared stone. The stone was coated with gold leaf.

Like every other child in Founderston, Laura had wished she was allowed to climb high enough to stand on one of the little iron balconies below the dome. She had occasionally caught sight of someone up that high. And she — like every other child in the city — had noticed that a ladder ascended from one of the balconies up to the golden turret. Laura remembered her childish wondering as she emerged from the long climb up the spiral staircase and found herself on the balcony below that ladder.

The balcony wasn't big enough to hold four people, so one sister lingered at the top of the stairs while Father Roy edged around Laura and stepped onto the ladder. 'Please follow me,' he said.

The dome was like a horizon. Laura felt that she was nestled up to the moon. Below, the accordion music and the metallic slither and clanging of a tram sounded far away. All noise was sucked up into the blue air surrounding them.

'It's completely safe,' said the sister behind Laura. 'Just go carefully.'

Metal loops enclosed the ladder at every fourth rung. Laura saw that she would be inside this protective spine of iron. She began to climb. Father Roy's black coat flapped and crackled above her. The ladder vibrated. They ascended the curve, till they weren't climbing but crawling.

Laura put her head down and watched her hands. The more shallow the slope became, the more precarious she felt. When the curve had been steeper, gravity had seemed to hold her on the ladder, now it seemed all too easy to slip through the protection of the bars beside her and slide away down the smooth marble skin of the dome. Laura stopped. She clutched the ladder and closed her eyes.

'Come on, you're nearly there,' the woman behind her said.

'What's the hold-up?' said the sister bringing up the rear; she sounded anxious.

'Lift your head, Laura,' said Father Roy.

Laura raised her head and opened her eyes. She saw that Father Roy had emerged from the ribbed tube and was standing at a doorway in the gold wall. There was a room behind him. A room! An enclosed space. Safety.

Laura scrambled towards him. He gripped her by the collar of her coat and drew her into the room. There was a step down, and Laura stumbled and caught herself on the edge of a big round table. The sisters piled in behind her, the second sister with a basket on her back filled with bundles, blankets, candles. The woman heaved the basket off her back and tipped it out onto the table, then lunged to catch the candles as they rolled towards its centre.

In the little bit of light coming through the door Laura saw that the table was about ten feet in diameter, so big that it nearly filled the round room. Its surface was concave, so anything set on it slid into the middle.

The sister sorted some candles from the pile of blankets. She placed them on the ledge above the door and lit one. Then she began to arrange the blankets into a bed on top of the concave table.

Father Roy faced Laura. 'You'll be safe here, and sufficiently removed that other people should be safe from you.'

Laura looked out of the door at the blue air, then down at the floor, as if it were transparent and she able to measure the distance between this isolated, elevated room and the nave of the cathedral below. She considered how far she'd climbed, but still wasn't sure if it was far enough.

Father Roy said, 'Someone will come to wake you before everyone else's usual bedtime. Any parishioners nodding off during the sermon will just have to take their chances.' The priest studied Laura's face. 'We can't warn them,' he said, then, 'His Eminence has spoken to your aunt, and has read your letter. It *is* your letter, isn't it? Anyway, we know what dream you have.'

The nuns were waiting at the door, flanking it like black sentinels, their hands concealed in the folds of their habits.

'Sleep now,' said Father Roy.

'Don't lock me in,' Laura said.

He nodded and went out, followed by the sisters. The door was closed. Laura walked around and checked it — it gave when she pushed the latch. She fastened it again, then peered around the cylindrical chamber. There was a mirror suspended in one corner of the room, high on the wall, angled down, a round mirror about forty inches in diameter. Beside the mirror was a handle and meshed cogs and wheels. Laura went closer to inspect this machine and experimentally pushed the handle. It was stiff, but slid half a turn. She heard a rolling noise of machinery moving in the ceiling, and thought she saw a coloured shadow swimming in the surface of the mirror. She leaped back. The whirring stopped, and the mirror showed her only the table top and the blot of her makeshift bed.

Laura took her aunt's coat off and added it to the bedding. Then she pushed down the rolled sleeves of Marta's nightgown. The sleeves dangled from the ends of her arms; they would do to trap her hands and save her face from scratches. Laura pulled the nightdress off, knotted the ends of the sleeves, then put it back on. Then she clambered onto the table, burrowed into the blankets and closed her eyes.

Before long she was drowsy. She could sense the nightmare suspended in her sleep like a monstrous fish hanging motionless beneath the surface of a dark pool. It wanted to swallow her. She was afraid, but so worn out that she simply gave in, and went under.

* * *

Laura struggled up in pain. Her tongue hurt, as did the roots of her nails, which she'd bent back by clawing at the table top. She lay still. There was salty blood in her mouth. She opened her eyes. The room was filled with bright light. By the light she saw first the small tears in the sleeves of her nightgown, and her fingers hooked through the cloth, nail tips split and nail beds white with prolonged pressure. She closed her hands, hid her abused fingertips in her palms. Then Laura saw that the sleeves of her nightdress were covered in colour — blurred scales in warm terracotta — and that there was movement in the colour, a tiny flapping splash of vivid red, and shapes that crawled in a grid of brown and grey, through which — *within which* — she could see the shape of her own arm.

She felt dizzy. She felt that she had woken up to find herself lying on a window. She was in a big wheel of light, in which she could see tiled rooftops, a silver river split by streets, and one familiar roof, oval with a jewelled dome — the Rainbow Opera.

Laura sat up. She found that she was sitting within a circular image of the Isle of the Temple. It was a projection. She turned to the source of the light and looked up into the mirror. Through its dazzle she thought she saw the island, impossibly bright, impossibly compressed.

The candle above the door had gone out.

Laura climbed off the table and pulled the door open. She looked back at the table. The image had disappeared. When she closed the door again, sealing out the light, the image came back.

Laura pushed her blankets off the table, and looked down on the round bird's-eye view of the Isle. She made out the movement of vehicles in streets, pedestrians in the plaza, the quick alteration of sunlight across the face of the river, the streaming speed of a flock of birds passing over the rooftops. She gazed at this small circle of the world surrounded by darkness. She was turned inwards, but looking out. She watched without being seen. It was eerie and wonderful. And, as she circled, peering down, the image very gradually grew darker. The windows of the Isle bristled with gold light, then the streetscape and river turned ghostly and, finally, the chamber went black.

Laura felt her way to the door and opened it on a square of dark-blue twilight air. She fumbled about on the ledge above the door and found another candle and a box of matches. She lit the candle, set it upright and sat on the floor to wait.

Later there was noise and vibration from the ladder, and one of the sisters reappeared, a basket on her back.

Laura gave the sister a hand and helped her into the room.

The nun unpacked food and drink. She said, 'I'm here to feed you and prevent you from sleeping.' And 'Here' — she passed Laura a chamber pot, and a bottle of water.

'Thank you,' said Laura. 'Where's my aunt?'

'I won't answer questions. Would you like to make yourself comfortable now, then replace the lid, rinse your hands and have something to eat?'

Laura did as she was told. She emptied her bladder and washed her hands. The nun had found two seats under the table. She set food before one and watched as Laura ate. Then she lit several more candles, got out some darning and passed Laura a Bible. She asked that Laura read to her as she plied her needle. Acts. Then the Gospel of St Thomas. *'His disciples said to him: On what day will the Kingdom come? Jesus said: Not with watching. They will not say, Lo, here! Or Lo, there! The kingdom of the Father is spread out upon the earth, and men do not see it.'*

Some time during the night Laura picked up a blanket and wrapped it around herself. And some time during the night the nun gave her a lesson with needle and yarn and darning egg. Laura hadn't darned before — nor had she ever worn a darned stocking. She was clumsy; her hands were sore. The sister read to her while she worked.

When they heard the bells in the tower ringing, the sister stopped reading. 'Matins,' she said. 'I'll go now. I was told you could be safely left by morning. I suggest you push that chamber pot well under the table so that you won't risk knocking it over with your foot.' She gathered her darning and the remains of the meal, leaving Laura several apples, a bottle of water and the Bible.

Laura left the door open. She reassembled her bedding, knotted the sleeves of her nightdress again and lay down. She made no attempt to fight sleep. She'd managed perhaps five hours in all — five hours in five days. The nightmare didn't let her stay asleep. She'd had it three times now, when she'd first caught it, then at the Rainbow Opera, then in the late afternoon of the day before. Each time she'd fought her way out, fought as the buried man strained to escape his coffin.

This time her body's need for sleep anchored her in the dream. Her struggle was horribly prolonged. When she was finally able to free herself she could scarcely move. She lay in her twisted bedding and howled with shock and despair.

Once her shuddering had subsided to shivers, Laura's eyes kept trying to shut themselves again, so she got up and went to sit on the sill of the low doorway in the cold morning air. From there she watched the Isle come to life, its bridges fill with cars, carts and pedestrians. She watched the men at work on telegraph poles, putting up wires for the new telephone system that was slowly spreading its way around the city. She watched the smoke of trains passing across the two bridges that linked the west bank to the Isle, and the Isle to the east. This was a commuter line: it came in from Founderston's western suburbs through villas and parks, then past Founderston Girls' Academy. It passed through the district that held the museums, galleries, libraries and government buildings, after which it crossed the river, went through a tunnel built under the wide plaza before the tower of the Regulatory Body and left the Isle by a bridge to the east. The line then passed through the Old Town and terminated at Founderston Central Station, with its marshalling yards, warehouses, station hotels, circling cabs and railway lines on to long-distance destinations. Laura watched all the traffic, and birds passing above and below her. The sun came out of the clouds and warmed her where she sat. She ate an apple.

Mid-morning she felt the vibrations on the ladder and, shortly afterwards, a head appeared over the horizon of the dome. It was Father Roy. He was followed by a man in a white robe, with a golden beard and a square, brimless white hat.

Four

Father Roy remained by the door and the Grand Patriarch, Erasmus Tiebold, advanced around the concave table — the screen for his *camera obscura* — till, realising that the girl would continue to drift away from him, trailing her damaged fingertips around the rim of the tabletop like someone house-proud checking for dust, he came to a standstill and started to talk. He spoke softly. 'I thought I would give you some time to reflect,' he said.

Laura Hame had reached a point equidistant from Father Roy and the patriarch. She stopped and looked at him. 'Where's Aunt Marta?'

'She is at home with Downright and the estimable Mr and Mrs Bridges.'

'So, she left me to you.'

'Yes. You do know that we are kin, Laura? Your Tiebold grandfather was my cousin.'

The girl nodded.

'And, when you sent me a letter you gave me a certain amount of responsibility for you.' The Grand Patriarch produced the letter and laid it on the tabletop. Then he told Father Roy to close the door. Laura stumbled against the wall away from them. But once the door was sealed and the image from the twenty-four-inch lens and forty-inch mirror of the *camera obscura* flowed in full, brilliant colour, the girl came back and stood staring at him, her face lit from below. The Grand Patriarch pointed at the camera housing. 'Can you reach that handle above your head?' he said.

She put her hand on it.

'Give it a turn.'

She had to use both hands, and hang her weight on the handle to bring it down. The camera moved with a hollow rolling noise. The image swam, and the east bank of the Sva swung into the light as the bridges to the west slid away into darkness. Laura stopped winding and looked down on a slightly different slice of the city.

'Does it make you feel godlike?' The Grand Patriarch asked. 'Like a hidden and disembodied witness?'

'No,' said the girl.

The Grand Patriarch touched the image on the tabletop. 'Why did you write to me?'

'I wrote to the director of the Regulatory Body and the editor of the *Founderston Herald* as well.'

'And none of the letters was signed with your name?'

'No. They are all signed "Lazarus", and I had someone else copy them out for me.'

'Why disown what you chose to do?'

'I did what my father asked me to do. It was his idea. There wasn't any other way.'

'I can't question your father about his motives, but perhaps you can answer for him.'

'I want to *go*!' Laura said, plaintive. 'I need to go In and overwrite this nightmare. I'm so tired my heart won't slow down. What will happen when I can't make myself wake up? I don't know what happens in the *end*. But the man in the coffin never gets out. He dies in there. He takes a long time to die. I don't want to go on and dream that.'

'So — is that what you caught? A man trapped in a coffin until he dies?'

Laura Hame blinked at him. She looked surprised and momentarily relieved. 'No. I didn't catch the nightmare to its end. I woke up before I got there.'

'Then I don't see how you can dream a death you didn't catch,' the Grand Patriarch said, practical. 'Laura, I want to talk to you about what you've done.'

The girl sighed and shrugged. 'My letter explains it.'

'Well then, according to your letter, you wanted to gain support for people who were being terrorised?'

Laura nodded.

'And in order to do that you chose to terrorise people?'

She stared at him, sullen. 'What other way was there to show them? How else could I prove it? I didn't have any evidence. I couldn't take *photographs* of what was happening.'

The Grand Patriarch paced back and forth for a moment, thinking. He ran his hand along the table through rooftops and courtyards, streets, flights of steps, waterways, hurrying people. 'In my grandparents' day no one was taking photographs. Do you think that the people back then believed that testimony — to any crime — needed photographic evidence to support it? Are people now any less inclined to listen to testimony? To listen in good faith?'

'You would say "faith",' the girl said, insolent, but without any great energy.

'Faith doesn't just mean faith in God, Laura. It means faith in people, in the truth, in truth-telling. Faith in your own ability to make yourself heard. Faith that people will understand what you take the time to explain to them. Faith that people don't need to be tricked, or *sold* the truth.'

'I wanted to do what Da told me to. He left me a letter asking me to do what I did. I followed his wishes. I kept faith with him.'

The Grand Patriarch studied the girl before him. 'Do you think you did the right thing?'

'I was *asked*. And it wasn't just Da. I kept catching dreams about convicts. Why would I dream about convicts unless the Place wanted me to help them too?'

'You caught dreams about convicts?'

'I found convicts in dreams. Sometimes it seemed they *found me*. I did what I could. I could only think to do what Da asked me to.' Laura sounded quite desperate. She pressed her forearms into her stomach so hard that she stooped. She seemed to be trying to hold herself together. Then she took a deep, shuddering breath, straightened up and said, 'Besides, if you could do something that no one else could, wouldn't you have to find your own way of acting in the world?'

'I can't think what you might mean,' said the Grand Patriarch. 'Unless you're boasting — as dreamhunters do — about the size of your penumbra?' He shook his head, and saw that she was echoing his gesture. 'Tell me, how does "finding a new way" match up with "just doing what your father asked you to do"?'

'Maybe I found a new father,' she said, and gave a little wild laugh.

The Grand Patriarch's assessing stare was so prolonged and intent that Laura dropped her gaze. Then she heard Father Roy shuffling his feet. When the Grand Patriarch resumed his questions his tone was careful, almost gentle. 'Your aunt says that the letter you sent me was not in your own hand. Did you therefore mean to get away with it?'

Laura nodded.

'And you involved someone else in your plans?'

'Someone copied the letters for me.'

'Your cousin?'

'No!' Laura was horrified. 'I wouldn't do that to Rose! This was my responsibility. But I've done enough now and I don't want to do any more. Everyone knows now. Someone else can figure out what to do next.' She stamped her foot, in petulance and frustration and weary misery.

The Grand Patriarch told her to calm herself. Father Roy approached her and handed her a handkerchief. She took it, spread it open, and held it against her face. The wounds on her lips had reopened, and they printed the white cotton with bright red blotches.

'There are dreamhunters who get on the wrong side of the Regulatory Body,' the Grand Patriarch told her. 'And I've tried to help them. They've confided in me — misgivings, fears, rumours.'

Laura removed the handkerchief and licked her bleeding lips.

The Grand Patriarch said, 'Have you ever heard of a dream named Contentment?'

She shook her head. 'It doesn't sound like a nightmare.'

'No, it doesn't. Have you heard of the Depot?'

'That's a funny name for a dream,' she said. 'Dream names tend to be descriptive.'

'I don't know that it *is* a dream.' The man regarded her steadily. Laura could see he was weighing something in his mind. He said, 'Do you know what a master dream is?'

'No, not really.'

'You may have "done enough", Laura, but you don't *know* enough.' The Grand Patriarch shook his head. 'The Regulatory Body sends you off into the Place with signal whistles, but without a full education!'

The Grand Patriarch watched the Hame girl, feeling vexed and sad. He found her lack of shame deeply offensive. The sullen set of her battered mouth, the stubborn ego looking out of her eyes.

But when she answered back he was less offended than surprised by her coldness. 'This isn't about what I know,' she said. 'What I did at the Opera will open a public discussion. We will all soon know more.' She spoke as though she were an angel guarding the gates to Eden.

The Grand Patriarch took a deep breath and began to rethink his approach. He wanted to help this girl more than he wanted simply to ease her misery. She had been left to find her own way — orphaned, and formidably gifted. She had gone off the rails, as they say, but in her own peculiar way. She might have gone looking for love and ended up in some unsuitable entanglement. She might have gone looking to forget and drugged herself with dreams or drink. Instead she'd found refuge in this hard, self-righteous autonomy. Though she was clearly suffering, in a way her heart had stopped. To Erasmus Tiebold it was clear that he must find some way to start her heart up again. And he must do it before he sent her to her father. Hame could help his daughter just by turning out to be alive. Finding her father should restore the girl's faith in the general shape of her life. But, right now, looking at Laura, Erasmus Tiebold felt that he was watching water set into ice. There were forces at work, altering her soul — the nightmare itself, the act of sharing it and her obvious terrible loneliness.

The Grand Patriarch had an inspiration then. He said, 'Laura, you haven't injured me. But I'd like you to explain to someone you have injured why you felt you had to do what you did.'

'I'm sure I couldn't make any worse job of it than I already have,' Laura said, brisk and unfeeling.

The Grand Patriarch retrieved the letter. He turned away, touched Father Roy's arm and conducted him out. Once they were down the stairwell Erasmus Tiebold said to his secretary, 'She'll need clothes for her journey. Let's have her cousin deliver them to her.'

Five

The dreamhunters were huddled in a dispirited group at one corner of the porch of the rangers' station at Doorhandle. No one was standing anywhere near them. Around their feet were their dust-covered packs and bedrolls. They had been In to get Beautiful Horse. But none of them had been able to catch it.

Buried Alive *was*, it turned out, a 'master dream' and could not be overwritten. It had to be endured for six to eight nights at least. The dreamhunters were waiting to be escorted out to the Regulatory Body's dream retreats, cabins on the near slopes of the Heliograph Ranges. They were 'guests of the Body', detained, and guarded by rangers.

The Chief Ranger appeared to explain the delay. He was having trouble finding volunteers. Rangers were not normally so skittish, but the combination of newspaper reports on the riot, and the sight of these dreamhunters emerging from the Place with freshly bleeding mouths, had proved a little too much for some. 'They're behaving like novice dreamhunters with superstitious tales of fatally indelible dreams.' He spread his hands, made a gesture of helplessness. 'I'm sure you'd rather *not* be escorted by men I had to force.'

Grace asked if she'd have time to send another wire.

'Certainly, Mrs Tiebold.'

Sandy asked if he could go with Grace to the telegraph office, then said, as he fell into step with her, 'I want a word with you in private.'

Grace pulled a paper from the pocket of her long silk coat and handed it to him. It was a message she'd received earlier. Sandy smoothed the paper out against his chest. He read:

LAURA IN MARTAS CARE STOP SHE DID NOT SLEEP STOP ONLY FRIGHTENED STOP ROSE

Sandy read the telegram twice then hurried to catch up with Grace. 'Where is Mr Tiebold?'

'I don't know,' Grace said. 'And Rose didn't bother to tell me where *she* is — though I'm told she's back at school. Still, that is what you wanted to know, isn't it? Where Laura is?'

'When I found Rose outside the Opera I could see she hadn't slept. She said Laura hadn't, either. I guess they were talking.'

The telegraph office was brightly lit. There was one keyman and two clerks in the booth. Grace stood at a counter in the centre of the room and wrote her message. 'Do you have any money on you?' she asked Sandy.

'Yes.'

'Have you wired your parents? They might be worried. They'll have seen your Uncle George's name in the papers.'

Sandy shrugged. He said, 'I'm reluctant to wire my parents. My father's attitude will be that since I've decided to take up a "frivolous and unproductive" life, I deserve any difficulties my decision brings me.'

'He'd really say that?'

'Probably.'

'We'll be detained for a week,' Grace said. 'Or, at least, *you* will.' She went up to the cage and pushed her message and money under the bars. Then she and Sandy trailed back to the others.

Maze Plasir's apprentice was sitting on the steps, rocking back and forth, his face wet with tears. George Mason leaned towards Grace and said, 'If I were Plasir I'd be on my way here already to protect my investment.' He nodded at the weeping boy.

'Plasir seems to go through apprentices pretty quickly.'

'Do you think he will come?' said Mason.

'I've offered him a lot of money,' said Grace.

'For what?' Sandy was bemused.

His uncle said, 'Several of Plasir's dreams are master dreams. He can catch, say, Secret Room and overwrite this nightmare. Would you like me to send him on to you, Alexander? I've contributed something towards Plasir's fee, but obviously Mrs. Tiebold is first in line.'

'Plasir might not agree,' said Grace.

'Well, if he does decide to, you'd better make sure our guards know to direct him to us,' said Mason.

Grace nodded and went indoors in search of the Chief Ranger.

'I can't contribute anything towards Plasir's fee,' Sandy said. The idea of being alone in the forest with Maze Plasir made him feel queasy.

Plasir was a Gifter: he could take his own memories of real people's faces and manners and graft them onto the characters in the dreams he caught. He was often employed by people who wanted what they couldn't have, and his repertoire included dreams that weren't at all respectable. Plasir wasn't respectable, though he did have powerful friends.

Sandy said to his uncle, 'I'd better just tough it out.'

'It's your funeral,' said Mason, and chuckled at his own black humour.

Grace returned, followed by a group of grim-faced rangers. One clapped his hands to get their attention. The drooping, hollow-eyed dreamhunters started with fright. 'Get up!' the ranger ordered. His men scooped up their packs and bedrolls. They were led away from the station and out of the village. Five rangers walked before the dreamhunters, setting the pace, and five brought up the rear.

Sandy felt herded and corralled. But he was the son of a shop steward in a factory that made flax matting. He had been raised in a house with strong views on the rights of working people. 'You know what we need?' he whispered to his uncle as they tramped along. 'We need a union.'

Six

Rose came in alone with Laura's bag and pulled the little door to behind her, as if she didn't want what she had to say to get out into the open air. She at once began to speak — commencing an attack. A few moments later Laura, thinking to confound her cousin, wet her finger and thumb, and closed them on the wick of the room's single candle.

'Laura!' Rose was enraged. And then she looked down into the light on the table, the world in miniature, perfect but for the distortion at its edges. Laura monitored her cousin's face for amazement, waiting for Rose's set, righteous look to soften.

Rose stared at the streets, beetling traffic and brushstrokes of flocking pigeons. She continued to look grim, staring through the world as though it were an apparition. She said, 'To think I believed you were telling me everything. That you'd let me in on what you were planning. But all you told me was what you were *feeling*. If we are friends, do you imagine that our friendship is just made up of shared feelings?'

'If I didn't talk to you about my dreamhunting, that's only because I thought it was better not to speak about what you'd missed out on.'

'Do you think that's what I'm talking about? Your sparing my feelings by not tantalising me with dreamhunter stories? Are you listening to me? I'm not even talking about what you chose to do — you may have had very good, considered reasons for bringing that nightmare to the Opera. But, Laura, I can't believe that you didn't tell me about that — that *thing*!'

Laura thought it better to pretend that she didn't know what Rose was talking about. She knitted her brow. 'Thing?'

'The monster. The statue. The thing that carried you off.'

'That was the nightmare. Part of the horrible dream.'

'I didn't sleep, Laura! You made *sure* I didn't sleep. You put Wakeful in my musk creams. I was awake, and I know what I saw.'

'Do you? You have to realise, Rose, that my talent has made me different from you.' Laura said. 'I'm not as susceptible to —'

'Lots of people have talent. Lots of people have things that make them different. But, you know, even if we shared every aspect of our lives, the difference between you and me was still going to be huge, not because you're *talented*, but because you believe that our differences are more important than what we have in common.'

Laura looked at Rose and wondered whether her cousin was going to cry. Rose was so worked up. Laura had always been the weepy one. Now she felt dry, deadened and suspended.

'So, I don't want to hear about your God-given talent. Especially since you are just going to stand there lying to me!'

Laura stood silent, thinking about the Hame inheritance: 'The Measures', her servant. She fought her urge to explain and, fighting it, realised that she wasn't finished, that there was more to do. After a while she said, 'When I go to the Place I feel that I might be able to catch a dream that will make sense of my whole life. Not of other people's lives. Just my own. It isn't that I think I'm different. It's that I have to deal with actually being different — with things that have changed me.'

'Listen to you,' Rose said. 'Even now all you're doing is talking about your bloody feelings.'

Laura shook her head. She was too tired to properly understand what Rose was saying to her. She doggedly went back to her explanation. Why wouldn't her cousin just let her get this said?

'Try to imagine it was you. Try to imagine that your Ma and Da disappeared and all you were left with was a letter saying what you were expected to do. Try to imagine that you did something that you knew was impossible — but it felt right. It felt like gravity. Not like a mystery and a terror, but like a secret wrapped around its own solution. Rose, I *know* I can be impulsive. But I couldn't see to do anything other than what Da told me to. And setting out to do it was like crossing a narrow bridge over a chasm — I couldn't stop, I couldn't look down. And I had to think my gift came to me because *someone* thought I should have it. That it was God-given.'

Laura was aware that Rose did not believe in God. All her life Laura had wavered between her cousin and uncle's atheism, and her father's faith. Now she was firmly in her father's camp. If 'The Measures' had not come from God — where had they come from?

Rose said, 'You think you've stolen fire from Heaven.'

Laura waited. Then she nodded. She nodded to say she accepted that Rose's view was fair and might well be right.

Rose just looked at her, bleak. 'Laura, you haven't told me anything. You don't trust me. Clearly you're not the person I thought you were. Or you're not the person you once were.'

Laura said, weakly, 'People change.'

But Rose had raised a hand to stop her speaking. 'The point is — honestly — that I don't know whether I trust you any more. Or even *like* you.'

Laura's face clenched and two cold tears slid down her cheeks. 'I don't believe you, Rose.'

'You'd better believe me.' Rose pushed the bag across the table. 'Have a safe journey,' she said, then left the turret room.

Seven

Chorley found his daughter at her school. He met her in the principal's office and walked her out into the quad, where they stood under a peach tree whose buds had just cracked to show tight, spotless tips of pink blossom. Rose stood a little way from him, and slipped her hands under the bib of her pleated pinafore to warm them. She wouldn't meet his eyes. 'You're going to ask me where Laura is. You know, if I had a dollar for everyone who's asked me that, I'd be rolling in it.'

'I know where Laura is. I've been to the Temple. Father Roy told me that at his request, you delivered some of her clothes.'

Rose was looking at him now. It was a careful, self-contained look, and very grown-up. 'For her journey,' she said.

'Yes. They're sending her off somewhere safe. To join her father — whom I've seen.'

'Oh,' said Rose. She blinked. She stretched out the toe of one highly polished shoe and pushed it through a puddle to make ripples. 'Laura didn't know about *that* when I saw her.'

'They plan to tell her when she's well on her way. They're worried about her state of mind, and I think it suits them to keep her subdued.'

'Yes, I can see that.'

'Darling?' Chorley said. He felt as if he'd dropped a stone down a well and hadn't heard either a clatter or a splash.

'So Uncle Tziga's alive?' Rose said, then she looked into Chorley's face, her expression open and wondering. Chorley reached for her and drew her to him. His earlobe brushed across the top of her head and he realised she'd grown since he'd last held her. She was hugging him now — hard — so that his breathing was a little constricted. 'I've been worried that Ma will be really angry with you,' Rose said. 'And with Laura.'

'I doubt your mother will be angry with me when I tell her I've found Tziga. I'd have come home sooner, only where I was they get five days' worth of newspapers only every five days. When Tziga read about the riot and nightmare, he said, "It's Laura." And I shouted at him.'

A sharp gust of wind swept over the roofs around the quad and altered the air pressure in the enclosed space. The peach tree seemed to throw up its branches in surprise, and drops of water rained down on father and daughter.

Chorley said, 'Tziga has a head injury. He has fits. It doesn't do to upset him.'

Rose drew back and looked into his face. 'How did he hurt his head?'

Chorley looked away. He couldn't meet his daughter's eyes. He tried to control his face and his feelings.

'Da?'

'I don't expect your mother back for several days yet.'

'Da?'

'No,' said Chorley. 'I'll tell you when I understand more.'

'Uncle Tziga is hiding from the Body,' Rose said. 'The Body supplies the Department of Corrections with nightmares.'

Chorley was startled. 'How do you know that?'

'Maze Plasir told Laura and me. We went to see him. That letter Laura tore up suggested she talk to Plasir. And it told her to do what she did — to catch a nightmare and overdream Ma at the Rainbow Opera. It was Uncle Tziga's idea. But, Da, Laura *lied* to me.' Rose's voice went high and tight. 'She lied to me,' she said again. Her father could see she was fighting tears. 'She didn't trust me enough to tell me what she meant to do. She mixed Wakeful into my Farry's musk creams so that I wouldn't sleep. She thought she was doing me a big favour, but she kept me out of everything, and when I confronted her she lied. *To me!* And I can't even talk about it properly till I have proof about what she's hiding. It's like I have to lie too, or look crazy.'

'The Hames —' Chorley began, trying to organise his thoughts about the Hames, the three he knew, anyway — morbid, dramatic, close-mouthed and apt at times to act like divinely appointed judges. 'You can't be too angry at Laura. Her father left her, and wrote a letter saying do this and do that. It was as if he'd told her she'd failed him somehow and had to make it up to him. She can't have wanted any of this.'

'I don't know. I didn't have the nightmare, Da. It made everyone crazy, but Uncle Tziga could always hold big, forceful, awesome dreams in his head without going out of his mind. For all we know, Laura might *not* have hated it.'

'Rose, Tziga *did* go out of his mind.' Chorley touched her arm. He wanted to reassure her. And he didn't want to tell her that her uncle had tried to kill himself. 'Besides,' he said, 'it wasn't just that Laura's father told her what to do, it was also a matter of her conscience. What the Regulatory Body and Department of Corrections are doing is *wrong*. Within the letter of the law, but wrong. And there's more to it. They must be up to illegal things as well — more than just forging Tziga's signature in the Doorhandle Intentions Book. I'm hoping the Grand Patriarch will eventually trust me enough to let me know all he suspects.'

Rose shuffled her feet and scowled at her father. 'Those bloody pledge-takers,' she said. She was talking about the swelling ranks of those who, inspired by the preaching of the Temple, had sworn off sharing dreams.

'The Grand Patriarch calls them his Ark.'

'So we'll all be drowned and they'll be saved?' Rose was exasperated. 'The Grand Patriarch thinks sharing dreams is sinful and we'll all be punished one day for doing it — struck down by a righteous God. The Regulatory Body may be up to no good, but there's nothing wrong with Ma or Mr Mason or the Rainbow Opera. *I'm* not throwing the baby out with the bathwater on the recommendation of some bearded ninny!'

Chorley burst out laughing.

Rose glared at him. 'Truth and justice are scarcely *ever* the property of religion!' she snapped. 'You taught me that! And if a pack of mangy convicts needs our help, let's help them because it's the right thing to do, not because God loves them!'

The school principal, a tiny woman, rushed with brisk little steps into the quad. 'Rose Tiebold! I hope you are not shouting at your father. Academy girls *do not* take that tone with their elders.'

'Bearded ninny,' Chorley muttered, sniggering. 'Mangy convicts.'

'I'm sorry, ma'am,' said Rose to her principal. Then, irrepressible, 'but he's a sore trial to me.'

'That's enough of that, my girl!' The principal shot the sniggering Chorley a quelling look. She said to him, 'It would be far better for Rose if, when she's rude, she weren't so confident that she's also amusing.'

'Yes, I see.' Chorley wiped his eyes.

'Is this interview over?' the principal inquired, tartly.

'Yes,' said Chorley. 'I have to go home and burn my Darwin.'

'Da!' Rose squeaked, and they both started giggling again.

'Rose! Mr Tiebold! Please!'

Chorley took the principal's hand and shook it. 'Thank you for your time, and your concern,' he said. He gazed into her eyes.

'Well — er — yes,' the principal said, then stood blushing and flustered as Chorley turned and left them.

Eight

The man in the chair before Cas Doran's desk was tired of answering the same questions, of giving answers that couldn't satisfy anyone, even himself.

'The assailant smashed the lights and broke the doors,' he said. 'He was wearing a mask. Or he had dirt on his face and a black mask tied across his eyes. He was wrapped up in something thick and squishy. His body felt soft when he knocked me down. He was there one moment, then gone the next. It was dark all along the second tier. Mrs Tiebold was shouting at us because a mob was after Mr Mason. I sent my men down to see what they could do for Mason — then, shortly after that, the police arrived. I didn't see where our assailant went.'

Secretary Doran was silent for so long that the former head of the Rainbow Opera's fire watch finally raised his face.

'Whoever he was, he was awake before the dream ended,' Doran said. 'Or he hadn't slept at all.'

The man nodded.

'A coat, a hat, padded clothes, well built, masked, perhaps six and a half foot in height, you say?'

'Yes. And he was gritty, as though he'd been lying on the ground.'

'The doors were hanging off their hinges. The door frames were splintered. How do you think that happened?'

'I saw that later,' the man said. He looked miserable. 'I don't know how it happened. I should have ordered the alarm bells rung as soon as the screaming started. We just watched Mrs Tiebold fighting it — the nightmare. We couldn't understand at first that everyone was doing the same. I've never seen a dreamhunter with a nightmare.' The man made claws of his hands and touched his pallid, unmarked cheeks.

Cas Doran's hand went to his own face and the stiff rows of adhesive bandages.

'It was an emergency. We weren't meant to stand by amazed,' the man said — then, 'Will I be prosecuted?'

'That's up to your manager, and the police.'

Grace arrived home earlier than Chorley expected, battered and dirty. He was able to tell her that Laura was no longer at her Aunt Marta's, but was safe, and Rose was back at school.

'I'll want to talk to Laura,' Grace said.

Chorley opened his mouth to explain that that might be difficult, and why, but Grace interrupted him. 'I'm going to have a bath,' she said.

Half an hour later Chorley carried a tray upstairs — soup in a cup, buttered toast, coffee. He put a stool by the tub and set the tray on it.

Grace said, 'I'm going to catch the express to Sisters Beach tonight. I've got a copy of Secret Room. It's somewhat spicy, so I'd better not give it to our neighbours. Summerfort is far enough from other houses. The dream isn't at my full size — something to do with Plasir's teensy-weensy penumbra, which I might say may be tiny, but is as black and deep as a well.'

'You slept with Plasir?'

'Yes, dear. Out in the woods, too.'

Chorley took deep breaths.

'Only a master dream can erase a master dream,' Grace said. 'I was lucky. Plasir already had Secret Room. He went In on St Lazarus's Eve, apparently. He told me that St Lazarus's Day is a good day for him to go dreamhunting since no one wants his performances on family holidays.' Grace smirked. 'Anyway, I checked the Intentions Book before I caught the coach from Doorhandle. Plasir did go In shortly before midnight, almost as though he wanted an alibi.'

'You can't seriously think Plasir had anything to do with the nightmare? With his parlour-sized penumbra?'

'I don't know what I think.' Grace emptied the soup cup and started on the toast and coffee. She told Chorley she wanted him to come to Summerfort with her. 'You'll enjoy Secret Room.' She looked at him, cool. 'You should be grateful that I want you to come. You must know I'm angry with you.'

Chorley nodded. Then he smiled. And it wasn't a smile of gratitude or reassurance, but of plain happiness. 'And I bet you could do with some really good news,' he said.

Nine

Laura left the Temple after five days. She promised not to sleep on the train. She was accompanied by the nuns who had looked after her, and by Father Roy, who said — once they had boarded the train and closed the door of their compartment — that they were going with her only as far as Westport.

'Is this an express?' Laura asked. 'I had hoped we'd stop at Aunt Marta's.'

'Your aunt has been included in every decision made on your behalf,' said Father Roy. 'She knows where you're going.' He watched the girl withdraw into a corner of the seat then into the folds of her black winter coat. She looked like some animal backing into its burrow.

Shortly before the express passed Marta Hame's station Laura got up and went out into the corridor.

Father Roy observed her.

She stood, her cheek laid on the window, and watched the stop come up. Her eyes were fixed on a hill near Marta Hame's house, a hill with a crest of black pines. Laura stared as the hill loomed, then flicked a glance at the compartment. Her eyes were bright and furtive. She left the window and hurried away along the jostling carriage.

Father Roy jumped up, threw open the compartment door and ran after her. She was at the end of the carriage hauling with her whole weight on the red-painted handle of the emergency brake

— which, fortunately, had not been designed with a child's strength in mind.

Father Roy threw himself at Laura and tore her away from the handle. She turned on him, hitting him with her fists.

The sisters joined him and helped him subdue her as gently as they could. As they hustled her back into the compartment, her head turned to follow the sight of that hill, sliding from window to window then retreating back along the track.

They closed the compartment door, and sat her down.

'I have to see him,' she said.

'You will be allowed to write to your friends. So long as you're careful what you say,' Father Roy told her. He thought: 'And we will read your letters. And perhaps discover who is in this with you. Whose strength you're looking to now. Who the *real* Lazarus is.'

Part VIII
Foreigner's North

One

Four weeks after the Rainbow Opera riot, Sandy Mason received a letter. Its envelope was postmarked 'Westport Central Post Office'. The letter was sent care of Mrs. Lilley at Sandy Mason's boarding house in Doorhandle, and he had to retrieve it under the watchful eye of his landlady's daughters.

The Lilley girls had a constant parade of young and homesick dreamhunters pass under their noses. They were choosy about whom they would pay special attention to, offer treats and flirt with. Alexander Mason at nineteen already had one good dream registered in his name. He had good prospects, and the Lilley girls were determined to cultivate him. When the letter arrived the sisters at once got their hands on it. They had a look at the handwriting on the envelope and decided it was from 'that Hame girl' — that sullen, flat-chested thing whom Sandy Mason, for some unfathomable reason, admired. The Lilley girls didn't hide Laura's letter, for they were principled schemers. But they did make sure they were present when Sandy retrieved it from the stack of mail on the hall table so that they could watch his reaction.

Sandy Mason was big, but surefooted. And yet, the moment he glanced at the envelope, he stumbled and knocked his knee on the newel post. He stood frozen at the foot of the stairs and gazed at what he held in his hand. Then he tore the envelope open, while bounding on up the stairs. A second envelope dropped out on the landing and he stooped to pick it up, then straightened slowly, staring at its address. Then he began to read the other pages while still stopped on the landing. His hand trembled. He walked slowly out of the Lilley girls' sight.

The girls' mother came out of her sitting room. 'Was that Mr Mason? Did he get his letter?'

'Yes, Mother.'

Mrs Lilley regarded her girls sharply. The girls were at their most refined when dealing with — or even thinking about — Alexander Mason. She wasn't sure which one of them had decided to snare him, or whether they were still sorting it out between them.

'Mother?' said one. 'Are Miss Hame's aunt and uncle still paying for her room?'

The letter was from Miss Hame, of course. Mrs Lilley had recognised Laura's handwriting. 'Yes. And that's their business — but I must say that girl's had the slowest start of any dreamhunter I've ever lodged.' Mrs Lilley went into her kitchen, leaving her girls in peace and smirking at one another.

Laura's letter was careful, coded and chatty.

> *Dear Sandy,*
>
> *I'm sorry I didn't have more to say to you last time we met. I just hadn't expected to see you there. I'm sorry for the trouble, and for any worry I caused you.*
>
> *I am mostly quite contented just now. It is very peaceful here. And I keep myself busy. Today, for instance, we all took a cart out along the shore to pick up the seaweed that came up with the spring tide on the last full moon. It's had a week now to dry and reduce. The men bale it up and store it all summer under the houses. It sits between the house piles in stiff tangles with shiny glass fishing buoys among it. They use seaweed as kindling and burn coal all winter. There's hardly any firewood.*
>
> *I was on light duties with the seaweed. It was more my job to keep an eye on two little girls — six and eight. They really know more than I do about (for example) the quicksand one*

should never walk on, or how one should never get between a sea-lion and the sea. (There are sea-lions resting up along the coast here. Sick or injured ones among them. We saw one seal yesterday with huge gashes from a shark, or a killer whale.)

There's a big boy here too — actually he's about my age, but seems younger. He applauds diving gannets as if they are performing for him. He is a little odd and wrapped up in himself. He talks and talks and never seems to know when anyone has had enough. On the seaweed expedition we girls were supposed to be having a sleep under the cart, but he kept us awake telling us that this was why motor cars were no good and how Southland could never have been settled at all if people on the plains hadn't been able to take shelter under their wagons. He reminds me a little of you in that he is so full of information. But you are far better at imparting it!

I will write to Rose too, and Aunt Grace, but it is you I have chosen to trust with a task. I want you to do one thing for me. I want you to take the enclosed letter to a certain place. You must catch a train going out towards Westport and get off at the little station at Glass Eye Creek. Then walk up the road past my Aunt Marta's house. As you come past the house you will see a hill with a pine plantation. I want you to climb up to the forest and go a short way into the pines and leave the letter lying on the ground. Then go away immediately.

Will you do that? It would mean the world to me.

I promise that I will see you again before too long.

You are my dear and trusted friend.

Laura

Sandy read the letter through several times. He realised Laura had given him enough clues for him to guess that she might well be at the lighthouse on So Long Spit. But was she giving him directions? Did she want him to visit her?

As he stood reading, a blush of pleasure had crept through him, heating his skin and robbing his legs of strength. He sat down on his bed, and turned his attention to the second sealed envelope, which was addressed simply: 'From Laura'.

Sandy stared at the white square, the two black-inked words. *From Laura* — as if Laura were the only real attachment the intended recipient of the letter had in all the world.

Sandy thought: 'Someone walks up to the wood every day to check for a message from Laura.' But surely not Marta Hame, whom, after all, Laura had mentioned in her instructions for the letter's delivery.

Sandy's skin began to cool. He seemed to cool and congeal all over. He went sour, sitting there.

Eventually he got up, stuffed the unopened letter into his pocket, and went down to the kitchen, where he was fed titbits by Mrs Lilley, and courted by her daughters, and where he helped peel potatoes till, finally, he was left alone with the steaming kettle.

Sandy held the envelope in the fume from the kettle's spout until the already dimpled paper dimpled more, and its glue softened. He unsealed the flap of the envelope then fled upstairs, shut himself in his room, drew out the single sheet of paper and unfolded it with hands that were shaking so violently that the Lilley girls would have been amazed by it — and frightened of him.

He read:

> *I'm sorry to take so long to get word to you. They carried me away. Please come to me. I am where the boy on the shore was in the dream I told you about. My first dream.*
>
> *I want you to come at once. I feel I must say 'please' and call you 'my dear' because you will no longer take orders from me.*
> *My dear. Mine still. Please.*
>
> *I should have gone with you. I should have listened to you on the train. I should have let you look after me. Without you I'm afraid of everything. I think I have put my heart outside of my body.*

Partway through reading the letter Sandy went cold, and his gorge rose, and he had to press his hand to his mouth. He tried to control himself, but couldn't. A moment later he was grovelling under his bed after his chamber pot, which he never used and which was covered in dust. He vomited into it. He stayed on his hands and knees till the retching had passed. Then he began to cry, dropping clear tears into the mess of regurgitated tea and toast. He hadn't cried in years, so did it perilously, like a busted machine whose cogs no longer meshed; painfully, straining his scalded throat; helplessly, because his feelings possessed him completely — grief, and jealousy as burning and bitter as acid.

Two

The troublemaker was taken on a long train journey from his prison in Canning to another, a prison at the end of a long pier. He knew he was in the north because it was warmer. Westport was where they sent all the hard men. Westport and the government mine.

The prison governor had a look at him, then he was left in his shackles, sitting before a desk in a locked room. After a time a man joined him: a man in a suit and bowler hat with one of those gold fraternity pins winking in his lapel. The man sat down and studied the papers in the file he carried with him. Then he closed the file, folded his hands, fixed the troublemaking convict with the clouded jellies of his eyes and began to talk. He talked about 'the rehabilitation of an ailing character'. He talked about 'criminality' and 'being tempted to take shortcuts to prosperity'. He talked about 'the cleansing sweat of honest work'. He said, 'You have shown an antisocial resistance to what, however *demanding*, amounted to a course of treatment. And so your treatment must be more aggressive, and tailored to your particular difficulties.'

The troublemaker's particular difficulty was that he didn't understand why this person was talking to him. Was the man a warden, or a doctor?

The man put his hat back on, gathered his papers and left the room. The wardens returned and took the troublemaker to another solitary cell. This one had a barred window, a covered bucket, a table and chair — dinner already there, lukewarm, but plenty of it — and a bed with a rolled mattress.

The convict ate. His tray was removed. Just before the lights went out a warden came by and told him he could now unroll his mattress, and bed down. The convict liked the look of the mattress — it was thicker than any he'd had before, and they had given him an extra blanket, though it was the warmest night he'd felt in a long time.

He lay down. Whatever was to come next — the coal mine, or more puzzling talk — it wouldn't come till tomorrow.

The Lifer was part of a work gang who were building a bridge. For twenty years he had laboured on the roads, in the coal mine at Westport, and in the copper mines on Shackle Island. He had worked till he couldn't straighten his fingers any more. Now he was among men on light sentences: the odd character who had strangled all his neighbour's hens, a light-fingered storeman, and a young man who had smashed the window of a pawnbroker's in order to steal his own hocked violin. He was a murderer among milder men, but old and harmless now, and on easy work. The others laughed when he told them this. One asked, 'What easy work is there these days even for free men — with convicts building all the roads and bridges? I started my sentence picking fruit. So who would pay wages to fruit pickers?'

There was something in this. When the Lifer had worked in the coal mine, the only free men were skilled labour: engineers and those who set explosive charges. He told his fellow convicts this. Then they were all talking about the savings a mine owner made and profit pouring back into the penal system.

'The whole country's a prison,' said the violin thief. 'I didn't know that before. But I won't forget it again.'

The violin thief was a month from the end of his sentence. The guards trusted him. He was the one who got to work in the tent in the water meadow by the bridge site. They even trusted him to sharpen the mason's chisels. The thief was fresh that afternoon because he'd been in the mason's tent and out of the worst of the heat. (When he'd come back to the bridge he'd stood smiling at the Lifer while the guards reattached his shackles. The smile really wasn't for anyone, but only seemed to say, 'Nearly now. I'm nearly free, nearly home.')

The Lifer was faint with the heat. It was April, and the farmers in the valley had been burning stubble, and the stumps of trees in fields freshly cut from the forest. Smoke hung over the valley and magnified the sun rather than filtered it. The Lifer asked for water. A guard brought the dipper. The water had a tang of burned blackwood. The old man tried to take his time but the dipper was snatched out of his hands. Half the water splashed onto the ground.

'Get on with it,' the guard said, and gave him a shove. The Lifer went back to work. He and the violin thief lifted another shaped block from a stack, they checked its number, and carried it to the balustrade, to the gap it was made to fit.

'Are you all right?' the young thief asked.

And that was when it happened. The Lifer's head was swimming in the heat, his cramped hands were slippery with sweat and spilled water. His grip on the chiselled sandstone failed and instead of easing the stone into its slot, he let it go so that it slammed down on one corner. The thief's hands lost it too, and it teetered, then tipped over the rail and into the river. It disappeared into the weeds that grew on the river bottom. Weeds that flowed like combed hair in the river channel and, nearer the bank, pressed against the surface of the water like hair bundled into a hair-net.

The guards heard the splash and came to look. They craned over the rail. 'Where did it fall?' one asked.

'How do you suppose you are going to fetch that up out of there?' said another.

The guards pushed the Lifer and the thief, jostled them about between their fists and feet and rifle butts.

The mason appeared to inspect the damage. The stone beside the gap was cracked. 'The one in the water is probably chipped too,' he said. 'They'll both have to be replaced.'

'Do you hear that?' a guard said, and shoved the thief again. 'You'll both have to be replaced.'

'The stones,' the mason said, dogged and irritated. 'I meant the stones.'

'We could have this scum wade in from the riverbank to get it out,' said the overseer.

'Yes. I would like to take a look at it,' the mason said.

'But if you're sure it's ruined . . .' the thief began, and was struck in the mouth. He was quiet for a while after that, his top lip skewered by a broken tooth.

The guards turned on the Lifer and pushed him along the bridge and onto the road. He scuttled, pursued by blows, down the bank to the river's edge. He protected his head with his arms, then fell to his knees on the soggy ground and stared at the water. Its shallows were thick with curdled weeds. The thief dropped down beside him. The young man's chin and throat were coated red. Over their heads a guard said, 'Which of you was it dropped the block?'

'It was him,' said the young thief. 'Look at his hands. He can't keep a firm hold of anything.' He sounded desperate.

'All right, old man. Get in there.' The guard put his boot in the small of the Lifer's back.

'Remove his shackles, for God's sake!' the young man pleaded.

'Fine,' said a guard. 'You can go, since you're so concerned for his well-being.' The guard kicked the thief, who splashed into the water's edge and caught himself on his hands. Black mud oozed up between his fingers till his hands were buried. The young man turned to the guards, eyes glimmering with fear. He edged around so that his feet and shackled ankles entered the water first. He crept backward, his hands groping and slithering on the sopping turf. He was looking into the Lifer's eyes, and his gaze said, 'No. Not now. Not when I'm nearly free.'

When he was up to his hips in the weeds his feet slipped. His eyes flared with terror and he sank his fingers into the turf. He heaved and grappled his way back up the bank, clawing the thick coating of moss from the ground. He came out wallowing in mud, his front coated and face dappled. He lay on the bank, gasping, his hands still full of gobs of mud. He stared at what was in his hands, his face quite mad for a moment, both horrified and exultant, as though he'd discovered them full of human flesh or the makings of a dreadful weapon.

The Lifer could see the thief's face, and his expression, but the guards couldn't. They were laughing, staggering with mirth, their feet slipping in the mire the thief had made. When they stopped laughing they turned their attention to the Lifer. 'Let's see how he does.' They *didn't even put it to him.* Only agreed among themselves that it was his turn. Then they began to kick at him, not hard, only coaxing, but they didn't stop till he turned to try backing into the water.

'No!' The thief came to life, gave up nursing his handfuls of mud, shook his hands empty to reach — but was struck down.

The Lifer edged back into the river. The water was warmed by the sun, and by the vegetation. He went carefully, searching for safe footings. He went down in a fresh place, not in the muddy slot the thief had made in the bank. He looked over his shoulder and saw water textured by floating weed then, beyond that, smooth, its skin twitching only where touched by pond-skimmers. He glanced up at the guards, who were quiet now, and at the bridge, the still forms of all the staring convicts, the beautiful carvings, the lucent scales of sunlit water reflected on the underside of the sandstone arch. He looked around, and then he slipped, slithered back, his hands tearing at the weeds. He saw the thief lunge forward and splash onto his belly, hands stretched out.

The weeds came loose in the Lifer's grasp. He was holding onto them, but they had let go at the root. There was nothing behind his feet. The weeds parted and he went back into the water, his eyes open. Billowing clouds of mud followed him and he lost sight of the surface for a moment. Then it was back as brackets of black ripples on a hot blue sky. His shackles drew him down into the channel, and the weeds closed over his head. He was engulfed in caressing green gloom.

He held his breath. He stretched his arms up. He felt the cool lightness of air on his knuckles so opened his hands, forced his gnarled fingers straight up into the air. He waited for a grip, a rope, a breath

—

The green light turned red, the still water turbulent. His lungs ached, then opened. He sucked in water. There was nothing behind it, or beyond it. No air.

In a room beside the troublemaker's cell, Maze Plasir pushed back his eiderdown and turned up the flame of the lamp by the bed. The light was like a reprieve. The dreamhunter leaned back on his pillows and breathed deeply. He felt weak with gratitude just for waking up. It was absurd to feel that way, and Plasir waited patiently for the feeling to fade. While he waited he hurried his recovery by saying to himself, 'It's my nightmare, and so *I am* the river.'

Once the force of the nightmare's end had faded, Plasir again began to feel dissatisfied with it. It wasn't particularly strong, as far as nightmares went. But the Department of Corrections had chosen it from its description in the Regulatory Body's *Dream Almanac*. The man next door, the troublemaker, had done something that Corrections thought would best be treated with a nightmare in which submersion and the weight of iron figured heavily. Plasir picked absent-mindedly at a loose thread on the silk cord trim of his bolster. In a moment he'd settle down again and begin another cycle of the dream. He caught himself holding his breath as he strained to hear sounds on the other side of the wall. He remembered that there had been one subject who, for some reason unable to wake up, had stopped breathing.

The dream, Sunken, did end with a death. It was one of only a very few dreams that did. Hame's nightmare Buried Alive was so terrible that it was said no dreamhunter would be able to stay asleep long enough to see its end. Plasir wondered what would happen if an unconscious dreamhunter was set down on the site of Buried Alive. That would be an interesting experiment. But, sadly, no one could experiment with the nightmare since no one knew where it was to be found. Tziga Hame had concealed the dream's site, and Lazarus — whoever the hell *he* was — wasn't volunteering information to any Body.

Plasir liked to experiment with dreams. He had learned to like it as he'd become more experienced, and as he began to notice how much some dreams changed.

Second Sentence, for instance, was a split dream. For years Plasir had caught it, but hadn't known it was a split dream. Then the Body had had Jerome Tilley, one of the rare Novelists (as those who caught split dreams were called), take a closer look at all its most effective 'think again' dreams. The Body had wanted to check that, for instance, a dream Plasir had been catching, about a young woman attacked in her home, might not also have something from the point of view of the husband who discovered her bleeding body at the dream's conclusion. It turned out that it did have, and the dream Violated became Violated and The Husband's Horror. The Body then had all its dreamhunters with Corrections contracts catch the dream till they found one who could reliably catch only The Husband's Horror. Jerome Tilley's experiments were all part of the Body's plan to develop more 'targeted' treatments for hardened offenders.

Noting Tilley's experiments, Plasir had begun to wonder about his own speciality dreams. After a time, just wondering seemed to make it possible for him to open some of them up. He never did catch a split dream — he wasn't a Novelist — but he found that a few dreams suddenly switched their point of view. And so it was that Second Sentence had thrown up the nightmare Plasir named, simply, Sunken. Sunken had the same setting as Second Sentence — a bridge under construction in a country town, on a hot day after harvest time.

Maze Plasir stopped pulling threads on the bolster and held his breath again. He had realised something. That Alexander Mason's Water Diviner was *also* set in the country town and valley full of the haze of smoke. Plasir concentrated; he looked very hard at his memory of the country town. It wasn't anywhere he knew in life, and there was something about its reality that was off kilter. There was the whittled elegance of the woman's skirts — skirts with higher hemlines than women ever wore. There was the lack of jitters in the sleek motor cars. The town seemed real and not real at the same time. (Though, of course, all the dreams were *factual* — none had monsters, or unassisted flight, or any of the things true human dreams had.) The country town of The Water Diviner, Sunken and Second Sentence was strange to Plasir, yet, if he squinted through the brown haze at its distances, he thought he could see familiar hills, hills he'd seen somewhere he'd been as a child.

Plasir concentrated. He strained to know. Then he gave up, sighed and settled himself down on the bed and went back to his first train of thought.

Second Sentence was from the point of view of the violin thief. The young man began the dream happy, because his sentence was nearly up, and because he'd been working with the mason, a man whose skill he admired. The heat wasn't draining the young thief dry — he had his health, and hope. He had learned his lesson. He was full of a resolve to stay out of trouble, to spend the rest of his life out of the power of the law. The smoke-stained skies made him think of music, the slow, green, waving weed made him think of music. Second Sentence was a constructive, reforming dream. It had lessons to teach, like 'stick to your resolve' and 'keep your temper'. After the old Lifer drowned, straining up into the air, straightening his crippled fingers, the young man stared for a few seconds at his mud-caked hands and a thought flashed through his mind — or more a feeling than a thought, for the dreamhunter Plasir had never been able to make much sense of it. It was a thought about a belief or a story and, like most of the thief's thoughts, it had a kind of tune to it, a musical chant. 'I'm not helpless,' the thief thought — as people in desperation do sometimes think the exact opposite of what is true and being proven to them. And then, in the dream, the young man lost his temper and surged up, took hold of a rifle from the hands of the nearest guard, the one standing slack-jawed and sated with cruelty. He seized the rifle and tore it away from the man, swung it, clubbing and clubbing, till the other guards hauled him off. The guard had a broken skull, and the young thief, only weeks away from freedom, was then looking at years, at a second sentence.

Second Sentence was very effective — less nightmare than a dream with a nasty, sobering turn at its end. But now that he was catching its other aspect, the dream seemed a lot less useful and positive to Plasir. The old man of Sunken had next to no experience of pity, and yet how desperately he looked about him for it. He looked into all the faces. But what he saw was what he already knew about the world — that it didn't make any difference if you kept your temper or stuck to your good resolve, for there was malice, always close, and always ready to lend its icy hand.

Second Sentence showed a way out of trouble — though the young man didn't take it. What Sunken showed was that it didn't matter what you did, because accidents happened, and accidents were opportunities for evil. Second Sentence was a warning dream. Sunken was a nightmare. Taken together they were horribly incompatible, and Plasir couldn't help but wonder what a Novelist like Grace Tiebold would make of the dream — for it was *one* dream, and Grace Tiebold would catch it intact, the old man and the young together. She'd catch both the terror and despair of one, and the rage and crushed hope of the other.

Maze Plasir closed his eyes. He would go back to sleep. He would give the troublemaker in the next room another dose. And he'd try to take a better look at the other thing about the dream that troubled him.

Plasir had *been* the thief, on and off, for years. He'd seen everything through his eyes. The thief knew his own past, of course, but wasn't really thinking about it on that morning. For instance, Plasir had known from Second Sentence that the thief played the violin, but only learned from Sunken that he had stolen his own instrument from a pawn shop. Plasir knew about the thief only what he'd managed to gather from the young man's thoughts on that afternoon at the bridge. Then, when he first caught Sunken, the old Lifer had shown Plasir the *face* of the person through whose eyes he'd formerly seen everything.

There was something about that face. Something familiar. The thief looked healthy and happy, and wary and furtive — none of this strange in a criminal on light duties and near the end of his time. But when the stone fell into the river, and the guards turned their spite into sport, and the two convicts were driven to the river's edge, and the old Lifer gazed into the young thief's face and saw fear and pity —

'*I know that person*,' Plasir thought. 'I've seen that sensitive, stubborn mouth before. Not in a dream.' Plasir pictured the mouth and the eyes. Eyes full of sadness and shame and resignation and, behind that, power: pitiless, cold power.

Three

Chorley told Grace that he'd promised the Grand Patriarch he'd be back to see what he could do for 'the Cause'.

'What cause is this?' Grace asked. 'Tziga's? Laura's? The cause of stirring up trouble between dreamhunters and their public?'

'The Grand Patriarch offers refuge to renegade dreamhunters. He thinks the Body is up to no good. Tziga's ideas and Laura's actions have nothing to do with him. You can't blame him.'

Grace glared at her husband. 'Am I allowed to blame anyone? Or is it best for me to just bite my lip?'

'Better than biting me, dear. It's not my fault that Laura and Tziga are out of reach.'

'No, but it is the fault of Erasmus Tiebold.'

Chorley gave a sigh of put-upon patience, kissed his wife on top of her head and went out.

The Grand Patriarch thanked Chorley for his visit and asked him, since no one expected him to denounce dreamhunting, did he think he could investigate the Place?

'Rangers go there and make maps and call it exploration,' the Grand Patriarch said. 'Philosophers muse about it as a phenomenon and call that — rightly in some ways — *thinking* about it. But none of us is getting any nearer to knowing what the Place really is. You've been close to the subject for years, you are familiar with all the distracting facts already. You have a reputation as something of a scientific mind, and independent thinker. So please, Mr Tiebold, look into it for me.'

Chorley went away from this interview and, for days, hadn't been able to imagine where to start. He reread some of those philosophers and was struck again by how they all seemed to talk about the Place as if, by coming up with the right metaphor for it, they might be able to say what it was. He found that he liked Dr King's account in *A History of Southland*. King's approach to the Place seemed practical. He tried to find evidence of its earliest appearance. Chorley mused on King's speculation that the dreams might be memories of people who had lived in its geographical vicinity. And on his own idea that the Place was like a mirage. Chorley considered all this — as, no doubt, the Grand Patriarch already had.

And then he remembered the telegraph line that had once run through the Rifleman Pass, from Doorhandle to Sisters Beach. A line that was long ago abandoned. The wire, though intact and visible throughout its entire length, was finally deemed hopelessly unreliable. Signals were either lost, or there were strange interferences in them — such as a patterned tapping that didn't match any known telegraphic code, or bits of code that could be deciphered but that gave the keyman on the receiving end bad, mad messages.

And so it was that, several days after remembering the abandoned telegraph line, Chorley found himself waiting in a poky room beneath the mosaic floor of Founderston Central Post Office. The man Chorley waited with didn't have much to say, but stood at his desk sorting through a bunch of keys on a string. The room was dingy. There were windows only at the top of one wall. Through them Chorley could see people passing — or their feet at least — on the street: scuffed shoes and polished ones, the wheels of a pram, a woman in a hobble skirt and the lower legs of a small girl in flimsy blue sandals.

'It's summer already,' Chorley thought.

A second clerk shuffled into the room — a man with a coat and complexion the colour of manila cardboard. The first clerk stopped sorting his keys and tossed them back into an open drawer. He said, 'I was just telling Mr Tiebold here that if any of the bad transcriptions from the Wry Valley to Sisters Beach line had been kept, you would know where to find them.' He turned to Chorley and said, 'Mr Nevis was a keyman at Doorhandle twenty years ago when the trouble started.' Then, to Mr Nevis, 'Can you help?'

Mr Nevis nodded and held the door open for Chorley.

As they descended into the cold subterranean corridors beneath the Central Post Office Mr Nevis told Chorley that yes, he had been a keyman and had sent and deciphered messages to and from Sisters Beach. In fact, he had been at his post in the telegraph office on the evening when the Doorhandle innkeeper came in to wire for a surgeon.

'For the boy with the broken leg — who later became your brother-in-law, Mr Hame,' Mr Nevis said. 'The line had been complete then for three years. It was working well, except once when the road washed out and took half a dozen poles with it. The weather in Rifleman Pass was a challenge, but we hadn't yet encountered the problem that closed us down. That problem started after Tziga Hame's fall.'

Mr Nevis opened a steel door, located a light switch and let Chorley into a room containing long avenues of shelves filled with files. The air was chilly and undisturbed.

'We kept those messages separately,' said Nevis. 'We had a special file for them — several by the time the Post Office abandoned the line, which they didn't do, despite the problems, till the Founderston to Sisters Beach Railway opened, and the new telegraphic line with it. Those files had red tape on their spines. I remember making up a new one myself.'

'How many were there?'

'Mad messages? Hundreds. We had to have a special short key code for "Corrupt. Send again."'

Mr Nevis made a noise of discovery and dropped into a crouch, his knees creaking. He pulled files from a shelf, bundled them into his arms and got up with Chorley's help.

At the back wall there was a bench under a bare bulb in a wire cage. 'I'm afraid you won't be very comfortable, Mr Tiebold. My manager doesn't really like anything brought up from underground. But I'm sure you'll find you won't need to look far for a good example. For nonsense of a special kind.'

'Is it formless nonsense? Or nonsense only in the context of the message?' Chorley asked. He longed to edge the man aside and look himself.

Mr Nevis was patting the pile of files, tidying and talking. 'I never thought madness terribly interesting myself, whether it was Lady Macbeth wringing her hands, or Lucia di Lammermoor wafting about in her bloodied bridal gown. I never looked at the corrupt messages with any real attention.'

Chorley stepped up beside the elderly clerk and seized the stack and slid it along the bench till it was under his own nose. 'Has anyone ever gone through these looking for a pattern?'

'What kind of pattern? All the Post Office did was try to fix the problem. It even had men camping out at night under every tenth pole in order to catch the pranksters.'

'And all this happened before the Regulatory Body was formed?'

'Yes. Otherwise it would have been their problem. The Post Office blamed us keymen at first, said it was our mischief. *We* blamed the fellows on the other end. But it was the Place. That line was unbroken from Doorhandle to Tricksie Bend — it ran outside, not Inside — but the Place used the telegraph to try to talk to us. Look!' Nevis snatched one file, flipped pages and found a message:

MOTHER FAILING STOP DOCTOR SAYS ONLY MATTER OF DAYS STOP PLEASE RISE UP I SAID RISE UP COME AT ONCE STOP ANDREW

'That's more or less typical. That "Rise up!" stuff.' Mr Nevis sounded triumphant. He peered at Chorley, waiting for a reaction.

Small hairs were bristling on Chorley's nape, his whole scalp tightening. The 'interruption' in the telegram was a plea, like the cry of a king besieged on a battlefield. Chorley licked his dry lips. 'Does this sort of thing turn up often?'

'"Rise up", you mean? Yes. We got that one all the time. Come to think of it, perhaps that's the pattern you're asking about?'

'Yes.'

Mr Nevis sighed. 'I suppose, then, that you'll want to read through all of these?'

'I will.' Chorley was engrossed already, leafing through the first file.

'Shall I see if I can find you something to sit on?'

'Thank you.'

On the afternoon of the last day of classes, Rose brought Mamie home with her so that her friend could help her choose what she should take on her proposed four-week visit to the Doran family's summer residence in the Awa Inlet. The girls came in with the Dorans' chauffeur and Rose's school trunk.

'You can put it down here, thank you,' Rose said to the man. 'Mamie will stay for dinner and someone will deliver her home later.'

'Have you even checked that anyone is home?' Mamie said. 'Or are you too busy being decisive?'

Rose ignored her friend, thanked her friend's chauffeur and sent him off. 'I could take hours choosing what to take,' she said. 'I think I've exhausted my decisiveness.'

'Well then, while you're weak and easy to influence, shall we start by deciding what you'll bring to read?'

They went to the library, where they met Rose's father, who was standing in the doorway with a notebook held open on the top of his head like a small pitched roof. 'Girls!' he said, in a tone of happy discovery. 'You know your poetry, don't you?'

Mamie said, 'Yes, poetry is the proper province of girls.'

Rose said, 'Mamie is here to help me choose what to pack. I'm going away on Monday. You won't see me again till Christmas. You have taken that in?'

'Yes, darling, and we mean to spend the weekend at your beck and call. Your mother is coming home tonight. And there's a letter from Laura on your dresser.'

Mamie looked at Rose, curious. Rose hadn't mentioned her cousin for ages. 'Where *is* Laura?'

'Staying with relatives,' said Rose and her father simultaneously.

Chorley wandered over to his cluttered desk and moved books and papers about to find something. Rose came and peered over his shoulder at a notebook. She read:

HOME FRIDAY NINE FIFTEEN STOP SHE IS COMING MY OWN MY SWEET CAN YOU MEET ME AT STATION STOP PHILLIP

and:

OFFER ACCEPTABLE STOP SHE IS COMING MY OWN MY SWEET WERE IT EVER SO AIRY A TREAD SETTLE TODAY STOP YOU HAVE MY FULL CONFIDENCE STOP WELLES

'"She is coming, my own, my sweet, were it ever so airy a tread",' Chorley quoted.

'Yes, that is almost certainly poetry,' said Rose.

'It's *Maud*,' said Mamie. '*Maud: A Monodrama*, by Tennyson. We did it last year. You remember, Rose, you kept saying, "Come into the garden Maud, the black bat night has flown", whenever you wanted a word with someone in private.' Rose had always been with Laura then, and Mamie had not been her friend. Mamie had watched Rose's joking intimacy, amused and a little envious of Rose's many 'Mauds'.

Rose went to the bookshelf to look for Tennyson. 'What do you want the poem for, Da?'

Chorley glanced at Mamie then said, 'I'm writing a scientific article and I thought I'd give it some polish by adding a little verse.'

Mamie couldn't conceal her look of scorn.

Rose found the collected works of Tennyson and passed it to her friend. Mamie could find the right lines far quicker than she. Rose went to look over her father's shoulder at his notes again. He flipped the book to show her its first page, and its title: 'Bad code from the obsolete Founderston–Sisters Beach telegraph line, 1886–1893.'

Mamie said, 'It is *Maud* — chapter twenty-two, stanza eleven.' She read it out.

> She is coming, my own, my sweet;
>   Were it ever so airy a tread,
> My heart would hear her and beat,
>   Were it earth in an earthy bed;
> My dust would hear her and beat,
>   Had I lain for a century dead;
> Would start and tremble under her feet,
>   And blossom in purple and red.

'That's so strange,' Rose said. 'What do you make of it, Da?'

'I think that's the least strange bit of the whole overwrought poem,' said Mamie, who didn't know what they were talking about. She shut the book with a snap.

'I'm still working on it,' Chorley said to Rose.

Four

Sandy caught Convalescent Two and took it to St Thomas's Lung Hospital. But his dream was of a very poor quality, his copy of it somehow murky and strained. He was sent away again. He returned to Doorhandle and Mrs Lilley's house and tried to pull himself together — he felt scattered, jumpy and lumpish at the same time. He couldn't seem to fix himself. He thought about Laura all the time. Laura and her unknown suitor. Her letter to him was folded small and tucked into the lining of his wallet. As for the other one — the same night he'd opened it, Sandy had torn it into tiny pieces and thrown it out of his bedroom window. It was gone, so he couldn't now decide to be honourable after all and just deliver it.

Sandy's room in Doorhandle was his only home. When he was in Founderston he was working, and had a bed at one of the hospitals. But at Mrs Lilley's he hadn't much in the way of privacy. He couldn't just go to ground and nurse his broken heart, or his bad conscience — he wasn't actually sure which was troubling him most. Mrs Lilley's other young tenants were in and out and kept asking him about Laura. 'Where is she? Is she coming back?' And the Lilley girls, seeing him silent and morose, would try to cheer him up with kind little attentions. Sandy was sure his linen was changed more often than his rental contract stipulated (and he was someone who read and remembered every clause of any contract he signed). The younger girl kept waylaying him in the hall, darting out of the kitchen perhaps with a stirring spoon for him to lick — the sort of treat he'd once begged his mother for. He got clean linen, food, flattery, flirtation.

And, on a Saturday night when Mrs Lilley's bed of outrageously pink carnations had all turned modest and furled for the night, the eldest girl came and sat beside Sandy on the back steps. She said, 'What a shame it is, Alexander, that you can't take up a pipe. A pipe is a peaceful, manly sort of habit, I think. My father enjoyed a pipe. But of course I know dreamhunters don't bother to smoke, since they can't keep a pipe alight when they're In the Place.' She was showing concern, and what she knew. She leaned forward at the waist and tried to look into his lowered face. 'Still, I would like to see you light up, Alexander.'

'Why carry around another craving?' Sandy said, brooding.

The Lilley girl laid a hand on his back.

And Sandy turned his head and kissed her, because she wanted him to, and because she wasn't Laura.

Five

So Long Spit's 'Blinking Bob' was not one of those lighthouses that people lived in, a tower of mortared stone, containing a series of cylindrical rooms and topped with a room holding the lamp. All there was to Blinking Bob was four steel legs, four long flights of steps going up between them, and a square room with glass around the top half of all four walls. The room housed only the lamp, the mechanism that made the lamp revolve and several tins of benzene spirit. The lighthouse keepers and their families lived in three weatherboard and corrugated iron houses that stood around the tower. The houses were in a wind-break, the tower on a slight rise, its legs anchored in concrete. Blinking Bob was the second tower built on the Spit; the first had been wrecked by drifting sand.

On a summer day, a few weeks before the solstice, Laura sat with her back to the rivet-studded wall of the lamp room at the top of the lighthouse.

Laura's father, Tziga, was cleaning smoke stains from the lamp. The lamp was bigger than her father's torso, a structure of cut crystals in a copper frame, four bull's-eyes surrounded by curved ribs of crystal. The whole thing was shaped like a glittering bishop's mitre.

Laura's father's hands were gloved with rags. He was running them back and forth between the crystal ribs. It was rather like trying to clean the blades of an egg-beater without first immersing it in water. He worked with the sun behind him, so as not to be dazzled by the light shining through the lamp. And in that light his scars seemed nothing but the shadows his hair threw across his face.

Laura had been with her father, sleeping and waking, almost every minute since she'd arrived six weeks before. She was beginning to be used to the changes in him.

She had been warned, as well. A priest called Father Paul had taken charge of Laura at Westport, and had brought her to So Long Spit. She hadn't crossed paths with her uncle Chorley — he'd left several days before she arrived. Chorley had apparently been there when Tziga read the newspaper accounts of the riot at the Rainbow Opera. He had witnessed Tziga's fit. He had talked to Father Paul about Tziga's frailty, and Father Paul had prepared Laura.

It was only when they boarded the schooner *Morningstar* at Westport that Father Paul had told Laura who was waiting for her at the lighthouse. Her *father* — who she'd been allowed to think was dead. Who had been kept from her, and on whose behalf she'd acted, hurting Aunt Grace and Sandy, infuriating Rose and earning her cold shoulder. If only she'd known her father was alive. If only someone had told her. Laura had said all this to Father Paul — raging at him, at first too resentful to feel relief.

And Father Paul patiently explained some things to her.

He told her that, over the last few years, a handful of dreamhunters had come to the Church — the institution most loudly critical of dreamhunting — to express their worries about some of the Regulatory Body's uses for dreams. 'We lost touch with a few of them,' Father Paul said. 'They disappeared. Too many dreamhunters disappear. So, Laura, when your father turned up, his famous face swollen beyond recognition, at the Magdalene Charity Hospital in Westport, in what doctors call a "coma", but still able to infect other patients sleeping near him with terror, we thought it best to report him dead, and spirit him away. It was cruel to his family, but after the other disappearances, the Grand Patriarch deemed it necessary. When we heard that Tziga Hame was supposed to have "vanished" while attempting a crossing of the Place, we knew he had to *stay* hidden.'

The other thing Father Paul had said to Laura, just before they climbed down the rope ladder from the deck of the *Morningstar* to the platform by the lighthouse, was that her father's health was very fragile and she must take care not to upset him.

Laura had been forewarned. She'd treated her father tenderly, waited on him and, whenever he just sat staring into space, would sit pressed up against him. Her Uncle Chorley had dispatched a doctor to the lighthouse — and paid a fortune to keep him quiet about where he was going and whom he treated. The doctor prescribed Laura's father drugs that dampened down the intensity of his seizures, if not their frequency.

Father Paul had stopped by only the day before with letters for Laura and Tziga. He told them that Chorley wanted them both back at Summerfort by Christmas (Christmas was three weeks away, a few days after the summer solstice): 'The Grand Patriarch says that now that the government has set up its Commission of Inquiry into the riot, if the Regulatory Body wants to speak to either of you — to question you, or call you to account — then, equally, the *Commission* might subpoena you. The Grand Patriarch thinks the Body will think twice about doing anything to call Tziga Hame's existence to the Commission's attention.'

Of all this, Laura's father had only seemed to take in that he'd be back at Summerfort by Christmas. He seemed baffled by anything beyond immediate practicalities. For him it seemed there was only ever the task at hand — the crystal clouded by smoke coming clean under his cloth. He'd become slow and remote. There were people to smile at, or listen to with sombre attention. There were things that must be remembered — for instance, he was always reminding Laura not to go out in the sun without her hat. But there was no larger world for him any more, no public life, nor any matter of real consequence.

Laura stood up and looked through the lighthouse window. The tide was out along the Spit and the few patches of scrub in the dunes showed as black flaws on the horizon, wobbling in the heat haze. Scarves of dry sand blew along the surface of the wet. There was sand high in the wind, for Laura could hear the whisper of its grains in the gusts buffeting the window-panes.

'Da?' said Laura.

Her father looked at her, then rotated the lamp on its housing so that the cleaned crystals spun scintillating in the sunlight.

'Do you remember I told you about Sandy?'

'Your friend? You mention him often. Did you tell me something particular about him?' Laura's father frowned at her, anxious perhaps that he'd forgotten something she'd said.

'No.'

'I liked his uncle, George Mason. As a singer, I mean. Marta and I often went to the opera. We would sit up in the gods with all the other students. Mason was about twenty-five when I was sixteen. He was young, but he had a big bass voice, like the father of all fathers.'

Laura laughed at this story, because it was something new, and related to Sandy. And because her father seemed so collected in speaking about his past — his past before the Place.

'Lots of the early dreamhunters were musical. I don't know if that was ever noted as a tendency. No one would think to notice now, since there aren't too many distinguished musicians at fifteen. When George Mason became a dreamhunter it really was a loss to music.' Laura's father knelt to gather the cleaning rags into a bucket, and Laura could see he was actually concentrating on grasping, lifting and releasing. But he kept talking, his memory of twenty years ago exact, even if his movements were not. Laura had wanted to hear his thoughts on Sandy — on Sandy's bewildering prickliness — but she didn't want to interrupt his remembering.

'What about you, Da? How good were you?'

'Marta was a better musician than I was. So it was probably just as well it was I who fell.' He hauled himself up, gripping the housing of the light. Then he turned to Laura, and she was forced again to regard the ruin of his face, and that frightening look in his eyes — a kind of tremulous pulling together of his attention. He said, 'Laura, you know I wasn't in my right mind when I wrote you that letter.'

Was this an apology? Laura wondered. 'That letter was all I had left of you,' she said. 'Of course I took it seriously.'

He touched his scarred forehead. Then he reached for Laura and put an arm around her and held her.

Laura closed her eyes and simply basked in being held. She shouldn't ask any more than this. He couldn't answer — wasn't answerable any more. When she looked into his eyes now, she saw watchfulness and uncertainty. His love for her was intact — but his understanding wasn't.

Tziga released her.

She said, 'Here, let me give you a hand,' and took the bucket from him. They left the lamp house. Partway down from the tower, Laura stopped. She had spotted something. She shaded her eyes and squinted into the wavering air.

There was someone out there, standing still and straight on the beach. The figure was far off, but Laura felt that he or she was looking at her.

Laura clattered down after her father, checking now and then on that watching figure. At the foot of the steps she returned the bucket to her father, then took a few bounding steps away backwards, making excuses, 'I'm just going for a walk, Da —' Then she was off, running barefoot on the springy stems of beach grass, under the pines, then onto the sand. She ran in a long curve, for the watching figure had moved off the beach and into the dunes, and she had to alter her course in order to intercept him.

As she came closer Laura could see only bright skin, no clothes. It was Nown, and he was waiting for her, leading her in among the dunes where they wouldn't be seen. As she closed the distance between them, she could see his head was lifted and he was checking the lines of sight between himself and the top of the lighthouse.

Laura came to a skidding stop before him. She staggered about, panting, then folded over a stitch in her side. For a moment all she could hear was her own breathing. Then she heard the sea, and a tern crying as it flew along the line of low breakers. She straightened up and faced her sandman. He held out his arms to her.

She looked over her shoulder at the lighthouse.

'There must be things you want to say,' he said.

She went to him and let him pick her up.

He stooped over her and hurried away, skirting the base of the dunes till they were screened from the lighthouse, and also from the sound of waves on the western shore.

Nown stopped within the shade of a high, crescent-shaped dune. Below the dune was a salt pan, and when Nown set Laura down, her feet cracked its crusted surface and she found herself standing in a shallow trench surrounded by sliding, dirty-white plates of salt.

Nown stood watching her and waiting for her to speak.

She said, 'You got my note?'

'No.'

'I sent a note enclosed in a letter to Sandy. I asked him to leave it in the forest.'

'I left the forest as soon as you moved west. I followed you.'

'How did you know where I was?'

'You made me, Laura. You are my compass.'

Laura sat down abruptly in a patch of smashed salt crust. The air was uncomfortably hot nearer the ground, but Laura wasn't able to get up again. She had thought of something, and her thought had taken the strength from her legs.

Nown was speaking, volunteering his story — something she imagined he wouldn't have done before she freed him.

'There were many rivers to cross,' he said. 'I followed the foothills of the Rifleman Mountains, and struck only tributary streams. Sometimes I crossed over into the Place, but the distances there are too great. And at the coal mine beside the river — I don't know its name — there were miners, and barges coming and going, and a river ford with a ferry on a rope. I had to wait till it was dark and disguise myself under a blanket. I had to steal the blanket. The ferry man was drunk. There was one threatening deluge on my journey — and I had to burrow in under a bank. It took time, but I got here without getting my feet wet.'

'Your literal feet,' Laura said.

'The feet you gave me.'

For some reason this sounded like an accusation. Laura couldn't tell whether she was being blamed for the shortcomings of Nown's feet, or for failing to respect them *as* feet. 'Nown,' she said, 'if you knew where I was because I made you, does that mean that you knew where my *father* was — I mean the eighth you — when he went missing?'

'Yes.'

Laura took several deep breaths before asking, 'Why didn't you tell me?'

'I did tell you that since *I* still existed, then he was still alive. And you strode ahead of me smiling and crying. You didn't ask me where he was.'

In the shelter of the dune, the salt filled the still air with its dry fumes. Laura was having difficulty thinking. She got up and kept walking. Her sandman followed her. His weighty steps made wider circles of cracks in the crusted salt.

After a time Laura said, 'Does anything I say matter to you the way it did before you were free?'

'I don't yet know.'

'But you followed me here.'

'Yes.'

Laura led him out onto the beach again. The tide was coming in and, as she looked back between the gap in the dunes, Laura could see that it was making more progress on the western shore than where they were, so that the sea seemed to pile up against the barricade of the Spit.

She was more comfortable in the open air. Nown had come close to her until she was standing in his shadow. She was sure he'd done it deliberately — had noticed that she was panting and that she'd put up a hand to shade her eyes. Without looking at him, she pressed her hand against his side, his gritty skin and mock ribs and ridges of muscle. She said, 'From now on could you please tell me anything you think I might need to know?'

He was silent.

'Nown?'

Laura could have sworn she heard him sigh. She glanced at him, but his face had no expression, or none she could interpret. Perhaps she had only expected to hear a sigh. He was looking at a bank of cloud closing in on the Spit faster than the light sea-breeze. Or at least, he seemed to be looking at it. She asked, 'Can you see that?'

'There are layers of wind. One is warmer,' he said. Then, 'Laura — my experience of freedom is limited. So, therefore, is my experience of making judgments. I cannot yet know what I will have to consider each time I am considering what you need to know. My knowledge of your needs has been guided by your instructions. At times I have tried to imagine, without guidance from you, what you might need. I have made mistakes. After you caught the nightmare you were weeping and I picked you up to rock the tears out of you — I had seen that done. You did stop crying, but you didn't approve of my action. I cannot trust the sympathy I have for you to guide me. We are too different, you and I. If you ask me to mind your needs, are you then giving me *your* freedom? Why would you free me only to hand over your own freedom?'

'Nown!' Laura had to stop him. He was retreating into a thicket of philosophical complications, and she was sure it was a deeper and thornier thicket than either of them could imagine. She stepped onto one of his feet in order to stretch up and cover his mouth with her hand. 'Shh,' she said. 'That's enough.'

He pulled her hand away. 'Besides,' he said, 'if you ask me to tell you anything you might need to know — to remember to tell you from now on anything you might need to know — are you asking me to *promise*? I think a promise must be like a law. I understand laws. They are what I've lived by. If a promise is like law, then, even free, I think I might do whatever I promise. Come what may.'

'But no — I released you,' Laura said. 'You're free.'

'I'm free to promise,' Nown said. 'And if I choose to make promises, I'll honour them.'

'Don't promise, then! *Don't* tell me what I might need to know.'

Nown's eyes blackened and glittered. 'Don't say that.'

'You can't possibly still be susceptible to my orders.'

'I find I am. I still want to do what you want.'

'Well — stop!' Laura ordered, exasperated.

'No,' Nown said.

She started to laugh, stood laughing, turned into the sunlight, which was fiercely hot, concentrated by the encroaching cloud. She felt happy, in a crazy way. Nown was a fearful responsibility, but when she was with him the feeling she had of being trapped and baffled disappeared. He was so contradictory — scrupulous and untamed at the same time — that in his presence all the things that had hemmed her in seemed to melt away. Her father was broken and beyond reproach, Rose was right to hate her, and she had been wrong to keep her own promises. But Nown made her feel like God on the first Sabbath — he was a great responsibility, but he was *good*, like the world, and being with him made Laura sleepy with happiness.

They kept wandering on along the Spit, away from the sentinel lighthouse. They didn't talk. It seemed that Nown had nothing further to tell Laura, and she, finding herself so content with him, stopped thinking altogether.

The massed grey clouds closed in on them, and a wind came up, a constant, cool, gritty wind. It scalped the dunes and scattered sand into the waters of Coal Bay. As the tide came in, and the waves grew bigger and steeper, water began to sieve through the Spit itself, so that the dunes grew damp and gave differently beneath each step they took. Nown hiked up to the spine of the dunes, and walked there. Laura followed him with difficulty, till he picked her up again and went along with her, rocking her as he swayed.

'Can you see the sea at all?' she asked.

'No.'

'Is it like walking on a bridge, then? A bridge over nothingness?'

'But there are birds,' Nown said.

Laura looked where she supposed he was looking and saw the diminishing dunes and bleak, choppy sea and, at the very end of the Spit, flashes of white — not foam on whitecaps, but the myriad bodies of roosting gannets. Even in the stiff wind there were gannets out over the sea, weaving back and forth, scanning the water for prey. Hard-pressed and hopeful now, for it couldn't be easy for the birds to spot fish under the agitated waves. Still, every few seconds one of the great gliding creatures would pause, and close its wings, and fall, an accelerating white dart, into the water. The bird would disappear, and would surface some time later, shaking itself off, clutching at the air till the air shouldered its weight, flying up to rejoin the rest of the hungry patrol.

Laura asked Nown to set her on her feet. She leaned against him, sheltered from the worst of the wind, and watched the gannets fish. She felt she should applaud these dives as the lighthouse keeper's son did.

They stayed watching for a long time, till it was too cold and grey, and the birds became hard to see because the day was coming to a close. Then Laura held out her arms and Nown picked her up and set off along the narrow backbone of the Spit towards the pale streak of the distant lighthouse.

Laura had her sandman crawl in under the keeper's house, where tangles of harvested seaweed were drying among its timber piles. She told him to stay still and hidden.

In the early hours of the morning, when the dependable westerly had dropped again, Laura climbed out of her bed — a mattress on the floor beside her father's — and crept out of their hut and under the keeper's house. She found Nown by touch. She lay down with her back against his body, and drew his arms around her. Then she went back to sleep again, cradled in a nest of shaped sand and snarls of seaweed.

At dawn Tziga woke and let his arm drape off the side of his bed to feel for his daughter's head on her pillow. He couldn't find it. He ran his palm over the cold, empty dent where her warm curls should have been, and then leaned up on an elbow to look at her bed.

Tziga put on his patched fisherman's jersey and went out to find her. He looked on the outer shore, and found only a flock of terns standing by the tide-line turned into the breeze. Then, as he was crossing the windbreak to look on the Coal Bay shore, Tziga noticed a smear of pallor between the piles of the keeper's cottage. As he got closer, he recognised Laura's white nightgown. He steadied himself against the wall of the cottage and stooped to look.

Laura was asleep, but the sandman's eyes were open — always open, made that way — and looking at him.

Tziga felt himself recognised. He felt the sandman's calm, alien interest. He saw how the thing's arms enfolded Laura's slight body, how her head was pillowed on its shoulder. The thing looked nothing like his own roughly made and rather grotesque servant.

Laura had been late for dinner, pink with cold and exertion, and very happy. Now here she was, asleep in these inhuman arms. The sight terrified Tziga. He wanted to crawl in among the seaweed and haul her out. He wanted to make the thing disappear.

She didn't need it any more.

Tziga looked for the letters of its name and saw an unmarked brow, and below the brow the eyes, watchful, but with no sign of concern, or of challenge in them. The thing was simply waiting for him to go away. It seemed to know that he wouldn't want to wake Laura, and to understand that he wouldn't want her to find out he'd seen it.

Laura woke up when she heard stirring above her, the keeper's wife opening the stove-top to drop kindling on the embers of last night's fire. She turned to Nown. 'My Uncle Chorley is sending a boat to take me and Da to Summerfort. For Christmas — so soon. I'll want you there, Nown. I'm sorry to have to send you off, but if you're going to get there in time you're going to have to start walking. I know you do most of your walking by night, and the nights are getting shorter.'

'Yes.'

'What are you saying yes to?'

'The nights are shorter. You'll want me. I should start walking to meet you there. I believe you are sorry. I'm saying yes to all that. And, yes, I will go now, I will do what you ask.'

Laura extracted herself from the accommodating hollow he'd made in his body. She said thank you. She crawled out from under the keeper's cottage, picked stiff fragments of seaweed from her nightdress and crept back to her cold bed.

At breakfast Laura's father asked her whether she'd written again to her friend Sandy.

'He didn't reply to my letter. It wasn't much of a letter, I'm afraid. I'm no good at writing them.'

'Have you written again to Rose?'

'She's given up on me, Da.'

'Don't be silly, Laura.'

Laura scowled at her plate of porridge.

'You're just nursing a grudge,' said her father. 'Rose told you off. A telling-off isn't a real breach, darling.'

'But I can't say what I need to say to Rose in a letter.' Laura knew there was nothing she had to say to Rose before showing Rose Nown. He'd still be her secret, even if she showed him to Rose. Rose was Rose. The only reason she hadn't told Rose everything was that she wasn't *telling herself* either.

Her father was saying, 'I may be an invalid, but you're not. You aren't even a fugitive. No one can prove you had anything to do with — with anything. You can take up dreamhunting again. You can catch new and useful dreams, build up a career, team up with your friend Sandy, look after one another and play the bigger venues. You're still in the world, Laura. You belong to the world. You don't belong with an invalid. You can't stay sequestered. You should be with *people*.'

Laura nodded. 'All right,' she said. She gave his hand a squeeze. 'But until I see Rose I won't know what to say to her. And Sandy — Sandy prefers telling people what to do to taking suggestions.'

'Fine. But when we go back, you can be a dreamhunter. You can have friends. You can have a pretty dress made and go to the Presentation Ball with your cousin.'

'And you can be poked and prodded by Uncle Chorley's expensive physicians.'

Six

Grace was buying a new pack at an outfitter's on the Isle of the Temple when she ran into Sandy Mason. Sandy was picking up and putting down sale-price water bottles, working his way along a shelf. None of the bottles seemed to pass his inspection. He looked dubious and sour, as though he were suffering from indigestion.

'Hello,' said Grace. 'How are you?' Grace wasn't just being polite, she really wanted to know. She was sure that Sandy would have suffered some kind of trouble after taking a print of Buried Alive. She had. Her own suffering had taken the form of a marked dip in the popularity of her performances. She had been forced to catch old favourites, and to travel with them to some of the smaller provincial dream palaces: the Beholder at Sisters Beach — before the summer season had filled it with its big audiences — and the Second Skin in Westport. She'd even sat up on an overnight train to the first sizeable town south of the Corridor. Eventually Grace had returned to the Rainbow Opera for a performance at reduced rates; the Opera was paid, but she wasn't. It had taken her weeks, and cost her money, but she had finally worked her way back into public confidence. Her audience had forgiven her.

Though Grace was back on form, she had found that she couldn't relax. When she was busy wooing back the public, she'd been able to put other thoughts and feelings out of her mind. Now these suppressed feelings had returned in force.

It had been written in newspapers: '*Grace Tiebold should be ashamed of herself.*' She had read it, and imagined other people reading it — her neighbours, the workers at her favourite cake shop, the man who trimmed her hair. She'd gone around with her eyes cast down for fear of finding herself looked at — not by those she had offended or disappointed — but by people who had only heard it said: '*Grace Tiebold should be ashamed of herself.*' She was afraid she'd notice those people looking at her to see how she was taking it.

Grace had done the hard work, had shown humility and was back in favour. But now she wondered if she'd ever again feel her former happy confidence in her power to please people. And if she'd ever be able to forget the *relish* she'd sensed in her public telling-off.

So, when she asked Sandy Mason how he was, Grace wasn't just being polite, but was genuinely concerned.

Sandy just grunted in reply to her question. Then he looked guilty and tried again. 'I'm fine now. There was a short period when I was catching poor-quality dreams. St Thomas's turned me away. I nearly had to give up my room, though Mrs Lilley was good about waiting for my rent. All the other lodgers kept asking me about Laura, as though she were mine.' Sandy had begun his account in a brisk, no-nonsense voice but ended sounded bitter. He was frowning at Grace. 'Laura's room just stands there empty,' he said.

'I can get a message to her, if you have one,' Grace offered.

Sandy's frown deepened; he shuffled his feet. 'I mean — it's *wasteful* to keep a room empty week after week.'

'Never mind that,' Grace said. She was puzzled by his behaviour. He'd been so concerned about Laura after the riot. 'I'm sure Laura would be interested to hear about your union plans,' Grace said.

'Oh, that.' Sandy sounded disgusted. 'There was a meeting. We should have been talking about a charter and how to collect dues. Instead, it was an orgy of whingeing, dreamhunters slighting dream-parlour managers, or complaining about the state of the dream trails. I saw how much had to be done. And I saw that I was going to have to do it all myself. Besides —' Sandy paused '— I want to be a great dreamhunter. And I've only got seven months of my exclusive left on The Water Diviner. I don't have time to waste.'

'Fair enough,' said Grace. Then she persisted. 'You could give me a letter and I'd pass it on to Laura. I'm going to see her at Christmas.'

'I know where she is,' Sandy said, so blunt he was almost brutal. 'Not that she really meant to let me know.' He emphasised the 'me'.

'Oh well,' Grace said. She picked up her pack and hoisted it onto her shoulder to test its empty weight.

Sandy seemed to be having a struggle with himself. Grace thought that he might have realised it was against his self-interest to be rude to the most famous dreamhunter. He began to talk again, stiff and expressionless. 'I did set out to visit her. I caught a lift on a barge from Tarry Cove — you know, the last stop on the Sisters Beach line?'

'Where the fishing fleet anchors.'

'And coal barges. I caught a lift on a barge going to Debt River, the mine at the base of So Long Spit.'

'And?'

'And I thought about it as I went.'

'You thought about going to see Laura?'

'I thought about whether I really wanted to see her.'

'Oh, Sandy, what did she do to you? I mean, apart from —' Grace stopped, not wanting to talk out loud about Laura and the nightmare. She put her hand on his arm. 'Was it you who copied the letters for her?'

Sandy was startled. 'What are you talking about? What letters? Laura sent *me* a letter — she wanted me to pass it on to some other person.'

'Who?'

'The letter didn't say. I was supposed to leave it somewhere. I didn't do it.' Sandy was struggling to dampen down the fury in his face and voice. He ended up looking prim. 'She was trying to get me to be her go-between.'

Grace looked about them. The outfitter's wasn't busy. They had an aisle to themselves. She lowered her voice, trying to encourage him to do so too. 'Where is this letter now?'

'I tore it up. Bits of it are still plastered to the guttering outside my bedroom window. A nice reminder of Laura, and my limited usefulness to her.'

Grace touched his arm again, tentative. 'Sandy, I want to apologise for Laura if she —'

'She's just a *child*,' he said. 'Self-centred, feckless and childish.'

Grace shook her head. She had once thought that way about Laura, but Laura had changed.

'Anyway,' Sandy said, 'at least I didn't totally waste my time. When I got to Debt River I met a ranger who was walking the border from Tricksie Bend, mostly on the outside, only ducking In at those earth ramps they use as lookouts. Do you know what I mean?'

Grace nodded. She'd seen the ramps on the border the few times she'd gone along it rather than heading straight In. The ramps were about ten to fifteen feet high, and made of piled earth tamped down by spadework. Each ramp was a vantage point over the surrounding country.

'The ranger told me about a dream on Foreigner's North,' Sandy said.

Foreigner's North was a landmark on maps of the Place. It was on the furthest western border, just Inside. It was in the north as well as the west, possibly also the furthest northern point of the invisible territory — Grace would have to check a map of Coal Bay to be sure. She had always presumed it was a compass reference of some kind.

'The dream — Quake — is something only a few dreamhunters can catch. The ranger told me that it was alarming, but not exactly a nightmare. No one has their name on it, because it isn't commercial — supposedly.' Sandy looked smug. 'Though I think I've uncovered its commercial potential.' Sandy laughed. 'I saw that, Mrs Tiebold — your eyes lit up.'

'I'm intrigued,' Grace said. 'How can a dream be "not exactly a nightmare"?'

'Well — if something alarming happens in it, but the person whose point of view it is isn't alarmed. Quake is from the point of view of a child, like The Water Diviner. I'm wondering whether that's my affinity: dreams where the audience gets to be a child again. The boy in The Water Diviner is about ten. This is a much younger child, maybe four or five.'

'That's very unusual.'

'Perhaps you'd like to come to my performance tonight? I've spent the last two days chewing Wakeful and getting together an audience — mostly scientists from the University. Geologists and so forth. I've rented a whole floor of a hotel here on the Isle. Eight bedrooms. I'm charging twenty dollars a head.'

Grace was a little embarrassed for Sandy — standing in the aisle of an outfitter's and advertising his prices. But she still asked for the name and address of the hotel, and when the doors closed before the performance.

'Will you come?' Sandy asked, keen to impress her.

Grace considered. She closed one eye. She took her time. She very much wanted to come and try Sandy's Quake. She'd not been four or five since she was four or five, and couldn't remember it very clearly. She'd been to a performance of The Water Diviner and had thought that although Sandy's penumbra was still quite tight, his dream was very clear, and exact in all its details. He was a promising talent, and he was catching new things, which the majority of dreamhunters didn't even try to do. She said, 'If I attend, then you'll be boosted.'

'Then perhaps you could come at a reduced price.'

'Reduced?' Grace didn't believe her ears. He was so brazen. He'd even folded his arms and tilted his head back. He was bargaining. He wasn't going to be flattered by her interest. She said, 'A discount then, for me and my husband.'

'Done,' said Sandy.

'We're fashionable people, you know,' Grace said.

'Yes, I do know. And I know I'm supposed to fawn upon all the fashionable people.'

He was thinking of Laura, Grace thought. What had the girl done to him? What was in that letter he tore to pieces? She said, 'We'll see you tonight then. I'm looking forward to it.' She patted his arm, and took her new pack up to the counter.

'A letter! And he destroyed it?' said Chorley. 'Was it a letter to some man?'

'He didn't say it was to a man. You're jumping to conclusions — the conclusions you're always jumping to these days. One moment you're fretting about Laura and Sandy Mason, the next you're fretting about Sandy's supposed rival. Honestly, Chorley!'

'Young men can't be trusted with girls.'

'This is the voice of experience, I suppose?'

'Rather remote experience, but still.'

'You're turning into such a reactionary. It's that old man with the beard — your new best friend.'

There was a scorched silence from Chorley. He put his coat on over his silk dressing gown. He put galoshes on over his tasselled slippers. He fumed. 'The Grand Patriarch is not a replacement for Tziga,' he said.

'I'm sorry, dear. But you can be so silly about Laura. She's no more likely to be seduced than Rose. Less likely, since she's sequestered on So Long Spit. Conveniently,' Grace added, 'till I cool off.'

Chorley ignored this remark. 'Laura hasn't many barriers left in her behaviour. That seems to be something dreams do to some dreamhunters. And — let me remind you — I was *right* to worry about Tziga.'

'You weren't worried he'd be *seduced*.'

'I was worried that none of us, and nothing he had, would ever be enough for him.'

'I'm like that too,' Grace said.

'No, you're not.'

'Yes, I am. The only difference between Tziga and me is that I love all the dreams I catch. I love them. And without them I'd be nothing. I'd be a withered apple on a windowsill.' Grace pulled her image from a dream, one of her sad ones, in which a widow returned home after her husband's funeral, and after a short time staying in the houses of relatives, to find nothing much changed, but her house empty and stale, and her stored apples withered.

Grace said, 'I love being borne up by my big audiences — everyone breathing together, breathing in time with my breathing. It's not just that I enjoy what I do, or that I'm proud of how good at it I am. It's this — when I'm carried up on the high tide of a full house at the Rainbow Opera, when I'm *not myself*, that's when I'm most fully alive.'

Chorley put his arms around his wife and kissed her. He said, 'Dear, none of that is under threat. Your audience fell off for a time, but you got them back again. You had a bad patch, but it's over.'

They quietly held one another. Then Grace said, 'Shall we go and see what this boy has, then?'

Sandy's twelve guests gathered together in the larger suite to have a drink before they retired. They pulled dining chairs into the space before the hearth, between the sofa and armchairs already there. A waiter wheeled in a trolley with hot chocolate and cakes, port and brandy.

It fell to Grace to play hostess — she was the only woman present and the collection of crusty geologists were clearly used to being waited on. Grace poured chocolate, and handed around cups and glasses, and spooned cream onto slices of cake. Then she gathered her white silk dressing gown around her bright yellow silk pyjamas, and sat down with her own cup of chocolate.

Sandy stood with one arm on the mantelpiece and one foot up on the hearth. He was giving an account of his journey. He seemed to be enjoying himself, speaking well and with a natural authority.

Chorley leaned towards his wife to whisper. 'How old is he?'

'Eighteen or nineteen, I believe — he Tried late.'

Chorley nodded and continued his haughty scrutiny of the boy Rose referred to, jokingly, as 'Laura's suitor'.

'The further west I went, the poorer the land was. When we think of Coal Bay we think about Sisters Beach or the dairy flats around Whynew Stream. But beyond Whynew Stream there are only wet paddocks rusty with dock leaf. I slept where it was dry, just Inside the border. But I didn't walk along on the Inside. It's pointless to do that.'

'Yes!' One geologist removed his pipe from his teeth with a loud clack. 'The Inside to outside ratio is miles to yards, I gather.' He put his pipe back in his mouth with another punctuating clack of tooth enamel on polished walnut. 'It's simply incredible.'

Sandy said, 'Because the Place is so vast, its explorers have tried to make landmarks, as well as recording the landmarks they find. One of the first explorers was a legendary figure — legendary among rangers at least — a man known as "the Foreigner".'

'They think he was French,' said Grace.

'He tried to walk the border before anyone else,' said Sandy. 'The first mapmakers kept finding his marks. Foreigner's North is a landmark — a compass mark carved into the ground on the border, at the point furthest north and west, though I understand his west is somewhere else.'

Grace said, 'It's because of his west that they suppose he's a foreigner — west is *ouest* in French.'

Sandy said, 'A ranger took me to Foreigner's North. The dream Quake is right on top of it. The compass mark — a big N — looks like it's been hit by a quake too. It's cracked right across.'

'There was a sizeable earthquake in Coal Bay in 1886,' a geologist said. 'That's what first uncovered the coal at Debt River. Lumps of it washed downstream and began to turn up on the tide. The forest is very thick in the north-west, but prospectors went in and found the slip, and the seam of coal. Of course, folks had already found coal at Whynew Stream over a hundred years before. But that seam was soon exhausted. However, that's where the name comes from — Coal Bay.'

'The quake was twenty years ago?' said Chorley.

The geologist nodded, then turned to Sandy and asked, 'Is the quake in the dream a good-sized one?'

Sandy straightened and took his arm off the mantelpiece. 'Shall we go and see?'

The boy was practising his violin on the porch of the cottage when he saw something pouring out of the dead tree trunk in the yard. He put his violin down — his child's violin, a fine thing, as precious and clever as he was himself — and brushed his itching jaw against his shoulder. The rosin made a mark on his shirt. He stepped off the porch and wandered across the yard to look at the flood of — what? Sap?

From far away the substance looked like chocolate sauce from one of his Ma's 'self-saucing puddings'. (His Ma used to say that she was a 'self-

saucing pudding', which was a joke about how in their family there was no 'Da', like in other families.)

The boy squatted to look at the brown substance. The air was hot nearer the ground, as though the ground were cooking something.

He saw that the oozing mass was ants, thousands of them, flowing in a twisting, glistening brown rope down the grooved tree trunk. He could actually hear them. The ants were making a noise like bursting bubbles in sea foam — only much quieter. The boy could only hear them because the sounds of the world had dropped away. Even the birds in the bushes were silent.

His mother came to the cottage door to ask what he was doing. She was wiping her hands on her apron. He wanted to say to her that the ants were leaving their nest. But he didn't get to say it. He saw her hands grow still, though she continued to hold her apron gathered before her.

They both listened. The boy wondered why the horses in the paddock behind the house had decided, all at once, to gallop down to the back fence.

But the thunder wasn't horses.

The ground began to move — it lurched sideways, and then jolted up in shudders. The boy fell forward onto his hands and knees. He heard his mother shout. He saw her rush across the porch. At the same time the cottage chimney slammed down onto the corrugated iron roof, then came apart and slid — bricks and boulder-sized chunks of mortar and brick — down the curve of the roof and off its edge. The boy's mother rushed out between the falling bricks. None of them struck her.

She staggered across the yard and picked him up, then stumbled under the yard's one tree, a cabbage tree partly smothered with honeysuckle. The honeysuckle was in flower and as they stood — he in her arms — the tree dropped honeysuckle blossoms and a thick veil of floral scent down over them. His mother spread one hand over the crown of the boy's head and held him sheltered in the curve of her body. She leaned back against the tree trunk and struggled to keep her feet.

There were crashes and thumps from the cottage — scarcely audible in the thunder from everywhere. And there were high-pitched sounds — the squawk of nails pulled loose from timber, and the painted weatherboards splitting with a sound like gunfire.

Water was jumping up out of the puddles and into the air.

Then the heaving and juddering stopped. The yard went quiet, though the air seemed to torque and rustle.

The boy's mother held him tight. Her heart was beating so hard the boy could feel it pushing against him, fierce and powerful. Her heart was strong, the boy thought, but not nearly so strong as the ground, the angry ground.

Grace was shaken awake by the bed heaving. Beside her Chorley was sitting up. She heard him fumbling around on the nightstand. He lit a candle.

Grace made a muffled noise of irritation. The bed sheets were uncomfortably starchy and the room was stuffy. She remembered that she was in a hotel — the sort of hotel young Sandy Mason could afford to rent for his performance.

'That was Verity,' Chorley said to his wife.

Grace's next annoyed grunt had, at its end, a mild tone of inquiry. Verity was Chorley's dead sister, Laura's mother.

'The woman on the porch,' said Chorley.

'Sandy isn't a Gifter,' Grace said. She was waking up, reluctantly. She could feel herself shrinking away from something.

Maze Plasir was a Gifter (or, impolitely, a Grafter). He could graft the bodies of real people onto the characters in his dreams. That was why he was in demand by the sort of men who would send him out to watch — say — their daughter's school friends and then have those school friends stand in for the obligingly friendly females of Plasir's speciality dreams. Gifting was a very rare talent. Some dreamhunters, at certain times in their lives, did make their own substitutions. As a young woman, Grace had found herself replacing the anonymously handsome faces of her dream's heroes with Chorley Tiebold's after she first saw him at a ball. It just happened, and was beyond her control.

'But why would Sandy think of *Verity*?' Chorley said, bemused. 'Where would he *get* her from?'

'Laura.'

'How could he get her from Laura?'

'No. It *was* Laura.' Grace sat up so quickly she threw the covers off them. 'It wasn't Verity — it was Laura.'

Chorley screwed up his face. 'Why would Sandy want to imagine himself as a child and Laura as his mother?'

Grace put her hands over her face. She was very confused, appalled and, at the same time, deeply moved.

'It's perverse,' Chorley was saying, his voice strained.

Grace put a hand on his arm. She was worried he might leap out of bed and wake up Sandy Mason, and start demanding explanations. 'Calm down,' she said, though she was very far from calm herself.

'It's so perverse I can't even imagine what kind of perversity it is!' Chorley said. Then, 'Why are you laughing?'

'You're funny.'

'Grace, Sandy Mason finds he's an angelic, violin-playing little boy, so immediately supplies himself with my niece as his mother. And you're laughing. I'm a liberal man. I have an abundance of tolerance for dreamhunters and their peculiarities. But this is going too far.'

Grace wiped her eyes. 'Shhh,' she said.

Chorley shut his mouth and only radiated indignation.

Grace took his hand and met his eyes. 'That was Laura. She wasn't tall or fair like Verity, but she had Verity's sweet, queenly face. Sandy Mason isn't a Gifter. And if he recognises the woman in his dream he'll be very upset and angry with himself and suppose it's because he can't get Laura out of his head.' Grace kissed her husband's hand. Her own heart was pounding as hard as the heart of the woman in Sandy's dream, but she tried to be calm for her husband's sake. 'Listen, love,' she said, 'the convict in Laura's first dream remembered being a boy racing a schooner along the shore of So Long Spit, and you saw the lighthouse keeper's boy doing just that. The dreams are set in the future. And that was Laura, grown up and with a little boy of her own.'

Part IX
Summer and Christmas

One

When on holiday in Awa Inlet, Mamie preferred to spend as little time as possible with her brother and his friends. Mamie told Rose that the boys were boring. She preferred to give them the slip. Straight after breakfast she and Rose would often walk up the stream and into the beech forest, or set out along the hot mud track through the reed beds at the eastern end of the inlet. Mamie would tell anyone who was listening that they were going to gather shells on the sand bar. Or she'd say they were going swimming and then *would* go to gather shells.

Ru had once confronted Mamie about it. 'You told us you'd be down by the rocks,' he said, aggrieved.

'So?' said Mamie. 'Why do you suddenly want *my* company?'

Ru had coloured up and hadn't complained again.

Mamie was, in her own brutal way, trying to look after Rose, who had discovered that it wasn't at all fun to be admired by someone she didn't like, especially someone you had to share a roof with. When Ru Doran looked at her, Rose felt at odds with her own body. She felt that there was something amiss with her. She didn't want Ru to think she was beautiful. She felt that she should be able somehow to show him that he wasn't allowed to have opinions about her appearance — or, at least, that he wasn't allowed to show them. Being openly admired by someone she found unattractive made Rose feel that her beauty didn't belong to her, was in fact something tricky, a demon hiding inside her, prompting and making offers, and emitting strange odours when she'd rather just go about being her usual self.

Mamie and Rose's favourite beach in the inlet was towards the western end, quite some distance from the Doran house.

On a day two weeks into Rose's visit, the weather was very hot, and the girls had swum for over an hour, jumping from the rocks over and over until their ears began to ache. Then they lay on the sand. Salt prickled on their warming bodies as their skins grew dry and tight.

'How long can we stay away?' Rose said to her friend. Her room got the afternoon sun and would be too stuffy to hide in.

'I'm going to have to have a word with Ru, aren't I?' Mamie said.

Rose shrugged, her shoulders rasping on the sand.

Mamie picked up Rose's skirt and fished in its pocket for the letter Rose had received that morning.

'Hey!' Rose said, but didn't move.

'It's only Patty — Patty is a weakness we share, Rose.' Mamie pulled a face, then quoted their classmate's letter: '"I am deprived of society here in the South. I see no one I like."' She laughed. 'But see, a paragraph later she's dancing the military two-step with her cousin. You know, I think they're all cousins in Canning. Which is a shame, since poor Patty is one of those girls who is longing to be able to say to someone things like "An introduction for the purposes of a dance does not constitute an acquaintance." Instead, she knows absolutely everyone. And Rose! It says here she already has the pattern for her Presentation Ball gown. Hasn't she got *any* other interests?'

'Making fun of what other people are thinking doesn't actually constitute "an interest", Mamie,' Rose said.

Mamie tossed the letter down. 'Let's go back,' she said. 'I'm not going to be kept from the house by my brother and his tedious admiration.'

Rose got up and dressed, while Mamie tried to think of a plan to discourage Ru. 'You could propose marriage — that ought to sober him up.'

'I could start scratching myself all the time, so he thinks I'm infested.'

'Or you could clear your throat every thirty seconds like Miss Toop at the Academy.'

'I could make a three-pronged attack, clearing my throat, scratching *and* proposing,' Rose said.

'Or you could just attack his three prongs!'

'Mamie!'

Shrieks of laughter.

That night, in the small hours, Rose woke and lay listening. She heard a disturbed bird twittering in a tree near her window. Perhaps its calls had hooked her out of sleep, or perhaps she'd been roused by the same thing that had made the bird cry out in alarm. She felt that something remarkable had happened only a moment before. The curtains in Rose's room were thick, the room black and the bird calls were bright in the darkness.

She got out of bed and shuffled to the window, slid the curtains open and squinted into brilliant moonlight.

Outside all the colours of day were present under a smoky filter. It was late, and a dewfall had softened and silvered the grass.

Rose decided to go out. She left her room and crept down the stairs. She went out by the French doors in the dining room. They were locked, but the key was in the lock.

She set off down the flagstone steps of the terrace, then veered away through the orchard and headed for the best path to the sea, the bed of the narrow-gauge railway that ran from the shore to the house.

The Doran summer house was on a slope at the back of the inlet. It was grand and solid, built of blond sandstone, its roof tiled with slate. It had been a big project, in a remote spot, and had presented its builders with some challenges. Labour hadn't been a problem, for the hill had been terraced and the foundations laid by convict labour. The difficulty had been in getting the materials from the shore to the site across the boggy paddocks of the former farm. The farm already had a rough road that ran, plumb straight, from the shore to the foot of the hill, along an avenue of great mature plane trees. Cas Doran's solution to the transportation problem was to have a narrow-gauge railway line built along the road. A small engine ran on the line. In many trips, over many months, the engine hauled stone and timber, marble and parquet flooring, roof tiles, window glass and finally furniture from the landing to the site.

When Rose had first arrived at the Awa Inlet, the train she was on made a special stop at the end of the trestle bridge that crossed the mouth of the River Sva. Rose then got into a small boat, and was rowed up a broad tidal channel, through the reed beds, to the Doran jetty. There she was greeted by the sight of a butler sitting in the cab of a little engine. A footman stowed her bags in the single truck the engine was pulling. Then she climbed into the engine behind its driver and rode up to the house.

The engine had been stoked up several times during her visit — to pick up Ru's guests and their luggage, and to carry supplies: baskets of fruit and vegetables; sides of pork and beef; cages of live chickens; blocks of ice; and hampers of dry goods, preserves, cheese and wine.

Rose emerged from the orchard and went into the avenue of old trees. She patted the engine, which was sitting in its shelter, cool, still and breathless.

In the daytime the avenue was a shady tunnel; at night it was like a cathedral, a ruin with a broken roof. Rose walked beside the tracks, her face turned up to the moonlight that fell, almost warm, through gaps in the foliage high overhead. She only glanced down now and again to step over tree roots that snaked almost all the way up to the railway line.

Rose intended to go to the shore. The tide would be out, and she wanted to see what the bare sands of the inlet looked like by the light of the moon. But, as she came near the two stacks of rails left over from the time the line was laid, Rose saw something that made her stop and stand still, and then slink off the track and behind a tree trunk.

She stepped up onto a tree root and peered around the trunk to check that yes, she *had* seen a light. There was a lamp sitting, unattended, beside the piles of rails. Nothing moved in the circle of its vaporous white light. And then a moth appeared and began a colliding orbit.

Rose, craning around the trunk of the tree, saw four rangers appear. The men flickered into existence beside the pallets and their loads. The rangers were working in pairs, picking up several rails each and carrying them out of sight, Into the Place.

For two weeks Rose had walked by the stacked rails — and, for that matter, the pile of 'surplus' wooden sleepers a few paces away, concealed in a patch of fennel. She had walked past them and hadn't wondered how Doran's builders had made such a huge overestimation when buying for what was, after all, less than a mile of line. Nor had she wondered why the rails, after sitting there for years, lacked even the faintest freckle of rust.

Now she knew. The piled rails never rusted because they were replaced: new ones were landed on the shore — probably when the house was empty — and were carried by engine to this spot, and then, by rangers, Into the Place.

Rose knew nothing about the country In from the Awa Inlet, but she knew that she'd never heard *anything* about a railway in the Place. Where would a railway line go? And what would run on it, if a flame couldn't be kindled and put to coal, to heat a boiler and make steam? If there could be no spark in the valves of a combustion engine, if only muscle could move things?

As Rose considered all this, the rangers came and went, and the stacks of rails were gradually reduced. She remained where she was till she worked out, from snatches of the rangers' talk and their gestures, that next they meant to start transporting the wooden sleepers from the fennel patch to the border.

She couldn't keep edging around the tree in order to stay out of sight. She'd have to make a break for it, wait till they were all In, then break cover and run as far from the lamplight as she could. She hoped that the light had formed a kind of capsule, and had sealed the rangers into it so that they would be as blinded as people coming into a dark room from a bright outdoors. She hoped that the moonlight would seem weak to their dazzled eyes and they would miss her running form, her pale hair and white nightgown.

Rose waited till all four rangers were out of sight, then sprinted flat out for the next tree. She slid behind it before they reappeared. Again she waited, ducked out, dashed on, scrambled under cover.

When she was five trees further up the avenue, she looked back to see the lamp moving, then passing into the fennel, casting giant feathery shadows on the smooth trunks of the nearest plane trees. The shadows leaped to engulf the trees as the lamp was lowered to the ground.

Rose sprinted through the orchard and up the steps to the house. Her feet and the hem of her nightgown were wet with dew, the cloth clinging to her ankles. She didn't pause to catch her breath, but made straight for the unlocked dining-room doors.

Then she stopped dead.

Ru Doran stood on the veranda beside the only unlocked door. He looked at Rose, then past her at the lamplight along the railway line. He craned, and came forward. Rose edged away a little, so he stopped. 'What was it?' he said.

'Rangers,' said Rose.

He regarded her. 'You know, most girls would be more cautious about wandering at night.'

Rose shrugged. She met his eyes, but only briefly.

'But you aren't like most girls, are you, Rose?'

'What do you mean?' Rose said. She felt uneasy. Ru was standing between her and the door.

'Well — your mother is a dreamhunter. And so you've been exposed.' His tone was insinuating.

Rose tossed her head, snorted and started forward briskly.

Ru intercepted her. He put his shoulder against her, backed her into the wall and caught hold of her wrist.

'Please let me go,' she said.

'You're still whispering.' He sounded amused. 'Very sensible. It would be a shame to be caught. Out of your bed. Snooping.'

'Let go of me,' Rose said, angry but ineffectual. She found that she was feeling more indignant than frightened, though she knew that perhaps fear was the sensible response to being cornered and threatened.

Ru Doran *was* threatening her. He'd decided she was a certain kind of girl. A girl somehow spoiled by 'exposure' to freedoms and excitements most girls hadn't had. He thought she was fair game. And he was laughing at her: chuckling in a superior, indulgent way, and shaking his head. How dare he be so comfortable about making her uncomfortable?

'Let go of me,' she said, 'or I'll get my father to sort you out — or, better, I'll get *your* father to do it!'

Ru Doran's face went hard with anger and, immediately following the anger, spite. He put his free hand to her face, perhaps to press it over her mouth. But Rose had had enough. She moved towards him, and let herself fall forward. One of her feet thumped onto his instep, and her wrist wrenched free of his grip. She plunged through the gap between his body and the wall of the house, caught herself on her hands, sprang up, ran to the door. She jerked the door open and rushed inside.

Rose hurried back to her room, closed the door and locked it. She climbed into bed, and lay fuming and shivering till the birds started up, legitimately this time, to greet the dawn.

Two

The following day, shortly after lunch, Cas Doran was in the library, having a fine time marking different-sized circles on a map of Founderston, when he heard raised voices in the hallway. His wife's voice, and his daughter's. He opened the library door and put his head out to hear.

'You're not doing anything, mother! I'm sorry I lost my temper at breakfast, but as far as I can tell the day's just ticking over as usual.'

'Be quiet and go back upstairs, Mamie.'

Cas Doran went out to investigate.

As soon as she saw him, Mamie hurled herself at him, though stopping short of actual contact. 'Father, Rose is leaving!'

'What on earth is going on?' Cas Doran demanded.

'Ru assaulted Rose!' Mamie said.

There was a moment of blank, burning silence.

Cas Doran looked at his wife. She appeared pained and put out. 'Mamie,' she said, coldly, and pointed at the stairs, 'please go, before you do any more damage.'

Mamie looked at her father and clasped her hands together to make a gesture of pleading. 'I don't see why Mother must believe Ru!' she said.

Doran held up his hand. 'I don't see any point in your offering your opinion, Mamie. I'll wait to hear from your friend.'

Mamie started to cry. 'Don't do that,' she said. 'Don't do that thing where you start talking about someone not using their name.'

'Mamie, you're being oddly abstract,' said her father. He wasn't used to seeing her cry — in fact, he hadn't seen her shed a tear since she was quite small.

'She's "Rose", not "your friend",' Mamie said. She turned around and stomped back upstairs, wiping her eyes on her sleeve — mottled, stout, ugly, angry.

Cas Doran asked his wife to please step into the library. He held the door open for her and closed it firmly after them.

His wife told him that Mamie had been in her room since breakfast, after tipping a plate of black pudding and grilled tomato into her brother's lap.

'What did Ru have to say?'

Doran's wife folded her hands into one of the pleats at the front of her lace tea-gown and looked trustingly and calmly at her husband. She waited for him to take charge.

'Yes, I suppose I should ask him myself,' said Doran. 'Will you fetch him for me? And I'll want to speak to Rose too. Perhaps you should dispatch Mamie to find her?'

Doran's wife said, 'It's my opinion that since taking up with Rose, Mamie is showing signs of becoming a rather passionate and dramatic girl.'

'So you think Mamie is exaggerating?'

'Yes, I do.'

Doran said, 'Please send Ru to me.'

Ru Doran looked astonished when his father asked him what he'd done to upset Rose.

'Some time last night?' said Doran, prompting.

'Oh.' Ru touched his forehead, tapped himself several times between the eyebrows. His father knew this gesture — Ru was organising his thoughts. 'I thought Mother had this all in hand. Very well. Last night I couldn't go to sleep,' he said. 'So I went out onto the terrace to have a cigarette. I'm sorry, father, I know you don't like me to smoke.' He looked contrite. 'While I was there I noticed a light in the avenue. A lamp of some sort. I was about to go and see what it was, when I saw Rose hurrying back up the lawn. I guessed she'd been meeting someone — perhaps her cousin — since the light was just about where the border is.' Ru looked earnestly at his father. 'Whatever she was up to, I caught her at it.'

Doran nodded.

'When she saw me, she wasn't pleased. She tried to push past me. I grabbed her wrist and asked what she was doing. Then she stepped on my foot — I can show you the bruise if you like. She rushed inside and the lamp went out a few moments later.'

'And that's all there was to it?'

'Yes, father. Rose was startled because I caught her up to something. But it is my fault she's upset. I was having a bit of fun, pretending to want to interrogate her.'

Doran nodded. 'Thank you, Ru. You may go now.'

Ru gave his father a tight little smile, and left.

Rose had her dress back on over her wet bathing suit. Her hair was dull and full-bodied with salt. She was walking back along the railway when Mamie met her. 'Good God, Mamie! Have you been crying?' Rose asked. She reached out for her friend, then thought better of it and only gave Mamie her shoes to carry. They fell into step, Rose still occasionally mounting a rail, her toes curled to grip, swaying as she balanced along it. She told Mamie she'd gone out to get away from everyone. 'You were so upset when I said I'd be leaving. I thought I should cool down and think about it. Anyway, I've given it some more thought and I think the sensible thing *is* to cut my visit short.' Rose gave her friend a careful look.

There wasn't much Mamie could say to Rose's plans. She did say, 'Father wants to speak to you.'

'Did you tell him?'

'No, I —' Mamie's mouth worked, then she smiled. 'I tipped Ru's breakfast on him. I mean, on Ru, not Father. Then I had to explain to Mother. Then Mother spoke to Ru. Then she spoke to Father. I've spent most of the morning shut in my room.'

'Oh, hell,' said Rose. She came to a stop and her foot slipped off the rail. She tumbled and only just caught herself, then stood rubbing the knee of the leg she'd landed on awkwardly.

Mamie said, 'I'm supposed to deliver you to Father in the library.' Then, 'For goodness' sake, Rose, can't you walk and think at the same time?'

Rose started walking again. She said, 'I may have to go home, but you should come and stay at Summerfort. Make a return visit. Do you think your parents will let you?'

'One minute you're upset, the next you're arranging your social calendar.'

'So?'

'You don't nurse grudges, do you?'

'Mamie, I'm not going to let my feelings about Ru contaminate our friendship,' Rose said, then thought, rather surprised: 'Yes — friendship. Mamie *is* my friend now.' She went on: 'I'd like you to come to Sisters Beach in the New Year. We can visit a dressmaker together. We can pick patterns for our Presentation Ball gowns.'

'Oh, I can see that happening — after your father has chastised my brother.'

'My father needn't know a thing — if *your* father knows his business.' With that, Rose strode off towards the house with her head held high.

Mrs Doran came into the library. 'I have Rose,' she said.

'I asked Mamie to fetch her,' said Doran.

'And Mamie did so. Then she went back to her room. I can't have her creating scenes at the breakfast table, even in defence of her friend's honour.'

'Very well,' said Doran. 'Mamie can remain in her room. But only until this evening.'

'That Tiebold girl likes attention,' Mrs Doran said, in a warning tone. She opened the door, ushered Rose into the library and left, closing the door after her.

Doran got up and gestured the girl to a seat near the window. She sat and he remained standing, his back to the bright sunlight. 'Well, Rose,' he began, 'you want to leave us early?'

'I think I must,' she said.

'Mamie tells me that you're upset.'

Rose began to fiddle with her hair — picking up the ends and inspecting them. 'Um, not so much now,' she said. 'Now I'm feeling fairly resolute.'

'May I ask what you mean by "fairly resolute"? Do you mean that you're approximating resolution? Or that you're being fair?'

'Mamie gets it from you,' Rose said.

'Gets what?'

'Hair splitting.' Rose was frowning at the ends of her hair. She dropped the crackling golden mass and looked up at him. She began to tell the story — her side of it. 'I went for a walk last night and saw some rangers shifting the surplus rails and sleepers. I wondered what was In from the Awa Inlet and why you were building a railway there.'

'I see.' Cas Doran blinked and rubbed his jaw. He felt his scalp prickle as blood pumped up into his head. He said, 'To put you right on that score — directly In from here are the Pinnacles, a range of steep, crumbling hills. They are by far the most extensive known barrier in the Place. Last year a group of rangers built a gate to block the entrance of the only pass through the Pinnacles. They did all the welding here, on the shore, then they carried the gate In and set it up. The gate is often locked because the pass through the Pinnacles is unstable and unsafe. Rangers struggle to keep it in reasonable repair. Lately the Body has had rangers building retaining walls on the worst cliff faces in the pass. As it happened I had surplus rails and timber, and thought they might like to make use of them.' Doran spread his hands. 'So there you go,' he said.

Rose had listened, but towards the end of his speech her face had gone taut with watchfulness. She looked ten years older and superbly intelligent. Doran regarded her with wonder. He thought: 'What on earth is she thinking?' He began to check his story for faults. In a moment he had it. Of course there were new rails all the time, the pile almost always refreshed the moment a load was removed. The rails never sat there long — so they didn't rust. Rose Tiebold could guess he was lying — but Doran didn't feel in the least uncomfortable. He only felt very alert. He had a strange urge to ask her what she thought of his explanation, and an even stranger desire to know what she'd think of his whole plan. He put these odd ideas aside and prompted her. 'You were watching the rangers, and —'

'And when I came back to the house I met Ru, and he said I shouldn't be wandering about at night.'

'And so you shouldn't.'

Rose frowned at this interruption and went on in a rush. 'And then he said I was different from other girls, and that it was because my mother was a dreamhunter and I'd been exposed. That was his word: "exposed". Then he squashed me into the wall and grabbed my wrist. I told him to let go. He was laughing. Then I told him that Da would sort him out, and then that *you* would. He got a mean look — so I stood on his foot and got away.'

Cas Doran was as intrigued by the similarities between Rose's and Ru's stories as by the differences.

The sun had moved and Rose's eyes were now no longer in a strip of shade formed by the window frame. They were watering. She got up and stepped out of the patch of sunlight. She remained standing. 'I hope you believe me,' she said, dignified.

'Ru has a very different story.'

'I'm amazed he feels he needs a story.'

'Do you think it's at all possible you're taking this too seriously?' Doran asked.

'I've been thinking about that. When I talked to Mamie this morning I was very angry. Then I took a step back. Now my head tells me it wasn't really serious, I wasn't in any danger, I was just being nervous. He did keep laughing as if he hoped I'd get the joke.'

'Well, I'm relieved to hear you say that.'

'Wait,' Rose said. She held up her hand. 'Ru made me feel bad. My head may say that I'm being oversensitive. But my head is timid. It wants to hide itself in the sand. My gut tells me that maybe Ru would have taken his teasing as far as he wanted, even if he only thought of it as teasing.'

Cas Doran listened, nodding.

'I hope you believe me,' Rose said again.

Cas Doran turned away from her and thought — disconnected thoughts. He thought that his son must learn how to behave. Ru must not break the law. No child of his could be a criminal. Doran thought that he must pack Rose off back to her home. His wife had said the girl was a troublemaker. It was better to simply remove her. 'I'll have Ru apologise to you,' he said, after a silence.

'Must I be embarrassed further?'

Doran looked at Rose sharply. 'You haven't mentioned embarrassment before. And, Rose, when you told Mamie your story she caused a scene. You must have known she'd do something. You say, "I hope you believe me," but really you're asking me to *do* something. You want to exercise your power, but only up to a point, apparently. You don't want to be embarrassed. But I think you are obliged to hear my son's apology.'

He watched her grow pale.

'Rose, I think I can rely on you to be reasonable.'

Rose burst into tears and sank to her knees. She pressed her face into the seat of the chair she had been sitting in. She wept, totally abandoned — as if in an ecstasy of misery.

Cas Doran was startled. 'Come now,' he said, hovering ineffectually over her. Then, 'Do you want me to fetch my wife?'

'No!' Rose howled. Then, 'Why do *I* always have to be reasonable?'

'Well, think how you'd feel if I'd said I depended on you to be *un*reasonable,' said Doran. He was gratified by the result of this remark. Rose stopped crying to think, as tantrum-throwing tots will if some imaginative effort has been made to distract them. He added, 'It's a compliment, you know.'

Rose wiped her eyes, and hiccuped. 'People are always trying to control me with compliments.'

'I'm not trying to control you. I'm trying to do right by you. I'll have Ru apologise, and you'll hear his apology. It might do him some good to see how upset you are. You will listen to what he has to say, then I'll have you seen safely home.'

'Can Mamie come and stay with me after Christmas? Even if her mother is angry at me.'

'I'm sure that can be arranged.'

'Thank you.'

'And I'll deal with Ru. I'm sure you're right that he doesn't really see how he troubled you. But I'll make him see.'

Rose muttered something that Doran didn't catch. He told her to dry her eyes and compose herself. 'I won't be too long,' he said, and left her.

Alone in the library, Rose considered blowing her nose on the curtain — its nice brocade. It was a spiteful thought. As she considered it, Rose thought of Mamie's mother's rich skirts, and imagined the curtain was the hem of a skirt. She seethed with fury till she felt she was breathing smoke. Her nostrils were pricking and stinging.

Rose got up and paced. She laughed at herself, at what she'd nearly said aloud when Cas Doran had said of Ru, 'I'll make him see.' 'Yes, I bet there's a nightmare for that,' she'd muttered. Thank God Doran hadn't heard her.

Rose was annoyed with herself for crying. But she'd wanted to go home without having to see Ru Doran again. She longed to be with her family at Summerfort. They would all be home for Christmas. Uncle Tziga too. Rose wanted so badly to put her arms around them all — Uncle Tziga, Laura, her Ma and Da — that she could almost smell them, the different smells of their clothes and hair. She felt like an animal — simple, and crazy with homesickness.

In her agitated state Rose had been pacing round the room and had stopped before the library desk. She stood a while in a trance, then happened to notice what she was staring at. In the low, angling sunlight Rose could see that the inset leather surface of the desk was printed with different-sized circles. Many circles, like raindrops in a puddle, except that only some of them were overlapping. And, as she had only a short while earlier, listening to Doran's story about the use of steel rails for retaining walls, listening and thinking 'That's plausible' and also 'But why is there no *rust* on the rails?' Rose found herself in two minds. One — the mind on top — was uncomfortable and unhappy and worried about having to face Ru Doran. The other mind, the one underneath, was shouting like a siren, 'Look! Circles!'

There were other things on the desk: piles of papers, folders, an inkwell and a jumble of pens, pencils, geometry instruments. There was also a large rolled canvas. Rose saw that the roll was embossed with curved lines, like scales, marks that showed clearly in the low sun.

Rose swooped on it, unfastened the string that kept it closed and let it fall open.

It was a map of Founderston. A detailed map, with a scale of six inches to a mile. Rose saw that the central city was covered in circles, some drawn in pencil, some in ink. In the middle of each circle, in neat, particular handwriting, was a street address. Rose read: '121 Courtesy Street'; '15 Fuller Grove . . .' Some of the circles with street names and numbers also had surnames. And some of these names seemed vaguely familiar to Rose.

As her eyes roamed over the map she heard footsteps in the hallway. She hurriedly rolled the map, twisted its string around it several times and set it back at the side of the desk. Then the door opened, and she spun around to put her back to the desktop, and her face to the window.

The low sun was hot on her cheeks. She heard Cas Doran say, 'Rose —?' and turned around, her face burning, to peer blindly through a fog of green, the after-image of the bright window. In her head she was reciting the few facts she'd gathered: '*121 Courtesy Street, 15 Fuller Grove . . .*' And the names: '*Langdon, Polish, Swindon, Pinkney.*'

'Ru,' said Cas Doran, cueing his son.

Rose saw a shadow step forward. She could scarcely see Ru through the haze of after-image. He looked like a monster floating in a jar of brightly coloured spirits — methanol stained by the monster-colour leached out into it. Rose continued to recite silently: '*121 Courtesy Street, 15 Fuller Grove . . .*'

Ru said, 'I'm very sorry I frightened you, Rose. It wasn't my intention to cause you any distress by my clumsy teasing.'

'Rose?' Doran said, as if he wanted her to make an argument, or ask something. He was prepared to let Ru make light of what had happened, but he was still offering her a chance to put up a fight.

Ru said, 'It was only supposed to be a bit of fun. It was thoughtless of me.'

'All right,' Rose said. She wanted to get out of the room. Her sight was clearing. She'd felt concealed by her temporary blindness. Now she could see Ru Doran's smirking, false humility, and his father's searching stare.

Rose realised that the names were those of dreamhunters — Langdon, Polish, Swindon, Pinkney. She was sure of it. Gavin Pinkney was Plasir's apprentice. And she was sure that the circles represented penumbras. Overlapping penumbras, covering much of central Founderston.

'May I go now?' she said.

'Yes, of course,' Doran said. But as she walked by him he detained her, put out a hand and touched her arm. 'Thank you for hearing him.'

Rose shrank back, involuntarily. Then she gave a stiff nod and went out.

The following morning Rose and Mamie, and several of the Doran household's numerous all-purpose servants, walked at low tide to the station by the trestle bridge over the mouth of the Sva. The men put out the flag for the westbound local, then put Rose's trunk on it when it came. Rose kissed Mamie goodbye, and got on the train.

At Sisters Beach station she left her trunk with the stationmaster and walked around the waterfront and up the hill to Summerfort. She found her mother and father sitting on the wicker chairs on the veranda, in their robes, and with damp hair, though it was past noon.

'Hello, Rosy,' said her Da. 'Is it next Friday already?'

'What happened, darling?' said Grace.

Rose opened her drawstring purse and passed her father Cas Doran's letter. 'I'd like to read that after you,' she said.

Grace got up and read over Chorley's shoulder. Partway through she took a deep breath, and puffed up all over like an angry cat. Chorley handed the letter to Rose and ran his hands through his hair.

Rose read:

My dear Mr Tiebold,

Your daughter cut short her visit, though I understand from both her and Mamie that there is some plan for a reciprocal visit some time after Christmas. I will leave it to you to decide whether or not that should be permitted.

Rose asked to leave because she had some trouble with my son, Richard. I questioned Rose and Richard and unfortunately received differing accounts of the incident. I do intend to press my son further, and deal with him as I find he deserves. For now, I am very sorry for Rose's distress, and I hope she will soon be comfortable and cheerful again.

Yours sincerely,
Cas Doran

'What did the boy do, darling?' Grace asked.

'Nothing much. I did think he might hurt me. Though it could have been only a nasty sort of teasing. He grabbed me and kept hold of me even when I told him to let go. I had to stand on his foot.'

Rose looked into their concerned faces. She remembered how when she got up in the morning after her scene with Ru, she had checked for a bruise on her wrist, and was disappointed not to find one. Then she recalled the bruises encircling Laura's wrists — black bands of bruising, marks she'd noticed as her cousin stood, unbinding her hands on the balcony of the Rainbow Opera, on the night of the riot. 'Oh, Laura,' she thought.

She said to her parents, 'I wish I'd known for sure that I was in danger.'

'You *did* know.' Grace got up and put her arms around her daughter.

'I was more angry than scared, Ma. It doesn't seem right to cause so much trouble out of anger.'

'The boy deserves trouble,' Chorley said. 'You can't go around grabbing girls.'

'Yes, Professor,' said Grace.

'I'll follow it up,' Chorley said. 'I'll make sure Doran does deal with him.'

Grace frowned at Chorley and gave a small shake of her head.

'My trunk is at the station,' Rose said.

'I'll go and get it,' her father said, and stepped off the porch before remembering he was still in his dressing gown.

As her mother led her indoors, Rose asked, 'Is Laura really coming home for Christmas?'

'Yes. Everyone will be here,' said Grace. 'The whole family — just the same as last year.' She smiled at Rose. 'Isn't that amazing?'

Three

By mid-afternoon on the day that Laura and Tziga were due at Summerfort, Rose had completed almost all her tasks. She'd been to Farry's to buy cakes. She'd purchased coloured crêpe paper to make paper chains. She'd sorted through the boxes of old Christmas decorations for whatever was salvageable. Since the family weren't to have a tree that year, Rose rejected the glass balls and birds. She was glad she wouldn't have to sit about with a bar of white soap and cheese grater making snow to sprinkle on the branches. Rose's Ma had always liked to dress the tree. Grace also liked roast goose and brandy-soaked puddings. But Rose's Da had put his foot down several years ago about the midwinter menu, and Summerfort's cook would now roast a couple of ducks the day before and spend her own Christmas at home while the family dined on cold meat, salads and fresh berries with cream.

'It'll be just like last year,' Rose thought, as she hung paper lanterns. 'Only without a tree.' Rose rather missed the tree, which always smelled lovely, though it had seemed like some magnificent and neglected altar, glittering in the dark indoors, ghostly with its soap snow, and at many removes both from what it commemorated, Christ's birthday, and where it was, a beach house at the height of summer.

After she had hung the decorations, Rose tried to settle and read a book. Not only was she unable to concentrate, she also found it impossible to sit still. She mooched about the house, till her mother told her to either sit down or go outside. Rose went out and ambled about Summerfort's grounds, circling the house at the edge of the lawns. When the sun had gone, she lit the lanterns. Then she ran down to the beach and stood at the water's edge looking out over the smooth bay for a boat. There were several lit masts. Some were moving across the water — fishing vessels heading into Tarry Cove — and some were apparently stationary, though any of those might actually be headed towards their end of Sisters Beach. Rose strained her eyes. Then the dusk-loving sandflies found her and she had to move again.

She left the beach and walked around the base of the headland to the lagoon. The tide was out. When Rose stepped onto the sand it bubbled, as small basking crabs scuttled back down their water-filled holes. Rose strolled out into the quiet arena of damp sand. There was no traffic on the road beyond the lagoon, or the railway line further away against the base of the hills. The night seemed enormous. Rose was used to being alone in rooms but not in a landscape. As she paced out into that space, her bare feet on warm silt and rotted shells, she felt that she was taking a little look at the lives of some of those people nearest to her — Laura, her Uncle Tziga, her own mother. 'How far away they must be,' she thought, 'whenever they take one of their walks.'

When she and Laura were children and complaining that they were bored, Rose's Da would say, 'Don't you have any inner resources?' Having 'inner resources' meant having a lively mind, interests, appetite. It meant that you should go and get a book or draw a picture. It meant *'Entertain yourselves'* — preferably quietly. Rose had always been able to entertain herself, and Laura too. Laura wasn't as keen a reader, and was less inclined to think up projects, or start a new game. 'Given an audience, I expand,' Rose thought, 'but given space, I shrink.' Yet Laura — Laura had found space because she wasn't always with noisy, definite Rose, and because she'd left school and become a dreamhunter, and because her father disappeared. 'She's grown so much,' Rose thought. Then, 'Will I *ever* catch up with her?'

Rose turned around and tried to find the break in the trees where the track went up behind the headland. She couldn't see it at all. She walked to the trees and went along beside them, stumbling sometimes and barking her ankles on driftwood, till she found it. Its soft, sandy surface was cold now. There was dew on the trees flanking the path, and dew on the lawns of Summerfort. All the lanterns were still alight, but several of their candles were guttering. The glass doors were closed on the rapidly cooling air.

Rose went in and ran upstairs. There was a light in Laura's room. Rose pushed the door open.

Laura was standing at her bureau patting one of the furred, silvery lamb's-lugs in Rose's flower arrangement. She was wearing a darned jersey; it was too big for her. She was also wearing heavy cotton trousers and rope-soled sandals. Her hair had grown, so that its uneven lengths made a wide black halo around her face.

'Hello,' Rose said. Then, 'The flowers were Ma's idea,' for some reason finding herself unwilling to admit to all the trouble she'd taken.

Laura looked wistful. 'She scarcely said a word to me when we came in — which I suppose I deserve.' She frowned at the flowers. 'Doesn't your Ma usually just cram them in a vase and leave it at that?'

Rose didn't want to talk about her mother's long-postponed show of resentment. She said, brightly, 'Your hair looks nice. You should let it grow,' then immediately regretted her bossiness.

Laura wandered over to the window and eased the sash up a few inches. She looked out into the blackness. Her look was expectant and yearning. Without turning around Laura asked, 'How was it at the Doran summer residence?'

Rose plonked herself down on the bed. She began to talk breathlessly about the map she'd spotted in Cas Doran's library, its circles representing penumbras, and how, in some of the circles, there were names of dreamhunters who had disappeared. 'Or dreamhunters who were supposed to have taken "early retirement",' Rose added. 'Gone back to their towns south of the Corridor, or gone abroad. There weren't any big earners among them, no one really distinguished. Da and Ma looked up the names I'd managed to memorise. Ma tried to find them by chasing up their friends and relatives. She'd turn up to supposedly return something she'd borrowed. And Da's planning to reconnoitre one of the properties. He wants to see who is in residence. I'd like to do it. I could throw my schoolbag over the wall of 121 Courtesy Street and then sneak in, and if someone caught me I could say that one of my friends tossed my bag over the wall. Da can't do that. What's he going to say? "I'm sorry, but my silly friend Mr Brown threw my umbrella into your garden"?'

'Do you think Cas Doran wants to get a whole lot of dreamhunters colouring Founderston's dreams?' Laura said, frowning. 'I thought Colourists were rare, not just because colouring is illegal, but because it's difficult.'

'We have no idea what he means to do. But whatever it is, he's working on getting coverage of the whole central city.'

Laura came and sat on the bed too. Rose smiled to see this, but didn't pause in her talk. She felt that she was trying to lure some shy animal. She told Laura about the constantly replenished piles of narrow-gauge rails beside the border. 'Ma immediately decided to take a trip to the Pinnacles, but when she made inquiries at the Tricksie Bend ranger's post about the state of the pass she was told it was closed for repairs.'

'Which would support Cas Doran's story about the rails being used to reinforce collapsing banks.'

'Except he said that the rails were leftovers. That there was just one lot. In which case they've been sitting there for two years without rusting.'

Laura nodded.

'Taken together with the circles on the map, the rails just seem —'

'Yes, there's a railway line.' Laura seemed certain. 'A railway line Inland. But why? And when the pass is closed, is there just a sign saying "Danger. Closed for Repairs"?'

'There's a locked gate, apparently. A big spiked iron gate.'

The girls looked at each other, wide-eyed. Rose was so curious about this theoretical railway she was practically urging Laura to go and check it *right now*.

'I'll go after Christmas,' Laura pronounced, as if she were reading Rose's mind. 'I'll take Nown with me, to see how he manages the gate.'

Rose's hands went numb, then her feet followed. For a moment she thought she might faint. She stared at her cousin, dumb. 'Noun' was the word Laura had yelled at the Rainbow Opera. A monster had come running in answer to Laura's call, and had carried her away. The monster had 'NOWN' inscribed on the back of its neck.

After a moment Laura seemed to realise what she'd said. She glanced at Rose's face. She looked startled and sly.

'Your monster,' Rose said. 'Whose name is Nown.'

'He's not a monster. He's a —' Laura paused and pondered. 'He's a soul called into different bodies, time and again, throughout history. Bodies made of sand, or earth, or fired clay. And once of ash — or so he tells me.'

Rose sat with her mouth hanging open. She wanted to ask why Laura was telling her this now when she'd denied it before, at the risk of Rose's great resentment. She said, tentative, 'Why did you —?'

Laura didn't let her finish. She seemed keen to talk, eager now to tell. 'Why did I make him?'

This wasn't what Rose had intended to ask, but she was distracted by the question. 'You *made* him?'

'Yes. That's how he comes to exist. He's made. I *said* that. He's made of sand, or earth, or fired clay, and once of ash. And I think whoever makes him has to need him very badly. And they have to give something up. When Da got on the special train last summer, and I learned he wouldn't be at my Try, I just gave up some of my faith in him. I think I understood that even without knowing it himself, Da meant to leave me. He meant not to be there for me, at my Try, and then not at all.'

'Wait. What do you mean?'

'Da jumped off the pier at Westport. Didn't anyone tell you that?'

'I thought it was an accident.' Rose was horrified.

Laura shook her head. 'No. And I think I knew. I thought he was letting me down, but I *felt* he was leaving me. I gave up my faith in him. Or rather, my faith left me. But it didn't just blow away like smoke. I saw that rock on the track bed, the rock I just had to pick up. I think I put my lost faith into it, without knowing what it was for. And without knowing what wanting to do that was for. What being *able* to do that was for. Then, much later, I put the rock into Nown's chest when I made him.'

'Oh my God!' said Rose. To her eyes it seemed that her cousin was framed by brackets of blue light. Then black patches bloomed on Laura's face and obliterated it altogether. Rose stooped and pressed her face into the coverlet. She felt nothing — for a moment saw and heard nothing. Then her sense of touch came back, and the texture of the embroidery under her cheek. Laura was stroking the back of her neck. 'Oh my God!' Rose said again, muffled.

Laura reminded her cousin that she was an atheist.

Rose wriggled violently, like an infant trying to avoid being dressed. Then she sat up. 'So your monster doesn't just smash things and run off with girls?'

Laura smiled. It was one of her rare very happy smiles, which having reached its physical limits in terms of crinkling eyes and curving lips, then seemed to go on to pump light into the air around her. She said, 'No. Mostly he just does what I say, but all the while noticing the world in a way that's entirely his own.'

Rose opened her mouth to ask something further, but was disturbed by a knock on Laura's door. Rose's Ma put her head around it. 'Rose,' Grace said, 'you should come and say hello to your Uncle Tziga. He has to go to bed straight after we've had dinner.'

Rose clapped her hands to her face. She felt the heat come into her cheeks. She got up and ran downstairs. Laura and Grace came after her, talking — Rose caught snatches of their exchange. 'You've grown an inch or so,' Grace said. 'You'll need new shirts and trousers.'

Rose's Da and her uncle were sitting in the unlit living room in armchairs by the window. The moon was coming up over the headland at the eastern end of the beach. Rose went to kiss her uncle and first saw the changes in his appearance by moonlight —

which made them somehow less terrible. She crouched by his feet and he took her hands in his.

Chorley said, 'We've just been discussing Doran's map and surplus rails.'

'Us too,' Rose said. She glanced at Laura. 'That's what we were talking about.'

'That's nice,' said Grace, droll. 'Now you two pairs of conspirators can get together in a pack. I almost feel sorry for Secretary Doran.'

Four

The family had several days during which, in the spirit of the season, they were very careful with one another. Rose was now keeping Laura's secret and already felt she wouldn't have much trouble doing so. She was hardly likely to talk about something she had such difficulty even thinking about. When she thought about how Laura had said, 'He's not a monster, he's a soul', Rose would get dizzy with astonishment.

On Boxing Day the cousins ambled along the seafront to Farry's. They sat at their favourite table, looking out on Main Street and its traffic of holidaymakers in summer finery, ladies in new hats or gowns, men either dutifully or proudly wearing Christmas-present ties and tiepins. The children had new toys — dolls and doll's prams, bats and balls and sailing boats — but were blotchy and fretful, still recovering from Christmas Eve sleeplessness.

The cousins ate white chocolate and cardamom ice-cream, and Rose told Laura about what she was now referring to as her 'run-in with Ru Doran'. She said, 'I don't want to exaggerate how upset I was. Especially not with Mamie coming in a few days.'

'I would have been upset, too, if it had been me,' Laura said.

'I keep feeling I should have known how to handle him better. And I shouldn't have complained to Mamie. It was Mamie who made a fuss. She's very loyal to me.' Rose touched the high collar of her shirtwaist dress. 'Anyway, the whole thing has me dressing differently.'

'There are nice boys, Rose. You might want one of the nice ones to notice your figure.'

'Maybe nice boys don't notice those things,' Rose said.

'Huh!' Laura said. 'What's the first thing you notice about a boy?'

Rose scanned the room. The only young men in Farry's that day were the waiters. One caught Rose's eye and came over. 'Can I get you ladies anything more?'

'Manners,' said Rose to Laura, answering her question.

'Manners are off today, I'm afraid,' the waiter said.

The cousins giggled. Laura asked the waiter to bring them some lemonade.

Rose looked sly. She asked Laura, 'Do you think Sandy Mason notices your figure?'

Laura said, 'I wrote to Sandy and he didn't write back.' She sighed. 'I hoped at least he'd tell me off about the nightmare. I'm sure he must have known it was me. Your Ma hasn't said anything yet either.'

'Perhaps *you* should say something.'

'I can't say sorry without making excuses.'

'Yes, I know, you were only doing what your father told you to do.'

'Yes.' Laura laced and unlaced her fingers. 'That's my excuse. I followed my father's instructions. But I wanted what came with his instructions. The spell. I wanted to make myself a sandman.'

Rose touched her brow. She could feel it coming — the dizziness, chills, a clench of disgust. It was as if her whole body wanted to shrink away from the altered reality of the world she found herself living in.

Laura studied Rose's face, then turned her eyes down to the table top. 'I don't have a figure,' she said, reverting to their earlier subject. 'I think Sandy only liked me because I come from a famous family.'

'No, Laura, he really liked you.' Rose remembered Sandy Mason's fiery blush, the intensity of his attention when he looked at her cousin. 'You should write to him again. You could ask him to visit us at Summerfort. You need all your friends, Laura.'

Laura studied her cousin, then said, 'I need people.' Cool and bland.

'Yes,' Rose said, innocent of her own meaning, and of the fact that Laura had understood her meaning — that Laura needed people rather than her monster.

The lemonade arrived and they drank it and went back to their traditional summertime occupation of watching the world go by Farry's big bay windows.

That evening Grace surprised her family by announcing over tea that it was time they all heard what she had to say. Chorley was possibly the most startled of all of them. He stared at his wife with the white-eyed look of a shying horse, but kept his seat.

'Pass your father the sugar bowl,' Grace said to Rose.

Rose handed the sugar to Chorley, who helped himself to five lumps and sat back stirring his tea. The sugar lumps thunked and the spoon rattled sharply.

Laura got up, and went to sit on the footstool beside her father. She took his hand and faced her aunt.

'Right,' said Grace. Then she set her cup down and stood up.

'Are you making a public announcement?' Rose said.

'Hush,' Grace said to Rose. She looked at her brother-in-law. 'Tziga, now that you're not catching those horrible, distorting nightmares, you must be thinking more clearly.'

'Yes,' Tziga said. 'Though sometimes I forget what it is I've thought clearly.'

'I know that. But my point is — you must be able to see now that your plan, such as it was, wasn't a very good one.'

'The papers didn't publish Lazarus's letters,' Chorley said, defending Tziga.

Grace stamped her foot. 'I don't want to hear any of you refer to "Lazarus" *ever* again. I might have to maintain that silly fiction in public, but I refuse to do so in my own home!'

Laura said, 'I'm sorry I overdreamed you. It's not Da's fault.'

Tziga squeezed Laura's hand. 'It *is* my fault. I asked you to do it and I wasn't thinking straight.'

'But it is wrong to give a nightmare like Buried Alive to convicts to make them behave, and slave away in the Westport mine,' Laura said.

'Yes, Laura, but is giving the St Lazarus's Eve patrons a nightmare about being buried alive any way to change that?' Grace said.

'I think you're being naïve, Ma,' Rose said.

Grace flushed. She glared at her daughter.

'Think of Doran's map,' Rose said. 'Think of what he's planning to do.'

'What *is* he planning to do?' Grace set her hands on her hips.

'Use your imagination.'

Grace rounded on Chorley. 'Are you going to let your daughter talk to me like that?'

'Rose, please be more polite to your mother.'

'And you —' Grace went on, speaking to her husband now. 'You could ask your good friend the Grand Patriarch what *he's* planning to do about Doran and the Regulatory Body. Except, of course, it isn't the Body the Grand Patriarch dislikes, it's dreamhunters.'

'That's not true,' Tziga said, softly.

'The Regulatory Body has been around for a little over ten years,' Chorley said. 'Have you ever heard of any institution that has become as powerful as the Body has within such a short space of time? Even Christianity didn't manage it.'

'Napoleon?' said Rose, as though she were doing a quiz. She was ignored.

'That's beside the point,' Grace said. 'You seem to think Doran has a plan. And you also think — rather trustingly — that the Grand Patriarch has a plan too.'

'He has vigorous suspicion,' Chorley said. 'He acts on his suspicions. He hides dreamhunters who come to him for help.'

'And how many of those "disappearing" dreamhunters that you and Rose have been talking about have been disappeared by the Church rather than the Regulatory Body?' Grace said. 'After all, the Church didn't tell us where Tziga was.'

'They weren't sure I'd recover,' Tziga said. 'And the Body didn't tell you what had happened to me either.'

'True,' said Grace. 'And the Church did help you. I understand that you feel you owe the Grand Patriarch. And I know you're a churchgoer — a believer. It *is* different for you, Tziga. But Chorley thinks he's doing research for the Grand Patriarch. He's taking it all very seriously. When really it's just another one of his bloody hobbies!'

There was a moment of silence, then Chorley dropped his teacup into its saucer, got up and walked out.

'Ma!' Rose said.

Grace's eyes glazed over with tears. 'Why doesn't anyone ever listen to me?'

'Please don't cry, Ma,' Rose said, distressed.

'You're going to start trespassing on properties in Founderston looking for clues,' Grace said to Rose, and began to sob. 'Your father has you thinking that it's all right to break the law if it's for a good cause.'

Rose went to her mother and hugged her. 'Well, I won't, Ma. I'll let Da do it.'

'You all act as though you've been appointed to save the world,' Grace said, still sobbing. 'The world doesn't need saving.'

'I was only trying to mend my mistakes — mistakenly,' Tziga said, sadly.

Laura just sat there, wearing a dazzled, radiant expression.

'There, there,' Rose said to her mother.

'What's so wrong with our lives, anyway?' Grace said, querulous. 'Why do you all have to be such damn rebels?'

'I'm not,' said Rose.

'It does,' said Laura. 'The world does need saving. Or, at least, I *think* it's the world.'

Everyone looked at her. Then Chorley came back into the room and everyone looked at him instead. He was carrying one of his notebooks and a pen, so vigorously dipped in ink that the fingers of his right hand were tipped brilliant scarlet. He gave the notebook to Grace and said, 'If you will, dear, could you please read out aloud the passages I have underlined?'

Grace gave him a look of dread, but did as she was told. She spoke softly, stammered once or twice, but read: 'Rise up! Rise up! I said to rise! Crush them! Rise up and overturn everything! Find your feet and get up! Shake them all off! I said, Get up! I said, Rise up now!'

Chorley said, 'I found those within only seventy pages of bad messages from the abandoned Founderston to Sisters Beach telegraph line. Sometimes there's just the odd, plaintive "crush" or "rise" or "shake". Plaintive is the right word. These are complaints — angry complaints.'

'What about the poetry?' Rose said.

'It seems there are two voices,' Chorley said. 'One complains, the other seems to be in an ecstasy of anticipation.'

Grace held the notebook out, and her husband took it.

'Dear,' he said, 'I do feel that I'm blundering about in the dark. I do feel like a dimwitted dilettante. But I don't think I'm wasting my time.'

Tziga added, hesitantly, 'What Laura did to you, Grace, and to the rest of the Rainbow Opera's patrons, she did because I told her to when I wasn't in my right mind. I don't trust my judgment any more, but I do trust Chorley's.'

'It may all really matter, Ma,' Rose said. 'What we choose to do might make a big difference.'

Chorley kept his eyes on his wife's face. 'I promised the Grand Patriarch my time in exchange for knowing where Tziga was. I'm honouring a promise.'

'Marta knew, too, and she chose not to tell you,' Tziga said. 'They thought I might not live. And they thought I knew more about the Body and Doran than I did, that I was in deeper with the Body than I was. And they supposed I knew more about the Place, as though it were a deity and I were its prophet. An evil deity, with an evil prophet,' Tziga added, then put a hand over his face.

Chorley started and hurried to him.

'It's all right, Da,' Laura said.

Chorley said, 'You should be resting, Tziga.'

They helped him up and walked him slowly from the room. For a time they could be heard making soothing sounds as they helped him up the stairs.

Rose and Grace looked at each other.

'You do know I'm not siding with Da against you,' Rose said. 'Ma, you're only determined we stop snooping because you're afraid we'll get into trouble. You're scared of what the Body will do to us because you're just as sure as we are that they're up to no good.'

'But why does it have to be *our* problem?' Grace said.

'Because we know about it.'

Five

Just three days later Grace found herself presiding over a very different household.

Chorley came in with an armload of parcels while the girls were having their breakfast. He turned back the cloth at one end of the table and put the parcels down, and Grace laughed as Rose practically climbed over Mamie to grab one and tear it open. Dress patterns and samples of cloth spilled out onto the table top, some of the swatches of silk crêpe so light that they seemed to skate on cushions of air, speeding across the polished table and onto the floor. Mamie and Rose snatched and tussled. Laura gathered up the dropped swatches and started to hand over the pearls, and pure whites, and oysters, and creams.

'I'll look awful in all of these,' Mamie said, with no hint of her usual aloof sarcasm.

'Oh no, let's see, there must be something suitable.' Grace got up to join them.

'I'm going to choose a plain pattern.' Rose was sorting through the patterns. 'Something only I can wear.' She drew herself up to her full five foot ten. 'And I am *not* going to show off my bosom.'

'At least you have a choice about that,' said Mamie, and crossed her arms over her large breasts, pressing them flat as though hoping to push them back into her body.

Rose shuffled dress patterns. 'I'm sure we can find something pretty and becoming for you.'

'But am I becoming?' Mamie raised an eyebrow.

Grace and Rose nodded earnestly.

Mamie looked away. 'I'm becoming bored.'

Laura, who had been standing stock-still and staring out of the glass doors of the dining room, spun around and said, 'Excuse me, Mamie. Could I borrow Rose for a moment?'

'She's not mine to lend,' Mamie said.

Laura grabbed her cousin's hand and opened the doors.

'"Come into the garden, Maud,"' muttered Mamie as the other two went out.

'What is it?' said Rose, then found herself performing a little hop to avoid tripping over some stones — five of them — that had been laid in a neat row on the bottom step of the veranda.

Laura let go of Rose to push the stones under the step.

'*What?*' Rose demanded.

'I'm sure that's a sign,' Laura said. She took hold of Rose, led her to the margin of the lawn and began stooping to peer under bushes.

'What are we looking for?' Rose said, and began to search too — pausing once to dive into a bush and retrieve a croquet ball.

Laura continued to work her way around the house. Then she started down the track to the lagoon. She said, over her shoulder, 'He won't be too near the water.'

A moment later Laura had to double back for Rose, who had stopped following.

Her cousin pulled at her, but Rose planted her feet and stood firm.

'Don't be scared,' said Laura. 'He won't hurt you.'

'No. No. No,' Rose said, and wriggled to shake off Laura's grip. But she didn't make any move to go back up to the house.

Laura let go and faced Rose. 'You wanted to know. This is the only way you are ever going to come near to knowing.'

Rose said, 'I've seen it. I can believe my eyes.'

'You should *meet* him.'

Rose could feel the blood in her head — indignation, fear and fury. She told her cousin, 'People don't meet monsters. No one offers introductions to monsters.'

'Aren't you even curious?'

Rose was quiet, thinking about that. Laura waited. She looked so anxious for approval that Rose wanted to smack her. Rose started down the path again. Laura gave a little gasp of relief and darted on ahead, searching the trees. Rose felt she was out walking a silly young dog.

Laura's monster was hiding in the filmy gloom under a tall weeping willow. At first it was hard to see, utterly still, and of a dun shade similar to the tree trunk. But when Laura flung the willow fronds aside, it stirred and the light scintillated on its sandy skin. Rose saw Laura take one of its hands, her fist closing around a big thumb. She drew the monster out.

Rose backed away as it approached. Laura was between them, her face glowing with love, but the monster was so huge, so competent in its movements, so uncanny, that Rose could not hold her ground.

'This is Rose,' Laura said to her monster, who continued to look down on the top of Laura's head, then into her face as she turned back and *glowed* up at it.

'She looks so proud of me you'd think she'd made me too,' Rose said. She heard how steady her own voice was and felt a little braver.

Laura laughed. She said to her monster, 'Were the rivers and streams a problem on your way back?'

'It hasn't rained, and they are smaller,' the monster replied.

Rose thought that no one could ever mistake that voice for human. It was too dry. There was no moisture, no *flesh*, involved in it. The sound wasn't even animal — yet those were words. Rose shivered, but continued to stand her ground.

'Let your cousin go back to the house,' the monster said. 'You must have things you need to tell me, Laura.'

Laura looked disappointed, as if she'd hoped they would all sit down together and have a conversation. She looked at Rose, then back up at her monster. 'But the things I have to tell you are about discoveries *Rose* has made. We think that the Regulatory Body has built a railway line into the Place. We thought that you and I should go and look at it, and see where it goes.'

The monster did not move its eyes. It didn't glance at Rose for confirmation, as any person would have. It hadn't looked at her at all, she was sure. The only indication she had that it knew she was there was that it had spoken to Laura about her. It wasn't as though the monster was being rude — Rose didn't feel snubbed, as she would have if a person had treated her this way. She just felt that she wasn't the monster's business — that she was *so* not its business that her existence was minimal to it. 'Laura,' she said, 'you talk. You make plans.'

'Am I to set out somewhere?' the monster said, to Laura. 'Tonight will be safer than today. Where shall we meet?'

Laura clutched the monster's arm and pulled. It didn't lean into her. It was immovable. Her feet slid on the gritty ground till she was pressed against its side. 'Don't go right away,' she said. 'You only just came.'

'I said tonight, not today.'

'You must be tired.'

'Now you are being silly, Laura.'

Laura laughed again. She sounded very happy.

Rose said to her cousin, 'I will leave you to give your — sandman — directions.' Then, 'He does follow orders, doesn't he?'

'Oh,' Laura said, and laughed some more. Then she collected herself and said, 'Well, obviously. He's here, isn't he?'

'Here,' thought Rose, 'and shouldn't be. Shouldn't exist.' But she said, 'I'll leave you to talk.' She backed away from the willow. She kept backing, kept the monster in sight for a time before turning and hurrying up the hill to the house.

Part X
The Depot

One

Ten days later, Laura made her rendezvous with Nown a little east of the last regular station at Morass River. They began their journey, weaving In and out across the border. Inside, they tramped through dry but untouched and upstanding meadows, Nown going before Laura and treading the grass stalks down. The going was easy. Every few minutes they would stop and stand still and listen for signs of other travellers. The trail was deserted.

As they went, Laura gazed Inland, across the grasslands to a line of low hills, all in graduated shades of beige. Sometimes she turned her eyes towards what she could see beyond the border, an endless haze of meadow that faded away to a creamy sky. Laura knew that if she walked in that direction she would cross back into the green world. But, as she gazed, she began to imagine facing a second kind of Try in which she would find that the reliable border had vanished, and she'd never be able to get out again. She saw this so clearly that she had to check, to walk towards the border —

— where she found herself on a path that ran along a bluff above one of the many brilliant blue coves in Coal Bay's notched curve. The sun was hot and had raised all the perfume of the forest.

Nown stepped out beside her. Almost onto her, since she hadn't moved to make room for him. She teetered and he caught and steadied her.

A light wind was hissing through the flax between the track and the coast. The sea was calm, the waves idle and sleepy. But it seemed noisy after the Place. Laura said, 'We won't hear anyone coming along this track. We'll be caught. And your eyesight is better In there, isn't it?' She said all this, but didn't really want to go back In.

'It's only because there's less to see that people are highly visible there,' Nown said. 'Laura, we'll make better progress on this side of the border. And if I carry you, then you can listen while I walk.'

Of course Laura went to sleep in Nown's arms and didn't wake till his gait changed. He was stepping from boulder to boulder along a beach heaped with stones ranging from fist-sized to elephantine. 'I think I'll stay where I am for now,' Laura said, and tightened her arms around his neck. 'Don't drop me.' She knew he wouldn't, only said it to savour how safe she felt.

Nown said, 'I want to beat the tide. To get around that headland before the sea comes up.'

Laura wondered what it was like for him, stalking along the edge of a sea that was invisible to him except as a hole in the world, a void that gradually came up to engulf the path on which he made his way. She asked, 'Does the sea frighten you?'

'The tide is reliable. And none of these bluffs is too steep to climb.'

'But doesn't it unnerve you? Don't you feel threatened? Don't you think, "What if a big wave comes?"'

'No,' Nown said. 'I don't know that I have an imagination.' He gripped Laura firmly and vaulted up a rocky spur in several strides, launching himself across gaps lined with kelp and thickly beaded with green-lipped mussels. A high swell pushed into a gap and, white with trapped air, lunged at Nown's legs. Laura squeezed her eyes closed and pressed her face against his gritty neck.

By late afternoon they had rounded the headland at the western end of Awa Inlet. The tide was still high, and they faced a wide sweep of water. Far away across the inlet was the lacework of a railway trestle across a river. Beyond that they could see the thick forest in the rain shadow at the back of the inlet and, against the dark hills, the blond stone of the Doran summer residence, shining in the low sun.

'We should go as far as that long bridge over the river mouth, then turn back In,' Laura said. 'If I sleep soon I can be up again before midnight. And I'm sure we can get from the bridge to the house between four and dawn, at your speed.'

Nown pointed at the water directly below them, at a channel, blue between two submerged sandbars. 'What is that?'

'I don't know what you mean,' Laura said, looking at it. Then she realised. 'Oh, damn — there are *two* rivers. That's the Sva letting out through the reed beds way over there. The Rifleman must be hidden behind this headland. I've gone past here in the train dozens of times, but it all looks different.' She could see that the water in the channel was moving very fast. Even if they waited for the tide to go right out, the river would still be there, pushing against the cliff on the far side of the headland.

'The channel is a colder nothingness,' Nown said, to explain how he'd picked out the river from the surrounding seawater. 'It is even more nothing.'

Laura said, 'The railway line is in a tunnel here. After the tunnel it runs along a ledge above the river, and turns onto a bridge.' She pointed through the hill they stood on. 'The tunnel runs through this hill and the bridge must be just beyond it.'

She knew the view out of the train windows very well: the long curve of graded track that passed down a channel of rock roughly formed by dynamite then chiselled out by the pickaxes of, she now knew, convict labour. The bridge over the Rifleman was iron, and very strong. It had to be. The Rifleman was a short river, fed by streams draining from a range of rainy mountains. It arrived at the sea swift, chilly and full. Ten miles further along the railway line was the other structure, of bleached ironwood, that picked its way across the braided channels and low sandbanks of the Sva mouth. The Sva, where it reached the sea, was depleted by miles of farmland and was a much gentler river than the Rifleman; its stream only hastened a little as its valley narrowed between the foothills and solitary Mount Kahaugh.

Laura said, 'Put me down.'

Nown lowered her to the ground, and she leaned against him and stretched and shook her legs to get her blood moving again. Then she took his hand to encourage him, and began to scramble up the hill through the scrub, grabbing at the slender trunks of hebes, and brilliant waxed sea laurel. She let go of Nown to haul herself up the steepest slope of the hill. She could hear him following her, the foliage making a flinty scraping against his hardened body.

Laura reached the top of the slope and went carefully after that, peering, till she saw where the scrub abruptly came to an end. She crept forward and arrived at a drop. She craned over and saw the brick buttresses of the tunnel mouth and the railway line twenty-five feet below.

She turned to Nown. 'If we climb down beside the tunnel we can go along the track and cross the bridge. It's the quickest route.' Then, 'Can you see in the dark?'

'I don't know dark, Laura. "Dark" is what you say to explain not being able to see.'

'Oh,' said Laura. She lay down on her stomach, unscrewed the copper cap of her water bottle and held the bottle under a steadily dripping fringe of moss. Her arm got tired, but she managed to get a drink.

'I have water,' Nown said, and shook one of the two big skins he carried.

'I'll need that later, when we go In.'

Laura rolled back from the bluff and onto her sandman's feet. She pulled at his arm to let him know she wanted him to sit. He folded himself carefully into the little space there was, branches snapping as he lowered himself onto them. 'I'm going to sleep for a while,' Laura said. 'Please make sure I don't roll off the drop.'

He lifted one leg and placed it, crooked, over her body. She rearranged herself, her back to the drop and her head pillowed on his other foot. She said, sleepy, 'You know to stay still, don't you?'

'Yes, Laura.'

She closed her eyes and let herself drift off.

Laura slept for a few hours and woke up, stiff and cold. The sun had gone, and Nown was nearly the same temperature as the air.

It was summer, but she had let herself fall asleep on the ground without wrapping herself in her bedroll.

Though all the sunset colour had gone, the sky in the west had a pithy pallor, and there was still enough light for Nown and Laura to climb safely down the bluff onto the track.

The tunnel mouth breathed at their backs, smelling of wet brick and coal smoke.

They began down the long shallow incline of the track — both were walking as far from the drop as they could, Laura leading and Nown following. They stepped from sleeper to sleeper and built up quite a rhythm, hurrying, only sometimes steadying themselves against the pickaxe-pockmarked rock of the cliff face.

They reached the place where the track turned away from the cliff. It ran onto an iron trestle that curved around to join the span of the railway bridge. There was nowhere to pause and step off the track. Still, Laura put her hand back to halt Nown. He stopped instantly at her touch, didn't blunder into her as most people would. She glanced back and saw him frozen with one foot raised. He looked like a photograph of himself.

Laura listened to the night. She couldn't hear the river. The tide was high, slack and silent. She heard one of the little rainforest owls giving its musical two-note cry. She heard oystercatchers out over the inlet. She didn't hear any trains.

Laura stepped onto the bridge. It wasn't a very long span, probably no more than fifty yards. It was easier to walk on than the track by the cliff had been: there were girders under the wooden sleepers of the bridge, a firm skin of rivet-studded iron. It was a good surface, and Laura hurried.

Then she stopped again to listen. The headland behind them was booming. Laura looked back at Nown, her eyes wide.

An engine burst from the tunnel, braked on the incline and came sliding and panting down the track towards them.

Laura took off. She closed the distance between herself and safety — but then her foot slipped and she sprawled across the tracks, slamming her elbow hard. Her arm lost all feeling, then seemed to fizzle back into existence as if it were breaking out of a numbing foam.

Nown reached her, scooped her up and ran with her. She saw the train over his shoulder, looming onto the bridge, its light sweeping an engine-length ahead of its long cowcatcher. Laura screamed. Nown swerved off the tracks and pushed her through two crisscrossed girders onto the outside of the bridge. He stretched up and over one girder to lower her onto another that jutted from the plane of the bridge. Laura's feet touched the girder, then took her weight. She stood balanced. She tried to pull herself free from Nown's grip. Her arms were stretched up over her head, wrists closed together in one of his hands. She could see his face through a gap in the bridge structure, close to her own, and side-lit by the growing yellow light of the train. She shouted at him: 'Get off the bridge!' She couldn't hear her own voice over the thunder of the train.

Nown released her arms and she folded up into a crouch, her palms and boot soles clinging to the girder. The bridge was jolting under her.

Nown stooped and began to ooze through the gap below the one he had rolled her through. Laura saw his head and arms emerge whole and shapely, then his chest and hips following, extruded like icing piped through a square nozzle.

Laura closed her eyes against the glare of the engine. The train sounded its whistle then blasted past. Laura was sprayed with sand. The train's violent jolting dislodged her from the girder. She slipped, scrabbled for a hold, then dropped off. She opened her eyes as she fell, glimpsed the underside of the bridge and a cloud of sand fanning out into the air and already drawing back in thickening eddies towards the shadow that was Nown.

Laura fell into the river. It was cold and salty. Her eardrums stabbed with pain and her back felt slapped red even through her jacket and shirt. Her pack and bedroll were pulling her down, so she wriggled out of their straps, let them go and kicked up to the surface. She blinked the water out of her eyes and looked back at the bridge.

Nown was visible, in silhouette, back-lit by the flashing yellow squares of carriage windows and the straight, sweeping shadows of the bridge structure. He seemed to be poised, looking her way, as if about to jump into the water after her.

She opened her mouth and shouted at him: 'No!' Then realised as she shouted that Nown might imagine she was calling for help. She trod water for a moment longer, then turned and struck out at an angle for the far bank. She headed away from the middle of the stream and — she could tell by the solid power of the water — the current pushing by the bluff and out to sea, even against the full tide.

The train had passed on over the bridge. Its thunder diminished. Laura stopped swimming and looked back again. Nown was still there, leaning out over the water, looking after her. Laura swam on.

Suddenly there was a solid shelf under her hands — her hands first, her feet couldn't seem to find it, as if it were really a shelving ledge rather than the bank. It couldn't be the bank, anyway — Laura could see the bank, still some twenty yards from where she was, a pale beach scalloped by the river and tide and topped by a tangle of driftwood. But there was *something* under Laura's hands, something solid and strangely furry, like thick dust. She heaved and scrambled up onto it. The crown of her head was touched by heat, then she tumbled out into the bright, diffuse light of the Place. She was soaking, and water ran from her hair and clothes and made thick fawn mud of the dusty ground she lay on.

Laura stood up. She started to laugh. She stood, dripping and hiccuping with mirth. Of course she had known that the bridge was built as far upriver as it could be without crossing the border, but she hadn't imagined that the railway line she had travelled on so many times, back and forth to Summerfort, was only yards from that border.

Laura gave herself a good shake. She wondered how far she'd have to walk along the border to have cleared the river. She made an arbitrary decision — an hour would do it. Before she set out, she held her watch to her ear and was relieved to hear it making its usual sharp, dry tick — it hadn't been damaged by its dunking.

Two

Laura stayed In long enough to dry off. She finally emerged above the beach by the river. The tide had dropped and the moon had come up. Laura could see the river's current muscled in the moonlight.

Nown unfolded from the beach, shedding sand that wasn't his. As he came towards her, Laura saw at once that he was a little shorter and more slender than before. 'Did the train hit you?' she asked.

'My feet,' he said. 'I lost some of them.' He spoke as though he were a centipede and had plenty to spare. 'The train carried part of my feet away with it. When I continued along the track I found some sand — but I couldn't persuade it that it was me any more.'

'You look younger,' Laura said.

Nown's head reared back with surprise. 'How?'

'Less bulky, I suppose.' Laura ran a hand down his arm. She stepped close to him to measure herself against him. The top of her head had formerly come to his sternum; now it came to his collarbone.

Nown said, 'I saw you disappear. But I was sure that you didn't go under — then certain of it when I went on.'

'Went on *where*?'

'Went on existing, Laura. I waited not to exist — though I did think you had gone Into the Place, not under the river. Then, when I did go on existing, I went on walking too, along the bridge to look for the rest of my feet.'

Laura shook her head. They were always having these strange conversations. She asked him, 'Do you still have the water skins?'

Nown pointed at a single water skin on the ground nearby. 'When the train came I flung them over onto the far shore. One burst.'

'Damn.'

'And you've lost your pack and bedroll, Laura.'

'Yes.'

'Then shouldn't we go back?'

'Oh no! Let's go on to the Doran property. Rose said there was an orchard. I can steal some fruit. We should at least take a look In to see where those rails have gone.'

Nown picked up the surviving water skin, then Laura, and began to make his way around the shore of the inlet.

Near dawn they crossed the ironwood trestle over the braided Sva mouth — without encountering another train. Then they turned towards the back of the inlet, walking on the hard-packed sand beside a channel through reed beds, where the warmth of the previous day was still trapped in the thick fur of stalks.

At sun-up they found the Dorans' jetty, and the beginning of the narrow-gauge railway. A little while later Laura spotted the orchard. She asked Nown to put her down, and sprinted towards the trees. She could see clusters of apricots, and black plums with a white bloom on them.

But before she reached the orchard she ran through the border and Into the Place. She swore. Her voice came back at her instantly, a single flat reverberation, from a mass of crumbling grey land forms that rose abruptly about a quarter of a mile from the hummocky meadow where she stood.

The Pinnacles — eroded, crooked spikes — stretched out along the horizon, a barrier made, apparently, from heaps of sculpted ash. The peaks looked as fragile as piles of old leaf-litter held together by spider web.

Behind her Nown said, 'I can't climb that.'

Rose had said there was a gate. Laura guessed that she and Nown had come In beyond where it was, simply by turning off towards the orchard rather than continuing on up the avenue of plane trees. She asked, 'How much water do we have?'

Nown handed her the water skin and she weighed it — it was several days' ration. But she was without food.

Laura fished in her pockets and found only a tin of Farry's Extra Strong Liquorice Pellets (Recommended for Regularity). 'Oh, great,' she muttered. Why couldn't she have been carrying mints or barley sugar? She said, 'I'll have another nap here, then see how far we can get on this much water and without food.' Laura stared at Nown, her finer-limbed and slightly less overbearing sandman. 'And I suppose I could send you on further to take a look *for* me.'

'You could,' he said.

'We'll see.'

'Yes, we will see what you decide,' he said.

Laura hadn't expected him to respond at all. And she was even more surprised when he expanded. 'You are the one who needs to eat, Laura. And you are the one who needs to know.'

Perhaps he was telling her off for saying 'we' — saying it and not meaning it, because she was the one with a mission, and he only had to look after her. She said, 'Are you angry with me?'

'I'm never angry.'

'Then I don't understand what you're trying to say.'

Nown was silent, and Laura knew he was thinking, because the ironsand gathered in his eye sockets and on his brow. After a time he said, 'If you send me to look, you may not be satisfied with my report. You and I see everything differently.'

Laura nodded. She was only partly paying attention, while casting about her for a bit of ground without bumps, somewhere to bed down. The grass around her was in a very bad condition, not just flattened but shredded. As she scuffed at the humps on the ground Laura listened to Nown once more giving examples of things he saw. Because she was listening with only half an ear it took her a while to realise that he was almost singing. Singing without a tune.

'You are a web of light,' he said. 'You are the shape you are. Trees stream upwards, grasses lance, fire billows and makes a flaw of light. The sea is where there isn't anything, but gannets go like spears into it, and fly up again from nothing —'

'You made a poem!' Laura said.

'— sometimes with a fish,' Nown concluded, less poetically.

Laura chose a relatively even patch of bare ground. She asked for the water skin, swallowed a few mouthfuls and lay down. She yawned till her jaw joints cracked. She tried to remember the poems she'd learned for examinations in elocution lessons, and those she'd learned at school. She lay with her eyes closed and recited the few fragments she had by heart. '*A slumber did my spirit seal; I had no human fears . . .*' And '*. . . she is coming, my own, my sweet, were it ever so airy a tread . . .*' Then, as she drifted off to sleep, she heard Nown repeating it all back to her, word perfect. And she thought: 'He really does remember everything I say.'

Laura woke later, in the Place's unchanging light. Nown was standing sentinel beside her, facing west, the direction from which people could most likely be expected to appear. She got up, said, 'Stay here,' and wandered off to find a bush to crouch behind.

Instead, she found a grave.

It was a long, low mound, of the same size and shape as earth piled up on a fresh grave.

Laura shouted for Nown. Her shout echoed from the Pinnacles.

Nown came at a swift run. He saw that she wasn't in any danger and stopped beside her, anxiously searching her face till he noticed the direction of her gaze.

They contemplated the grave together.

'Why would anyone choose to be buried in the Place instead of being taken back to their family?' Laura said, haunted and horrified. 'To their family,' she thought, 'and trees, grass, rain, day and night, church bells and birdsong.'

'This might not be choice, Laura.'

'Do you mean that someone was murdered? But this isn't a secret grave. It's here in plain sight — even if only dreamhunters and rangers can see it.'

'There's no marker.'

'No.' Laura's skin was clammy and her scalp tight. 'Nown — could you see if there was someone *alive* in there? Could you see their — web of light under the earth?'

'No. I can't see the gannets once they go into the water. I couldn't see your body in the river, only your head, and your arms moving in and out as you swam.'

Laura moaned.

'Are you thinking of your nightmare?'

Laura clenched her jaw and nodded once, sharply.

'Shall I dig it up for you?'

Laura grabbed her sandman's arm, though he'd made no move to start digging. She shook her head. She didn't want to see any corpses. Since grass didn't grow in the Place there was no way to tell how long ago the earth had been piled up over whatever lay beneath it. 'Let's just go,' Laura said. She turned away to find somewhere else to make herself comfortable. She didn't look back. She didn't see Nown pause, long, his gaze apparently penetrating the disturbed earth as if, perhaps, he could see what lay there.

Who lay there.

Three

The gate to the pass through the Pinnacles was closed. There was no one beyond it on guard — no one anywhere about. It was made of iron, a plain, workmanlike thing, bolted together and set into two short walls of mortared brick. The walls were pressed right up against the sides of the pass.

The Pinnacles themselves were perhaps only a hundred and fifty feet high, but steep and unstable. No one with any sense would think to set foot on their mealy grey slopes. There was no grass or scrub. It was as though they, like the grave, had come into existence after the grass had grown (and had stopped growing), as if they had bubbled up through the ground and set, a belt of brittle peaks.

A length of chain was wrapped around the joined sides of the gate. The chain was fastened with a padlock.

Laura put her face to a gap in the bars and looked along the pass at a road sprinkled here and there with hunks of fallen earth, but otherwise swept smooth.

Behind her Nown said, 'If you step out of the way I'll break it open for you.'

Laura took several steps back. Nown seized hold of the bars and began to shake the gate, pulling back and thrusting forward with his whole weight. At first he moved as if he were a body with muscles, and then began to move faster than any human body could. The gate clanged and boomed. The noise set off slips on the sides of the pass. It looked as if the Pinnacles were melting. Laura glanced around, but saw no one. The din the gates were making would be audible for miles.

Finally, in the racket, there came a sharp metallic crack. One of the hinges had broken, so that half of the gate sagged. Nown said, 'Can you climb that?'

She nodded.

He picked her up and boosted her into the gap. She scrambled, then lowered herself over the top of the gate, hung on for a moment and dropped. She backed away and waited for Nown to join her. He tossed her the water skin, then swarmed up the slope of the bars and tumbled over, landing with a thump that shook the ground. He got up. They stood still for a moment listening to pattering falls of earth. Before them the surface of the road was no longer smooth but blistered with debris.

Nown and Laura started along the path, she now and then jumping and scuttling aside from small rushes of dislodged pebbles. They walked softly for fear of shaking down the walls above them. They didn't speak.

Laura thought it was reasonable to assume that the gate was closed only for safety, when the Pinnacles Pass was in a state of poor repair, or when the Body was transporting materials for the secret railway of Rose's theory. So, Laura realised that because the gate was closed, she and Nown were likely to encounter other people — rangers making repairs, or carrying rails. At any moment, they might round a corner and run into a party of rangers hurrying back to see what had made all the awful noise. She should have a plan in case someone appeared. Things had been going badly: she'd lost her bedroll, her food, one water skin; she'd missed the fruit; and Nown had lost part of his feet — though the ones on which he was walking looked almost exactly the same, if a little smaller. She should decide what to do if she and Nown did run into rangers. She racked her brain. Eventually, 'Nown?' she said.

'Yes, Laura?'

'If we meet any rangers, could you — um — render them unconscious?'

He was silent.

'Could you —?'

'Are you sure?'

'Unconscious. Yes.' Laura was annoyed. Nown was acting like a responsible adult again. 'Do you have any other suggestions?'

Nown was quiet for a long time, then he said, 'You could shout at them: "Run for your lives, my nightmare has got loose!"'

Laura laughed. It was silly, but seemed less chancy than her plan.

Her sandman added, 'I'm not sure that I know how hard to hit a man to make him unconscious. I could try putting a hand over his mouth and nose, but then I could only deal with one man at a time.' He sounded practical.

'All right. We'll try your idea. Maybe that should be a contingency plan if ever we meet another dreamhunter or ranger.'

'Even your friend Sandy?'

Laura fell silent, thinking of her unanswered letters. She was going along with her head down and so missed the branch in the path. She stopped only when Nown called out to her. She looked up and saw that he was standing beside another closed and locked iron gate.

The path they had already travelled had twisted and turned so much that Laura had lost her usual vague eastwest orientation (the feeling that, since she was on this border of the Place, and facing In, Tricksie Bend lay somewhere west on her right-hand side.) From the map she'd studied, Laura was sure she was on the trail — a trail that led to Sanctuary Valley, a spread of open grassland containing a handful of commercial dreamsites, the only official destination beyond the Pinnacles, and the only reason the Regulatory Body maintained a pass through those dangerous peaks. There'd been no sign on the map that the trail branched anywhere beyond the gate. And yet Nown was standing by another gate, which blocked the way onto another trail.

This gate had a sign on it: *Detour Route. Closed April* 1905 *by order of Eugene Parker, Chief Ranger.*

'Break it open,' Laura said.

The second gate was far stronger than the first, and Nown had to resort to rushing at it, crashing into it with his shoulder. Laura was forced to remain standing near the path of his run-up, in the centre of the intersection. Even then, the myriad slides set off by her sandman's booming impact on the gates spilled debris right to her feet. Every hillside was shivering and shedding stones and earth. The air filled with grey dust. Laura closed her eyes, covered her mouth and crouched down, coughing. She felt the wind of Nown's swift passage again. There was a louder crash, the squawk of iron tearing, the singing rattle of a chain unravelling, a series of ringing clangs, then nothing but the bubbling whisper of crumbling earth.

Laura staggered up and peered through the dust, her eyes streaming.

Nown was extricating himself from the fallen gate. He turned to her and held up the broken chain, which appeared to be giving off a fine blue film of smoke, quite distinct in the dust-filled air. 'Smoke, without sparks,' Nown said, apparently impressed. 'And the old saying has it that there is never smoke without fire.'

Laura laughed, then coughed and pulled her shirt collar up over her mouth. She went to her sandman and pushed him forward. He stepped onto and across the fallen gate, and turned back to give her a hand.

The supposedly abandoned detour route was narrow, its sides so close together that they seemed to arch over the trail. It was gloomy in the winding pit of the pass. Because there was no direct sunlight in the Place there were never any shadows, only degrees of bright misty obscurity. But here, between the close walls of the Pinnacles, shadows seemed to have pooled, a thin stain of gloom.

Laura followed Nown, one hand against his back, which was warm, as if, in all his recent furious activity, the grains of sand in his body, chafing together, had woken heat. He felt the same as he did when sun-warmed. It was reassuring and kept Laura from — from whatever it was that seemed to live along that squeezed trail.

The dread Laura felt seemed alive, and to come from outside her. She'd felt it earlier, when she'd stood looking at the grave on the border. She had thought then that her dread was only the memory of the nightmare Buried Alive, and of the howling, thumping, flower-covered grave in The Water Diviner, the dream she'd caught with Sandy. But the atmosphere in the abandoned detour trail was exactly like that of the grave. It had a sense of something stopped, and powerless, and profoundly miserable, but still *there*, like the afterlife of despair.

'I hate it here,' Laura muttered to Nown.

He said, 'I hope I won't have to break another gate. The walls are too close.' Then he spun around, gathered her into his arms, and carried her. She closed her eyes and pressed her face into his neck.

After only another half-hour Nown came to a halt. He stood so still that it was as though he'd become inanimate, a real statue. Laura lifted her head and saw that he had stopped before a platform built of timber and bolted steel, and topped by some kind of apparatus. Laura wriggled, and Nown set her down.

There was a cage on the platform, a chest-high box covered in steel mesh. It had a gate at the front, and rods rising from its top corners. The rods joined in an apex above the box. There was a hook attached to the apex, and the hook was locked to a cable.

Laura tipped her head back to follow the cable up from the platform to another identical platform, diminished and distant on the levelled summit of a high pinnacle.

The rangers had built themselves a cable car.

In the widening of the trail before the platform, lying about, were chains, a small pile of rails bundled in thick straps, large, heavy canvas sheets with steel-reinforced eyelets at all four corners, and all sorts of other signs — a multiple, overlapping mêlée of boot prints, greasy rags, dropped work gloves — that rangers had been hard at work here lifting loads to that summit.

'The winch has two handles,' Nown said, 'with double grips on each handle. Four men can work it at any one time.'

Laura saw that he was right. She stood quietly for a moment, thinking. The cable car looked very sturdy. Nown was as strong as four men — at least — and could probably manage to winch up the slope as much weight as the cable could bear. She was slight. She'd be safe. She would only have to go to the top and take a look. Then she could come straight back down.

Although Laura was thinking of a quick trip and a little look, still she said to Nown, 'May I have the water skin, please?' Her words came out with brittle politeness.

'No,' he said.

'Nown!' Laura stamped her foot, sending out a small puff of dust that hovered around her ankles. 'Look — there's probably no way down the far slope. Or, I mean, there is probably another cable car and no one to wind it for me. You don't need to worry.'

'If there's no way down the far slope, you won't need water.'

'You're supposed to do what I say!' Laura said.

Nown didn't reply to this.

'May I just have a drink then?'

Nown passed her the water skin. Laura screwed off its copper cap and took a long drink — more than she wanted or needed. She replaced the cap and wrapped her arms around the water skin, cradling its sloshing, damp bulk. She knitted her brows at her sandman, then turned on her heel and went up the steps onto the platform. She opened the gate of the box cage, stepped in and fastened it after her. 'Now you will winch me up there,' she said.

Nown followed her up onto the platform and studied the winding mechanism. He didn't touch it. He looked at her, waiting.

Laura glared at him. A minute went by, then she burst out, 'This might be our only chance! I should go as far as I'm able!'

'Yes.'

'Well — get winding then!'

'I can be made again, you can't. This is your only chance.'

Nown was telling her that this was her only *life*. Laura lost her temper. 'Let *me* make the decisions! I'm in charge!' she yelled.

Around them again came the rustling whisper of falling earth. Laura slumped, her knees gave way. She crouched down in the cage, her fingers gripping its mesh, and the water skin pressed between her thighs and belly. She began to cry. She pressed her face against the grid of wire and sobbed. She cried because she was frustrated and tired, even of crying — she had spent a whole year in tears.

The cage quivered, then swung free. It was ascending. Laura stood up. Nown was winding the mechanism's great drum. The handles squeaked and the greased cable wound in on itself with a sticky, kissing noise. The sounds gradually receded. Then Laura could only hear the cage creaking as it swung. Nown and the platform grew small and the cage slid up above the grey slope. The ground below Laura was as pockmarked as a glacier honeycombed by sun-heated dust and pebbles. It looked treacherous.

Laura went up, but felt no wind. The air temperature remained the same — warm and dry. The view opened up around and then below her, revealing a series of peaks back the way she and Nown had come, then all around, to the eastern and western horizons along the border — but not extending beyond the border into that visible but inaccessible hinterland that all dreamhunters looked into before crossing back into their own world. The Pinnacles were clearly a feature of the border itself. Laura could see the opening to Sanctuary Valley, several hours' walk along the branch of trail they'd not taken. Flanking the valley, and stretching away Inland, was a forked tongue of grey pinnacles thrusting out from the main mass of peaks. The furthest fork was thick, a real barrier, like the main range. The other was slender, in places perhaps only three peaks wide. From ground level this fork might appear to be a real barrier, but from high on the cable car it showed as not much more than a fence or screen. For these peaks screened the eastern hinterland from anyone on level ground.

As the cage swung gently up, Laura looked into the land beyond the narrow barrier. She saw grasslands with, here and there, stands of dry trees like clutches of stilled smoke. And, as the cage bumped against a wall at the back of the platform, Laura saw the railway line that ran, plumb-straight, through the grasslands, till it faded into the vaporous brightness of the Inland horizon.

Laura opened the cage door and got out onto the platform. She waved at Nown. He didn't acknowledge her gesture.

Laura went to the far end of the platform and looked down. There wasn't another cable car. There was a flying fox. The rangers could let gravity do the work of carrying down loads of rails and other goods bundled in the canvas slings. For themselves, however, they had built a tower. It was made of steel, and had many flights of steps. The tower stood out from the base of the pinnacle and could be reached from the summit by a twenty-something-foot span of bridge.

Laura went back to the cage and waved to Nown again, this time not to say, 'I'm all right,' but, 'Goodbye, I'm going.' She thought she saw him shake his head, then knew he had, because he raised a hand to wave her back. Laura held up her wrist and touched her watch face. She spread her fingers, counted them off with the pointing index finger of her other hand. 'Give me five hours,' she signed. She hoped he would know that she didn't mean five minutes. Laura waited for her sandman to react, then turned her back on him and struck out across the bridge to the tower.

Four

Since first coming to the Place, Laura had seen some roads so smoothly surfaced that bicycles could be ridden on them. She'd seen rudimentary steps on slopes, latrines, well-levelled camping grounds and even one stubby lookout tower. She had never seen anything that showed the purpose or industry of the cable car, tower and railway line. All showed signs of heavy use, so that, looking at them, Laura knew that somewhere, at the other end of the line, there would be a settlement of some kind, buildings and people — for the railway was a supply line.

When Laura reached the foot of the tower she found a handcar, sitting on the rails and up against buffers. The handcar was a simple contraption, a platform with plenty of room for freight and two seats set facing one another with a couple of levers between them. The levers, if pushed up and down, would make the wheels turn. Once the handcar built up momentum Laura imagined that it would go quite fast — perhaps as fast as a sprinting man.

Laura set out along the railway line. She didn't mean to go far. She was thinking she'd just go far enough to find herself even with some landmark, like a stand of trees, that she could later use as a sighting from the tower in order to make a rough estimate of the length of line she could see. If it took her an hour to reach — say — *that* stand of trees, the one that looked to her novice dreamhunter's eye about an hour away, then later she'd perhaps be able to make a rough estimate of how many hours there were beyond that. Laura knew that the Regulatory Body would never have bothered to build a railway line for anything that rangers would regard as a reasonable walking distance. The line must be at least longer than a day's walk. Its final destination was, most likely, days away.

Laura ambled along, remembering the sorts of things that were at the end of secret trails in books she'd read. 'A diamond mine,' she thought, 'something precious that they don't want to share.' After all, there was no reason to suppose that there weren't pockets of precious minerals In the Place, and that prospecting rangers might not have turned something up. She imagined Cas Doran and his friends with a growing reserve of undeclared wealth. She imagined a fortress and a vast army of soldier rangers training in manoeuvres. A secret army. Then she remembered that guns wouldn't fire in the Place, so the soldiers of her imaginary army would have to be lying on their bellies, pointing rifles and making gun noises with their mouths.

She giggled.

The stand of trees that Laura had picked as a landmark was getting closer, but only very slowly. She sighed and picked up her pace. She was hungry, but that was no excuse for dragging her feet and daydreaming.

A while later, when she'd raised a sweat, and her mind was just idling, the thought that had been trailing her for days — possibly since Rose first told her about the 'surplus rails' — finally caught up with her. She remembered that the Grand Patriarch had asked her about 'the Depot'.

Laura raised her head and squinted up the line. 'The Depot' wasn't the name of a dream: it was a destination, where something was stored.

What else had the Grand Patriarch said? There was something else, a name from a rumour, because hadn't the Grand Patriarch said that most of his intelligence came from rumours?

Contentment.

Laura stopped walking when the word came into her head. She stood still, shivering and short of breath. The world darkened around her as the pupils of her eyes contracted. Dread had crept up and pounced on her. And, now that she was still, she understood that her footsteps had masked a vibration. A sound.

A steely rolling was coming from the line behind her.

Laura spun to face back along the line. She saw the handcar bearing down upon her, fast. Riding on it were six rangers.

Laura jumped from the raised track bed and sprinted away across the meadow. She heard a shout, then the handcar braking. She looked back and saw four men pouring off it after her.

The rangers came tearing through the dry grass with a sound like a grass fire. They ran her down and grappled her. Laura fought them, punched and kicked. She was lifted up into the air and then dumped onto the ground. The wind was knocked out of her. For a moment, her only thought was how to fill her lungs. They ached and struggled to expand again. She was making a sound like one of those enraged sea-lions she and the lighthouse keeper's girls had disturbed sleeping on the sands of So Long Spit. She drew breath in a prolonged, barking howl, rocking with pain and effort. She wheezed, and tears poured down her cheeks and into her ears.

One of the rangers tore her shirt open and grabbed her licence on its chain. He put his head down to read the copper tags.

'We haven't had anyone escape,' another ranger was saying, 'and look at what she's wearing.'

'She's not one of ours,' said the one who had hold of her licence. 'This is Tziga Hame's daughter.'

Five

They tied her wrists and ankles with their bandannas and carried her back to the handcar. They set her down among boxes and baskets and tall zinc milk cans that Laura guessed were full of water. She could smell oranges and apples, bread and the sharp perfume of the cocoa and cinnamon in dreamhunters' strong bread.

An argument was conducted over her head. Someone poked her with a boot, not hard, but carelessly. 'Who broke the gates?'

A second man said, not to her, 'Whoever it was must have heard us coming and run off along the trail to Sanctuary Valley.'

'That's only conjecture. Still, I guess someone should go back and track them. Look — I'll go. And you come with me, McIndoe. The rest of you get on and raise the alarm.'

Again the boot prodded Laura. 'Who are they? Your accomplices?'

The second man said, 'How did they know what they were looking for? What have you got to say for yourself, girl?'

'Let her alone,' another said. 'She'll tell us afterwards, anyway.'

After what? Laura thought, and bunched herself up into a tight, defensive ball.

The handcar bounced on its suspension as two men jumped off it. Laura heard the sloshing of water skins being settled. One of the men who was leaving said, 'Be as quick as you can. Those gates will have to be fixed as soon as possible.'

Laura wondered where her sandman had hidden. The cage would have been on the summit when the rangers reached the cable car — after passing through two broken gates. Not just broken, but exploded. Laura remembered the stretched-liquorice look of the tortured links of the smoking chain. Nown would probably be burrowed in somewhere, with only his roughly made back exposed. He could look as natural as a big stone whenever he really needed to.

The four remaining rangers settled themselves on the handcar. Laura heard a spring squawk as someone sat, preparing to work the levers. She mustered her courage. She unclenched her body, rolled onto her back and looked up at one of the men.

He met her eyes, and his face creased with worry. 'You're really only a baby, aren't you?'

'How far is it if you go around the long way?' Laura asked him.

'How far to where?' one of the others said, impatient.

The handcar was moving now. The landscape slid by, faster every second. None of the crankshafts or levers made a noise; all were too well greased. The only sound was the creak of springs in the seats as the rangers' weight shifted while they worked. That, and the ponderous, rolling noise of steel wheel-rims on steel rails.

The man who was looking at Laura said, 'She means, is there another way around the Pinnacles. She's hoping her friends will be able to follow her on foot.'

The other man laughed. 'There's no long way, girlie,' he said. 'Only a wrong way.'

Laura never did learn how long the journey was. They removed her watch, so she couldn't tell the time. They didn't try to talk to her any more. She sat slumped against a basket.

The rangers worked the levers in shifts. The Pinnacles faded into mistiness before they fell behind the horizon. The plain across which the handcar moved was bald, and seemed to swell up towards the sky as though showing the curve of the planet. Hours went by and Laura fell asleep. She ran through some coloured rags of dreams, too fast to take in anything of any of them.

When she woke up, stiff, her face numb on one side and printed with a pattern of basketwork, one ranger remarked, 'It would have been easier for you if you stayed asleep for just another half-hour.' He pulled her to her feet. She stood propped and teetering between the stacked baskets as the handcar reduced speed and rolled in among some buildings.

The ground of the compound was dusty and lightly embossed all over by footprints — boot prints and bare feet. The compound consisted of a cluster of huts, several long barracks-like buildings and shelters with canvas roofs and walls, the walls rolled up like window blinds to reveal rows of pallet beds. Some of the beds were occupied by people either sleeping or reading. They were all wearing yellow cotton pyjamas. More yellow-clad figures sat about on benches, or stood where the grass began again, facing away from the buildings, or lay on their backs gazing up into the unremarkable white sky. There was even a group of pyjama-clad young men playing a not very energetic ball game, all barefoot and scuffling in the dust.

The handcar pulled up at a platform. More rangers appeared, and began unloading the supplies, carrying everything into one of the huts. Laura was picked up like baggage and put down on the platform. She waited as people went by her with boxes and baskets. She ignored the rangers and tried to catch the eye of one of the people in yellow. Most were men, but Laura did see a few young women among them. They all looked well fed, well rested and reasonably clean. They were not at all interested in Laura's appearance. Their eyes went across her as though she were no more surprising than anything else they looked at.

Laura didn't like their yellow uniforms, or their vulnerable, unshod feet. But she could see that none of the people seemed sedated. They were all active and coordinated and clear-eyed — only strangely calm.

Several more rangers emerged from one of the barracks and came over to Laura. The one wearing a white coat and stethoscope frowned as he came up, and said, 'Untie her immediately.'

When her hands were free Laura pulled the gaping front of her shirt together.

'There's no need to do that, young lady. I want to look at your licence,' the doctor said.

'She's Tziga Hame's daughter, Laura,' one of her captors said.

The doctor gave Laura a careful, appraising look.

'She was walking Inland along the railway line about an hour from the tower. The gate at the beginning of the Pinnacles was broken, hanging off its hinges. The detour gate was smashed to bits. But the girl was on her own when we found her.'

The doctor looked into Laura's eyes. 'Did you break the gates, Laura?'

'They were already broken,' she said. 'I wondered whether there was some emergency. I went in to see if I could be of any assistance.' She lifted her chin and stared at him, cool and defiant.

One of the rangers snorted in disbelief. 'Who worked the cable car, then?'

Laura said, 'I was so determined to help I went up the cable hand over hand.'

The ranger hissed in anger, and reached for her, but the doctor fended him off. 'There's no need to press her. We'll know her story soon enough.'

To Laura he said, 'I'm sure you understand that you're in trouble. You've trespassed. And there's the matter of damage to property.'

Laura didn't like to meet his eyes. There was a look in them, a cold, stripped-down look. It frightened her. Instead she turned her attention to the railway line which, she saw, didn't end at the platform but went away, dead straight, Inland. She asked, 'Is this the Depot?'

'Yes, it is. But where did you hear that name?'

'I don't remember. What's out there?' Laura pointed along the line.

'The railway is being extended solely in the interests of exploration. Believe me, the further you go the less memorable it is. But I suppose you are one of those dreamhunters with romantic ideas about the hinterland? About a dream like Koh-i-noor? A big matchless diamond of a dream.'

He was making fun of her. He was all scorn and cynicism: a fortress, defended, but defending only emptiness. That was what she could see when she looked into his eyes. He knew he was doing wrong, and meant to go on doing it, but was still capable of feeling resentment when anything reminded him of it.

Laura remembered seeing a similar expression in Maze Plasir's face when she'd asked him about supplying nightmares to the Department of Corrections.

As these thoughts went through her mind, Laura began unconsciously pursing her lips and shaking her head.

'Are you about to *scold* us?' the doctor said, sarcastic.

The look she gave him — the doctor remembered it all his life. She met his eyes, her expression icy and knowing. It wasn't bravado. She didn't strike him as brave. She was still shivering and clutching her torn shirt closed over her tiny breasts. Fear was there in her body, frank fear in her tremors and whitened knuckles. But she looked like someone who couldn't feel her own fear, because it was being interfered with by faith. Faith was pouring out of her face at him, bigger and louder than anything. She looked like a saint.

It was very impressive. But being impressed only made this man feel spiteful. He leered at Laura Hame. He said, 'I'm pleased to see you're not afraid. You have no reason to be, as you'll soon learn.' He nodded to the rangers he'd come with, one of whom laid a hand on her shoulder, while the other knelt to unlace and remove her boots. The doctor smiled wider and added, 'I know you'll be very happy here.'

The hut had a wooden floor, and white dust had gathered in its corners. It had a window with bars on it, but without glass. There was no need for glass: no cold to combat, nor wind to screen. A thin mattress was set square against one wall. There was a bucket: clean white enamel, with a lid. There was no other furniture.

An hour after Laura was put into the room, the door was unbolted and a tray delivered to her. On it was a mug of water, and oatcakes topped with honey. There was a bowl full of some kind of cold tomato concoction, and an orange.

Laura sipped the water slowly. She wasn't so much planning an escape as just meaning to. Because she meant to escape she would take every opportunity to store water in her body. She drank slowly, with the idea that she, like an indoor plant, would absorb more water if watered gradually. As she sipped she looked through the window at the people in yellow.

She saw one she recognised. It was Maze Plasir's apprentice, Gavin Pinkney. Oily, snide Gavin — who had passed in the Doorhandle Try last autumn, and who was licensed before Laura since he didn't catch dreams about convicts.

Gavin was sitting, holding his bare toes in either hand and rocking gently back and forth.

Laura put her face against the bars and called to him. 'Gavin!'

He was slow to react to his name, but turned to her smiling already, then beamed. He got up and came over wearing a goofy but completely genuine grin. 'Hello,' he said.

'Gavin, how long have you been here?'

Gavin shrugged. 'It's great here,' he said. 'Though I could *murder* a bit of cooked meat.'

'A while, then?' Laura said.

'I'm so glad you've come,' he said. 'You'll find you feel better almost immediately.'

Laura nodded to encourage him, and he began to echo her nod, his eyes creased with smiling. 'It's wonderful that we're together,' he said.

'You and me?' Laura was astonished. He'd shown no sign of liking her before.

'All together,' he said, in a singsong voice. 'It was all worth it.'

'What was?'

'The work, the chances I took. Time well spent, to end up with this — this full well of time.' Gavin's voice was nasal — his usual quacking voice, but his tone was so serene he sounded mesmerising. 'And we have the whole day ahead of us,' he said. 'This beautiful day.' He looked around, his face shining, as if illuminated by brilliant spring sunshine.

Laura covered her mouth with her hand. She retched, and some of the water came back up from her gullet tainted with bile. She swallowed, and tried to control herself.

Gavin went on. 'There's my mother waiting for us — still in the best of health. And my grown children, favoured by fortune, he prosperous, she generous. How foolish I was to worry about them. And the grandchildren — here they come up from the beach, the girls practising cartwheels and the boys carrying the canoe paddles . . .'

'It's a dream, Gavin,' Laura said, to put a stop to his rapturous chanting.

'A dream . . .' His eyes flickered.

'Contentment,' Laura said, guessing.

'Yes.' His face cleared. Then he said, puzzled, 'Don't you want to be happy?'

There was a clanging from one of the buildings. It sounded like a dinner bell. Gavin got up, dusted off his backside and left without saying another word. Laura watched all the yellow-clad figures making their way, orderly and eager, towards the sound of the bell.

There was no fence around the compound. There was no need for one — the barefoot, captive dreamhunters wouldn't want to run away from decent food and the blessed company of the dream.

Before they had put her in the hut the rangers had made Laura turn out her pockets. She'd said to them, sneering, 'Do you suppose I'm carrying a lock pick? Or a knife?' But of course they'd been looking for Wakeful. Wakeful was what Laura wished she had now — the drug, or a lock pick, or a knife.

She knew that her captors had only to wait for her to sleep. Then they could ask her their questions. Once she had taken a print of the dream, and had been drugged by its bliss, they would ask their questions and she'd answer them, trustingly. Nothing would matter. It would be a beautiful day, and she'd have the whole day ahead of her.

Before she could have second thoughts, Laura began to feed the oozy oatcakes through the bars, then she poured the tomato stuff out after them. As she did this she whispered, 'I don't want to be happy. I don't want to be happy.' She didn't put the food in her slops bucket, because it was still empty and clean and she might be tempted to fetch it out again. Her captors might not be patient, she reasoned: they might drug her food to make her sleep sooner. Laura could still see how the smashed gates had looked. If they were *her* gates and she had found them and hadn't known how they had been broken, she'd be very keen to find out as soon as possible.

Laura ate only the orange. She chose to believe that it was protected from tampering by its peel. She stopped whispering to herself as she ate, but went on once she'd swallowed her last bite, in a slow, burning panic: 'I don't want to be happy.'

She went to the window again to stare out into the grasslands. She imagined she saw a far-off figure, a dark speck. But it was only a dust mote sliding down the surface of her eye.

Her mouth shaped his name.

A ranger found the food. He picked up the oatcakes and went away. The doctor appeared a few minutes later at her door. 'You're being very stupid,' he said. 'Unless you want to answer our rather pressing questions now.'

Laura shook her head and backed away from him.

He signalled to the rangers waiting behind him. The men stepped into the hut and grabbed her. The doctor advanced on her. He pulled a square black leather case from the pocket of his white coat. He snapped its lid open. Laura glimpsed the gleaming glass and steel of hypodermic needles. 'No!' she shrieked.

'No?' The doctor hesitated, the case open. He tilted it back and forth so that bubbles slid in the glass barrels of clear chemical.

'I'll be good, I'll eat, I'll lie down.' She was babbling. Then she burst into tears. She sobbed in rage and fear, her voice dropped a full octave and she said, 'I'll kill you,' sobbing.

'You'll be good, and you'll kill me?' the doctor said, cold and sweet. But he must have made a silent command too, for the rangers released her. Laura cowered away from them against the wall. Through the distortion of tears she saw the doctor point down, at the mattress she was standing on. She obeyed him, lowering herself onto her knees.

'I'll send in more food. It isn't drugged, Miss Hame. You'll sleep better with something in your stomach.'

'Yes,' Laura said. 'Yes, all right.' She held her hands out, palms up, pushing them away.

They left. She heard the bolt on the outside of the door slide into place. Someone gave it a rattle for good measure. Then it was quiet. She could hear footsteps in the yard, the occasional murmuring voice. She thought she could hear the other captives having dinner, the clack of spoons on enamelware. She covered her ears and squeezed her eyes shut and tried to push back the panic that was threatening to annihilate her, prematurely, since Contentment was poised to wipe her out as soon as she slept. The dream would replace herself with itself, her desires with its self-satisfaction. It would replace her family with its family, its cartwheeling granddaughters.

Laura found herself singing. She sang to stay sane. She sang the school song of Founderston Girls' Academy, a song about striving and virtue and setting forth together. Then her voice trailed off and she stared through the striped mattress cover in front of her.

She had come up with a plan.

The ranger sent to look in on Laura Hame stopped by her cell window and took a quick peek. He didn't know quite what he expected: to surprise her at something, perhaps — but what?

The girl had her back to the window and didn't notice him. She was kneeling in one corner of the room and seemed to be busy sweeping up the dust gathered in the angle of floor and wall. She was using her hands, and was in danger of picking up splinters from the rough planks flooring the hut. The ranger thought: 'So — she's decided to keep herself awake by doing housework.' She looked like a penitent, on her knees and grubbing away at the dirt.

'It's futile, you know,' he said.

She stopped what she was doing, stiffened, but didn't turn around.

The ranger waited for a moment, then went away.

When, over an hour later, he came back to check, the Hame girl was sitting cross-legged in the centre of the room, with her back to the window. She'd removed her jacket and spread it out before her. The dust she'd swept up was gathered in a tiny pile on the jacket. This was odd, but he was reassured to see that she had in her hand the small seedy loaf from her second plate of food.

'Good girl,' he said.

She turned around and gave him a cold look. 'Don't gloat,' she said. Then, 'My clothes are uncomfortable. I'd sleep better in a pair of those yellow pyjamas everyone is wearing.'

He went away and found a clean pair, a little too big for her, but she could roll up the sleeves and ankles. He returned to the hut and found her standing at the window. Over her shoulder he could see her jacket, lying humped in the middle of the room. There was no sign of her housekeeping dust-pile. The bread was gone, the water cup empty and on its side.

He pushed the pyjamas through the bars. She thanked him and he went away once more.

The ranger stayed away over an hour. When next he looked in on the Hame girl, she was still up, but was in the pyjamas — their yellow highly visible in the gloom of the hut.

She was singing.

The ranger opened his mouth and drew breath to say something to startle her, and a familiar, lovely odour hit his palate. The scent seemed to come billowing out through the bars in the window. Ozone — summer rain on warm earth. The ranger shook his head, and shouted, 'Girl!'

Laura Hame broke off her singing with a cough like a sob. Her shoulders slumped.

'Do you want me to tell the doctor to come and pay you a visit?'

'Go away!' she yelled. She didn't jump up or twist herself about. She spoke vehemently but only turned her head to look back over her shoulder. 'I want to sleep,' she said. 'I have a sore stomach. I'm waiting for it to pass.'

'Better be soon,' he threatened, then went away once more.

Laura put her palms over her eyes to catch her tears. She rocked back and forth in her own darkness. There was only *this* to do. It would either work or it wouldn't. She had to empty her mind of all fear and expectation. She had only to remember that it did work — that she, Laura, was already living in a world in which she'd succeeded at this. The only rule was the spell. The only effort, faith.

She set her wet fingers on the drying surface of the little man she'd made out of dust and chewed bread. She made the surface of the mix tacky and pliable once more. She began to sing again, from the beginning, 'The Measures' — that chant made of *koine*, demotic Greek, and nonsense sounds, glossolalia, the tongues of angels. Every word was different from the one before.

The power began to build and spin around her. She sang on in her tired, sweet, young voice, and this time no one came to interrupt her. When she finished singing the room seemed to vibrate — it was so stuffed with energy. Laura picked up the second of two small crescent-shaped slivers of fingernail, her own, and stooped over the tiny, tacky form of the bread-and-dust man. She scratched the letters onto the broadest part of his anatomy, his chest. The other bit of fingernail was already buried in that doughy chest, as a heart. Laura etched 'NOW,' but left off the final 'N.' She didn't need him to speak to her, only to follow her orders.

For a second the tiny bread-and-dust figure lay inert. Then suddenly, his stillness looked like surprise. He flexed his legs, and got up, and turned his little, roughly formed face up to hers.

Laura laughed and smiled down at him.

His attention was so focused and expectant that it pulled her out of her brief moment of rapt relief. 'Look,' she said, 'I'll just go and check the window to see how many people are out there. We need plenty of people in yellow, and fewer rangers. A while ago I heard a bell ringing at that building farther off — so perhaps the rangers are having *their* meal. I hope so.' She bit her lip to stop herself talking. She needn't explain her whole situation. He was so tiny that she thought she'd better keep her instructions simple. 'His brain can't be very big,' she thought, nonsensically. Then she recalled that he didn't have a brain anyway, so maybe his size didn't determine his mental capacity.

Laura made herself stop thinking it all through. She went to the window, saw there were now plenty of yellow-clad people about — as many as there had been when she first arrived, hours ago. Perhaps this was their roster of daylight. The camp might very well run with a 'day' and 'night' for the convenience of the rangers. So, it was 'day', and there were people about. There were even a few wandering quite far out from the camp — maybe as far as they'd ever want to go on the invisible leash of the dream.

Laura turned back to the room. She picked up her bread-and-dust man and put him on the windowsill between the bars. 'I want you to jump down, run around the hut and find some way to climb up and unbolt the door.'

The tiny Nown didn't hesitate. He jumped out of the window. Laura heard the pattering sound he made landing. She didn't hear his footfalls.

Laura went to the door and waited. Eventually, she heard noises, as if someone with sticky fingers were touching the door. She put her ear to the wood and concentrated till she could hear that the noises were progressing up the outside surface of the door. Then she was deafened by the loud rattle of the bolt. She pulled her ear back and the door swung in, the little man riding it, his elbows locked around the loop of the bolt and his legs braced against the sleeve of it.

Laura poked her head around the door. A few of the yellow-clad people looked at her, some smiling, but none with any real interest. Laura put out her hand, and the bread-and-dust man stepped onto her palm. She slipped him down inside her shirt, where he clung like a lizard.

Laura stepped out of the hut and bolted the door behind her. Then she put her head down and ambled away, smiling to herself and swinging her arms as though she were filled with some private, sunny monologue. She imitated the other people. As she went past one of the tent dormitories she petted its canvas wall. She walked in a weaving, indirect way, in the opposite direction to the isolated rangers' barracks. She didn't attempt to keep the railway line in sight — she would have to find it later.

She sat down for a time where the bare beaten earth of the camp compound began to sprout grass again. She kept her back to the buildings and tried to look relaxed, drizzling dust through her fingers and talking to herself. Now and then she glanced back till — at one glance — she saw the buildings, the yellow-clad bodies, but no rangers nearby or facing her way.

Laura immediately ducked down and stripped off the yellow pyjama top and trousers. She was still wearing her own clothes underneath. She pushed the pyjamas down the front of her trousers then rolled and wriggled away into the thin grass, headed for the scrub. As she went she rubbed herself in the dust — her face and hair, her dark trousers and pale shirt — till she was as dun-coloured as the ground she crawled along.

For a long time she slid from bush to bush. Her bread-and-dust man now nestled in the small of her back, holding onto her belt. The heels of her hands, her fingertips and the skin on her feet dragged on the ground till they were scraped and burning. Her palms filled with splinters of dead vegetation. She didn't dare put her head up until she could no longer hear any noise from the Depot. Finally she got to her feet and, stooped right over, hurried away.

It was hours before Laura let herself turn back towards the railway line. She took a course only tending towards where it lay. At every few steps she glanced around, looking for rangers on foot, or riding on a handcar. When the handcar did appear Laura was surprised how close it was. She threw herself down on the ground and lay completely still. Her bread-and-dust man tumbled off her back and lay still too, by her ear, with his cracked and drying hand against her cheek.

When Laura looked again the handcar had travelled out of sight.

Laura went on, parallel to the railway. She just kept putting one foot in front of the other, hour after hour. She walked, straining her eyes, looking and looking for any sign, however far off, of the Pinnacles and the tower.

She slept for a time, but badly. She was thirsty and feverish.

A nosebleed woke her. The blood only oozed, sluggish and tacky. While she held her nostrils pinched, trying to staunch it, her bread-and-dust man leaned against her knee and watched her.

'He knows where I am. Wherever I am,' Laura said to him, in a pinched, croaking voice she scarcely recognised as her own.

Eventually she got up and went on, not noticing that she'd left the little man behind, till she felt him leap and cling to the leg of her trousers. She scooped him up and put him on her shoulder.

She walked. Nothing moved but her. Hours went by, transparent, emptied out, even of time.

Laura's lips cracked. Her tongue gradually grew a coat of some thick salty stuff. Then it began to swell.

Many hours later her bladder began to cramp. She fumbled at her trousers and squatted to urinate. It burned. There were only a few drops, and it went on burning deep inside her.

Laura sat down and cried — cried without producing tears.

The bread-and-dust man tugged on her hair.

She got up and went on.

Later — a long time later — Laura had a lucid moment. She thought: 'I'll die unless I let the rangers find me.' She lifted her head and took a good look about. She could see no sign of the Pinnacles, not even a smudge on the horizon. She turned and saw she had wandered close to the raised track bed. The steel lines were shining at her like water. She went towards them, clambered on all fours up the little slope and sat there, slumped.

Her bread-and-dust man scrambled off her and onto the track bed. He doubled up and pressed his whole little length against the steel.

Laura thought: 'He's listening for a handcar.' Then she lay down.

Someone touched her. It hurt. A hard something rasped across the stinging fissures on her mouth.

Wet parted her lips. At first she could taste only water on her tongue, then as she took more, its true taste came: musty, warm, stale water.

It was taken away from her before she was full. She croaked a complaint, and drooped, her head lolling against the yielding, creaking arm that held her.

With a ghost of decision, she whispered, 'I don't want to be happy.'

She was lifted up. She was gathered in her loose skin, in her own weakness; she was gathered in his strength. She was lifted, cradled, carried in safety.

And they went so fast there was wind to cool her skin.

Six

Laura and Nown emerged from the Place just west of the railway bridge over the Sva. It was dawn, but the air seemed to cool only Laura's skin, not to reach the parched, burning core of her body. Her chilled skin had formed a shell around her. She'd lost touch with the world. She was being carried, but the motion seemed only to pantomime walking. Perhaps Nown was only pretending to move. Yet, when Laura opened her eyes, she saw that they were further out on the tide-bared sands of the inlet.

Nown sat her down by a channel of the river and slid her forward so that her feet dangled in the stream. Its cold burned her blistered skin. She cried out and tried to flex her knees, but was too weak to withdraw her legs from the water. Nown held her in place until her feet went numb. Then he picked her up again and carried her back to the station by the bridge. He put her down on the gravel of the raised track bed and lifted the metal flag that would signal the next train to stop. He came back, hunkered down and drew Laura into his lap. 'I have nothing with which to wrap your feet,' he said, then, 'From now on I'm going to put things that might be necessary to you into my body.'

Laura puzzled over this remark, but couldn't make any sense of it. Minutes later he said, 'I've filled the water skin. The tide is going out and the stream flowing seaward, but its water might be tainted by salt. I wouldn't know. I can't taste it.'

Laura tried to answer him, but only croaked. It seemed to her in her fever that her sandman was brooding on his shortcomings. The water skin pushed against her. She fumbled for it with her hands and scabbed mouth, but it was too heavy for her to lift. Nown raised it and eased the nozzle into her mouth. The water was a little salty, but Laura liked its taste. Perhaps she needed salt.

'Not too much at once,' Nown said, and they had a little tussle, she clinging to the skin and he trying to take it away without upsetting her. The water gushed out onto her face and shirt. Laura felt the cascading coolness, then the panicked scuttling motion of the creature who — all this time — had ridden clinging to the inside of her shirt. Laura's bread-and-dust man emerged, and clambered up her, finding handholds on her collarbone, then the ends of her hair. For a moment he swung bumping against her jaw, then Nown closed a fist around him and plucked him from her.

The bread-and-dust man surveyed Laura, the railway line and inlet from his perch in Nown's fist. His mitt-like, fingerless hands were folded across the top of Nown's thumb. His flat and vestigial face looked mild and perhaps curious.

Nown stretched back the arm that held the little creature, then punched it into his own chest. Laura had one glimpse of a tiny gaping mouth and kicking legs, then both Nown's fist and the bread-and-dust man vanished, buried in the sandman's chest.

'No!' Laura rasped. She was horrified.

'It is better if there are not too many of us around at one time,' Nown said. His buried wrist began to sort itself out from the sand of his chest, and he withdrew his hand, whole and empty.

'Is two too many?' Laura's eyes were stinging, but no tears would come.

Nown didn't answer her.

'Why did you do that?' Laura knew he could hear her, however insubstantial her voice had become.

'There were too many of us.'

'Is two too many?' she asked again, and again Nown didn't answer her.

'Can you do that?' she said. 'Destroy him? Don't *I* have to do that?'

'It isn't destroyed; it is only swallowed.'

Nown put his hand on the railway line. He announced that there was a train on its way. He set Laura on her feet by the station signal, then lifted her arm and hooked it around the signal pole. 'Stay there. Stay standing,' he said, then he left her. He picked his way down the embankment and strode along a reed-lined beach beside one channel of the river. Some distance from her he hunkered down and wrapped his arms around his legs, dropped his face onto his knees and imitated a tide-worn stone.

The train was a local headed towards Sisters Beach.

On a clear day the red-painted steel flag of the stop signal was visible to the driver from the lowest turn of the Mount Kahaugh spiral. He had miles to slow and stop. The Secretary of the Interior had a house in Awa Inlet — and it was Doran who most often used the station. There was never any question that the train would pause, though stopping always put at least ten minutes more on any journey.

It wasn't until he was going very slowly, and approaching the bridge, that the driver saw the small ragged figure by the signal. As he pulled to a halt he saw that it was a girl, her clothes torn at the knees and elbows and white with dust.

A conductor got out to inspect the prospective passenger. He took in her bedraggled appearance and lack of luggage. He went up to her ready to ask whether she even had the fare but, when he reached her, he saw how young she was, and how she trembled, and how she was holding herself up against the signal pole. Instead of demanding money the conductor placed his strong hand under one of her elbows. 'What happened?'

Passengers were pushing down their windows and poking their heads out to take a look.

'Are you a dreamhunter?' the conductor asked.

'Yes. I got lost,' the girl whispered.

'Can you walk?' the conductor said, then looked at her feet and gave a little yelp of sympathy. He put an arm around her and took some of her weight. They tottered together towards the nearest door. Another conductor leaned out and lifted her up. He said to the first, 'The only house here is up beyond that border.'

'Yes,' the girl whispered. 'I couldn't look for help there.'

There was a clatter of stones behind them as someone came running along the track beside the train. It was a passenger, who had jumped from one of the second-class carriages. He was wearing a dreamhunter's long duster coat. The young man said, 'I'll take her.' He sprang onto the steps behind the girl and scooped her up.

The second conductor retreated into the carriage ahead of him. The first followed, only leaning out to wave all-clear to the driver.

The train exhaled and began to move.

'We have an empty compartment in first class,' the first conductor said to the young man. 'She'll be more comfortable there.'

The girl had her eyes closed and her head on the young man's shoulder. Perhaps she had fainted.

'I can't pay.' The dreamhunter looked stricken and stiffly angry at the same time.

'Was anyone asking you to pay?' The first conductor was irritated. 'If you'll please just carry your friend this way.' He set off up the carriage. The young man followed.

The other man went to find towels and soap, bandages and ointment, food and drink.

Laura woke up to find a man in a brass-buttoned uniform bandaging her blistered feet. Her head was in someone's lap. She looked up, and said, 'Sandy.'

'Laura,' said Sandy. Then, 'Love.' Then, 'What have you been doing?'

'I got lost,' Laura said, and closed her eyes again.

Seven

Laura didn't really come back to herself till she and Sandy were in a taxi taking them from Sisters Beach Station up to Summerfort. The driver was sitting out in the open air. They were in the back and she was leaning heavily on Sandy. He thought she was still faint and feverish, then she started to speak.

As she talked he realised she'd postponed answering his question, 'What have you been doing?', and that what he was now hearing was her answer.

'The Regulatory Body has built a railway line beyond the Pinnacles at Z minus 16.' The map reference made her sound lucid, despite her ravaged little voice. She said, 'They run handcars on it. They move supplies. There's a kind of camp far Inland along the line. A camp they call the Depot. It's full of dreamhunters, missing dreamhunters and, I guess, a few no one misses — like little Gavin Pinkney. Rose told me she saw Gavin on St Lazarus's Eve after the riot. And Aunt Grace saw him before she went into quarantine in the forest near Doorhandle. I bet if you asked Plasir where his apprentice was, he'd say Gavin had suffered a breakdown and was under treatment.'

Sandy saw Laura's eyes glimmering at him in the gloom of the cab. He saw her tears spill and how her skin grew instantly red where the tears were running. She wasn't sunburned — no one ever got sunburned in the Place — but her skin was so parched and damaged that it flared wherever salt touched it. Sandy drew his cuff up over his hand and dabbed gently at her cheeks.

Laura went on. 'The camp is on the site of a dream, a master dream called Contentment, which makes people perfectly happy. Perfectly, slavishly happy.' She shuddered.

Sandy put his arms around her.

'I didn't sleep,' Laura said. 'I got away.'

'Good girl.'

They had arrived at their destination. Sandy opened the door, dropped his pack onto the shell driveway. He pulled money out of his pocket and paid the driver. He said, 'Keep the change,' which felt as strange as anything else that was happening, since it was something he'd never said, or been moved to say, before. He eased out and lifted her up — she was so light, so small.

Sandy watched the taxi backing around the corner of the drive, its tyres kicking up clanking scallop shells. He asked Laura, 'Is anyone here?' Then turned to the house in time to see someone appear — a small man with greying black hair and a badly scarred face.

The man looked alarmed and hurried down off the veranda.

Laura croaked, urgently, 'It's all right. *I'm* all right!' She sounded even more worried than the man looked.

The man reached Sandy and for a moment, despite his slightness and fragility, looked set to snatch Laura out of Sandy's arms.

'I can walk,' Laura said. 'Don't try lifting me, Da. It's only my feet that hurt.'

Sandy finally recognised the man. He was Laura's father, Tziga Hame — reported missing a year ago, declared dead shortly after that.

'Take her inside,' said Tziga.

'I'm all right, Da,' said Laura.

'Shhhh,' said Sandy and Tziga together.

Sandy carried Laura indoors. Tziga Hame went ahead. He led Sandy up to Laura's room and pulled back the covers on her bed. Sandy put her down and Tziga shook out an eiderdown and draped it over her, leaving her bandaged feet uncovered.

Laura lay looking at Sandy then her father. Her gaze went back and forth between their faces and her eyes began to close. For a moment longer her eyes went on moving behind their shut, smooth lids. Then she was asleep.

Tziga Hame said, 'It's probably best just to let her rest. I'll sit with her. I have a nurse, who is out at the market. When she returns, could you please send her up to me? Laura's Aunt Grace went In yesterday to catch something for the Beholder. Laura's cousin is in Founderston with her father for a dress fitting. I'll cable them tomorrow. You can help yourself to something to eat. The kitchen is on the right at the foot of the stairs. And Sandy, if you would be so good as not to go off anywhere before I've had a chance to talk to you.'

Sandy was puzzled that he was known to this man he'd never met, and by Tziga Hame's tone, which wasn't just gratitude, but a kind of warm eagerness that Sandy knew he didn't deserve. 'Um,' was all he managed to say.

'Good,' said Tziga, as though Sandy had said, 'Yes, Sir.'

Sandy retreated from Laura's room and went downstairs and wandered about examining everything. The house wasn't at all what he had imagined — what he had been imagining since the day the previous summer that the two beautiful, forward, tangle-haired girls had edged up to him when he was lying on a sun bed on Sisters Beach in order to read over his shoulder. They had talked about their libraries — two libraries in two houses. They had talked about their town house in Founderston and their beach house, Summerfort. Sandy had spent the following few days looking up at the big house on the headland. And, more recently, he'd looked to see it from the sea when he sailed into Tarry Cove on a coal barge. Sandy had thought Summerfort would be full of brocaded chairs and tasselled lamps and furniture darkened and gnarled with carving, with gilded mirrors and brass firescreens and Turkish rugs and crystal lamps. Sandy wandered about looking at the bare floorboards — oiled timber — the few rugs, the faded, comfortable sofas, everything showing the wear of sun and sand. Everything except the books in the library, whose windows were shaded by white

Roman blinds. The chairs in the library were studded leather, but so aged and scuffed by use that in some places the leather was pink not red.

Sandy sat down and gazed up at the spines of the books. After a moment he heard the front door open and went to relay Mr Hame's message to the nurse.

Later, the sun went down and Sandy followed the light out onto the veranda in order to keep reading a book he'd found, a book with a title irresistible to him. Laura's father found him frowning over *The Seven Principles of Self-Reliance*. Tziga Hame sat in a chair opposite him.

'How is she now?' Sandy said.

'She's sleeping. Her feet have been lathered with some smelly ointment and properly, professionally bandaged. When the nurse left us she told me about her ordeal.'

'She told me too.'

Tziga nodded. 'I hope you'll stay, Sandy. I mean — you must.'

Sandy bit his lip for a moment, then his irritation and the sense he had of himself as being salt of the earth got the better of him. 'I can't just hold my breath, even when someone I care about is convalescing,' he said. 'I have to earn a living.'

'I wanted to talk to you about that. And about Laura.'

Sandy was speechless. Was Laura's father trying to talk to him about his 'prospects' — whether he could support his daughter? Laura's father didn't sound stern, or prying — he didn't seem embarrassed either, and if he was joking he was being remarkably deadpan.

Tziga Hame went on, 'There's a dream I'd like to have again. I doubt I can catch it myself. I don't have the strength any more.'

Sandy realised that he wasn't being asked about his intentions towards Laura. He also understood that Tziga Hame's scars and stove-in cheekbone were signs of a more serious, invisible injury. 'I must be kind to him,' Sandy thought — though the notion of trying to be kind made Sandy feel he was trying to stuff his big feet into small shoes.

'Just listen.' Hame smiled a sweet, fey smile. 'Let me finish before I forget how I began,' he said. Then, 'Master dreams are all somehow brutal, even when they're beautiful. I couldn't manage The Gate now myself, but Laura certainly can. And Grace tells me you show great promise . . .'

Part XI
The Gate

One

When Laura was up and about again, and Chorley, Grace and Rose were back at Summerfort, there was a family conference.

Sandy Mason sat in on it, looking at once embarrassed and pleased with himself.

For a time they talked about the Regulatory Body's secret railway and the happy captives at the Depot. Laura hadn't told anyone but her father that she'd been caught, and held, and how she'd made her escape. She did tell them she'd been seen, and recognised, but didn't say that Cas Doran and his cronies might be surprised to see her alive after she'd vanished from the remote and isolated compound. Laura and her father hadn't discussed the possibility that she might be in danger. And it crossed Laura's mind that her father — still sometimes muddle-headed with fits — hadn't even considered it. She didn't raise the subject, because she didn't want to have to hide again.

Laura's father was himself tired of hiding. At the meeting, Tziga said, 'If I reappear in Founderston the Regulatory Body will, no doubt, feel uncomfortable. But since I only want to visit medical specialists, and not darken the Body's doorways, it'll soon get over it.'

'We should all return to Founderston,' Chorley said. 'You'll get better care. And Laura must talk to the Grand Patriarch about this Depot. We should put the problem in his hands — for now.'

Grace pulled a face. She said, 'I agree that Laura should go back. Late summer is a very good time for her to return to work. All the regular healing dreamers supplying the hospitals and nursing homes are out of the city enjoying their holidays. It makes sense for Laura to go back when there's less competition, and when she can do so in a kind of disguise.' Grace looked at Sandy. 'And this is where you can help. The best thing you can do for Laura is form a temporary partnership with her. You can catch the same dreams and sell yourselves together — two dreamers for the price of one. You can say you're boosting one another and then maybe — with smaller houses, and less supervision — your performance won't strike anyone as *too* remarkable. Laura's Buried Alive pushed her penumbra out to about five hundred yards. I think it must have blown her wide open.'

Tziga said, 'At some point Laura's figures must become official.'

'Yes,' said Grace. 'And just because we have to deal with Cas Doran and his bloody Depot and whatever the hell his plan is, that doesn't mean that Laura's future is finished. Or mine, or Sandy's. When the Regulatory Body is sorted, there will still be — well — a Regulatory Body. We'll all still be dreamhunters. Laura will have to work according to the advantages and constraints of her power. What we need for now, so that nobody will suspect she acquired her big penumbra by catching Buried Alive, is a way for Laura to ease into work until she's recovered enough to catch The Gate — which, when I shared it twelve years ago, gave me another twenty-five yards.'

'When you catch The Gate, you can offer it to the sanatoria at Fallow Hill,' Tziga said. 'I can make the arrangements for you.'

Grace and Tziga had, it seemed, taken their cue from Laura. Young Mason was now completely in their confidence. Chorley trusted Mason — up to a point — but resented the fact that his own fatherly authority had been usurped by Laura's actual father. Tziga seemed to think he was up to making decisions for his daughter, despite the fact that he'd always been impractical, and was now confused and forgetful.

Chorley watched Grace and Tziga handling Sandy Mason and

thought: 'Grace is ambitious for Laura. She's so focused on Laura's future that she's overlooking present problems.'

'So,' said Grace, to Sandy. 'Will you work with Laura for a time? Does that suit you?'

Sandy blushed and nodded.

Laura looked at the floor and smiled. Then she got up. 'If that's settled, may Sandy, Rose and I go to Farry's? There's only *invalid* food here.'

'Fine, fine,' said Grace, and waved them off.

When the young people had gone, Grace said, 'I'm so pleased Sandy's got over the business of the letter. Now that he's seen Tziga, he thinks he got it all wrong and she was writing to her father.'

'Why do you say "he thinks she was" instead of "he knows she was"?' asked Chorley.

Grace looked irritated. 'Fine — *knows* she was, if you like.'

Tziga said, 'The point is that Sandy isn't angry with Laura any more, and can be called on to help her.'

Chorley did agree that Laura's well-being was important, and that the young man seemed to be important to her well-being. He dropped the subject of the letter Laura had asked Sandy to deliver. Though, no matter which way he looked at it, some things refused to become clear. Sandy supposed now that Laura's letter must have been to Tziga. But the letter had come from the lighthouse where Laura was staying *with* her father, so she would hardly have been writing to him.

Chorley had always supposed that Sandy Mason was the one who had helped Laura carry his movie camera from Y-17 in the Place back to Summerfort the previous winter. But, if so, why wasn't the boy *with* her when he and Rose arrived? Sandy Mason didn't strike Chorley as particularly well bred or bashful. Laura had been in the bath when Chorley and Rose arrived and Chorley was convinced that if he arrived at Summerfort *now* to find Laura bathing he might well find Sandy Mason in the damned tub with her!

So, the question remained, who was Laura's letter to? And who had carried the camera? Apparently there was some shadowy agent whose existence no one but Chorley seemed ever to notice, as someone sensitive to draughts notices the least touch of cold, moving air.

Grace got up and stretched. 'I'm so glad that's all settled. It's time Laura got on with actually being a dreamhunter — instead of a spy for the Church.' She gave her husband an indulgent smile. 'And how *is* your investigation going?'

'Slow, puzzling and possibly pointless,' Chorley said. 'I have one more person I want to talk to. Then — like the Commission of Inquiry — I'll ponder my findings. Such as they are.'

Two

On a warm day in early February, Chorley sat in a café in University Square. The establishment was surprisingly busy, even though commencement was still over a month away. Chorley had an appointment with Dr Michael King. He'd reached the stage in his investigations where what he wanted was to chew the fat with any intelligent person prepared to really *think* about the Place. He'd decided that the historian Dr King was his man.

King arrived at the café half an hour late. He bustled in, scanning the tables, spotted Chorley and gave him a wave, his raised hand making a little upward wriggle as if to mime smoke going up a flue. Then he swerved and pounced on a table near the door, and one student at that table. 'Mr Jones! Where is that thesis you're supposed to have finished and turned in?' he said, in a loud, friendly tone.

The young man got up. 'I came to see you about it —' he began.

'Yes — and a colleague of mine caught you putting curses on my closed door!'

'I wasn't cursing you, sir. I was just vexed not to find you there, because I wanted to personally put my paper into your hands.'

'Mr Jones, did you, or did you not, wish a pox upon me?'

'No, sir. I only wished a pox upon your closed door.'

King laughed. It was a silent, wheezy laugh, but his shoulders bobbed up and down. He put a hand on the young man's shoulder. 'If you don't have your paper with you, why don't you run off and get it? I'll be here for the next hour talking to this gentleman.' He pointed at Chorley.

The student hurried out. King came over to Chorley, beamed at him and offered his hand. They shook hands. King called for more coffee. 'That lad,' he said, 'wants to see his paper safely in my hands. He must think that he's done something astounding.' He chuckled some more. 'Now, before you tell me why you wanted to meet me, I must pass on a hello from Judge Seresin. He said that you were one of his cleverest students. And the laziest.'

Chorley remembered his old professor, Seresin, who was now a judge at the Supreme Court and, incidentally, the head of the Commission of Inquiry into the Rainbow Opera riot. Chorley had disappointed Professor Seresin. 'I didn't complete my degree,' he said. 'I fell out of a third-floor window while drinking with some friends. I don't remember it at all. I wasn't hurt. Apparently I landed in a freshly turned flower bed and got up and wandered away. There were dozens of witnesses, and a fuss, and my father put me on a boat to Europe. And that was the end of my studies. I had a full year in parts foreign, then my father died and it turned out we didn't have any money.'

The coffee came, a double order, since Chorley had ordered for himself shortly before King arrived. Chorley had also ordered a large oat biscuit. King eyed it. 'Please help yourself,' said Chorley, pressing the plate forward.

'No, no,' said King, and slid the plate back beside Chorley's elbow. 'And so, when you discovered that your father hadn't left you anything, were you ever tempted to Try?'

'I arrived back during the first of the rush. It was rather like a gold rush, wasn't it?'

'Yes and no. So many people were stopped right away. It was as if they discovered that despite there being gold in the ground, they weren't physically able to *dig*.' King's fingers fluttered then made a little foray towards Chorley's biscuit. They broke a piece off. The fingers conveyed the fragment to his mouth; he glanced down at it, apparently surprised, then opened his mouth to accept it.

Chorley said, 'I thought then that the whole dreamhunting thing was a little vulgar. I mean — citizens were carrying blankets and pillows into the People's Park on summer nights. Founderston was my town, and it changed almost overnight. I felt somewhat resentful.' He shrugged. 'So I didn't go near the border till I went with my wife, shortly after we were married.'

'And you found that you couldn't go In.'

'That's right, I couldn't.' Chorley piled three sugar lumps into his coffee. 'I read your chapter on the Place in your *History of Southland*. It struck me as one of the most lucid things written about it.'

'You flatter me. And surely there are dozens of even more lucid paragraphs buried among official twaddle and statistical stuff in the Dream Regulatory Body's records?'

'I'm not going to bother the Body.'

'Why not?' King was giving Chorley a shrewd appraisal.

'The Grand Patriarch has set me this task. I'm supposed to think about the Place.'

'That's fine. That's not a novelty,' said King, and his hands pounced again on Chorley's biscuit. He broke off a big piece and continued to talk, gesturing with the fragment and scattering crumbs around the table like a priest scattering drops of holy water in blessing. 'Plenty of people have *thought* about the Place. But really intelligent debate hasn't been possible because feelings run so high. The Church preaches against dreamhunting. Dreamhunters feel defensive. And the Regulatory Body tries to smooth things over by behaving like a strict parent towards dreamhunters — in public, at least. All the discussions are about whether the Place is good or bad, and how it should be used.'

'Yes,' said Chorley, eager.

Dr King seemed startled at the interruption. He slapped the table top. 'Exactly! We know how the Place can be used, but not why it's there. Do you realise that that is opposite to our views on human life? For instance, as a man who believes in the material rather than the spiritual, I know that my fundamental *purpose* in life is to father children and teach them the skills for survival. To, in short, do what a mother cat will for her kittens. A human version of that. So, you and I must continue the species —'

'Oh dear,' said Chorley, 'you and I?'

Dr King patted Chorley's hand. 'No, my dear man, you with your charming wife, and I with mine. But that description of why we are here doesn't give any clues as to how we should actually live our lives — the *uses* of our lives. How many times are we confronted with a thing for which we have a use, but no knowledge of its nature? Its purpose? That's what the Place is to us.'

Again King made a raid on Chorley's biscuit. Chorley didn't dare take a bite of it himself. He was momentarily distracted by this, and when his attention returned to what King was saying, he found that the man was talking about Aristotle.

Chorley was bemused. Hadn't they agreed that there had been enough theological and philosophical thinking about the Place — and now King was bringing up a philosopher?

'You are familiar with Aristotle?'

Chorley, in his impatience, quoted part of a song he'd learned at university — or rather in the bars and cafés around the university. 'Said Aristotle unto Plato, have another sweet potato.'

Dr King gave him a wry look. 'Was that the version you learned?'

'No, it was "you're my little sweet potato". Of course I know Aristotle. Greek philosopher. Taught Alexander the Great. Disapproved of plays, because he thought that if people enjoyed the villains in plays, that would encourage them to behave badly. The Grand Patriarch would like him.'

King laughed his vigorous, shoulder-shaking laugh and reached for some more biscuit. 'Would you like your own?' Chorley said, and turned to seek a waiter.

'Oh no! No!' King desisted. 'Now — why I mention Aristotle is that with the Place, investigators are reduced to the same state of knowledge as the ancients. We really haven't any scientific methods we can apply. There are so few fruitful experiments. Yes, we have brought out bottled air and burned it. Yes, we've collected soil samples and performed chemical tests. But what of it? Chemistry won't do it.

'Aristotle invented an early system of classification, with a place for everything: animal, vegetable and mineral. For instance, in

Aristotle's system, put simply, man is a two-legged animal without wings. A chicken, on the other hand, is a two-legged animal *with* wings —'

Chorley, annoyed by this detour, said flippantly, 'And Long John Silver, having only one leg, wouldn't be a man?'

'Well, yes — but do we count his parrot? Its legs *and* wings?' Dr King chortled and took some more biscuit.

Chorley wondered whether he dared to call a waiter over and order *himself* another biscuit. He didn't want to embarrass King, whose trespasses were rather charming. In most situations Chorley was the one licensed to be less formal. But King was making him feel a little starchy. That was why he'd made his silly remark about Long John Silver — only to get a witty comeback.

King said, 'Aristotle is useful in the case of the Place because we can use him to ask very simple questions about it. Shall we try?' He began, 'What is the Place made of?'

'Land,' said Chorley. 'Plains, hills, riverbeds — land.'

'Good! What does it contain?'

'Vegetation. Dead pasture, brush and trees. There are no animal remains, which is very strange.'

'No, no!' Dr King waved his remnant biscuit back and forth as if by sowing the table top with crumbs he might encourage a crop of little biscuits. 'Let us ignore what the Place lacks. Aristotle would have you start with what a thing *has*, not what it lacks.'

'So the missing leg doesn't count, but the parrot does?'

'Quite so! And therefore Long John Silver was a three-legged creature with wings. Now — let us say that the grass and trees in the Place are land too, shall we? We don't normally exclude grass and trees from any purchase of a property, do we?'

'All right. Then what the Place contains is dreams.'

'And what are dreams?'

'They are like thoughts. An activity of our sleeping brains.'

'Dreams are thoughts,' Dr King said, and made a coaxing motion at Chorley. 'Thoughts suggest consciousness. So what do we have, so far, as a classification for the Place?'

'Land — with consciousness,' said Chorley.

'Yes,' said Dr King, then, 'Do you mind?' as he took the very last piece. It was the first time he'd asked. 'The mediaeval scholars who were Aristotle's heirs had the whole of creation in ranks, with ideal examples at the top of each rank. So in the category of animals there were noble animals, like lions, "the king of the beasts", man above that, and above man, angels. Even gems were ranked, not according to rarity, but all sorts of other ideas, mostly religious.' King paused and then glanced guiltily at Chorley's empty plate.

Chorley had to struggle not to laugh.

King brightened again, and said, 'So, in those old categories, the animal world rises into the spiritual through man. But the mineral world does not rise into the spiritual. So what is the Place? It's invisible to most people, like a spirit. It's land — so mineral. And it has dreams — so it's conscious.'

'Conscious, and mineral,' Chorley said. 'Which leaves us none the wiser.' Then, because he felt he owed it to Dr King, Chorley told him what he knew so far. About the telegrams, and how some of the dreams seemed set in a time further on than now. He talked about the convicts in Laura's first dream, and the ones Tziga would edit from the end of Convalescent One. The newspapers hadn't printed Lazarus's letters — but Chorley knew what at least one had said, the one Cas Doran showed Grace when he questioned her. The newspapers only claimed that a dreamhunter 'assailant' calling himself Lazarus had sunk the audience at the Rainbow Opera into a nightmare as a protest against the use of convict labour. This claim had started all sorts of public discussions about, for instance, how miners' wages were low because some mines were worked by convicts. But no one was talking about the Department of Corrections' use of nightmares in prisons. Chorley told King about the letter Grace had seen, in the hope of getting him talking to others. The man was a talker, and a lecture theatre in the university might not be as good as a newspaper at getting word out, but it was as least as good as the pulpits of Southland's churches.

When Chorley had finished, Dr King shook his hand, and said, 'You will let me know how you get on with your investigation, won't you?'

'I will.'

King signalled the waiter, paid the bill, then rearranged himself — his scarf, handkerchief, crumpled papers, wallet and spectacle case — in the distorted pockets of his white linen summer suit. He shook Chorley's hand again, started away from the table, swerved, came back, asked Chorley if he was intending 'to write it all up in a book', insisted that Chorley *must*, patted his pockets again, shook Chorley's hand once more and wandered out of the café — disappearing only a few minutes before his student returned, panting, with the essay he was so proud of.

Chorley left University Square and turned onto the riverbank, heading towards home. It was a sunny day and the cafés on the embankment were full. Chorley found himself enchanted by these sultry, under-populated squares. It was years since he'd spent any time in Founderston in summer. When he was young his parents and sister Verity would go to a hotel at Sisters Beach, and he and his friends would have the townhouse to themselves. They'd stay up all night and sleep all day and roam about looking for adventure.

Chorley was ambling along in a mild fever of nostalgia when he spotted his niece and Sandy Mason at a table outside a café. They had pulled their chairs together. Laura was leaning on Sandy.

Chorley veered off his path and stood over them.

Sandy straightened up and said, 'Good afternoon, Mr Tiebold. Please join us.' He jumped up to get a chair from an adjacent table, and placed it for Chorley. 'Will you have something?' He reached for his wallet.

Chorley placed his palm on Sandy's breast pocket and patted him firmly and discouragingly. He wasn't about to let this boy buy him anything.

'We're flush, Uncle Chorley,' Laura said.

'It's going well, then?' Chorley caught the eye of the waiter. He said to his niece and her friend, 'What will you have?'

Sandy went red.

Laura, oblivious, asked for a scone and another pot of tea, then excused herself and dashed off to the bathroom.

The young man waited for the waiter to go away and said, 'Mr Tiebold, please don't act as if you're paying for me to take care of Laura.'

Chorley gave Sandy a look of wounded innocence. 'I don't mean to make you feel that,' he said.

'My money is as good as yours,' Sandy said. 'You can enjoy my hospitality, can't you?'

Chorley raised an eyebrow.

'Laura's *father* approves of me. Who are you to disapprove?' Sandy seemed furious.

'Laura's father is brain-damaged,' Chorley said.

When Laura returned to the table she couldn't fail to notice that Sandy and her uncle were glaring at each other. 'What's the matter?'

'Apparently my money isn't good enough for your uncle,' Sandy said.

'Uncle Chorley always pays for everything,' Laura said. She sat down and nestled up to her friend again. 'You'll just have to get used to it.'

'I think it's very good for old dogs to learn new tricks,' Sandy said.

Laura chuckled. 'He's calling you an old dog,' she said to her uncle.

'Woof,' said Chorley.

The waiter brought tea and Laura's scone. 'I'm still so hungry,' she said. 'My dressmaker keeps having to let out the seams of my ball gown — which is good, because it's quite fitting in places, and before I started filling out again there wasn't much to tell between me and the cloth still on its bolt.'

'We're going In again in three days to get The Gate,' Sandy said. 'Laura's ready.' He put his arm around her waist.

'We have to go,' Laura said. 'It's not working out — performing together. We're just too big. I've been doing midnight at Pike Street and Sandy's doing midday at St Thomas's. We're booked at both places together and go along together, then I stay awake in my room next to his. They always supply separate rooms, did you know that?'

'No. And good,' Chorley said.

'Sandy has to stay awake all night, which is hard on him. The only problem I have is making sure I hang on to consciousness when Sandy goes down. He's a bit of a Soporif now.'

Sandy said, 'Buried Alive did that to me. Once I'd got over the patch where I couldn't catch dreams at all.'

'That was emotional,' Laura said, and swayed against him — bump, bump, bump — till she got a faint, conceding smile. Then she looked back at her uncle. 'Anyway, the doctors at Pike Street, where I sleep, think they have two real talents, and a great bargain. St Thomas's is happy enough to have two for the price of one, but one of the doctors said to Sandy, sadly, that while our Convalescent One is Hame quality — soothing and significant — even with Sandy helping me I seem to be only getting the sort of range that can be expected from any reasonably talented young dreamhunter.'

Sandy said, 'We can't go on with our ruse. Sooner or later the different hospitals will compare notes.'

Laura said, 'Sandy's very pleased that we've been able to work these day and night bookings because we're earning twice what we would otherwise.'

Chorley smirked at Sandy. 'That must have been very gratifying for you,' he said, and watched the young man suppressing objections.

'So, it's time for us to go and get The Gate,' Laura said.

Chorley looked across the Sva at the dome of the Temple, perfect in actuality, wrinkled in its reflection on the river. He thought about The Gate, a dream Tziga had had twelve years before, and had claimed not to be able to find again; a dream other dreamhunters had looked for in vain.

Tziga had caught The Gate when his wife, Chorley's sister Verity, was dying. Tziga had carried the dream back for her, only to find she had died while he was away and without his, or *its*, help. Tziga fought sleep for two days after the funeral. He'd gone down fighting, as though he'd meant to die with the dream and take it to Verity. Tziga was a religious man and may well have been able to imagine meeting his wife in the afterlife. But he'd succumbed to exhaustion — and to his brother-in-law's tender determination to comfort him. He'd slept and dreamed and a good proportion of his neighbours had shared his dream.

Chorley remembered the dream as one of the most wonderful experiences of his life. He understood why Tziga had kept it hidden all these years. No matter how anyone else who shared it experienced The Gate, to the bereaved Tziga the dream might have seemed only an unbearably beautiful lie, not an answered prayer.

The Gate was different from every other dream. All the Place's other dreams were based on natural laws, and possible facts. No one flew in a dream, breathed underwater or met a minotaur. The Gate was, however, mystical, transcendent and unreal. It promised an afterlife.

'But it isn't either true or false,' Chorley thought. 'Because what it *is* is a wish. And wishes aren't either true or false.'

'I'm looking forward to this dream,' Laura said. 'I remember the feelings it gave me when I had it when I was little. It'll help Da.' She rested her head on Sandy Mason's broad shoulder. 'Besides, I want to fall asleep with Sandy. It's perverse to keep resisting it.'

Chorley knew she meant that it was hard to keep herself awake and reading a book while Sandy dreamed Convalescent One, but, when he glanced at Sandy, Chorley could see the young man feeling the effects of her unintended double meaning. Sandy flushed, clenched his jaw and crossed his legs. Laura had picked up his hand and was playing with the soft flesh between his thumb and finger — childish and intimate. Sandy was having trouble with this, and Chorley saw, at last, that the young man was in love with Laura, not just drawn and possessive. Sandy was trying to control his desire, and having trouble with it. Chorley could see that the young man too thought that Laura wasn't ready for things to go any further between them. She was in danger of getting in too deep too young, not because Sandy was older and infatuated with her, but because of her own behaviour. Something — Chorley could not imagine what — seemed to have stripped away all the normal caution she should have about just touching another person, any other person. The attention she was lavishing on Sandy's hand was playful but intense. She stroked and pressed his hand as if in search of a secret mechanism that would make it open up, or turn into something other than a hand.

Chorley said, 'If you don't mind, Sandy, I'd like a word in private with my niece.'

Sandy retrieved his hand, nodded curtly and got up. 'I'll be in that bookshop on the corner,' he said, and took himself off.

Laura dropped her hands into her lap and assumed a blank, wooden look.

Chorley cleared his throat. 'Judging by your expression I think perhaps you know what I'm about to say. You must be careful with that boy.'

'I'll try not to *lose* him, Uncle Chorley, if that's what you mean.'

'You know that isn't what I mean. He must be several years your senior.'

'Three years. Which is nothing,' Laura said. She sounded dry — not exactly impatient.

'At your age that's a big difference.'

Laura laughed.

'What?'

'I see difference differently,' she said. Then she sighed, a sigh like a yawn, as if she was sleepy. 'Sandy suits me.'

It seemed a strange, cold thing for a girl to say, and Chorley shivered to hear it.

'I like to be with him,' she added. 'I'm safe with him.'

'Yes, I think you probably are. And he does seem to sincerely care for you. But even if no one is mistaken in their feelings, feelings get hurt. And there are physical dangers of intimacy.'

'Uncle Chorley, you're talking to someone who nearly died trying to see what was at the end of a railway line. Intimacy — as you put it — is safer than half of the things I've had to do.'

'*Did* you nearly die?' Chorley knew she'd been sick — 'knocked back' Tziga had said — but Tziga understated his own injuries too.

'We'll have some film soon of the Depot,' Laura said.

'What?'

'Da and I arranged for someone to go In at the Pinnacles with one of your movie cameras, to film those buildings and people. We need documentary evidence.'

Chorley supposed he shouldn't be surprised that Laura and Tziga were communicating independently with the Grand Patriarch, and calling on his help. Of course the Grand Patriarch must have dreamhunters who would act as his agents.

'We'll show the film to the Commission of Inquiry,' Laura said. 'That's probably the quickest, simplest way to get questions asked, and to cut Cas Doran off at the knees.'

Chorley reached across the table and waited for her to take his hand. She did — hers dry and calloused, a smaller version of his wife's and Tziga's. 'Dreamhunter,' Chorley said, wonderingly, and squeezed her hand. 'You changed the subject,' he said. 'Don't think I didn't notice.'

'Yes, I did. But, back on that subject, Aunt Grace was only Sandy's age when you met her.'

'Your Aunt Grace was a powerful woman.'

'Uncle Chorley, *I'm* a powerful woman,' Laura said.

'Or girl,' Chorley said.

'Don't worry. Sandy is loyal and kind, and I think maybe I do love him.'

Chorley sighed, then got up and helped her up too. He opened his wallet and dropped notes onto the table. 'All right then, honey.' He took her arm, 'I'll deliver you to your destiny.' They set off towards the bookshop on the corner. As they went along, Laura said quietly and fervently, 'Oh — I wish he were.'

Three

Laura was late for her final ballgown fitting. Grace and Rose had been there for half an hour. Rose had her dress on and was standing between two canted mirrors. Sunlight came in through the high fitting-room windows, and there were electric lights on the walls, but Rose managed to look like candlelight and moonlight combined, like the central panel of some devotional altarpiece, haloed with radiance.

She had wanted a high-necked dress, and the design she'd chosen had a Chinese-style collar that circled her strong throat. The bodice was fitting, boned and tapered in at the waist — then followed the swelling curves of her hips. The fabric was heavy bone-white silk. The sleeves and bodice were sewn with a filigree of seed pearls. The skirt of the dress had a train that Rose would have to fasten to one arm in order to dance. Rose was practising this when her cousin came in.

'You'll do very nicely,' Grace was saying. 'And we must put your hair up.'

Rose arched her back and neck and threw off light.

Grace grinned at Laura. 'I think there will be displays of dumb admiration and the falling over of feet.'

'It's not too tight?' Rose said.

'No,' said everyone.

The dressmaker nodded to one of the seamstresses. 'Please go and get Miss Hame's dress.'

Laura had toyed with pale blues and greens, and Rose had nearly persuaded her to wear pink. But her aunt had insisted that since she wasn't a debutante, and didn't have to wear white, she should decide that for the purposes of fashion she wasn't a young girl and could choose a strong colour, one that would set off her tan and dark hair. Laura's dress was also silk, of a vibrant coral red. It was sleeveless, with a low square neck, fitted at the bust and flaring under it. It was a simple dress of a rich fabric, and Laura was going to wear it with long black gloves and her mother's jet choker.

Laura put her dress on and shared the mirror with Rose while her hem was pinned. They stood looking solemnly at one another.

'Do debutantes wear white so that men can imagine the brides they'll be?' Rose asked her mother.

'I'm not sure,' Grace said. 'I didn't have a coming out.'

'It's for *you* to imagine the bride you'll be,' said the dressmaker.

'I don't look like a dreamhunter,' Laura said. She wished that Nown could see her in her ball gown — which was silly, since he couldn't see colour anyway.

Her tall cousin walked out of the mirror's frame. 'Can I get out of this now?'

'Certainly. And we should look at your friend's dress. She's due in for a fitting tomorrow at three. Her mother has already given the dress her provisional approval.' The dressmaker looked worried.

Rose had finally taken it on herself to design Mamie's gown, after they had held every variation on white — icy, bone, cream, pearly peach, salmon, beige, fawn — up to Mamie's face, and every shade, without fail, had made Mamie's mauve, mottled skin look corpse-like. Grace and Rose had found a pattern Mamie liked, a dress that would let her bare shoulders and the tops of her breasts rise up out of it. A dress with belted waist and a skirt with two generous pleats at the back and two at the front. Rose's innovation was to make the shawl-neck and sleeves of black silk — to add a black belt, and to make the recessed pleats black also. The silks were the same weight, the white brocaded, the black with a sheen rather than a gloss. The black made Mamie's skin look better — a lilac-tinted pallor, rather than fishy.

When the dress was produced, Rose, Laura, Grace and all the seamstresses gave it their full attention.

'Mamie's mother can't mind if we come to her next fitting,' Rose said.

'I'm sure she won't,' said the dressmaker.

'It's a big responsibility — making this ball less of an ordeal for Mamie,' Laura said.

'She'll enjoy it,' Rose said. 'You wait and see. As for me, *I'm going to have* — a ball!'

Four

Sandy only stopped in at Mrs Lilley's to smuggle some blankets off his bed and stuff them into his pack. He hid the pack outside, then went back into the kitchen to fetch Laura, whom he'd told to keep Mrs Lilley and her girls chatting.

The Lilley girls were scarcely responding to Laura's polite patter. They were cool and monosyllabic. The eldest shot Sandy a wounded looked and spun back to scrubbing the stove top.

'Well, ladies — good day,' Sandy said. Then, 'Come on, Laura.' He put an arm around her shoulders and ushered her out of the door. He picked up his pack.

'We're only going In for one night, so what's all that?' Laura said, then, 'Do those girls hate me just because they had to keep airing my room?'

Sandy grunted. He listened to Laura's patient silence. He felt that she was waiting for a confession. He said, 'I took one of them to a dance held by the Wry Valley Young Farmers. The girls sat one side of the room and the men the other, like a school dance. And a good part of the men were out among the cars and carriages drinking whisky.'

'Which one did you take?'

'Patricia,' he said. 'The eldest.'

'I knew they liked you,' Laura said.

On the way back from the dance Pat had pushed Sandy against a tree trunk and put her hand down his trousers. He liked that too, rather helplessly, but the very next day he'd set out walking the border — the walk that finally took him to Debt River and the site of the dream Quake.

'One of them even said to me that you weren't really my sort,' Laura said.

'I'm not,' Sandy said, sulkily.

'I don't have a sort. Do you think you do?' She sounded breezy. 'What's she like then, your sort of girl?'

Sandy thought it was best to be quiet.

'Taller, I suppose,' Laura said, musing.

They walked hand in hand into the rangers' station and made straight for the line before the big ledger of the Intentions Book. Several older dreamhunters smiled at them in an indulgent way.

'What are we going to write?' Laura whispered as they shuffled forward.

'That we're walking a short way east along the border.'

'Is that what Da said?'

Tziga Hame had given Sandy directions on the day he delivered Laura to Summerfort. He told Sandy that The Gate was just inside the border, about two hours east of Doorhandle. 'It's easy to find because it is right on a landmark rangers refer to as Foreigner's West — for some reason.'

'I've been to Foreigner's North,' Sandy said. He wanted to impress Laura's father with what he knew, to tell him all about the supposed French explorer and his crazy attempt to map the Place, and his odd compass bearings, *Nord* and *Ouest* — 'north' and 'west' in French. It was interesting, Sandy thought, the whole question of who the man had been and how the hell he'd got himself so turned around, since *Nord* may have been in the north, but *Ouest* was more south and east — east of Doorhandle anyway. But Sandy hadn't launched into a dissertation on what he knew, because he'd worked out that it wasn't a good idea to interrupt Tziga Hame, whose concentration was ragged, and who got upset when he lost the thread of his thoughts.

'The Gate is in plain sight,' Laura's father had said to Sandy. 'But scarcely anyone would think to bed down there, because the ground is hard and uneven and cut up. The dream is in a tightly confined spot, actually in the circle. You'll find a circle on the ground. I knew the dream was there when I first saw the site. I don't know how I knew, but my need was so great, I suppose, that some instinct led me to it. The confined site, the bad ground and the rarity of dreamhunters who can catch master dreams — all have guaranteed that The Gate has sat there untapped since I caught it.'

Nearly two hours after they went In, Sandy and Laura ran into a ranger with paint brushes in his pockets and carrying a pot of paint. He had been refreshing signage, he said.

'Are we anywhere near Foreigner's West?' Sandy asked.

The ranger laughed. 'You young dreamhunters are so funny, with your little alliances, and your sightseeing.' He raised one brawny arm to point with the hand holding the paint pot.

'Is there a latrine near here?' Laura said. She didn't like to squat behind bushes when she was with Sandy — and knew that dreamhunters and rangers disapproved of such behaviour in the Place's more populated areas. She asked her question peering out at the ranger from behind the shelter of Sandy's shoulder. The Body employed at least a thousand rangers so she knew she shouldn't expect that every one she met would know about the Depot, or that she'd escaped from it.

'The trail branches by those trees up there. The Inward branch leads to a latrine then back to the landmark. I've painted the latrine too, so be careful, it might still be wet.'

'Thank you,' Laura said.

'What are you planning to catch?'

'We're not dreamhunting. We're just sightseeing, as you guessed,' Sandy said.

'And spending time together.' The ranger winked at them, and went on his way.

They walked on till they reached the branch in the trail. Sandy let go of Laura. 'I've been watering the bushes along the way,' he said.

'Yes, you have,' Laura laughed. 'You're nearly as bad as a dog.'

'It's because we spend all our time in cafés, drinking tea,' Sandy said, resentfully. Then, apparently without any thought of the connection in ideas, he said, 'I'll make a bed for us with these blankets. Your father warned me that the ground was bad.'

Laura went on peering up into his face, waiting to see some sign of self-consciousness, for him to relent and acknowledge what everyone else could see, and was teasing them about. They *had* been spending all their time in cafés when they weren't shut up in separate rooms in hospitals. She never went home. He never used his key to his uncle's flat. They sat in cafés — together.

Sandy looked down at her. Laura noticed that his jaw was hastily shaven and scratchy in patches. She looked into his eyes, saw resentment and, behind that, baffled, patient misery.

A sharp shiver passed over him. And then he bent his head and kissed her.

They were kissing, wrapped together, upright, his hands on her face, her hands covering his. His lips were full and firm, his chin was rasping and rough.

Laura's bladder gave her a stab.

She broke away from him. 'I have to go,' she said, and waved her hand in the direction of the latrines, and sprinted off.

Laura's bladder was full, but shy. She was a long time in the box smelling of fresh paint before anything came. She kept giggling and shivering. The little byway was quiet — as deadly silent as anywhere else in the Place, but Laura had the impression the shelter she was standing in was in the middle of a stampede.

When she'd finished, she uncapped her water bottle and spilled water over her hands, patted her cheeks with her wet palms, then ran back along the path to find Sandy.

He'd made a bed of his purloined blankets, and emptied his pack of all the tins and hard-edged packages to make one pillow. He was sitting down, setting out a picnic, but he jumped up when she appeared. He grabbed her — or she collided with him — and they continued kissing, more involved with each passing second.

Laura thought: 'Do people do this?' She'd never seen anyone kissing like this. Books said things like 'He rained kisses on her face.' But suddenly they seemed tied together, mouth to mouth. She felt his skin, the wiry hair on his chest. Her hands had got into his shirt. They seemed to have minds of their own. No — she *agreed* with her hands. Sandy's skin was smooth, his muscles springy and supple. He was lovely to touch, warm and dewy.

He was saying her name, into her mouth.

'What should I do with your clothes?' Laura said. Her throat was so tight she wanted to cough.

Sandy caught her hands and held them away from him. 'Laura, we shouldn't. We have to be careful.'

'I don't care!' she said fiercely. 'I love you.' She began struggling with the buttons of her own shirt. She pulled its halves apart — sending one button spinning.

Sandy caught her hands again, then pulled her against him. Their bare skin came together and Laura sighed. Sandy was saying yes, all right. 'But go slower, Laura.' He began to help her with her clothes. She attacked his belt buckle, then responded to his 'slower' and let go, leaned into him, kissed his shoulders, as high as she could reach when his head was raised.

He took her face between his hands again. 'I love you, Laura. I mean it. I don't want to be without you, ever. Can you — would you — do you think we might get married? Please say you will.'

'Please, Sandy, let's lie down together.'

'I don't really know what I'm doing,' he said. 'Neither do you. That's why we have to go slow. And I wish you'd *promise*.' He sounded as though he might cry.

'Oh — look at you,' she said. She'd uncovered some more of him and thought he was beautiful, and that made her tearful too.

Sandy gave a gasp and grabbed her and they fell down together onto the ground, which was still impossibly lumpy even under all the blankets. They writhed around, trying to get comfortable, and to get at each other, clumsy and hasty. They slowed down and stared at one another, their eyes moving, and sometimes meeting, with bright, searching, softened looks.

Inside Laura's great excitement, there was a kind of peaceful expectation. She had felt big and powerful before, and she had felt small and lost. Being like this with Sandy seemed the best way to discover what size she *really* was, and where she belonged, both in her body, and in time and space.

He found himself in what he supposed was the garden of one of the farms in the valley. An ordinary garden, made glorious by his exhaustion and the glow of final things.

He had somehow lost his shoes and the grass was tender on the soles of his bare feet. It was twilight, some time in the half-hour after sunset when the sky still fumes with the sun's power, but the earth is drowsy. The garden was giving off vapour, scents, ghosts of dewfall in the soft air.

He wasn't dreaming. No one could fall asleep while in flight, stumbling and singing, every breath a phrase of the song. And why bother to fall asleep before a thing you might not survive?

Ahead of him a path wound through rhododendrons. The bushes were not in flower, because it was summer. Because it was summer there had been a bonfire on the beach — three days ago, was it? Three days ago, when he still had his strength, and shortly before he'd lost all hope.

He became aware that someone was ahead of him. A woman was winding her way through the rhododendrons. He could see the pale streak of her skirt disappearing around the curve in the path.

He followed her onto the clearing of a lawn. Around the lawn's dusky green arena were citrus trees: lemons and limes, mandarins and kumquats, glowing like lanterns among the glossy darkness of their leaves.

The woman glanced back, and lingered as though he were lagging behind and she must wait for him.

There was a gate before her. It had white-painted posts, and a peaked roof like the gate to a churchyard. Beyond the gate was another green room.

The woman waited, and he caught up with her, then she went ahead and he fixed his eyes on her hand, the hand held back to him. He would know it anywhere. It looked like his mother's.

She beckoned, trailed her arm like a rope he could catch. She walked on, caressing the petals of flowers, the quilted foliage of a humble hydrangea, and a tibouchina, its purple flowers haloed with cerise.

There was too much colour to take in. His prison-ruined eyes watered, and made after-images, a halo around every object. The woman's pale skirt reflected the colours, as though she stood in the light of a stained glass window.

She stopped at the gate and waited. He could see a little of the garden beyond her — its piled flower colours and flower lights.

It seemed to him that the fierce currents of heat had been only momentarily calmed. The sun had gone, but something had electrified the atmosphere. Something impossible was about to happen to the twilight.

The woman who might be his mother smiled at him, as if to say, 'Wait till you see this.'

The sun had gone, and the birds had soothed themselves down, settled and roosted, shadows nestled into shadows. But suddenly they began again to make expectant noises, like dawn birdcalls.

The sun was coming back.

Because the sun was coming back, the day would return and take him through it again. Not his real yesterday, but something better. Every hour would brighten back to noon, and then on towards morning. With every hour he would be cleaner and fresher and more full of the certainty that is health and youth. There was no hurry. It was the first time for everything. That was her promise, that was where she meant to take him — through the gate, into all that was sweet, and easeful, and good in the green fathoms of a garden.

Then the sun came back and covered them both, and carried them off to the first time for everything.

Five

Cas Doran was still in his office, his back to the oval window and its view of the Isle of the Temple and its three domes. Nearest was the green, copper-clad dome at the top of the offices of the Dream Regulatory Body. In the middle distance was the scintillating skin of the Rainbow Opera. Farthest off the Temple shone, so pale that the sky seemed to show through it, as the bruise of a slight tumble will show on a petal of fallen plum blossom.

Doran had for some minutes been peering out from under a steeple made of his hands at a cable on his otherwise clean and empty desktop. He looked as if he was developing a headache.

'Are you going to tell me what it says?' Maze Plasir was sitting across the desk from Doran and sipping wine.

'Laura Hame has finally signed in at Doorhandle in the Intentions Book. I've already had reports from St Thomas's and Pike Street. I knew she was back in Founderston, dreamhunting, peddling Convalescent One with her friend the Mason boy.'

'Why is her signing in worse than her continuing to hide?'

'She's mad,' Doran said. 'She escaped from the Depot — God knows how. She was threatened, deprived of liberty, and she simply comes back to Founderston and picks up where she left off late last winter. She's insane. Or she's very simple.'

'I'd love to talk to her,' said Plasir.

'Why?' Doran looked up, sharp.

'To sound her out. She's not simple, Cas, though she may be mad.'

'Is she trying to draw me out somehow? Is this the advice they've given her?'

'*They*, Cas?'

'Them — my opponents.'

'Do you mean "Lazarus"?'

'I mean the Grand Patriarch,' Doran said.

Plasir nodded. He twirled his glass, looked at the lozenge of light spinning in the wine. 'How did the Hame girl escape?'

'Incompetence,' Doran said. 'My allies are incompetent.'

'Not all,' Plasir said, mildly.

Doran scowled. He thought of Rose Tiebold in the library at his summer residence, tearful, but cool underneath. Rose asking him about the surplus rails in the Awa Inlet. Rose after the riot, saying, 'Laura didn't sleep, we were talking.'

'Courage isn't cleverness,' he said, thinking aloud. 'They can't outwit me.' He opened one of his desk drawers and produced the rolled scroll of his map of Founderston. He spread it open and peered at the circles that represented the penumbras of dreamhunters — dreamhunters loaded with Contentment. None of them were in place yet, but could soon be.

Plasir said, musing, 'I remember how I would sometimes see people stop Tziga Hame in the street, to kiss his hands. Do people like Hame need to resort to anything as vulgar as using their wits?'

Doran studied his map, and thought of the fortress that was the Temple — how he hadn't been able to buy, or rent, any property in its vicinity, so wasn't able to get one of his dosed dreamhunters near it. 'What I need is a Soporif,' he said.

'Then we must acquire one, by all means,' Plasir said, and sipped, then smacked his lips. 'Perhaps we should separate Miss Hame from her friend the Mason boy. The reports from Pike Street seem to suggest he is one, like his uncle. What do you say to that, eh, Cas?'

Six

After the dream Laura and Sandy were still in its deeps, waiting to sleep again. They talked, and kissed; they rested, and slept and went back to The Gate. After a time — hard to measure how long with no night and day — they exhausted their food supply and their ability to sleep. They got up, groggy, and began stuffing their rubbish of wrappers and empty jars into their packs. Laura stepped off the muddled blankets and Sandy began picking them up, one by one, to shake them. Together they folded each blanket. When the last one was lifted Laura looked down on the bared earth. At that moment it seemed to her that the most significant things that had ever happened to her — The Gate, and Sandy — had happened in this uncomfortable spot. She stood looking reverently at the ground, her face soft with serenity and bodily tiredness.

There was a circle carved in the dirt. Much of their discomfort had been due to this deeply scored mark. Laura frowned at it. 'What's this?'

'Foreigner's West,' Sandy said. He was busy fastening a belt around the bundle of blankets so they'd be easier to carry.

'Pardon?'

'You know how rangers have their own legends, like we dreamhunters do? Theirs are about exploration rather than dreams.' Sandy got up. His knees creaked. 'Rangers talk about "the Foreigner" more as though he's a good story rather than a historical fact — a pioneering ranger who didn't make maps but left compass marks.'

'I don't understand,' Laura said.

'Does it matter? All it means for us, Laura, is that no one tries sleeping here because it's too uncomfortable. And, since The Gate is only on this confined site no one has ever caught it. Your father said he only found it because he was always able to sense where healing dreams were. When he walked by Foreigner's West he knew the dream was here.'

Laura began to twist her hair. Her curls had felted at the back, she had been lying down for so long. 'But this isn't a compass mark,' she said. She spoke softly and Sandy leaned forwards to hear her. Finding himself near, he kissed her on her earlobe. He said, 'The idea that these are compass marks is the only reason rangers suppose the pioneer was a foreigner. *French*. They think the marks stand for north and west in French. The dream Quake is right on top of Foreigner's North. Foreigner's North is an N carved in the ground — *Nord*. This is an O, for *Ouest*.'

Sandy went on with what he was doing, lengthening one shoulder strap of Laura's pack so that he could carry it for her. It took him a moment to notice how still and silent she had become. He looked up at her.

'It's a Nown,' Laura said. 'The Place is a Nown.' Her voice was almost inaudible.

Sandy tried to figure out why she had chosen this moment to correct his grammar. He reviewed what he'd been telling her and couldn't recall having mentioned the Place at all.

Laura still stood as if entranced. The colour had drained out of her face.

Sandy put his hand under her elbow. He was afraid that she was about to faint. But she didn't sway or crumble, she simply stood frozen.

Nerves made Sandy giggle. He said, 'Love, you are looking like Lot's wife, white and fixed to the spot.'

Laura could hear Sandy only as a murmur through a wall, one of those sounds that wakes you — a late-night conversation, or muffled crying. She was lost in the past.

She remembered the day she had made Nown. He had stood up out of the dry stream bed and shown her his true face, a face she had longed to see. He had got onto his knees before her and had made his pledge and introduction: 'Laura Hame, I am your servant.' She was exhausted after making him, and had slept for a time. When she woke up she had lain admiring him. He'd stood, surveying the grasslands Inland, engrossed. When she'd asked him what he was doing, he had answered, 'Listening.' When she asked what he was listening to, he'd said, 'I can hear now.' And she had stupidly, wooden-headedly, imagined that just as she'd made a more handsome sandman, she had also managed to make one with better hearing. He had even repeated himself in an effort to explain what must have bewildered him. 'I can hear now,' he'd said. 'I am here with myself.'

I can hear Now. I am here with myself.

They were *all* his selves — the Nowns, and speechless Nows. He'd come alive again and discovered he was standing *inside* himself — another self — a Nown who hadn't had its final letter added, the letter that, in the spell, 'gives speech'. He'd tried to tell her, but she hadn't heard him. She hadn't heard his name when he used it. 'Now' was only a word, and Sandy had just heard her say that 'the Place' was a noun. It was an easy mistake, an obvious mistake. One word for another: 'noun' for 'Nown'.

And to invent some surveying French ranger to explain an N and O carved on the ground was an irresistible mistake. Because whatever logic such mistakes lacked, they still made some kind of daft sense.

What was the alternative? That someone had walked in a long loop around miles and miles of ground, singing The Measures and stopping occasionally to inscribe the letters of the spell: N O W. Someone had brought the land itself to life and tried to make a slave of it.

Sandy found himself holding Laura up. She was overcome, by exhaustion, or the elixir-like power of the dream, or with trepidation about how far they had gone. Sandy couldn't tell exactly what it was that had thrown her into a state of shock. He didn't know what he could do to help.

She clung to him. Her skin was cold and she was shivering. Sandy coaxed her to sit back down, and she all but collapsed on him. But then she was asking questions again, and her voice sounded rational. 'The N on the site of Quake — is it in one piece?' she asked.

'Never mind that now,' Sandy said, soothing.

'Please tell me.'

'No, it isn't. The letter is cracked right across. There really was a quake there at some point.'

'It's free, then,' Laura thought. 'Its first N has been erased, as I erased Nown's in the small hours of St Lazarus's Day. It is its Own. And I've always felt it was talking to me because it *was* talking to me, or *trying* to. It knows me. If the dreams are set in the future, it must once have known me. My father's sandman was the eighth Nown, mine is the ninth. The Place must be a later one. But whose?'

Then she thought of the angry demands from the bad telegrams: '*Rise up and shake them all off! Rise up and crush them!*' She didn't understand it at all. What did the Place want?

'Laura, please stop crying,' Sandy begged.

She held her breath, hiccuped, struggled.

Agonised, Sandy burst out, 'You should be happy!' But he was asking too much for himself and that scared him. 'Because of The Gate,' he added. 'How can you be unhappy with *that* inside you?'

Laura shook her head, choked. 'This is just a reaction. Don't mind me.'

He put an arm around her waist. 'Can you walk? Let's go home. Let's go and do your father some good, and start making our fortunes.'

Laura nodded. She let him help her up. They stepped out of the circle, and went slowly away from that place.

Seven

Five days before Founderston's Presentation Ball, the director of the city's largest sanatorium, Fallow Hill, was shocked by the sudden visit of a man he'd thought was dead.

Called to his office, the director found Tziga Hame sitting in front of his desk.

For nearly twenty years Hame had a contract with Fallow Hill. When the dreamhunter disappeared it had been a great loss to the sanatorium. The director was surprised, and delighted, to see Hame. Then, looking harder, he wondered whether the man had come seeking treatment. In the minute it took the director to process these impressions, he noticed his office was full of Hame's relatives. He shook hands all round, then sat down to hear what Hame had to say about his injuries.

Hame and his sister-in-law were sitting. Grace Tiebold's husband, her daughter and Hame's daughter stood at the back of the room, with a dreamhunter unknown to the director, a young man with tired eyes and several days' stubble on his jaw.

The director leaned forward and focused on Hame, or tried to, because his eyes kept wandering and he found himself counting them: *one, two, three, four* — four dreamhunters in the room. He imagined he could feel them, like storm pressure, an inaudible roar coming off them and an invisible fire raging around them.

'As you know,' Tziga Hame began, 'it isn't often that any dreamhunter catches anything new. The almanac gains perhaps fifteen to twenty dreams in any year, and most aren't of any great consequence.'

The director nodded, then was distracted by Rose Tiebold, who was pulling a quizzical face, touching her own chin then pointing at her cousin's, miming a question about the grazes on Laura Hame's chin and top lip. The marks were nothing much: scuffs from gorse prickles. Laura Hame touched her face, looked away from her cousin and kept her fingers pressed against her mouth. The young man glanced at her, then his hand found hers, and the director saw them move their arms to conceal their entwined fingers behind their backs.

Tziga Hame was saying, 'If we go straight to the Body with this, it will be classed as "a dream for the public good". But I think it should be tested before it's classified. I think it needs expert witnesses. You and your doctors are experts on dreams, long-term illness and palliative care.'

The director sat up straight. 'Good God!' he said. He had realised that it was *the dream* he could feel, in the room — an endless cascade of high feeling. He looked into the faces of all the dreamhunters. He should be able to *see* it.

'My daughter, Laura, and Alexander Mason here have a dream the like of which has never been felt,' Tziga said.

Grace Tiebold coughed. She covered her mouth with her gloved hand.

The director said to her, 'You've sampled it already?'

'Yes. We both have,' Hame said. 'And I'd very much like to have it again. So, if you could include my board in their five-night contract?'

'The Presentation Ball is in five nights,' Laura Hame added, as though to explain something vital.

'Laura wants to stay till the very end of the ball,' the young man said. He blushed and looked about nervously as though he had no right to speak. Then he squared his shoulders. 'But I will sign up to play the night of the ball, and for however long the dream lasts after that.'

'I can come back too, and sleep with Sandy — only not on the night of the ball,' Laura said. Her chafed cheeks dimpled.

Alexander Mason looked stony.

Grace Tiebold turned around in her chair to look at the young dreamhunters. She froze, staring, then said, 'You should shave, Sandy.' She sounded wrathful. The director couldn't imagine what the boy had done to offend her, or what his position was among this talented and high-handed family.

Grace turned back to the director. 'These young people should go and wait outside while Tziga and I settle details.'

'It's been a pleasure to meet you, Miss Hame, Miss Tiebold, Mr Mason,' the director said.

The young people left, the girls whispering fiercely. The director busied himself with the paperwork.

Rose said to her cousin, 'I hope you can get rid of that rash by Saturday night.'

'What rash?'

'On your chin.'

Laura touched her chin. She gave a secretive smile, then she looked at Sandy. 'Aunt Grace is right, you should shave,' she said.

'Oh — it's a *kissing* rash,' Rose said knowledgeably. 'I've heard about those.'

Eight

Rose stood in the lower hallway of the Founderston house, ready minutes before everyone else, though hers had been by far the most involved preparations. Her hair had been washed and loosely curled in the morning, then pinned into apparently artless whorls and tendrils shortly after lunch. After dinner it was decorated with real pearls, both fixed pins and drops, that shimmered and shimmied every time she moved her head. Rose had been sponged down, powdered and perfumed by eight o'clock, and had got into her stockings and slip, then finally her dress. She'd had a maid to help her, hired specially for the occasion, since the household had ordinarily no need of lady's maids. The maid had worn cotton gloves to protect the lustrous silk of Rose's ball gown from her hands. Rose was gloved now too, in one of the five pairs she had got for the season. She had covered herself with her white velvet cape. She was ready — ready to be presented to society, and to make a spectacle of herself. It was 9 p.m. The ball was to begin at nine-thirty.

Where was everyone?

Rose tapped her foot. She didn't touch anything. She began to imagine that the dust and cobwebs would jump off the walls, that fingerprints would float off the banisters beside her and drop greasily onto her clothes like smuts from a ship's funnel.

Rose heard a door latch. It was the back door. Laura pushed through from the kitchen, walking backwards, her brilliant skirt bunched in one hand. In the other she had a large canister of film. She had her gloves on, but her hands were poking out through the unbuttoned openings at her wrists. There was a small spray of dark mud on the back of her skirt.

'This is it!' Laura said, panting. She opened the door under the stairs and went into Chorley's workshop. Rose followed her, stopping in the doorway when she caught a whiff of all the chemicals.

Laura put the film canister on the table and opened the drawer where Chorley kept his pasteboard labels. She uncapped a bottle of ink, dipped her pen.

'Be careful,' Rose said.

Laura stopped, pen poised. 'You're right. What should I put? I can hardly write "Damning Evidence", can I?'

'I meant don't get ink on your gloves.'

Laura laughed, overexcited. She had been like this for days. At times she was deliriously happy, at other times she seemed paralysed by gloom. The dream alone couldn't explain it. Rose supposed that it was whatever Laura and Sandy were up to — more than kissing, maybe. She felt left out, and left behind. It wasn't that she saw herself as less grown-up than Laura, because Laura wasn't acting particularly grown-up — she wasn't acting like anything, except perhaps a string of firecrackers lit at both ends and dropped in the street. It was just that Rose found she couldn't imagine what it took to generate this crazy pitch of feeling.

'I've come home every day just to watch for his sign,' Laura said.

She meant her monster's sign: his five stones in a line. Rose said, 'There I was thinking you'd come home to bathe in buttermilk, like me.'

Laura hadn't spent the last few days washing her hair in camomile (or rosemary in her case) to brighten it, or having manicures and pedicures. Instead, she would come back from Fallow Hill mid-morning, with Sandy Mason in tow, and they'd sit in the library or parlour, alone together. Chorley had pointedly opened the door the one time they'd closed it.

'I came downstairs about fifteen minutes ago and heard a knock on the door, then someone tormenting the pump in the yard. He'd come in the back and had left the film on the steps. With a note.' Laura pulled a paper out of the top of one glove and passed it to Rose.

The handwriting was in smudgy charcoal, the letters evenly sized and backwards sloping. The note read: 'I am under Market Bridge.' Rose turned the paper over and saw that it was a paste-scabbed strip from some bill advertising a dream.

'I have a bone to pick with him,' Laura said. 'It's almost as if he knows and is avoiding me.' Then, 'Damned ball.'

'Damned inconvenient Presentation Ball,' Rose said. 'Damned untimely debut.' Then, waspishly, 'Our big milestones are very different these days, aren't they?'

'Yes.' Laura was blunt. 'But you want this film to see the light of day just as much as I do.'

'True,' said Rose. She came right into the workshop, forgetting her fear of the contaminating chemicals. She took the canister from her cousin and stowed it in a drawer. 'We'll hand it over to Da tomorrow. He can deliver it to the Grand Patriarch. Or straight to the Commission of Inquiry. His decision.'

From the hallway Grace called, 'Rose! Laura! Where are you?'

Rose swept out of the workshop, clutching her cape about her. Laura followed, struggling to stuff her hands back into her tight kid gloves. Grace started fussing. 'Where's your wrap, Laura?'

Laura dashed into the kitchen to retrieve it. When she returned to the hall her father had appeared. He kissed her on the forehead and said, 'Have fun.' He kissed Rose too and wished her the very best of luck. 'I wanted to go, but I don't think I can manage the excitement.'

Grace was flustered. 'Rose — are you all together under that cape? I didn't get to inspect you.'

'Ma, I'm a work of art,' Rose said.

Grace hustled her family down the front steps.

Rose was muttering mutinously that it was silly to take the car when the People's Palace was only five minutes' walk away.

'You must be delivered to your debut, Rose. You can't walk there,' her mother said.

'Here, let me help you with that,' Chorley said to Laura. He'd been watching her attempts to fasten the buttons on her right wrist with her left hand. He helped her into the car, sat beside her and bent over her hand. She felt his fingertips on the inside of her wrist and said, dreamily, 'Sandy will be there.'

Everyone laughed. 'Yes, we *know* Sandy will be there,' chorused Rose and Grace.

At the People's Palace there was a separate entrance for the debutantes and their mothers. This took Grace and Rose straight up the building's secondary staircase to the debutantes' dressing room. It was, in fact, a series of rooms: one where they left their coats, then a large mirror-lined room with love seats and ottomans, then an innermost room, with attendants in black and white uniforms, and lavender-sprinkled towels, big bottles of cologne and a seamstress — should one be required. Rose looked at all these elaborate comforts and mused on the value Founderston put on the female offspring of its first families. It all made her feel rather like a prize racehorse being transported to an important horse sale.

The rooms were crowded with slender girls in white, and their generally more substantial mothers in every conceivable colour. Grace, accustomed to dream-palace finery, had welcomed the chance to get into something plain. When Grace removed Rose's white velvet cape she felt that she was indeed unveiling a work of art. She stood beside Rose and basked in her daughter's glow. Rose shone, she scintillated, and she towered over most of her peers, even in her flat-heeled dancing slippers. Grace saw various mothers bridle at the sight — the shock — of Rose's beauty. The reaction of Rose's friends was quite different. As soon as they caught sight of her through the crowd, they squealed and rushed over. Rose collapsed into their cluster, hugging and bouncing about, a giggly girl again. Grace blinked away tears. She was glad Rose couldn't hold her composure — it was just too much too soon, and could only serve to isolate her, to set her apart, alone, among older male admirers. Grace could imagine it already: the sterile triumph that was waiting for her daughter who, she judged, was too young to escape the traps of flattery.

* * *

Mamie's mother was determined to make the best of the ball, to put on a brave face and to show her daughter how to do it. As she said to Mamie when she was making her final, short-tempered, motherly adjustments to her hair and wrap, 'There are some things that are simply expected of ladies, and that is that.' Mrs Doran wasn't blessed with docile children, but Mamie could usually be relied on to be calm — if only as a result of being chronically unimpressed. However, for the past week Mamie had been stuffing herself shamefully, and for the last twenty-four hours, on and off, she'd been vomiting. Mrs Doran was determined that her daughter wasn't actually ill, but was only giving way to nerves.

Everything necessary had been done for the girl's debut. She had a double strand of pearls — a gift from her father. She'd had five hair appointments till they found a style that suited her. And she had got her way over her deviant black and white gown. She had her black gloves, her crown of flowers. Mamie's interests had been served with the greatest possible care, attention and expense. And now, her mother thought, it was time for Mamie to show that she could make the best of her lot.

What Mamie's mother couldn't see was that while the ball was still far off, Mamie had been happily scornful about it, and anyone who hoped to enjoy it. She'd gone along with plans, scoffing at all the fuss. Then, one night a week before the event, she woke up with a heart full of dread. *This was it*, the first occasion in her life on which it would matter that no one much liked her. She wouldn't fit in, wouldn't be just one more goose in the gaggle of girls. She was too serious, too ponderous. She wouldn't be sought out. Her dance card had a number of names on it — friends of Ru, who understood what was expected of them — but no one would actually want to dance with her, or sit with her.

Mamie knew Rose had done her best for her. She also knew Rose understood that Mamie was unattractive — and it seemed to matter to Rose, though perhaps only as a *problem* with possible, partial solutions. Rose had served her friend — Mamie knew that.

But now Mamie was on her own, with her transformed classmates, and all the people who knew how to behave, how to enjoy themselves, how to rise to occasions.

The Doran family were half an hour late. Cas Doran let his wife, son and daughter sit in the car for minutes before he joined them. He finally left the house flanked by officials passing him telegrams and taking dictation. Then, when they got to the People's Palace, Mrs Doran spotted *more* officials in black bowler hats. 'Cas, this is impossible,' she said, as she eased her wide self, and wider skirts, across the seat. 'Why must the government be in crisis on the night of the Presentation Ball?'

Her husband's fingers closed like claws around her wrist, crushing the links of her diamond bracelet into her flesh. 'The government is not in crisis, my dear. You must not say such things. And have you forgotten that you and Mamie do not get out here? That the car will take you around to the north door, and that it is only for reasons of security that I have been delivered before you?'

'I hadn't forgotten.' Mrs Doran settled herself again and rubbed her wrist. She heard Mamie whisper, 'Stop it. Just stop it.'

Cas and Ru got out. Ru stood waiting for his father at the foot of the staircase. He kept adjusting his uniform tunic, pulling at its hem, twitching its collar. Mrs Doran wanted to shout at him. The car wasn't moving. It was in a queue. And, for all his nonsense about security, Cas was standing on the steps holding court — with no one of any consequence, only his bowler-hatted underlings. She heard him say, 'I have no use for another report. I want to see the man. Bring him to me.' Then he summoned his son to his side and went up the carpeted steps, pulling on his gloves.

Up in the dressing room the society matrons presiding over the ceremony of the presentation were marshalling the girls.

Grace kissed her splendid daughter on the little patch of bare arm between her sleeve and the top of her gloves. Then she let Rose go.

A matron said, 'You young ladies all know which row you'll be in. Please remember that the order of your presentation will be determined by the alphabet, not by any sentiments of friendship.'

Grace heard her daughter from among the white, glistening throng. 'Yes, girls, we can put friendship in our glory boxes and get it out again after we're married.'

There was laughter. One of the other mothers applauded — perhaps someone young enough to remember the society dragons herding her.

Another mother sidled up to Grace and whispered, 'This is all very strange.' As they followed their daughters down what seemed like endless hallways and staircases to the ballroom, Grace and this woman, whom she'd never met before, talked about their very different comings of age: Grace at twelve in an apron behind the counter of her father's shop, and the other woman a governess at seventeen.

The debutantes and their escorts bustled into the Founders' Hall before the ballroom. As they passed under the forty-foot lintel carved with the names of the founders, the woman beside Grace touched her hand and pointed out the name at the centre of the shallow arch: *Tiebold*.

Mamie and her mother only caught up with the cavalcade of debutantes at the entrance to the Founders' Hall. The matrons were lining the girls up — one hundred and five of them, in fifteen rows, seven abreast. The girls had practised, and the manoeuvre was quickly accomplished. Mamie was in the fourth row, Rose the thirteenth. Mamie craned over her shoulder to see her friend, highly visible because of her height and radiance. Inadvertently Mamie caught Patty's eye. Patty was babbling to any of her neighbours who would listen that she shouldn't be nervous, she'd been to all sorts of assemblies all summer in the south. 'Fancy dress balls, cricket club balls, the Masonic Ball in Canning. Girls who know how to dance don't have to wait to come out. And all the married ladies dance because women are still so outnumbered by the men in our town . . .'

'Shhhh . . .' said someone.

'Mamie, you're wearing *black*,' someone hissed.

'Perhaps she hopes to start a fashion.'

Simpering.

A matron clapped her hands. 'Girls!'

'Bloodstock. Brood mares,' Mamie muttered at her feet.

'Oh God, I need to go again!' squeaked the girl behind her.

From the ballroom came the sound of trumpets and drums, cymbals and violins — their processional music.

Cas Doran left his son in the company of several young naval cadets. (Ru had a commission, and was now at the naval academy at Westport.) He joined the throng around the President. There was a flurry of handshaking among the powerful men of the government. Cas Doran watched the master of ceremonies at the far end of the room conferring with Mamie's grandmother, Eugenia Chambers — a woman like some imposing public building that has been flounced, frilled, tucked and draped with lace.

Doran had the sense of some threat looming behind him and turned to see a long black slab of a body — the Grand Patriarch in his robes, his beard combed and oiled and glistening golden-white.

'Secretary Doran,' said Erasmus Tiebold. 'Are you and your family back in Founderston for the entire season?'

'Yes. My daughter Mamie is out this year.'

'Congratulations.'

There was a silence, then Doran, pricked by curiosity and a cat-like delight in hunting, tried to continue the conversation. 'Were you able to get out of the city yourself over summer? New Year was very uncomfortable, I hear.'

'Alas no. I must always look forward to the ball season — when the churches are full.'

'Indeed? The theatres and dream palaces too, I gather.'

Erasmus Tiebold shot Doran a look of scarcely veiled contempt. Doran, inspired by this, went on. 'And can you manage to have a quiet season by stocking yourself with sermons well ahead of time?'

'Sermonising is the least of my work.'

Cas Doran nodded, a polite, understanding nod. 'And yet I hope you may discover some leisure in the coming weeks. As I say, I predict a peaceful season. And surely if the flock is contented the shepherd is also?'

The Grand Patriarch was silent for a moment, then he replied, 'With too much rest I fear I should not know myself.'

Doran had to turn away from the old man's cool, keen scrutiny. He thought: 'How much can he know? And what can he prove?' Then he recalled the telegrams and second-hand news, the wild reports he'd had all evening, and he shivered. He shivered, but his skin went hot and his muscles hardened and he was filled with a wish for combat and the bodily joy that always came with it.

The master of ceremonies drummed his staff on the floor. The crowd drew back towards the walls of the ballroom and the orchestra struck up a processional tune.

Cas Doran was surprised at how taken up he was by the ceremony. He had always thought that the whole idea of the presentation of girls to society relied on that society's being more limited than that of the Republic of Southland. Families rose and fell in the Republic. People made fortunes, and their daughters were presented — by now, often only to other fortune-makers. It was a transplanted tradition, and Cas Doran only took it as seriously as his wife's insistence that the family dress for dinner. The ball was just another silly social exercise that it was pointless to resist. Yet as he watched the As, Bs and Cs, Doran was gradually overcome by a sense of suspense. Something important *was* about to happen. Then came Lillian Danvers, and Rebecca Deal, and Penelope Dische and finally Mamie Doran, who didn't stumble or falter, passing from one state to another — schoolgirl to Society — with no visible embarrassment.

Doran relaxed. His mind idled for a time. He refused to think about the mad, fragmentary reports that had come in from the rangers who had arrived in Founderston shortly before he left for the ball. One of these rangers — whichever his officials judged would be the most coherent — would be delivered to him here at the People's Palace. They would find a quiet room, he'd get the stories straight and he'd make plans. In a short while, he'd make plans.

The entire population of the room held its breath, then sighed collectively as Rose Tiebold dropped into her curtsy and came up again, graceful and glistening, holding up her coiled golden hair like a heavy crown on her slender neck.

Several young men thought to themselves sadly that Miss Tiebold's dance card was bound to be full already.

Minutes later, when the first chords of the first dance had sounded, and all the debutantes had taken to the floor, some with their fathers, some with brothers, some with suitors already, one of Maze Plasir's best clients caught him on his way to the refreshment room. The man clutched Plasir's sleeve and stood close to whisper in his ear. 'Rose Tiebold,' he whispered, his breath wet on Plasir's earlobe.

'No,' Plasir said. 'I'm terribly sorry, but no.'

'Surely, Maze, you can't suddenly have developed scruples?' the client said, bunching his round face so that it looked like a deformed apple that has grown pressed between branches.

'Get away from me!' Plasir hissed.

In the breather after the second dance — a maxina — Rose went back to her mother and showed her card, full but for one space. 'I'm about to meet twenty new people,' she said. 'But if I like any of them I won't be able to get a second look.'

Grace threw up her hands. 'I don't have any advice.'

Mamie's grandmother, the formidable Mrs Chambers, leaned across Grace and told Rose that tomorrow the calling cards would come in. 'And a parade of young men's mothers. Next Wednesday there is the President's Ball, then after that Founders' Day Ball, the Naval Ball, the Grand Social and the Carnival Social — and a dozen other private functions. Anyone you like you are bound to see more than enough in the coming weeks.'

'That's why you have five pairs of gloves, Rose. And another gown coming,' Grace said.

'The girl has only *two* gowns?' exclaimed Mrs Chambers.

'Oh dear,' said Grace, and laughed. 'I'm no good at this.'

Rose's next partner came to claim her. She gathered up the hem of her dress, and he took her hand and led her onto the floor and into a crisscrossing, lively *contredanse*. It was fun, and all Rose's hours of practice came back to her. No one on the floor seemed lost or clumsy. The girls were all weaving their way deftly backwards past their partners, their hair bouncing, their heads turned back over their shoulders. Rose saw Mamie, wearing a look of determination and concentration, but doing well. She saw Laura, who was dancing not with Sandy but with a tall, faired-haired army lieutenant. Laura was easy to spot, in her vivid dress, flying, light on her feet.

The next dance was a waltz. And Laura danced with Sandy, scooped against him, so that he seemed to support half her slight weight. Rose's partner was a proficient dancer, but so shy and formal that Rose had a hard time not laughing her way through the whole thing. He talked about the weather, and the heat of the room. She wished he hadn't mentioned the heat. Her close-fitting, pearl-encrusted gown was proving hot and heavy. She was going to be cooking before the night was through.

One of the ushers delivered a note to Cas Doran and pointed out the men standing, bowler hats in hand, partly concealed by pillars in the entranceway. Doran made his way around the edge of the dance floor.

His daughter galloped past, part of a group of couples skipping anticlockwise within the clockwise movement of a greater circle of dancers. Mamie looked at him as though he were guilty of some terrible treachery to her. He slowed down and stared after her as she was swept away. He was annoyed — his wife had promised and assured him that, *ultimately*, Mamie would enjoy this ball. It didn't appear to him as though she was enjoying herself.

The Regulatory Body officials had delivered one of the rangers who were the source of the reports that, all evening, had been aggravating the Secretary of the Interior. They had secured a quiet room in the palace. Their chief closed that room's door and they all gathered around the tired man.

'I want you to explain these reports,' Doran said, and produced two of the telegrams. 'I know you've been told to be careful in your communications. But in this instance you've been so careful that you've left us in the dark.'

He placed the telegrams in front of the ranger. The top one read:

AGENT SEEN FILMING THE DEPOT STOP GAVE CHASE BUT LOST INLAND

'How is it possible that your people pursued this cameraman but didn't manage to catch him?' Doran said. 'You were, after all, selected for your strength and stamina as well as your discretion.'

Every ranger had once hoped to be a dreamhunter. All had enjoyed a moment of elation at their Try. They had crossed the border! Each one of them had imagined being rich and famous, but all had found themselves unable to catch dreams. There were no famous rangers, and all were wage workers for the Dream Regulatory Body. Some did a little better in private deals they made with various dreamhunters, but none was rich. Rangers did tend to suffer from a sense of thwarted ambition, so it had been no trouble for Secretary Doran to recruit men keen to take on extra risks — and vows of secrecy.

'The man was faster than we were, even carrying his camera,' the ranger said. Then he straightened in his chair. 'I want to give a report, Mr Secretary, not offer excuses.' He began: 'At 5.30 p.m. on February the twenty-eighth, rangers McIndoe and Butler first spotted a man, standing around one hundred and fifty yards from the outbuildings of the Depot and cranking the handle of a movie camera. As we watched he came closer. Rangers McIndoe, Butler, Carter, Hollander and I —'

Cas Doran looked at one of his officials, who supplied the ranger's name: 'McIntyre.'

'We approached him,' said McIntyre, then paused and passed his hand across his face, pressing hard, as though to wipe something off. 'Secretary Doran,' the man said, 'the cameraman seemed to be wearing some kind of suit.'

'A uniform?'

'No.' The ranger seemed reluctant to say what he'd seen.

'Please go on,' Doran said.

'He was wearing an all-over, skin-tight, glistening grey suit of some kind.'

'Knitted,' one of the officials added; he had obviously heard the story earlier.

'I didn't say knitted,' the ranger snapped.

Doran knew that the navy was trying to develop garments to keep bodies warm in cold water, and supposed it was possible that someone enterprising might have invented a protective, water-conserving suit to be worn deep Inland.

'Not knitted, not rubber, not any of those things you've speculated about,' the ranger said, glaring at the Body officials. 'I want to say that it —' He broke off and scoured his face with his hand again. Then he finished, very softly, '— that it wasn't even a suit.'

'Wait,' said Doran, though no one had spoken. He walked around the room a few times.

After the riot at the Rainbow Opera several members of the fire watch claimed that a 'glistening, grey, monstrous man' shorted out the alarm board and smashed all the doors on the private balconies. Cas Doran paced and thought. He thought that Conan Doyle's 'hound of the Baskervilles' was only a dog daubed with luminescent paint and howling with pain. He didn't believe in monsters — he *traded* in them, at least in monstrous dreams. He knew that impressionable people could be made to believe things that weren't true, could be tapped for fear of the unknown — as if dread were the groundwater of humanity and all any intelligent master of men had to do was to sink a well.

Doran rounded on the ranger. 'You've been manipulated. You're a superstitious lot, you rangers and dreamhunters. You make myths faster than you make money.'

'All right,' said the ranger, then added, 'Sir.'

'Perhaps you couldn't catch him because you were afraid of him,' Doran said, insinuating.

'We ran after him. He slung the camera over his shoulder and took off like a — horse.'

'Oh — not like a flying horse?' Cas Doran's voice dripped sarcasm.

The ranger went red. 'He went Inland, west, at a forty-degree angle to the railway line. He didn't have any water with him. Or none we could see. He may well have had a cache of supplies somewhere. But we immediately posted guards at the tower, and over the cable car. He can't possibly have got his film out again. There's no danger of that.'

'Laura Hame is out there in the ballroom, dancing, a picture of health. And yet I was assured that she couldn't have used the cable car either.' Doran swooped on the ranger, slapped his hands down on the arms of the man's chair and leaned over him.

The man cowered back into his seat.

Doran shouted, 'There is obviously another pass through the Pinnacles that you lazy incompetents couldn't find! A route that wouldn't have required years of work and thousands of dollars of engineering to open!' He snapped upright again, releasing the arms of the chair so quickly that it teetered and the man flailed for balance before the chair came down again on all four legs. His voice quiet again, Doran asked one of the officials to fetch Maze Plasir. 'As for you,' he said to the ranger, 'you can get back to the Depot, immediately. And I will arrange for you to supervise several months' worth of supplies on your journey.'

'Are we to be under siege, then?' the ranger asked, and flinched when Doran looked at him.

'There you go again,' said the secretary. 'Imagining yourself surrounded by monsters.' He signalled to several officials, who helped the man up and led him out.

Maze Plasir appeared, fanning himself with a lady's ivory and rice-paper fan. He took one look at Doran's face, sat himself down, and waited.

Doran said to his men, 'I want that Soporif you've been promising me.'

'We've had him under constant observation since he began performing at Fallow Hill. But he's never on his own. He's even been sleeping in the same bed as the Hame girl.'

'Ah, young love,' said Plasir. 'How inconvenient.'

'He dressed for the ball tonight at his uncle's apartment. His uncle was there.'

'You could always have taken his uncle too,' Doran said.

'We didn't have the manpower, Mr Secretary.'

'Tell your detail to be a little more daring,' Doran said. He dismissed them.

When the door closed, Plasir said, 'Are you about to put your plan into action?'

'Yes.'

'And you will tell me when you need me to go In and catch a master dream to provide your household with some shelter?'

'My house and the houses of my allies are safe. Out of range. I'll need you to have some strong dream as a safety measure. In case some dreamhunter actually thinks to go on the offensive. I imagine that a small capsule of one of your master dreams could withstand the wide sweep of Laura Hame's?'

'Yes. If you keep me close I can keep you safe,' Plasir said. 'But, Cas, I'd much rather we made a slow start and experimented with the dosage of Contentment. This has all been so long in the planning that you should only act on *your* timetable.' Plasir's posture and tone were casual, but he was trying to warn his friend.

'I haven't time.'

'This isn't about Tziga Hame's return, is it?'

'No. I've made inquiries. He's under treatment for epilepsy. There are no epileptic dreamhunters.'

'True.'

'The Tiebolds and the Hame girl are out there dancing, bending their knees to the seasonal social rituals. The Grand Patriarch is bestowing blessings on debutantes. Whatever measures they are taking against me, they must suppose they'll work. They must suppose they have me somehow. The Hame girl may be simple. She might not have had the imagination to see what the dream at the Depot could be used to do. She might just have run back home wiping her brow with relief that she'd avoided charges of trespass. She might believe she's a naughty girl and be thinking nothing much about Contentment and what it can do. But I can't count on that, can I?'

'No.'

'They've forced my hand.'

Nine

Shortly before midnight the orchestra stopped for a supper break. The debutantes came off the dance floor, and some found their mothers waiting for them with plates. Grace beamed at Rose and handed her one on which cold meats and salads were heaped in a perilous pile.

'Ma!' Rose passed the plate to her father. 'I have to go upstairs and cool off. This dress is magnificent, but it's killing me.'

Grace looked crestfallen. 'We didn't really think it through, did we?'

'Never mind.' Rose squeezed her mother's hand and smiled at her father, who was foraging through the green salad with a fork, chasing chunks of meat and potato.

Rose left her parents. She spotted Mamie in the slow queue making its way into the supper room. Mamie was with Ru, but Rose still went up and asked her friend whether she was enjoying herself.

'I'm hungry,' Mamie said.

'You stood up for nearly every dance,' Rose said, congratulating her.

'That would explain why I'm hungry, wouldn't it?'

Rose glanced at Ru and saw that he had his back to them. She relaxed a little.

Mamie said, 'I know you want me to say it's not so bad after all, and I'm having a fine time, because really, Rose, it's you who persuaded me into all this.' Mamie gestured about her at the crowd in their finery.

'You always intended to come out this year.'

Mamie screwed up her face. Her cheeks began to show webs of red — her skin never flushed evenly. 'Who says I intended to come out at all? Why would I want to? This ball is nothing but a way for a girl to declare that she expects to get married.'

'Can't it just be fun?'

'It could be fun if it *were* fun,' Mamie hissed.

Rose lost her temper. 'Why do you always have to be above everything? You're acting as though this whole occasion existed as a slight to you. You're not enjoying it, so it must be no good!'

'It's easy for you, Rose,' Mamie said, with quiet contempt.

'Yes, it's true, some things are easy for me,' Rose said. Her voice was cool, but Mamie stepped back from her stare. 'Yes, nature has been kind to me. But that's no reason for my friends to think they should act like checks and balances to nature.'

Mamie was on the back foot, and breathing hard, but she held her ground. 'I don't need your charity,' she said to Rose.

'It was just help, Mamie. It's what friends do.'

Someone touched Rose's shoulder and she jerked, knocking whoever it was back.

'Ow!' said Laura.

'Watch it, Rose,' said Sandy.

'Do you want me to go up to the powder room with you?' Laura asked her cousin.

Rose looked at Laura sheepishly, and all the fight left her. 'Yes. Thanks,' she said.

'I'll be down again to say goodnight before you go,' Laura said to Sandy. He was going to dream The Gate in the small hours at Fallow Hill. She had opted to stay on for the whole ball. ('Rose will want to talk about it,' she'd explained to Sandy. 'It's a big thing. And I'd like to be there in the morning to see the first calling cards come in.')

The cousins strolled away, arm in arm.

Mamie turned her face to her brother's back, her lips pressed together hard.

Sandy joined the line and shuffled along. He pretended he hadn't heard a thing. He expected Ru to comfort his sister, but Ru kept on chatting to his new Navy School friends. Those young men were peering at Mamie, some embarrassed, some concerned, some spitefully amused — but no one uttered a word. Sandy tried to think of something to say. Something kindly. His mind was blank. If he'd meant to stay, he could have asked her to dance; but he didn't mean to stay.

Chorley Tiebold went past, gave Sandy a friendly nod, then glanced at Mamie and stopped in his tracks. He came over. 'You shouldn't have to stand in line,' he said. 'You girls are supposed to have plates waiting for you. And trainers who can toss a blanket over you so you won't cool off too quickly while they walk you around.'

Mamie snorted.

'What can I get you?' Chorley said. 'I've eaten. There are plates all over the seats in there.' He jerked his thumb at the ballroom. 'I managed to balance mine on the bust of President Broughton, with the help of his laurel wreath.' He drew a circle around the top of his own head, then mimed balancing something.

'I'd like some trifle and cheesecake,' said Mamie. 'My mother has had me on lemon and barley water for two days.'

'Time for a mutiny,' Chorley declared.

'Yes.'

'You stay there, I'll be right back,' Chorley said, and sailed off to the head of the queue.

'Mr Irresistible,' Mamie muttered. But she was prepared to accept charity, so long as it came with cake.

Laura unfastened the hundred small pearl buttons at the back of Rose's dress. Rose sat slumped in front of one of the dressing-room mirrors, while Laura and an attendant fanned her face and bare back. Rose's head felt impossibly heavy, weighed down by her high coif of humid hair. A drop of sweat trickled down behind one ear and the attendant dabbed it away with a towel. Someone brought her an iced tea.

Debutantes were in and out to make themselves comfortable, and repair their looks. Some appeared with their mothers — they were already being debriefed about whom they had met, whom they had liked and who had seemed to like them. Several sat miserably and listened to anxious motherly advice. Most didn't stay long. By the end of supper time the powder room and cloakroom were almost empty. The attendants were gathering discarded towels and dropped hairbrushes. One senior from the Academy, her mother in attendance, was lying on a sofa, overcome after dancing every dance. Another girl had a blistered foot. She had spent the supper hour soaking it in briny water. Her mother had bandaged the blister and the seamstress was now busily unpicking a seam on the girl's dancing slipper so that she could stuff her bandaged foot back into it.

Rose told Laura she wasn't yet ready to go. She'd have a bit of a wash and splash on some witch hazel.

'I'll just go down and say goodnight to Sandy,' Laura said, 'and be back to help button you up.'

Laura hurried out to the second staircase and down one floor — where there was access to the main staircase and she could find her way back to the ballroom.

Sandy was waiting for her in the entranceway. She grinned at him, grabbed his hand and dragged him back to the stairs. 'Surely I'm not allowed up there?' he said, but went with her.

She scampered ahead of him, sometimes going backwards and holding him with both hands. They got up to the second floor and she took him along a hall and onto the secondary staircase. She led him down it to the low-ceilinged hallway by which all the debutantes had entered earlier. Laura whispered, 'Rose told me it might be quiet here, but it's even better — there's nobody at all!'

The gas lamps on the stairs had been lit, but the ones near the street doors were out. Neither Sandy nor Laura wondered about this unguarded entrance, only embraced it as an opportunity to be alone. They stopped to kiss, Laura with her back to the wall. They broke apart when they heard running footsteps on the stairs, but then, when no one appeared, they melted together again.

'I wish I'd known more of the dances,' Sandy said.

'But Captain Goodnough's *Useful Guide to Ballroom Dances* says that good taste forbids a lady to dance too frequently with one partner.'

Sandy stroked Laura's curls. 'You like dancing. I didn't know that.'

For minutes more they leaned together, sharing breath and not speaking, then Sandy said, 'I'm late already.'

'And I've left Rose all unbuttoned.'

Sandy pushed her gently away. 'Goodnight,' he said.

Laura left him, skipped into the light and, turning every few steps, went back to the stairs, then vanished up them.

Sandy straightened his tie, and checked that his shirt was tucked in — Laura had the habit of pulling its tails out of his trousers.

He heard faint music, the orchestra striking up again.

Light appeared on the dark street beyond the door, lamps carried low and making a grid of shadows on the cobblestones. Then there were men in the doorway, who held their lamps so that their faces were concealed and only their shapes could be seen, their suits and bowler hats.

'Alexander Mason,' said one of the men.

Sandy began to back away.

'You are to come with us.' They advanced into the hallway. Their pressure lamps reflected off the lustrous oiled-silk wallpaper and revealed their faces and shrewd, stony expressions.

Sandy turned to flee and heard the men break into a run behind him. They caught him at the foot of the stairs. He struggled and yelled. The bar of an arm closed on his throat and silenced him. He grappled with it, but couldn't get his fingers under it. Someone hissed, 'Be still!' in his ear.

But Sandy continued to fight, he kicked and threw his weight forward. He was wrenched upright by the arm pressing on his windpipe.

'Subdue him!' a man ordered, in a fierce whisper.

'*No!*' said another — the only man among them with any sense or foresight.

Sandy couldn't breathe. He was blacking out. He clawed at the arm. His fingers fizzed then went numb. Everything went white — like sheet lightning without a thunderclap to follow it.

* * *

The man who'd remained at the door to watch the street wasn't the one who had foreseen what would happen. He saw what *did* happen but, for several long moments, didn't understand what he was seeing. The dreamhunter was putting up a fight. Five men were clustered around him, grunting. The man in charge was issuing orders. Finally the dreamhunter slumped —

— and all the men around him dropped to the floor, like marionettes whose strings had been severed. The man at the door felt a stunning blow, violent lassitude that seemed to come from the core of his own body, a warm explosion of sleep. It struck him down onto his knees. Nearer the floor the air seemed full of the smell of flowers and freshly fallen dew.

The man shook his head to clear it. When he looked up he saw that two of the dropped lamps had shattered and spilled kerosene, and that the floor was on fire. A liquid fire crept towards either side of the corridor. It didn't look dangerous. It looked like the flames over a pool of brandy cradling crêpes suzette. Nothing bad could happen. Not in a world that smelled like a beautiful garden.

The man shook his head again, and staggered up. He could see a heap of inert bodies beyond the pool of fire. The flame reached the walls, licked at the oiled-silk wallpaper, then streaked upwards and spread flowing onto the ceiling.

The man hurried towards the fire, his arms over his face. The corridor had become a squared tube of flame. The flames were bright, but black at their bases, consuming their smoke before it fumed from them.

The man jumped over the pooled fire. He fumbled at the fallen bodies, got hold of one by an arm and thigh, hoisted it onto his shoulders and stood up. He turned back to the exit, and ran through the fire. The kerosene coated the soles of his shoes, so that he left fiery footprints behind him.

Ten

When Laura arrived back in the powder room she found Rose sitting straight while one of the attendants closed her back into her pearly carapace of dress with the help of a button hook. Rose was relieved to see her cousin. She opened her dance card and found the name of her next partner. She showed it to Laura. 'Could you find him and give him my apologies? I'll be down shortly.'

Laura took note, nodded and rushed out again. She was enjoying this dashing about. She wasn't hot, she was very fit and she liked the way the gilded panels and mirrors and her own vivid reflection flashed past her as she ran. She liked leaping soundlessly down the carpeted stairs.

Laura sprinted down one flight of the lesser stairs, then along the hall that came out onto the main staircase. She loped down the wide steps of its outer curve, raced through Founders' Hall and into the ballroom. She slowed down and looked about for the young man; saw him between the rows of a Scottish dance. The expression on his face suggested indigestion to Laura. She worked her way around the dance floor to him and touched his arm. 'Rose says sorry. She's still upstairs. It's the heat.'

'Oh,' he said.

For a moment they stood awkwardly side by side, then it finally occurred to him that he could dance with this girl. 'If you're not engaged?'

'No. I'd love to.' Laura beamed, and held out her hand.

For the next few minutes, whenever the open, weaving figures of the Scottish brought them together, he'd babble about his university studies, the horse his father had in the Founders' Day Cup and so on. Then he remembered to introduce himself. Then he lost his tongue when he realised he was dancing with Tziga Hame's dreamhunter daughter. Laura flew through the dance smiling at everyone, aglow with happiness.

She had only just come off the dance floor and caught her breath when another young man introduced himself and engaged her for the mazurka. During it Laura looked around for Rose, but it seemed her cousin had missed another dance and again left someone standing.

Then the music faltered: a horn sounded a farting note, a violin swooped into a discord. The dancers slowed and turned to the orchestra. Someone had hold of the conductor's arm. The conductor's baton was pointed at the floor. The musicians were setting aside their instruments, and some were on their feet — those nearest the conductor, who could hear what was being said to him.

The master of ceremonies released the conductor and turned to the crowd. 'Ladies and gentlemen, I must ask you to leave the building immediately. Could you please make your way in an orderly fashion through the Founders' Hall and down the stairs, and depart by the main doors? Would you then please assemble on the west side of People's Plaza? Do not collect your belongings. Do not look for your family members. They will find you — this message is being repeated in every other room. Now go at once, and peacefully.'

The crowd began to move, with more speed and elbows than had been suggested. The murmur of questions became a rising buzz of alarm, then someone yelled, 'There's a fire!'

Laura and her partner had come together when the music stopped. They went along together, turning slowly in an eddy of pressing bodies. 'My mother is in the supper room,' he said. He began to push his way against the current, aiming at the high door of the supper room, visible over all the flower-decked and brilliantined heads.

People were shouting the names of relatives, and receiving answering shouts. The hall was ringing with calls, and throbbed with a swelling clamour of fright. But everyone kept their feet, and the hall was clearing. Laura went with the flow. She wanted to locate her uncle and aunt and was sure the quickest way to do that was to get out of the building and into the plaza. She was simply too short to see over the heads of the crowd.

Laura was in the Founders' Hall when she smelled smoke. Somewhere in the building someone opened an external door and let in a breeze, the air pressure changed, then the scent of smoke swept across the crowd. The people started and shuddered and, as one, shied away from the smell.

An elbow collided with Laura's head. She saw stars. When she managed to get her bearings again, she found she was facing backwards. Her feet weren't touching the ground. She was being carried along by the crowd. It was terrifying and she began to cry out for help.

She caught a glimpse of a bunch of bodies in black formal wear on a dais at one end of the hall. Men who had fought their way free from the crowd and were now scanning it, looking for their own people. She saw her uncle among them, taller than most. His head was swivelling back and forth — he had heard her screaming, but wasn't able to find her. She lifted an arm and waved to him and he launched himself off the dais and into the thick of the people. He shoved and swam his way towards her. He picked her up and lifted her over his head, then let the crowd carry him onto the sweeping curves of the wide staircase and down into the street.

Chorley put Laura down. He hurried her clear of the main doors. Once free of danger, the crowd seemed to collect itself and begin to cooperate — for the most part. People hovered, waiting to see who came out, while the police tried to get them to move out of the path of the clanging fire engines and horse-drawn water tenders.

'Rose was still up in the powder room,' Laura said to her uncle.

He said, 'Can you see your aunt?'

They kept hold of each other and turned this way and that, searching for the little figure in the grey silk dress. Then Chorley snapped upright and cried out. He pointed. Laura followed his pointing finger and saw that her aunt was on the terrace outside the ballroom, with dozens of other people, all clustered at the stone balustrade and calling down to the crowd. None of them seemed terribly worried and, as far as Laura was able to tell, they were asking for news, not help.

Chorley gripped Laura's arms and fixed her with his sternest look. 'You stay right there,' he said. 'Grace should be fine. It'll be possible to reach all those people with ladders. I'm going back in to get Rose.'

Laura hung on to him.

'Laura!' he yelled in exasperation, broke out of her grip and ran back to the still-choked exit, dodging firemen unravelling hoses and opening fire-nets. He found his way up the steps and through the main doors and vanished from Laura's sight.

Laura looked up at the People's Palace. Streetlights caught on the woolly underside of a pall of smoke that didn't seem to have come from any exterior part of the building. Perhaps it was oozing through the roof, or up an internal air shaft. The smoke hung, quite still, and coloured only by the lights from the square. It looked so innocent, so anticlimactic after the crush of escape. The sounds of human frenzy were dying down. People still called out to loved ones, and there were orders, from police and firemen, and the pounding of pumps and rattle of hose reels and extension ladders.

Then came a deep, bright smash from the building, and flames burst out of an exploded window on the second floor. The crowd shrieked, then moaned. Arms went up, pointing. The innocent fleece of smoke above the building now had the light of fire at its heart.

It was one of the attendants in the dressing room who first noticed the smoke. She supposed it was the smell of scorching, and went to check that the two irons had been returned to the stove top. The irons were where they should be, the kettle was still half-full, its base in no danger of burning through. For a few moments the woman stood frowning at the stove and sniffing.

Somewhere in the large building a door opened to the outer air, and the faint whiff shifted and became a strong odour. Then, in the cloakroom — the room nearest the hallway — an attendant shrieked as a wisp of smoke coiled in and spread thinly across the ceiling. She ran into the powder room, screaming, 'Fire! Fire!'

'Be quiet, child!' her superior commanded.

Rose was before one of the full-length mirrors giving herself a final checking over. Her face was still too pink, and she was very uncomfortable. She heard the shouting, and at the same time, the lights wavered as a film of smoke covered them.

Rose picked up her train and hurried out towards the hallway. Everyone else followed her.

They found the hallway filled with a haze of grey-white smoke. But halfway down its length, pouring along the ceiling, as though gravity had reversed itself, was a brown pall, oily and thick.

It was Rose's instinct to move away from the sight. But she didn't know what lay the other way. There were no signs pointing to exits — like at the Rainbow Opera. This was a much older building. It still had gaslights on its upper floors, and Rose couldn't remember having ever noticed fire escapes bolted to the heavy carving of its stone exterior. She pulled her train up, pressed it against her mouth and, with a quick glance at the woman beside her, set off into the smoke.

After she'd gone a short way she realised that only three other young women had gone with her. Her eyes were streaming. She began to cough through the cloth muffling her mouth. She, and the women who had followed her, turned around and retreated.

Chorley ran up the steps of the palace at the same moment as some shift in the air inside the building — a window breaking, a door opening — gave the conflagration a breath of fresh air. He was in the entranceway, pushing through firemen towards the stairs, when the main staircase seemed to open like a dragon's throat and vomit fire. The flames spat down the stairs and sailed free from their bases, touching curtains and carpet, the beautiful oiled-silk wallpaper, and the deadly, glistening Cellophane decorations. Everything flammable caught fire. The firemen staggered back. Chorley was knocked over, and the back of his head hit the marble floor.

* * *

Grace was waiting to one side of the jostling group of people who had gathered at the balustrade of the terrace where, they judged, the first ladder would touch down. The people were craning over, watching the ladder swivel and expand as men on the back of a fire engine cranked it up into place.

Grace wasn't in any great hurry. She thought it would be safer to hang back than to join the shoving bunch. Besides, from where she was, she had a better view of People's Plaza.

Her eyes hadn't yet found Rose. She'd spotted Chorley and Laura as soon as they appeared. Chorley's greying gold hair and height made him easy to find in a crowd, and Laura's dress was highly visible. A moment ago she'd seen Chorley leave Laura and run back to the palace, passing out of her sight under where the main entrance was. She knew he was looking for their daughter. Rose wasn't in the plaza.

Grace's eyes went back and forth, back and forth.

There was Mamie, standing with her mother, grandmother and brother. Cas Doran was on the steps of the State Library, with the President and other ministers and dozens of bodyguards and police. It made Grace furious to see all those able bodies in uniforms forming a fence around dignitaries instead of doing something.

Grace looked over her shoulder and into the ballroom, the far end of which was on fire. Only a few moments before, fire had come, following the smoke. It had climbed the vines of Cellophane streamers that festooned the entrance to the ballroom. The Cellophane went up like a fuse, and dissolved into drips of flame. The velvet hangings behind the orchestra ignited.

The fire was more than sixty yards from where Grace stood, but she could hear it. The sound it made was solid and soft, like a huge audience clapping with gloved hands.

Grace tilted her head back and looked up at the façade of the People's Palace. She saw smoke wafting through only one window on the third floor, a few threads straining up into the air above the window's deep moulding then dissipating. It looked so innocent.

It looked like smoke coming from the window of a busy working men's bar.

Grace walked along to the corner of the terrace. She joined a man who stood with his coat held up over his head, as if it could protect him from anything that fell from above. He seemed to sense her approach. He turned and said, 'Careful,' and pointed at the tiles beneath her. Smoke seeped between the slabs, and Grace could feel heat through the thin soles of her dancing slippers. The man turned back to the balustrade, dropped his coat, and pointed. Grace looked and saw what he'd been watching.

In the side street facing the State Library the whole wall of the People's Palace was ablaze. Smoke poured through every window, and fire through a good half-dozen of them. A fire engine and a water tender were in the street, and the cobbles were already submerged. The stream from one hose played in spurts on the building, but reached only as far as the second storey. The other hose was trained into the side entrance of the palace. As Grace and the man watched, something moved or collapsed inside the building and a gout of fire spat out of the entrance. It swallowed the men holding the hose, then retreated again, leaving them rolling on the street, their uniforms and skin smoking.

Grace put her hand over her mouth.

The man shouted to her that his mother and sister were up in the third-floor dressing room. 'I'm sure of it!' he shouted.

'I think maybe my daughter is too,' Grace said, then burst into tears. She gripped the hair at her temples and held on to it as though it were her only handhold and she were hanging over an abyss. She could see the young man had begun to cry too. He was saying, over and over, 'That's where they went in,' about the red maw of the side entrance. 'That's where I left them.'

Some of Grace's hair came away in her hands. It hurt. She looked at the smoke seeping through the tiles, and said, 'We should move. The fire is under us.' She took his arm and led him away, back to the balustrade, but not into the crowd. A window exploded over their heads and showered them with glass. The crowd on the terrace howled and a number of people scrambled up and knelt balancing on the stone coping of the balustrade.

* * *

After her uncle left her, Laura stood for a few moments watching her aunt, a little isolated figure, head turning back and forth, back and forth. Laura knew that if Rose were anywhere to be seen, Grace would see her. Laura watched. She held her breath, let it go, held it again. But no matter how long or keenly she stared, she didn't see her aunt seeing Rose.

Laura came back to herself. She looked around for a gap in the crowd and went through it, away from the burning palace. When she reached the street that led to the river, she began to run. She ran alongside a hose, not yet fattened by water. She burst out onto the west embankment and swerved to avoid the firemen and their big pumping appliance. The firemen had a hose in the river.

Laura set off towards Market Bridge.

None of the busy firemen noticed as the little fleet figure in coral-red silk sprinted by.

The women shut the cloakroom against the smoke. They retreated from the outside door. Rose ran into the powder room and hauled open the curtains covering one window. She threw up the sash — ignoring the sudden shrieking behind her — and thrust her head out. The window opened onto an airshaft. The airshaft had a jumble of rubbish at its bottom and was already full of smoke.

Someone hauled Rose back and slammed the window. It was the head attendant. The woman was more stern than frightened. Rose saw that there was more smoke in the room than before she'd opened the window, and instantly understood that by opening it, she had offered the smoke free passage into their sanctuary. 'Sorry,' Rose said.

'The only windows on an outer wall are those above the toilets,' the attendant said. 'And they only open a gap.'

Rose ran to look. She made sure she shut the two doors between the dressing rooms and bathrooms. Her caution was unnecessary. The toilet windows were already ajar. They were of frosted glass, about fifteen inches in height and twenty-five across. Metal catches were firmly screwed into the frames on either side of each window, allowing them to open at an angle, with a gap of perhaps seven inches at their tops.

Rose lowered a toilet seat and climbed onto it. She reached around the cistern and gripped the top of the frame with both her hands. Then she lifted her feet and hung her whole weight from the frame, which creaked and buckled. The glass cracked and most of it dropped out. A large piece scored a cut in Rose's cheek as it fell. She released the frame and dropped back onto the toilet seat, then tumbled onto the floor of the stall. She pressed the back of her gloved hand to the cut and looked up at the angled window frame — still firmly in place, though empty of glass. She picked herself up, shook her gown free of glass and left the toilets.

In the dressing room the head attendant and the one mother were soaking hand towels in a basin and handing them around.

The head attendant passed Rose another basin and told her to fill it with water in the bathroom and, before she did that, to thoroughly wet her own gown and hair.

Rose went into the bathroom and turned on a tap. Water came in a dribble, then stopped altogether.

The gaslights in the room flared, then dimmed, and were extinguished. Rose dropped the basin, and it shattered with a sound like the single stroke of a big bell.

The room in which Rose stood was now dark, except for a fluttering, sullen glow one way, and the rectangles of faint light from the high windows over the toilets.

'Rose!' the attendant shouted. 'Come back!'

Rose wasn't surprised to be known. But it did seem strange and lonely to hear herself summoned out of the dark by a stranger's voice.

'Nown!' Laura's shout reverberated in the hollow of the first arch of Market Bridge. She had come only partway down the steps from the embankment. The light from the nearest streetlamp reached no further.

A shadow appeared out of the blackness and resolved itself into her sandman. He mounted the steps. She held out her arms and he picked her up. His limbs felt coarse and very cold. She realised that she was making a comparison between the feeling of being held by Nown, and by the warm and pliant Sandy. 'Run,' she said, and held on tight.

Nown bounded up onto the embankment, and Laura let go of one arm to point at the pall of red-lit smoke several blocks away above and beyond the buildings. 'Faster,' she said. She was out of breath after her run. She wanted to say, 'Why didn't you tell me that the Place was a Nown?' and, 'You said you were with yourself, but you never said what you meant.' But Nown had picked up his pace so much his running jolted her and she had to press her head against his shoulder so she wouldn't suffer whiplash. His body began to heat up and smell like rain on hot stones.

He ran in the shadows of buildings backlit by fire. He bore down on the firemen with the hose in the river, went by them and turned to follow their hose, turned so fast that a snap of white sparks outlined one of his flexed feet. Laura's stomach lurched.

He slowed as the street opened out onto the People's Plaza. He came to a stop and set Laura down.

'Rose is on the third floor,' Laura said. 'North side. But you'll have to shout for her.'

Nown looked at her and Laura saw the black band of iron sand drain away from his eyes, like dampness seeping through him. The black settled beneath his cheekbones and over his mouth and jaw. She didn't know what it meant, the shadow passing down his face, but it made her think of sorrow. Then he jumped away from her and plunged through the crowd, straight at the building. He scattered people — all of whom had their backs to him and their faces towards the fire. The people left reeling in his wake were perhaps only able to get a look at the missile of his body when he was yards beyond them. He sprinted in a straight line and with inhuman speed to the main steps of the building, through the firemen, who at this distance were only strokes of black against a maw of flame. Some of the firemen took a step or two after this mad figure, but stopped when he ran straight into the flames on the blazing staircase.

* * *

Grace saw Chorley carried out of the People's Palace. She saw him placed on a stretcher and borne away through the crowd. She had lost sight of Laura. She could see the debutantes. Many were draped in borrowed coats, but still all their lustrous white dresses reflected the fire as faithfully as polished silver.

The air between the terrace and plaza was distorted with heat. Grace could no longer recognise any of the faces below her. She stood, frozen in place, till someone took her arm, drew her to the balustrade, lifted her up and lowered her onto the ladder. Her feet and hands found its rungs. She looked over her shoulder, saw others well below her making their way down. She began to follow them.

Grace was fit and nimble and her skirt was a manageable length. She soon caught up with the person below her. Then someone pulled her off the ladder and for a moment she stood on the vibrating rear deck of a fire engine. The air smelled of steam and hot steel. A fireman took her arm and showed her where she could climb down. The cobbles were drenched. Another fireman drew her back from the engine. She was in the way.

Suddenly Laura was standing beside her. Grace put her arms around her niece and together they walked away from the palace, the pounding engines, the torrents of cold and warm water. They stopped at the edge of the crowd and stood, clinging to one another. Grace was drenched and shivering, but her feet smarted, as though they'd been sunburned.

When Rose returned to the others she found the head attendant had finished passing out wet towels. 'There's no more water in the taps,' Rose said.

'There's no time,' the other woman replied, and passed Rose a towel. Then she walked out of the only illumination — smoke-bruised firelight — and fumbled her way across the room. Her workmates began to bleat at her. 'Come back!'

She returned carrying scissors. She squatted and began to hack at the train of Rose's gown. She made a sizeable hole, then wrapped the cloth around her hands and ripped the train away from the skirt. Then she picked up her own towel, went to the cloakroom door and opened it.

For a moment all they could see was smoke — they'd made way for it, and it came towards them, twisting and black, as solid and supple as bull kelp in a fast-moving tide. The women and girls instinctively ducked, cowered on the carpet in the hallway, where they found that the air was clearer.

The head attendant choked out, 'Hold on to one another's skirts.' She began to crawl towards the staircase. The others followed her. Rose came last, and reached back to pull the cloakroom door closed behind her. She wasn't sure why she did it, but she had the sense that the fire was behind the smoke, pushing it, hungry for draughts, like those coming through the high windows in the bathroom.

The women crawled quickly along the hallway to the head of the secondary staircase. The smoke there was like black mud, obscuring everything. The women stopped, coughing through their muffling towels. Then there was a flurry among them, a galvanising panic, as the head attendant rolled away into the muck, without a word or sign. The girls behind swayed with indecision, then followed, one after another. Rose hesitated a little longer. She hadn't seen the head attendant go — she'd been too far back. If she had, she might have thought — wrongly — that the woman had fainted and fallen. As it was, she followed the others into the smoke-filled stairway, followed them because it simply seemed better than being alone.

Rose tumbled down; she knocked against the walls, and against something soft. She kept her eyes closed, but felt sparks touch her face when she reached the bottom.

She found herself on a flat surface. She'd been turned around and wasn't quite sure where she was. The head attendant seemed to know, though, because she was gathering them together, crawling in a circle around the entire group. Rose was relieved to be able to see again. Here the smoke only poured blackly along the top half of the hallway, and was transparent below that. The clearest air was near the floor. It was as though the smoke were sediment, and had settled on the ceiling because the ceiling had its own gravity.

Rose felt the head attendant pulling at her, driving the decorative seed pearls on her gown into the flesh of her arm. It hurt, but when Rose turned back to detach the hand, she saw she was being hauled away from a drop.

The lower flights of the secondary staircase were entirely gone. The women were on a landing that ended in hanging strips of smouldering carpet and charred floorboards. Below that was a shaft full of fumes and sparks and rags of floating fire.

Now that she'd shown them what to avoid — and where they couldn't go to escape — the head attendant continued to crawl the other way, along the corridor that, Rose recalled, should join the main staircase.

Rose paused to fold her skirt up and stuff its hem under the boning of her waistband. She bared her knees, then picked up her wet towel and followed the others. She'd gone only a little way when a sensation brought her up short. A *memory* of a sensation she'd felt just a few moments before, and hadn't fully registered. On her tumble down the stairs she had struck something soft. Now she knew that it was a body in a dress and petticoats — a girl like her.

Rose dropped her towel, turned around, got her feet under her and plunged past the open shaft and back up the stairs. She ran up five, eight, ten steps, her arms out wide, touching the top of each step. She held her breath. Then she felt silky cloth, and a solid body under it. She followed the shape of the limb, and closed both her hands on one of the girl's ankles. She threw her weight backwards, and dragged the girl down the stairs.

Once Rose had the girl out in clearer air she saw it was another debutante, a girl from a class a year ahead of hers at the Academy. Rose found her towel and slapped the girl's face with it. She shouted her name. The girl didn't stir: her face was a terrible colour, waxy, her lips tinged black as though the smoke had been kissing her. Rose shook the girl, who flopped, her head banging on the carpet.

Then, through her own hoarse shouting, Rose heard her name: 'Rose!'

Rose dropped the girl — the *dead* girl — and retreated. She scuttled along the hallway in the direction she'd seen the others go. The smoke seemed to be thinning, streaming away faster behind her, and sucked into something ahead of her. It was as if where she was — perhaps halfway along the hallway that joined the two staircases — were at a tipping point, a summit with solid avalanches of smoke breaking loose on either side of her.

'Rose!' The call came again. It was a deep voice, like an echo out of a dark cave. It wasn't the voice of the head attendant.

Suddenly Rose saw the others. They were a distance away, their faces and figures brightly lit and stripped of their individuality by the colour of fire. The head attendant was signalling to her, Rose was sure. Then, the next moment, she was equally sure the woman was trying to call another of their number back to her. Rose recognised the mother of the girl who had been left behind on the stairs. She recognised her by her finery — all the other women were attendants, not guests at the ball. And Rose recognised her too by the expression on her face — one of horror and despair.

Rose lurched up and ran towards the woman. She didn't want the mother to see her daughter. She knew that if the woman went back she wouldn't stir again, she wouldn't make any further efforts to escape. Rose saw all this at once, her mind making calculations full of people instead of figures. The face and name of this woman's younger daughter, a cheeky junior at the Academy, came instantly to Rose. Her memory of the existence of this girl seemed to jump right into her body and drive her forwards, so that she collided with the woman and sent her hurtling back across the landing and into the others, who were crammed in the doorway of a room — a room that was dark, though only with night, not smoke.

Rose struck so hard that she rebounded. Her weight shifted. And then the whole landing moved too, under her. It tilted and tipped her towards —

— *heat*. Rose flung out a hand and caught hold of the edge of a decorative shield, part of the high-relief carvings on the wall panels of every one of the palace's main chambers. The shield was only gilded plaster — it crumbled under her touch — but it helped her regain her balance.

Rose saw that below her the whole main staircase was on fire. Fire had climbed its sweeping curves, consuming every atom of carpet and curtaining. Flame flowed over all the carvings, a film of fire like some spiritous liquid. All the shields, crossed swords, wheat sheaves, bunches of grapes, lions, griffins, cherubs, ribbons and bows — everything retained its shape beneath its fiery double. It was as if the fire meant to make a mould of all the baroque glories of the palace so that it could be formed afresh one day.

Rose saw all this in flashes, her eyes squeezed down to their narrowest and pouring tears.

The other women were shouting at her. She couldn't make out their words. The fire was too loud, as loud as the engine of an express train blasting through a country station — but a roar without rhythm.

Rose heard her name once more. The sound came from below her. Shielding her face with her hand she looked first at the women — they were signalling her to come to them, to dare to run across the tilting landing. And she then squinted down into the maelstrom of fire.

Laura's sandman was below her, pressed against the wall on the curve of the staircase. He hadn't been there a moment ago. The fire was licking the panels and the wooden treads of the great stairs, but it shunned his body, finding nothing of interest in it. Laura's monster had always appeared to Rose as a shadow, a shapely, shadowy body — now he shimmered in the light of the flames, as though his skin were covered in frost. He moved another two steps up, in one bound.

The landing jolted and tilted further. Rose fell to her knees and dug her fingers into the crumbling plaster. Her cousin's sandman stopped and stood still. Rose imagined that his eyes were directed not at her, but at the underside of the landing visible to him. He dared another step, but it was *his* weight disturbing the fragile equilibrium of the staircase. He stepped, and it shuddered and gave more.

Above the roar and sharp cracking of the fire Rose caught the thread of a call. She looked at the women again and saw that the dark room beyond them had opened up. From where she hung Rose could see along a series of rooms, through several doors, to a window. The window was open and one of the women — the head attendant, Rose thought — was standing before it. Beyond her was the façade of another building. Rose recognised its arched windows as those of the State Library. There was a window directly opposite the one where the woman stood. It too was open. There were men at it, leaning out and slowly feeding a ladder across from one building to the other. Rose could see that the ladder had wheels on the end pointing her way. It was a library ladder. The head attendant reached for it, pulled it towards her, then flipped it over so that the wheels locked onto the edge of the windowsill. She turned Rose's way — Rose saw her face flash orange in the firelight. The head attendant began to call and signal to the clustered women. They had been facing Rose, but then they all turned away and ran towards the window and ladder — without a backward glance.

Rose slid her hands along the wall, and edged a foot along the sloping floor. It shuddered. She glanced at Laura's sandman. He was motionless. Then he slowly raised an arm and pointed towards Rose's avenue of escape. He was encouraging her to go, to try it.

She edged forward. The landing quivered again as something beneath it wrenched and dropped. Then the floor suddenly bucked and pitched Rose forward. She caught herself on stiff extended arms. The floor had turned into a flat chute pointing Rose down at the fire. The heat blasted her face. She smelled burning hair and scorching fabric and scrabbled backwards. Then her hands were on her slippery skirt and she lost her grip on the slope. She slid forward, crying out, the hot air slamming into her mouth. Her fingers found carpet and again dug in. She spun around and went up the slope, her eyes wide open. She saw handholds, whatever would give her purchase. The floor was moving, but not one of her lunges missed its mark. She seized every safe hold just an instant before it gave way, just long enough to propel herself upward.

Finally she found herself suspended, her hips and legs hanging over a drop, her arms, head and shoulders on the firm floor of the hall beyond the landing. She heaved herself all the way onto the landing, then beat out the fire on her skirt with her hands, still in the remnants of her ripped gloves. Her dancing slippers were smoking, her stockings were a web of shrivelled silk through which showed utterly hairless, pink skin.

Rose swarmed back from the drop, but the floor was firm. A series of supporting walls beneath her had held up (and, in fact, would still be standing more than a day later, when the fire finally burned itself out).

Rose looked across the gap at that faraway window. She could see two women still waiting to cross, and another hunched shape crawling slowly along the ladder. She could see the urgent faces and beckoning hands of the librarian rescuers. Rose looked away. She turned her eyes down to Laura's sandman, who stood, his face turned up to her. As she watched he set his hands back against the wall behind him. He flexed his knees. He was preparing to jump — to try to join her.

For a moment Rose went weak with hope and relief. She wasn't going to be left alone and have to save herself.

Nown leaped. The steps came loose from the wall and dropped away behind him, robbing his leap of any impetus. He arched out and up towards the edge of the landing, his body stretched as though each particle could provide propulsion to the one above it and force him upward. He hung in the air. Then his snatching hands fell short, and he went down. His lower body fell first, his arms and head and blank face followed. Far below, and still falling, he condensed back into a proper human shape against the fire. Then the fire swallowed him, and he was gone.

Rose got to her feet and fled, back along the hallway to what remained of the secondary staircase. There was less smoke in the hall now — the fire below had finished burning carpets, curtains, paintwork, whatever would produce a lot of smoke. It had moved on to consuming the dry and seasoned timbers of the palace's interior. The heat funnelled through the hall behind Rose and propelled her along. She hesitated at the sight of the black-lipped body of her schoolmate, then averted her gaze and ran up the stairs.

The third floor was hot and full of smoke. The air wasn't moving, the fire wasn't being pulled that way. But as soon as Rose threw open the cloakroom door she felt, behind her, the fire belch and take hold and vault forward, moving up towards her.

The marble tiles of the bathroom were warm, but not smoking. The toilet seat she'd stood on perhaps only ten minutes earlier was still down. Rose lifted it and dipped her scorched feet in the bowl — but was still too inhibited by years of habit to cool her hands in the water. She kept her tattered gloves on, dropped the lid once more and stepped up onto it.

She was going to try to squeeze through the empty window frame. She thought perhaps she'd fit, but she'd done a lot of growing over the past two years and her sense of her own true size was with her only sometimes. At this moment she felt small, like a child who should be able, seeking safety, to cram itself into little spaces or escape through tiny gaps.

She found she needed something else to stand on. She thought of the dark dressing room and cloakroom behind her. She examined her memory and rejected the footstool — its legs were set too wide — the chairs (same problem), the basin (she had broken that). Then she remembered the seamstress's wicker sewing basket.

Rose ran out and felt her way around the side of the room where she knew the basket must be. She touched the stove — it was still hot. As she snatched her hand back, she knocked over the poker. If only she dared to open the door to the hall there would be more light — from the fire, the fire she mustn't let find her —

A moment passed when nothing happened. Rose coughed and didn't think. The clang of the falling poker echoed in her brain. Then she bent over, felt for it and picked it up. Holding the poker, she continued in her search for the sewing basket — round, wickerwork, sturdy enough to stand on. Then she felt the texture of plaited willow beneath her tattered glove. She put her arms around the basket and hurried back into the toilet. She placed the basket on the toilet seat and stepped up onto it. It creaked and rustled but held her weight. The window was right in front of her now. She measured the empty frame with her eyes, saw how the light caught in a few jagged bits of glass sticking up out of the cracked putty like teeth from gums. Rose thought: 'Laura could fit through this.' A silly thought, but Laura was the person with whom Rose had shared every moment of wriggling through places only children could wriggle through: the ventilation grille in the Academy cellars, some time in their junior year, and the wood-box at Laura's Aunt Marta's.

Rose pulled the empty frame down till it stopped against its catches. She shoved the poker into the gap and wrenched it back and forth. The frame gave suddenly, splintered at one corner. Rose began to work on the right angle that had remained firm. She demolished the frame, till it was a disjointed mess of splintered timber hanging from its hinges.

Rose dropped the poker and pushed her head and shoulders out through the window.

She found herself high above the gravelled back yards of several small buildings. There were signs of fire there — or of people's attempts to combat it. The back doors of all the buildings were open and the empty yards were full of dropped buckets and big puddles near the pumps. Even from where she was, Rose could see that all the walls were drenched.

She called out, her voice hoarse from smoke.

No one appeared.

She wriggled and writhed to get her hips out through the window. Her dress caught and tore as she moved. It scattered pearls. The window was too small for her to perch in it without a handhold. But it wasn't until she was almost all the way out that Rose found one: the guttering above her.

She stopped to catch her breath and cough, her legs still inside, her back to the drop. Without her grip on the guttering she would have fallen. Next, she knew, she would have to heave herself up over the lip of the guttering and onto the roof. She would need to keep her legs straight to get her knees out of the window.

Somewhere inside the palace something caved in with a series of crashes. The whole building shook. Far away, a crowd of people screamed together.

Rose sucked in the fresh air. She inched one hand forwards, feeling for a handhold beyond the guttering. It was a big square gutter with a high lip on its inner edge. Rose hooked her fingers over that and then began to pull herself simultaneously out of the window and onto the roof. Her shoulders and elbows popped, the muscles in her back stretched to snapping. Then her knees came out of the window and she was able to get her feet onto the sill, not to balance — there was no possibility of a pause to find her balance — but only to push up. She moved her other hand to the back lip of the gutter and, painfully scraping her breasts, forced her head and shoulders and chest onto the roof.

After that it was easy. She swung a knee up and was suddenly kneeling in the guttering set into the stonework. Ahead of her was a flat expanse of roof sealed with bitumen, and set with several skylights. The big skylight over the central staircase was like a greenhouse in which fire was growing and running riot. Around it the roof tar bubbled and smoked.

Rose got to her feet and made a long circuit around the big skylight. She went gingerly, because the tar was hot and soft, and because she was afraid the roof might collapse under her, sending her down — like Laura's sandman — into the heart of the fire.

Laura and Grace stood in the crowd and watched fire rise to fill every window of the front façade of the People's Palace. During those minutes someone came and draped a blanket over Grace's shoulders. She said, 'Thank you,' but her eyes never strayed from her watching. The engine and tender backed out of the side street on the north side of the building, retreating, the firemen hauling the heavy hoses back with them. More fire engines had arrived and hoses were in play over the whole front of the building. The smoke flowed straight up now, pushed by superheated air.

Someone put a hand on Laura's shoulder and she looked around and saw that it was her uncle. Chorley stood behind them, almost supporting himself on them. There was a bandage wound around his head. He caught Laura's look of horror and said, 'It's nothing. A bump.' He bit his lips. He didn't say, 'Where's Rose?'

Grace was weeping, and trembling from head to foot.

Some stranger first spotted Rose. He shouted and pointed at the figure in white, glimpsed through the smoke streaming from the plumes of fire that belched from every window. Then the whole crowd saw her and made a sound, a rumble of anxiety that gained volume and turned into urgent yelling. The firemen moved almost as one, turning their hoses on the windows directly beneath where Rose was standing.

Chorley and Grace ran into the confusion of water, shouting their daughter's name. The firemen rushed to hold the couple back. A fire engine was being moved. The fire-nets had been laid aside, unused. Now a group of firemen converged on one net. They spread it out, pulled it taut, lifted it and hurried across the plaza to stand beneath the corner of the building, the only place without windows, and so too without fountains of fire.

Laura could see that Rose was watching the firemen. She'd seen the net. She came nearer to the edge and picked up her skirt to climb out onto a jutting cornice.

It was then that the big skylight exploded. It sprayed glass in every direction. The crowd howled in terror, but the girl on the roof only dropped into a crouch and covered her head. Then she got up again, slowly. Her hair had come loose, and was floating straight up from her head like a bright flag. She stood looking down at the net, a slender figure in white, apparently utterly composed.

It was a long way down. The circle of the fire-net seemed a small hope. A twisting column of flame had erupted from the gap where a skylight had been. Rose could hear tar sizzling, she could see where the roof was sagging. The heat behind her was terrible. In a moment she'd be on fire.

Rose took a couple of steps back. She wanted to be sure she could jump far enough to clear all the masonry below her. Only two steps should do it. She kept her eyes on the circle of the net. She lined it up with her gaze, as she'd line up the deepest water when she was jumping at high tide from the rocks below Summerfort.

The crowd saw her retreat, and howled. Rose heard her parents' voices rise above the cacophony of the fire, the roar and splash of hoses, and all the other voices. Their despair made them audible — those cries could be heard through anything, it seemed, even through the rules of the universe.

Rose ran forward and jumped. The air rushed past her. Her feet flew up over her head so that she slapped, shoulders and back first, into the canvas. Her breath was knocked out of her. She bounced up once, then the canvas caught her and she lay tumbled on it, her elbows smarting.

Through the faces bent over her and the hands reaching for her, Rose looked up at the roof, which didn't seem so far away now. It really wasn't any surprise that she'd made it.

Then her Ma and Da and Laura appeared. The firemen laid the net down, so Rose was on solid ground. Her father scooped her up. He was crying. Her mother was crying. Laura was crying. But why on earth were all the other people crying, even the firemen? Weeping and touching her as though she were a holy relic.

Part XII
Epidemic Contentment

One

The fire burned for a night and a day, fuelled by coal stored in the palace cellar. When it was out, the smell of it hung, horrible, over much of the central city. There were no calling cards, no parade of mothers, no preparations for later balls. For a day Rose lay upstairs and coughed, then her cough quietened. Laura went out and called for Nown under the dark arch of Market Bridge, looked for him among the broken glass, rags and human waste. Then, when Rose was able to tell her story, she told Laura she'd seen Nown fall.

Laura lost track of time, but did wonder why Sandy hadn't come. Then, on the afternoon of the second day after the fire, George Mason arrived with red-rimmed eyes and his bad news. He stood in the library and showed the family what he had wrapped in his handkerchief in a nest of soot — the broken chain and charred copper tags of his nephew's dreamhunter's licence.

The next day, when Laura was sitting at the dinner table and her father was trying to persuade her to eat, even cutting up her food for her, Rose saw that Laura had a look like the façade of the People's Palace: stony, and still standing, but burned out inside.

Rose went to visit Mamie. She waited in the entrance hall and overheard Mrs Doran say to her daughter, 'Really, Mamie, it's so *common* of your friend just to turn up unannounced. It's to be discouraged.'

Rose heard Mrs Doran coming and darted away from the door. Mamie's mother emerged, gave Rose a smile with no buoyancy, and said, 'Mamie is waiting for you, please go in.'

'Thank you.' Rose opened the door a crack and flitted through it, trying not to touch anything as she went.

Mamie didn't get up, but did begin to fidget. She said, 'What's under the scarf?'

Rose touched her silk bandanna. 'My hair is frizzy at the front. I'll have to let it grow a bit before it can be fixed.'

'You look sphinx-like,' Mamie said.

'You mean I don't have any eyebrows. Frankly, being a sphinx stinks.'

Mamie said, 'Do you want tea?'

'No, thanks. Do you want to play hostess?'

'Not really.'

'Aren't you pleased to see me?' Rose said, pushing it rather.

'Yes.' Mamie straightened her spine; sat as a lady should. She looked like her grandmother, without that woman's supporting corsets. 'I saw you jump. There was even a picture of it in the papers.'

'I'm sorry that you felt I bossed you about the ball,' Rose said.

'Don't think about it. You meant well. And I couldn't have resisted Mother, anyway.'

Rose wriggled forward on her seat. 'Just because everyone imagines that coming out means we're advertising ourselves as available for marriage, that doesn't mean we have to experience it all that way. We don't have to take any of it seriously.'

Mamie shrugged. 'But have you thought what you're going to do with your life apart from getting married?'

'No. I've only thought what I might do for the next year or so. Have a final year at school, then travel around the country staying with all my classmates and distant relatives — really get to know the whole country, not just resorts like Sisters Beach and the spa in Spring Valley. Then, when I'm twenty-one, I can go to university.'

'To study what? And why?'

'Something for its own sake. Or law — for justice.'

Mamie gave Rose a slow smile. 'I'm going to eat until I'm so fat that everyone will leave me alone.'

'No, you're not,' Rose said, impatient. 'Da is going to teach me to drive. He can teach you too, if you'd like.'

'What on earth for?'

'Independence. Get up and go. Honestly, Mamie, complaining doesn't make you a rebel, only action makes anyone a rebel. We girls have to do what we can. Take whatever opportunities we're offered.'

'Tea?' Mamie offered again. 'There's some lovely almond cake.'

Rose laughed.

Mamie continued: 'What you have to realise, Rose, is that I'm not adventurous. Laura is your natural companion for adventures. You can't jolly me into joining you. It's not that I'm timid, it's just that I hate failure, and hate to be uncomfortable, and I don't particularly enjoy effort. I'm a lost cause.'

Rose looked at the floor. She thought: 'Whereas Laura is just lost.'

The day before, Laura had gone with Grace to see George Mason off at the station. Mason was taking Sandy's remains — a collection of carbonised bones — back to his family. Afterwards Laura had talked to Rose, in a wispy voice. She told Rose what she knew about Sandy's home — his six brothers and sisters. One brother was the head of the night shift at the sawmill. Another was an engineer in a railway workshop. His father was a shop steward at a factory that made flax matting. Laura talked about the year Sandy had spent working in that factory, about his school with its tattered books and sour hallways. Sandy's mother was a teacher at a similar girls' school. The family had tenuous respectability — all of them had stayed at school till fifteen.

Rose said to Mamie, 'Laura has had adventures I can't even imagine. She's even been in love. Her heart is broken.'

'Laura hasn't been lucky, has she?'

'No — Sandy, her mother . . .' Rose looked hard at Mamie. 'I suppose you've heard that her father's back?'

'I've heard that he's ill.'

'Yes. That's what has finally roused Laura. In a couple of days she is going In to get The Gate.'

'The miracle dream.'

'I've had it three times now.' Rose could feel her face softening. 'It's extraordinarily beautiful. It is proving a little controversial, though. At Fallow Hill it carried off any of their patients who were close to death, or ready to die. It can't be dreamed near anyone critically ill or injured who has any chance of recovery. What it does is tell whoever dreams it that there's something beautiful to go on to after death. It tells it with such conviction that very sick people just let go of life. But it's excellent for chronic illness, pain, madness and misery. I'm glad Laura's father has persuaded her to get it for him. Of course he's hoping it'll help *her*.'

'Is your mother planning to catch it too?'

'No. Ma is going further In to get End of the Drought. She's going to perform it at the Rainbow Opera. What Founderston needs after the fire is a balm of rain — and the dream's sloppy romance, and little white horses.'

'You forget I haven't had any of these dreams.'

'Oh,' said Rose, feeling awkward. She did keep forgetting that Mamie's mother hadn't let her daughter go to a dream palace.

Mamie was looking sly and thoughtful. 'Is End of the Drought a master dream?'

'I didn't know you knew anything about that.'

'I know *all* about it, despite my lack of first-hand experience.'

'I don't think it is a master dream.'

Mamie rearranged herself and seemed to change the subject. 'Well,' she said, 'I'm getting on a train tomorrow night. My father is sending me off to our summer residence.'

'Alone?'

'The servants will be there.'

'Does your father think you need a holiday?'

'No.' Mamie stared into Rose's eyes.

Rose searched her friend's face. Mamie was looking sphinx-like, though she still had her eyebrows. She was trying to tell Rose something, to tell without actually saying.

'Or,' said Rose, 'does he just think you'll be better off out of Founderston?'

And Mamie said, 'That must be it.'

* * *

It was Rose who remembered the film, five days after the fire. Chorley developed it and they all sat down to watch it.

Laura saw that Nown had cranked the camera a little too slowly, so that the film's action was fast, the captives and rangers jerky and insectile in their movements. There was shutter-flicker, as though the camera were peering through eyes that were blinking away tears. But there were the huts, the barracks, the canvas-walled rooms of the Depot.

'How did you get this?' Chorley said.

'I didn't,' Laura said. 'I was here.'

'We sent someone,' said Tziga.

When Nown had been shooting the footage Laura had been lying in Sandy's arms within the circle of Foreigner's West. They had got up and folded the blankets and she had given up one life for another. Nown had betrayed her. He was heartless. He should have told her what he must have known. He'd always carried her but — in a way — he'd made her walk. Her long, hard journey might have been simple and short if only he'd said, 'The Place is the same thing I am, a Nown — that's something you need to know.' The Place had been showing her convicts long before her father left her his letter saying she must do something for them — a letter that told her to catch a terrible nightmare, and share it with innocent citizens. She'd hurt people, and wasted the little time she had had with Sandy, when if only she'd known, she could have asked Nown what on earth was it that his other self must want from those it gave its dreams?

Chorley said, 'I'll take this to the Grand Patriarch. I imagine he'll want to present it to the Commission.'

'Make a copy first,' Tziga said.

Grace said, 'I hate having to rely on that old man to get things straightened out.'

'We're not relying on him, we are consulting with him,' Chorley snapped.

Laura thought how strange it was that her aunt was still able to imagine things being 'straightened out', as though all that had to happen was that Cas Doran be exposed and the Regulatory Body be encouraged to mind its own business. Grace seemed to think that if those things were accomplished then dreamhunters would be able to get back to their prospecting and performing in peace. Rose and Chorley and Tziga wanted Doran stopped and punished. They wanted to weed out corruption. Was Laura's aunt right to look to a time beyond that, to order and everyday life?

Laura thought nothing could be mended. And she was sure she was thinking just as straight as her Aunt Grace. So which of them was right?

The family agreed that Laura shouldn't be left alone. But only Rose understood what that meant. As soon as her cough eased, Rose had taken to climbing into Laura's bed. She didn't try to watch with Laura, to stay awake and stare into the dark — she slept, but she was there.

The night they screened the film, Rose fell asleep almost the moment she put her head on her pillow. She woke after an hour or two, from a dream in which she wandered along red-painted hallways, unable to open any of the doors because their handles burned her hands.

'Nightmare?' said Laura, from the other side of the bed.

'Yes. There's never any fire in my nightmares. Just heat.'

'I still have nightmares where I'm thirsty.'

Rose turned over and tried to see her cousin. There was a little light coming in the window from the street, enough so that the shadows of the flowers on the frosted-glass lamp on the nightstand were visible. Rose could see the lumpy shadow that was her cousin, and the glimmer of Laura's eyes. Because it was dark Rose felt a little daring. She said, 'Have you thought that you could make your sandman again?'

'He let me down,' Laura said, her voice flat.

'He couldn't help it.'

'Not in the fire. Before that.'

'So you won't make him again because you're angry with him?'

'I won't make him again because I can't make Sandy.'

Rose thought about the logic of Laura's statement. Of course it was flawless. It made perfect sense. Rose knew that her cousin had loved both of them, Sandy and the monster. Laura wouldn't resurrect one if she couldn't resurrect the other.

'It's not just a decision,' Laura said. 'I think it's prohibited. My need is great, but I can't feel the song. When I found Da's sandman, but before I knew "The Measures", I could feel this storm of music around me. Now I don't feel anything.'

Rose found one of Laura's hands under the covers and held it.

'I'm just going to be good and do what I'm asked. Then maybe I'll stop feeling so sick and tired. Sandy felt like my family and my future.'

Rose squeezed Laura's hand.

Laura said, 'Wouldn't it be terrible if none of us had futures, only fates?'

'I don't believe in fate,' Rose said. It was true — Rose believed in the poker, the sewing basket, the broken window, the rooftop, the fire-net, the way out. She believed in reprieve. And she was sure that, sooner or later, she would think of some way to help Laura. Something would come to her — it was only a matter of time.

Two

Saturday evening. Two men, one tall, the other small, walked slowly back across Market Bridge from the Isle of the Temple. The evening was autumnal and there was a white fume rising from the surface of the river.

Other pedestrians they passed glanced, then turned to stare after them.

'It's taking a while for the word to get around Founderston that you're not dead,' Chorley said.

'I've been sequestered at home, or at Fallow Hill.'

'After Monday we'll be able to deal with the reports of your death. We can bring up the matter of the forged signature in the Doorhandle Intentions Book.'

'After Monday that will be an even smaller matter than it is already.'

Chorley and Tziga had shown the film of the Depot to the Grand Patriarch. On Monday afternoon the Commission of Inquiry was due to convene again. Their report would be published soon. All submissions had been read, all witnesses questioned, all arguments heard. But the seven men of the Commission were due to meet again to discuss their findings — and the Grand Patriarch intended to deliver the film to them, with Laura and her testimony.

'I wouldn't like to be in Doran's shoes after Monday,' Chorley said. 'Though he must have been forewarned. Your cameraman was spotted. In the final seconds of the film a ranger points at him.' Chorley was quiet for a moment, then added, 'He'll have to testify too, I expect.'

Tziga was silent.

'Tziga? Why did Erasmus ask you how you got the film? I thought the cameraman was his agent.'

Tziga looked vague and baffled, and Chorley was once again overcome by nervous tenderness towards his damaged friend. 'Never mind,' he said. 'Don't worry about it.'

They came off the bridge onto the west embankment. The air was still, but nevertheless carried the smell of damp, burned timber.

When they arrived home they were met by a one-girl whirlwind. Rose was wrapped in a thick shawl. She said the house was cold. She said there were fires laid already, kindling and coal under a summer's worth of dust. 'Could someone else please put a match to them? I'm allergic to matches. Temporarily, I hope.' She followed her father into the parlour and, as he knelt to light the fire, she stood behind him, ranting. 'I'm sick of salad and eggs and bread,' she said. 'Now that Uncle Tziga's no longer a big secret, could we *please* get back our cook and maids?'

'Cook left last year. She retired to nurse her sick sister. Remember?' Chorley said.

'Why would I remember? I wasn't here. I was boarding at school, and eating boiled bacon and boiled broccoli and boiled bloody potatoes.'

'We can summon the maid back any time. She's only on leave. Paid leave.'

'This family is hopeless!' Rose raved. 'Renting rooms they don't use. Paying maids to take holidays. Throwing money at problems!'

Chorley got up and stared at his daughter with wide eyes. 'What on earth has got into you?'

'The Doran house is packed with servants. Mamie and her mother can sit around being ornamental. What would we have done if gentlemen *had* come calling for me? Fed them dried fruit and boiled eggs with their black tea?'

'Sorry,' said Chorley. 'I'll place an advertisement for a cook on Monday. After Monday everything will be different. We'll sit down and talk about the future. You and I. We'll make some plans.'

'Fine,' said Rose. She came to stand beside her father and leaned against him, not to be friendly, but to edge him aside so that she stood directly in front of the fire's warmth. She said, 'So it's to be Monday, then?'

'That's when the Commission reconvenes. Would you like to go with us — Laura and Tziga and I, and the Grand Patriarch and his people?'

'No. I don't want Mamie to hear I was in on the kill. She'll probably never speak to me again anyway.'

Chorley put an arm around his daughter. 'Are you warmer now, dear?'

'Yes.'

'I'd better go and see what Tziga is up to. Part way through your tirade he headed for the kitchen.'

'Oh no!' Rose rushed off to rescue the food from her uncle's absent-minded efforts.

Chorley was in bed by eleven, but it took him a long time to go to sleep. He would be drifting off but would wake up with his heart pounding, startled by the memory of his daughter's plunge from the roof of the People's Palace, or by panic at all the little things he'd left undone. He hadn't talked to Rose about what she wanted to do this year. And how was Laura? Just how involved with that Mason boy had she allowed herself to become? Was Tziga any better? Would Grace be safe walking Inland alone?

Taken together, all these little worries and serious frights kept rousing Chorley till around three in the morning, when he fell asleep in the midst of a memory of the Depot film — the pyjama-clad figures in flickering black and white, an agitated picture of serene sleepwalkers.

The man was with his family. They were trailing up from the beach after an early morning swim. The blond sandstone of his house caught the light of the lifting sun. In the high tide, the forest seemed to come right down to the water, so that the headland spilled over its reduced shoreline like a gem bulging with light above a gold setting. In the scoop of the bay, two sails were visible, and one far-off smudge of smoke from a steamer's funnel. The man gazed at the horizon and had a sense of the world beyond his peaceful property going on, industrious and in good order.

As he strolled and looked about him the man was filled with satisfaction at everything he saw. He realised that this was one of those moments when it seemed the world itself stopped him and clasped his hand and gave him its congratulations.

He stopped walking. He took a cigar and his cigar trimmer from the pocket of his dressing gown. He trimmed his cigar to his satisfaction, then lit it, and blew out smoke of a creamy texture and bluish tinge, the taste of which reminded him of other pleasures he'd taken — meals eaten, deals struck, rivals beaten. He planted his legs and stood in his orchard, his bearded chin tilted up, blowing smoke into the branches above him.

Wasps had burrowed in the hanging shells of the last apricots of the season. The smoke dislodged them and the man watched, delighted, as the insects kept on seeking the lost sweetness through the smoke, dogged and stupid.

'It was all worth it,' thought the man. 'All the risks I took, all the sacrifices I made.' Before him — yesterday, today, tomorrow — was the proof of the good he'd done himself: his beautiful house and happy family.

He could see his mother on the terrace, with her silver tea service, and old-world shawl. She was ninety years of age, and still straight-backed and sound of mind. With her was his second wife. She'd seen him. She was coming down the terrace steps. In a moment she'd join him and he'd put his hand in the small of her slender back.

His son and daughter passed him, in friendly conversation. He watched them with gratification. He'd been wrong ever to worry about them, since, true to their mother's habitual saying, they were the cream that had risen to the top of society. His son looked every inch the prosperous businessman he was — a major stockholder in the nation's largest utilities company.

The man detected that advice was being offered, brother to sister, and that it was a happy exchange. His daughter had mellowed, had grown up generous and grateful and good. He had been foolish to worry about her too — though he could always say to himself now that worrying about her was part of doing well by her.

One of his granddaughters stopped beside him. 'Look, Grandfather!' she said, and did a cartwheel.

'Very good,' said the man, then, 'Watch out for the wasps.'

She did. She was careful. She called out the same advice to her younger sister. There were no mishaps. He could hear them, their laughter broken up by grunts of effort as they practised all the way to the house.

The eels the boys had caught yesterday would be smoked and boned and ready for breakfast. The man had a good appetite. He ground out his cigar on the trunk of the apricot tree.

The girls had gone indoors, and the inlet became for a moment a silent arena in which the future — his future — breathed like an expectant audience. Yes, it had all been worth it, the brinkmanship, the qualms of conscience. He had taken things on himself, had made hard decisions for others, and had been rewarded by this peace — and by being right. He was the architect of the prosperity of his nation. It had all turned out for the best. And he knew that he was, in the balance of time, a better man than most.

The orchard grew warmer, and the wasps took themselves off to their bush nests.

His grandsons came last, gingerly walking barefoot by him. They were strong boys, sun-browned, carrying their canoe paddles.

For another moment the man was by himself in the warm morning. He was utterly content. Whatever wrongs he'd committed were only, in the end, part of this loveliness, this life he'd made, this nation he'd shaped, this whole beautiful day ahead of him.

Three

On that same Saturday, Grace drove Laura to Doorhandle, their bones shaken by the bad early autumn roads. Before either of them went In, they asked for a claim form at the Chief Ranger's office, and filled it out. Laura staked her claim on The Gate. They made a note of where they were going in the Intentions Book, then walked In together.

They went to Foreigner's West and Grace sat beside Laura as she slept. Then Grace kept Laura company again to the coach stop at Doorhandle, before heading back In herself on a three-day round trip to the site of End of the Drought.

Laura was in the waiting room by the stagecoach stop when she heard an announcement that, because of a cracked wheel-rim, departure would be delayed an hour. She looked at her watch and then went out. She wasn't hungry, so she wandered up and down the short boardwalks browsing shop windows. She was doing this when she saw from a distance one of the Misses Lilley coming her way, and decided that she simply couldn't face *any* Lilleys.

Laura ducked into an alley between the draper's and butcher's and came out on the slope down to the banks of the Rifleman.

There was a bridle path by the river. Laura walked along it, away from the border, until only Doorhandle's church steeple was visible over the riverside trees.

Most of the flowers had gone to seed, but the Queen Anne's lace had lasted and stood waist high. There were big dragonflies zooming back and forth across the path, and whenever one passed close, Laura would warily stop to see what it was going to do. They had always liked to fly into Rose's hair and Laura was worried that since Rose and her hair weren't present, the insects might find *her* attractive instead. But the dragonflies swerved around her as if she were protected by an invisible barrier.

It was very quiet on the path. The native birds had, for the most part, gone back into the forest — everything they liked to eat was over. With the bullying parson birds gone, the thrushes were back and singing. Laura stopped to listen to one, its song a flow of joy so sure it was almost matter of fact.

The breeze dropped altogether and the sun seemed to kiss the tops of Laura's ears.

Then there came a vibration — footfalls on the path behind her. Laura remembered that she wasn't supposed to be alone. That there were reasons other than her bereavement why her family was sticking so close to her. She turned — and threw up her hands. She was dazzled. The low sun shone, magnified, through a volume of glass. The sun melted as the glass moved.

Laura closed her eyes and cried out.

Someone spoke, said her name in a deep, melodious voice — a voice she didn't know.

Laura opened her eyes again and looked at where the voice had come from. The patch of magnified, blinding sunlight had gone. The thing between her and the sun had moved. She could get a better look at it now. What she saw was a human-shaped volume of glass. She could see trees and grass and the river through the body, distorted, twisted like the petals of colour at the heart of a glass marble.

Laura backed into the cloud layer of Queen Anne's lace and didn't stop till she met the trunk of a tree.

He approached her slowly, the glass Nown, and as he came she saw a smear of dirty bread dough in his abdomen — all that remained of her little bread-and-dust man. She saw the solid lump of dark matter in his chest: a rust-stained rock from the track bed.

She saw that he wasn't completely, limpidly transparent but had, in his human-shaped volume, here and there, bubbles hanging like frog spawn in pond water. She saw that the different thicknesses of his different parts made shadows within him, and that these weren't shadow-coloured, but bronze and indigo and blue-black. The shadows and distorted world melted in him as he came towards her — *moved*, a glass statue that was flexible, as if still molten.

As he came close, Laura saw that the soles of his feet were frosted by the wear of walking. Up close his hand was white too — or, because he put his hand up to touch her face, the white might only have been her breath misting the glass of his palm.

Nown stooped. He brought his head down to hers so that their foreheads were pressed together. Laura didn't say anything. She only rubbed her face against his. Her cheeks were wet with tears and squawked against his smooth glass skin.

He put an arm around her to support her. She could scarcely stand, and couldn't speak. His skin was warm from the sun, but unyielding. Her hand against his jaw felt a fake sinew like a seam of some harder mineral in a sea-worn stone. His jaw moved, but stayed as hard as any stone. He said, 'Rose?'

Laura cried harder.

'I called,' he said. 'And I was lucky, she was near. It didn't take me too long to find her in the fire. But the staircase was eaten away by then and I did more harm than good. I'm sorry. I promise in the future to do more, to do — *I know not what* — to save whomever you love.'

Laura clung to him. She had the feeling that something blocked had burst open and she was being swept towards the future she had thought she'd lost. She choked out, 'Rose saved herself,' and felt him relax — as much as anything unyielding could be said to.

'Sit down,' Nown said, and lowered her to the ground. He knelt before her. His body became the yellow-green of grass and flower stalks, his head milky with flowers — filled, and surrounded, and crowned with flowers. Laura touched his face again. It was a little unclear where he began and ended. He was there, and not there. And it was more difficult than ever to read any expression on his face.

After a long while, when the light was turning gold and midges had gathered under the tree, Laura was calm enough to tell Nown what had happened. She told him about Sandy. 'Men must have been lying in wait for him,' she said. 'The Gate had turned him into an even more formidable Soporif than his Uncle George. His uncle thinks he was knocked out in a struggle, and took everyone down with him. The men who attacked him were carrying lamps. None of them would have been conscious when the fire started.'

Nown sat still and seemed to be thinking. Laura watched him and considered how she'd felt betrayed by him. How she'd given him up in her heart, and wrapped herself in Sandy — Sandy's warm flesh, her sense that Sandy was a real life, a true future. She considered that some of her willingness to fall into all that — love, and promising her life — was made up of fury at Nown. She had felt spiteful and righteous. Now she didn't know what she felt. Her feelings were so strange, beyond relief, or reprieve, or gratitude.

She took a deep breath. 'The site of The Gate is on the border and inside a big O that someone has inscribed on the ground. For years rangers have supposed that the O stands for *Ouest* — the French word for west. They suppose that because there's also a big N on the ground in the north. N for *Nord*, they think. But when I saw the O, and Sandy told me about the N, I knew what it really was. What the Place really *is*. Why didn't you tell me that the Place was a Nown?'

'You didn't ask.'

'That isn't an answer. Once I'd freed you, why didn't you tell me? You must have understood that it was something I needed to know.'

'Yes.'

'Why didn't you, then?'

'I didn't know what would happen.'

Laura reached out, put her knuckles against his rock-hard shoulder and gave him a hard shove. He didn't stir.

'I couldn't foresee the consequences for you and me if I told you.'

'Couldn't you just act in good faith?'

'My freedom isn't like yours, Laura. I think that whenever I have to choose what to do, I have to know what will happen. My free will has laws, it seems. Because I cannot lose my soul, my free will must have laws.'

This somehow all made sense to Laura. It made her feel terribly tired, but better. She'd been wrong to resent him — she was always wrong when she expected him to act like a human. She sighed — she had just realised that she'd missed the coach. She asked Nown, 'Why didn't you come to find me in Founderston?'

'It was only yesterday that I was able to dig myself out. They had finally moved enough of the debris to make the ash loose around me.'

'I thought you'd been destroyed.'

'I fell into a pit of coal. It was burning. There were hours when I thought I might not be able to go on. To go on distinguishing myself from the burning coal. We were the same temperature and I became confused about where the coal ended and I began. Then I felt myself melting, and as I melted I reduced, and found myself, my limits. I drew some air into me so I wouldn't shrink too much. I didn't want to be small. And, as I took that breath, I remembered that Laura had made me, and that I'd promised to watch Laura, and never to hurt her. I kept myself together, and cooled. And then I had to wait.'

Laura looked at him. The sun was bristling through him now, broken by the shadows of the trees across the river. 'All right,' she thought, 'this is my life.' What she said was, 'Father needs me, I have The Gate for him. Can you get me to Founderston before midnight?'

'Yes.'

She studied him. He'd not be too visible in the dark, but by daylight he was conspicuous. He could no longer pretend to be a stone. She was sure that although he could move, he could no longer stretch or flatten, or make a comfortable sling of his arms to carry her in. Then she had an idea. She knew where she could find clothes he could wear. She had a moment of confusion about her plan — it was practical, but it made her a little queasy. 'You stay here,' she said. 'I'll be right back.'

Laura left him. She hurried back to the village and to Mrs Lilley's boarding house.

She asked her landlady about the trunk she was storing. George Mason had asked Grace to tell Mrs Lilley that he would drop by in a day or two to collect his nephew's belongings. Laura said to her landlady that George Mason had told her she could have one or two of Sandy's things. Conveniently, tears filled her eyes as she spoke.

Mrs Lilley patted Laura's shoulder, took her to the box room and gave her the key to Sandy's trunk.

Half an hour later Nown was clothed in trousers, a knitted hat and Sandy's long dreamhunter's duster coat. Laura saw that her sandman hadn't wholly managed to combat the shrinkage caused by his change from river sand to glass, despite the frog-spawn skeins of bubbles he'd drawn into his body. He was nearer to Sandy's size now: a little over six foot, and as slender as a young man. He'd kept all his proportions, but there was less of him.

As Laura stood gazing at Nown and wondering about the change, he finished buttoning the coat and slipped his glass hands into his pockets, to see how much bright surface he could hide. Something in the pocket rustled, and Nown drew out a piece of paper. He gave it to Laura.

It was a yellowing newspaper clipping. It was a photograph of her, looking fearfully through the veil of her new hat, into the blast of a photographer's magnesium flash, on the day of her Try.

Laura folded the picture and put it in her own pocket. Then she held her arms out, and Nown picked her up and began to run with her, upriver, away from Doorhandle.

Four

Laura didn't get to Fallow Hill till after midnight, so missed speaking to her father. It was Nown who held her up at the end of their journey, by arguing about leaving her. She had to insist that she'd be all right, she'd be with her father. Nown finally let himself be persuaded, and took himself off to Market Bridge.

Laura settled in the room beside the one she'd always shared with Sandy. They'd liked the room whose single bed was against a wall, so that they could share it with less danger of tumbling out. Laura chose to sleep in the adjacent room, in a narrow iron bed. She dreamed The Gate and woke to find sunlight filling the room, because she'd forgotten to close the curtains. She got up and went to find her father, who, it turned out, *hadn't* checked in the night before.

Laura was alarmed. She said no thank you to breakfast and set off home.

She caught a tram. It was early, but the usually packed Monday morning coach was as empty as a Sunday evening one. Laura got off in the market. The farmers' stalls were full, but the market wasn't. Laura didn't notice the anxious stallholders — she was intent on getting to her favourite pastry shop, on a corner near her house.

When she arrived at the shop, she was disappointed to find the trays under the counter almost empty.

'Do you have any pinwheels?' she asked the woman behind the counter.

'I have cream cornets, almond puffs and Eccles cakes. All the ones *I* like best,' the woman said, and beamed.

'All right, I'll have eight almond puffs.'

The woman slipped them into a bag. She passed them to Laura and left Laura's money lying on the counter, though a little change was due.

'What a beautiful day,' the woman said.

Laura said, 'Mmmm,' and waited a moment longer for the woman to ring up the sale and give her change. Then she blushed, and left.

The awnings were still closed on the newsagent's kiosk opposite Market Bridge. Bundles of the *Founderston Herald* lay beside it, the strings fastening them still uncut. Laura steered around the bundles and dashed down the steps by the bridge. Before she got to the first arch she saw a pile of clothes lying in the bottom of a boat tethered to a ring by the steps. She recognised the knitted hat on top of the pile. Then she saw, against the submerged steps below her, a clear patch in the river, like raw egg-white dropped into milky tea. The patch stirred and unfolded, and water rose up out of the water, shedding water. Nown walked up the steps.

'It can't matter to you that your clothes stay dry,' Laura said, pointing at the bundle in the boat.

'They're not my clothes,' said Nown.

Laura went back up onto the embankment and looked about, both ways. She could hear traffic on the bridge, but there was no one in sight. She told Nown to put his clothes — *the* clothes — back on.

She took him home and into the back yard. She planned to smuggle him up to her room later. 'I can always run a bath and hide you in it,' she said. Then, 'Can you *see* water now?'

'No. I can't see through it either. I felt you on the steps by the river. I can always feel you as you come towards me.'

Laura stood with him, thinking about what he'd said. She knew she should go in. She needed to know what had happened to her father to keep him from his appointment at Fallow Hill. But the yard was quiet and familiar and private — and she wasn't unhappy. She laid her palm against her servant's side. His shirt — Sandy's shirt —

was damp, having blotted the river water from his surface. He felt like stone under the cloth. 'And what do I feel like as I come towards you?'

'Laura,' he said.

She removed her hand and went towards the back door.

'Laura,' he said again, and she turned back to him. But he was only finishing his answer. 'Laura, who is life,' he said. 'But not *just* Laura.'

'I should hope not. There's life everywhere,' Laura said, somewhat primly. She lifted the latch, pushed the door and went inside.

'Laura and someone else now,' Nown finished, speaking to the closed door.

Laura found boiled eggs, broken and mashed into the flagstones of the kitchen floor. She stopped and stared at them, then hurried on into the hall. She called, 'Hello!'

'Hello, darling!' Rose called back.

Rose was lying on the window seat in the morning room, in her dressing gown. She was playing with the tassel of the curtain, catching it and tweaking it with her toes.

'Are you all right?' Laura asked.

'Yes. Isn't it a lovely day?' Rose stretched, arched her back, subsided, continued to pluck at the cord.

'Have an almond puff.'

Rose sat up and took one. She tucked in. She gave a little grunt of happiness.

'Where's Da?'

'Don't know,' Rose said, muffled and scattering flakes of pastry.

'Isn't he up yet?'

'He was up for breakfast,' Rose answered. Then she giggled. 'We forgot the eggs and they almost boiled dry. They were bouncy.'

Laura went to look for her father upstairs. His door was open and he was asleep in a pickle of bedclothes. He looked peaceful, so she left him.

Chorley was in the library, listening to his gramophone. He too was in his pyjamas and dressing gown. He had little purple dots of spilled jam on his front. The top of his desk was clear, but for a row of gramophone cylinders lined up across it. All his papers, notebooks, even his inkstand had been pushed to the floor.

'Laura, listen to this!' Chorley said. He raised a hand to conduct the tenor's squeezed voice for a few bars of the song. 'This music reminds me of eating dinner outdoors,' he said. '*Alfresco*. Surrounded by family. How wonderful it is to be surrounded by family.'

'Well — yes,' Laura said. She couldn't believe she was looking at her uncle wearing food stains. She didn't think she'd ever seen him drop food on himself. He could even eat ice-cream without mishap in a stiff wind.

He kept his hand up, conducting, his arm moving just a little off the beat. 'It was all worth it,' he said, dreamily. 'I put in the time, and ended up with this — all the time in the world,' he said.

Laura backed out of the room and into the hall. She leaned on the wall, her legs watery.

A few minutes later Laura was back in the yard. She was carrying a pair of her uncle's slippers and a long scarf and gloves. She gave them to Nown. He sat down to put the slippers on. She had to help him with the gloves.

'Your hands are shaking,' he said.

'My family have had that dream. Contentment. They're all blissful and silly,' she said. Her voice had a tremor too.

Nown wound the scarf around his lower face. He was overdressed for the weather, which was still warm. He looked a little sinister — or as sinister as anyone in slippers could. Yet no one would imagine his bundled figure was anything but human.

Laura walked out of the yard. Nown followed her. He didn't ask where they were going, or what they'd do.

As Laura walked she saw all the things she'd not noticed before, like how quiet the streets were — a Monday like Sunday. And that none of the people who were out and about were in a hurry, and all looked friendly and happy.

The motorists on Market Bridge were the same as ever, jostling and impatient. Most were from outlying suburbs. They were going about their business and perhaps felt just as baffled as Laura by a choice of only three pastries in their favourite patisserie, and the *Founderston Herald* printed, packaged, but not on sale.

Laura and Nown crossed the river to the Isle of the Temple. They made their way to Temple Square. Laura told Nown to wait for her in St Anthony's Chapel, which was on the northwest corner of the nave and always full of shadows in the morning.

Laura went to the Grand Patriarch's palace and told one of the caped guards at the gate that she wanted to see His Eminence.

After a long time, over an hour, Laura rejoined her glass man in St Anthony's Chapel. It was gloomy and uninviting, but Nown wasn't the only one there. There were two women at the altar, silhouetted, heads bowed, in the light of the candles they'd lit.

It turned out that Nown could no longer whisper. His voice had been a deep, dry rasp. It was deep still, but now clear and melodious, and even when he spoke quietly it was like listening to water falling into a stone basin in a still garden. 'St Anthony is the patron saint of the lost,' he said, informatively.

'We should say a prayer, then,' said Laura. 'I couldn't get anywhere near the Grand Patriarch or Father Roy. Apparently they are either out or terribly busy. The people I spoke to wouldn't disturb them just to say a little dreamhunter had come to see them. I'm a person of no consequence, and I've been snubbed by pompous functionaries. I did get to leave a note for Father Roy. I hope he jumps out of his skin when he reads it.'

'It's because you're a girl,' Nown said, matter of fact.

'Yes,' said Laura. She put a coin in the honesty box, took a candle, lit it and said a short and not terribly coherent prayer. Then she took her glass man by his gloved hand and left the Temple.

Five

Minutes after Laura had left her house, a car pulled up in front of it. Three men got out. Two were in pinstripes and bowler hats, and had heavy, swinging bulges in their jacket pockets. The third was the red-haired, waxy-skinned Maze Plasir.

Plasir tugged on the bell chain for several minutes before Chorley opened the door. 'Hello!' Chorley said, cheery. 'Visitors! Isn't it a lovely day, visitors?'

Plasir took Chorley's arm and propelled him back indoors. The other men crowded in after them.

'Shall we sit down?' Chorley said. 'My papers are all over the place in the library. Let's go in here.' He threw open the parlour doors and swept into the room ahead of them. He flopped onto a chair, draped his legs over one of its arms and let his slippers drop off his feet onto the floor.

The Regulatory Body officials perched together on the edge of a sofa, ramrod-straight and ready for action.

'I must go out and buy some more music,' Chorley said. 'I've listened to everything I have here.'

Plasir nodded sympathetically. 'This afternoon, perhaps,' he suggested.

'Isn't it afternoon yet? I'm looking forward to a nice nap later,' Chorley said.

'A capital idea,' said Plasir.

One of the burly officials sniggered.

'I've come to ask about one of your films, Mr Tiebold,' Plasir said.

Chorley's face lit up. 'That's something else I could do later. Watch my films. That would be fun. Those films are certainly one thing I've done that was worthwhile. I've been thinking a lot about that lately — what is worthwhile.'

'Yes. Taking stock. Very healthy,' said Plasir.

'That's right, humour him,' said an official.

Plasir gave the man a cold, quelling look. 'There's one film in particular that interests me,' Plasir said to Chorley. 'A film of the Place.'

'I have two of those,' Chorley said. 'No one in the world but me has a film of the Place.' He looked thoughtful. 'Excepting Cousin Erasmus, I suppose.'

'Cousin Erasmus has a film of the Place?'

'Yes.' Chorley swung his legs down and when his bare feet touched the floor he looked at them and laughed. 'Why *do* people bother with shoes indoors?'

'He's full of opinions. True to his character,' said one of the officials.

'Be quiet,' Plasir said. 'Mr Tiebold, where do you keep that film?'

'It's in my workshop.'

'Would you fetch it for me?'

'Do you want the other one too?'

'Cousin Erasmus's copy?'

'No. *He* has that. I mean, the one Tziga took — it's only two or three minutes long, but it's very beautiful in its way.'

The officials were nodding, so Plasir said, 'Yes, I think we'd better have both of them.'

One of the officials got up. 'I'll help you, Mr Tiebold.'

The other said, 'Is Mr Hame at home?'

'Yes, is he?' said Plasir. 'And when do you expect your wife back?'

'Tziga was here at breakfast,' Chorley said, vague. He left his slippers and wandered to the door. 'I can't remember what Grace said about when she'd be back. Does it matter? We have the whole day ahead of us. This beautiful day.'

Plasir pulled a face and shook himself. This dream of Cas's was horrible — incomparably horrible. Cas was making adjustments, moving his loaded dreamhunters about, and making sure the capital kept on ticking over, that its civil servants and politicians were soothed and full of generosity, but not as lost as *this* — or as desperately lost as the dosed dreamhunters themselves. The Hame–Tiebold house had been two nights at the intersection of overlapping penumbra, under the spell of no fewer than three vivid dreamhunters. And this was the result. Chorley Tiebold had always sneered at and snubbed Plasir, and yet here he was being good-natured and cooperative without giving his actions a moment's thought.

When Chorley disappeared into his workshop, Plasir went looking for the house's other inhabitants. He found Tziga upstairs asleep, and smiling. He found Rose in the morning room, playing with one of those toys where a clown climbs a ladder and does flips. She had an empty biscuit tin before her and her dressing gown was speckled with crumbs. She looked up at Plasir and gave a shriek of laughter. 'I wasn't thinking about *you*,' she said. 'I was daydreaming. I thought my daydream might conjure someone. But not you. Yuck!'

'I'm wounded, Miss Tiebold,' said Plasir. Then, 'Your cousin didn't stay for breakfast at Fallow Hill. Where do you think she is?'

'Um,' said Rose. She squeezed her toy so hard that the little clown flew right off it.

'On such a beautiful day, where might Laura have got to?' Plasir coaxed, since Rose was a little more feisty than he'd expected.

'She was here shortly after breakfast,' the girl said. Then she grinned. 'Uncle Tziga and I bounced boiled eggs.'

'That sounds like wonderful fun,' said Plasir. 'But where is Laura?'

'Laura is alone,' Rose said, blankly. 'Alone. All alone.'

'Do you have any idea *where* she is alone?'

'Everywhere. She doesn't have to be, though. She could make herself another monster. She's being stubborn about it.' Rose looked up at Plasir and a little frown marred her smooth brow. 'Doesn't she want to be happy?'

Maze Plasir shook his head in sympathy. He went out to check on the progress of the search for the film and found both of the men he'd come with in the library. One was pushing together a pile of paper under the bottom of a long damask curtain. The other had a reel of film tucked under his arm and was holding a box of matches.

'What the hell are you doing?' Plasir demanded.

'What we were told to do, Mr Plasir. We have the film. We are meant to take care of everyone who has seen the film.'

'Doran told you to "take care" of them?'

'Yes, Mr Plasir.'

Maze Plasir was stunned. 'No! Stop!'

The man who was standing put his hand up, in warning.

'At least let me take the girl. Doran can't possibly want Rose Tiebold killed. She's a friend of his daughter.'

'Nothing was said about that.'

Plasir pushed forward and there was a scuffle. He was shoved from the room. He heard Chorley calling in a plaintive voice from the workshop, 'Hello? I seem to be locked in.'

Plasir hurried in to Rose, grabbed her and pulled her to her feet. 'Come with me,' he said.

At that moment there was a knock on the front door. Plasir froze. Rose wriggled her shoulders and got out of his grasp. 'Don't be so rough,' she said.

The officials ran out into the hall. Both men were carrying revolvers.

The person on the front step called, 'Rose! Why is this door locked?'

'It's Laura Hame,' said Plasir.

'Good,' said an official. He rushed at the door. But just before he yanked it open the shadow of the girl left the glass. She had bolted. He chased her out into the street.

Plasir saw his chance. He made his choice. He'd leave Laura Hame to her fate — but he'd save Rose Tiebold. He hustled her out of the front door. He was in time to see the Body man sprinting through the side gate and into the alley that led to the back yard of the house. It seemed that the Hame girl had boxed herself into a dead end.

Plasir gripped Rose's arm and dragged her along the embankment.

* * *

Laura skidded into the yard and pushed past Nown. She yelled, 'Look out!' She didn't even look back, just rushed to her family's rescue. She banged through the back door, stumbled across the kitchen, skidding on mashed eggs, and fell through the kitchen door.

A man with a revolver jumped forward and seized her. He thrust its muzzle into her ribs. She twisted, and then a gap appeared beside her — the workshop door had opened. The gunman's grip loosened momentarily and Laura flung herself through the workshop door, crashing into her uncle, who was saying, 'I remembered where I put the spare key.' Then '*Ouch*' as she trampled him, though he didn't sound very perturbed.

Laura crashed into the work-table, and turned to see what was coming. For an instant the workshop doorway was full of the Body man, his gun raised and pointed right at her, then a shadow slammed into the man, snapping him in the middle so that his knees bashed his head. The doorway was empty.

Laura emerged to find Nown standing over the felled man. Nown was still, erect and calm, not like a combatant but a ceremonial sentry. He said, 'I have rendered them unconscious.' He'd clearly dealt the same way with her pursuer.

From the street Laura heard an unmistakable noise: the squeal Rose used to make as a child whenever she was angry at not getting her own way. Laura looked for the revolver. She picked it up and went to the door. She peered out.

Plasir was struggling with Rose, who'd sat down like a stubborn toddler and was kicking her legs.

There was a barge out on the stream of the Sva. The man at its wheel was watching the struggle. Laura heard him shout, 'Hey! You there!'

Laura ran down the front steps, hurried up to Plasir and pointed the gun at him.

Rose stopped struggling and stared at Laura with big eyes. 'He's a nasty little thing, but I don't think you should shoot him, Laura,' she said.

'She won't,' said Plasir. His eyes were darting about, between the gun, the barge and the door to Laura's house. 'What did you do with those Body men?'

'I shot them,' Laura said, and eased the hammer back a little.

Plasir released Rose and backed away, his hands raised. 'I didn't hear any shooting,' he said, but looked uncertain.

'Don't go another step,' Laura said. 'You're to come with me.'

'You won't shoot me.' Plasir continued to edge away. 'There are too few of you,' he said. 'You can't win. You'd better just leave the city.'

Laura raised her voice, and called, 'Nown!'

Rose said, 'Oh — your monster! Do you have him again?' She cackled and shook her finger at Plasir, then began to call too, 'Nown! Nown!' Gaily.

Nown came along the embankment. He noticed the agitated bargeman, gave him a wave with his gloved hand, then advanced on Rose, Laura and Plasir. Laura kept her eye on Plasir, who saw that the reinforcement she'd summoned was a man bigger than he was. He turned to run.

Nown passed Laura, gently relieved her of the gun, then closed in on Plasir, caught him in a few swift bounds, pinned him, picked him up and carried him back to the house.

Laura put her arm around her cousin, helped her up and followed.

Plasir had gone completely limp. Nown carried him to the workshop, took the key from Chorley and put Plasir inside. Laura saw that Plasir was shocked and passive. He was staring at Nown, trying to penetrate all the wrappings to see why the body that had grappled him had been so unnaturally hard. He peered, but seemed to wince away too, as though, as much as he wanted to know what was under the wrappings, he was also afraid of knowing.

Nown picked up the unconscious official and put him in the workshop too. He closed the door and locked it.

'Who is this?' Chorley said to Laura. 'Why is he wearing all that? Is it snowing?' Then, distracted, 'Rose, your dressing gown is torn.'

Laura took her uncle's arm. 'Let's get something to eat and drink. My friend here will check on Da and bring Rose a clean dressing gown.'

'All right,' said Chorley, and contentedly went with his daughter and niece into the kitchen.

A few minutes later Nown came through the room, handed Rose a dressing gown and said, 'No, thank you, I'm a little busy,' to Chorley's friendly offer of a cup of tea. Then he went out into the yard, returning with the other unconscious man. He disappeared with his bundle into the hallway, this time to stay out — out of range of Chorley's happiness-hampered, but still too lively, curiosity.

At three in the afternoon Father Roy turned up with several cars as an escort. Laura let him in and showed him her father, Rose and Chorley, who had opened every tin and jar of preserves and were at the kitchen table enjoying a long, large, messy lunch. She told Roy about Plasir and the two unconscious officials locked in her uncle's workshop. She handed over the revolvers. 'I'm putting all this in your hands,' she said. 'I have a dream that will clear space in Doran's grid of Contentment. I only want to get my family back. Please, can you tell someone to meet Aunt Grace when she comes out of the Place? Can you bring her to me so that she can be safe too? The dream she's gone to catch isn't a master dream.'

Father Roy sat down at the kitchen table and spoke in a very gentle voice to Chorley, Tziga and Rose. 'Come on, we're all going for a ride.'

'If I'm going on an outing I should get dressed,' Chorley said.

'Naturally. Let's see how quick you can be,' Father Roy said.

'Race you!' shouted Rose to her father. They jumped up and jostled their way out into the hall and thumped up the stairs.

'I'm an invalid,' Laura's father said, and drew his dressing gown protectively around himself. 'I'm excused from making efforts.'

Laura closed her eyes and rubbed the bridge of her nose.

Father Roy summoned his escort, unlocked Chorley's workshop and manhandled Plasir and the one limp and the one groggy official to the cars outside. He then went back to the workshop and gathered up an armload of film canisters, including the one the Body officials had located. 'I'm taking all these in case we need decoys at some stage,' Father Roy said.

Laura was alarmed. 'Didn't the Commission reconvene today? Isn't this almost *over*?' Her throat began to hurt. She was going to cry again.

'No. That's why we missed you when you came to find us. His Eminence and I were cooling our heels at the palace of Justice. When your uncle and father didn't turn up with you, we simply imagined you'd had word.'

'Word of what?'

'Word that the meeting was postponed because the convening judge, Seresin, was "unavailable".'

'*No*,' said Laura. 'No. This can't go on. Someone has to put a stop to it.'

Chorley and Rose came downstairs. Chorley looked very spruce, as usual, but reeked of cologne. Laura could see that his jacket was dewed with it. Rose had her shirt buttoned up wrong and was wearing all her favourite necklaces — amber, coral, carved ivory, crystals, jet, pearls — all together. She said, 'I ate so much I had to be sick.' She spoke in a loud whisper, perhaps only meaning to speak to Laura.

Chorley looked at the stack of films in Father Roy's arms. 'Are we having a screening?'

Laura went to fetch her father, and while she was in the kitchen she poked her head around the back door and told Nown to follow her. 'There are steps down to the river around three sides of the Temple. You'll be able to find a place to hide. My task now is to sleep and sort out Da and Uncle Chorley and Rose.' She spoke to the space between his hat and the top fold of his scarf. His glassy surface was in shadow, and without reflected light the visible segment of his head was just an absence, something watery rather than airy, on which the hat seemed to float.

'There were weapons,' Nown said. 'When there are weapons I should stay at your side.'

'I don't feel safe without you, true. But I think I *am* safe at the Grand Patriarch's palace. And his people need my protection.'

'Yes,' said Nown.

Behind Laura, Father Roy said, 'Miss Hame, we should go.'

Laura gave Nown a beseeching look, then pushed the door shut.

She helped Roy get her father up. Tziga walked, slow and shaky, leaning on both of them. As they went along he said to Laura, 'The thing about this dream, darling, is that even though the man is blissfully pleased with himself it's the wasps eating the apricots that are most *present*. Those wet shells of fruit still hanging on the branches. It's as though the dream uses the man's eyes like a camera to show us something more real than the story he's telling himself about what a fine person he is.'

'Da!' Laura was floored by surprise and admiration. 'You're yourself.'

'Not really. But I am a dreamhunter.'

Laura kissed her father's hand.

'Also — when Rose and I were bouncing the eggs I had a seizure. Didn't she tell you?'

'She didn't.'

'She and Chorley must have carried me up to bed. The fit seemed to shake the dream loose a little.'

Father Roy handed Tziga into his car. Laura climbed in beside her father and cuddled up to him. She whispered, 'The dreams *are* memories, Da, like Uncle Chorley always thought. Human memories from a time in the future. But the Place itself uses them to try to talk. It shows us what *it* finds meaningful.'

Laura's father peered at her, puzzled.

'The Place is a Nown, Da.'

Tziga opened his mouth, but didn't say anything for a long moment. Finally he said, 'Whose?'

'I don't know.'

Six

On Tuesday morning Laura woke from a long repeated cycle of The Gate. She opened her eyes. She felt her whole body breathe in and exhale the dream's radiance. Then the person beside her in bed said, 'Am I where I think I am?'

Laura sat up and studied Rose. Rose looked affronted. She lifted the covers and said, 'You let me get into bed wearing shoes.'

'Sorry,' said Laura. 'It was an emergency. *You* were an emergency.'

'I certainly was,' Rose said, with feeling. Then, 'Who can I sue? Who can I kill? Show me my enemies and I will burn them to the ground!' She propelled herself out of bed, and then had to throw the blankets over her head and burrow into the covers for a shoe.

Someone knocked on the tall double doors of the gloomy bedchamber. A nun put her head around the door and said if they would wash and dress she would see them in to breakfast.

Rose began to sort herself out. She ran her fingers through her tangled hair. She rubbed her mouth, which was still crusted with food. She found a mirror and inspected the crocodile skin on her neck — the indentations of all the beads she was wearing. Then she stood stock-still. 'You pointed a gun at Maze Plasir!' she said. And then, in an elated squawk, 'You have your monster back! He was dressed like a cabbie on a cold night. He *scragged* Plasir!' She laughed.

'Come on,' Laura said. 'I want to hear what the adults are planning. Dear God, let them have a plan.'

The adults looked grim. But they were all there — everyone Laura could have hoped to see. Her father, in pyjamas and a knitted grey shawl. Uncle Chorley, his jaw set and nostrils white. Grace, who looked frightened.

Laura's Aunt Marta was there, and her Mrs Bridges, who was taking plates from servants at the door and carrying them to the table.

George Mason was there too. The car sent to meet Grace at Doorhandle had passed him in the village. He had been on his way to Mrs Lilley's for Sandy's trunk. Grace had persuaded him to come along with her. He was sitting beside Laura, and as he passed her a plate of muffins, he said, 'The Regulatory Body stalked Sandy — I know it. I don't care what it takes, I'll see Doran pay.'

The rest of a crowded table was taken up by Erasmus Tiebold, Father Roy and half a dozen other priests.

Maze Plasir was at the breakfast too, though Chorley had pointedly removed his butter knife from beside his plate.

Plasir wasn't eating.

Erasmus Tiebold was asking Plasir questions. 'I imagine Doran has himself, his allies and the Founderston Barracks at least out of the range of this dream, or covered by other dreams. But how long does he mean to keep it up? My cousin Chorley's household had it very strongly — were they targeted? Or are all Founderston's citizens lying about moon-gathering and gorging themselves?'

Plasir leaned back in his chair and looked at his hands. He said, 'You can't win.'

'If the whole city is in the same shambles as my cousin's house, then I can't see what Doran hopes to gain, or how he hopes to get away with it.'

'Can't you? For a start the film and the girl can be kept from the Commission. You might still have the evidence in your possession, but who will be interested in it?'

Father Roy had a lightweight edition of the *Founderston Herald* open before him. He also had yesterday's papers from

Westport and Canning and other smaller towns in the south. He said, 'It is reported here that Congress passed a vote to abolish the two-term limit on the presidency.'

'And then there's *that*,' gloated Plasir. 'You're in the Temple, and the dreams you need to catch to keep people safe are in the Place — two localities far apart. There are only four dreamhunters in this room, and one of them is an epileptic.'

Laura put down the muffin she was picking at and pushed aside her teacup too.

Plasir looked around the table, his eyes glittering. He said to Erasmus Tiebold, 'And, unless I'm mistaken, Your Eminence, you have been chewing Wakeful. Why? Are you so reluctant to share *any* dream that you're drugging yourself to save yourself from Miss Hame's charming speciality?'

Laura gazed at Plasir with amazement. He could make anything sound corrupt. The Gate was her 'charming speciality'.

'Please remove him,' Chorley said.

The Grand Patriarch nodded to one of the priests, who called on some of the Temple guards. Plasir got up, and gave them a nasty smile. He said, 'Face it — you're finished.' He was led out.

When the door had closed Grace said, 'He's right about some things. All they have to do is get *us* — me, George, Laura. Then we're finished. You can't go on chewing Wakeful for ever.'

'I thought that Wakeful could give me eighty sleepless hours,' Erasmus Tiebold said.

'Not safely,' said Tziga. 'With a dream inside you it can. Without a dream you'll become gloomy, angry and possibly dangerous within sixty hours.'

'Then you'll develop an irregular heartbeat,' Chorley said. 'It's hearts that need sleep.'

The Grand Patriarch looked worried. It was his first sign of it.

'End of the Drought is useless,' Grace said. 'I have to catch a master dream. Laura's The Gate will be good for another four days, possibly more. I have to catch something to spell her, and buy us some more time.'

'My penumbra won't go anywhere near protecting the whole palace,' George Mason said. His face creased with unhappiness.

Chorley said, 'We have to focus on the film.'

'The Commission is — out of commission!' Grace shouted. 'What good is your bloody film?'

The Grand Patriarch winced. 'Please, Mrs Tiebold.' There was something about his expression that made Laura think he was telling Grace off for a lack of refinement.

Laura put her hands over her ears. She sat for a moment and listened to her blood roar. She concentrated on not being sick. All the food on the table smelled awful: the eggs sulphurous, the muffins soapy with baking powder, the milk fatty. Food had been tasting funny for days, but now it was as if it were poisonous.

'Hey!' said Rose suddenly, very loud, and interrupting everyone. She leaped up and put her fists on the table, and leaned across it and over the newspaper Father Roy was reading. She grabbed the paper and turned it — she had been reading it upside down. 'Listen,' she said, and read out a death notice:

Seresin, Kathryn (née Kralls). 10 March 1907, at the age of 55, after a short illness. Beloved wife of Judge Mitchell Seresin.

Rose looked around the table. 'The Commission didn't reconvene because its head wasn't in town. He would have been at his wife's deathbed. And he'll be at her funeral, in Castlereagh, this coming Friday. We can take the film to him!'

There was a short, electrified pause. Then everyone started talking.

Seven

No one who saw the large party that arrived at Founderston Central Station the following day would have thought they were engaged in a desperate plan. The group stood under the great clock suspended from the cavernous ceiling of the main concourse. They were well dressed, and well equipped with bags and picnic baskets and travel rugs. Among them they had a number of large film canisters, fastened in buckled carrying straps.

As they waited, they were met by men who, it seemed, had been sent ahead to buy train tickets. The men approached the group, tickets were produced, words exchanged — but no money, no tips.

The party stood watching the clock, then they moved as one out onto the platform and, after a quick round of farewells, dispersed to different trains.

George Mason wasn't with them. He had left in the early hours by car. He was to travel by the back roads of Wry Valley to the border west of Doorhandle, where he planned to go In and catch Plasir's speciality dream, Secret Room — a master dream.

Marta and Tziga got on a train going south. Their tickets would take them to the spa in Spring Valley, where invalids often went to bathe and drink from the mineral springs. With the Hames were a priest, one of the Grand Patriarch's most trusted men, and a stolid Temple guard. Marta carried a copy of the film, the long strip of nitrate removed from its reel and wound in a figure eight into the false bottom of her narrow valise — a bag of a shape that no one would suppose could store a reel of film. Marta and Tziga intended to check into the spa at Spring Valley, where Tziga would stay as another decoy. Marta would take a boat — supposedly for a day trip across the lake — escorted only by the Temple guard. On the far side of the lake was a small but picturesque mountain village, from which a road wound down fifty-five rough miles to the far side of the mountains that divided Southland. A weekly coach service ran on that road, delivering mail and other goods to farms and settlements along the way. Marta and the Temple guard would catch that coach, then the train again from a small station south of the Corridor. The train would get them to Castlereagh by Friday evening.

Two priests carrying a reel each boarded the express to Westport. Both reels were unexposed film — decoys.

Chorley and Grace got on the Westport local. They too carried films. One was of the sand-sculpting competition, and the other of a pod of blackfish stranded on So Long Spit. The couple would leave the train at the small stop near Marta Hame's house, where they would be met by Marta's Mr Bridges, with a car. They would take the car, skirt the capital on country roads and meet the border to the Place just east of Doorhandle. Grace would go In and try to catch The Gate. Chorley meant to drive on through Rifleman Pass to Sisters Beach, where he would stay with his daughter and wait for news.

Rose represented the group's back-up plan. She left the concourse of Founderston Central Station, and boarded a local for Sisters Beach — alone. She carried an overnight bag and a hatbox containing a wide-brimmed, flower-trimmed hat. She was in first class, as usual, and as soon as she got on the train she locked the door of her compartment.

Laura was to stay in Founderston, at the Temple, to dream The Gate and hold the fort till Grace relieved her — or George Mason if Grace was unable to make it back in time.

That was the plan.

Laura was allowed to accompany the others to the station to see them off. When they got to the divider between platforms five and six she hurriedly kissed her cousin, then turned to plead with

Father Roy. 'Could I please, *please*, see my father onto the train and settled in?'

'Very well,' said the priest. 'But be quick.'

Laura unfolded a travel rug and tucked it around her father's knees. She gave Marta some hasty instructions on how to mix elderflower cordial to his taste.

'Yes, yes, child,' Marta said. She gestured at the priests waiting for Laura on the platform. 'You should go. You must understand that if this were a game of chess, you would be the king.'

'I don't play chess.'

'Don't draw it out,' her father warned. 'It only makes saying goodbye more difficult.' He caught her eye. She was still fussing around him, rearranging his pillows. Their heads were together. He said, 'What's on your mind, Laura?'

Marta said, musing, 'Founderston must be full of dreamhunters wondering why business is falling off. If Erasmus could only gain their confidence . . .'

'Contentment will have erased any dream that isn't its near equal,' Tziga said to his sister. Then, to his daughter, 'What is it, love?'

She kissed his cheek. 'I should go.' She kissed her aunt too, and wished them both good luck. Then she said again, to her father, 'I must go.'

Laura left the compartment and turned away from the door she'd come in by. She hurried up the train, into the second-class compartments, which were full. She went along, peering into the compartments and through their windows, which looked out onto the train on the track beside theirs — the Sisters Beach local. Finally Laura saw what she was looking for: her cousin, a solitary figure clutching a candy-striped hatbox. Laura pushed into a compartment. She said, 'Excuse me,' to its occupants then stretched over them to haul down the window. She leaned out and waved.

Rose got up and opened her window.

The people behind Laura were protesting and pulling at her clothes.

'Wider,' Laura said, to Rose.

Rose leaned her weight on the window and forced it open. Laura gripped the luggage rack above her, stepped onto the windowsill and climbed out of the window of the train she was on. She straddled the gap. Rose leaned out and helped her through. They tumbled together into Rose's compartment. The hatbox fell off the seat, lost its lid, hat, loose satin lining and reel of film. Rose got up and slammed the window shut to cut off the sounds of indignation: 'Well, I never!' and 'Of all the nerve!'

The train beside the local began to move, the annoyed faces slid out of sight, then the dining car with its 'Spring Valley' legend. Laura pushed Rose back into her seat. She said, 'Don't look,' and ducked down herself as one of her father and aunt's escorts hurried along the corridor of the moving train, looking and looking, no doubt alerted by the people Laura had left behind on the platform.

Then the windows were empty, the train gone. Rose pulled down the window blind. A minute later their train jerked and began to move. It slid out of Central Station, jostling through the points in the railway yard, before finding its way onto the line north.

Laura got up off the floor. She gathered the hatbox and its contents.

'I thought there was a fishy lack of ceremony in your leavetaking,' Rose said.

'The Grand Patriarch will have to make do with Plasir and his Secret Room,' said Laura. 'He can pack everyone he really needs into a few rooms with Plasir and they'll be safe from Contentment.'

'He'll have them all chewing Wakeful, Laura, before he ever shares one of Plasir's sleazy dreams.'

Laura grinned at the thought. 'Well, a sleazy dream might offend him, but so would The Gate. It's blasphemous. It says that paradise is only time running backwards. And someone's mother guards the gate instead of St Peter.'

Rose gave her cousin a careful look. 'The woman in The Gate isn't "someone's mother", Laura — she's you.'

'Yes, I know.'

'And all those years ago your Da must have mistaken her for

your mother. He'd have thought that the dream really was meant for Verity, to ease her dying.'

Laura nodded. 'I thought it was Sandy's doing that she looked like me. Then I caught it without Sandy, and she still looked like me.'

Rose put up the window blind again, in time to see the birch-lined playing fields of Founderston Girls' Academy slide by. She said, 'Do you think Uncle Tziga and your Aunt Marta have a chance?'

'Not much of one — not if they're followed.'

Rose plucked at her skirt, patted its lace-edged pockets. 'I hope you have a plan, then.'

'No.'

'You climbed between trains without a plan?'

Laura did know where she was going. And she knew that Nown would feel her leaving Founderston and would follow her as fast as he was able. There was a place she would go to, and he would join her there — then they would see. She said, 'I have this much of a plan. You should go out and find a conductor and pay my fare. And you should tell him that we want to get out at the stop in the Awa Inlet.'

'We're visiting Mamie? That's the plan?'

'You are.'

Rose nodded, and got up to do as she was told.

It was dark at the train stop. The tide was out and the only light came from the breakers, a mile away at the mouth of the inlet. Gulls roosting on the sandbar made a warm clucking out in the dark.

Laura and Rose sat on the stony bank. They didn't dare go on till there was more light. Rose had her bag and hatbox. Laura had Rose's coat, and in its pockets a bottle of lemonade and some biscuits from the train's dining car.

'I can't think what you're planning,' Rose said, to the patch of solid darkness that was her cousin.

'Neither can I. I don't mean I don't know — I mean I can't think about it.'

'Don't do anything self-sacrificing.'

'I think I have to, Rose. But it's not that bad. I promise you'll see me soon.'

'There's only that railway line and the Depot over the border here. Do you mean to make your monster wreck the cable car?'

'I hadn't thought of that.'

'It would be a pretty desperate measure. The people at the Depot might starve.'

'Yes. That's a good argument against it.'

Rose shuffled next to Laura and put her arm around her. She was seeing certain things very clearly now. She saw that there were decisions that people had to make, alone, for other people. And that sometimes there was no substituting for whoever had to decide. There were torches that couldn't be passed on. Laura's light would go out in Rose's hands. Rose saw it now — and it made her feel very old and lonely.

A band of light, the shade of a ripening lemon, outlined the eastern headland. The world came back, bit by bit, till the girls could see water glimmering in the channels of the reed beds, and the white streak of crushed shell that was the path to the Doran summer residence.

Mamie woke when a maid knocked on her door, came in, opened the curtains and started talking. 'Miss,' she said. 'Your friend Rose Tiebold is here. She must have arrived on the five o'clock train. She was waiting on the terrace when the boy went out to get milk from the spring-house.'

Mamie got up and found her dressing gown and slippers. She stumped downstairs scratching her scalp.

Rose was at the breakfast table. A maid and the butler were bustling around her as though she were in danger of dying in the next several minutes for lack of jam, honey and hot rolls.

Mamie sat down too and waited for the servants to leave. When they had gone, she said, 'Did you have some kind of disagreement with someone, Rose?'

Rose hesitated, then looked amused. 'Yes.'

'And you came here to me?'

'Yes.'

Mamie was pleased. She nearly told Rose she was honoured, only that wasn't quite right. She'd been so bored. Now she felt useful. Then she frowned. 'I'm not any good at drying tears and so forth.'

'You won't have to do that. We can sit on the terrace drinking cider, and playing cards, and reading books all day. That will fix me.'

Mamie pushed the plate of rolls towards her friend. 'My perfect day,' she said. She missed seeing the pained face Rose pulled.

For much of the day they did sit on the terrace, sipping cider cooled by luxurious ice. They read mostly, for Mamie hated cards, and every other game of chance.

In the late afternoon, alertness pulled Mamie out of her book. She looked up.

Rose put her own book down and stood. She walked to the edge of the terrace and slowly, tentatively, raised her arm.

There was a man striding up the avenue of plane trees. When he passed through the bands of sunlight, Mamie saw that he was wrapped, head to toe, in an odd assortment of garments.

The man saw Rose, broke stride and raised a hand to return her greeting. Then he strode on, and vanished into the air.

Mamie said, 'Do you know that dreamhunter?'

'No, I don't know him at all,' Rose replied.

Eight

Nown was twelve hours behind Laura. He travelled by day and night and many people saw him — the motley, bundled man who ran as fast as a horse. He was a sign and a wonder to many, who were able to say thereafter: '*Only the day before, I saw . . .*'

Laura, waiting, was afraid of being seen. She was out in the open. She hid herself as best she could by lying down beside the long, low mound of earth. Her wait was long, and she fell asleep.

It was late in the epidemic and the boy knew what to expect. He'd seen things at other houses along the country road on which they lived. He'd seen how the letterboxes at the breaks in poplar hedges would have a white tea towel tied to them. That was what people were told to do if they needed help. The Boy Scouts would come by to deliver cooked meals and clean linen.

During the sickness the boy's mother had said that he was allowed to go out for exercise, but shouldn't go near anyone. He'd sometimes lie in wait in the culvert by the crossroads, and would emerge when the Boy Scouts went by. He'd follow them, fishing for news. From them he heard of the houses — two neighbouring — where only silence greeted the visitor's knock, and everyone inside was discovered dead. 'With their faces and fingers turned black,' one Scout said.

When his mother became ill and banned him from her sight, the boy would sit outside her bedroom door and listen to her cough. And at night he'd wake up in his own bed and would listen for silence — the silence he imagined coming, as eloquent as speech, from a blackened face. Then he'd hear her cough again.

The third night he woke up because the cough was dragging itself along the hall. The boy lay straight in his bed, like a body in a coffin. He was cold because he didn't have enough blankets on his bed. He was cold because he was feeding himself and had let the stove go out. And he was cold within himself, all the way through, as though he were an orphan already and had to think first what he could do for himself.

He got out of bed and followed his mother into the kitchen. She had carried her writing box from her bedroom to the table. It was open and the boy saw her many packets of letters, bundled with ribbons that had faded over the years, and grown brittle.

His mother's face was white. Her hair was plastered to her neck by sweat. She knelt on the floor pushing handfuls of wood chips through the stove door. Then she got a match and lit the stove. Tendrils of smoke came out of the door, then were sucked back into the stove as the fire began to draw.

The boy was practical. Since there was a fire, he filled the kettle and put it on the stove. He reached over his mother to set it down, and she pushed him back, her hand hot on his leg.

The boy sat on the other side of the kitchen and kept his eyes fixed on the spout of the kettle, waiting for steam. He'd make some beef tea. While he waited he picked up his violin and tuned it. He didn't watch his mother burn her letters, or only glanced once and saw the fire turn one packet into a black-striped brick, then a kind of paper chaff, flakes of soot circling in the stove.

She burned all of them — the letters from her cousin who lived in another country. One letter a week for eight years. She had never read the boy any of the letters and so it didn't matter, nothing was different, the cousin in another country knew all about him and he knew nothing about her. But his mother was burning the letters, and that mattered. And then she didn't want beef tea, and she wouldn't let him touch her or help her as she dragged herself back to bed.

He washed his few dishes, because there was hot water. Then he returned to his bed, where he tried to stay awake and listen, as though *his attention were a rope — a rope that keeps a boat tethered to a jetty as the river rises. His waiting turned into a dream. In his dream the rope wasn't long enough to keep the boat afloat when the river came up. It was the rope that drowned the boat.*

In the morning the house was silent, so silent that as he strained to hear, the boy heard a plum fall from the tree in the yard — landing with a soft thump on the neglected lawn.

After the dream Laura didn't go back to sleep. She stayed down, her cheek turned away from the bulk of the grave and her eyes on the bleak, ashy peaks of the Pinnacles, so near, but hazy, standing in a white ground-mist of dead grass.

Time went by. Then the ground vibrated, and Nown said, 'Laura,' in his low, musical voice.

Laura sat up. Nown pulled off his hat, as if removing it out of good manners. Then he began to undress. He stripped off and abandoned all the clothes, but handed her Sandy's coat and told her to put it on.

She didn't argue with him, even though the request was strange. She had a coat on already. And she somehow knew he didn't mean her to take off the one she was wearing first. Laura simply put Sandy's coat on over hers. It was hot and heavy, and she knew she wouldn't be able to walk anywhere dressed like that. But she obeyed Nown because it was the first time he'd ever told her to do something.

She rummaged in her now-blanketing clothes for the apples Rose had picked for her in the Doran orchard. And for her bottle of lemonade. She pulled on the wire that loosened its china stopper and took a mouthful. 'I wish we could sit down and share a meal,' she said to Nown.

'With this grave as a table?'

Nown was easier to look at in the light of the Place. The light was even, and his skin threw off no dazzling reflections. He did kneel by her, kept quiet as she ate an apple, and the crack of each bite echoed off the Pinnacles.

Once the apple was gone, Laura licked its juice from her fingers and touched Nown's chest. She saw her fingers suspended only inches from his heart. She could recall distinctly the velvety feel of the rust-stained lump of gravel she had picked up from between the railway lines at Sisters Beach Station. 'Nown,' she said, 'this grave is the heart of the Place. Its unhappy, horrible heart.'

'My heart isn't me,' Nown said. 'It's only what you put into me.'

Laura closed the space between them and leaned on him. He held her tight. After a time he started to speak, in his beautiful new voice, as clear as he was. It was like hearing fresh air speak.

'Laura, this Now — the Place — is so immense and powerful, what must it have as its heart?'

Laura shivered.

'A person,' Nown said.

Laura pressed her face against his shoulder and opened her eyes wide. She saw her own arm through his body, its bone bent as though she'd suffered poor nutrition in childhood.

'Someone is buried here,' Nown said.

Laura whispered, 'I knew it.' Though her nose was pressed against him he had no smell. When he was sand he'd sometimes smelled of heat and moisture, now the air near him was empty of odour. She said, 'I hated this grave when I first saw it. I thought of the grave in The Water Diviner — rustling and moaning.'

'Yes. What is buried here isn't a body, it's a living person.'

'Buried alive!' Laura said, and began to cry. 'But I don't hear anything.' She mashed her mouth and nose into Nown's hard, impossibly flexible shoulder. He didn't taste of anything either, left neither flavour nor matter on her tongue. 'You're not *there*,' she grieved. 'And I can't change you.'

'My own,' he said. 'My sweet — you must try to be calm.' He said, 'Listen, leaves don't fall from the trees here unless someone walking by them brushes them off. Nothing is alive, and nothing is dead.'

Laura pushed herself away from Nown. She propelled herself backwards and knelt, her arms wrapped around her stomach, stooped so that the crown of her head touched the dirt of the graveside. 'I can't bear this,' she said. Then, a moment later, 'What will happen?'

'What will happen when you ask me to dig up this grave?'

Laura laughed, wildly. 'You'll refuse me, because you can't *know* what will happen. Isn't that the rule for you?'

Nown was silent.

'Your free will has laws. That's what you told me.'

Nown said, 'I think this Now is keeping promises I made to you.'

Laura clenched her body into a tighter ball. She cried out as though he had struck her. Above her head, dulcet, clear, the glass Nown kept on with his pitiless reasoning. 'I promised to do everything to save whomever you loved.'

She gasped for air between sobs. The pressure of tears behind her eyes was so great she thought she might literally cry her eyes out. She shouted at Nown, '*Who* is being saved? *Whom* do I love?'

Laura had often imagined Nown's sighing, but this time he did sigh and she heard it. 'You know that it is difficult for me not to answer your questions, Laura. It is in my nature to answer whatever I can. So I will give relief to my nature and answer you — though I'm tired of it, tired of my routine obedience.'

Laura looked up and saw through her boiling blur of tears that Nown was counting off the fingers on one of his hands. 'Whom do you love?' he said. 'You love your father and your cousin, your uncle and your aunt. And you love me.'

'I do love you!' Laura said, in the voice of someone begging for mercy.

And still he went on, and she heard him say, 'And you *will* love that child you're carrying.'

Laura bent over again. She howled like an animal. She thought: *God, let me die now. God,* she thought, *if it was God at the beginning and end of all this, in the tomb at Bethany opening Lazarus's ears when they were stuffed with the silence of death and, somewhere, not too long from now, please God, when this music finally falls silent for my cursed family. God,* Laura begged, *let me not have to choose.* Because Laura did feel she was being asked to choose between her friend, and her future.

Nown gathered her up again and held her while she cried, and while the jagged remnants of sobbing shook her, and when she was worn out and looking listlessly through her swollen eyelids at the blue shadows inside his body.

Close to an hour passed that way. Finally Laura stirred and sat up and looked into her servant's face. 'When I ask you to dig up this grave I'm afraid the world will end.'

'But, Laura, we already know that it doesn't.'

It was true. They knew that an invalid would ride on the roof of a train, and convicts fleeing through a forest would look down on a bonfire on a beach like the beacon of a better world. They knew that friends would ride together down a wild river; a boy would find a spring pushing through a seam of coal on his father's property; a drought would end; and a mother would shelter her child as an earthquake shook the scent of honeysuckle down over them. And they knew that some lost, grown child would wish so hard for salvation that he'd have a vision of his mother waiting for him at the gate to paradise.

'Laura,' Nown said, 'you came here and waited for me so that you could ask me to dig up the grave. You didn't need me to tell you any of this.'

Laura nodded. He set her away from him and began to delve in the dry earth of the mound, digging quickly with his hard, transparent hands.

'Wait,' she said. There was more to say. She had said it already, but it was one of those things that couldn't ever be said enough. 'I love you.'

'Yes.' Nown waited, reasonable, peaceable, his dust-gloved hands poised above the crumbling rent he'd made in the piled earth. Then he set to digging again.

The man lying on the shallow hollow in the earth looked dead, his face grey with dust over black grime, coal dust in the pores of his skin. His face was familiar. Curiosity made Laura daring. She licked her palm and ran a lock of his hair through her wet hand. His hair was grimy too, but showed a trace of a true bright red.

'I've seen him before,' she said to Nown. 'He was building a wall in a dream. He crept over to me and pulled a paper from his mouth. It was the bottom part of the letter Cas Doran wrote asking the ranger to follow Da. He was also the man who stopped to help that crippled convict up when they were being hunted by dogs through the forest. And I think he's one of the convicts working on the stone bridge in The Water Diviner. And he's one of the convicts in Convalescent One, in leg irons, standing on the causeway.'

Nown seemed unmoved by Laura's wonder. He only said, 'Remember what I told you about the final N? You cannot end this Nown until you have first given it its voice.'

'Have pity,' Laura said.

'I will.'

Everything she asked her servant to do trapped her further in what had already been done. Nown's pity was a promise fulfilling itself over time — a long, inhuman time.

'Here, I'll help you,' Nown said. He took her hands and assisted her down into the shallow trench so that she perched above the body. She kicked toeholds in the wall of the grave, steadied herself and stooped over.

The man had his hand on the wall, his index finger curled to make a mark. Laura glimpsed the wings of the letter W beneath the hand. She turned her eyes up to her servant, tried to find his eyes in the glowing, glassy nothingness of his face. She said, 'What will happen?'

'Ask him,' Nown said.

Laura bent to her task. She scratched an N into the wall beside the man's hand.

Nothing happened. No one spoke. The Place was as still as ever, a silent desert.

Laura thought of her family, separated, trying desperately to fix things.

She took the man's thin wrist in her hand. It was like touching a fresh corpse. The temperature of his skin was tepid, too cool for life. She moved his hand away from the wall, so that the W was exposed. Then she used his fingertips to wipe the letter away.

Far inland the compound of the Depot imploded. The buildings rushed together like matter in water pouring towards a drain. The timbers of the huts and barracks split as a slope thrust up under them, and all their bolted doors burst open.

Greenery — ferns, trees, vines — burst like fireworks amid the splinters and billowing dust. Fireworks that froze into permanence, startled trees above gouged wet earth. Forest birds fled shrieking from the mess and circled up over a towering tangle of metal — fifty miles of narrow-gauge railway line concertinaed into fifty yards of mangled mountain forest.

And yet, by some miracle, this violence spared the few people there. A miracle of care and intention. When their barracks and dormitories exploded, the yellow-clad bodies were momentarily cradled in huge fists of dust — dust as soft as talcum powder — then released and spilled into the tree ferns on the forest floor.

Grace lay in the circle of Foreigner's West, a dusty blanket thrown over her for camouflage. She was asleep, despite the lumpy ground jabbing into her hip bones.

. . . the woman waited for him at the gate. He saw that her eyes were red, ruined by weeping. She stretched out a hand to him, and clasped his wrist. He remembered that he was dreaming. He knew that the twilight was a landslide, and its silence his deafness.

The woman, small, young, strong for her size, tightened her grip and hauled him towards her through the arch of flowers, through the gate — to where it was cold and someone was whistling, and someone else was angry, slamming a teacup down into its saucer.

A fly made a six-point turn, tickling, landing on his face . . .

Grace touched her face. The blowfly took off, bounced from her arm like electrified thistledown and zoomed away. When its buzzing had faded, Grace heard a parson bird whistling above her, spitting and clanking in its characteristic mix of music and disharmony. She opened her eyes on green leaves, and the blue sky between them.

Part XIII
Lazarus Hame

One

Rose and Mamie were having breakfast when the first figure came out of the forest. A man in yellow pyjamas made his weaving way through the stream below the spring-house where the valley narrowed.

Mamie got up and opened the door to get a better look.

Another man came out of the trees. This one seemed eager. He blundered through the stream and raised his arms as if rushing to embrace someone.

'What do you make of this?' Mamie said.

Rose had watched the film and listened to Laura's description of the captive dreamhunters. But these men had come from the forested foothills of the Riflemans, not appeared at the border on the avenue.

Mamie flicked Rose an anxious look. More figures were walking down the valley. They were mostly men, but there were a few women among them. They all seemed disorientated, then very excited. They saw the house, and hurried towards it.

'They don't seem to be together, as such,' Mamie said.

Rose joined her friend at the door. They waited. Several servants joined them — two footmen, one carrying a cricket bat, and a maid with a feather duster, who had seen the people from an upstairs window and now looked as though she wished she'd remained upstairs.

There were more yellow-clad people arriving all the time.

'I don't like this,' Mamie said. She drew Rose inside and shut the French doors. She shot the bolts.

As they came upon the house the people began to babble. At first they were speaking only to themselves, rapt with relief. 'This is my house,' Rose heard one cry. 'I'm home!'

'My beautiful house!'

'It was all worth it, for this!'

Several paused on the terrace, puffed out their chests and gazed about them with proprietary satisfaction. Others made straight for the front door. The footmen repelled two — then retreated inside and slammed the door. 'Miss Doran! What shall we do?'

'Don't let them in!' Mamie looked terrified. She and Rose joined the servants gathered in the entrance hall. They listened to the voices beyond the door. Raised, contending voices. It didn't sound like an argument, it sounded like a group of children all clamouring for attention.

'This is *my* house.'

'No, it's mine. I built this house twenty-eight years ago.'

'Both of my children were married out of this house. My grandchildren visit me here.'

'What should we do?' Mamie asked the butler.

He looked desperate.

Rose grabbed her friend. 'Let's leave. We can get out by the back door.'

Mamie moved immediately to do this, but Rose detained her. 'I mean, we should grab what is necessary, then set off.'

'What?' Mamie wrung her hands. 'What is necessary?' She jumped when the door knocker sounded.

'Wife?' said a voice outside. 'Is that you?'

'Where is everyone?' said another.

And, 'Why don't you come out? It's such a lovely day.'

Rose dragged Mamie upstairs. She pushed the hatbox that held the film to the back of the wardrobe in the guest bedroom. She found a sun hat, a coat, her good walking shoes. She went through Mamie's wardrobe. She tossed a heavy coat onto the bed, and a soft bag. 'Change your shoes.'

Mamie sat down to swap her slippers for her school shoes. 'Shall I take my jewellery?'

'I don't think they're here to loot the house. Only to live in it.'

'Why?' Mamie was in an agony of incomprehension.

Rose heaved a sigh. 'Your father has been dosing kidnapped dreamhunters with a dream that makes people happy and compliant. He's filled half of Founderston with it. That's why I'm here. Mamie, you *knew* something like this was going on.'

Mamie began to cry. 'But why do they think that this is their house?'

Rose considered. 'Well — I've had Contentment and, come to think of it, this *is* the house in the dream.' It was so strange. Rose realised she had seen Mamie as a middle-aged woman, and Ru as a middle-aged man. She had seen their children — either his or hers or a mix of both — turning cartwheels and carrying canoe paddles and hurrying indoors for a breakfast of eels they'd caught the day before.

'Please pull yourself together,' Rose said to her friend. 'This is frightening, I agree, but I've been living with alarms for some time now and do you see me carrying on?'

Mamie made an effort. She took up her coat and bag and followed Rose to the kitchen, where Rose rifled the cupboards and drawers for cans of fruit, a can opener, biscuits, ginger beer, sweets, matches. She stuffed their bags, and lifted them to test their weight.

Mamie jumped and cowered at every noise. But the noise was only voices and the door knocker. The dreamhunters were puzzled at not being let into their own house, but were in too good a mood to force doors or break windows.

Rose checked the servants' entrance. There was no one in sight. She went back to Mamie, gave her a bag to carry and led her from the house.

Two

Laura and the buried man were in a forest of tea-tree. The sea was visible downhill as brightness through the tangled black trunks. As the minutes passed a bird dared to speak up again. 'Peep?' it said — perhaps asking some other bird, *Did you notice that? What was that?* 'Peep?' it went, each time a little bolder, till it was answered, and the whole hillside began to gossip.

The man sat with dry dust smoking away from his hair and clothes in the slight breeze. He turned his head slowly to face Laura, moving like someone half-frozen and very depleted. He whispered, 'Why are you just sitting there?' Then, 'Why aren't you running away?'

Laura searched her pockets, found her remaining apple and offered it to him. His hand came out, tentative, then snatched. He hunched and bit into the fruit, then gave a little grunt that seem to say that although the food pleased him he'd rather not let himself in for being pleased again. He gobbled the apple and wiped his fingers on his shirt.

'I don't know any way over the Rifleman,' Laura said. 'Except by the railway bridge. It's best crossed in daylight. So we should set out now.'

He raised his head again and peered at her, suspicious.

'After that we can follow the coast. We can be at Sisters Beach in a day and a half.' Laura got up and removed Sandy's coat, which Nown had asked her to put on over her own. He'd been right to do that. The slippers and trousers and scarf and knitted hat seemed all to have vanished with the Place. So had Nown. Nothing cataclysmic had happened at the grave. Nown had only become more transparent, till he wasn't there. The beige grasslands and ashy barrier of the Pinnacles vanished, and the tea-trees came, in a close crowd, and stood like dark spirits around them, not quite still, a sea breeze sieving through their aromatic leaves.

Laura gave the man Sandy's coat.

He got up, with difficulty, and put it on.

Laura saw that his feet were wrapped with strips of cloth torn from the bottoms of his trousers. His shirt was blue cotton, a work shirt, but the ragged trousers were printed with prison arrows. He covered himself up with the coat.

Laura pulled out a lemonade bottle and let him have the last of its contents. 'We'll need the bottle for water,' she said. 'You can carry it.'

She set off towards the sea, without waiting to see whether he'd follow.

Three

Shortly after leaving the village of Doorhandle, the Sisters Beach coach pulled up for someone who stood in the road, both arms raised, a fan of ten-dollar notes flourished in one fist. Naturally the driver let the woman on.

It was autumn, not quite the low season, but still the coach had plenty of room to take on another passenger. The other travellers made a few rearrangements to accommodate the woman. She crammed herself into a corner and sat biting her fist and staring out of the window as the coach went on up Rifleman Pass.

There was mist on the summit. Dark, lumpish shapes loomed at the roadside, the stumps of trees from a forest burned off years before, and limestone outcrops.

The woman, though at first despondent, eventually seemed to be taking a great interest in the view.

Finally one of her fellow travellers asked her, 'Is this the first time you've been through the Pass?'

'Yes.'

'Are you — forgive me if I'm wrong, and I must be — the dreamhunter Grace Tiebold? You do look like her.'

'I am her.'

The passengers exchanged looks. 'But how?' one said, for they all knew the famous story of 'Tziga's Fall' and how any dreamhunter on the Sisters Beach stagecoach would find themselves falling out of a suddenly immaterial coach at the border to the Place.

'How can you be here, Mrs Tiebold? We're beyond the border.'

'The Place has gone,' Grace Tiebold said. 'It just went.'

Four

Laura didn't relax until they had crossed the railway bridge over the Rifleman and climbed the cutting to the tunnel mouth. It wasn't a long tunnel. When she looked through it, the far opening appeared the size of one of her own fists. Still, she didn't like to venture into it. She turned to the man who was limping behind her. He stopped and stood at some distance from her.

She called out to him: 'I don't think either of us is in a fit state to have to run.' She wanted to complain that this did concern him too, and why should she have to be the leader? She gestured at him to join her.

He came up, reluctantly, and peered into the tunnel.

Laura saw that he was as pale as ever, and slick with sweat. His shirt was open and she could have counted all his ribs.

'We can go over the headland,' she said. 'It takes longer, but we can just creep along.'

'This is your stamping ground,' he said. 'Lead on.'

'I'll need a leg up,' she said, and went to the side of the buttressed tunnel mouth to show him where they'd have to climb.

It was a struggle, but eventually they both managed the steep bit and got into the scrub. From the top of the headland Laura pointed out the beach, where there was a fresh stream. 'No more than two hours,' she promised. 'We'll rest there.'

The man looked back at the Awa Inlet. His slack, exhausted face registered surprise.

'What?' Laura said.

'The causeway,' he said. 'It's not there.' He was terribly puzzled. He rubbed his eyes and squinted. 'I'm short-sighted, but even I couldn't miss a strip of black across the inlet. That *is* the Awa Inlet?'

'Yes.'

'I don't understand. I helped build that bloody thing.'

Laura put out a hand and touched his forearm. He flinched and snatched it away. She said, 'Tell me your story.'

He glared at her. 'And I don't understand why you're not running away from me.'

'Tell me your story,' Laura said again. She kept her gaze level and calm. She stared into his eyes — eyes the colour of oil, and hot with hatred and suspicion and hurt. She said, 'We're going to have to help each other all the way down the slope. So, as we go together, you can tell me your story.'

He put a finger in the outer corner of one of his eyes and pressed the eye into a slit. Laura had seen one of her spectacle-wearing school friends do that when she'd put her glasses down somewhere and was looking around for them. 'How old are you?' he asked, trying to get a good look at her.

'Five months ago I turned sixteen.'

'You're just a kid.'

'A *kid*?' She was unfamiliar with the usage.

'A kid.'

'I suppose you think I just flaked out in the forest?' said the man. 'I guess I must have. I was trying to do something. Something incredible. Of course it didn't work. It wasn't ever going to work. I must have been crazy. I had strange ideas in my head that I guess I resorted to in a time of need. I should be dead. I should have keeled over dead and deluded. Gone off in a happy fantasy.'

Laura interrupted him. 'No, I wish you'd start at the beginning.'

'I was starting at the point where I'm dead and discover there's no heaven.' He sounded as though he hated his story — and himself.

'Please,' Laura said. She held the branch of a bush so that it wouldn't flick back into his face. When he took it she saw his tattered nails and bloody nailbeds. He must have dug his grave using only his hands.

'All right,' he said, and began again. 'You can see by my trousers what I am.'

'No,' said Laura.

'Do you mean no you can't see that I'm a convict, or no don't start there? Maybe you want me to start with my birth?' He was sarcastic.

'Yes. Start there.'

'Well — how is your history, girl?' he asked. Then, without waiting for an answer, he just began.

'My mother was a dreamhunter, but the Place disappeared before I was born. I didn't have a father. I lived with Mother and Grandfather, who wasn't ever a well man. He taught me to play the violin. We lived on a small trust fund my mother had. She'd had a famous uncle. Her uncle made films. But when I was still an infant he went to the Ross Sea with one of those expeditions, and died there. His daughter, my mother's cousin — they were very close, they wrote one another letters every week for years. This cousin had married a man no one in the family much liked, and she went with him to live in another country. It was a kind of exile, I think. After the Ross Sea, my mother's uncle's widow joined her daughter. I can just remember her, the widow — she used to bring me expensive chocolates whenever she visited.

'Grandfather died when I was eight. After that we lived quietly. I went to a little country school. My mother died in the Influenza when I was ten. When she was dying she burned all her cousin's letters. I was left to suppose that she hadn't wanted me to know them — her cousin, and her cousin's husband.

'After she died I went to live with her other aunt, a strict spinster, who sent me to school and gave me more music lessons. Even after its lonely beginning my life should have been not too bad, but I got into trouble because people did, in the years when things were at their worst, with the bread lines and men walking the roads looking for work. You see, even with all those men out of work, and willing to work for the price of food, the bloody government still had its Prosperity Measures — the penal code.'

He broke off. 'I don't expect you to agree with me about this. You're a well-dressed girl with rounded vowels.'

'I'm glad I've got something rounded,' Laura said.

They had stopped in a patch of shade. Flies had found them — or him, for he was rank with filth. They were too tired to go on right away.

He said, 'How do you like my story so far?'

'I hate it.'

'Not enough romance?' he said, acid.

Laura burst out laughing. He sounded so like Sandy. Her laugh was affectionate, and he was rather thrown by it. 'Oh — just go on,' she said, wiping her eyes.

'If you stepped over the line back then,' he said, 'you'd end up contributing to the economy in some involuntary way — believe me. I got into trouble during the worst years of the Depression, the very worst. My violin was my means of making money — but no one was hiring musicians. I pawned my violin to buy food. But I couldn't bear not having it. I'd patrol the pawnshop window looking at it. And one evening, I just broke the glass and took it.

'I got caught and sent to prison. I had a light sentence, I was with the chicken-chokers and the disgruntled men who set fire to their employers' wheatfields. The work they gave men on light sentences wasn't exactly hard labour, and I was young and fit. But the wardens were sadists. One day I witnessed something very cruel. Impossibly cruel. I lost my temper, attacked the guard and injured him badly. After that I was in for twenty years. I was only nineteen and at first I didn't understand twenty years. What young person understands twenty years?

'I worked building the causeway, and on the Howe Peninsula digging bird-shit for the nitrate trade. I worked in the coal mine at Westport. Over time I lost all hope, except of escape, which isn't much of a hope on an island, even a big island like Southland.

'Then, six years after my second sentence, came the riot in the prison, and the fire. I escaped with a couple of dozen other men. We took a sloop from the wharves, but none of us was a sailor and we foundered off Pillar Point on the west coast of So Long Spit. The search party and their dogs hunted us up the Spit and, at some point, I left the others and took to the sea. I was lucky. I was carried by the rising tide back along the shore of Coal Bay to Debt River.

'And this is where my story will become incoherent to you — or very interesting, possibly, because you're a bit of a strange girl, aren't you?'

'Yes,' Laura said. Then, 'Let us go on and find that stream and get a drink.'

Telling his story seemed to have calmed him, and helped him to regain some sense of consideration. As they went on he stopped now and then to see how she was — though he was in far worse condition than she. Nothing further was said between them till they reached the stream.

It was a quick, small stream that came onto the beach and cut a sharp-edged channel in the sand. The man lay down on his stomach and sucked at the water. Laura scooped out a hollow in the sand, waited for the grains to settle, then dipped the lemonade bottle into the pool she'd made.

The sun was setting over the mountains on the far side of Coal Bay. The dark was coming, so when they finished drinking, they crawled up the beach and flopped in the fringe of salt-burned scrub. Without consultation they had decided together not to try to traverse the beach of boulders in the dark.

'After this stretch it's all easy going,' Laura said. She dropped her head and closed her eyes.

She heard him say, 'Why are you doing this?'

She shook her head; her hair rasped on the sand. She nestled into its cold softness.

'Strange girl,' he said. Then he went on with his story.

'The search party wouldn't have expended any energy mopping up one stray convict. They only had to wait for me to turn up somewhere where I couldn't give a good account of myself. They only had to wait for someone to turn me in. But I decided they were still in pursuit. It was because I felt special. Specially hated and feared. Even when I was a free man I felt that some people I met would act as though I were a tiger pretending to be a schoolboy or a musician. It was my name, you see.'

'Hame,' Laura said.

There was a long silence. Finally he said, testing, wary, 'But you're not chasing me, are you?'

'No,' Laura said.

Another long silence. Laura broke it. 'You're someone I've just met. Someone I feel for.' She thought: *'Family.'*

'You don't think I'm mad?'

'No.'

'You wait,' he said. 'We're not there yet. Wait till I tell you what I did — what I tried.

'Some guards had been killed in the riot, and the prison was razed. I imagined they would kill us when they caught us. It seemed to me that just running wasn't enough. I wanted to defend myself. And later, once I'd lost my mind, I just wanted revenge. I should have gone to a farm family and trusted someone to have pity. But I was in a bad way in my head: wet, and cold, and hungry. I didn't feel human, or entitled to fellow feeling. I hated everyone free. It seemed to me that whoever was free had let us convicts be beaten and broken, and driven into the river to drown. They'd stood by and let it happen.

'Something came into my head at Debt River. A story I'd heard my great-aunt tell, between music lessons, about magic. She'd taught me a song, though I was only interested in tunes I could play on the violin. The song was supposed to be a spell that would make a little portion of the earth come to life — be alive and *obedient.* At Debt River I remembered the song, and I remembered an earthquake that had frightened me when I was little. No one we knew was hurt in the earthquake, but I remembered going into the city afterwards, once they'd replaced all the bits of wriggly railway line. I remembered seeing heaps of tumbled stone in the street. There were little aftershocks. I'd wake up crying and my mother would sing to me. She too had sung that song. To comfort me she told me that she and I — if we *wished* hard enough — could make the earth itself listen. Listen and lie still.

'At Debt River I was hiding near the mining camp, eating fern shoots — stripping off the black fur and eating them raw. After a short time I'd exhausted the food supply: I'd found every freshwater crayfish in the stream, and had gouged out the heart of every tree fern. The sounds from the camp made me sad rather than keeping me company, and so I just *began*. I began without thinking. It was as if something in my head had more use for me than I did for it. I took the first steps of the spell I'd been taught and had thought was only a quaint folk ritual. Or rather, I began the spell, but adapted it to my purposes.

'I'd decided to show everyone. The men hunting me, the oblivious miners, the families on the farms I didn't dare go to. I'd show them, I thought. I started to sing and made a mark on the ground and began to run again. I travelled up Debt River and into the mountains, then I crossed over into Wry Valley.

'I travelled like that for more than a day. Then I slept, dreamed the song, woke up and kept on singing. That's how I went along. And at one place I slept I made another mark on the ground. The song seemed to be consuming me — and I dreamed impossible things. I dreamed of being saved and starting over.'

The man fell quiet.

Laura waited. She was too afraid to prompt him or comfort him. She did want to know his story, and she wanted to help him, but she didn't know what to do.

When the man spoke again his voice had changed; it was remote and resigned. 'I did die,' he said. 'But there wasn't another garden beyond the gate, there was a whole world, the same again. More thirst and cold and hunger. Here. Here with you — you strange girl.'

'You dreamed something impossible,' Laura said. 'But that isn't the end of your story.'

'No. I woke up.' He stirred. Then he sounded faintly amused. 'You know, that's what is comforting — that parts of what I recall, even after I lost my mind, still seem logical and real and practical. I remember wrapping my feet in strips of cloth after I lost my shoes. I remember singing and walking many more miles, mending my makeshift shoes as I went. I remember how my last meal wasn't much of a feed, because wasps had spoiled the apricots left hanging in the orchard by a grand mansion. I remember deciding that it was altogether too big a gesture to dig my own grave with my hands, and spending some time finding a flat stone to serve as a spade.'

'You dug your own grave?'

'After days, and miles — and the same thought in my head for days and miles. I didn't have to survive it. All I had to do was keep singing, and come to a place where I'd feel that I'd closed a circle. When I did come to that place, I scratched out a hole in the ground, a hole big enough to lie in. I lay down in it. I was finished. I wanted time to stop, and to let *me* stop with it. And I wanted revenge.

'I made the final mark that finished the spell — a W — and then said to the land, "Bury me, and rise up. Rise up and crush them all."

'And then I felt you brush the earth from my face.'

The outdoor night-time quiet had a stealthy quality, as though it were listening to both of them, stalking them with its attention. Laura thought of Nown, and could almost feel him, far, far away, reaching for her, his wish to touch her so strong that she felt touched.

This man's vast servant had obeyed him. The earth of his excavation had fallen in to cover him, and had piled up over him to make what he'd imagined for himself: a low grave-mound. His servant took him to its heart, as its heart. And then it rose up. There was an earthquake — and back along the miles of its master's journey the ground moved and cracked and *broke* the N that came to be known as Foreigner's North. By its master's own actions the first letter of that Nown's name was erased. It was its Own, and it remembered an earlier promise it had made: *'I promise in the future to do more, to do — I know not what — to save whomever you love.'*

Laura knew she would love her as yet unborn son. She *had* loved him — she, the woman who had lived a quiet life caring for him and her invalid father. Laura's servant, the ninth Nown, had loved her, and so the giant, immobile, speechless tenth, the Place, remembered having loved her, and went looking for her to ask for help. To say, 'Here is one you love who has asked me to stifle him. What should I do?' It moved its territory of stopped time back in time. It went too far, went on until it found the first someone it felt it knew — Laura's father, who had taught its heart music. It tried to tell him. It showed him his grandson, standing in chains beside a railway line. It tried by the only means available to it — the memories of the lives its territory had encompassed — to tell anyone who would listen. To show them not just the injustices, but also the beauty of human life against which injustice is a blasphemy: the joy of the boy on the shore racing the schooner, the happiness of the singsong around the beach bonfire — dancers, banquets, desires, balloon rides, the miracle of rivers. *Life.* It said, though not in words: '*There is something underneath all this; someone buried alive.*' It was like a person talking in his sleep — speaking urgent nonsense. It waited, and it felt Laura as she came towards it, through time, being born, growing up, reaching the age of her Try. And sometimes it would rap out its faith and rapture on the Founderston to Sisters Beach telegraph line, singing: '*She is coming, my own, my sweet . . .*' Singing a song she had taught it.

'Why the hell are you crying?' the man asked. He seemed offended. 'It wasn't my intention to make you cry, girl. Look, if I was crazy, it's passed now.'

'Shut up!' Laura said. And cried.

He got up and shuffled down the dark beach to drink some more. When he came back, she said, 'I'm glad it's so dark. It's easier to talk to you without seeing you.'

'I guess I am a pretty pitiful sight — especially for anyone in prime condition.'

'I'm not feeling guilty because I'm healthy and you're half-dead!' Laura shouted. 'You idiot! And the condition I'm in is *pregnant*!'

'You've run away from home because you're pregnant?'

'Shut up!'

He did, and she knew that was perhaps because he felt sympathetic — if exasperated — and that he wasn't at all the hard and heartless person he made himself out to be. She couldn't help but feel for him — he was so like Sandy, and he had her father's beautiful black eyes.

After a time she said, 'Do you think you can stay awake long enough for me to tell you *my* story?'

'I think I should hear your story. And I'm not sleepy, only hungry and weary. I feel as if I've slept for ages.'

'Well, you have,' she said. And then she told him her story.

Five

There was a rough track from the Awa Inlet across the saddle. It wasn't one dreamhunters knew, of course, since it was within the section of the map they couldn't enter. Mamie was familiar with a few miles of her end of it. Her family sometimes went along it to have picnics at the lookout. Beyond the lookout, sparse foot traffic meant that the track was overgrown. Gorse shoots grew out of the path, and the bare patches were stippled by the holes cicada nymphs had tunnelled out of. It was rough going, and the girls stopped walking when it got dark. They curled up in their coats, back to back, and Mamie shed more tears about 'her stupid situation' and Rose's 'exaggerated ideas' about her father's scheming. Rose let her friend cry and complain, and they were both soon asleep.

The following morning they were walking along the spine of a hill over the sea when they spotted two figures far below, making their way around a cove, stepping from boulder to boulder.

Rose stopped and shaded her eyes. Then she cupped her hands around her mouth and shouted, 'Laura!' She saw her cousin hesitate and cast about, then wave to her. 'Stay right there!' Rose shouted. 'Come on,' she said to Mamie. 'We're going down there.'

Mamie moaned, but when Rose set off downhill she hurried after her.

The man Laura was with had filthy red hair and was wearing Sandy Mason's coat — Rose was sure of it. The coat was wet. The strips of cloth wrapping the man's feet were oozing blood-tinged seawater. He'd been pulling mussels off the rocks at the tide line, and was smashing them open and eating them raw.

'I told him you'd have some food,' Laura said. 'But he has a somewhat independent disposition.'

Rose put her arms around her cousin and held her close. Mamie began to burble, more excited than complaining, about the dreamhunters who had swarmed to the Doran summer residence. 'Rose thought it best to run off. But I'm beginning to suspect there's a strong streak in your family of fleeing the scene.'

'Huh!' said the man smashing mussels.

'Who is he?' Rose asked Laura. She could see that he was wearing arrow-printed trousers and that his ankles bore marbled purple scarring caused by years of wearing leg irons.

'This is my cousin, Rose,' Laura said to the man.

Rose was intrigued by how gentle and respectful Laura sounded when she spoke to him. The man looked up at Rose with great interest. It made her blush. Then he dropped the shell-and-mussel-flecked stone and, looking decisive, said to Laura, 'How many people are there who need to know?'

Laura said, 'There's Da, Uncle Chorley, Aunt Grace and Rose.'

'But not this girl,' he said, and pointed his chin at Mamie.

'No,' said Laura.

'Well, I'll wait till they're all in one place. I'm only going to tell my story once more. Then, if I'm going to have any kind of life, I have to keep my mouth shut. I'm sure you agree.'

'Hell — you're a bit forceful,' Rose said to him. She had a very strong urge to pick a fight with him. It made her feel like a blowfly trapped under a glass.

'Do you have food?' he said, and gave Rose an up-under-the-brows look, as if he was the kind of dog who nips your fingers while snatching meat.

'Only if you tell me your name,' Rose said.

'Lazarus Hame.'

Rose looked at Laura, who said, 'Yes, it turns out there was a Lazarus after all.'

Six

In one of the fashionable terraces above the bay at Castlereagh there was a house where all the mirrors had been covered, and where, in the late afternoon following the funeral, only a few family members and close friends remained. The servants were gathering glasses and plates from under the chairs, on the windowsills and from the top of the piano.

No one expected a caller, given the time and the funeral wreath on the front door.

One of the dead woman's daughters went to answer the knocking. It was something to do. Something to distract her from her nagging misery.

On the steps stood a small, severe-looking woman, and a man in a long cape, who had his arms folded under it in a way that made an imposing triangle of his upper body.

The dead woman's daughter stood aside and let the two in. She took them in to her father, who was tucked in the house's smallest downstairs room, drinking whisky with his best friend. Then, because the room was so small, the daughter went out and closed the door.

'Judge Seresin,' said Marta Hame, 'I'm very sorry for your loss. I hate to disturb you at this time, but I've come a long way and on desperate business.'

'Mitch, this is Marta Hame!' Dr King said to his friend the judge.

The caped man took a pace back and leaned against the door. He let his hidden rifle dangle, so that its muzzle appeared from under his cape, pointed at the floor.

'With a Temple guard!' said King. He was intrigued.

Marta Hame put her valise on the table, opened it and lifted out her folded clothes balanced on the flat false bottom. She put the pile down, then produced the figure eight of film. 'We'll need to put this film back on a reel. It's footage of the Depot, a prison camp in the hinterland of the Place, reached by a secret railway line. Cas Doran and his Regulatory Body have been loading captive dreamhunters with a dream that makes anyone who has it stupid and incautious with happiness. Doran has begun to use this dream to control people in the capital.'

The two men stared at her, mouths open.

'So far he's contrived to have a dream-narcotised Congress pass legislation to extend the presidential term. And he is hunting down and trying to eliminate, or permanently dream-drug, anyone he thinks will spoil his plans.'

'I told you that vote was rigged,' Dr King said to his friend. 'And I'm sure the earlier appointment of the Speaker of the House was somehow rigged too.'

Marta said, 'My niece Laura has been to that camp and can testify to its use. And anyone who has had a strong dose of the dream can testify to the fact that it is a gross abuse.'

'But, Miss Hame . . .' Judge Seresin said.

Marta blinked at him in surprise. She was already worried that he hadn't leaped into action of some kind. Didn't he believe her?

'Have you not heard?' he said.

'Haven't you seen the newspaper?' Dr King said.

Marta's hand crept to her throat and clutched her crucifix. 'I've been travelling by back roads and in locked railway compartments. I've had no news.'

'The Place has gone,' said Seresin. 'It just melted away. Any plan of Doran's that requires dreams is doomed. Finished. Doran's empire has fallen.'

'Poor sod,' said King, then chuckled.

Then the judge jumped up and stuffed a chair under Marta Hame's sagging legs. Dr King poured her a stiff whisky.

Marta knocked back the whole glass, grimaced and said, 'God be praised.'

They refilled her glass and shook the decanter at the Temple guard, who set his gun against the door and joined them.

'I'll cable Wilkinson — who will quickly work out which side he's on,' said Seresin.

'I'll cable the Grand Patriarch, and my brother at Spring Valley,' Marta said. 'And could you issue a warrant for Doran's arrest?'

'I shall certainly be doing that,' said the judge. 'But perhaps we should all get on the next train to the capital?' For a moment he looked defeated and exhausted.

King said, 'Yes, Mitch. That would be best.' He put his glass down, and touched his friend's hand.

The judge nodded. He looked at Marta with solemn dignity. 'I think I should see to this myself,' he said.

Seven

The President, Garth Wilkinson, regarded the men in his outer office: the Grand Patriarch and his secretary Father Roy, Supreme Court Judge Seresin, Dr King and the resurrected dreamhunter Tziga Hame. He straightened his waistcoat over his trim stomach, said, 'I will be with you shortly, gentlemen,' and walked back into his own office, his inner sanctum, where his friend, the Secretary of Labour, was waiting for him.

'Karl,' said Wilkinson. 'There's one thing I think we should do right away, and that is get Doran's name off the Prosperity Measures Bill. We needn't lose the ground we've made there.'

'So — you're letting them have him?'

'I don't have any choice.'

'And what about the repeal of the Presidential Term Limits?'

Wilkinson sighed. 'Well — we've landed on a snake there. But it need not be a long snake, it might only take us back twenty places, since only the last vote will be discounted. The vote under the influence of that dream — about which you and I know nothing whatsoever.'

'What if Doran's Colourist talks?'

'If Plasir keeps quiet about the colouring, then he's guilty of nothing but having a criminal friend. Or having misplaced his trust — as we have, Karl. We trusted Doran. How were we to have known he was such a villain?' Wilkinson put his hand over his heart and practised a look of great disappointment. 'And I doubt we're in danger from Doran himself. Cas won't say anything to further jeopardise his achievements.'

'What makes you think that?'

'He's a patriot,' said Wilkinson.

They left the Presidential Offices in a cavalcade of motor cars and men on horseback.

Dr King and Judge Seresin rode in the President's own car. It was a five-minute drive to the palace of Governance, where the Secretary of the Interior had his offices.

Wilkinson said to the two men opposite him, 'I do not relish this task. Cas Doran is a personal friend.'

The car turned onto the embankment. Across the Sva, on the upstream end of the Isle, the tower of the Regulatory Body seemed to be throwing off seed. Paper was being tossed from at least two of its top windows. Sheaves of paper that fanned as they fell into the swampy garden below, or blew out over the river to lie, white, on the water.

'I wish someone would put a stop to that,' King said, mildly. 'That's history.'

'The real tragedy is that thousands of people will be out of work,' Seresin said. 'Everyone in those offices, and dreamhunters, rangers, the staff of dream palaces, and proprietors of dream parlours. All will be ruined.'

'Indeed. The social consequences are dreadful to contemplate,' said President Wilkinson.

The cavalcade pulled up at the palace of Governance and they went into its lobby, which was already full of police. Garth Wilkinson and his bodyguard got into the first elevator. The Grand Patriarch, Father Roy, the judge and Tziga Hame all waited patiently. King rocked back and forth on the balls of his feet saying, 'Oh — to be a fly on the wall!'

Doran was alone in his office. When the door opened and he saw Wilkie he was pleased — and even more so when the President stepped into the room and shut the door on his escort, the police and the handful of pallid and pop-eyed officials who were helping the police put Doran's papers into crates.

'His Eminence and Judge Seresin will be here soon,' said Wilkie. 'I'm very sorry, Cas.'

Doran opened his mouth to speak, but his friend held up a hand. 'We've only a moment,' Wilkie said. 'And I want you to know that I regard this failure as bad luck. Who could have guessed that the Place would choose this moment to vanish?'

Doran kept quiet, but went on nursing the murky suspicions he had, because he didn't believe in coincidences, only in hidden influence.

'Very bad luck,' Wilkie said, sounding like someone consoling a punter after their favourite has taken a tumble at the Founders' Day races. Then he said, 'Oh — and that Hame is with them. I thought I should warn you, since I know you regard him rather superstitiously.'

'He's nothing now,' Cas Doran said through clenched teeth. 'He's a cripple, a fiddler from the old town. Curse him and his family.'

And then the door opened and that man came in with the other men. The Grand Patriarch was all dignity, and so were his secretary and the judge. The historian King was present too, which was something of a surprise to Doran. King — the bumptious twit — was so excited he was having to suck in his lips to keep from smiling. Tziga Hame had his eyes cast down as though he was embarrassed or ashamed.

Wilkinson said to them, 'Secretary Doran was just saying that he has hopes of house arrest.'

Doran flushed. He wanted house arrest even less than he wanted to be shut up in a cell in Founderston Barracks. At home he'd have to endure his wife's tears and recriminations. He didn't want that. He didn't want *her*. So — Wilkie was going to act sympathetic in private, then subject him to indignities. Like the indignity of having Seresin say to him, 'Your charges will include abduction and conspiracy to abduct. They are too serious for house arrest.'

Doran gave the judge a polite nod.

'How did you hope to get away with it?' the Grand Patriarch said.

Doran thought for a few moments about a possible defence —

and saw it was impossible. He thought about making Wilkie's life uncomfortable — of all the people he could take down with him. But he liked what he'd achieved too much to undo it all just because he couldn't enjoy it. Knowledge was enjoyment. Knowledge of a few lasting successes. And, since he didn't plan to defend himself, he at least had the satisfaction of being able to answer the Grand Patriarch: 'I would have succeeded had the Place not disappeared.'

'The Place is not the whole story. There will be other changes,' said the Grand Patriarch, in the tones of a crusader. 'This society cannot continue in its callous willingness to base its wealth on suffering.'

Doran laughed. 'Oh yes, Your Eminence? And what are *you* going to give up?'

Garth Wilkinson smiled ever so slightly and inspected the fingernails on one hand.

'Do you think I might be taken off to gaol now?' said Doran. 'My lawyer is here already and wants to go along with me.' He touched the solitary paper on his desk and looked at Wilkinson. 'This is my resignation — though I don't know why I imagined it was required.'

'Thank you, Cas,' said the President.

Father Roy opened the door and stood aside. Doran came around his desk and walked past them. He stopped beside Tziga Hame and tried to catch the man's shy gaze. He asked, 'Do you know why the Place disappeared?'

'I don't know anything,' said Tziga Hame.

'And you *are* nothing now,' said Doran. 'You and your famous family.'

Tziga Hame gave Doran a beautiful smile. 'Yes, please God,' he said, 'let us be nothing — for a time, at least.'

Doran stared into that wavering black gaze and sought understanding. Understanding didn't come to him. 'What I tried to do *had* to work,' he said to Hame, very quietly, and with desperate puzzlement, 'because there I was, twenty-six years later, congratulating myself on my successes. The dreams were the future.'

'Oh — you knew that?' said Tziga Hame.

Doran nodded, then walked out to the waiting police.

Eight

When they finally reached Summerfort, Laura drank a large glass of milk and went straight to bed, never mind that her hair was tangled, or that her feet would make her sheets filthy. She left any explanation to Rose, who didn't know much, but did explain why Laura was so tired.

For days Grace had alternated between silence, weeping and clinging to Chorley saying, 'What will we do now? What can I do with my life?' Rose's bit of news gave Grace something to think about. 'Laura's *pregnant*!' she said. 'How far along?'

'Well — it must have been before Sandy . . .'

'Oh, the poor girl,' Grace said. She jumped up.

Rose grabbed her. 'No, Ma. Let her sleep. She told me that's all she wants for now. I'll go and make up a bed for Mamie.'

Mamie had remained outside. She'd picked up one of the folded rugs from the wing-backed wicker chairs, and was sitting, cocooned, gazing out at the view.

'And then I'll run a bath for that man,' Rose said, and jerked her thumb at Lazarus.

Lazarus waited in the doorway. He stood very still, and his extreme exhaustion only added to his presence. His face was cadaverously thin and pale, and Chorley, looking at him, was tempted to make some joke about Poe's raven — because the man really did look like he might start croaking, 'Nevermore!' at them.

* * *

Rose took Lazarus to the upstairs bathroom. She put the plug in the tub and turned on the taps. The water splashed, then began to chime as the tub filled. 'I don't think I've ever seen Laura so sad,' Rose said.

'Laura is sad because she believes in fate,' he said.

Rose was trying to work him out. She kept staring at him, and the longer she stared the longer she wanted to stare. He was grimy and abrupt and, she thought, violent in some way she couldn't quite work out, but he was mesmerising to her — the mysterious *fact* of him.

He said, with a kind of exhausted eagerness, 'But I think what happens is that when anyone does anything absolutely extraordinary — great or terrible — when they change the world, they make *another* world. When God separated light from darkness and made the world, perhaps he left the dark world behind him. And, because the dark world is still there —'

'You really are a Hame, aren't you?'

A little colour came into his cheeks, rosy grey under the dirt. 'Meaning?'

'Quaintly religious.'

'Who are you calling quaint? You old-fashioned girl,' he said.

Rose turned off the taps and tested the water. She couldn't tell whether it was a comfortable temperature. Her hands still felt warm as hot, and hot as burning. But this man wasn't an infant and could look after himself. 'Throw your clothes outside the bathroom door and I'll bring you something to wear,' she said, and bustled out.

Mamie was in the guest room, sorting through some of Rose's clothes to see what she could fit. Chorley had gone out to send a telegram to Mamie's mother, saying she was safe and staying at Summerfort. Laura was still asleep.

Rose had taken up the task of listening to her mother's lamentations, which were a little less keen now and interspersed with thoughts about Laura's baby. 'If I weren't so worried about how we're going to make a living, I'd be happier about it. Your father and I always wanted another baby, but it didn't happen. I do love babies.'

'Ma, we don't owe anyone money. And we have two properties. Everything is freehold and there's money in the bank. We're not going to be poor.'

'But I don't know who I am if I can't catch dreams,' Grace said.

'Then you'll find out, Ma.'

'Hello!' Chorley called from the front door.

'He has good news,' Rose said. 'He sounds really happy.'

A moment later Chorley appeared, his arm clasped protectively around the waist of a figure in yellow pyjamas.

'*Sandy!*' Grace and Rose shouted together. They rushed him and hugged him. Grace cupped his whiskery, grinning face and cried. Rose held his hand, noticing as she did the shiny, red, hairless patches that resembled her own scorch marks.

'He was limping doggedly barefoot along the promenade,' Chorley said.

'I'm all right,' Sandy said. 'I only walked from the Awa Inlet to Sisters Beach.'

'Forty-five miles,' said Grace. 'Nothing for a dreamhunter.'

'Are you all Contented?' Rose said.

'A little. I feel much less serious than I know I should. I *should* feel like tearing off Secretary Doran's head.'

Chorley gave a gleeful laugh and pulled a telegram from his pocket. He gave it to Rose. It was from her Uncle Tziga. It said that Cas Doran was under arrest on charges of abduction.

'That's a start,' Rose said. She felt only grim relief. She knew that she'd have to carry this news to Mamie, and that Mamie might feel that she should go back to Founderston at once, to stand by her mother. And Rose knew that some time in the near future there would be a trial, and that her family would be called to give evidence against her friend's father. Mamie already had difficulties with the world and its expectations, and this could only make it all worse. Remembering how she'd said to Mamie, proudly, that she would go to university to study 'law — for justice', Rose thought that it was all right for *herself*, she had committed herself to a struggle, had spied, plotted, carried a copy of the damning film. But Mamie hadn't made any choices, yet would have to suffer for those her father had made.

Rose touched Sandy's arm. 'Laura is in bed,' she said. 'You know where her bedroom is, don't you?'

'Um, yes,' Sandy said.

Chorley poked Sandy in the arm with a stiff finger. He said, with a prod for every word, 'She-is-with-child.'

Sandy opened his mouth, swallowed, then shut it again.

'Precisely,' said Chorley, and pointed to the stairs. 'Go,' he said.

Laura woke up, still tired, with the heavy, sickening feeling that comes when you know something terrible has happened. Then she remembered that the terrible things were still ahead of her — her whole future mapped out already in the story Lazarus told her. She longed to speak to Nown. She badly wanted to tell him what it was like to *know* what would happen. To know, and to have to choose to be alone in knowing.

She opened her eyes — and looked straight into Sandy's. He had been lying with his head beside hers, waiting for her to wake up. He smiled and touched her cheek.

And in that moment everything changed for Laura. The world became world-sized again, and full of surprise.

Sandy said, 'There's a strange man in the upstairs bathroom. A strange man who looked at me strangely.'

'Well, he would,' Laura said.

'I wasn't dead,' Sandy said. He gathered her in his arms.

Laura took a deep breath of Sandy's own odour — with its overlay of dust and sea salt. 'It's not *true*, then,' she said, through her tears. 'Here you are, my baby's father. I thought I was going to have to go through with it all — do all the lonely things. Say *bon voyage* to Uncle Chorley. Let Rose live in another country with the man no one much liked — whoever that is. Nurse Father. Live quietly. Wait to die. I thought I had to do what fate dictated. Follow its laws as my poor Nown had to follow my orders.'

'Ssh, darling,' Sandy said, stroked her hair and tested her forehead for fever. 'It's all right.'

'Yes,' she cried, 'it *is* all right. Here you are. That poor man out there must come from a different world from this one — a world without you in it. God is merciful. God has given us all a new world to live in — like The Gate. There *is* a first time for everything.'

Sandy smiled at Laura, moved by how moved she was, but completely bewildered. 'I have no idea what you're talking about, love.'

She laughed, and her last two tears were squeezed out of her eyes by a smile. 'I'll tell you,' she said.

When Lazarus came downstairs, wearing some of Chorley's clothes, he found Grace, Chorley and Rose waiting for him. He seemed unable to look at any of them for long. His gaze flitted away around the room and finally lighted on Tziga's violin, sitting on its stand and covered in a peach-fuzz of dust. Lazarus crossed the room — so thin in his borrowed clothes that he seemed to drift, bodiless. He picked up the violin and put it up to one ear. He plucked at its strings with his scabbed thumb, then began tuning it — plucking, listening, twisting its pegs. 'This is mine,' he said, softly, lovingly. 'The last time I saw it, it was "produced in evidence".'

'*Excuse* me?' Chorley said, outraged.

Rose said to Lazarus, 'I know this isn't everybody, but I promise I'll pass on faithfully anything you say if you don't feel like saying it again.'

Lazarus nodded. Then he said, 'My name is Lazarus Hame.'

Chorley narrowed his eyes. 'Explain,' he said.

'Give me a moment,' said Lazarus.

And it was amazing what Lazarus could do, given a moment.

Nine

The city was bigger, and so were all the other settlements. There were more roads, better roads, with many more cars on them.

But Nown kept away from the roads. He travelled cross-country, and often by night. He walked so far that his feet turned as white as old ice.

Laura had been his compass — she was north, south, east and west to him. He couldn't find her, but kept on looking in all the places he'd found her before.

His pilgrimage finally took him along So Long Spit. He walked on past the lighthouse, then further, beyond where he'd been that day with Laura.

At the end of the Spit, a sandbar pointing out into a thousand miles of empty ocean, Nown found the gannet colony. He stopped at the edge of the throng of black and white birds and gazed at the pattern they made, a glow going away into nothing. He thought: 'Laura,' her name like a prayer. 'Laura, I am not in the same world as you.'

He started forward and moved delicately in among the roosting gannets. The birds weren't at all afraid of him. They shuffled aside, clucking tetchily.

Eventually Nown stopped and stood surrounded by the warmth of the colony. He looked out over the sea, gazed into nothingness and waited. He began his waiting.

The setting sun shone though his glass body, and showed up the dark matter at its heart — his heart, a rust-stained rock from the track bed.

Epilogue
1912

It was three days before Christmas and the family was at Summerfort. Chorley had just finished shooting a film, his first two-reeler, and was shut up in his workshop, editing it. His three jacks-of-all-trades — Sandy, Sandy's brother the engineer, and Lazarus — were kneeling on the lawn around a newspaper on which rested a dismantled camera. The camera had been responsible for some edge-fog on the film, and they were trying to work out where the light had leaked in.

The newspaper, disregarded by the men, carried a headline that, three days before, had made everyone in the family very happy: 'Prison Reform Bill Passes — Hard Labour Abolished'.

Grace was upstairs, getting her granddaughter off to sleep, so that her daughter could study.

The afternoon was still and humid, the air filled with the abrasive music of hundreds of cicadas, and one violin. The violin belonged to a four-year-old boy, who stood, shoulders back, his instrument tucked under his chin, playing. He was practising legato, his bow moving smoothly and never leaving the strings. His performance was watched by his grandfather, who sat on a stone seat at the edge of the lawn, back to the hazy, hot blue of the bay.

The cousins, Laura Mason and Rose Hame, were on the veranda. Between them was a table covered in books and papers.

Laura was using Rose to test the wording of title cards for the finished film. Chorley liked to use as few title cards as possible. That morning he and she had watched a rough cut, and worked out where it was absolutely necessary to add those six or so seconds of darkness and white words.

Laura hunched, chewing on the end of her big, flat builder's pencil. Then she pounced, scrawled for a moment and raised the sheet of paper to flash it at her cousin.

Rose read: 'Pat Slocum — General of the Heroes of Dog Alley.'

'That's not bad. But is it worth interrupting the action for?' Rose said.

'He's a dumpy little dandy who swaggers, so we know "General" and "Heroes" are ironic,' Laura said. She frowned at what she'd written, chewed her pencil some more, then had another inspiration. She scrawled more words and held them up.

Rose read: 'The Commander-in-Chief of the mighty forces of Dog Alley — General Pat Slocum.'

'Change his name to Pat Potts or something,' Rose said. 'Unless Da's done the cast credits already.'

Laura was about to answer when Rose lifted her book and flashed its title: *Southland Constitutional Law*. She said, 'I'm having enough trouble with this, without the Dog Alley Gang.'

Laura gathered up her bits of paper. She went in search of another victim. She stood behind her son and flashed title cards at her father.

'I've forgotten the film's plot, darling,' Tziga said, 'so I'm not much use. But I like "mighty forces".'

And, at that moment, the ground began to shake.

Laura dropped into a crouch and put her arms around her son. She watched her father's slow realisation that this violent noise and vertigo weren't the beginning of one of his fits, but external to him. Tziga didn't try to stand up. He clamped one hand on the edge of the stone seat, and rode it as it rocked and juddered.

Laura could hear glass breaking. She looked back at the house.

The panes in the dining-room windows were exploding, one by one. The windows had jammed in their warped frames and were bent and bowed. Laura saw that Rose was trying to crawl to the front entrance. Trying to get into the house and upstairs to her baby. But Laura could see Grace already had the baby. Grace was sheltering in an open door on the upstairs balcony, her back against the door frame, her head and shoulders curved protectively over the lace-swathed bundle of her granddaughter.

Chorley staggered out the front door, and pulled Rose back in under its solid frame.

The ground between Laura and the house cracked, the fissures only inches wide, but showing stretched fibres of grass roots. The gravel on the new driveway jumped like popcorn in a hot pan.

And then the shaking stopped. Sound seemed to ebb all the way out of the world. The silence that followed the quake was like a presence — some vast, demonstrative, living thing.

In the Sisters Beach fire station, a siren wound up into a long wobbling shriek.

Laura saw that her father had only held on to his seat with one hand — he still had the book he'd been reading in the other, his finger shut into it as a place marker.

Sandy ran up to her. They both took a good look at their boy, Sandy squeezing his arms as if to check for injuries, she brushing his fine red hair back from his face and peering into his black eyes.

Rose was already up on the balcony. Grace gave her the baby, who was howling louder than the fire siren.

Lazarus called, 'Is she all right?'

'She's fine,' Grace shouted down. 'She was fast asleep. She's only angry because I woke her.' Then, 'Where's Chorley?'

Lazarus and Sandy's brother pointed at Chorley, who came out to where his wife could see him and waved to her. 'I'm going to go down into town and take a look about,' he said.

'Take your camera,' Grace and Rose said together.

Laura's son was trembling. She chafed his arms. 'Wasn't that strange?' she said, in a bright voice, hoping to reassure him.

'It's all over now, son,' said Sandy.

The boy looked from one parent to the other, his eyes round and bright. He said, 'Was the ground angry? Was it trying to get up?'

Glossary of Dreamhunting Terms

Claim Whenever a dreamhunter finds a new dream, he or she must register it with the Dream Regulatory Body. A claim will give a dreamhunter a one-year exclusive. However, any dream that the Dream Regulatory Body chooses to classify as 'a dream for the public good' cannot be claimed.

Colourist A Colourist is a secret persuader, who will insert into another dreamhunter's performance some impressions at the dream's beginning or end, when the audience is less fully absorbed in the performance. The audience, taking on a Colourist's impressions, think they are their own thoughts or feelings. A Colourist's dream is usually a print of a dream taken from a **Gifter**, who has altered it to deliver its desired message. Colouring is illegal.

Dream Almanac Published by the Dream Regulatory Body, a guide to dreams, by content, type and location.

Dream for the public good A dream deemed too valuable for commercial use alone, usually a healing dream. The Department of Corrections also classes **Think Again dreams** as 'dreams for the public good'. Any dreamhunter may catch a dream for the public good, and can perform it in a dream parlour or a dream palace. But each time the dream is caught the dreamhunter's contract with the Regulatory Body rules that several nights must be spent dreaming it in a hospital. Exceptions to this are dreams like Convalescent One and Starry Beach, discovered before the formation of the Dream Regulatory Body.

Dream palace A large building, often purpose-built, in which dreams are performed. According to Dream Regulatory Body regulations, to qualify as a dream palace the building must have over fifty beds. Dream palaces are often round or ovoid and consist of several tiers, balconies with bedrooms opening off them. In the centre of the palace's auditorium is the dreamer's dais, where the dreamer sleeps. Only dreamhunters with a large **penumbra** perform in dream palaces. Dream palaces are a vital part of the life of Southland; attendance is a social occasion and most fashionable people will own formal nightwear. The Rainbow Opera is Southland's largest and most magnificent dream palace. It was built for Grace Tiebold.

Dream parlour Any place with fewer than fifty beds dedicated to the performance of dreams. Many of the hotels and the pilgrims' hostels on Founderston's Isle of the Temple became dream parlours during the early years of the industry. Tickets to attend general-exhibition dream parlours are much less expensive than those to dream palace performances, though there are specialist dream parlours with prices dependent on the market for their dreams. Maze Plasir, a **Gifter**, is the proprietor of an expensive and exclusive dream parlour.

Dream Regulatory Body Established in 1896 under the Intangible Resources Act, the Dream Regulatory Body (also known as the Regulatory Body or just the Body) is a department of the Secretariat of the Interior. As such, it is the responsibility of the Secretary of the Interior, Cas Doran. Cas Doran was the main author of the Intangible Resources Act.

The Regulatory Body employs **rangers** to patrol the Place. The Regulatory Body also holds Tries and undertakes the testing and training of successful candidates of each **Try**. All dreamhunters, dream palaces and dream parlours must be licensed by the Body. The Body also has contracts with other government entities, to supply dreams for health care and for programmes of education and rehabilitation in Southland's prisons.

Dream sites Dreams are sometimes found in general areas, and can be caught by a group of people. This is the case with

Wild River, and is one of the reasons why the dream is used to test the successful candidates of each Try. But some dream sites are very confined; their dreams are hard to discover, and can often be caught only by a particular kind of dreamhunter. Maze Plasir's Secret Room is a confined-site dream. So is Tziga Hame's The Gate. That dream's site was so confined that Hame claimed never to be able to find it again.

Dream trails Roads, paths and scratchy routes in the Place, dream trails usually lead to popular, tried and tested dreams.

Dreamhunter Anyone able to enter the Place, catch one of the dreams to be found there, carry it back into the world and share it with others. Dreamhunting has been an industry in Southland for twenty years, and is a major form of entertainment and therapy.

Gifter (or **Grafter**) A dreamhunter who can take his own memories of a real person's face and manners and graft them onto the characters in the dreams he catches. Gifters are usually employed by people who want what they can't have, or who have lost someone they love.

Healer A dreamhunter who can catch and convey vividly the great healing dreams.

Hame Any dreamhunter with a big penumbra. The name comes from Tziga Hame, possibly the greatest dreamhunter.

Map references in the Place On maps of the Place the main references are bands and sections. Because the Place is vast, and its interior unexplored, it is mapped in bands from either end. Each band represents a three- to five-hour journey on foot, depending on the terrain. From Doorhandle the Place has been mapped from bands A to I. The Tricksie Bend end is less thoroughly explored, and has only been mapped from Z to U. From the Doorhandle border one enters Band A, from the Tricksie Bend end one enters Band Z. Each band is divided perpendicularly into sections. The sections are a kind of longitude to the latitude of the bands. The sections began with 1 to the west of Doorhandle and minus 1 to the east, and the same at the Tricksie Bend end, so that the map would work if its references were ever to join in the as yet unpenetrated interior. Grace Tiebold's first dream, Pursuit, is at A minus 1, In and a little east of Doorhandle. The stream bed where Tziga leaves Chorley's movie camera is at map reference Y-17, seventeen sections west of Tricksie Bend, and just over three days' walk In.

Master dream Any dream that will erase another, and cannot be erased by anything other than another master dream. Examples of master dreams are Secret Room, Buried Alive, The Gate and Contentment.

Mounter Any dreamhunter who can **overdream** another and erase the dream he or she is carrying.

Novelist Any dreamhunter who can catch a **split dream**. The people who share a Novelist's dream will sometimes pick up one point of view, and sometimes another, or switch back and forth all night between the two. Split dreams are richer and more complex than other dreams. Grace Tiebold is the most celebrated Novelist dreamhunter.

Penumbra A dreamhunter's projection zone is known as his or her penumbra, a term borrowed from astronomy, where it describes the partial shadow that the moon casts on the face of the earth during a total eclipse. (The 'umbra', or totality, is the dreamhunter himself or herself, asleep and haloed by the shade of a dream.) An average public performance sized penumbra is around eighty yards. Some dreamhunters, like Maze Plasir, have small penumbras yet still have good careers because they have other specialities, and their projection zones deliver hypnotically intense dream experiences. Grace Tiebold has a three-hundred-yard penumbra. Tziga Hame's, at four hundred, is the largest on record. Grace Tiebold and Tziga Hame cannot sleep just anywhere when loaded with a dream.

The Place The territory where the dreams come from is called the Place. It is infinitely more vast than the hundred or so square miles of the mountain range it encompasses. Only a very few people can enter the Place. Of these, some become dreamhunters, and can make their fortunes from dreams caught, and carried out, and shared with others. No one has established how long the Place was there before being discovered. Protected by remoteness, and the sparse population of the Rifleman Mountains, the Place had its first verifiable appearance on a day in November 1886 when a young violinist named Tziga Hame disappeared from a coach travelling between Doorhandle and Sisters Beach.

Rangers Employees of the Dream Regulatory Body, rangers patrol the Place, maintain its trails and, when necessary, perform search-and-rescue. **Rangers** are those who find that although they can enter the Place, they can't catch dreams.

Soporif Soporifs often work in hospitals, enhancing the effects of anaesthetics. They enter the operating theatre before the surgeons and their assistants, and bed down near the prepared patient. Anyone who is close to a **Soporif** when he falls asleep will fall asleep with him. George Mason is Southland's best Soporif.

Split dream A dream that has two points of view. Only a **Novelist** dreamhunter will be able to catch both points of view at the same time, and deliver them to the audience. Examples of split dreams are Second Sentence/Sunken and Grace Tiebold's famous first split dream, Pursuit.

Think Again dream A dream used in Southland prisons for educating prisoners.

Try Twice a year, in the autumn and spring, the Dream Regulatory Body holds Tries, at which people, the majority of them teenagers, attempt to enter the Place. Only one person in three hundred will cross over into the Place.

Wakeful A powerful stimulant that dreamhunters chew to stay awake when they have walked days Into the Place to catch a dream they don't want to waste before they have an audience. Wakeful is a purple-red fibrous paste with a pleasant perfume. It is dangerous if used for too long or in large doses.